Effigy

Book One of the Coileáin Chronicles

M.J. FIFIELD

FAVORITE SPOON PUBLISHING

Printed in the United States of America
First Printing, 2014

ISBN: 978-0-9961074-0-2

Favorite Spoon Publishing
78 Grove Street #1031
North Conway, NH 03860

Book Design: Judy Maenle; www.mosaicbookworks.com

Cover Design: Ravven; www.ravven.com

To my village.
Thank you for taking care of this idiot.

Pronunciation Guide

Aelhaeran: Al-har-an

Amatheon: A-math-eon

Auryn: Awe-rin

Brollachan: Bro-lach-han

Bronagh: Bro-nah

Ceallach: Kay-lock

Coileáin: Co-lee-ain

Darragh: Dar-rah

Eamonn: A-mon

Einar: I-nar

Eluned: Elle-in-ed

Fáinne: Faw-in-nye

Faolan: Fay-lawn

Haleine: Ha-lane

Idris Fein: Ee-driss-feign

Iollan Iuchar: Yoll-an Yuch-are

Laorans: Law-rans

Mairéad: Ma-raid

Luisiúil: Louis-shoo-elle

Maoilriain: May-oh-ree-ain

Mireille: Me-ray

Piala: Pea-a-la

Revelin: Rev-lin

Rhoswen: Rose-when

Rhydwyn: Hrid-win

Rhys: Hress

Saoirse: Seer-shuh

Seoras: See-or-as

Sighle: She-la

Acknowledgements

As a writer, I always worry that I don't know enough words. Never has this fear been more fully realized than now, as I attempt to thank those without whom this novel would only exist in a three-ring binder under my bed.

For example, my brilliant cover artist, Ravven, who overcame and forgave my complete ignorance of the cover design process in order to produce a gorgeous cover with which I am absolutely in love. Thank you, Ravven, for saving me from having to use stick figures.

A mountain of gratitude belongs to Judy Maenle at Mosaic Book Works for her tireless efforts to turn this manuscript into a beautifully designed book. Thank you for your guidance and endless patience.

There's also Callie Leuck, my grammar guru, whose expertise was invaluable as I navigated the contentious waters of comma placement. Thank you for keeping me from running aground.

And then there is my bevy of beta readers. From typos to plot holes, you keep me from making too large a fool out of myself, and I thank you for it. I want to give a special shout out to the following four: Jacob Jordan, Elizabeth Mannette, Mike Fox, and Heidi Fox for having the fortitude to survive multiple drafts as well as countless crazy, rambling emails concerning those drafts.

Last, but not least, are my friends and family—the people whose love and support mean the world to me. You keep me in cupcakes, cookies and smarties, notebooks and pens, and kicks in the ass. I am especially grateful to Joe, Jacob and Alison who have spent so long on the front lines of this mission, laughing with me and occasionally laughing at me, but always loving me and encouraging me to keep moving forward. It can't have been easy, and I thank you from the very bottom of my heart for hanging in there.

Prologue

Darian Coileáin didn't mind killing. The sound of a well-made blade slicing through flesh and bone didn't bother him. The blood he wore at the end of a battle washed away as easily as dirt gained from a day of plowing. When others vomited or sobbed over the atrocities they had seen or committed, Darian prepared for the next encounter. He never doubted it would come. King Nathan Maoilriain desired above all else to expand his already-great demesne, and Darian desired above all else to give his king what he wanted.

It was a more profitable endeavor than plowing. He knew this after watching his father and his father's father break their backs tilling an unrewarding earth, but Darian had never plowed a field. He had never done anything other than train for his role in his majesty's army. He went where his king sent him, fighting his king's cause without question. The causes never mattered to him, but they mattered to his king, and that was why he went and served and killed. He knew eventually it would lead to reward.

The king didn't care about Darian's reasons any more than Darian cared about the king's. Nathan kept him around because Darian had proved to be a talented soldier and a brilliant strategist who understood what was fundamentally important. Success mattered above all else. The king wanted it and Darian provided it.

Currently, the king wanted Quatara, a small country that lay west of Tanuba and continued on to the far reaches of the Endellion Sea. Nathan wanted to control Quatara's seaports and wanted Darian to control them for him.

Their campaign had been successful thus far. There was one remaining rebel cell holding out in the city of Parthalan, but it would fall. They all did. Darian had come too far to allow any other possibility to come to pass. He knew a victory here would lead to the grandest reward of all. A grateful king would name him Quatara's seneschal, a title he much coveted.

And so it came to be how Darian was not in Tanuba when his daughters were born. Instead, he was in the middle of a war-torn land, following his king. The war was important enough to Nathan that he had come himself, to lead his own men, and Darian would stand beside him until the end.

When the letter bearing the Coileáin crest came, Darian stood in the king's tent examining maps and making plans for the next morning's attack. A page entered the tent and handed Darian the letter. He tore it open without seeing the wax seal on the envelope. He read it, expecting to see the enemy's position as reported by his scouts but instead saw that he had become a father.

"Well, what is it?" Nathan asked.

"It is from Darragh," Darian said. "He writes to tell me I am a father."

The king laughed and clapped his hands together. "Well done!" he exclaimed. "A son, I hope."

"No." Darian could not take his eyes off the letter sent to him by his own steward. "Daughters. Twins."

"Two daughters?"

Darian could hear the disappointment in his king's voice. Nathan already had two young sons of his own, and the possibility of daughters never had crossed his mind. Neither had it crossed Darian's mind, but he found he did not care that instead of a fine healthy son he had two fine healthy daughters. He would still raise them to be his heirs.

"Well," Nathan continued, "you will have your son next. He will still inherit your holdings."

Darian nodded, knowing that was what the king would like. Nathan Maoilriain embraced tradition. A man's holdings were always meant to pass to his eldest son. If Darian's father had had anything to his name, Darian would have inherited it when the man died. In spite of the king's own views, Darian did not care for that custom. Why should his newly born daughters not inherit all he held when the time came? His wife, after all, was the only reason he had anything worth speaking of.

The Lady Rhoswen, the daughter of one of the king's most trusted nobles, had been presented to Darian as a gift for his years of dedication to Tanuba and her king. With their marriage, Darian gained wealth, lands including an estate just beyond the king's city of Mairéad, and a place in society that, despite all his victories on the field of battle, he had always been denied. With her, he was more than a soldier; he was a lord—one who held the king's ear on all matters. Indeed, it had been a most advantageous match.

What he had not anticipated to gain, though, and what he found he occasionally feared, was love for the woman. He had not expected it. He had not expected to care for her at all, but in the year they had been married, he had grown to love her. Darian had seen what love could do to a man were he not strong enough. He did not want to fall victim to that.

"You'll have quite the homecoming when this is through, won't you?" Nathan commented.

Darian knew better. He was surprised his king had made such a suggestion. When the battle for Quatara ended, Nathan would be the victor, and Darian wouldn't leave the country unless a matter of the crown called him back to his king's side. His time spent in his native Tanuba would become limited indeed.

But there would still be a homecoming of sorts. When Tanuba's rule was established, his wife and daughters would join him in Quatara. Rhoswen would not like it. She would not want to raise her children in such a place but it would not matter. She may have considered him a lord, as did everyone, but regardless of title, Darian was still the king's servant and would remain in Quatara as long as Nathan desired. When it was safer, Darian would have his family join him.

His wishes were carried out, and when his daughters, Mireille and Haleine, were six months old, they came along with their mother to Parthalan. Rhoswen's reaction was much how he expected it would be. After being separated for the better part of a year, he was met with calculated displeasure. She was careful to keep herself in check and held her tongue for nearly three months as they adjusted to a new life in this still wild country. He appreciated the effort, for as soon as his daughters were first placed in his arms, he ceased to care what she thought. He was captivated by his daughters. It was as dangerous, he supposed, as loving his wife.

"I do not like it here, my lord," Rhoswen said when she finally broke. "It is not my home."

They were in the library, as it was their custom to retire there after the evening meal. Rhoswen would sew while he worked on the problem that was Quatara. After she spoke, Darian lifted his quill from the letter he composed to the king and glanced at his wife.

"It is now," he said.

He returned to his work. The air was suddenly thick with their silence, but he didn't look up again until he heard the doors open.

"Where are you going?" he asked.

"To look in on our daughters."

"They are well," he said, sensing her uneasiness. "We would have heard, otherwise. The nurses are with them, and there are guards outside the nursery."

"Yes, my lord. It is for my own peace of mind that I go. However," she said as if reminding herself of his position in the household, "if this displeases you, I will remain."

He sighed and rose from his chair. "You do not displease me, my love. I will come with you and we will see that our daughters sleep peacefully."

Darian nodded to the two guardsmen at the entrance to the nursery. They bowed and opened the doors for the couple. He and Rhoswen walked inside, and the doors closed behind them.

His heart almost stopped when he saw what was before them. The two nurses were dead, brutally slaughtered. Even after the horrors he had seen during his years on the battlefield, the sight of it turned his stomach. Rhoswen immediately fainted, Darian catching her just before she fell to the floor. He yelled for the guards as he turned his head toward his daughters' cradles.

Two large cloaked figures stood there, each one bent over a cradle. The children were screaming.

Darian passed his wife to one of the guards and dove toward the kidnappers. He grabbed the man bent over Haleine's cradle by his shoulders. The second guard joined Darian, attacking Mireille's aggressor.

With a great effort, Darian pulled the man away from the cradle and his daughter. The man grunted and swung back with his arm, hitting Darian's face with his elbow. Darian's head snapped back from the blow, but he recovered quickly and prepared to face the man who threatened his daughter.

But the man wasn't a man at all. Darian staggered back from the shock as he looked at his opponent. It wasn't human. It was—Darian didn't know what it was. It towered over him—a wolf of some nightmarish sort. Its face was dark, except for its yellow eyes, and was horribly misshapen. The creature opened its mouth and snarled, exposing rows of sharp and stained teeth. Saliva dripped down, and the stench of its breath was awful, reminding Darian of dying men on a battlefield. He felt bile rise into his throat and swallowed hard to force it back into his stomach.

What manner of creature was this?

Upon hearing his daughter's cry, Darian looked past this wolf-ish monstrosity to the cradle where Haleine lay. Then he focused back on the creature, determined to rip the beast limb from limb. He sprang at the monster, his hands outstretched. The animal raised an arm and blocked Darian's assault.

But as Darian hit the floor, he realized the animal in front of him had done much more than defend itself against the attack mounted against it. Darian saw the gleam of knife-like claws pro-truding from the creature's paw and looked at his chest. The wound was grievous. Darian was surprised he had not yet felt the pain. He pressed his hand against it and looked up again.

The monsters were gone. The guard was dead, mutilated as the nurses had been. There was no noise coming from either cradle. Why was there no noise? With the commotion—why weren't they still screaming? Darian struggled to his feet and stumbled over to see his daughters' fate.

Haleine was safe and appeared to be unharmed. He nearly sobbed at the sight of her. He touched her head gently before turn-ing to the second cradle. Mireille was not there. Darian cried out in agony as he fell to the floor.

"My lord?" Darragh called, coming into the nursery. "Oh my lord, you are injured!"

"They've ta—they've taken Mireille," he gasped. "We must send men out imme-immediately and bring her back."

But they did not bring her back. Against Darragh's wishes, Dar-ian himself led the search until his wound drove him to the ground. He cried out his daughter's name in anguish before directing the others to continue on. They searched for days. They searched for weeks. They searched for months, but still they could not find her nor the creatures that had stolen her from her cradle.

On the day they would have celebrated the first year of her life, they buried her memory, since that was all they had of her.

Darian's physical wounds healed, leaving purple scars across his chest.

And in Quatara he remained.

Part One: Catalyst

CHAPTER 1

Darian was in the middle of the latest report on Quatara's rebel movements when the sudden sound of his youngest daughter's laughter stole his attention. He glanced at the opened window that overlooked the garden and smiled as more of her mirth reached his ears. At twelve years of age, Sighle was more noted for being silently solemn; to hear her laugh with such abandon was a rare sound. Darian dropped the parchment on his desk and moved to the window to see what caused his daughter such delight.

She was dancing, spinning and twirling as though the garden were a stage. Her elder sister, Haleine, stood in the center of Sighle's circle looking bemused with the girl's actions.

"Sighle, come sit," Haleine implored.

"Come dance," Sighle countered.

Haleine laughed. "I will do no such thing."

Sighle stopped spinning and walked toward Haleine with the grace of a drunkard. Haleine laughed again and tried to direct her sister to a bench, but Sighle was not yet finished. She grabbed Haleine's arms and tried pulling her into play.

"I do not know what has gotten into you, but stop it," Haleine said as she broke free of her sister's hold. "I will not dance."

"You will," Sighle said. "You'll see."

"I won't."

Darian was not surprised. Haleine was eighteen and no longer a child. She had grown into a lovely young woman, tall and slender, with her mother's blue eyes and the same thick auburn hair. Though more prone to humor than Sighle, Haleine remained well grounded and had more sense about her than a great many of the king's advisors. She would not be the sort to frolic in a garden.

"You'll dance at your wedding," Sighle said.

"Mayhap," Haleine said. "But I'd have to have a wedding first."

Darian frowned. The truth was she should have been two or three years married by now. She should have been running her own household, and the child she chased after should have been her own. The problem was not a lack a suitors. No, the girl's grace and beauty alone would have seen Parthalan overrun with men seeking a bride, but in infancy she had been promised to the king's second son, Revelin. The betrothal had been a reward for Darian's capture of Quatara, but Nathan wouldn't see the marriage done until his eldest son, Zoltano, had been wed. Darian's daughter could—and would—wait.

Which meant Sighle would wait as well. There was time yet. She was only twelve, after all, and he was in no hurry to see her married. When the time came, though, he thought she would do well enough. The girl had inherited his darker looks and likely wouldn't grow to be the beauty her sister was, but the Coileáin name alone would secure her a fine match.

However, those were concerns for another time, another day, perhaps even another year. All that mattered now were his bright and beautiful girls and the joy they had found on this day in this place.

Darian Coileáin considered himself fortunate to have two daughters, but his heart still ached for the third.

Sighle had resumed her dance, and Haleine her exasperation, when the door behind him opened. Darian ignored it and kept watching his daughters.

"My lord, a letter from the king has arrived," Darragh said.

Sighle spotted him watching in the window then and stopped spinning. Her arms fell to her side and she stared at him.

"Leave it on the desk," Darian said. "Find the king's man a meal and a place to rest until I have a response ready. Assure him it will not take long."

"The messenger is Lord Cathal," Darragh said.

Darian turned from the window. Adomnan Cathal was anything but a common messenger. He was a nobleman, born and raised, and the closest thing Darian ever had to a friend. Darian had come to know him when they were both trying to carve out a name for themselves in the king's army. They had fought together in several battles, including the one that had given the king Quatara. While Darian had stayed in Parthalan, Cathal had gone back to Tanuba to inherit his father's titles and lands. He now acted as Darian's eyes and ears in the king's court, but never once had he personally delivered a letter. If he were here now, it could not be good news he carried.

"Then you best let him in," Darian said.

Darragh bowed his head and opened the library door. Cathal walked in, still wearing his mud-spattered cloak and boots. Darian silently took in the man's appearance and closed the window.

"My lord Coileáin," Cathal said.

"You're the king's messenger," Darian said.

Cathal produced the folded parchment. "Today, I am."

Darian looked at the letter in Cathal's hand. Nathan trusted Cathal because Darian trusted him. Whatever was written on that parchment, Darian wouldn't like it.

Cathal crossed the room and held out the letter. Darian took it. He turned the letter over in his hands and looked at the king's seal. How many letters like this had he opened? How many times had he broken this seal to find requests for counsel or an appearance at court? How many times had Nathan sent a summons to war? None of them had ever been delivered by a nobleman. None of them had ever filled Darian with even a fraction of the dread he felt now.

"What tidings does the king send?" he asked. "Something extraordinary must have happened to warrant you standing here."

"Just read it, Darian."

Darian nodded and broke the seal. He opened the letter and saw it was written in the king's own hand. Even a summons to war had been written by a scribe. Darian read what the king had written and then read the words a second time. He read them a third time, hoping he had somehow misunderstood their meaning.

"Darian," Cathal said.

He looked up. Cathal had removed his cloak and now sat in one of the chairs in front of the fire.

"Do you know what this letter says?" Darian asked.

Cathal nodded. "It is an honor."

There was no doubt about that. It was an honor so great that even a man as ambitious as Darian Coileáin had never thought it possible.

He went and sat in the chair opposite Cathal. "Rhoswen will not like this."

Cathal shrugged. "You will make her understand. You have before."

He had done that. He kept her from leaving after Mireille's loss. He kept her from leaving after Sighle's birth. She loved him enough to stay in a land she hated, but would this latest request of the king's be asking too much of her? Would she still agree to stay?

"Would you want this for your family?" Darian asked.

"Every man would."

"Even knowing what we know, you would want this?"

"Even then. Yes," Cathal said. "But the king chose you."

"Where is the king now?"

"On a ship bound for Lira."

"He's not wasting any time, is he?"

"He never has," Cathal said. "He has his agreement signed and now he wants it sealed."

Lira was the island nation to the south of Tanuba, on the other side of the Endellion Sea. Long had the monarchs of both countries worked toward an alliance. The last round of negotiations had occurred two weeks earlier. Darian had been summoned to the king's side for the event, but the Quatari rebels had kept Darian from going. He had heard nothing on the subject since. Now he knew why.

"And for that he needs me. He needs this," Darian said. He held up the letter, and Cathal nodded. "You are to act as escort?"

Cathal nodded again. "He thought it would make it easier. He knows you cannot leave."

"He does not want me to leave."

Cathal shrugged. "They are the same, are they not?"

Darian was spared answering by his wife's arrival. He was not ready to see her yet. He was not ready to share the letter, but he should have known she would come as soon as she heard of Cathal's arrival. She considered Cathal just as much a friend as Darian did. As she entered, Cathal rose and crossed the room to greet her. Darian stood and turned in their direction.

"Adomnan," Rhoswen said, warmth infusing her voice. "I did not know you were coming. Darian didn't tell me."

"Your husband did not know," Cathal said. He took Rhoswen's hand and kissed it. "I'm imposing upon his good will."

Rhoswen stood on her toes to kiss his cheek. "You could never be an imposition. For how long will you be with us?"

"Just a day," Darian said. "His ship leaves for Lira in the morning."

"And the other matter?" Cathal asked. "The king will be expecting your answer."

"The king already has my answer," Darian said, "and he knows it. You'd not be here, otherwise. Find Darragh and tell him to make the arrangements."

Cathal nodded. "I'll leave you to it," he said, offering Rhoswen a bow. "My lady."

Rhoswen didn't notice the bow. She didn't notice Cathal as he left the room. Her eyes were locked on Darian.

"What arrangements?" Rhoswen asked when Cathal had gone. Her cheer from earlier had disappeared. "Why is Adomnan here?"

"The king sent him with a letter."

"The king sent him," Rhoswen said. Her voice showed she understood the implications. "Why? What does Nathan want now?"

Darian held out the parchment. "Our daughter."

Rhoswen crossed the distance between them and snatched the parchment from his hand. While she read the king's letter, Darian went to the window to look again at his girls. They sat together on a bench, the younger reading aloud from a book. He turned away when he heard Rhoswen gasp. She still gripped the letter but appeared to be reading it through again. How many times would she do that? Would three be enough, or would she need three times more?

"No," she said finally. "Nathan cannot do this. Haleine is already promised. She's to be married to his own son."

"That will not happen now."

"*This* will not happen," Rhoswen said, shaking the letter at him. "You cannot allow it."

"This will happen. It is happening and I cannot stop it," Darian said. "The king wants this. He wants Haleine for this."

"Well, he can't have her."

"Of course he can have her. It's already done."

Rhoswen shook her head. "Make all the arrangements you want. I won't let her be sent to that place. I won't let her be married to that man."

"That man is the crown prince of Lira."

"Yes, and I know all too well what is said about him," Rhoswen said. "For eighteen years, Darian, you fiercely guarded that girl from all threats, and now you're willing to just give her over to him? To that?"

"Not willing, no."

"But you'll do it anyway," Rhoswen said, "because you have always given the king what he wants."

"I have."

"We lost Mireille because Nathan wanted this godforsaken land that still fights against you, and now we've lost Haleine because Nathan has no daughters of his own. What will he demand next? When does it end?"

"It doesn't."

"No," she said. "This isn't happening. There has to be a way—there has to be someone else. Haleine isn't the only girl in his kingdom. He can—"

"This is an honor," Darian said. "Nathan chose Haleine to honor us."

"Well, I don't want it. He can keep his honor. I'll keep my daughter."

"No, you won't," Darian said. "She was never yours to keep. She has always belonged to the Maoilriains. I know you do not want this, but the king—"

"I'll not call that man my king," she said, "and if you do this, I'll not call you my husband."

"You may do as you wish," Darian said, forcing himself to say the words. "It won't change this. The king has decided, madam, and we will obey."

"You are no better than a slave," she spat.

Darian sprang forward and took the letter from her. He tore it in half and half again before throwing the pieces to the floor. Rhoswen watched them fall before kneeling to pick them up.

"That is true," he said. "And you are no better than a slave's wife, but our daughter will be queen."

Rhoswen stood and lifted her head to reveal her tears. Darian placed his hand on her cheek.

"It's not so very far away," he said.

"Only the other side of the ocean," Rhoswen said as she walked away from him.

"She is your daughter. She is my daughter," Darian said. "She is strong enough for this. She is strong enough for anything she may find there. She'll not be lost."

"No. Just given into the hands of a monster."

Rhoswen stopped in front of the fire and dropped the pieces of parchment into the flames. Neither of them said anything as they watched the king's will burn.

"I do not want this," Rhoswen said when it had been reduced to ash.

Darian nodded. "Pretend."

—◈—

The day, though still young, had been rather exhausting. It began when Haleine awoke to find her sister had joined her in bed some time during the night. When questioned about her presence, Sighle responded by saying, "It's cold."

It wasn't cold. It was the warmest day of the year yet, uncommonly warm for the spring season, but Haleine did not scold her sister nor call her out for her lie. She suspected Sighle to be lonely, and there was no one else with whom she could keep company. As it was a feeling with which Haleine was all too familiar, she resigned herself to being her sister's constant companion.

But now that they had reached a lull in their activities, Haleine sat on the bench with her eyes closed and her face turned to the sun. Sighle was all but in her lap, reading aloud from whatever book her tutors had assigned her. Her voice was thin and hesitant but still rhythmic enough to lull Haleine to an even more somnolent state. Haleine was nearly asleep when one of her father's pages interrupted.

"My lady?"

Haleine opened her eyes and looked at the boy who stood before them. As none of the servants ever referred to Sighle as anything other than the 'young miss,' there was no question the boy had been sent for Haleine.

"Your father summons you," the boy said.

Sighle dropped her book, and he immediately bent to retrieve it while both Haleine and Sighle lifted their heads to look at the library window.

"My lady?" the boy said.

Haleine nodded and gently eased Sighle off her. She stood, smoothed her skirts and took the book from the boy. She held it out to her sister, but Sighle still stared at the window.

"I'm not yet finished," Sighle said.

"You're finished for now. Here," Haleine said. She took her sister's hands and placed the book between them. "Take this."

Sighle looked at her. "Do you know what he wants?"

"Not in the least," Haleine said, "but I imagine only that the queen summons me again to court."

Sighle launched herself off the bench and wrapped her arms around Haleine. "What do I do without you?"

"One of the maids can listen to you read," Haleine said.

"None of the maids know how to read."

Haleine worked her way out of Sighle's grasp. "They can still listen."

"My lady," the boy pressed. "Your father waits."

Haleine leaned in and kissed the top of Sighle's head before following the boy out of the garden and into the castle. She did not know what had happened, but from the way the servants moved about, it was clear something had. She wove her way around them as she walked to the stairs.

She stopped at their base when she saw Adomnan Cathal. She knew him well but had never seen the man outside of Nathan's palace. Never before had he come to Quatara, but now he stood across the room with her father's steward. Both men had their heads bent over a piece of parchment. Lord Cathal lifted his head first and saw her watching him. He bowed then, bending far deeper at the waist than her status required. She nodded in return and hurried above stairs to the library.

Both her parents waited there. Her mother sat by the fire, silently crying and trying desperately to stop. Haleine couldn't stop staring at her and didn't until her father said her name. He stood at the opposite end of the room, leaning against his desk. Haleine couldn't recall ever seeing him lean before. A perfect soldier was her father, always at the ready. It was his life's pride, but now he used the desk as though he lacked the ability to stand on his own.

"What has happened?" she asked.

"You are to leave us."

"Have I been summoned to attend the queen?"

"Not the queen, no."

"Then what is it? Why are you so defeated? Why is Mother crying? And why is Lord Cathal below stairs bowing to me as though I were someone other than a nobleman's daughter?"

Her father lowered his eyes to the floor. "I have told you of the possible alliance between Tanuba and Lira, haven't I?"

"Possible?" she asked. "It must be signed by now, isn't it?"

"It is," Darian said. "Part of the agreement states Tanuba will provide a wife for Lira's crown prince, Maddox Aelhaeran."

Her mother gasped then, the sound of someone trying too hard to hold back a sob. When Haleine looked at her, Rhoswen wiped her cheeks as though it would erase what Haleine already knew. She turned back to her father.

"Do you mean for me to be that wife?"

"The king does, yes."

"But Revelin," she said. "What of Revelin? Does the king forget that I am—?"

"The king forgets nothing." Darian brought his head up. His eyes were the only part of him that showed any life. "And I will not have you showing such familiarity with the prince of Tanuba."

"We have been betrothed since the day of my birth, Father," Haleine said. "Why would I ever call him by his title and not his name?"

"Because he is your betrothed no longer," Darian said. "A new match has been made for you. A better match."

It wasn't possible. Revelin was handsome and kind. He was a good man whom she loved and who loved her in return. He was a man she would be proud to call husband.

Haleine shook her head. "There is no better match."

"There is one," Darian said. "And this is it."

Her mother stood and walked toward her. Haleine put her arm out to discourage Rhoswen from coming any closer.

"Father," Haleine said. "You can't—"

"Do not fight me on this," he said. "It is done, and you will go."

"I don't want to go," Haleine said. "I do not wish to do this."

Darian looked away. "I don't care."

The words were a slap in the face. Haleine recoiled and came up against her mother. Rhoswen put a hand on her shoulder. The touch, meant to be reassuring, had quite the opposite effect, but Haleine was too stunned to shrug it off.

"When?" she asked.

"On the morrow," her father answered.

On the morrow. Emotion rose inside of her, and Haleine laughed before it could come out as anything else. She had waited years for her wedding, but it couldn't be happening like this. Not to a stranger in a strange land. Not to someone who wasn't Revelin.

Her stomach lurched, and she put her hand over her mouth. She couldn't stand there anymore watching her father stare at the floor. She left the library. Her mother called her name, but Haleine ignored her and ran to her own chamber. She burst through the door to find four servants packing her things into a pair of trunks.

"Out," she said. "All of you, out!"

They curtsied or bowed and left the room. When she was alone, she emptied each trunk, throwing every carefully folded garment haphazardly and letting them fall where they may. Afterward, she sat on the floor between them and looked at the shambles her life had become.

On the morrow. Good God.

———∽∽∽———

Haleine didn't see her parents or her sister again until the next morning when it was time for her to leave. She entered the court-yard and saw her mother and sister waiting there. They were not dressed for traveling.

"You're not coming," Haleine said to spare her mother the task.

"Adomnan will see you safely there," Rhoswen said.

Haleine looked past her mother to see Lord Cathal standing with her father beside the carriage. He bowed to her. Her father did not.

"Very well," Haleine said. "He has never failed Father. I am sure he will see this chore done."

"Haleine," Rhoswen said. "Your father cannot leave. You know this."

"And you do not travel without him. Yes, I do know this."

"The king will be there," Rhoswen tried. "The entire royal family, as a matter of fact."

"But not my own."

Rhoswen struggled to respond. Haleine didn't want to look at her mother anymore and focused instead on her sister. Sighle watched the activity with quiet understanding, and Haleine wished she felt as calm as her sister looked. She reached out and touched Sighle's cheek.

"I will miss you."

Sighle looked directly at her. Haleine was taken aback by how dark her sister's eyes were. She was their father. Haleine hadn't noticed before just how alike they were.

"You'll find love," Sighle said.

Her mother smoothed the hair on her youngest daughter's head. "Yes, yes, of course she will," Rhoswen said, her voice unnaturally cheerful. "I did, didn't I? The prince will assuredly be as fine a man as your father."

Haleine nodded, but she knew she could not allow herself such hope. She understood that she left love behind. Her mother cried now and came forward to hug her. Haleine allowed it but was incapable of reciprocating any emotion. Sighle did not hug her nor touch her in any way. She stayed attached to their mother's side.

"You'll dance now," Sighle said.

Haleine could feel tears forming behind her eyes. She didn't want Sighle to see them, so she turned away before they had a chance to manifest further and walked to the carriage. Cathal bowed as she approached, but her father stood rigid. When she was close enough, Darian took her hand in his. He kissed it and then her cheek.

"Remember it is an honor to have been chosen," he said.

But the honor did not belong to her. The king had given her to Lira to honor her father. The words were on her tongue but she did not say them. Instead she allowed him to help her into the carriage. She slid along the seat to the opposite corner. Cathal climbed in and sat near the door. She felt his eyes on her but she refused to look at him.

"My lady?" Cathal said once the carriage started moving. When she didn't respond, he tried again. "Haleine?"

"How long?" she asked.

"Ten days, if the weather holds. If it doesn't, I don't know. But you will be quite safe. I promise you that."

She thought back to her mother's tears in the library and nodded. She would see.

Haleine had never sailed before but found it to be an agreeable-enough experience. If she hadn't been journeying to a foreign land to marry a man she had never met, she might have even called it pleasant. Her only companions were Lord Cathal and a maid whose name Haleine did not know nor cared to learn. Whenever in their presence, they would try to engage her in a conversation in which she had no interest, so early on she found a refuge at the bow of the ship where neither of them would seek her company.

She spent as much time there as she could, enjoying the wind and the sun and the salt air while watching the ship cut through the water. The endlessness of the ocean was soothing, and there was nothing more fitting than not being able to see anything upon the horizon. One morning that would cease to be true. The ocean would give way and her future would remain. She returned to her cabin each night another day closer to discovering what awaited there.

The weather stayed favorable, and the ship arrived in Lira on the tenth day. As it was too large to dock at the port itself, the anchor was dropped and a skiff prepared to take both Haleine and Lord Cathal ashore. While the sailors prepared, Haleine stood on the bow and took in the sight of her new country.

Two piers stretched into the water. Several small vessels were tethered to one. The other was empty of both boats and people. The people, instead, walked along the tawny beach. Some moved toward the water while others made their way to a modest settlement established even farther away from the sea. Beyond that, there was the green of trees and grass, all plush and lovely. But as pretty as the scene was, Haleine was surprised by its simplicity. For such a rich country, Lira did not seem like much.

"This is the port of Eoten," Cathal said as he joined her. He leaned against the rail. "It's certainly not the largest port in Lira, but it is the closest to Parthalan. King Amatheon's palace is located in the city of Eluned. We'll travel the rest of the way by carriage. It'll take most of the day, but we should be there before nightfall."

She was disappointed it would not take longer but did not say so.

"Princess?" Cathal said.

Haleine looked at him. "I would prefer you not address me as such."

"Why is that?"

"I am not a princess."

"You will be soon enough. Why wait?"

"I am not a princess."

"Are you nervous? You needn't be," Cathal said. "A marriage to Revelin would have given you the same title."

A marriage to Revelin wouldn't have made her mother sob, nor would it have made her father unable to look her in the eye.

"I do not marry Revelin," she said. "The prince."

"No," Cathal said. "Instead you're marrying the crown prince of a country richer than your own."

"How fortunate," Haleine said dryly.

"Yes," Cathal agreed. "Quite."

She did not know if her tone had been missed or ignored but did not care to ask.

"Are you afraid?" Cathal asked next.

"No." She didn't know if it was a lie.

Cathal nodded and pushed off the rail. "Good girl."

———∿∿∿———

Cathal, in an attempt to tease a conversation out of her, sat by the carriage's window and described everything they passed, but she sat in the opposite corner and let him ramble without comment. Despite knowing very little about Lira or Eluned apart from their location on a map, she didn't care what any of it looked like. It didn't interest her. She wanted only to hide.

Her opportunity to do so was lost when the carriage stopped within the palace walls. The door opened for them, and Cathal exited first. He reached for her, and she slid across the seat and took his hand. He helped her out of the carriage, and she took her first look at her new home.

The courtyard was dry and dusty, filled with scores of soldiers and their mounts. Servants stood to the side, all with bowed heads. Only the pages moved as they sprang forward to take horses from their riders. In the distance were the rooftops of two other buildings that likely belonged to the stables and the soldiers' barracks, but in the center stood the palace, looming over all. Built from white gray rock, it was beautiful and frighteningly immense. Four tall towers seemed to scrape the sky. Closer to earth, ivy-laden trellises climbed the walls and wrapped around balcony railings. The windows reflected the late-day sun, casting a glow about the castle. Cathal moved to lead her inside, and she hesitated, feeling both unworthy and unwilling to set foot in such a structure.

"My lady?" Cathal asked.

She looked at him and took his arm. "I am ready."

Inside, they were greeted by an older man of average height, graying hair and a subdued though not unkind smile. He dressed well, but the quality of the fabrics told her he was Amatheon's man.

The man bowed. "Lord Cathal."

"Ceallach," Cathal said. "May I present Lady Haleine Coileáin?"

Ceallach turned to her and bowed again. "My lady."

She nodded but looked away to examine the banners hanging from the walls and ceiling. Some of them she recognized as Lira's crest, a rearing unicorn against a background of silver and blue. Others featured the emerald-and-gold-backed lion of the Maoilriains. A third banner showed the unicorn and the lion together on a sea of deep purple. It was, she realized, a symbol of the alliance. She was a symbol of the alliance. She frowned and redirected her attention to Ceallach.

"The king asked me to greet you," the man was saying. "I apologize I was not in Eoten. I did not mean for you to travel here alone."

"It is no matter," Cathal said when he saw Haleine would not respond. "Where are our masters?"

"The royal families—both of them—are not here now. They're on a hunt," Ceallach said. "We did not know when exactly you might arrive. But don't fear; you will have a proper presentation at dinner this evening, my lady. It'll give you ample time to rest."

Haleine again said nothing. The smile on Ceallach's face dimmed. Cathal gave her a look that suggested he was disappointed with her manners.

"I think rest would be an excellent idea," Cathal said. "We thank you."

His tone reinforced his look. He wanted her to thank Ceallach as well, but she did not. She would not. She didn't care what either man thought of her manners.

"My lady?" Ceallach said. "This way, if you will?"

She considered the request and nodded. Better to hide in the privacy of a chamber than stand stubborn in an entry.

Cathal excused himself, and Ceallach alone showed her to her chamber. He led her through the hall to a flight of stairs and up them. As they walked, he talked to her about the palace and the king and queen. The only thing of interest to her was how Ceallach did not once mention the prince.

"And these shall be your rooms, my lady," Ceallach said, opening a set of doors. "I hope you will find them to your liking."

He stepped aside to allow her to enter. She did so and gave the room a perfunctory glance. There were candles and flower-filled vases on tabletops. Beautifully crafted furniture and lovely woven rugs were scattered throughout. A large fireplace had been built into a wall to her right, and to her left were a pair of tall glass doors that opened onto a balcony. It was indeed lovely and by far the most luxurious bedchamber she had ever seen, but she didn't care about any of it. She wanted to know about the man she was to marry.

"Your maid is called Bronagh, and she will be here shortly to attend your needs," Ceallach said. "She will fetch you anything you

16

require, and I will return to collect you for dinner when it is time. Have you any questions?"

She looked at Ceallach. "When will I meet the prince?"

What little smile he had left disappeared completely. "Soon, my lady. You will meet him soon."

Ceallach bowed then and backed out of the room, closing the doors behind him. Haleine sank into a nearby chair and stared at the doors as she contemplated his statement and the regret that had dripped from his voice. It was not how she thought he would answer, but she shouldn't have been surprised. More and more did she understand her mother's tears. Something was wrong with Lira's crown prince.

Why hadn't her father prepared her for this? To what fate had she been condemned?

She didn't know how long she'd been sitting when Bronagh arrived. Her maid was short and stocky but not fat. She wore a simple gray dress and shoes. The scarf meant to cover her head had slipped to her shoulders, revealing straight brown hair. She entered the room through a side door and carried with her a tray bearing a decanter and a goblet. She placed the tray on a table near the fireplace, picked up the goblet and came to stand in front of Haleine.

"My lady," she said, bobbing a slight curtsey. "My name is Bronagh and I am—"

"My maid, yes," Haleine said. "Ceallach told me to expect you."

Bronagh nodded. "Good. Well, I've brought you some wine and I've ordered a bath. We'll get you refreshed before the feast tonight. I imagine you must be tired from your travels."

Haleine supposed she was but what she really felt was lost. Bronagh held out the goblet.

"Here," Bronagh said. "Drink this. It will help."

As Haleine drank her wine, a barrage of maids arrived, using the same door Bronagh had. They were different shapes, sizes and ages, but all were dressed in the same simple garments. Each woman carried a bucket and they paid her no mind as they disappeared through yet another door. When they filed out again, each took the time to curtsey before leaving.

"This way, my lady," Bronagh said, gesturing to the side chamber.

Haleine put her goblet on the floor and followed Bronagh. The small room was a bathroom with an oval tub of white marble at its center. Haleine had been raised in a household of wealth and privilege, and still she marveled at the luxury of it all. She was certain it was not what she should have done but she could not help herself.

"Come," Bronagh said. "This will help you find yourself again."

Bronagh helped her undress and then into the tub. Haleine assured the woman she was capable of washing herself and Bronagh withdrew into the bedchamber, closing the door behind her.

Haleine sank into the warm water until it lapped her chin. The grime and dirt from her journey soaked off her skin, and the sensation was marvelous. She never had had a bath quite as glamorous as this one felt. She used the soap the maid had left for her and washed herself thoroughly from head to toe.

When that was done, she relaxed. She laid her head against the side of the tub and closed her eyes. How long might she rest here before Bronagh or someone else came to fetch her? She endeavored to find out, but the water grew cold before Bronagh returned, so Haleine climbed out and wrapped herself in the robe Bronagh had left behind. She cinched the robe around her waist and returned to the bedchamber.

Bronagh had gone but not, Haleine noticed, without laying out a gown and the proper accessories for her to wear. She walked to the bed to examine the ensemble. The gown was not one of her own.

"You must be Haleine."

She was surprised and scared by the deep male voice. Apparently she wasn't alone after all. She looked around the room to see who had spoken.

She spied him in the corner, sitting in one of the room's multiple chairs. He was young, unmistakably handsome and richly dressed. His hair was black and neatly trimmed. His eyes were a cool blue and he looked her over with interest. She desperately wished she wore something more than the thin linen robe. He stood and walked toward her.

"Who are you?" she asked even though she was aware this would be Maddox Aelhaeran, the crown prince of Lira and the man she was to marry.

"I think you know," he said.

She nodded. "I do."

"Then perhaps you are smarter than I thought you would be. Most women I have known can hardly think for themselves."

"That is not the case with me," she said.

He stopped just inches away from her and took her in with one long, probing look. He tilted his head to the side and licked his lips. Haleine felt her stomach churn, and she breathed deeply, willing him to leave.

"Really." He took a small step back. "How old are you?"

"Eighteen, my lord."

"Old to be as yet unmarried."

"Yes, my lord."

"And unspoiled?" he asked. "I won't have another man's leavings between my sheets."

Her face flushed. "I am a virgin."

"Your father couldn't marry you off? I can't imagine there wasn't some man somewhere hot for you."

"I was before promised to Prince Revelin Maoilriain."

"Were you? Why didn't you marry him?"

"It was determined our union would not come about until after Prince Zoltano had been wed. They sent me here first."

"Revelin," Maddox laughed. "Well, that certainly settles the question of your purity. I can't say Revelin would know what to do with a girl, whether he was married to her or not."

Maddox continued to chuckle, obviously impressed by his cleverness. Haleine bit her lip and looked away.

"You may thank me if you like," he said next.

She raised her head. "Thank you, my lord?"

"For saving you from a life of tedium with that honor-bound prick. Just in time too, I wager. I hear they've nearly agreed on a dowry for that cunt Feond considers a princess. Considering the amount of whoring Zaide Romanza's done, I didn't think there would be enough in her father's coffers to get Nathan to take her as his daughter-in-law."

She stared at Maddox in wide-eyed shock. She had met the princess on several occasions at Nathan's court, and though she had never cared for the woman, she never would insult her in such a manner. Haleine didn't know what she was to think about this man so cavalier about such crudeness, this man who would soon be her husband.

"How he must have hated to give you up," Maddox said. "Come, let's have a look at Tanuba's finest offering."

His hand rose and moved to untie her robe. She covered his hand with her own.

"You will not, my lord," she said.

19

"Who are you to tell me no?"

"You will not, my lord."

"I want to see what I marry."

"And you shall, for after we are married, I will not have the power to deny you," she said. "But until that night you will not see anything."

The look in his eyes changed and he smiled. The sight of it turned her blood cold. He put his hand behind her head at the base of her neck. She let out a small gasp as his fingers dug into her skin.

"You have spirit about you," he said. "It doesn't matter though. I'll beat it out of you soon enough."

She felt sick, far more so than she had when her father announced her betrothal to this man. She looked at him now in horror and tried to escape from his hold, but his grip only tightened. The pain caused her to relent until she felt his other hand work the tie at her waist and slip inside her robe.

"You will not!" she cried and pushed him away.

"The hell I won't," he hissed. He grabbed her by the throat and pulled her close. "I will look and I will touch and I will take whatever I desire."

He stripped the robe from her body and released her. She stood there, the robe piled at her feet, as he examined her. He circled her, running his hands over her skin. When he faced her again, he touched her breasts and squeezed them. She stepped back then, but he didn't allow her to gain any distance from him. She was desperate to be free of his touch and fought against him any way she could. He laughed at her efforts, pinned her arms to her side and used the weight of his body to force her back toward the bed.

"Maddox!"

He stopped at the sound of his name. She took advantage of his distraction and broke free of his hands. She swept her robe off the floor and put it on. She held it closed, pulling the material as tight as she could manage, before seeing Ceallach advancing toward them.

"You are not to be in here," Ceallach said sharply. "You will leave at once."

"You do not have the power to order me about, old man," Maddox said, focusing once again on Haleine. "I am pleased with what I see before me and I will do as I like."

Her face flushed again but this time with anger. "You are alone in your pleasure, for I have seen what is before me and it pleases me not."

He slapped her across the face and she fell to the floor. Tears started to come, and this time she could not stop them.

"You will not speak to me like that!" he shouted. "Ever!"

"Your highness," Ceallach said. "I must insist you leave immediately."

She rested on her knees as she waited to see Maddox's reaction to Ceallach's request. To her surprise, he walked away and left the room. Ceallach knelt at her side and reached for her.

"You will not touch me!" she declared.

She lurched to her feet, feeling both dizzy and ill. Her throat ached and her cheek stung. Ceallach again made an attempt to help her, and she lashed out at him until he got to his feet and backed away.

"I must apologize, my lady," Ceallach said. "He was not—"

"I am owed more than an apology," she interrupted.

"I am sorry, my lady, I—"

"Stop!" she screamed. "You saw what he was doing, and you know what he would have done had you not come through those doors! And knowing this, knowing the sort of man he is, you—your masters—will still have me marry him?"

Ceallach looked to the floor.

"He is a monster," she seethed.

Ceallach still did not speak.

"Go," she said.

"Please, my lady—"

"Go."

"They await your presence in the dining hall."

The absurdity of the statement made her laugh. "I am not going. Please extend my apologies to the king and his wife. Tell them of how I have met their son if you deem it appropriate, but I will not come to dine with them this night."

"You should eat."

"What does it matter if I eat? If you will marry me to that monster, you already sentence me to death. Starvation would be a kinder way to see it done," she said. "Now get out."

Ceallach nodded and left without another word. When he was gone, she collapsed again to her knees, placed her head in her hands and cried.

CHAPTER 2

James ap Seoras was not the sort to take risks. Perhaps it was the reason he was well into his twentieth year and had yet to find himself a wife. That, in his grandmother's eyes, made him a family failure. Sarai had been married with children at the age of fifteen. His parents, Seoras and Mahree, married at sixteen and he was the result. A daughter had followed, born when he was two. Her name had been Saoirse and she lived but two years before fever took her. A stillborn lad soon followed, but when James was five, his parents had another child, another boy, and named him Aaron. Aaron had thrived and now spent as much time as possible away from the farm chasing after the village girls. Aaron would not fail his family the way James had.

The whole thing was wearing on him. It wasn't that he hadn't been presented with opportunity. His family's farm had grown over the years into quite a thriving homestead, one of the most prosperous in Enimode, and, as a result, his father had been approached by more than one man looking for a good match for his daughter. Seoras brought each proposal to his eldest son and laid it before him with the same terms. James wouldn't be forced into anything he didn't want.

His father, as well intentioned as he was, didn't understand James's objections. The problem wasn't that he was opposed to marriage. He wasn't. It was more that he didn't want to be married simply because he had reached a certain age. He wanted there to be more to it than that. He didn't know exactly what was missing but knew all the same it was something each prospective bride had lacked.

The latest girl had been no exception. She had made such an impression on him that James couldn't even remember her name now. She was of a good family from the village of Kewe, one of Enimode's neighbors, and would have brought with her a substantial marriage portion. Seoras never said a word, but James had been able to tell that his father had given considerable thought to forcing his first born into accepting the offer. Mahree had remained quiet, but Sarai, however, had been significantly more vocal. It was his duty to marry the Kewe lass, she had said. He needed to set aside the nonsense of there being something more—of wanting something more—and settle for what had been offered.

Duty or not, nonsense or not, that morning, James still had dashed all their hopes when he had given his answer. The rest of the day had been rather intolerable, spent doing chores while warding off his grandmother's lectures and his parents' disappointment, and both James and his brother had disappeared as soon as the opportunity had presented itself. Aaron had gone to the village on an errand for their father, and James had taken to the forest.

He had wandered along the paths he'd traveled since boyhood and ended up on the edge of a secluded pond located not far from the homestead. James walked to the end farthest away from home and sat with his back against a willow tree. Occasionally, he leaned forward to select a pebble from the ground to throw into the water, but mostly he just absorbed the peace around him. He suspected he would need all the calm he could muster were he to return to the farm that day. The sun was starting to set when his solitude came to an end.

"Your mother told me I'd find you down here."

James smiled. He didn't have to look to know who was there. It was Dana. They had been friends for as long as James could remember. So long, in fact, Dana was more a brother than anything else. And when James did look, he saw Dana hadn't changed much from the last time they had seen each other.

They were the same age, height and build, but their similarities ended there. James had inherited his parents' darker features, brown hair and eyes. Dana's hair was blond and his eyes blue. Mahree often called those eyes a sort of net and waited for the day when Dana came back to their homestead with a wife on his arm. That day hadn't come yet, and James thought it never would. Dana wasn't the sort to settle. He never had been.

James couldn't remember how old they were when Seoras first discovered Dana asleep in the barn. Aaron, he recalled, was still in his cradle, so they couldn't have been more than five. However, he did remember clearly the awe in which he had regarded Dana when his father first brought the boy into the house. James had stared at

Dana, a boy his own age, with no parents of his own, no home of his own and perhaps no fear of anything as he spoke to Seoras and Mahree as though they were old friends and not complete strangers.

Mahree immediately adopted Dana. She tried to hold onto him for as long as she could, which, as it turned out, wasn't very long. Even with a family willing to take him in, Dana was still prone to disappearing for increasingly long lengths of time. At first, Mahree worried incessantly about her surrogate son, but every time he disappeared, he returned eventually to the family's homestead.

In between visits, Dana roamed around as he pleased, his only companions his horse and a tiny pegasus named Faolan, and no one seemed to be nagging him to find a wife. When James would ask why his friend would willingly submit himself to such torture as a visit, Dana said he liked the company because it sometimes got lonely traveling from place to place with no one to tell him what to do. Some days, James didn't think that sounded too awfully bad at all.

James threw a pebble into the water. "My mother wasn't supposed to know I'm down here."

"I know," Dana said. "Better luck next time."

"Next time I think perhaps I'll just run far, far away," James said, "never to be heard from again."

"I've been trying to get you to do that for years now."

"Aye, well, I mean to do it now."

"We'll see," Dana said as he sat down on James's right. "I saw Aaron at the tavern."

James nodded. "Since he was supposed to be at the mill, it only makes sense that he'd be at the tavern. What was he doing there?"

"Drinking, when I saw him," Dana said. "But Rhiannon tells me he was meeting a secret lover."

"Another one?"

"Your brother's a young man in love."

"In lust, more like it."

"Nothing wrong with that."

James snorted. "Do you know how many secret lovers that boy has? None of them, by the way, secret."

Dana shrugged. "You know how those things go," he said. "A village like this, everyone knows who's doing what and who they're doing it with."

"Aye. I know that all too well." James sighed. "What are you doing with Rhiannon anyway?"

24

"What do you mean?"

"I mean I like going to that tavern, and for now her father likes us being there. But if you start carrying on with his daughter, I suspect our welcome will quickly come to an end."

Dana grinned. "There is a precedent for that, isn't there?"

"Several."

"She brought me ale and gossip, nothing else, I swear. The tavern wench remains untouched. At least by me," Dana said. "Now do you want to tell me why you're in such a foul mood, or shall I guess?"

"If you've seen my mother, I doubt very much you need to guess."

"She might have mentioned something about another rejected marriage proposal," Dana said. "A promising one from the sound of things, and Sarai is looking to pitch a fit for your treachery."

"Did my mother tell you that too?"

"She didn't have to," Dana said. "Your grandmother started in on me before your mother took pity and sent me after you."

"If Gran found fault with you, she must really be angry. God, you'd think I was doing something a lot worse than refusing an offer of marriage."

"Well, you're twenty years of age and have no lads of your own," Dana said. "It's odd."

"You don't have any lads either."

"None I know of, anyway," Dana said. "What was the lass's name this time?"

"Damned if I know," James said. "Awful, isn't it? I met the girl, and I can't even remember what she was called."

"Well, you're a man of some property. No one expects men of property to remember every pretty face."

"Some property? There's a barn and a two-room cottage."

"You forgot the root cellar."

"The root cellar, aye," James said. "That does make it one of the grand halls, doesn't it?"

"In Enimode, anyway."

James laughed and gave Dana a sideways look. "What are you even doing here? We weren't expecting you back for a week or more."

"Something's come up, you might say."

"Oh aye? And what's that?"

"A cure for your ails," Dana said. "For a time at least."

"Another feast in another lord's hall?"

"No."

"Then you must have found a new house of ill repute."

"No. There's hardly time for that now," Dana said, "which is too bad because I think you could really benefit from it. But again, time's short, and what I am about to tell you is very serious."

"That would be a first," James said. "The only thing you've ever been serious about is not being serious."

"Well, that's not true anymore."

"And why not?"

"Because things are going to change."

"What do you mean? What things?"

Dana picked up a small stick and began to strip the bark from it with a dagger he removed from his belt. He shrugged.

"The world to which we are accustomed is going to change very soon," Dana said. "And not for the better, I'm afraid."

"What makes you say that?"

Dana sharpened one end of the stick to a fine point. "A unicorn told me."

James didn't know what he thought Dana might answer but never would have guessed that. It was true that unicorns existed in Lira, but they were more than elusive, and sightings of them were rare. In his twenty years, James only had caught a glimpse of one such beast and was the singular member of his family to be able to make that claim. He certainly had not been aware unicorns were willing to talk to anyone or anything but their own kind. He honestly had not been aware unicorns even talked.

"A unicorn?" he asked.

"Seems strange, I know, but I swear it's true. I was camped out in the forest, not too far from Labhras, when a unicorn approached me and asked if he might have a word."

"And you said yes."

"Of course I said yes. Why would I ever say no? You hardly ever *see* unicorns to begin with, forget have a chance to converse with one. We had a very interesting talk."

"About what?"

"About how the world will be changing. Prince Maddox is scheming."

"A member of the nobility scheming. How unusual."

"This is different," Dana said. "If we're not careful, the king and queen will not live much longer."

James stopped leaning against the tree and stared at Dana, who was still whittling down the stick as though he had said something commonplace.

"That is a hell of a thing to say, Dana."

"I know, but the unicorn swore it was true."

"The unicorn swore it was true. Right," James said. "Why exactly was the unicorn telling you this?"

Dana took a deep breath. "Because we are to lead a rebellion against Maddox."

"You and the unicorn?"

"No. The unicorns will lend their aid, but I was speaking of you and me."

"You and me," James said and Dana nodded. "Lead a rebellion against the royal family?"

"Aye."

James laughed and threw another stone into the pond. "Aye, all right. Let's do that. Let's lead a rebellion against the royal family. That's a brilliant idea, Dana, really. Don't know why I never thought of it."

"James, I'm serious."

"You're not. And do you know how I know? Because you're not an idiot, and only an idiot would ever consider rebelling against the royal family."

"That's not true."

"Have you hit your head? Have you fallen and hit your head very hard somewhere along the way?" James asked. "A unicorn tells you to rebel, and here you are, ready to go through with it?"

"It's not just the unicorn," Dana said. "Faolan—"

"Faolan? Your bloody pegasus is involved in this?"

The question had been asked in surprise, but now that James considered what Dana was telling him, he wasn't astonished at all. He had long thought there was something more to the pegasus.

For as long as he had known Dana, he had known Faolan. The little pegasus had been a part of the initial admiration in which James had regarded Dana. He had never seen anything like Faolan before, nor since, and had been instantly jealous that he himself had only dogs and no pet so exotic as a pegasus. Dana had told him that he'd come across Faolan one day in the forest, and the pegasus hadn't stop following him since. This had led to James spending more than one day wandering the forest in the hopes of coming across a pegasus of his own.

The color of smoke and just as elusive, Faolan was small enough to stand in a man's hand or perch on his shoulder. Apart from his wings, he was the perfect model of a horse in miniature. James had said as much to Dana once, only to be stunned when the pegasus rolled his eyes in a manner that could only be described as annoyance and said, "I am *not* a horse."

What he was, Faolan had continued, was one among a colony seldom seen in these lands. There was a place where that wasn't true, but James didn't know its name nor its location. Faolan refused to say more about his origins, but whatever this mysterious land was—*wherever* it was—Faolan and others of his kind were held in the highest esteem. James himself had never felt the need to pay any sort of homage to Dana's pet, but he had seen men, mostly sailors, in Eluned's marketplace lay eyes upon Faolan as he stood upon Dana's shoulder. Their eyes first flashed with recognition before their hands, in a seemingly compulsory manner, rose to touch their forelocks. The gestures disappeared quickly, especially if the men spied James looking at them, and James always was left wondering if he'd imagined it. Dana had thought so. Faolan, James recalled, had echoed the sentiment.

"Aye," Dana said. "Faolan's involved in this. More than you know. More than *I* know. He serves Laorans. Did you know that? I swear you can live your whole life with someone and still have no idea who he is."

"Laorans?" James asked. "The goddess?"

"Aye."

"The goddess who doesn't exist?"

"Well, I don't know about that."

"Well, I do. Dana, she's a myth. She's something put in children's stories to explain why grass is green or the sky is blue. She's not real."

"I think you'll change your mind on that."

"Do you hear the words coming out of your mouth?" James asked. "You show up here going on about talking unicorns and rebellions and goddesses and—"

"There's just the one goddess."

"This is insane!"

"I know it is," Dana said. "God, I know it is, but it's the truth, James, and it's our destiny."

"You believe in destiny now, too, do you?"

Dana shrugged. "I guess I do."

"Well, that's...brilliant," James said, "but Dana, I'm a *farmer*."

"I'm aware."

"And still you think we have this shared destiny to bring down the royal family?"

"Just the prince," Dana said. "But, aye, I do."

"I don't know how they convinced you, how they made you believe, but I won't be a part of it."

"Of course you will. You can't deny destiny."

James leaned back against the tree. "No."

"What?" Dana looked at him for the first time since they started talking about rebellion.

"No. I'm saying no. I'm not doing this. If I have a destiny, it's to find a girl to marry and farm my own land and die from old age and not—"

"That's as much your destiny as it is mine. You've never wanted that."

"Well, I don't much want to swing from a gallows either," James said. "And as unexciting as farming may be, I still prefer it to death by hanging."

"I don't really intend for that to happen."

"Does anyone ever really intend for that to happen? No. I won't do it. I don't want to be a part of this lunacy, and I don't care what you say. My mind's made up, and my answer's no."

Dana nodded. "All right then. Tell the unicorn that."

"What unicorn?"

"The one standing behind you."

James leaned forward and to the left to look around the tree. Standing there, impossibly quiet and still for a creature so large, was a unicorn.

"Oh bloody hell," James said as he scrambled to put some distance between himself and the beast. He stood ankle-deep in the pond before he stopped and faced both Dana and the unicorn.

Dana tossed the stick away and stood, wiping his hands on his breeches. "James, meet Lorcan."

"James ap Seoras," the unicorn said. "We would speak with you."

"We?" James said.

Other unicorns appeared then, stepping out of the forest and into the small clearing. They stood behind and beside both Dana and Lorcan and continued to emerge around the pond until they surrounded it.

"Oh bloody hell," James said as he looked at them all.

"That's exactly what we hope to prevent, and we need your help to do it," Dana said. "I need your help to do it. I'll go it alone if I have to, but I'd much rather have you with me."

"Dana—"

"Don't say no. Not yet. Just give us three days. Give *me* three days," Dana said. "After that, if you're still not convinced, you can say no."

"Three days," James said. "And then you'll let me say no?"

"If you like," Dana said. "But you won't."

"I will."

"You won't," Dana said. "Now get out of the pond, will you? We really should be going."

"Going where?"

"Eluned."

—⟶⟵—

Haleine awoke the next morning with a headache. At first, she was reluctant to move, but gradually the pain subsided, and she turned her head to the right in order to look out the glass doors that led to the balcony. The sun hid behind a wall of clouds, and a steady rain fell over the kingdom. She could not have imagined a more appropriate setting to accompany her mood.

Finally, she slid off the bed. She still wore naught but the robe from the previous night. The room was rather cold, and she shivered as her feet touched the stone floor. She stepped immediately onto one of the rugs and leapt lightly from one to the next until she stood in front of the fire. When she was warmed, she moved to the balcony doors and gazed out over the city before her.

Eluned was not like Parthalan at all. Parthalan was mainly a city with buildings on top of buildings, all designed without imagination. There wasn't the expanse of land that was before her now. There was the city just below her and forest beyond the city walls. She could not see it, but she knew somewhere was the sea and the mountains that marked the border between Lira and her neighboring country, Feond. Lira was a kingdom abounding with life and possibility. But for all the opportunity the land held, she would experience none of it.

Her father had seen to that.

Her interest in the landscape lost, Haleine went to the vanity and sat in front of the mirror. Her reflection was miserable. For the first time, she saw the bruises on her throat. She touched them gently before picking up her comb. She had finished working out the tangles from her hair when Bronagh entered the room. Her maid bowed her head and kept it down.

"My lady," she said. "The queen has requested your presence at the morning meal. I am to help you dress."

Haleine put the comb down. "And if I do not wish to go?"

"Forgive me, my lady, but I do not see where that matters."

She nodded, appreciating the maid's truthfulness. "Neither do I."

She wore the ensemble Bronagh had laid out the night before. The dress was made from a heavy violet material. It lacked any additional embroidery, which surprised her, but Haleine liked the plainness of the dress. Even her jewelry was simple. She wore none apart from a gold belt around her waist and a gold pendant around her neck.

"Now for your hair," Bronagh said.

"No need."

"My lady?"

"I shall wear it down."

"But, my lady," Bronagh said. "It's—"

"It's what? Improper? Look at my neck, Bronagh. I think I'll take the chance."

"I'll cover the bruises. No one will know they're there."

Haleine touched her neck. It did not bode well that her maid was trained in such an art.

"No," Haleine said. "Let all of them look upon what her son has done."

She left Bronagh standing there, the maid's mouth gaping. Haleine crossed the room and opened the doors. She stopped short at the sight of two guards. When they saw her, they parted and she walked between them. She had taken just a few steps when she saw Cathal leaning against the wall.

"My lady," he said, straightening only so he could bow. "You are well?"

"As if you care about that," she replied.

"You're angry."

"Can you think of a reason why I should be otherwise?" she asked, and he offered no response. "My father couldn't even look me in the eye. Now I know why."

"The king—"

"I do not want to hear about the king," Haleine said. "I do not want to hear about him nor this glorious honor he has bestowed upon me."

"What would you have me say?"

"Had you a daughter, and had the king selected that daughter for this, would you still want it? Would you still find it to be an honor then?"

"Yes."

She stepped in closer to him. "You are either a liar or every bit a monster as the man you'll have me marry," she said. "Whichever it is, it does not matter, for I have no use for either. Do not speak to me again."

She walked away. The two guards followed her. Lord Cathal did not.

Both Ceallach and Queen Michaela waited for her within the dining hall. It was the first time Haleine had seen it, and though she was fast becoming familiar with Lira's wealth, she still found herself intimidated by the grandeur of the room. The floors were made of smooth white stone and tall pillars carved from the same rock were evenly spaced along the room's two long walls. Great banners of a beautiful silver material hung from them. The Aelhaeran unicorn was seen everywhere but was especially prominent along the fabric covering the head table. It was here where Michaela sat, all alone. As Haleine approached, she took note of the other tables in the room, all abandoned. How many people would she share her meals with, and why were none of them in the room at that moment?

When she stood in front of the queen, Haleine felt her earlier bravado abandon her. She fingered her hair, suddenly wishing she had worn it up as she should have. She cursed herself for that then cursed herself for worrying about it. This woman in front of her would marry her off to the demon she called a son. Let her think what she wanted about how her future daughter-in-law wore her hair. Haleine did not care.

"The Lady Haleine, your majesty," Ceallach said.

Michaela smiled. "Yes, Ceallach, thank you. You may go now."

He bowed and backed out of the room, leaving Haleine alone with the queen.

Nearly alone, Haleine thought. The two guards remained, standing as still as statues. She glanced at them briefly, and when she looked back at the queen, Michaela nodded.

"Quite right," she said softly. Then she cleared her throat and addressed the guards. "Willem, you and your companion may also go."

The guards retreated to the hall, and Haleine was left staring at the queen.

"I can see your gowns fit," Michaela said after a moment had passed in silence. "If you do not like the fashion, we can have new ones made. We were not sure what you would like."

A multitude of responses flooded her mind, but Haleine bit her tongue to keep from speaking them.

"Do you have something to say?" Michaela prompted.

Haleine shook her head.

"Your control is very impressive," the queen said next. "No doubt your parents taught you well, but it is all right to speak your mind."

"The gowns are lovely," Haleine said. "Thank you."

"That's all?"

"Would you have me say something else?"

"I heard how you met my son. I thought you might have something to say about that."

"Is there anything I could say that would change the outcome of my arrival here? Is there anything I could do?" Haleine asked. Michaela shook her head. "Then I scarcely see the point, your majesty."

Michaela was quiet for a long time. Haleine stood still and waited.

"Would you care to sit and breakfast with me?" Michaela asked.

"I was told my presence was requested."

"As it was, but you are not a prisoner, Haleine," Michaela said. "If you do not wish to be here in this room with me, you are free to leave."

Haleine smiled. "Not a prisoner," she repeated as she moved to sit beside the queen. "How awfully amusing."

Michaela smiled. "You will do nicely."

—————

The day, as long as it had been, had somehow passed without sight of her betrothed. Haleine was relieved as she climbed into bed. She didn't know what caused the man's absence or who might have intervened on her behalf, but whatever the reason, she was grateful for the opportunity for one last night of peace.

During breakfast, Michaela had informed her that the wedding would take place the following morning. It was the culmination of a fortnight of celebration held in her honor but also in her absence.

Haleine did not care about the missed festivities, as she had no desire to celebrate a marriage to a man as evil as Maddox, but the announcement of her imminent nuptials had robbed her completely of her appetite. She had begged to be excused, but Michaela—despite her earlier sentiment regarding Haleine's freedom—had denied the request. There was too much to be done.

There had been a fitting for her wedding gown and an endless line of guests to greet, including King Idris Fein Brollachan of Feond and his daughter, Zaide Romanza. Haleine found herself quite unable to meet the princess's eyes and was glad when the most important guests of all, the Tanubian royal family, appeared, and Zaide Romanza fell back. King Nathan, his wife, Haraszty, and their three sons came forward. Haleine greeted all of them except Revelin. He avoided her.

He hadn't even *looked* at her.

She pressed her face against the pillows as she recalled the look he had worn on his face much of the day. Surely he did not find her at fault for their change of fate? He had to know the decision had not been hers and, if it had been, she would have gladly chosen him over any other in the world. It did not matter that Revelin would likely never ascend the throne. She wanted him, not a crown. She did not wish to be queen, not of Tanuba—and certainly not of Lira.

Tears rose in her eyes and she got out of bed. Sleep would be futile this night. She put on her robe and sat on the floor in front of the fire. There had to be a way to stop it, to save herself. Michaela was wrong; she had to be wrong. Mayhap there were no words to free her but there was something Haleine could do. One thing she could take.

But they thought otherwise. They believed they had taken that choice away from her, too.

She did not know from whom the order came, but earlier, while the guards watched, Bronagh and two other maids had gone through the room and removed anything with which they thought she could cause herself harm. Haleine had thought it absurd at the time, even embarrassing. Why would they ever think she would do such a thing? Had there been another girl? Some young Liran noblewoman selected to marry Maddox? Had she met him and decided to open her veins with a shard from a broken mirror or a shattered vase? Had she spilled her life to avoid spending another moment with the animal they called a man and considered a prince? Did they seek to defend against it now?

But did any of them truly suppose bleeding to be the only way to die?

Haleine glanced at the doors that led to the balcony. She could throw herself off it. Let herself fall like a stone and leave them to find her body broken and soulless and out of their reach.

Or there was the fire. She looked at it, losing her focus in the flames. Yes, the fire would lend itself well to her needs. Mayhap she wouldn't have to die. She could scar her face—her body—badly enough that Maddox would refuse to marry her. It would not matter to her if she were no longer beautiful, but Maddox could care. He was that sort.

She held her hand over the flames, just beyond their reach. Could she do it? Allow herself to burn? Even if it killed her, it would still save her life.

Her hand wavered slightly and dropped within the flames' reach. She gasped at the pain and withdrew her hand. She looked at her red and blistered palm before falling onto the floor. She cried and pounded the stone. She hated it; it wasn't fair. It wasn't supposed to be like this. The eve of her wedding, and there she was, crying and trying to work out her death.

No, no, no, stop it! She commanded herself. *You must stop this. You are better than this. Stronger. Prouder. You were raised to be better than this.*

She sat up, gasping now for breath. Her mother and father had abandoned her to this. Why did it matter how she was raised when this hell was to be her fate? She looked at her hand again and moved away. She removed a coverlet from the bed and retreated to the corner farthest from both the fire and the balcony, where she sat on the floor with the blanket wrapped around her body.

Her tears were gone, resignation planted in their wake, by the dawn. Haleine remained on the floor, gazing upon a pale sunrise, when Bronagh entered the room. She proceeded to the bed to rouse her charge, not noticing it was empty until she stood at its side. Haleine then watched her maid search the room in a near panic before spotting her in her corner. Bronagh required more than one deep breath before coming over.

"What are you doing on the floor, my lady?" she asked, poorly disguised relief in her voice. "Are you all right? Are you ill?"

"I am not ill. Nor would it matter if I were."

Bronagh extended her hand. "Aye, that's true. Now up with you before the others come in."

Haleine glanced at the servants' entrance.

"That does matter," Bronagh said. "You don't want them to see you like this."

She supposed that was true enough; her life would always be about appearance now. Haleine nodded and allowed the maid to help her to her feet. Bronagh took the blanket next and folded it neatly over her arm.

"Right then," Bronagh said. "Let's prepare."

The room was soon flooded by servants bearing food and bathwater and clothing. She followed their instructions and was appreciative of not having to think for herself, but their presence was suffocating, and—strength and pride be damned—she longed to return to the solitude of a corner and a blanket. What would happen when she stood in the cathedral, surrounded by even more bodies? How would she ever manage to breathe then?

It wasn't until the wedding gown was produced that Haleine was suddenly glad for the maids' presence. She was not yet convinced she would be able to walk in it unaided. The dress was crafted from layers of white silk and had probably required the revenue of a small country to make. It cut across her chest, leaving her shoulders bare. The sleeves were broken, allowing an undersleeve of pale blue to be pulled through. Pearl-adorned ribbons held the two materials together. The maids placed several strands of pearls around her neck, but pearls were not the only jewels she wore. One strand had attached to it a beautiful sapphire pendent. The shoes slipped onto her feet were encrusted with more of the same pearls and sapphires. It was overwhelming, cumbersome and heavy, and she was grateful when Bronagh directed her to sit.

Her relief was too brief and disappeared completely as Bronagh set to work disguising the prince's brutality. Haleine watched in the mirror as her bruises disappeared beneath the cover of artfully applied powders. Haleine carefully studied her newly flawless skin as the maids styled her hair. When they finished, Bronagh placed a delicate diamond tiara on Haleine's brow. The sight made her breath catch and her eyes water.

"None of that," Bronagh said quietly. "It'll not help you."

It would seem nothing would help her now. Haleine ignored the maid as she stared at the tiara. She hated it. She hated every-thing about it, everything it meant, but most of all she hated her parents for placing it there. She touched it as she studied her reflec-tion. The maids mistook her gesture and smiled at one another, congratulating themselves on a job well done. All, Haleine noted, except Bronagh. She looked directly at Haleine with caring—and perhaps even pity—in her eyes. Haleine frowned. She did not want pity.

"You have burned your hand, my lady," Bronagh said.

Haleine lowered her hand, barely glancing at the still-throbbing wound. "It does not matter. It pains me not."

A knock at the door caused the maids again to swarm around her. They helped her out of her chair, and a number of guards escorted her from the bedchamber to the palace's courtyard. There she was ushered into an open carriage decorated with more flowers than she had seen at any one given time.

The carriage started with a jolt and, upon its exit from the pro-tective palace walls, was surrounded by mounted guards. Cheers immediately erupted from the people lining the streets. She was momentarily surprised by the number of them. Some waved and called out her name. Some called her princess. She felt sick at the thought. Her hand rested against her stomach to quiet the unease rising there.

The carriage stopped in front of the cathedral, and the guards standing outside its doors created a pathway for her. The carriage door opened and a hand was offered to her. She took it without seeing to whom it belonged, paying attention instead to the sur-rounding noise and the panic swallowing her.

She couldn't do this; she couldn't. Did no one care for her? Would they all sacrifice her to this man—this terrible man—with-out troubling their consciences? Her answer came from the music swelling inside the sanctuary. She closed her eyes for a brief moment as she was led inside the church.

Once there, more women, new women, surrounded her. They were finely dressed, and Haleine knew they would be her bridal attendants and ladies-in-waiting. They fussed over her appearance as the maids had done, adjusting this and that, smoothing her train, and readying themselves for their march to the altar. They buzzed with excitement while hailing her good fortune. She once again stood still and allowed the commotion to happen around her. She closed her eyes and focused on nothing but breathing. She heard the bridal music and knew her time had come, but she did not move.

"My lady," the attendant on her left hissed. "They await you!"

Haleine opened her eyes and calm washed over her.

"How rude of me, then," she said as she took her first step, "to keep them waiting."

⚊〰⚊

Unless one counted taverns—and Dana knew some who would—he had never spent much time in places of worship. He certainly never had set foot in one as elaborate and imposing as Eluned's cathedral.

He was surprised to be standing there at all. In an unexpected gesture of largesse, Amatheon opened the doors to commoners who wished to view the nuptials, or at least as many as would fit. Dana and James had been among the fortunate few and were now crammed shoulder to shoulder and front to back at the very rear of the sanctuary.

In front of them, sitting on cushioned pews, sat the nobles. Those hailing from Tanuba sat to the right. Lira's own nobility sat to the left of the aisle. Dana had watched them enter, recognizing some from various alehouses. Others he knew from their hospitality. He had broken bread with them, drank and whored and laughed with them and spent nights at their hearths, but he knew that even if they happened to notice him amongst the masses, they would not acknowledge him here. Ale and mead were often equalizers in taverns and a lord's own hall, but this grand room about to witness a marriage that would represent an alliance between two powerful countries was a far cry from Dana's usual haunts.

He leaned against the wall as his eyes swept over the room and came to rest on the great stained glass window set in the wall high above the altar. Its design featured vibrant blues, greens, yellows and reds twisted into one of the elaborate knots favored by Lira's artisans. The pattern continued throughout the cathedral, carved into the altar and pews and walls. It was sewn onto the banners hanging from the rafters and woven into the stoles worn by the archbishop.

James nudged him then and called his attention away from his surroundings. Dana looked to see the arrival of the royal families.

38

People bowed as best they could, but the monarchs didn't notice as they glided past their subjects to take their seats at the very front. Dana had little more than a passing knowledge of Tanuba, gleaned from the men's tables at which he had supped, and he had never seen its king. He couldn't see much more now than the backs of the princes' heads, and their parents were completely hidden by their great chairs.

Only Maddox was openly visible as he stood at the front of the sanctuary. The archbishop stood alongside him, and together they awaited the arrival of the bride. Dana took the opportunity to examine his would-be enemy. He had heard tales of the prince's cruelty. Maddox, it was said, loved pain. He loved to inflict it upon those weaker than himself. Torture, mutilation. It didn't matter nor did his victims. He started with animals and graduated to servants and whores. They were disturbing rumblings uttered no louder than the quietest whisper because the lad was still his father's heir. The king's one fault, Dana thought.

When the music changed, Dana knew the bride had arrived. He shifted his glance from the prince to the girl.

Rumor had it the future princess was not an attractive woman, but as she entered the sanctuary and took her first steps toward the altar, Dana realized the problem with rumor. It was seldom accurate, and in Haleine's case, it couldn't have been more wrong. She was stunning. His hands fell to his side and he pushed off the wall, mesmerized by her appearance.

"God, James," he breathed. "Would you look at her?"

James didn't answer, but Dana didn't notice as he was drawn in even further by Haleine's presence. He felt as though time had slowed, perhaps even stopped. The noise filling the cathedral—the whispering, the music, all of it—fell away, and there was nothing but him and her. He was dumbstruck by the sight of her, but even more powerful than her beauty was the aura of serenity and strength surrounding her. Without realizing he was doing it, Dana elbowed his way through the people in front of him so he could stay even with her.

He wanted to call to her but couldn't find his voice. He wanted her to turn her head and see him. But her eyes were locked on Maddox. She walked toward him with death in her eyes. Dana saw it there, underneath her calm exterior. Recognizing it caused him to withdraw slightly from the reverie. He looked again at Maddox and saw the wolf. Would she become the lamb?

Dana was pulled fully from his trance when a hand landed on his shoulder. He expected to see a bewildered James behind him. Instead, there stood a frowning guard.

"You are making some guests quite irate, my friend," the man said.

"Had they moved out of my way, I wouldn't have had to push them."

The guard's frown deepened. "Perhaps you should remove yourself from the church. Or perhaps I should do it for you."

Dana considered this. Better to be in the same room with her than to not be able to see her at all. "Perhaps I'll just withdraw to the background."

"I think that would be wise."

The guard stepped to the side and Dana returned to James's side. Haleine now stood in front of the altar, and the service began.

—◊◊◊—

Haleine did not know for how long the ceremony lasted. She heard nothing the Archbishop said and did not know if she had even managed to speak her vows. She stood at the altar, watching everything with a sense of incomprehension—that it wasn't happening to her at all—until the ring was placed upon her finger. With that small gesture, reality caught up to her. She nearly fainted and would have were it not for Maddox's strong grip on her elbow.

It was done. Oh God, it was done.

Her husband turned her toward him in order to kiss her. He had not done so the first night in her bedchamber, and she was not prepared for it now. He pressed his lips hard against hers and forced her lips apart so his tongue could slip past. She wanted to gag, cry, scream and shove him away, but she pushed all urges back down within her and took his hand as he led her from the church. The carriage waited for them and she climbed into it. Her husband forced her down beside him and kept his arm around her to prevent her from moving away.

"You're hurting me," she said.

She was not surprised when he ignored her, and she looked at the wedding band and the burn on her hand. She folded her fingers into a fist as she closed her eyes and wished for a swift end to the day.

40

Her wish was denied, as the wedding reception turned into an everlasting event. First were the speeches. The kings praised and honored each other and wished their blessings for the newly made alliance between their countries and their children. Maddox lifted her hand with his and they drank their toast. Amatheon's noblemen honored them next, followed by Nathan's. Lord Cathal spoke as her father's representative but was careful not to address her—nor even look at her—directly. Haleine drank at the end of each speech and was feeling light-headed by the time the dancing began.

There seemed to be no end to the men with whom she was required to dance. First there was her husband—God, her *husband*—then Amatheon, followed by Nathan and Idris Fein. Prince Zoltano came next. He was as loathsome as Revelin was desirable, and his conversation was littered with innuendo inappropriate for anywhere other than a brothel. Still, she bore it because Revelin would follow his brother, and she would be able to speak with him at last. But at the end of the dance, Zoltano bowed and disappeared, and Revelin did not come. She was left alone for but a moment before Prince Eamonn approached. He bowed and requested the honor of a dance. Having no reason to refuse, she consented.

She continued the dance until she saw Revelin disappearing from the room and out onto the balcony. She immediately broke away from her partner, offered the young prince a hasty apology and followed Revelin into the cool evening air.

He leaned against the rail, his back to her, as he stared at the setting sun. She looked to see that they were alone before approaching him cautiously.

"Revelin?"

He lifted his head but did not look at her. "You should not address me so informally."

"Was I not made your equal this day?" she asked, stopping just behind him. "If I may not address you so now, when was it ever appropriate before?"

"You misunderstand, your highness."

"Please don't call me that."

He turned. "It is who you are now."

"No, it isn't."

"Yes, it is. You should be glad. He has made you what I could not."

41

She shook her head. "And if you think for a moment that matters to me, it is well and good our path has thus divided because you know me not at all," she said. "Revelin, I would choose a lifetime of wretched poverty with you over all the titles and riches in the world."

"Titles and riches you have, but you will find choice is not among your luxuries, your highness."

"It is not the only thing," she said. "I do not love him. I will never love him."

Revelin smiled then. "No one thought you would."

"And you?"

"And me least of all. Do not think so little of me. I know you did not choose this. I know my father desired it."

She went alongside him and looked over the city below. "When did you know I would be sent here? When did they tell you?"

"Before you. Before your father. It is an honor to have been chosen. Or so they tell me."

"It is my father's honor. It is my burden."

"You should not think of it like that."

"And why shouldn't I?" she exploded. "It is my life that has been sacrificed this day, not yours. Do you know this man to whom your father gave me? I would think you do, for even if you do not know him, you know your brother well enough, and my new husband makes your brother look cordial."

"Haleine—"

"You mustn't worry about me, *Prince* Revelin. I will serve my country as she has required me. I will leave my family. I will leave my home. I will leave my betrothed. I will marry a monster in his place. I will lie with my husband. I will bear his children, and all the while I shall do so with a smile on my face and my country's best interests in my heart. I will make Tanuba proud; you needn't worry about that. But here and now, with you and me, I will speak the truth, if never again, and if you ever loved me, you will do the same."

Revelin put his hand on her cheek. "You should never doubt my love for you. Doubt all else you know to be true but never that."

"How could I do anything but doubt when all you offer me is congratulations on my good fortune at having been selected to live this life?"

His hand fell from her face and gripped her arm instead. "Because any other words I would offer would be a betrayal to my crown," he said with an intensity she had never before heard in his voice. "It killed me to see you joined with that man today. It kills me now to know I will never call you my wife. Treat me as a villain if it appeases your anger, your highness. I would gladly suffer that and much more for you, but do not forsake the truth."

He released her, and she walked away, shamed by his reprimand. She hadn't meant to lash out against him. She hadn't meant it at all.

"This is wrong. It's all wrong, Revelin. I shouldn't be—I shouldn't be here. It should be you and me, and we should be—" she stopped as the unobtainable image flooded her mind. She didn't want to finish the thought. "I do not know how I will survive this," she said instead.

"You will find a way."

She looked over her shoulder at him. "How are you so sure?"

"Because I know you. I know your strength. You will not be easily defeated."

He sounded so confident. As sure of his statement as Sighle had been of hers. The only thing Haleine was now certain of was that there was no certainty. She envied them. She went back to Revelin.

"I am sorry," she said. "I truly am. Will you forgive me?"

"There is nothing to forgive, your highness."

She smiled. "You will make a woman a fine husband if you will allow her to rail against you as I have done and dismiss it as nothing."

"The second son of the king of Tanuba is no good match for anyone."

"Only ambitious noblemen's daughters."

He nodded. "I wish I could change this night for you."

God, how she wished it, too. She stared at Revelin but was painfully aware how close the sun was to completing its decent. She needed to go back to the feast. They would start to look for her soon, if they hadn't already. She sighed and placed her hand against his smooth cheek.

They didn't speak, only looked at each other in the dying light until she lowered her hand and walked away. She heard him move, but when she entered the ballroom once again, she was alone. He had not followed her. She saw him on the balcony as she had found him.

"My lady, it is time."

She turned to look at Ceallach and saw his hand on her arm. "What?"

"It is time for you to be conducted to bed, my lady."

She stole one last look at Revelin, his back still to her. Ceallach tugged on her arm, and she allowed him to lead her away. She looked back and searched the masses for Revelin, wanting desperately to see him. The other guests were crowding her, excited to see the princess led off to her bed. They were in her face and all around her. She saw her husband being carried away on the shoulders of loudly singing men. They would parade him around to allow the maids time to prepare his wife for him. As they passed, the room cleared, and she saw azure eyes. At first she thought it might have been Revelin, but the blue was not the same quality. Instead, it was a man who stood in stark contrast to those surrounding him. Other faces were flushed with wine, pleasure and exhilaration, but this man showed none of that. She found it preferable and even calming that at least one knew and was not amused by the obvious farce in front of him. She stared at him and his liquid-azure eyes until the doors of her bridal suite came to a close and he was gone.

CHAPTER 3

O nce they were free of the palace walls, James could breathe easier. Still it was not as effortless as it would have been were he home. He didn't know if such ease would ever come again. Now that he had seen his enemy, the magnitude of what Dana hoped to accomplish was starting to suffocate him.

James had watched the prince all during the ceremony at the cathedral and then followed Dana as they stole attendance to the wedding feast. At first, James had been terrified of discovery but quickly realized that with all the commotion and excitement and drink, no one—the guards included—was likely to notice him as long as he stayed out of their way. And so he had watched the prince of Lira.

He didn't like what he'd seen. There was something about the prince, something James couldn't name, but it was akin to evil. He now understood Dana's sense of urgency. To allow Maddox to gain the throne would be sentencing the country to death. He wouldn't love the people. He wouldn't love the land. James wasn't sure how he felt so certain but knew it just the same. And so he would fight. But God, the thought made him sick.

"What did you get me into?" he asked.

Dana didn't respond. He was deep in thought and walked through the crowded streets as though half the city's population wasn't surrounding him in thunderous celebration. He had been in such a state ever since the feast ended. Maybe the severity of what they planned had settled upon him, too, but James doubted it. Dana never felt the severity of anything.

They were now returning to the tavern where they had taken up temporary residence. The proprietor, a woman called Orla, was one of Dana's longtime acquaintances, so it wasn't the first time James had stayed under her roof. Each time, she had viewed his presence with disinterest, and this latest encounter was no different. It had bothered him in the past, but he thought he'd be able to overlook it now. Meeting his enemy had drained him entirely, and he looked forward to his bed.

But as soon as they set foot inside the tavern, James realized sleep that night would be an unlikely luxury. The barroom was louder and more crowded than the cathedral or the feast or even the streets had been. Everyone was red-faced, drunk and in excellent spirits. One toast to the newly married couple would barely finish before the next was called. Dana ignored it all as he made his way through the crowd of people toward the back of the room where a barely visible Faolan waited, perched on a tabletop in the farthest corner.

It wasn't until they were closer that James noticed Faolan was not alone. A man and a woman sat with him. More acquaintances of Dana's, James supposed, as he and Dana joined them.

"This is Lucius and Ilya," Faolan said once everyone was seated. "They'll be joining us."

James sat back to examine the two newcomers. They were related. He could tell that. Most likely brother and sister, he thought. It was hard to be sure when they were sitting in the shadows, but he thought they shared the same thick brown hair and eyes. James, thanks to years of farming, was far from weak, but both Lucius and Ilya seemed stronger. He wondered the sort of training they had had and how Ilya ever managed to be a part of it.

Dana nodded. "I'll say nothing here, but tomorrow, someplace else, we shall talk at some length, I imagine. There is much to be decided after all. Have you taken lodging here?"

Lucius nodded. Ilya watched James. He met her stare for stare. She smiled and even laughed to herself before she looked away.

"Good," Dana said as he stood. "Tomorrow then."

He left the table and went above stairs. When he had disappeared, James turned back to Faolan and the two strangers sitting across from him. Nobody spoke. After a moment, James didn't know why he remained and departed as well. Ilya's laughter followed.

When he entered the room he shared with Dana, he saw his friend standing by the one small window and watching the palace. James went straight to his bed where he could see nothing through the window. He did not need to see the palace. He already had seen enough.

"Who are they?" he asked.

"Who are who?"

"Lucius and Ilya."

Dana shrugged. "Second in command, I wager."

"You wager? You mean you don't know them?"

"How would I? I've only just met them."

"And you're still prepared to involve them in this?"

"Any reason why I shouldn't?"

"We might have to put our lives in their hands someday. It would be nice to know they could be trusted."

Dana smiled and looked at him. "You'd never know you grew up in Enimode, you know that?"

James frowned. "What is that supposed to mean?"

"Nothing. It means nothing. You don't have to worry about Lucius and Ilya, James. They can be trusted."

"How do you know?"

Dana turned back to the window. "Faolan."

The rest was unspoken, but James knew it was there. Faolan had brought Lucius and Ilya to Dana, and Dana trusted the pegasus implicitly. He'd trust anyone Faolan brought to him. James thought he could understand that. It was the sort of bond he had with Dana, and if Dana was willing to accept the two strangers, James supposed he could do the same. He could at least try.

"Is something happening out there?" he asked next, removing his boots. He set them on the floor at the foot of the bed and looked again at his friend. "Dana?"

"What?"

"What's happening out there?" James repeated. "I've not seen you like this before. Is it the prince? Your insane plans?"

Dana left the window and sat on his own bed. "I hate knowing he's touching her."

James hesitated. "The prince and his bride?"

"Aye."

"Oh."

"I hate it," Dana said. "You don't realize how much I hate it. That man is—you saw him, James. I know you can feel it. We shouldn't have left her there."

"Well, kidnapping the bride on her wedding night certainly would've been one way to make our mark on the kingdom."

The comment had been made without thinking, and James saw that somehow it had been the wrong thing to say. He held up his hands to acquiesce the fault.

"I didn't mean to jest, Dana. I'd pity any bride of his, but the truth is I don't think there was a thing to be done. Not if you want to do what you say you do. Besides, you don't even know that he'd hurt her," James offered, though he knew otherwise. Dana was right; he could feel it. "Why would he?"

Dana looked over his shoulder. "Because he can."

＊＊＊

Bronagh removed the tiara first. The gown followed. Haleine was hot and sticky with perspiration but shivered as she stood naked in the bridal suite. The maid wiped Haleine's skin with a damp cloth then drew back the sheet of the wedding bed. She looked at Haleine and nodded. Haleine stepped forward and climbed onto the bed to await her husband. Bronagh covered her with the sheet, just barely covering her breasts. She carefully arranged Haleine's hair before backing away. Haleine's eyes hardened upon seeing the pity in her maid's face.

The other maids in the chambers did not bother with pity. They busied themselves with other tasks. One stoked the fire while another lit several candles and spread them throughout the room. A third maid scattered rose petals on a path leading from the door to the bed. Haleine watched the girl sprinkle what petals remained over the sheet that covered her. The sight of it all made her ill. They worked to create a moment of romance, of budding love, but it seemed only Haleine and the man with the azure eyes were willing to recognize the night for what it truly was.

The maids withdrew, and Haleine was left alone to wait. Silence enclosed the room. It was stifling; she couldn't breathe. She longed for an open window—something, anything—to make her feel less trapped. For the longer she waited, the less she could breathe and the more the horrible truth of what awaited her—of what now approached—settled upon her.

He would want to punish her. She had denied him before and undoubtedly this was a man accustomed to receiving what he wanted when he wanted it, and she had denied him. But now she had no right to refuse him anything, and he would make her pay. He would humiliate her. He would make her suffer and he would find pleasure in it: every tear, every scream, every whimper. He was that sort.

She felt tears on her cheeks. She didn't realize she had been crying and wiped them away quickly. She barely knew her husband, but it was certain that he was a man in front of whom one could

48

not cry. To show him weakness or fear would be a mistake. He would pounce upon it, seeing it as prey, like a hawk to a sparrow.

She clutched the sheet in sudden resolve. She would not be the sparrow. She would never show him fear. When he came to her, she would not fight him. She would not struggle. She would deny him what pleasure she could.

The doors opened and jolted her from her thoughts. She sat up, holding the sheet closer to her chest. She did not see him nor anyone else. The bedpost and the curtains that hung from it obstructed her view of the entrance. She heard the doors close again but nothing else. There were no footsteps. There was nothing but the same oppressive silence from before. Had she imagined it?

"My beautiful, bonny bride."

His voice startled her, and she jumped when she saw Maddox at her side. He lunged at her and kissed her as he had in the cathedral, only now tasting heavily of wine and smoke. She dropped the sheet and put her hands on his chest to push him away. His clothing was warm and wet, and as soon as he released her and drew back, she turned her hands to see her palms stained red. She shook at the sight.

"You're trembling," he noted. "Afraid I won't be gentle?"

She looked at this man, her husband, who now undressed before her. He stared at her, his eyes heavy with drink and dark with desire. She looked away and saw his breeches, once pristine white, now blemished by dark patches.

"What is this?" she breathed as horror spread over her.

"Have you never before seen the blood of the innocent?"

"Oh God," she said, looking at her hands again. "What have you done?"

She was still staring at her hands when he attacked her. As the smell and taste of death encompassed her, she forgot her earlier resolution and fought him. She screamed at him to stop. Her bloodstained hands made fists, and she beat against his chest until he grabbed her wrists and held them down. She was undaunted and continued to struggle against him, determined to escape.

His knee pushed down between her thighs, forcing her legs apart. He rammed into her and she screamed again. The pain paralyzed her. Her arms fell slack and she fell silent.

He thrust into her again and again, encouraged, she supposed, by her resignation and his victory. His head bent low as he concentrated on his task. His wine-soaked groans choked her. She gasped for breath and squeezed her eyes shut as she waited for it to end.

When the end did come, they both cried out. His was a cry of triumph and pleasure. Hers was a strangled, worthless protest.

He collapsed on top of her and momentarily robbed her of breath. His hands loosened their hold on her wrists as his body settled. When his breathing slowed, she realized he had surrendered to his drunkenness.

The knowledge brought her some relief, and though she longed to distance herself from him, she did not move for fear of arousing him. She instead stared at the cherub-adorned ceiling. The fire distorted the paintings, casting dark shadows on naive faces. She thought if she could get to the fire, this time she would not hesitate.

But she didn't move. She lay still in the cruel silence, soaking in blood and waiting for the dawn.

———

Dana was standing by the window when the cathedral bells started to ring. It was rather early in the day; the sun had not yet fully risen, but there was light enough to see great black banners unfurled over both the palace and cathedral walls. He took a step back but kept the palace in sight.

"Dana?" James's still sleepy voice said. "Has something happened?"

He couldn't take his eyes off the banners. "Aye."

He heard James get out of bed and pick up his boots before crossing the room to stand behind him, but Dana didn't turn around. Instead he watched for Faolan. The pegasus didn't disappoint, flying in through the window. He landed on the sill and looked at Dana.

"It's happened," Faolan said.

"What's happened?" James asked.

"Amatheon and Michaela were murdered during the night."

"Are you sure?" James asked, and the pegasus nodded. "Was it the prince?"

"Yes."

"What do we do now?" James asked.

Faolan didn't answer. Dana thought he understood why. It was a decision to be made by Dana alone. Whatever view of the future the goddess had was somehow dependent upon him. Dana, blind to the future himself, was to lead them—the humans, the unicorns, all of them. He had never felt the weight of it as much as in that moment.

"Fight a king instead of a prince," he said and saw the pegasus nod his approval. "Faolan, get Lucius and Ilya. Tell them what's happened and tell them to prepare."

Faolan disappeared from the window, and Dana looked over the just-waking city. People came out of their homes, summoned by the clangor of the bells. They looked at the cathedral, then at the palace's similar trappings. They did not know exactly what had transpired yet, but the black banners would cause them to suspect it. More than one of them stumbled. Some fell to their knees. They clung to each other as the realization settled upon them. It was a startling contrast from the celebration that had just barely ended before the break of dawn.

James stumbled next. "God, we're really going to do this."

We. Dana almost smiled. "Aye."

"Are you frightened?"

He really wasn't. "No."

"How is that possible?"

He shook his head. "Maybe I don't know any better."

When she first opened her eyes, Haleine didn't remember where she was. It took only a moment to evoke the memory, for as soon as she tried to move, her body screamed its protest. Fresh tears appeared in her eyes, and she hurried to erase them before realizing she was alone in bed. She found, though, that not knowing where her husband was concerned her more than anything else. She sat up and scanned the room.

Maddox was gone, but Bronagh was there, tending the fire. The maid turned when she heard Haleine and curtsied.

"You must dress immediately, your highness," she said.

Bronagh's use of title gave her pause, but Haleine recovered and got out of bed. She moved slowly, feeling every bruise and yielding to every ache. As soon as her feet touched the floor, she reached for the sheet to use in the absence of a robe.

"Where is my husband?" she asked. "Do you know?"

Bronagh rushed toward her. "Please, your highness, you must dress."

"Bronagh, where is—?"

Haleine stopped speaking as she heard the tolling bells. She turned her head toward the window. She couldn't see the cathedral but she didn't need to. The solemn peal chilled her, and she let the sheet fall away to look at her hands. The blood of the innocent, he had called it.

"What has happened?" she asked.

"The king and queen, your highness," Bronagh said. "They were murdered during the night."

He killed them. Her fingers curled inward and she looked at Bronagh.

"Was anyone else harmed?"

"The queen's guards were slain. Both of them."

"But no one else?" she asked as though four lives weren't enough.

"No."

Four lives. He had taken four lives, among them those who had given him life. The shock started to settle upon her and her arms went limp. Her legs gave way next and she began to sink. Bronagh caught her by the elbows, preventing her from slipping to the floor.

"No," the maid said harshly. "You mustn't do this, your highness."

"He killed them," she breathed. "Oh God, he killed them."

Bronagh shook her. "You must never say that again. Never. Not if you want to live."

"Is that choice mine? How regrettable the king and queen do not share my good fortune."

"You can do nothing about that now. You must forget what you think you know."

Haleine shook her head. "I will never forget. How could I? I can't live this life. Not if this is what is expected of me. I can't pretend I don't know what he is or what he's done."

"But you must. You must show restraint. You must be smart. You must be strong. You must do all of these things and do them well, for our late queen was a powerful woman and ruler, and now you take her place."

"I do not wish to be queen."

"Whether you wish it or not, it is who you are."

The thought left her feeling more faint than before. "I do not know how to be queen."

"Then you will learn. You cannot show weakness, your highness. Not even for a moment. You must stand strong."

And silent. The maid didn't say it again but she didn't have to. It was a lesson of which Haleine was already aware. She could not hide and show her husband fear now any more than she could before. It was even more imperative in light of her failure from the previous night. It was a horrible way to live but she did not know what else to do. She gripped Bronagh's arms to steady herself and looked into the maid's eyes. There was no pity to be found. Haleine suspected she would never see it again.

"Then I must prepare," she said. "You will help me."

"Yes, your highness."

But Haleine didn't move. She stayed still and held onto Bronagh. She could not show weakness. It was simple to say but much harder to do.

"I do not know where to start," she confessed.

"I do."

Could she really trust the maid? Did it matter, now that she had said what she had? Haleine nodded and put herself in Bronagh's hands.

There wasn't time for a proper bath, but Bronagh brought her a basin of hot water and Haleine washed as well as she could. Afterwards she dressed in a gown of black silk and sat so Bronagh could attend to her hair.

Haleine watched her maid through the mirror. "Why are you doing this?"

"Your highness?"

"No other maid would do what you have done for me this day. Why do you?"

"Forgive me, your highness, but I don't understand," Bronagh said. "It is my place to see to your needs."

"I do not mean my hair nor my wardrobe," Haleine said. "You seek to protect me. Why?"

"The queen asked it of me."

Haleine caught Bronagh's wrist. "What do you mean she asked it of you?"

"Before you came, I served Michaela. When she knew you were to arrive, she bid me to serve you, to help you, to protect you."

"Protect me from what?"

"You already know, your highness."

"I am not helpless," she said, feeling precisely the opposite.

"I do not suggest it."

Haleine released her and Bronagh resumed her task. Haleine continued to study her. She was still watching when Ceallach came into the room. Using the mirror, she scrutinized him as he approached. Here was a man who exuded weakness. It rolled off him like a strong odor, yet Maddox backed away when Ceallach so ordered. Why would her husband ever listen to him? Had she truly misjudged Ceallach so badly? She inclined her head when he bowed to her.

"You may go," he said to Bronagh.

Bronagh bowed and disappeared through the servants' entrance. Haleine watched her leave, steeling herself for this confrontation, then shifted her position on the bench to face Ceallach directly.

"I want to know what happened," she said.

"Your highness?"

"I know the king and queen are dead. Bronagh brought me the news this morning."

"She had no right—"

"She had every right. My question is why you were not here to tell me yourself."

"I do apologize, your highness," he said, "but as I am sure you can understand, there has been much commotion to deal with this day, as young as it is, and I—"

"Were any others harmed?"

She wondered what he would tell her. He hesitated as he considered his answer.

"You do not trust me, do you?" he asked and shook his head when she offered him no response. "The queen's guards, as I am sure you already know."

"Do you know who is responsible for these acts?" she asked.

"Alas, we do not, your highness. There has been some speculation of a rebellion mounting against your husband. The king's advisor has told me—"

"I thought you were the king's advisor."

"No, your highness, that man is Lord Omur. The king has asked me to serve you instead."

"The king, Ceallach, is dead."

"I beg your pardon, your highness, but the king is not dead," he said. "And neither is the queen."

She understood his meaning and shook her head. "Their bodies are not yet cold."

"You will be crowned before they are."

"A coronation before the funerals?"

"Lira will not be without a king, your highness."

Maddox did not deserve to be king. The thought was on her tongue, and she opened her mouth to say it but stopped herself.

"I wish to see the bodies," she said instead.

Ceallach blanched. "Your highness, please, I must object."

She stood. "You may object all you wish. I will see the bodies."

"It is no place for you."

"I will decide that. Your only task is to bring me there."

"My task, your highness, is to bring you to the coronation."

"It will keep."

"The king awaits you there."

"He, too, will keep," she said. "Take me now, Ceallach. I will not be dissuaded."

He raised his head and looked at her. She thought perhaps he was weighing her resolve and was careful not to look away. She knew she had won when he let out a heavy sigh and bowed.

"As you wish, your highness."

He led her to the room in which the bodies had been laid. He told her guards to stay in the hall and opened the door for her himself. He came in after her, but she barely noticed him as she was riveted by the terrible sight of her husband's art.

Maddox had had a brutal death planned for them. She could not imagine the horrors these people had been subjected to at her husband's hand. The bodies were scarcely identifiable now. She wasn't even sure she would have been able to recognize them as human if she hadn't already known it. She sank to her knees and looked around in despair.

"Your highness," Ceallach said. "Why did you insist on this?"

She wanted to see what her husband had done. She wanted to know of what he was capable. Maybe it had been foolish, even stupid, but she needed to understand the depths of his depravity. She did not, however, wish to explain that to Ceallach.

"Their families?" she asked.

"Families?"

"Yes, Ceallach," she said. "Their families. The guards' families. Have they yet been informed of this tragedy?"

"I do not believe so."

"Of course not," she said as she gathered her skirts and stood. "You will find their families, and I will go to them personally."

"The king will not like it."

Haleine stopped on her way out of the room and glared at him. "What makes you think I care about that? Find the families, Ceallach, and do not present yourself to me again until you have."

He bowed and she walked past him into the hall where her two guards waited. She walked to the opposite wall and touched her hand to it. She closed her eyes and took a moment, only a moment, to gather herself. Then she continued on.

As there didn't seem to be a way for her to avoid it, she went to the cathedral. She rode alone in her carriage and thought as little as possible. It was a task easily accomplished as she sat dumbly upon the seat with her hands in her lap and waited for the carriage to stop.

When it did, she wiped her face clear of any tears before they could be seen. Her door opened, and the guard Michaela had called Willem offered her his hand. She took it and allowed him to help her out. She paused for a moment to look at the great black banners covering the cathedral walls. Then she turned to see the people who would now call her queen. They stared back with wide eyes and clenched mouths. Some huddled together while others stood tall, their arms crossed and their shoulders squared. They were frightened. They didn't know what had happened though they would hear the rumors soon enough. Neither truth nor rumor would assuage their concern. A new monarch, regardless of how the throne was gained, would cause unease. They didn't know what would happen to them, what changes would come. She didn't know either but she feared for them.

"Ah, here you are at last."

She turned to see a man standing where no one was only a moment ago. He was tall, dark and impeccably groomed. He was faintly familiar to her. She had probably seen him at the wedding feast, but she couldn't place him. He dressed as a man of the church, in long black robes, but it was the braided gold belt around his waist that told her his position was at the palace and not with the clergy. She did not yet know his place in court, though given his apparent confidence and smile, she thought he most likely served her husband.

"I am Lord Omur, your highness," he offered.

"My husband's advisor."

"Yes. We were concerned something had happened to you. I would scold Ceallach for your tardiness, but I do not see him."

She wanted to ask him about his rebellion. She wanted to see him lie.

"Nor will you," she said. "I appointed him to another task."

He smiled. "Very well, your highness. Might I lead you inside? Your husband awaits."

"Is my husband much grieved?"

"The king is as you would expect. The news of his parents' death has shocked him greatly, but he is eager to protect his kingdom from any further threat."

He was the threat. She wanted to scream it but swallowed the words and followed Omur inside. She lost sight of him as her ladies swarmed her in order to dress her for the coronation.

First they helped her into a black sleeveless surcoat embroidered with silver unicorns and clasped together by great silver buckles. Next they offered her a fur-trimmed cape of red velvet. She thought the color to be an affront to the woman whose place she was to take but did not protest, as the effort would certainly be wasted. The cape was heavy and awkward with a long dragging train. Two of the ladies were given the task of carrying the train and making sure it didn't touch the floor.

She hated the pageantry of the thing but forgot about it when the remaining ladies parted, and she saw both her husband and his advisor waiting for her. The hate rose in her throat like bile as she approached them. Omur bowed his head and Maddox held out his hand. She wanted nothing more than to hurt him as he had hurt her, as he had hurt the others. She wanted to scratch out his eyes, his cool, murderous eyes; she wanted to cut off his hands, cut out his heart, *anything* to cause him hurt, but she did nothing but put her hand in his and walk alongside him.

The pews were again crowded with the faces of those she had seen the day before, so she knew where to find Revelin. He stood just behind his parents, his head facing front but angled to the right so he couldn't see her approach. He was so close and her heart ached at the sight of him. God, how she wanted him. *Needed* him. Why wouldn't he look at her? Why didn't he know? Just a glance and mayhap she'd not be so desperate. Just a glance and mayhap—

He was so close and she needed—would she be able to touch him? If she reached out just a little, could she feel him beneath her fingertips? Would he feel her? Would he look at her then? Would he know that his words were true?

Maddox, indeed, had made her what Revelin could not. Would not.

She extended her hand as much as she dared. She stretched as far as she could, but it was not enough.

Her fingers fell short; she could not reach him.

The Archbishop, flanked by two crown-bearing pages, awaited them at the altar. Yesterday he had blessed their union as man and wife, and now he waited to bless their reign as king and queen. They knelt before him and bowed their heads. The Archbishop stepped forward and placed a hand on Maddox's head, then her own. He offered a prayer and when he finished, he lifted his hands. Maddox raised his head, but Haleine kept hers bowed. It was the only way she thought she might survive the revulsion of touching Maddox and being crowned queen of this land.

She did not raise her head until the Archbishop put his hand under her chin to force the action. Next, he waved forth the pages and crowned her husband first before placing a gold circlet upon her own head. She flinched as the metal touched her skin.

A final prayer followed, and the Archbishop backed away from them. Maddox gripped her hand, and together they rose and were ushered from the cathedral. Once outside, the guards hurried them into a carriage. When the doors were closed, she lifted the crown from her head and laid it on the seat to her left.

"They tell me you intend personally to deliver condolences to the guards' families," Maddox said as the carriage started to move.

She looked at him, unsure what to think. She didn't know how he would know that already. Ceallach was the only soul to whom she had announced her intention, and he had not accompanied her to the cathedral. How had he told Maddox?

"Yes, I do," she said.

"You will not. I forbid it."

She heard the warning in her head but ignored it. She didn't want to stay silent. She hated the very sight of him and now he would know it. There would be consequences; she knew that, but if only for this once, she would not stay silent. She laughed softly. His eyes darkened at the sound.

"I know what it is you did," she said. "Who are you to forbid me anything?"

Fury flashed in his eyes. "I am your husband. Do not forget that."

"I do not forget," she said. "It is a curse which will plague me all my life."

"Bitch!"

"Murderer!" she screamed as he brought the back of his hand across her face. "Murderer, murderer, murderer!"

"Shut up!"

He hit her again and she slid onto the carriage floor. She looked into his eyes, black with rage.

"You killed them. Your mother, your father, all of them. You slaughtered them as though they were pigs to be sold at market. And you will not get away with it," she said. "The law says—"

"The law?" he asked. "The law? I, madam, I am the law."

Their eyes locked. The moment was intense and unmoving until Haleine broke it by spitting in his face.

"You are a murderer," she said.

He kicked her stomach in retaliation. As she fell forward, he grabbed her throat and stopped her. He pulled her closer and closer to him until their faces nearly touched.

"I am king," he said. "I am king ordained by a power higher than you or your damned law!"

He screamed the last of it at her and pushed her away. She fell back against the carriage door and rested there for a moment before confronting him once more.

"You are a murderer," she gasped. "You are a murderer ordained by the powers of hell, and I will shout it from the rooftops until every living being on this earth knows it."

Maddox turned away. She started to move from the floor but did not get far. Without warning, he whirled around and struck her face with his elbow. She made no noise as she fell, nor did she make a sound as she lay on her back, stunned by pain and the taste of blood in her mouth.

"You will shout nothing," he said as the carriage came to a stop. "Am I understood?"

She closed her eyes and nodded. Once she had done so, he rose from his seat and left the carriage, pausing only long enough to crush her outstretched hand with his boot.

CHAPTER 4

For the third time in almost as many days, Dana was pressed against the back of the cathedral, held in place by the surrounding masses. Thus far, he'd witnessed a wedding and a coronation. This time however, the church had a much different air. Above them, monks chanted dirges, and, just to Dana's right, a group of guards carried the coffins containing the bodies of King Amatheon and his lady wife, Queen Michaela.

Following the dead were the new king and his new wife. Upon their appearance, people went down on one knee and bowed their heads. Dana did the same—James, Lucius and Ilya following his lead—but tilted his head in order to watch the couple's progress.

Maddox was a study in false grief as a smug pleasure danced in his eyes, but Haleine's face was taut and her eyes hard. Three days now had Dana seen her, and three days had she looked as such. Careful, composed and nearly emotionless. What would three days more bring? Or three weeks or three months?

The night of her wedding, he had stood sober amongst drunkenly complacent guests who didn't care what would happen to the girl being led to her wedding bed. He didn't know what had made her look at him or why she had continued to stare, but there had been a quickly fading moment right at the start when he saw—for the first and only time—an unguarded emotion. It wasn't happiness nor anything like it, but it had been honest.

There was no honesty now. There wasn't anything.

The king and queen reached the front of the sanctuary and disappeared from his view as they sat. The people rose and the service began. Dana stared straight ahead, hearing nothing and seeing nothing but her empty blue eyes. He looked up when Maddox rose from his chair in order to kneel at his father's coffin. The queen stood behind him. The king offered a prayer and turned to face his people.

"Mourn him," the king said. "Mourn him well."

Maddox took his wife's hand, and the king's subjects again went to their knees as their monarchs made their way along the center aisle. Dana was the last, breaking his stare and moving only when James pulled him down. This time he did not watch as the king and queen passed him. When they had gone, he stood and looked at the other three members of his still-secret rebellion.

"Let's go," he said. "We have work to do."

———

When the king and queen returned to the palace, the king got out first and walked away without another word to his wife. There was no need to speak. He had said and done all he needed to in the cathedral.

"Did I hurt you much?" he had asked as they walked down the aisle.

He squeezed her hand then, the hand he crushed just the day before. She didn't want him to see the pain in her face and turned from him until she could control it.

"You will never hurt me," she told him when she could again look at him.

"Give me time," he responded.

Now Haleine sat alone in the carriage and looked at her hand. It was ugly, swollen and bruised. It was the only part of her Bronagh couldn't hide with her powders and tricks. Rhys, the court physician, had wanted to put a splint on it to protect the newly set bones, but she had refused. She hadn't wanted to show Maddox how he had hurt her. She still didn't.

"Your majesty?"

Willem stood there. He had done the same the day before. She remembered seeing him then through lost eyes clouded by pain. If he feared for her either then or now, he did not reveal it. She nodded and moved to exit the carriage. When he held out his hand to help her, he was careful to reach for her uninjured one.

Bronagh waited in her chambers. She was unable to disguise her relief at Haleine's seemingly safe return. She ushered Haleine through the doors and into a chair by the fire. She moved away to fetch a goblet of wine. She set it down on the small table next to the chair and picked up Haleine's hand. She studied it and the consequent grimace on Haleine's face.

"I will have Rhys summoned," Bronagh said. "And after he sets your bones for the second time, perhaps you will allow him to splint it properly."

"Perhaps I won't," Haleine said.

Bronagh's shoulders fell. She opened her mouth to speak but said nothing. Instead she bowed and backed away. Haleine stayed by the fire, still cradling her hand as Bronagh asked Willem to send for the physician. She did not return to Haleine's side, and Haleine did not look up until she heard her new title.

"Your majesty?"

It was not the physician. Bronagh would have announced him, yet the maid had not moved. She lifted her head and saw Ceallach standing there. He bowed.

"I'll not have you entering this chamber unannounced," she said.

"Of course, your majesty. Forgive me."

"You have found the families, I presume."

"Families?"

"You know of what I speak. You are not a fool. Please do not present yourself as such."

"Again I ask for your forgiveness, your majesty, but the king has forbidden me from doing this for you."

"Why would the king forbid such a thing?"

"I do not ask the king to explain himself," Ceallach said. "You would be wise to do the same."

"I do not seek your council," she said. "If you have nothing else to offer me, I suggest you remove yourself from my sight, as I apparently have no further need of you."

"Your majesty, I have come here today on Lord Cathal's behalf," Ceallach said. "He intends to sail with the Maoilriains but hopes he might have an audience with you before he departs."

The Maoilriains were leaving. *Revelin* was leaving. Of course he was. She didn't truly expect him to stay. His life wasn't with her anymore.

"Might I show him in?" Ceallach asked.

"No. Tell him no," she said. Cathal was not the one she wanted to see. "I have nothing to say to him, and I very much doubt he has anything to say that I wish to hear."

Ceallach bowed again. "As you wish, your majesty."

She watched him go before reaching for the wine at her side. Her hand shook too badly to hold the goblet, so she replaced it on the table but knocked it over as she drew away. The wine spilled out, coating the table as it made its way to the floor. She looked at it before she pushed herself out of the chair. She started to cross the room to the balcony but stopped when she saw Bronagh abandon her corner to attend to the wine. Her maid knelt on the floor and used her apron to soak up the mess.

"You knew them, didn't you?" Haleine asked.

Bronagh looked up. "Your majesty?"

"The queen's bodyguards. You knew them."

Bronagh slowly rose to her feet, her apron now stained purple. "Aye."

"Did they have families?"

"Aye."

"I wish to offer condolences. I want you to find a way for me to go to them and do this."

Bronagh paled. "Your majesty, the king—"

"Has no need to know."

"Whether he needs to know or not, he will," the maid said. "And he will be furious."

"Then let him be furious."

"You cannot continue to defy him. He will hurt you," Bronagh said. "More than he already has."

"I know."

"Then why do you do this? Why will you tempt him to hurt you?"

"I cannot show him weakness. You yourself have said so."

"It is not the same," Bronagh said. "Forgive me, your majesty, but it is not the same."

"Will you do this for me?"

"He will hurt you."

"Will you do this?"

"He will break you."

"He will do it anyway," Haleine said. "He will break me and, when he wishes it, he will kill me. You cannot protect me. You are more worthless than I am, if such a wretched creature could possibly exist, and you know this to be true. You tell me to stay silent; you beg me not to tempt the beast because you think it will be the only way to save me, but you are wrong. All your actions do is prolong this existence, and what use have I for that?

"Now, as worthless as you are, you still serve me. You will do as I ask, and you will see it done immediately, or I shall banish you from this place, and you can see what work you will find on the streets. How many highborn families do you think will be eager to employ a maid dismissed from the queen's service?"

Bronagh hesitated slightly before she bowed. "I shall attend to it without delay."

Haleine nodded. "See that you do," she offered, her voice now barely above a whisper. She waited for the maid to leave before returning to her chair and collapsing into tears.

———

The next morning, Bronagh claimed she hadn't yet found the soldiers' families. Haleine didn't know if her maid told the truth but suspected it to be a lie to keep her mistress contained. Whatever the reason, Haleine didn't want to sit and do nothing, so after a discussion with Ceallach, Haleine went to the city's hospital where she used skills taught to her by her mother to tend the wounds and illnesses of Eluned's poor. When she returned to the palace, she found an unhappy Bronagh waiting for her in the courtyard.

"The king is displeased?" Haleine said.

"The king is more than displeased," Bronagh said. "You must be hidden. We'll—"

"No," Haleine said.

"Your majesty—"

"No," Haleine said. "I'll not hide from him nor anyone else."

She entered the palace and made her way to her chambers with both Bronagh and Willem trailing behind her. Maddox and his advisor waited in the hall not far from her doors. She stopped short at the sight of them and offered her husband a brief curtsey. Maddox's face revealed nothing as he stepped close to her and fingered the edge of her cloak.

"They tell me you've been working in the hospital," Maddox said.

"Yes."

"Perhaps no one told you, but you are the queen of Lira and not a servant," he said. "You won't do it again."

"Won't I?"

"I don't want you to."

She shrugged. "I don't want you to murder the innocent."

She never saw him move until it was too late. There was a flash of blue—the sleeve of his tunic—and she slammed into the wall.

She started to fall to the floor when he grabbed her arm, twisted it behind her back and pinned her against the stone.

"You cannot provoke me into killing you," he hissed into her ear. "Think long and hard, my sweet, about whether this is a game you wish to play. Continue to defy me, and I will make you regret each and every breath you take."

He let go of her. She staggered back but didn't fall. When she regained enough of her balance, she raised her hand to stem the blood flowing from her head, but Maddox grabbed her wrist.

"Let it bleed. Perhaps then you will remember who is master here," he said. He released her and looked at Bronagh and Willem. "Help her and I'll have your head on a pike."

Maddox walked away. Omur lingered a moment longer, fixing her with an unreadable glance. Only when he had gone did she allow herself to slide to the floor and laid her throbbing head against the stone. She could feel the blood running down her face but made no effort to stop it. She made no effort to do anything but close her eyes and slip away.

When she opened them again, she felt hands on her shoulders. Smaller hands belonging to a woman. Bronagh's hands. The maid's mouth was near her ear, whispering just as Maddox had. Haleine covered her ears with her hands, but Bronagh gently pulled them away.

"Your majesty," Bronagh said. "You can't stay here. We'll go back to your chambers and—"

"No," Haleine said.

"Willem will carry you."

"No," Haleine said. "He can't."

"He can," Bronagh said as she slipped her hands under Haleine's elbows. "Come, let's get you up and—"

"No," Haleine said. She pushed herself up and rested on her knees. Her head swam, her vision blurred and she pressed her hand against the wound as if it might help. "Neither of you will help me. I'll not have your head on a pike because of me."

Bronagh backed away and Haleine stood. She walked the remaining distance to her chambers, keeping one hand against her head while the other dragged along the wall. Bronagh ran ahead—to open the doors, to gather her supplies, Haleine supposed—while Willem hovered too closely behind her, making ready to catch her should she fall.

But she didn't fall, not until she was inside the walls of her bedchamber. She collapsed into the chair nearest the door and was content to stay there and let Bronagh come to her.

"This is why," Bronagh said as she worked. "This is why you can't go to the soldiers' families. This is why you can't—"

"This is exactly why I will go," Haleine said, grabbing Bronagh's wrist. "You will find them, and you will do it quickly, for every day you delay I will return to the hospital, and I will bandage more wounds and tend more fevers and take every beating the king offers me."

Bronagh freed her wrist from Haleine's grasp. "I will bring them to you."

It was a good compromise, and she should have agreed to it, but Haleine shook her head.

"I will go to them," she said. "Soon, Bronagh."

"Yes, your majesty."

Two days later, Haleine sat in the cathedral with two women and their three children. All five were wary of her and were unwilling to look her in the eye. Any questions she posed were answered with the least amount of words possible. Sometimes she did not receive more than a shake or nod of a head. Was it grief that prevented them from contributing more, or had Bronagh said something to them?

When she ran out of words to say and the silence grew too unbearable, Haleine gave each family a small pouch of coins. It was not much, only what she could convince Ceallach to give her. She apologized that she couldn't offer more, but neither woman responded. Haleine nodded then, extended her condolences one last time and returned to the palace.

She entered her chambers to find Bronagh standing against the wall near the servants' passage. Her head was bowed and her hands were clasped together in front of her. Haleine didn't understand why until she saw Maddox lounging in the chair Haleine had come to call her own.

"She returns," Maddox said.

"She does," Haleine said as she untied her cloak.

"And where have you been now?"

She removed the cloak from her shoulders and draped it across the back of a chair. "Delivering condolences to the slain guards' families."

Maddox rose and came toward her. "I forbade you from doing that."

"Yes, I know," she said as he came to a stop in front of her. "I didn't care."

She braced herself for his reaction, but all he did was take her injured hand in his own.

"Then I shall have to make you care," he said.

"Do your worst."

Maddox smiled. "I always do."

He squeezed her hand with enough force to drive her to her knees. She ducked her head and closed her eyes as she willed herself not to cry out. He lifted her chin with his free hand and ordered her to look at him. When she did, he continued.

"You will lose."

He leaned in and kissed her forehead before leaving the room. The doors had scarcely closed before Bronagh was at her side, helping her up and over to the chair in which Maddox had sat.

"I'll summon Rhys," her maid said, "and he'll—"

"No," Haleine said. "That's not necessary."

Bronagh looked at her hand. "Isn't it?"

"No," Haleine repeated. "Just—just bring me some wine."

Bronagh sighed and crossed the room to fetch the wine. Haleine looked at the fire as she attempted to straighten out her fingers. She was crying when Bronagh returned.

"Are you sure, your majesty," Bronagh said, holding out the goblet, "that you wouldn't like me to summon the physician?"

"Yes, I'm sure."

"It can be done without your husband knowing."

"No, it can't," Haleine said. "Leave the wine on the table and go."

Bronagh put the cup down. "You can't keep doing this."

"Can't I?"

"The king will not tolerate it. There will be a reckoning. You won't be able to avoid it."

"I have avoided it thus far."

"Look what he's done to you," Bronagh said. "You haven't avoided anything."

"This is hardly his worst, and you know it."

Bronagh shook her head. "It only means he plans something even more terrible."

"More terrible than killing me?"

"You can't help anyone if you're dead."

"Neither can I help anyone if I'm a prisoner in this castle."

"They're not worth it, any of them," Bronagh said. "Those dead guards, their families, the bloody poor in the hospital—they're not worth letting him do this to you."

"And the old king and queen?" Haleine asked. "What of them? You were willing to risk your head on a pike because Michaela made you promise to protect me."

"Aye, and if the new king kills you, I'll have failed you both."

"He won't kill me."

"No," Bronagh said as she walked away. "You'll just wish he had."

◆◆◆

As the king had ordered, the country—especially those in the city—mourned. In the week following the old king's burial, Eluned fell into a state of melancholy. Those who loved the old king bemoaned his loss and drank toasts to his memory. Those who had heard the troublesome rumors about the new king drank as well but more for fear of what would come.

Bereavement of any kind wasn't an option for Dana. His work was too vital, and there was so much to be done. There were maps to be made, information and supplies to be gathered, *people* to be gathered. James talked frequently about their numbers. *A number, really, Dana,* he would say. *And not a very impressive one.* Four. That was all they had. Dana knew he wouldn't be able to complete the mission set forth before him with only James and the two others. He didn't know yet from where the numbers would come but knew just the same they would be there when needed. And that time had not yet come. Four, as small a number as it was, was enough for now. Four people, four tasks. They could accomplish much in a day.

Lucius and Ilya, he learned, were children of a master blacksmith, and he had taught both of them his craft. They knew the quality of a blade or bow and could judge the talent of the one wielding it. Dana was glad Faolan had brought them to this task. His own knowledge on the subject was quite good, especially considering his lack of formal training, but it wasn't good enough. Lucius and Ilya would help that. Every moment they could spare was spent training in the tavern's storeroom. It was hardly a waste, as they would certainly have to fight. He and James had been in their share of bawdy house brawls but rebelling against the king was nowhere near the same.

He entered the storeroom now where James was in the middle of a lesson with Ilya. Neither of them noticed him, and he didn't wish to interrupt so he watched as James attacked Ilya. James was more than proficient with a bow and dagger but was lost so far when it came to the sword. Even with his more untrained eye, Dana could see the clumsiness of James's strokes but noted that the effort was much improved.

"You're dropping your shoulder," Ilya said. "Every time you do, I can tell exactly what you're planning."

James tried the attack again. Ilya watched him, and while she still blocked his attack easily, this time she nodded and smiled.

"Good," she said. "Better. There's no need to tell your opponent what you intend until it's too late for him to do anything about it. That's what dropping your shoulder like that does. But now let's talk about your footwork."

"What's wrong with that?"

"You're picking up your feet. It's better to slide them."

James was exasperated. "What does it matter?"

"Attack me again. I'll show you."

James was slow to lift his sword again. He may not have been sure what he'd done wrong, but he knew the lesson he was about to receive would hurt. To his credit, he didn't back down. He attacked her as he had before. Ilya leaned back to avoid the first slice, then rushed James, holding her forearm as though she carried a shield. James stumbled and, unable to regain his balance, landed on his backside.

Her point made, Ilya stopped and dropped her sword. She nodded at James and offered her hand to him. James rolled onto his side and got up on his own.

"That was a little unfair on my part because you're afraid you'll hurt me," she said, "but you won't. At least not yet, so stop holding back, aye? And don't pick up your feet."

James nodded.

"It's coming," Ilya said next. "You've got talent, can't deny that. Give it time, and you'll be fearsome."

"Do we have that kind of time?" James asked.

"We'll make it," Ilya said, then nodded at Dana. "You next?"

He shook his head. "Later maybe. Where's Lucius?"

"Visiting an old colleague of our father's," Ilya said. "He might be able to help us with weaponry, maybe give us use of his facilities if nothing else. We're not going to be able to find everything we need; we'll have to make some of it."

"What are we even going to do with it all?" James asked. "It can't stay here."

"No, it can't," Dana agreed.

Nor could they, once it began. It was something that would involve more planning. He would consult with Faolan and Lorcan, but Dana already suspected they would need to retreat to the forest.

"Orla would never allow it," Ilya said. "She barely tolerates the sword practice as it is. We'll have to get it out of the city."

"That'll be a trick," James said. "The guards at the gate can be prone to searching wagons."

"Aye. That's true, unless they know you. That's why we'll ask for help from someone just like that," Dana said. "We're not completely without friends."

Ilya opened her mouth, perhaps to ask who Dana had in mind, but James knew already and spoke first.

"You mean my family," he said. "On a market day."

"Several market days, I'm sure. We're going to need quite a lot."

James shook his head. "You can't involve them in this. It's too dangerous. What if they get searched?"

"Have they ever been searched?" Dana asked. "In your entire life, have they ever been searched? James, I know you're worried, but think about it. The farm families on market day always arrive with a loaded wagon of goods to sell and leave with a loaded wagon of goods needed at home. They never get searched; there's too many of them."

"It's a risk."

"Aye, it is," he said, "but it's a risk we need to take."

James didn't look convinced.

"We'll ask," Dana said. "They can say no."

"If you ask, they won't."

Dana nodded. He counted on it.

"They won't say no," James said, almost to himself. He looked at the sword in his hand for a moment before handing it to Dana.

"James," Dana said. "We have to ask."

"Aye."

James left the room. Dana passed the sword to Ilya and went after him. He caught up to James in their room. James was already in the process of packing.

"What are you doing?" Dana asked. "Where are you going?"

"Home."

"James, we have to do this."

James stopped. "And I know it, Dana, but I won't put my family at risk if I don't have to. I'll bring the wagon on market day. I'll get the weapons out of the city. You get them ready to go."

"You shouldn't do it on your own."

James picked up his pack. "Then Da will help. But not the rest. I'll protect them if I can."

Dana didn't think Mahree or Sarai needed protection, nor Aaron for that matter, and would more likely be angry with James for suggesting it, but he didn't say anything. There wasn't anything to be gained by it, so he nodded instead.

"All right. We'll get what we can to start. You'll find a place to store them on the farm?"

"There's a cave in the forest. You know it; we've been out there before. It'll be better to store everything there. I don't want it on the farm."

Dana remembered the cave well and nodded again. It was far enough away from the homestead that—should it be discovered—suspicion wouldn't fall on James's family. It was also secluded enough that it would be safe. Most people didn't even know it was there.

"Fine. I'll go down to the stable with you and see you off."

"No need," James said and left the room.

Dana closed the door behind him and retreated to the window to watch James leave. Faolan flew into the room and landed on the windowsill just as James mounted his horse.

"Where's he going?" Faolan asked.

Dana watched James ride out of sight. "Home."

"Is he coming back? What happened?"

"Why did you choose him for this?"

"I didn't choose anyone for anything."

Dana left the window and sat in a chair. "Why was he chosen? Is he meant to be my conscience?"

"No, you already have one of those," Faolan said. "What happened?"

"I told him I want to use his family to get supplies out of the city."

"Makes sense."

Dana nodded. "He went to do it himself. He thinks the risk to them is too great."

"Of course he does. They're his family."

"They're my family too," Dana said.

He waited for Faolan to tell him it wasn't the same. Seoras and Mahree weren't his parents, after all. It was true that they'd fed and clothed him for years, but they weren't the people who had given him life. Those people were gone. There wasn't even a memory of them, for he had never known them. He waited to hear it, but the pegasus said nothing.

"I don't want harm to come to them any more than James does," Dana said.

"You don't have to convince me."

And Dana knew it was true. Faolan understood what was needed, probably more than he let on. He knew there would be sacrifices to be made and that this was just the beginning.

"What does it mean that I'm willing to take the risk and he isn't?" Dana asked. Faolan again said nothing, and Dana looked at him and laughed. "I've never known you to be so silent before."

"He'll be all right," the pegasus offered.

"Will he? He's balking already, Faolan, and it's only going to get harder."

"I know."

"I don't think he has the stomach for it."

"He will."

Dana considered that. Somehow he thought that was worse.

———⧸∿∿⧹———

The morning after her visit with the soldiers' families, Haleine's body gave out. Her injuries had caught up to her at last and she could no longer ignore them. She was forced to spend several days recovering in her chambers. Bronagh, though she did not say so, was delighted that Haleine's excursions into the city had been—at least temporarily—suspended. She proved it by being as good-humored as Haleine had ever seen. She was even entertaining the notion of telling Haleine to where else she might go to help Eluned's citizens when Ceallach interrupted. When Haleine looked at him, he bowed.

"The king summons you to the great hall, your majesty," he said.

"Does he," Haleine said, ignoring Bronagh's gasp. "Who else is in the great hall, Ceallach?"

"The entire court, your majesty."

Haleine nodded and looked at Bronagh as she rose from her seat. "It would appear your reckoning has arrived."

Bronagh moved to stand directly in front of her. "Don't go," she whispered.

"There's nowhere else to go," Haleine said. She leaned in and kissed her maid's cheek. "Thank you for all you've done."

Willem stayed close as she followed Ceallach to the great hall. When they arrived, Ceallach announced her, and the members of her husband's court moved to either side, creating a center aisle. Maddox sat on his throne on its raised dais at the end of the room. Omur stood just behind him on his left. Haleine put her hand out to prevent Willem from following any farther and approached her husband alone.

"You wished to see me, my lord?" she said, dropping into a curtsey before him.

"Come," he said. "Sit."

He gestured to the empty chair on his right. She looked at it, then back at him.

"I have something I wish for you to see," he said. "The view will be better from here."

She didn't move. She shifted her gaze to Omur. Her husband's advisor watched her, seeming uninterested in what happened before him.

"Come now, Haleine," Maddox said. "You wouldn't want to be contrary, would you?"

She hadn't been anything else, and he knew it. What game was he playing? She recalled Bronagh's words. *It only means he plans something even more terrible.*

"I wouldn't dream of it," she said, moving to take her seat.

"We both know that's not true," Maddox said. He turned to Omur. "Bring him in."

Omur gestured to someone unseen, and the doors opened once again. A pair of guards entered, holding between them a young boy. The three of them walked toward the dais. It wasn't until they were much closer that she recognized the lad as the son of one of the fallen soldiers. She slid to the very edge of her chair and gripped the arms. Something more terrible.

"What are you doing?" she whispered.

Maddox didn't answer directly. Instead he stood and walked down the dais's three steps and claimed possession of the boy. He stood behind the child. The boy looked at her, terror etched on every inch of his face.

"You recognize him, yes?" Maddox said.

"What are you doing?" she asked.

Maddox caressed the boy's throat. "Don't you know?"

Haleine stood. "I defied you. Not him."

"Yes, I know."

She heard the sound of a blade being drawn then saw the change in the boy's eyes. She didn't understand what had happened until a rivulet of blood appeared at the corner of the boy's mouth. Next she saw the tip of a bloody blade protruding from the boy's chest. She flew down the steps, but Maddox came around and caught her by the throat before she could reach him. She couldn't see it, but she heard the boy's body hit the floor.

"There's more where he came from," Maddox said, his voice almost a hiss. "Will you make me kill them all?"

He held her too tightly to allow her to speak, so she offered a small shake of her head. It was enough to satisfy Maddox.

"Smart lass," he said and shoved her away.

She fell against the dais steps and landed on the floor. She stayed there until Maddox, with Omur trailing behind him, had left the room. The now silent members of her husband's court watched as she crawled to the boy and checked him for the life she already knew her husband had stolen. She pulled the dagger from his body and cast it aside before cradling him in her arms. She bent her head down until their foreheads touched and cried.

James thought it ironic that after waiting his whole life for a reason to leave the farm that now, when presented with just such an opportunity, he couldn't get home fast enough. He didn't spare the horse as he left the city. It was a road he had traveled many times before, but never with this sense of urgency.

There were two main roads that lead to Enimode. They came from the west and the south. The western road led to the farther regions of the country and eventually the mountains that separated Lira from Feond. James had never ventured very far down that road; he never really had any call to, but it was typically the route

Dana took whenever he left the homestead. The south road led directly to Eluned and was, therefore, more traveled. James knew it well as his family used it frequently during the year to get to market. He also knew his time on this road was coming to an end. He was certain to become an outlaw and, as such, he couldn't very well travel the king's roads. He'd have to resort to the forest paths. They would take longer, but they would be safer from the king's men. The wildlife would be another concern, but James thought he would rather confront a wild boar than one of the king's regiments.

The first sight of the village was always the church steeple. It was modest, like the rest of the settlement, but tall enough to be seen through the trees. He saw the mill next and behind it, the river from which it drew its power. The tavern followed, Rhiannon and her father standing in front of it. Rhiannon waved to him, and James waved back as he passed and guided his gelding off the main road and onto the path that would lead home.

His family's homestead started on the very edge of Enimode's boundaries. The forest acted as a border, as it abutted the farm on every side but the one facing the village. They were far enough away that it occasionally felt as though they weren't a part of Enimode at all, but even if James never again set foot in the town, he'd still be a part of it. Dana proved that.

He first saw the barn and, next to it, the year's fallow field. The animal pens followed. They were empty now, as the sheep, cows and horses had been turned out in the pasture for grazing. The dogs, Liam and Bari, lay in the fields with them, so there would be no one around to alert others of his arrival. James led his mount into an empty pen and removed the saddle and bridle before disappearing behind the barn.

As wheat brought in the most income, it was his father's habit to spend as much time as he could in the field, making sure all was well with the crop. It was an obvious place for James to start his search, and here it was he found his father. Seoras's face showed as much pleasure as it ever did as he clasped his son in a welcoming hug.

"You've come home," Seoras said.

"Aye."

"You said you'd be gone three days."

James nodded. "I was wrong about that. And I'll not be here long now."

"You mean to leave again?"

"Aye. There's something that I—that *we*—it can't be helped," James said as he stooped to pick up a handful of soil. "And we need your help, if you'll consent to do it."

"Are you in trouble, lad? Is Dana?"

Not yet, he wanted to say. He shook his head.

"All right," his father said. "Well, let us go inside and talk. Has your mother seen you yet? You'd think you'd been gone a year, the way she misses you."

"No, she hasn't seen me yet, Da," James said, "but we have to talk here and now because I don't want Ma to know what I have to ask you. I don't want any of them to know. And you can't tell them."

Seoras frowned. "You are in trouble, aren't you? What is it you and Dana have started? You hardly said anything of your plans when you left. I just assumed that you were—James, the king is dead, and his son sits on the throne. Do you know something about that?"

They hadn't said anything of their plans because there hadn't been anything to tell and no need to say anything. Dana explained his intended abduction of James by saying he was needed on a mission of utmost importance. It wasn't the first time Dana had done so. His father laughed about it because the missions of utmost importance constantly seemed to involve drinking and whoring for a night or two in a nearby village. Seoras always hoped James might come home at the end of it ready for a bride. But now there was more, much more. James knew the real reason would have to be revealed in some form, but still he was reluctant to tell his father all he knew.

"I might."

"And you don't want to tell me?"

"No."

"What are you doing, lad?"

"What I have to."

His father thought about that. James looked back toward the house. He could see Aaron heading toward the pasture and checked the skyline. It was time to bring the livestock in, a chore he had always shared with his brother in the past. Now he watched Aaron work alone.

"What do you need?" Seoras asked.

James looked away from his brother. "We need to get supplies out of the city. We want to do it on market day."

"What sort of supplies?"

"The sort we can't very well parade past a guardhouse."

"And we don't get searched."

James nodded.

"Well, of course we'll help if you say you need it," his father said, "but I'd like to know something of what you're planning."

There wasn't anything to tell him but the truth. James let the soil slip through his fingers. "We're going to overthrow the king."

Now his father thought about that. James watched him for a moment then motioned to his brother.

"I'll just go help Aaron with the animals, shall I?"

The evening passed without mention of why he had returned home. Mahree was so pleased to see her son again that he couldn't bring himself to tell her it was only a visit at best. He waited for his father to say something, but Seoras sat in his chair, watched his son and said nothing. James was grateful. It would be easier if she didn't know. The next morning, however, James climbed down from the loft he shared with Aaron and was met by his mother's worried face.

"I see Da told you."

"Aye," she said.

"Then I suppose Gran and Aaron know as well."

"They might."

He nodded. He wasn't mad. He knew, despite his hope for the opposite, his father would tell her, and his mother would likely involve Sarai. It was possible no one had said anything directly to Aaron, but Aaron was bound to overhear. His brother did that well.

"I didn't want Da to say anything because I was trying to protect you," he said. "If something happens and we—if I—I don't want them to come for you."

She said nothing, just stood there and stared at him.

"There's work to be done," he said and started to leave.

"It's treason."

She said it quickly but quietly, and he stopped and sighed. He didn't turn around.

"It's necessary."

"You're sure?"

"Aye."

Mahree sighed. "All right then."

On market day, he and his father left Enimode before dawn. The sun was trying to break through a thick wall of gray clouds as they entered the city alongside the farmers from the neighboring villages. The guards stood in their shelters, huddled in their fur-lined cloaks to combat the early morning chill, and waved the farmers on without another thought. They set their goods on display and the day began.

Later on, Dana appeared with Faolan on his shoulder. Even this wasn't unusual as Dana would occasionally see them on a market day, or even aid them in selling, if he were in the area. He and Dana greeted each other as though it had been months and not days since they'd last seen each other. In fact, the day felt entirely normal until his father spoke.

"Why don't you lads go and fetch the supplies," Seoras said. "James, you know what we need."

"Aye," he said. "We'll take care of it."

"Be quick, would you?" Seoras said, glancing at the sky. "It looks to rain, and I don't want to be out in it longer than I have to be."

James nodded and followed Dana back to the tavern. It was empty except for Orla standing behind the bar. She nodded at them as they passed through to the storeroom where Lucius and Ilya were packing provisions. He watched as they wrapped a number of daggers in cloth and stored them in a short barrel of grain.

"You'll ruin that if you're not careful," he said.

Ilya looked at him as she replaced the barrel's lid. "As long as the weapons are safe, I don't care if the grain gets ruined."

"Aye," he said, looking around at what they had accumulated in his absence. "You've done well."

"It's a start," Ilya said. "But there's still much we haven't come by yet."

"It'll come to us," Dana said.

"How? When?"

Dana shrugged. "I don't know yet."

"Glad to see you have a plan," Ilya said.

"Glad to see you have faith," Dana rejoined.

She laughed as she handed him the barrel. "Luckily for you, I do. I wouldn't be here otherwise."

James marveled at the camaraderie between them. From where had it come? It hadn't been there before he left, not like this anyway, and he had been gone for only three days. He took a step back as he watched the others before him, and for a moment, he could see it. The people would flock to Dana. He would draw them in just as he drew everyone in. They would fight for him, and they would die for him. James himself was prepared for that—at least he thought he was—and Lucius and Ilya were of a same mind. They hadn't known Dana nearly as long and still, they were prepared to follow him. The people, whoever they were, would gather around him too. It would work.

For a moment he could see it, he could believe it, then the sight of Lucius picking up a bolt of what looked to be linen canvas drew him back to the present. James looked at Dana in disbelief.

"Oh, that won't be suspicious at all," James said. "We have a lot of call for canvas on the farm, you know. We like to make little tents for the cows so we don't have to bother with the barn."

"No one will notice the fabric or anything else," Faolan said. "I'll make sure of it."

James looked at the pegasus next. "How are you going to do that?"

"Magic," Faolan answered.

"Magic?" James repeated.

"Yes," Faolan said. "Should the need arise, I can perform a cloaking spell that will—"

"Stop," James said. "Just—I don't want to know. God, I don't want to know."

"If you're sure."

"I'm sure," James said.

He was more than sure. He hated the idea of magic. It was unnatural and wrong, and to be suspected of wielding such skill was grounds for execution. It was worse, far worse, than acknowledging the existence of Laorans, but as James looked at the others, he knew he was the only one who thought so.

Ilya's expression was identical to the one she wore the night they first met. He hadn't thought much of it then—his head had been too muddled for that—but now it irritated him. Lucius's face held no expression, in that way reminding James of his father. James kept his eyes on Dana and Faolan the longest. Trusting Dana meant trusting Faolan. And trusting Faolan meant having at least the smallest amount of faith in magic and even Laorans. Could he manage it?

"If you can do this...this spell," James said, "why are we bothering to hide anything?"

"Because the spell is a last resort," Faolan said. "Using any sort of magic can attract the attention of...others who share similar skills, and there are some within the city walls I'd rather not alert to our exact location if I don't have to."

"Who are these others?" James asked. "What threat do they pose to you—to us?"

Faolan glanced around the room. "A conversation for another time. We do this first."

More mystery, more unanswered questions. Why didn't Dana see it? Why didn't Dana care? James clenched his fists. He'd come here for Dana; he stayed for Dana, but now James only wanted to leave them to their mad plans and blind faith. Let them deal with the magic and the unknown; he'd go home. He'd walk out and—

"James?" Dana said.

"You're just determined to kill us all, aren't you?" James said. "One way or another."

Dana smiled. "Just the opposite."

James nodded and picked up a second bolt of linen. It was much heavier than he thought it would be.

"Is there something in here?" he asked.

"Bows," Ilya answered.

"Right," James said. He had to stop asking questions. "Let's just get this over with."

❧

Haleine had been away from home for little more than a month when her mother's first letter arrived. A servant brought it to her chambers, called her by the title that had become her name, and held it out to her. Haleine sat in her chair and looked at the parchment sealed with her family's crest and addressed in her mother's writing but did not claim it. The servant repeated himself, looking flustered, and still she did not move.

She should have been pleased to receive a letter from her mother. She should have been pleased to have something from outside the palace walls. It had been two full weeks since she had allowed herself outside them, choosing instead to stay sequestered in her chambers with only Bronagh and Ceallach for company. Haleine was a prisoner, and a letter from her mother should have brought her joy, but she did not move. There was no room within her for joy.

There would be consequences; she had known that. There would be castigation for fighting him, for raising her voice to him and accusing him of doing exactly what he had done. There would be repercussions for openly defying him. Yes, there would be punishment for that. She established herself as a willful mare in need of breaking, and Maddox felt equal to the task. His verbal abuse, his physical abuse—that was no less than she expected.

But the boy—that beautiful boy with his wide, dark eyes—he was a loss she had not anticipated and now—now she was lost.

She knew what she needed to do. She wanted to fight Maddox; she wanted to stop him, but she didn't know how. How could she ever fight him? Helplessness was something to which she was unaccustomed, and the feeling was overwhelming her. She drowned in it as though she were adrift at sea, and with each passing day, it only grew harder to keep her head above the waves.

Revelin would be ashamed if he knew. He had spoken so well of her at their last meeting despite all the hate she had had for him. *I know your strength*, he had said to her. *You will not be easily defeated*. And yet, she feared she had been.

Though no one wanted her to, Haleine had tended the boy's body herself, washing him, dressing him and dragging her fingers over his face to close his eyes. He had looked at her for the first time that day, and she was the last thing he ever saw. Did he understand why?

And his mother—did she know? Did she understand? As much as she wanted to, Haleine had not spoken to nor even seen the woman. She stayed away, sending instead a trio of servants to bring the boy's body back to his family.

What had they told her? Did they tell an already grieving woman of how the queen had brought more loss upon her family? Did they tell her how easily it could have been avoided?

Maddox had warned her. Warned her not to fight him, not to defy him. Give him time, and he would hurt her. He'd make her suffer; he'd make her care. It was a game he promised she wouldn't win.

Why hadn't she listened? To him? To Bronagh? To Ceallach—any of them? There had been no shortage of warning, but she had not listened, and now that boy was dead while she was lost, haunted and afraid—so very afraid.

Fear, she knew, was as potent an illness as helplessness, and she was now badly afflicted with both.

And perhaps that was what lay in her mother's letter. Fear that her daughter might never forgive, helplessness over what had been done and what was still to come. What was worse was that Haleine suspected her mother's letter contained no such sentiment.

The servant repeated himself a third time, and Haleine brought him back into her focus. She should have been pleased, but the sight of the parchment filled her with anything but joy. She could not reach out for it. It was more than she could give.

All she had was anger.

She turned away. Ceallach stepped forward and took the letter from the boy. The servant was relieved and, after a hasty bow, disappeared through the servants' entrance. Ceallach remained at her side, holding the offensive parchment.

"What does your majesty wish for me to do with this?" he asked.

She didn't know how to answer him. Would her husband be pleased to know she refused a letter from her mother? Would he care? Would he find some way to use it against her? Beseech her mother for more letters? Or would he interpret it as another symbol of her resignation?

"Leave it on the table and go," she said.

He did as she bade and walked away. He returned to his plain, straight-backed chair in the corner. He had spent every day for two weeks now in that chair. He may have called himself her advisor, but she knew what he was really doing, why he watched her the way he did.

She looked at the letter and laid her hand on top of it. After a moment, she picked it up and moved to stand directly in front of the fire. She threw the parchment into the center of it and watched the flames engulf her mother's words. Tan changed to black and crumbled into ash. Behind her, Ceallach moved in his chair, but he did not speak and she said nothing to him. Let him tell her husband what he wanted. She didn't care.

She didn't turn from the fire until the sounds of trumpets startled her. She looked at the others in the room. Bronagh was equally surprised, but Ceallach sat motionless in his chair, his head turned toward the balcony. Following his glance, she went to see what was happening.

The army was marching, led by the cavalry with their high-stepping stallions. They moved though the city streets in perfect formation. She watched them pass through the city gates and lost sight of them as they marched into the forest. When the last column had disappeared from her sight, she turned to look at Ceallach.

"Where are they going?" she asked.

She received no answer.

CHAPTER 5

Newly arrived from Enimode, Dana and James sat at their usual corner table in Orla's tavern, sipping ale while waiting for Lucius and Ilya to return from a scouting mission. The barroom was crowded, more so than after Maddox's wedding or Amatheon's funeral, and buzzed with news. Dana watched it all with interest. Something had happened. He saw Orla leave the bar with two bowls in hand and come toward them. Stew wouldn't be all she brought. She placed the bowls in front of them and leaned forward.

"Did you lads hear this?" she asked, gesturing to the commotion behind her. "The king's army marched today."

"Where did they go?" Dana asked.

"Cinna. They destroyed it."

"What do you mean they destroyed it?" James asked.

"I mean they destroyed it. They burned it to the ground and killed everyone who tried to stop them," Orla said. "And then killed everyone else."

"Everyone?"

"Unless they had the good fortune to be elsewhere today, but from what I'm hearing, weren't too many that were."

Dana nodded. Why would there be? Cinna was a farming village, like Enimode. Without market, and with harvest looming, there would be little reason to be anywhere but their fields.

"Why?" James asked. "Did they say why?"

"They say they're looking for the rebels," Orla said. "The ones what killed the old king."

"Rebels," James said.

"Aye," Orla said. "The lads at the bar say the soldiers asked all the villagers about the rebels. When they didn't know anything—" she shrugged. "Thought you'd want to know, Dana."

He nodded again. "Aye. Thank you."

Orla went back to the bar. Dana focused on the table. He knew James was staring at him but kept his head down.

"Rebels," James repeated.

Dana still didn't look up. "They had to say something."

And it was true. They did have to say something. Maddox couldn't ignore the murders; he had to act, and band of rebels would be a perfect scapegoat. That didn't bother Dana. He expected it. He had expected it sooner.

What did bother him was the length to which Maddox carried the charade. Why go to such an extent? There were any number of criminals held in the dungeon. Any of them could've been found guilty of the crimes and hanged. The king could have produced any one, said they were guilty, and no one would've questioned it. But why would Maddox want to destroy his own people and land? Even if his lack of humanity prevented him from caring about that, why would he destroy the subsequent income? Was there something more to this of which Dana was unaware? Something Faolan hadn't told him? He frowned. He didn't like suspecting the pegasus of anything.

"It's more than coincidence," James said. "You think so, too. I can tell."

"I don't know what to think. Come on," Dana said as he stood. "We should talk to Faolan."

They returned to their room where Faolan laid, his eyes closed, in the center of Dana's bed. He looked as though he slept, but Dana knew better. He waved at James to close the door.

"Faolan," he said, advancing upon the bed.

The pegasus's eyes opened. He looked at the two of them for a moment before standing and flying to the window ledge.

"We should wait until Lucius and Ilya return," he said. "They'll have questions, too."

"Did they see it happen?" Dana asked and Faolan nodded. "All right then. We'll wait."

"Well, I won't wait," James said. "I can't. I have to warn them."

Dana sat on the edge of his bed, but James stood in the corner, looking about as angry and tense as he'd ever been. What would it take to make him stay?

"They're all right," Faolan said.

"For now," James said. "Cinna wasn't safe, and almost all its farms were owned by the king. Why will a free village like Enimode be different?"

"They're all right," Faolan repeated.

"They won't even know what's happened," James said. "I have to warn them."

"No, you don't," Dana said. "Word will travel a lot faster than you will, and I think we'll need you here."

"Dana's right," Faolan said. "We're out of time; we're being forced to act sooner than I thought we would, and you need to be here. We'll wait until Lucius and Ilya return. They won't be much longer. Then we'll talk. In the meantime, maybe you should pack. We'll have to leave the city in the morning."

"Where are we going to go?" James asked.

"Into the woods," Faolan said. "I know you've been planning it, Dana, and the unicorns will help with that. It's the right thing to do. You can't be associated with anyone or any place now. Names, homes, families—it's time to leave them all behind."

Dana didn't move as he waited to see what James would do. Leave your home, leave your family. It hadn't been put to James like that. Dana didn't know if James had even thought about it.

But whether he had, James just nodded. "I'll start in their room. You pack up in here."

He left the room, leaving the door open behind him. Dana looked around. There was nothing for him to do. He and James hadn't bothered to unpack yet from their last trip. He considered going to help James but thought better of it as he felt sure James wanted to be alone.

"Dana, ask Orla for some water," Faolan said. "We don't need much, just enough to fill a basin."

Dana didn't question the demand, but there was something he did want to know.

"How did you know what I was planning?" he asked.

"We're connected, you and I," Faolan said, "through Laorans and the unicorns. She knew, they knew, so I knew."

"You mean you read my mind?"

"Me? No."

"But the others," he said. "Laorans and the—the unicorns. They read my mind?"

"Yes."

"All of them?"

"No," Faolan said. "Go get the water, Dana. I'll explain everything."

He went below stairs and pushed his way up to the bar. Orla was at the other end, filling tankards as fast as she could. He waited for her to notice him. He had more freedom than anyone when it came to Orla's barroom, but she was very particular about the bar itself and didn't like others behind it. She also didn't like sword practice in her storeroom, and he was wary of pushing her too far. She hadn't become the tavern's alewife by being mild mannered.

As he waited, he listened to the gossip. Before he'd left for Enimode, they had talked about the queen. Her beauty, her kindness. They were growing to love her. It started with her visit to the hospital and continued with her audience with the families of the murdered soldiers. She'd not been seen since that day but, despite her public absence, they remained infatuated with her. They saw salvation in her, something to give them hope after the loss of their king. But now Haleine's name was far from their lips as they swapped stories of what the soldiers had done in Cinna. The tales were remarkably similar, unusual for barroom gossip, with a common theme of horrifying violence. Burning, looting, raping, maiming. Killing. And for what? A band of miserable louts who murdered a king and left the people to suffer for their terrible misdeeds.

He knew they were talking about him. He knew they were talking about James and Lucius and Ilya as well. What he didn't know was why or how, but after hearing himself described as a miserable lout, he decided he couldn't wait any longer. He looked to see where Orla was and leaned over the bar to find the jug himself. Let her be mad.

"Hello, lover," a voice said in his ear.

He straightened, jug in hand, and looked to see Piala standing to his right. She was an extraordinarily pretty whore with whom he had had the pleasure of sharing more than one night. She damn near set the bed afire every time he bedded her. It was what kept him coming back to her over and over again. She smiled and leaned in to kiss him. For the first time since he had met her, he didn't enjoy it.

Piala ran her fingers across his chest. "One of the girls told me you were back, that you'd been here days now. I called the stupid bint a liar because if you'd been in town for days, I would've known it because I would've been in your bed."

There was no anger in her voice, only mischievous flirtation. It was always the same with her. It was part of why he liked her so much. They had suited each other well in the past. It was different now, but he couldn't tell her that.

"Orla will skin you alive if she sees you," he said.

"Orla always allows your girls," she countered, running her hand through his hair.

"I can't."

He pushed past her and went to the storeroom to fetch water. Piala followed and watched him. She stood in the doorway and blocked his exit.

"James with you?" she asked. "There's no worries there. We can always send him next door. I do know a couple of girls who would be pleased to see him again."

"Not this time, Piala."

She frowned. "Something's wrong. What is it?"

"Nothing."

"Nothing? I know you, lover. You always come to call when you're around. You've even come here specifically to see me. I daresay I'm one of the few girls whose name you remember without prompting. And I know that if you've truly been in town for as long as they say that it's the longest you've gone without a girl in your bed."

"Jealous?"

She smiled. "I'm a whore. I don't get jealous. There's no profit in it. But I like you, love. I'm concerned is all. Why are you here this time? What have you got going on?"

He touched her cheek. "Be a good lass and forget you ever knew me."

She took a small step back, surprised perhaps that her wiles had failed her. He took advantage of that and slipped past her, leaving her standing alone. He wasn't worried. Piala was never alone for long.

When he got back upstairs, he saw Lucius and Ilya had returned. They sat on the bed, their eyes troubled and faces ashen. Whatever they had seen had shaken them greatly. They hadn't even bothered to remove their cloaks. Lucius's had a small silver unicorn embroidered upon it near the neck. Dana looked at it for a moment before closing the door behind him. The conversation to come was nothing anyone outside of the room needed to hear. He nodded at Faolan, who stood in the window near James, and held up the jug so the pegasus could see it.

"Good," Faolan said. "Pour some water into the basin and set it on the floor."

"In a moment." Dana put the jug on a table. "I want to hear what happened first."

"You were in the barroom," Ilya said. "You heard the stories. They're all true."

"Gossip, maybe," James said. "Exaggeration."

Ilya shook her head. "There was nothing to exaggerate. They burned it to the ground; they destroyed everything. Homes, barns, fields, everything. It's gone. They're gone."

"And you watched it happen?" James asked. "You didn't do anything to stop them?"

"There was nothing to be done," Lucius said.

"There must have been *something*," James said.

"We were two," Ilya said. "Two against an army. There was nothing to be done."

"And look at us now. Four against an army? It's not much better, is it?" James said. "Is that how it's going to be, then? Nothing to be done?"

"No," Faolan said. "Dana, the water."

Dana picked up the jug and did as Faolan asked. He put the basin in the center of the room. When he backed away, Faolan flew to the floor and stood beside the basin. He lowered his head and concentrated on the water. James, Lucius and Ilya looked at Dana. He shrugged. He didn't know what Faolan was doing.

"All right," Faolan said, returning to the window. "Look into the water."

They bent over the basin. A face belonged to an older man stared back at them with dark eyes holding no mercy.

"You've probably seen him at the king's side," Faolan continued. "He's placed himself as Maddox's advisor; he would've been at the wedding, the coronation, the funerals, all of it."

Despite their apparently close proximity, Dana didn't recognize him. It wasn't surprising. He had been so taken by the queen he had hardly noticed anyone else.

"Who is he?" Ilya asked.

"His name is Omur. And he is your enemy."

"What about Maddox?" James asked. "I thought he was the enemy."

"He isn't to be taken lightly, not by any means," Faolan said. "But this man here is the true danger."

Dana looked up. "I don't understand."

"Omur is the human vessel of the dark gods."

An already-silent room sank into a deeper silence. No one moved, but Dana felt three pairs of eyes settle upon him. He looked back at the basin as he considered Faolan's revelation.

The dark gods were not unknown to him. He didn't think there was anyone who didn't know about them. Much like Laorans, they were the stuff of legend, myths worshipped centuries ago by his ancestors' ancestors. Laorans was a goddess of the earth, *the* goddess of the earth, life and beauty, the sun and moon. The dark gods were just the opposite. They were sinister, evil beings who reveled in all that was ugly and brutal about mankind, death and war, hatred and suffering. And now he was going to fight them. He thought he'd probably have to rethink his strategy a little.

"The dark gods wish to kill Laorans," Faolan said, and all eyes shifted to him. "They've always wanted that. They think now they'll be able to accomplish that goal."

"Why now?" Dana asked.

"A combination of factors," Faolan said. "Some we know about, some we don't. What it means is that they believe Maddox's rule will weaken Laorans enough that they'll be successful."

James looked ill. "How is it possible to—to kill a goddess?"

"Tear her earth apart," Faolan answered. "Upset the balance any way you can and you weaken the goddess. The more turmoil, the weaker she becomes until she eventually dies. Coincidently, chaos is what the dark gods feed upon; the more there is, the more powerful they'll become. Any sort of strife, a famine maybe, a plague, a—"

"Rebellion," Dana interjected.

Faolan nodded. "Rebellion is particularly effective. It's not without risk, however, and Omur knows this. He's spread the rumors of a rebel group because he knows there will be people who will believe the king and will blame you for the hardship he brings to them. Those people will hate you and will work just as hard as the king's army to kill you. But Omur also knows there will be those who will join with you and fight against the king because of what they've lost. He's convinced he can tip the scale in his favor."

"That's where the numbers will come from," Dana said.

"Yes."

"If Omur wants this rebellion," James said, "why are we doing it?"

We. This time Dana did smile.

89

"Because we need it, too," Faolan said. "We can't stand idly by while they threaten to rip the country asunder. We have to fight for its preservation. It is Laorans's hope that Dana will be able to unite the people and ultimately end the dark gods' plans."

James thought for a moment and nodded. "Aye. If anyone could, it would be you, Dana," he said. "What happens now?"

"Omur has issued the challenge," Faolan said. "You have to answer him."

"Confront him?" James asked.

"Yes," Faolan said.

"How?"

The pegasus looked at Dana. "That's your decision, but I'd suggest something face to face. You want them to know who you are."

"I won't have to worry about them killing me?" Dana asked.

"Not yet," Faolan said. "Omur needs you now. He needs you to start this rebellion because rumor will only take him so far. And at least for a while, he needs you to be successful at it. You'll be safe."

"And the king?"

"I don't know what Maddox knows, or even if he knows anything; but, again, Omur needs you. He can't allow Maddox to harm you. He has ways to hold the king in check. Take advantage of it while you can."

Dana nodded. He would take any advantage he could get.

"Faolan," he said, "leave us for a while."

The pegasus nodded and flew through the window. Dana lifted his head and studied his companions. None of them looked at him.

"If you want out, if you want to leave, this is the time to do it," he said, "because tomorrow we give them reason to hunt us."

Ilya was the first to speak. "Then we'd better rest while we can," she said as she stood and walked out of the room.

Lucius followed her, and Dana and James were left alone again.

James finally looked up. "Did Faolan tell you any of this before now?"

Dana shook his head.

"Do you still think this is something we should do?"

"I never wavered. It's no different."

"No different? How is it not different? You heard what Faolan said as well as I did. There are forces at work here, primal forces, evil forces, worse than we could've imagined. Bloody magic and gods and—"

"And to think, just the other day, you wouldn't acknowledge the existence of one goddess."

"Damn you," James said. "Don't make light about this! Don't you dare do that! Gods, Dana. He wants us to fight *gods*."

"Aye, but it doesn't matter. Not really. Not when the people of this land are still under attack. If fighting to protect them aids Faolan's goddess, I gladly will serve her interests," Dana said. "But I will fight for the people first and foremost. Are you with me?"

James sighed. "You know I am."

"I do," Dana said. "Tomorrow I want you to take Lucius and Ilya and go to Enimode. You should probably stay off the main road, just in case, and stick to the forest paths. Get what we need there to set up a camp. Faolan and Lorcan and the other unicorns will know where to go. I'll join you when I'm done here."

"How will you know where we'll be?"

"I'll find you."

"What are you going to do?"

Dana stood and went to the window to look at the palace. "I'm going to answer a challenge."

"You shouldn't go alone."

Dana shook his head. "Alone is exactly how I should go."

———～～～———

His masters had made a habit of waiting. No, *habit* was too slight a word. To them, it was an art. Very specific were their plans, and precise timing was required. The prophecy, above all, was law, and to jeopardize it would be death. But Omur had no interest in endangering that for which he had worked all his life. These long years, decades and, yes, even centuries were all spent working to bring forth the time when his masters—Yelsneh, Lamak, Azia, Gargon—would return victorious from their exile and crush into oblivion the goddess Laorans who had banished them.

As long as they would wait, so would he. It had been more than a thousand years thus far. Omur had only been their servant for seven hundred of those years, a mere child when compared to Iollan Iuchar, the man who had first received the prophecy. He, like Omur, had been born mortal but was destined to be anything but, shedding his mortal existence to serve the will of the dark gods. He worked as Omur did, whispering into the ears of powerful men to push and pull them into unwittingly serving a higher, darker authority. Iollan Iuchar had gone by many names over the centuries, always keeping his true name and purpose secret. Omur was one of two on this earth who knew his true name, for Iollan Iuchar's life was sacred and his blood even more so. He was the man whose descendant would one day rip open the sky and rain fire upon the goddess's earth.

Yes, more than one thousand years had gone as they waited for this descendant and this moment, but now the time was growing nigh. Omur could feel it in his bones; he could feel it in the words his masters spoke. They were close, but still they would wait another century if need be, for what was one hundred years more to them?

But Omur did not think it would matter because he did not think they would have to wait another hundred years nor even half that number. Perhaps not even a decade more would hinder them from what they sought.

They were encouraged. That was why he had been sent to Lira to play act the role of servant to his puppet king. It was a loathsome task as Maddox was a loathsome man, but the king, too, had a role to fulfill, for without him, Haleine never would have crossed the ocean.

Omur did not know what his lords wanted with the girl, but they wanted her all the same. His few instructions had been clear. He was not to touch her. He was *never* to touch her. He was not to let Maddox kill her. The first was easy. The second, given the king's penchant for cruelty, was proving to be more worrisome.

Omur followed Maddox now as he made his way to his library. The king ranted as he walked. It was a common enough occurrence; he was always upset by something. Today, however, was different. The queen's maid had just informed him that the queen's courses had begun. He had failed to impregnate her. Maddox wasn't taking the news well.

"What use is she if she does not breed?" he demanded. "I married her to give me sons. God, what did Nathan do to me? I bed the frigid little bitch every night, and for what?"

The king required no response so Omur offered none. The maid's news did not surprise him. The king and his queen had only been married a month, and while Maddox frequented his wife's bed, there were many nights when he was too drunk from an evening of revelry with his nobles to even mount the stairs to the queen's chambers. The fact that the queen was not pregnant was hardly unexpected. The opposite would have shocked Omur more, for although Maddox was eager for a son, Omur felt no such need for an heir. As a squalling infant of either sex would only needlessly complicate his plans, he would prefer the queen remain childless and had taken the necessary precautions to render Maddox's seed harmless.

He thought the lack of an heir even more important now that the queen was steadily gaining favor amongst her subjects. Tales of her visits to the hospital and the cathedral had spread throughout the city and beyond its walls, and the people loved her for it. Her extended absence since had only added to their devotion.

He didn't understand it but he had feared it would happen. It was why he hadn't wanted her to go in the first place. He thought the only good to come from it was that the queen herself did not know how they loved her. The boy's death in the throne room left her defeated and ashamed. Omur had been pleased by that. He thought Haleine could be quite formidable an opponent if she only realized her true strength, but as long as he could keep her trapped in her self-made prison of fear and doubt, he shouldn't have to worry. Maddox's proclivities, held in check, would be more than sufficient for that.

Omur hated dealing with mortals. The idea that they were vital to his success was his only regret. They were ultimately unpredictable and tedious. He thought it wouldn't be so unpleasant if it were just the two of them, but the king and his lady wife were only part of what was needed. There was still Laorans's champion. Omur knew the man existed and was currently within the city walls. He had sensed Laorans's damn pegasus working its magic but hadn't been able to ascertain exactly where. They had kept themselves hidden well. Their interference was inevitable, even wanted, and while there was time to wait yet even for this, he was still curious. Too much depended upon Laorans's champion, and he wanted to know the sort of man with whom he was dealing.

So he had sent the soldiers to raze Cinna, partially because it was needed, but also because he wanted to draw the man out. Word would spread, the pegasus would know, and the man would act. He had not done so yet, but it had only been a day since the raid and perhaps still too early to expect anything.

Still ranting, Maddox stopped in front of the library doors and waited for the guards to open them. Omur followed him inside, and the doors closed before he realized that the king had stopped both talking and moving. Raising his head, he saw why. Sitting in the king's chair with his boots resting on the king's desk was the man who Omur knew would be Laorans's champion. It was not too early after all.

"Now who are you?" Maddox asked after he recovered from his astonishment. "And what are you doing in my chair?"

The man was perfectly calm and assured. Omur couldn't find a trace of fear about him. It would seem Laorans had chosen well.

"I'm the man you destroyed Cinna for," he said. "And I'm sitting."

The second part seemed lazy, almost an afterthought. It amused Omur and even the king to an extent. Maddox was not accustomed to people treating him with such nonchalance. It was a novelty of which Omur felt sure the king would soon tire.

"Really," Maddox said. "Does a whoreson like yourself have a name?"

"My name is Dana. It begs a question though. Shouldn't you already know my name? After all, you are trying to frame me for murder."

Maddox's face lost some of its humor. "What do you want?"

"I want you to stop the village raids. I know why you're doing it. You won't win."

The comment was directed at Maddox, but the rebel's eyes were fixed on Omur. Omur smiled and moved to sit in his usual chair. The king did not move.

"And why should I listen to you?" Maddox asked.

"I'll have to kill you otherwise."

Maddox was incredulous. "You enter this chamber unarmed and dare threaten to kill your king?"

"My king is entombed in marble, slain by your hand."

Maddox looked sharply at Omur.

"Oh. Did he tell you no one else knew the truth?" Dana continued. "Well, I guess he was wrong about that."

"How did you get in here?" Omur asked.

"Not important."

"That is true," Maddox said. "What I am more interested in is how you think you might get out of here."

"The same way I came in," Dana said. "Through those doors behind you."

"And you think I will allow that?"

"Aye, I think you will."

Again the comment was aimed at Omur instead of the king. Omur knew it even though this time, Dana's eyes never left Maddox. He tilted his head slightly to the side as he took in his opponent. The man truly did believe he was in no danger. The pegasus must have told him of Omur's need for him, and Dana had come here, trusting what the pegasus had said. It took a man of extraordinary faith to attempt such a thing.

"You're really quite something, you know that?" Maddox said.

Omur agreed with the sentiment. Dana stood and came around the side of the desk to stand directly in front of the king. They were near the same height, but Dana had a slight edge. Maddox noticed it as well. The two men circled each other, Maddox's hand hovered over his scabbard, Dana's poised where a scabbard should have been. When they stopped, Omur was able to look at Dana over the king's shoulder.

"Wait until we really get started," Dana said. "You haven't seen anything yet."

Omur smiled and nodded once. Dana stared at Maddox for a long moment, then turned his back and walked toward the doors. Maddox didn't turn around, but he didn't need to for Omur to be aware of the thoroughly unbelieving look crossing the king's face. Together they watched Dana walk out of the library, just as he said he would. Maddox didn't move until the doors had closed once more.

"Are you going to let him go?" he demanded.

Omur was going to do just that, but he didn't need to tell the king as much. He shook his head and rose from his chair. He would send men after Dana. They wouldn't succeed in capturing him— Omur couldn't allow it—but he thought it might do the rebel leader good to be nervous.

"He turned his back on you," Omur said, moving toward the doors. "He does not fear you. He could be trouble."

"Not if he's dead," Maddox said. "See to it."

And he would. In time.

———❧———

Haleine didn't know why, but the sight of the army rejuvenated her. Ceallach's silence only added to her interest. He had been tight-lipped and uncomfortable since she had asked where they had gone. Bronagh also knew what had happened. She would've heard it in the kitchens or the maids' quarters or even from the soldiers themselves. Throughout the day, she had been as uneasy as Ceallach and quite unwilling to look Haleine in the eye. Was she worried because of what had happened? Or was she more concerned over what Haleine would do if she found out? There was only one way to know.

"Bronagh," she said, "fetch water for a bath."

The order was carried out immediately. As she hoped, Ceallach bowed and took his leave of her. Willem came and stood near the bathroom's entrance while his companion remained in the hall. Bronagh helped her out of her gown and into a robe, then set her down to tie back her hair. Haleine waited until Bronagh was absorbed in her task before speaking.

"When the soldiers marched yesterday, where did they go?"

The question seemed to startle Bronagh, and she released the braid. She shook her head as she tried to restore order to her work.

"It is peacetime," Haleine pressed. "What reason would they have for marching?"

The maid still did not answer.

"Would you rather I ask Willem? Or my husband perhaps?"

"If your husband wanted you to know, Ceallach would have told you."

"Yes, that is true. Willem," she said, turning to her guard. "Suppose you tell me where the soldiers went."

"Cinna," he said.

Behind her, Bronagh made a slight strangled cry and let go of the braid completely.

"Where is it? What is it?" Haleine asked.

"Cinna is one of the king's farming villages, one of the closest to the city."

"Why would they have gone there?"

"Your majesty knows of the rumors of rebellion," he said, and she nodded. "The soldiers were given orders to search the village for the men responsible for the murder of the king and queen."

"But there was no—" she stopped and looked at Bronagh. The maid appeared as though she had ceased to breathe. Haleine sighed. "What did they find, Willem?"

"Nothing, your majesty."

Of course they had found nothing. What was there to be found? The rebellion was a lie, created by Maddox and his man to deflect guilt from those who deserved it.

"That's not all, is it?" she asked. "They did something else, something more, didn't they?"

"Willem, no," Bronagh said sharply.

"Willem?" Haleine asked.

He stood in his soldier's stance, staring straight ahead and avoiding the eyes of both women. He never flinched.

"They burned it to the ground."

Haleine's head was suddenly swimming. "And the people?"

"Dead."

"Why?"

"It was so ordered."

There was no sense in asking why such an order had been given. There would have been no answer. Tears filled her eyes as she thought of how they must have suffered. She covered her mouth with her hand to keep herself silent. She didn't trust what she might say.

Bronagh seemed to hold the same fear, for she quickly finished the braid and put her hands under Haleine's elbows and lifted.

"Come," she said. "You don't want the water to get cold."

What did the warmth of her bath matter when compared to the slaughter of a village of innocents? An entire village! And for what? A few tears spilled over and she wiped them away. The people of this land did not need her tears. They were useless, much like the rest of her.

"You cannot allow yourself to be upset so easily," Bronagh said.

"Am I to be made of stone?" Haleine asked.

"Aye."

She suspected her maid was right. She allowed Bronagh to lead her to the bathroom and waved her away. The door closed and she heard Willem move to stand in front of it. She slipped off her robe and let it fall to the floor before stepping into the water. Bronagh had placed a small pillow at one end of the tub for her use. Haleine rested her head upon it and closed her eyes.

There needed to be a rebellion, not only a rumor. There needed to be someone strong enough to do what she could not. Someone the people would love, and above all, someone who knew the truth. Unfortunately the only people she knew who knew the truth were the same people perpetuating the lie.

"Oh. I do beg your pardon."

Startled, Haleine opened her eyes and nearly screamed. The shock of seeing a man half-hanging in the window rendered her speechless. She lifted her head and stared at him. Willem. She had to call for Willem, but would there even be time? This man was here now, only steps away from her. He could slit her throat before Willem even got the door open.

The man jumped to the floor with hardly a sound and held up his hands. "Don't call your guard," he said, stepping closer to her. "Please. I mean you no harm."

She didn't hear all he said. She had stopped listening as soon as he came into the light. As soon as she saw his eyes. His azure eyes. It was not the first time she had seen them.

"You were at the wedding," she said.

"You saw me?"

"I saw you."

He smiled and lowered his hands. "And I thought I'd been so clever."

She didn't return his smile. She was still too stunned to do much of anything other than stare at her most unexpected visitor.

He stood at a height that rivaled her husband's and was as fair as Maddox was dark. He had a look of strength about him, slender but muscular. His clothing was that of a peasant, a worn leather jerkin over a fraying linen shirt, woolen leggings and leather boots. She looked at his eyes again and was stopped by his smile. It was genuine and disarming. She should've been concerned. She should've called for Willem, but she didn't make a sound. She didn't know quite what to make of this intrusion but, at the same time, felt it was something she didn't want to interrupt.

"Clever?" she asked finally.

"Here I thought no one had paid me any mind, only to discover the bride herself saw me. What gave me away?"

"Your eyes."

"My eyes?" He sounded surprised but interested and maybe even pleased. His smile widened. "I thought certain it would be my lack of velvet and fur."

She shook her head. "Your lack of joy."

The smile faded from his face. "Has he hurt you greatly?"

She couldn't look at him then and turned away but did not offer him any sort of answer to his question.

"Your majesty?"

"Might I be so bold as to inquire what it is you're doing here?"

"I did not mean to offend."

"Then tell me who you are and why you are here, or I will call my guard, and you can answer those same questions to him, provided he does not kill you ere you have the chance to speak."

"My name is Dana. I had an audience with your husband."

She looked at him. "Most people with whom my husband meets do not end up climbing through the window into my bath chamber."

His smile crept back. "I might have overstayed my welcome."

"Then climbing in a lady's window is not a habit?"

He grinned fully now. "No. If anything, I climb out."

It took her a moment to understand his meaning. When she did, she blushed and was immediately mortified to have done so.

"What business did you have with my husband?"

"I came to offer him a chance to surrender."

"Surrender to you?"

"Aye."

"Why would he do such a thing?"

"I wouldn't necessarily have to kill him then."

The color that had risen to her cheeks suddenly drained out. She stared at him again.

"I frightened you," he said. "I'm sorry. I shouldn't have—"

"Who are you?"

"My name is—"

"Not your name."

"I mean to lead a rebellion against the king," Dana said. "I mean to remove him from the throne. He's done things, your high-ness, terrible things, and—"

"How do you know?"

"I assure you my cause is just. The things he has done—"

"I know what he has done," she said. "How do you?"

He fell into a silent stare. "I cannot tell you."

"Cannot or will not?"

"Is there a difference?"

"Sometimes," she said, contemplating him. "Will the people follow you?"

"Enough of them."

She nodded. "Do you know what I was thinking when you so gracefully arrived?"

"I cannot say that I do."

"I was thinking of the need for rebellion. I was thinking of the need for someone, for you perhaps, who knew the truth of my

99

husband and was willing to fight against him," she said. "How is it that I lay here thinking this just as you fall through my very window?"

"I do not know."

"Neither do I but I think it must be fate, and I'll not turn my back on her," Haleine said. "Therefore I shall offer to you my service. Any help I may provide, you shall have."

"I would not presume to ask you to put yourself in such a position."

"You did not ask," she said, riveted to his eyes. "Tell me, when you offered, did you think he would surrender?"

"No."

"Then why did you do it? Why take the risk?"

He shrugged. "It made him angry."

"What did you gain by that apart from the opportunity to run for your life?"

"I don't know yet," he said, smiling again. "But if nothing else, I at least got to meet the queen."

"And I am worth risking death for?"

The smile as well as the look in his eyes changed. "Oh, aye. I am certain of it, Haleine."

She gave a little gasp at the sound of her name on his lips. He looked back at her, appearing tentative for the first time.

"May I call you that?" he asked.

"Considering the present circumstances I don't see how the use of my name will cause any harm."

He glanced down at her. "No. I suppose it wouldn't."

She blushed again. "I find this is not an auspicious place for conversation."

He smiled. "No, I suppose not. I should probably be making my escape anyway."

He backed away, never taking his eyes off her. Her blush disappeared as her body filled with an unfamiliar warmth. Unnerved, she looked away only to notice something new.

"You are unarmed," she said.

"Aye."

"Not even a dagger?"

"No."

"You stole entrance to the palace and threatened to kill the king without bringing a weapon?"

"Your husband also thought it odd."

"Are you mad?"

He started out the window. "We'll find out, I suppose."

His timing was impeccable. Just as Dana slipped out of sight, the door opened and Bronagh rushed in. Haleine kept her eyes on the now empty window and tried to keep a smile from crossing her face.

"Come on," Bronagh said, snatching the robe off the floor. "You're getting out."

"I'm not yet finished."

"Aye, you are. The palace has been breached."

Haleine looked at the maid. "Breached?"

Bronagh motioned for her to move. "Willem wants you where he can see you, and it's not safe in here."

Haleine rose. "And pray tell, with Willem standing at the door, how you suppose anyone will gain entrance to this chamber without his knowledge?"

Bronagh wrapped the robe around her and waved frantically at the window. "I don't know. A man could climb through that very window if he wanted."

Haleine looked at the window and smiled. She couldn't help it.

"Don't be ridiculous," she said. "What sort of man would do such a thing?"

CHAPTER 6

From a distance, the white-gray walls of the palace looked to be as smooth as glass, but to which Dana could now attest, they were actually rougher than a tradesman's hands. His palms bore the brunt of his discovery, as the rock bit into his skin every time he reached for and found a new hold. Despite the pain, he continued his slow progress because he was still too high to just drop to the ground.

Though, he had to admit, he was rather tempted to do just that. He wanted to test his supposed bond with the unicorns and their goddess. He didn't doubt Faolan's claim. He didn't doubt the connection was there—his jaunt through the palace thus far had proven that—but he was still curious about it. What would happen if he let go?

Please don't.

The voice in his head startled him and his foot slipped. His fingers curled around the unforgiving stone as he searched for a suitable spot for his foot. Once found, he rested his head against the wall and laughed.

The voice stayed silent. Dana wasn't surprised. The quiet and calm female voice who had been his guide through the halls of the palace was not the sort to waste words. She had spoken as little as possible as he made his way through the maze of nobles, servants and guards to the doors of Maddox's library. *Stop, go, turn here* was what she offered him. The people didn't concern her, nor, after he survived the first encounters unnoticed, did they concern him. Anyone he came face to face with merely looked at him as though they weren't seeing him, only looking through him. Even the two men standing at the entrance to Maddox's library paid him no heed as he passed between them on his way into the room. They didn't notice him when he left either.

In fact, he thought he would be able to just walk out of the palace with only the king and Omur having realized he was ever there. The idea was dashed when, as he made his way through a servant-strewn hall, he heard his name and turned to see Omur standing at the far end.

"Guards," the mage said. "Seize that man."

Time to go, Dana's guide said.

Dana smiled but didn't move as he looked at Omur, the horrified servants seeing him for the first time and, finally, the group of soldiers coming to arrest him.

Time to go, the guide repeated.

He'd gone then, now moving at a run, and followed his guide's still-unruffled instructions, only hesitating the slightest bit when directed to climb out a window in an empty chamber. That window had led to another window that had led to the queen of Lira's bath chamber.

She had seen him.

At the thought of Haleine, he lost his concentration. His footing followed. He grasped at the wall as he had done before, but his fingers failed to find a hold and he fell, landing in an overfilled hay wain. He wasn't hurt but still didn't move right away. Instead, he lay on his back and looked at the wall.

"Next time," he said, laughing, "let's try for a window nearer the ivy."

He rolled from the wain. His hands stung, scraped and bleeding. He flexed his fingers as he looked around. He stood in the midst of a ragtag collection of shelters. They were tents, hovels and some slightly better housing but nothing grand, everything serviceable. Men, women and children surrounded him, all engrossed in what they were doing: tending fires, cooking food, mending clothing. They were the king's retainers—landless knights, soldiers' families, craftsmen and the like, anyone whose skills the king found valuable and wanted to keep close. Dana walked among them on his way to the palace gates. They looked at him with the same blank stare that had been on every face at the start of his journey through the palace. Still he stayed on alert, ready to run again should Omur decide to resume the chase.

He spotted one woman removing strips of linen from a rope line where they had been drying. He approached her cautiously, but the woman did not react as he took right from her hands the two strips she held. He thanked her, though he knew she would not realize he'd done it, and walked away, wrapping his hands as he went.

He passed through the palace gates next, past the guards who paid him no more mind than anyone else had. He stood in the street and looked back at where he had been. He was physically intact but couldn't help feeling that he had left something behind.

"Hey, you there! Clear off!"

Dana looked to see one of the guards coming toward him. The man had the same look on his face as the guards who had chased him through the palace. Omur, Dana suspected, was working his magic again, but Dana wasn't worried about being captured. He had no name yet, and arresting him wouldn't do anything for Omur. But neither did he need to start anything with the guards at the gate. Dana stole another look at the palace before melting into the crowd around him.

He took his time in leaving the city. He walked randomly through the streets, turning suddenly and doubling back more than once, always checking to see if anyone followed him. Omur probably had other methods of tracking a person that Dana was quite powerless against, but he didn't want to lead anyone to the camp— wherever it was—if he could help it.

Once out of the city, he entered the woods and started toward Enimode, knowing it was the direction the others had taken. From there, he didn't know where he would end up, but that didn't concern him. He hadn't known the way to Maddox's library either, yet he had found that. His apparent connection to Laorans and the unicorns had guided him there as easily as if he had been in the palace a thousand times before. They wouldn't let him lose his way now.

Sunset had come and gone before he found the camp in a clearing deep in the Aerona Forest, well off any beaten path. It was a good location, southwest of both Eluned and Enimode, but as near to the middle of the country as they could get.

Torches had been lit, and a large fire burned in the center of the clearing. Faolan and the unicorns were nowhere to be seen, but there were more people than Dana had been expecting. He didn't know from where they had come, but he could guess. Ilya led a group erecting tents. He didn't know where the tents had come from either and couldn't guess their origin. Lucius and some others seemed to be taking stock of supplies while James tended to a small herd of horses. Dana headed toward him.

"What happened to your hands?" James asked in greeting.

Dana looked down at his linen-wrapped palms. "Nothing. Just bloodied them a bit."

James nodded and looked at him thoughtfully. "What's wrong with you?"

"What do you mean?"

"I mean, if I didn't know any better I'd say you just came from Piala's bed."

"What?"

"You're grinning like an idiot."

It only made him grin more. "Am I?"

James frowned. "You didn't just come from Piala's bed, did you?"

"No."

"Where have you been?"

The horse nearest Dana was nervous, pawing at the ground and tossing his head. Dana approached the animal and stroked its muzzle in an attempt to soothe it.

"Chatting with the king," he said. "I don't think he likes me much."

"Well, wait until he gets to know you. I'm sure he'll love you as much as the rest of us do."

"I'm sure he will," Dana said. "I notice our numbers have grown considerably since we parted this morning. Where did they come from?"

"Cinna. Faolan says the unicorns recruited them, whatever that means. The horses and the rest were what they managed to salvage and bring with them. The animals will be good for light use around camp and the like, but they'll be useless in battle," James said. "Maybe the people, too. I don't know. It's not as though I've ever..."

"Ilya will see to that," Dana said when James failed to finish his thought. "She's done all right with us."

"We're still untested."

"We won't be for long. Where is Faolan now?"

James waved in the direction of the forest behind him. "He and some of the unicorns went off to do something. I don't know what. They didn't say."

"I should go find them. Have you got this?" he asked, gesturing to the horses.

"Aye. Go on."

Dana gave the now-settled horse a final pat and walked in the direction James had indicated. He didn't have to go far to find Faolan. The pegasus, standing on a low-hanging tree limb, appeared to be holding court with six unicorns. They stopped talking as he approached.

"Am I interrupting?" he asked. "I could come back."

"No. Stay," Faolan said. He nodded to the unicorns and four of them left. "We were talking about the camp's defenses. We'll set up patrols for the perimeter, but we'll need something more than that."

"Something more meaning something magic?"

"Yes."

"Right. Well, I'll just let you handle that."

"Yes, you will," Faolan said. "Now let's talk about your visit to the palace."

"I suspect Maddox will attack another village now," he said. "Sooner rather than later."

"Of course he will," Faolan said. "You told him to stop. If he does, it looks as though he's afraid of you, and he isn't. So yes, he will attack another village. Probably even more than one before he's through."

"And when he does, it'll be because of me. Because I threatened him."

"You were threatening Omur."

"Maddox didn't know that," Dana said. "I was doing as you asked, Faolan. I was doing what you said needed to be done."

"I know."

"Look what happened."

"It would've happened anyway," Faolan said. "Don't tell me you're balking now."

"No, I'm not."

"Good. Things will get much worse than this before they get better."

"Are you trying to be comforting?"

"Realistic."

"Right," Dana said. "Do we have any way of knowing where Maddox will strike?"

"I don't know. Do we?"

Dana didn't understand Faolan's question at first but then nodded. He meant Haleine.

"You know about her, then. Because you read my mind?"

"Not me," Faolan said, jerking his head to the right. "Luisiúil."

Two unicorns stood there. Lorcan was one of them. The other was a much smaller mare who seemed impossibly white. The color was so pure she nearly glowed. Her mane and tail shimmered even in the shadow of the dense forest, and her forelock hung low, grazing her remarkably blue eyes.

"She's how you're connected to Laorans," Faolan said. "She's how you found your way here and—"

"And she's how you know what's in my head."

Faolan nodded. "The queen offered to help?"

Dana took a second look at the mare. If she knew of Haleine's offer, she likely knew of everything else he had experienced in that room. His thoughts, feelings, impulses. Luisiúil gazed back at him and revealed nothing.

"Aye," he said, aware Faolan was still waiting for a response. "In any way she can."

"And in what way can she help?"

He looked away from Luisiúil. "Right now she'd be a help if Maddox and Omur did all their planning in the middle of her bedchamber."

"You could convince her to leave her bedchamber."

"Aye," Dana said.

He thought he'd rather her just stay where she was. Nowhere in the palace would be completely safe, but staying away from the source of the trouble would be better than deliberately placing herself in its midst. He saw Luisiúil's head tilt slightly to the left.

"I don't know that I feel comfortable putting her at risk," he said, meeting the mare's piercing blue stare. "Maddox and Omur are both dangerous, and she's not Ilya. She may not be capable of handling herself."

"You don't know who she is or what she's capable of," Faolan said. "What was it you said to James? This is a risk we have to take?"

"You weren't present for that conversation."

"That doesn't matter," Faolan said. "Unless you suspect the queen of being in league with her husband—"

"No," Dana said, shaking his head. "She wouldn't."

"You should probably go back and see her," Faolan finished. "Sooner rather than later."

Dana nodded. He should return immediately. It would probably be easier to gain access to her chambers at night. But who would be there with her?

She's alone, a voice said from inside his head. *She's waiting for you.*

Dana once again looked at Luisiúil as he recognized the voice who had guided him through the palace. His idiot smile almost came back, but he held it in check.

"I'll go now," he said.

———

Haleine didn't move. She lay on her side and watched Bronagh feed more logs to the flames. When finished, Bronagh stood and examined the room to make sure all was in order. Haleine still didn't move. She didn't want Bronagh to know she was awake. It would lead to questions she didn't want to be bothered with, so she waited until Bronagh left before sliding out of bed. She slipped on her robe and went to stand in front of the fire.

She couldn't sleep. That particular experience wasn't unusual. She hadn't slept well since her arrival in Lira, but this night was different. Fear had been her unrelenting bedfellow, but tonight, she found something else inside her, something she had thought that perhaps she had left on the Quatari shore. For the first time, she was too full of hope.

It was foolish to put so much faith in a man of whom she knew nothing but his name. It was absurd to allow herself such a luxury as hope, but the response had been involuntary. He had disappeared from her window, but hope had stayed behind.

It couldn't be helped. He was a man who, after all, managed to both steal entrance to and escape from the palace without raising an alarm until he was as good as gone. He somehow knew the truth of what Maddox had done and would have the strength to right the wrongs.

She didn't know how she knew that about him. The physical strength was easy to see. It would take a man of considerable prowess to scale the palace walls as he had done. She thought of his arms and, for a moment, imagined what it would feel like to have those arms wrapped around her body.

She backed away from the fire then, feeling suddenly much too warm. She sank into a chair a safe distance away just as the sound of something tapping on glass reached her ears. She scanned the room and spied a figure standing on her balcony. The moonlight hid his identity, but she did not need to see him to know who it was. She went to the doors and opened them.

"I did not expect you back this soon," she said.

"Neither did I."

She stood to the side, allowed Dana to enter and closed the doors behind him. They stood and looked at each other for a moment before she gave a small jump and walked away.

"Please, forgive my rudeness and come by the fire," she said. "You must be chilled to the bone."

He laughed quietly. "Not really."

"Oh," she said, glancing at him over her shoulder. He hadn't moved. "Please, won't you sit?"

She chose her usual chair, situated to give her a view of whoever entered the room, be it servant or any other. Dana skirted around the edge and stood opposite her, the other chair between them. She gestured to the chair, but he shook his head.

"How did you know I would be alone?" she asked.

"I was watching, waiting. I saw the maid leave and took my chance." Dana shrugged. "And Maddox?"

"He's drinking and whoring below stairs. When he's done, he'll most likely be too badly off to make it all this way."

Dana nodded. He came around to the other side of the chair and sat. He stared at the fire for a time, then took a deep breath and leaned forward.

"Haleine, I need to ask for your help. I need you to do something for me. If you will."

Her heart fluttered at the sound of her name on his lips. "I told you I would do all I could."

"Why are you so willing to help without question? You know nothing of me."

"I know enough," she said. "But knowing what you do about me, you still have to ask why I would be willing to help?"

"There will be a cost."

"There always is."

"And if that cost is your life?"

"There would not be much to lament," she said. "Tell me what you need."

"Maddox will send men to attack another village," he said. "We need to know when and where."

She nodded. "I shall do my best to find out. Perhaps Willem—"

"Who is Willem?"

"One of my guards," she said. "The only one I know by name. He told me of the first attack."

"Because you asked him?"

"Yes."

"Is he loyal to you?"

"Loyal to me?"

"As opposed to your husband, aye."

She didn't know. It wasn't something she had thought of before. Willem was young but not so young as to lack experience. He was strong and sure and had appeared thus far to be wholly devoted to her care. He made her feel *safe*. She remembered the kindness he had shown her the day he reached for her uninjured hand or when he walked beside her, helping her in direct defiance of a king's command. He told her the truth when she asked for it. If not loyalty, what was it?

"Yes," she said. "I think he is."

Dana shook his head. "It's not good enough. If you don't know without doubt, don't involve him. It's really best if you don't involve anyone."

"Then I won't," she said. "How do I tell you if I learn anything? Will you be dropping in again?"

"When I can. But I don't want to establish any sort of pattern. Eventually, they'll want to arrest me."

"Eventually?"

He smiled. "I don't want to make it too easy for anyone to know where to find me."

"How, then?"

"Are you allowed to leave the palace?"

The question was a hand around her throat, and suddenly the boy stood in front of her, staring.

"I don't know," she said. "I've barely left this chamber since—"

A dagger appeared in the boy's chest, and the hand encircling her throat squeezed. She choked and closed her eyes, but the boy was still the only thing she could see, so she stared instead at the fire as though the flames might burn away his image.

"Since?" Dana prompted.

"Since I came here," she whispered when the memory faded. "The king is content to have me stay where I am."

"But you're not content."

Will you make me kill them all?

Haleine put her own hand on her throat. "Does it matter?"

"Only if you hope to help," Dana said. "Ask Maddox for permission to attend services at the cathedral, or ask him to go and pray. The reason doesn't matter." He paused a moment, looking at her as though he'd never seen her before. "Can you read? Can you write?"

"Can you?"

Her answer had been quick, automatic. The affront was heavy in her voice and Dana smiled.

"Enough for my purposes," he said. "How is it I always manage to offend you? It is never my intention. I just—I did not know what opportunities you might have been afforded."

"The queen of Lira is the daughter of the king of Tanuba's servant," she said. "There was opportunity enough."

He nodded. "Any information you have for me, write it on a scrap of parchment, as small as you can, and take it with you. When you go, the people will come to see you. They'll want to touch you. Let them, or at least some of them. When you come across my man, slip the parchment to him."

She had understood his instructions until then. Yes, she could read and write, but of espionage, she had no knowledge. Now she was forced to look at him blankly.

"How?" she asked.

Dana sat back in his chair. He smiled after a moment.

"I forgot subterfuge was probably not part of your upbringing, no matter the opportunity," he said. "Do you have parchment here? I will teach you if you like."

"Yes, of course," she said.

She went to the writing desk she had yet to use to fetch a sheet of parchment. She brought it back and held it out to him. He took it, tore a strip off one side and put the rest on the floor. He looked at her and beckoned her to come closer. She did and watched him fold the strip into a small square.

"How would you offer your hand to someone?" he asked. "To greet them, for instance, or offer a blessing?"

"Offer a blessing?" She wasn't sure she would ever need to know that.

"How would you do it?"

She thought for a moment and held out her hand as though he were a nobleman and this were an introduction at a ball instead of a clandestine encounter. He examined her hand from every angle, even tilting his head so he could look underneath.

"Good," he said. "Perfect, in fact."

He sounded so pleased, and she could feel her cheeks growing hot. They flamed violently when he reached for her outstretched hand and turned it over. Did the fire let off enough light for him to see?

"Here," he said. "Hold it like this."

He slid the folded square underneath her thumb and turned her hand over to reexamine it. He nodded, evidently satisfied. She drew her hand back and studied it for herself, making sure to carefully note the parchment's placement.

"Hold out your hand," Dana said.

She did. He grasped her fingers as delicately as any nobleman would. If they had been at a ball, the next action would be his lips brushing against her skin. She braced herself, fearing what that would do if the mere touch of his hand was enough to set her ablaze, but all he did was gently nudge her thumb aside to allow him access to the minuscule square held there. Then he let go of her, and his hand dropped to his side.

"That's how," he said, showing her the parchment. "Do you understand?"

She nodded.

"Do you need me to show you again?"

She shook her head. She should have said yes. She should have practiced more, but she was afraid of touching him again.

"Good. I'll ask my man to stay on your left. It'll make it easier to find him."

"Why not you?"

"I have followers who know how not to be seen," he said, "and I've been seen too much already."

"How will I know him?"

"By his cloak. There will be a single unicorn embroidered upon it. Near the neck. It will be small, so you'll have to look carefully."

"Yes, all right."

He nodded and looked at her for a moment. He had worn the same expression earlier, just before he asked if Maddox had hurt her greatly.

"I am sorry to ask you to do this," he said. "I know it will be, at the very least, difficult and unpleasant or—"

"It doesn't matter."

She didn't want to think about it yet. To ask Maddox for anything would prove to be a terrible thing. It would be horrible and humiliating. Difficult and unpleasant were the least of her concerns.

"It does matter. I won't forget," he said. "When you do go to Maddox, be sure Omur isn't in the room."

"Omur?"

"Your husband's advisor. Do you know him?"

"Yes, but I do not understand why his presence would matter."

"It may not seem like it, but Omur is even more dangerous than Maddox," Dana said. "He wouldn't want you to leave the palace."

"Why?"

"You made the people love you."

She shook her head. "No, I—"

"God, you don't even know it," Dana said. "Do you?"

"But I—"

"You made them love you, Haleine."

It wasn't possible; it *couldn't* be possible, and she wouldn't believe him. How could any of them love her? How could they hold any respect at all for her? After what she had done to that boy, why would they? She shook her head.

"Even if such a thing were true," she said, "why would it matter to Omur?"

"It is true. And it matters because you gave them hope. He doesn't want that."

"I do not understand. There is much more to this, isn't there?"

"There is," he said after a moment's deliberation. He stood. "And I will tell you, but not tonight. I've been here too long already."

She knew it was true, so she did not argue. Instead she extended her hand for him to kiss. He stopped and stared. She did the same, not knowing why she offered her hand at all, only knowing that she should rescind the invitation but couldn't bring herself to do so.

"I shouldn't," he said finally. "To stop after one chaste kiss would take a man of great restraint, and restraint is not what I am known for."

She withdrew her hand. "For what, then, are you known?"

She asked the question without thinking, and when Dana didn't answer, she looked up, afraid to see what was in his eyes. His gaze hit her, and for a moment, she felt as though she were floating. When she settled back in her chair, she found herself in desperate need of something to do with her hands and, in the absence of any better options, gripped the neckline of her robe with one and the arm of the chair with the other.

"You should—you should go," she said.

"Aye."

But he did not move. Several moments passed where they did nothing but stare at each other. She looked away first. She didn't even look up when he walked away.

"Be careful," Dana said.

She twisted around in the chair, but he was already gone.

—⁓—

As there was no safe way to leave Eluned at night, Dana stayed in Orla's stable. He left the city at dawn and found his way back to camp. It had been a considerable span since he had last slept, but he wasn't tired. He should be. His body should be screaming for sleep, but contrary to his understanding, his body was screaming for something else.

It was Haleine. It was knowing what she intended to do this morning and not wanting to think about how she would accomplish it. Whatever she did—however she went about it—would be because he had asked her. But there was even more to it than that. She had been in his mind ever since he first saw her across a crowded cathedral's sanctuary.

It was unusual for him to spend this much time thinking about a specific woman, especially one he hadn't even kissed. Piala was the closest he ever came to that, but the only time she crossed his mind was when he was near enough to the city for a visit. She was forgotten almost as soon as he rode away.

Haleine was different. He didn't suppose it was her status either. He'd known highborn ladies before and had found them to be little different from the girls in the brothels or the farmers' daughters or any of the rest. No, he didn't know what it was about her; he didn't know why or how it had happened, but his first glance at the queen of Lira had been like a single drop of rain falling from a seemingly cloudless sky.

It was a downpour now. He was almost afraid of her and the way she made him feel. He thought of her hand, outstretched in expectation of a kiss. God, how he had wanted to touch her, to kiss her, but he hadn't dared. He wasn't sure what that meant. Maybe it meant nothing. He'd been fascinated with women before, but the infatuation always faded. It would do so again. But even as he thought it, he knew it was untrue. Aye, he'd been captivated by

women, but he'd never feared one. He had never feared the consequences of a single kiss.

He had never thought of consequences at all.

He stopped once he realized he had walked into the middle of
a mostly deserted camp. The lack of activity surprised him. The
numbers he had seen the night before had dwindled, and now only
a handful remained. Where had the rest of them gone?

"Back again, then?"

It was Lucius, coming up from behind him and carrying an
armload of branches. Dana took half of the load and walked alongside him.

"Where is everyone?" Dana asked.

"Ilya has most of them on the training field. James is there."

"There's a training field? Well, I'll certainly have to see that."

"It'll be good if you do. The people are curious to meet you."

"I hope no one told them anything I couldn't live up to."

"Well, there was some discussion about dragon-slaying and
giant-killing."

"Is that all?" Dana laughed. "I think I'll go down there now."

"You won't sleep first? You've been gone all night."

"Not especially tired."

"Did all go well at the palace?"

He immediately thought of Haleine, her smile and her flushed
face. Was it because of the fire or something else? Perhaps he would
sleep. He imagined the dreaming would be spectacular.

"It did," he said. "It is fortunate that I've met you here, actually. I need you to do something for me."

———✺———

Haleine did not return to her bed that night. Instead, she stayed
in her chair and thought of how best to approach Maddox. When
morning came, she was no nearer an answer than when she had
started. It did not make her any less determined to carry out her
task. Her dread of failing Dana and his fledging rebellion outweighed everything else.

"Awake already?" Bronagh asked as she came through the servants' passage.

Since it was obvious she was awake, Haleine offered Bronagh
no response. Maybe there was nothing for her to do but go to Maddox and ask him what she would. She sighed.

"Are you all right?" Bronagh asked. "Are you ill?"

"What?" Haleine said, realizing that Bronagh now stood in front of her. "No. No, I'm fine."

Bronagh gave her a disbelieving look but walked away without further questioning.

"I'll have your breakfast brought up, then," she said, "unless you wish to eat in the dining hall."

"No. Don't bother, please," Haleine said. "I'm not hungry."

Bronagh turned and scrutinized her once again. "Are you sure you're not ill?"

"I'm sure. Please, Bronagh, I'm fine."

Bronagh went back to her chores when Ceallach came into the room. He used the main entrance, as the servants' passage was beneath him. Haleine caught a glimpse of Willem as the doors closed. Ceallach started toward the fire but stopped suddenly when he saw her sitting there. He offered a clumsy bow.

"Your majesty, good morning," he said. "I did not know you were awake."

She said nothing.

"What, may I ask, are your plans for the day?"

He always asked this. Every morning, it was the same. Next, he would suggest she join her ladies-in-waiting in the solarium where they were constantly at work on some insipid sewing project. She knew this because she had gone once. She hadn't returned since. She had no patience for the close needlework required and even less tolerance for the excessive gossiping in which her ladies partook. She much preferred the quiet solitude of her bedchamber.

"Perhaps your majesty would care to join your attendants in the solarium. They are hard at work embroidering banners for your husband's army."

"Perhaps later," she said.

She was not inclined to do anything for the benefit of her husband's army but thought the gossip might be worth hearing. The palace was buzzing with the news about this threat to the king. Maybe she could learn something Bronagh wouldn't want her to hear.

"But first," she continued, "I would like to visit my husband wherever it is he spends his mornings."

Bronagh abandoned her chores entirely and stared at her. Ceallach had a similar reaction.

"Visit your husband?" he asked.

"Yes, visit my husband," she said. "Alone, if he consents. I would prefer that pit viper of a man he calls an advisor not be privy to this."

Ceallach seemed even more concerned. "Might I ask the nature of this visit?"

"The nature of this visit is a matter between a wife and her husband," Haleine said. "However, you may tell him I have a request to make of him."

Ceallach stood dumbfounded.

"Ceallach," Haleine said. "Please feel free to go to the king now. Bronagh will help me dress, so I will be prepared when you return. We'll not want to keep the king waiting."

"Of—of course, your majesty," he said, bowing again. "I shall go immediately."

As soon as he left, Bronagh pounced. "What are you doing! You cannot mean to go there and—"

"That is precisely what I mean to do," Haleine said. "Now, Bronagh, if you please, I need to dress quickly. Ceallach will not be gone long."

Haleine tried to stand, but Bronagh was in the way. Haleine settled back down in the chair.

"Bronagh," she sighed. "You must help me."

"Tell me why you are doing this."

Haleine chewed on her lip while she contemplated her maid. If Bronagh knew, she would be able to help. Michaela had wanted Bronagh to protect her. She would keep Haleine's secrets, even if it was the last thing she wanted to do.

"Can Willem be trusted?" Haleine asked.

"What in the world does Willem have to do with this madness?"

"Can he be trusted?"

"Do you question his loyalty to you?"

"I am more concerned with his loyalty to my husband. Is he my man or Maddox's?"

"He is yours through and through. Michaela selected him for that purpose."

"As she selected you."

"Aye."

"Very well," Haleine said. She took a deep breath before continuing. "I have met the leader of the rebellion and have pledged to him my allegiance."

"You've done what? You met who?"

Haleine didn't repeat herself. She knew Bronagh had heard precisely what she had said.

"How could you possibly have met the leader of the rebellion? When would you have—" Bronagh stopped and nodded brusquely. "Don't be ridiculous? What sort of man would do such a thing as climb through a window in the queen's bath chamber? Perhaps, your majesty, it is the sort of man who believes himself to be a match for the king!"

"He is a match for the king."

"Are you mad?"

Haleine smiled. "We'll find out, I suppose. My clothing?"

"Why are you doing this?" the maid asked.

"It's going to happen again, Bronagh, what happened to Cinna. You know it, I know it, and I can't sit here and do nothing. I have to try to stop it. Do you understand? I do not wish to be broken."

Bronagh did not move.

"I know you do not think it," Haleine said softly, "but this will save my life."

Bronagh shook her head. "No, it won't, but I'll help you anyway."

As Haleine had predicted, Ceallach quickly returned with the news that Maddox would see her in his library. Ceallach still looked pale, but as faint as he appeared, it was nothing compared to Bronagh's complexion. Haleine imagined somewhere were ghosts with more color.

She left the two of them in her chambers, and only Willem and his companion accompanied her to the library. Lord Omur and two guards waited in the antechamber. All three of them bowed to her, but only Omur kept his eyes on her.

The guards opened the doors for her, and she entered the library alone. It was a good-sized, oval-shaped room with the same tall windows that appeared throughout the entire palace. The walls in between were lined with book-laden shelves. Only one wall was free of both books and windows but hosted instead the fireplace. It was darker than she thought it should be but reminded herself that it was unlikely her husband used the room for reading.

Finished with her assessment, her eyes settled upon the massive desk in the center of the room and her husband who sat behind it.

"My lord," she said, dipping into a curtsey. "Thank you for agreeing to see me. I know I have displeased you."

Maddox smiled. "You certainly have, but how could I resist finding out what it is you could possibly dare ask of me?"

There was a map atop a table to her right. She walked the room's outer edge with her head bowed and her hands clasped together and pressed against her mouth. She turned sharply and walked straight toward him. The table was now in front of her.

"Your forgiveness," she said, dropping her hands. "Your mercy."

"What makes you think I have either of those in me at all?"

"I thought perhaps your greatness would be limitless."

It was reckless of her to try flattery. She hadn't meant to try it so soon because she didn't know how he would react. He was a cruel man but far from stupid. Would he know what she aimed to do? She couldn't tell. His face was expressionless. She bowed her head, hoping to appear repentant, and took the opportunity to read the map.

Eluned was located in the northeast, not far from the Endellion Sea. Various towns and villages radiated in all directions from this point. She found Eoten but didn't recognize any of the other names until she saw Cinna. It lay nearby to the west, whatever was left of it. On the map, a great black slash had been drawn through it. Three other areas had been circled.

"Flattery, Haleine?" Maddox asked. "It'll not work with me. You were stupid to try it."

Trutina, south of Eluned, looked to be the closest target. The second, Piangi, located north of Eoten. Then Cerove, found even farther west.

"I said you were stupid to try it."

Haleine brought her head up. "Yes, my lord."

Maddox came around the desk to stand in front of her. "Why are you here? What do you want?"

He stood so close that she had to look up to see him. "I told you what I want," she said, biting her tongue hard enough to bring tears to her eyes. "Please, my lord, I beg you."

He cocked his head. "You want forgiveness? Mercy?"

"Yes, my lord."

"Do I frighten you?"

There was no answer to give him. She wouldn't say yes. She couldn't say no. She just stared back at him, unflinching. She didn't need to bite her tongue this time. The tears formed on their own. It was all the answer her husband required.

"Give me my son and I will give you your mercy," he said.

"And forgiveness?"

"Why, you nasty little jade. I really don't know how you dare."

Neither did she. The words were falling out of her mouth of their own accord. They were as new to her as they were to him.

"If you weren't such a pretty chit, I think I would've thrown you to the wolves by now for that tongue of yours. It's a shame I don't see this girl more in my bed; I wouldn't mind her presence there. I had her once—our wedding night, if you recall—but I haven't had the pleasure since. It's too bad," he said. "I'd certainly like to fuck her again."

Haleine couldn't breathe and didn't know how the next words made it out of her mouth.

"She's here now."

Haleine left the library looking far more disheveled and feeling far more shaken than she had upon her arrival. But she was also in possession of that for which she had come and did not wish to waste any more time. She gave an obviously angry Omur nothing more than a passing glance and escaped into an empty hall before turning to her guards.

"My husband requests that I go to the cathedral to pray," she said to Willem's companion. "I wish to go immediately, so please make the arrangements while I make myself presentable."

The guard bowed and left. She went in the opposite direction, fighting an overwhelming urge to run. Willem hovered just behind her, once again ready to support her if needed, and she swayed and started to sink. Willem immediately caught her and held her up.

"Trutina, Piangi and Cerove," she whispered. Willem's grip tightened. "Which will be first? How will it happen?"

He was silent for a moment, but then responded in a tone so quiet, she almost didn't hear him.

"Trutina first, followed by Cerove and Piangi."

"How many?"

"I do not know the exact number. I would not think many. They do not expect resistance."

"Thank you," she said, straightening. "To church, then."

The Archbishop had not been informed of her impending arrival and was not prepared to offer her a service. She assured him she did not require it, as she sought only a sanctuary for prayer. He bowed and left her in the company of Ceallach and her ladies.

She knelt in front of the altar but did not pray. She worried instead. Had she acted too rashly? Would Dana have had enough time to send his messenger? Did it matter? Now that she had Maddox's permission, she could return to the cathedral daily. If she did not find him this day, she would try again the next.

She stayed in front of the altar until her knees ached too badly to stay still anymore. She stood and motioned to her attendants.

"My cloak, please," she said.

As soon as it was draped across her shoulders, she drew her hands inside and reached into her sleeve for her secret. She held the small square in her hand the way Dana had showed her and walked out of the cathedral.

When she set foot outside, she had to stop and stare at the scene in front of her. Dana had spoken true. The people had indeed turned out to see her. They lined both sides of the stairs and waited for her. Was there anyone left in the city, or were they all here in front of her now? Why would they ever do that for her? She couldn't even fathom the number of them, or their reasons for being there. She looked from side to side, overwhelmed with the task before her. There were so many people. Would she be able to find the one for whom she was looking?

"Your majesty?" Ceallach asked.

"Yes," she said. "I'm ready."

She moved forward, taking the steps slowly. Willem stayed on her left, standing just behind her. Her other guard did the same on her right. As soon as she was within reach, hands sprung out from both sides, and the air was filled with the sound of her name. She hesitated as she looked at the outstretched fingers. Willem and the other moved forward. She knew they were going to force the people back, and she reached out to grab Willem's elbow before he could pass her.

"Please, Willem, no," she said. "It's all right."

Willem backed off, his companion following his lead. She stepped forward again, moving as slowly as she dared. She needed time to look the crowd over but didn't want to risk raising any suspicion.

Her breathing quickened and her chest tightened. Her stomach tied itself in knots, but she kept moving. She held out her hand, and her fingers grazed those reaching for her.

She was turning from her left to the right when a man in a russet cloak caught her eye. His hand came up, but instead of reaching for her, he scratched at his neck. It was then that she saw the tiny embroidered unicorn. She looked from the unicorn to the man, and his dark eyes held hers.

Now he held out his hand to her. "Please, a blessing, my queen."

Willem immediately moved to put himself in between Haleine and the man reaching for her, but she looked at her guard, shook her head and moved closer to Dana's messenger. She reached for him, and when their hands touched, she moved her thumb slightly to allow him access to the parchment. She felt his fingers curl beneath hers and pulled her own hand back. She stepped away from him and clasped the next outstretched hand as well. The people were clamoring for it now. She went to the people on her right and did the same.

When she finally reached the carriage, she thought she heard both Ceallach and Willem breathe sighs of relief. She settled on her seat and looked out at the people again. Dana's messenger was not among them.

chapter 7

James crouched low in the brush and watched the road in front of him. He had held the position for so long, his muscles ached, but he didn't move. There were five people on either side of him, all bent in the same position and all clutching a bow as though their lives depended on it. It was understandable, as their lives would depend on the weapon in their hands and how well they used it.

He took his eyes off the road long enough to look down the line of them. First those on his left, then the ones on his right. None of them saw him, as they stared at the road just as intensely as he had. Some of them wouldn't survive the day. Maybe none of them would. And he didn't even know most of their names.

He thought he should. He was responsible for them. When the fighting started, they would look to him for guidance because Dana had made him their leader. James thought that decision had been a mistake.

But he didn't share this with the ten people surrounding him. Neither had he shared it with Lucius or Ilya, nor even Dana, two days earlier when the four of them stood together in Dana's tent bent over a map and a scrap of parchment bearing the names of three villages. Cerove. Piangi. Trutina. One of them, all of them, would be coming under attack, and Dana was determined to save all three.

James had been so relieved to see Enimode missing from such a list that he neglected much of the discussion. He didn't know from where the information had come, only that it was taken as truth. He didn't know anything else either and had spent the rest of the time sitting back while the others debated the minds of the madmen.

What could he have added? Were they discussing plowing or planting or harvesting, he could've helped. Were they planning a barn raising, he could have contributed, but battle tactics and combat techniques were beyond him. The closest he came was hunting game. He'd hunted deer and other wildlife for nearly half his life, and Dana knew it. That was why James was in the forest, lying in wait for the king's army.

Dana was in the center of the village with Lucius, a small group of unicorns and the able-bodied citizens of Trutina. They intended to meet the army head on. The note claimed the king's men were not expecting resistance, and Dana wanted them to see they were wrong.

But first, the army would need to arrive. James had wondered more than once if their information was correct. The note had said Trutina would be first, but maybe the soldiers were bound for Cerove. Maybe they weren't leaving the city at all. He wondered if the same thoughts had crossed anyone else's mind. If they had, no one was sharing.

They couldn't afford to be wrong. Success was vital. What happened here would define the rebellion. Dana looked to send a message not only to Omur and the king, but also to the citizens of Lira. If they failed this day, if the army never came to Trutina and other villages were lost, their cause might be over before it truly began.

But Dana had taken the note to heart, and plans were made quickly. They estimated a regiment would need two days to reach Trutina. The rebel camp was maybe three days away, and they would be too late to prevent the first attack. No one wanted to abandon Trutina, but neither did anyone know how they would cover the distance in time.

Faolan and the unicorns provided the solution. They created a network of underground paths, lit by torches and lanterns, and entered and exited through altered trees. The paths crisscrossed from one end of Lira to the other, offering the rebels the means to move their own forces quickly and invisibly. They had taken this route to Trutina. James was skeptical that they would make up enough time, but upon their arrival, Trutina had been both unscathed and unaware of what lay lurking on their horizon. After that, James was convinced the unicorns had altered more than just the trees and the earth beneath his feet, but when he confronted Faolan about it, the pegasus declined to answer.

The unicorns had been instrumental in getting the town elders to believe Dana. They were awestruck by the beasts. Everyone knew the unicorns lived amongst them, but they were so rarely seen, and never like this: out in the open, in the middle of a village in such numbers. And what the unicorns failed to convince them of, the people of Cinna did. Word of what happened there had spread everywhere, and if the elders of Trutina had held any doubt as to the validity of the rumors, all they had to do was look at the people who had lived through it to know it was true.

So the rebels were welcomed and now they waited. James and Ilya had been sent to the forest to watch the road, to get word of the regiment's approach to the village and to flank the soldiers once they had passed. Ilya, a unicorn mare named Fáinne and ten others from Cinna waited on the other side of the road. James couldn't see them, but he imagined they were identical to the men beside him. They were farmers and hunters who had never so much as lifted a sword, so instead they carried daggers or axes along with their bows.

James had a dagger in his boot; a small axe meant for trees, not warfare, on his belt; and his sword on his hip. He hadn't planned on bringing the sword, as he was still learning its use, but Ilya had insisted and even made him practice removing the weapon from its sheath until he could barely lift his arm at all.

"Good," she'd said then. "Now practice more."

His last—and likely most effective—weapon stood behind him. It was the solid black unicorn stallion whose name Faolan had told him was Bearach. Bearach was a lethal beast, easily worth ten seasoned soldiers. James found himself intimidated by the animal and was grateful they were on the same side.

"Captain?"

James needed a moment to realize he was being spoken to. He hated the title and the implications it carried even more, but Dana had christened him as such when introducing James to the men he would lead, and the men had clung to it.

Why he was being summoned became obvious as the sound of a drummed cadence reached his ears. Another moment passed before he saw banners bearing the Aelhaeran unicorn flapping in the wind. He turned to Bearach who nodded and closed his eyes to send word to the village.

James adjusted his grip on his bow just slightly and felt for the quiver strapped to his back. His hand stayed close to the arrows so he would be prepared should the need arise, but he didn't take one. It was far too early. They had yet to see Dana.

The first of the soldiers were marching by now. One of the men on his right went for an arrow. His name, James knew, was Rhydwyn. He and his brother, Gair, had come to Dana's fight after their families had been slaughtered in Cinna. James reached over, caught Rhydwyn's wrist and shook his head.

"Steady," he murmured. "Patience."

He released the man and they waited, no one moving, until the last of the soldiers had gone by. James had counted a hundred men. They had a little more than half that. The unicorns almost made it even. Truly, it was better odds than he had thought they'd have.

"Captain?"

"Patience," he repeated.

When Ilya and Fáinne appeared on the road, he stood and motioned for the others to follow. Bearach came alongside him, and James handed his bow to Rhydwyn and climbed onto the unicorn's back. When he had reclaimed his bow, Ilya spoke.

"Arrows ready," she said, "but do not shoot. You wait for my signal. Understood?"

No one spoke. Some nodded, and everyone fitted their bow with an arrow. James looked over them, wondering what should be done next. Dana would've delivered a speech. He probably already had back in the village. It was too bad they had missed it; it would have been good, but James didn't say anything. Let Ilya do it if she wanted, but he didn't see the need to remind them why they were there.

"Forward," Ilya said. "For Trutina. For Cinna."

So she knew it, too. To say anything else would be a waste.

Bearach and Fáinne pranced. Ilya sat her mount easily, but James had more trouble and was forced to hold a portion of the stallion's mane to help him keep his seat. The unicorns were reluctant to accept human riders at all, only doing so out of necessity, and they had completely rejected the idea of saddles and bridles. James had grown up riding horses, and although he'd ridden bareback often, he'd never ridden without a bridle of some sort. It would take some getting used to.

They came up behind the soldiers and stopped. No one noticed them, as their attention was fixed upon Dana. The rebel leader sat on Lorcan's back, delivering a speech as the unicorn walked back and forth in front of the regiment. In spite of the terror he felt, James smiled.

"Turn back now, or this town will be your grave," Dana said.

The threat seemed extravagant, even laughable, and James made a note to tell Dana this later. Ilya motioned for the others to raise their bows. Bearach snorted and pawed at the ground. Several of the rear guard turned their heads at the sound and, upon seeing them, turned fully, surprise and fear filling their faces. Swears were uttered and swords were drawn, but the rebels held steady.

"Well, Captain Varro, was it?" Dana asked as Lorcan stopped. "Do you go?"

"I shall take great pleasure in severing your treasonous head from your body and delivering it to my king."

"Does this mean you reject my offer?"

As James rolled his eyes at Dana's glibness, he heard another sword being drawn and saw it held aloft. He could not see the man who wielded it but could only assume it was the captain. James slid an arrow from the quiver and nocked it quickly. He noticed Ilya did the same.

"Kill them all!" Varro ordered.

Ilya raised her bow and shot the soldier closest to her in the throat. She had the next arrow drawn and flying before the first man had hit the ground.

"You heard the man," Ilya said. "Kill them all."

Twenty arrows flew out in attack. Most hit their targets. Bearach reared before plunging into the confusion in front of him, and James landed on his back in the mud. He lost his bow in the fall and rolled to his left to retrieve it just as a sword was driven into the ground on his right.

"Lost your mount, boy," someone sneered.

James looked at the blade that had nearly killed him and then at its owner. It was one of the soldiers, a low-ranked man, judging by his lack of quality armor, but poor armor or not, he still held the advantage.

"Better off without him," James muttered, turning his head to look for his lost weapon.

His hand closed around it, and he immediately brought it up, swinging it in a wide arc to meet the soldier's second blow. It splintered the bow and rendered it useless, but since his head was still attached to the rest of him, James thought it a worthwhile sacrifice. He threw away the remains of his weapon and rolled again, removing an arrow from his quiver after he did so. Ilya had told them the armor would be most vulnerable at the neck and under the arms, so when his assailant raised his arms to bring his sword down a third time, James rose and drove the arrow into the man's side, just underneath his arm. The man screamed, and James released the shaft and stumbled back. He fell again, but it didn't matter. His blow had had the desired effect. James sat in the mud, more shaken now than when he had fallen from Bearach's back, and watched his attacker drop his sword and grope for the arrow protruding from his side.

It wasn't going to be enough. It wasn't going to kill him. James looked at the man's sword and lunged for it. His hands closed around the handle, and with a desperate cry, he swung the blade, defeated the armor easily and lodged the steel in the man's torso.

He saw what he had done and released the sword. The man fell in the mud, and James did likewise but he wasn't there long. A pair of hands lifted him to his feet and pressed the bloodied sword back into his grasp.

"Don't stop," Ilya's voice said in his ear. "You stop and you're dead."

He took one last look at the man he had killed and knew Ilya had never spoken a truer statement.

The battle continued, but James could later recall very little of it. Maddox's men floundered, unable to recover from their shock at the unexpected resistance, and the rebels were relentless. For his part, James knew he fought and killed, but, out of necessity perhaps, remembered nothing more than how it had started with a taunt and a drawn sword and ended with the king's captain and the remains of the king's army, hands bound behind their backs, walking alongside a unicorn escort to Eluned to deliver to his majesty a sobering message. The rebels had won.

Even when it was over, there was still more to be done. They could hardly leave Trutina in such a state and set to work tending the wounded, burying the dead and salvaging what armor and weaponry they could. It was gruesome work, all of it, and James was forced to stop more than once to vomit. He was not the only one.

"Look at you. You're hurt," a woman's voice said. "Come with me."

He felt someone tugging on the sleeve of his tunic and only then realized anyone had spoken to him. He looked to see his tunic torn and his arm bleeding. How it had happened, he didn't know.

He looked next at the plump, silver-haired woman who had been trying to gain his attention. She was one of the citizens of Trutina, their midwife and healer. He couldn't remember what she was called, though, and just stared at her.

She smiled. "Come along."

"Your name," he said. "I don't know it."

"Hanah. But that's hardly important. Let me look at your arm."

He nodded and allowed her to lead him to the other wounded where she directed him to sit on a log. She used a small knife to cut away his shirt sleeve and prodded the exposed wound.

"Your first battle?" she asked.

"Hasn't been much opportunity before."

"Aye, it was good of you to come, though I don't know that you've made Trutina any safer. I think maybe it'll be a bigger target now; our king is not one to let go of a loss easily, but it's good you came. You showed the people they don't have to lie down and die."

He looked over his shoulder at the freshly dug graves. "They died anyway."

"Some of them, aye. But this way was better."

"Was it? Does it really matter?"

"I think you'll find it does." She finished with her examination, picked up a rag and held it against his arm. Then she took his free hand and placed it on top of the cloth. "Here, hold this. It's not bad. You'll have a nice scar later. Women will love it; you'll see. I'm going to get a salve and a proper bandage, and I'll be back."

He held the cloth and watched Hanah walk away. He hadn't been alone for long when Dana appeared beside him, looking unfazed by everything that had happened. James thought he maybe hated Dana a little bit for that. Dana pulled James's hand away to look at the wound himself. He nodded, replaced the cloth and sat down beside James.

"Turn back now, or this town will be your grave?" James asked.

"Too much, then," Dana said with a hint of a smile. "Aye, I was afraid of that."

"Don't lie," James said. "You're not afraid of anything."

Dana's smile faded and he looked away. "Very nearly."

—◦◦◦—

The king and his court were sitting down to dine when there arose a ruckus that could not be ignored. Omur, seated at the king's right hand, kept his eyes on the back of the hall, awaiting Ceallach's arrival with word of what had happened. The man finally appeared, looking ill and concerned. He made his way to the king's table and bowed.

"Your majesty," Ceallach said, nearly gasping from a lack of proper breath. "You must come, you must see—"

Maddox, however, was far more interested in the queen sitting to his left to be concerned. He glanced lazily at Omur. "Deal with it."

Omur bowed his head and rose from his seat. "It shall be done, my lord."

He left Ceallach to recover in the hall and went, along with a handful of guards, out to the wall walk to see the disturbance. He barely glanced over the side before turning to the guard closest to him.

"Tell the king he must come immediately," he said.

The guard bowed and Omur peered over the wall again. He thought more men would have survived.

He would accept the army's failure much easier than Maddox. He'd known all along something like this would happen. What he had not expected was the rebel leader to experience such success this soon into his campaign. Dana had acted with such accuracy there was only one conclusion to be drawn.

There was a spy in the palace.

And if there was one, there was likely more than one, but he wouldn't share his suspicion with the king. His temper would be stoked enough by the scene below, and it would be the queen who would bear the brunt of it. Omur didn't mind that, but he did have to keep her alive.

Maddox appeared atop the wall, blustering about having been disturbed. Omur bowed and gestured to what waited below. Maddox looked and the remonstration came to a swift end.

"What is that?" he asked.

"The men you sent to Trutina," Omur said. "Or what remains of them."

"How?"

"My guess is, my lord, you have Dana to thank for this."

"How did he know of our plans?"

"I do not yet know, my lord," Omur said, "but I suspect there is a spy in our midst."

"Find the traitor. I want his head on a pike."

Omur bowed his head in agreement. The spy would be found, but he had no intention of mounting the head of any spy of Dana's on a pike. At least not yet. It would serve his purposes to know Dana's link. Knowing he could easily pass false information on to his enemy would be an advantage indeed.

"And I want you to discover from where that whoreson Dana hails," Maddox said next. "Burn it, and every soul within it, to the ground."

"I assure you it shall be done," Omur said and bowed as Maddox took his leave.

What he didn't tell the king was that it would be unlikely they would learn anything useful. He had been trying to ascertain Dana's origins since the man first appeared, but it would seem he did not have one village he called home. He was, at best, a drifter. Even after spending days reconstructing Dana's whereabouts, there was no discernible pattern to his travels. There was no one place in which he resided longer than others. The goddess's perfection in her selection of her champion was becoming irksome. Nevertheless, the man would have a weakness. Every human did, and Dana would be no exception. Omur would find what he needed.

"Go below and tell them to open the gates," he said to one of the remaining guards.

"But the unicorns," the man said. "The men—they fear them."

Omur looked once more over the wall. The largest stallion stared up at him.

"They have no reason to fear," he said. "The unicorns will return to the forest as soon as their prisoners have been brought inside. Tell the men to open the gates, and have Varro report immediately to my chambers. I have much desire to speak with him."

"Aye, milord."

Omur did not doubt that his wishes would be carried out and left the wall before the unicorns had dispersed. He went to his chambers to await the arrival of the captain. He knew Varro would loathe to be summoned so soon after his defeat. He would not want to answer for his failure before he had a chance to develop a reason for the rout, but Omur thought it best to move while the man's indignation was still fresh. He would not even have had the opportunity to strip himself of whatever armor he might have left. Omur didn't know how mercenary Dana's rebels would be, but he was interested in finding out.

He had poured himself some wine and taken a seat near the fire when Varro arrived. He had been stripped of all weapons and some choice pieces of armor. Mercenary, then, but practical. Varro came forward, bowed and waited.

"You seem to have lost your sword," Omur commented. He thought that loss would hurt the captain most.

Varro's head snapped up. "That misbegotten bastard—" he stopped and bowed his head again. "My lord, I deeply regret our failure."

Omur waved his hand. "It is of no consequence to me. The king, however, will likely be another matter, but he can be, and will be, handled."

"We did not expect resistance. None of us, my lord."

"And I freely include myself in that number, Captain. I did not summon you here to admonish you for your defeat. Instead, I have a task for you, should you be interested," Omur said. "Sit, if you'd like."

Varro remained standing. "Of course, my lord."

"How would you like an opportunity to reclaim your misplaced sword from the misbegotten bastard who currently holds it?"

"My lord, surely that is something for which you do not need an answer."

"I thought not," Omur said. "I would like you to select your very best men. You will go where I, and I alone, send you. I will give you instructions when necessary, and only when you are well upon your way will you inform the men who follow you of your destination."

Varro sat. "And what will you have us do there?"

"You will go to these towns, these villages, where Dana has been known to dwell at one time or another, and you will find his connection there. Start with taverns and brothels; my spy here in the city tells me he is that sort. Then I would like you to be as cruel as possible. Take days if you like; there will be no rush. When you are finished, and you have gleaned all you can from the people and the land, you will burn it, and every last soul within it, to the ground. Eventually, we will find the one that will break him."

"When will we begin, my lord?" Varro asked, a slight glimmer in his eyes.

"Not right away," Omur said. "The army will be marching again before long, and I want to wait until Dana is occupied elsewhere."

"We will make him regret ever coming here, my lord."

Omur smiled. "I certainly hope so."

—◦◦◦—

Haleine awoke with a start. She lifted her head from her pillow and looked at the moonlight-drenched balcony as she attempted to catch her breath. When she had, she shivered, realizing that the coverlets had slipped off the bed. She slid to the edge of the mattress and leaned over to gather them.

"Your majesty."

She turned toward the voice and saw Dana sitting by the fire but didn't relax entirely. How long had he been there?

She should've been more pleased to see him. She had thought and dreamt of little else in the days since their last meeting. Why she should have reservations about his appearance now, she did not know.

But he would have had a reason to come, one that would take precedence over her uncertainty, and she slid out of bed. She reached for her robe but didn't see where Bronagh had left it, so she took one of the coverlets instead and wrapped it around herself. She looked at Dana—still sitting, still watching—and walked toward him even though every part of her body called for her to move in the opposite direction. Perhaps he felt it too, because as she grew nearer, he rose and moved away.

"I require your assistance again, your majesty."

She sat. It was odd, his use of her title. He had used it so seldom in their previous meetings. His sudden sense of formality surprised her.

"I thought perhaps that was the case," she said. "You need to know what my husband plans now?"

"Aye. If you can find out."

"I will try."

He nodded. "I would very much like to stop him."

"I would very much like him stopped," she said. "I will do all I can, I assure you."

"Aye," he said. "I know you will. And you'll do brilliantly and find out everything I need, but it still won't be enough, will it? I still won't be able to stop them all."

"No one expects it of you."

"And what of the village that perishes because I wasn't there to prevent it?"

"You mustn't think like that. You can't think like that," she said. "You are at war with the king, and war is about sacrifice. Even the victors suffer loss."

He nodded again and stopped behind the chair but did not look at her.

"What happened in Trutina?" she asked. "Did all not go well? I thought the victory had been yours. Maddox was certainly angry enough for that."

His eyes flickered over to her and scanned her face. She knew what he was looking for, and if he were closer, he would have been able to see it, but the shadows the fire afforded her would keep her secret for now.

"No," he said. "The victory was ours."

"You never mentioned the unicorns."

He almost smiled. "Maddox received my message?"

"You know he did. How could he not? You paraded it through the streets and up to the palace gates themselves."

"I wanted to make sure the people would notice."

"Then success is yours once again."

He moved to stand in front of the fire and leaned with one arm against the mantle. His body held a tautness she hadn't seen in him previously. He moved so easily before, so fluidly and without care. She suspected the cause for the change but waited to see what he would say, what he would choose to reveal to her.

"It'll never be this easy again," he said, looking at the fire instead of her. "It was the hardest thing I've ever done, and I know it'll never be that easy again. He'll send more men next time. Better men."

"So you gather more men, better men."

"Gather them from where? He doesn't attack the nobles. He doesn't attack the larger towns."

She shed her blanket as she stood and walked across the room to where Bronagh had left a goblet and decanter of wine for her. She picked up the cask and poured the drink.

"Why does it matter who he attacks?"

"It matters because I gather farmers, Haleine. I gather bakers and shepherds. He preys on the weak, the small, the—" he paused. "The useless."

"They are not useless."

"No," Dana said. "Not if you want a field plowed or a cow milked."

She replaced the decanter and started back. "That is unfair."

His shoulders sagged. "Aye. I don't know why I said it. Of course they're not useless. But they're not soldiers either."

"They can learn."

"They shouldn't have to."

"No, but they do," she said. "And you can't change that. Not yet."

"But I will."

"Yes, you will."

She held out the goblet. He looked at her before taking her offering and sitting down. She stayed standing.

"You're not the man I met before," she said. "What happened to him? Where is the man who threatened the king with naught but the words he spoke? Where is the man who fell through my window while I was bathing and stayed to have a conversation? Where is the man who gathered a queen as one of his own?"

"Have I gathered you, Haleine?"

She sat across from him. "You know you have. Otherwise you would not be here in the dead of night telling me of your fear."

He stared into the goblet. "My fear," he said. "Aye, I do fear. What does that say about me?"

"It says you are human. Nothing more, nothing less."

"To be human," he mused. "Am I allowed?"

"You are allowed to fear," she said. "It is no weakness."

He slid forward and put the goblet on the floor. He was close enough to touch her and laid his hand on her cheek and the newly forming bruise Maddox had left there. She didn't flinch.

"Is that what you tell yourself?" he asked.

She said nothing. She had no voice with which to speak. She barely had breath, so she kept her eyes on his, hoping her silent stare would give Dana the answer he sought, the answer she longed to give, but a solitary tear escaped from the corner of her eye and gave her away. He nodded gently and moved his hand so his thumb could catch her tear before it fell.

She gasped out of necessity for air and lifted her head against his palm, causing his thumb to brush her lips. He pulled away as though he had been burned and stood.

"Mayhap we should absolve each other from our sin," she said when she was able.

"There has been no sin committed," he responded.

There was more to say, another word, but neither of them uttered it. They had said too much already, she thought, too much that now hung in the air as thick as smoke. They had spoken as confidants, as lovers even, making themselves vulnerable to each other to the point that, in any place else, it would mean their ruin.

She knew it alarmed him as much as it terrified her. They would never be able to go back, but would they have the courage to move forward?

They would have to wait to find out. He would leave her now; she knew he would. He would need to retreat and regain his focus, as did she, so she held out her hand to see what he would do. To her surprise, he came forward and took it.

In her dreams, when she offered her hand, he held it and kissed it. More than once he turned her hand over and laid a trail of kisses leading from her wrist to her neck. Her lips would be next, and then he would show her exactly for what he was known.

But here, now, he merely held her hand and rubbed his thumb over her fingers.

"I don't want to be afraid," he said.

She nodded. "Neither do I."

—⁓—

The following day found Dana sitting in his tent, staring at a map of Lira while trying to guess what Omur's next move might be. He didn't think he would have to try and guess much longer, as Lucius was in the city now, awaiting word from Haleine. She would've gone right away to find out what he needed to know; she wouldn't have wasted any time.

He expected Trutina to be a target once again. He didn't think either Omur or Maddox would be content with letting their defeat stand. Neither would be willing to concede that to him at this point. His rebellion was still too new and too untested for that.

Whatever Haleine's message read, Dana already knew he wouldn't be pleased. They'd been lucky before. Only one regiment had been sent, and they could fight those numbers. Omur would not make that mistake a second time. The youth of Dana's mission would be exploited again, for even if Omur only dispatched two groups of soldiers, Dana would be forced to make a choice between targets and which would be better to save strategically. The thought that one village could be worth more than another made him sick, but it was a choice he would make. War was about sacrifice, as Haleine had said, and Dana was learning that early on.

He left his tent in search of distraction. He should have studied the map further, but he couldn't sit still without lapsing into thoughts of Haleine.

He didn't know what possessed him to say what he had. Everything had just spilled out, and it surprised him still. He had been so careful. He needed everyone within his camp to believe he was without fear and knew without doubt they would be successful. Nor was it his practice to reveal weakness, any weakness. He never talked to anyone—not even James—the way he had spoken with Haleine.

He supposed he should have been more concerned about how often he now thought of all the things he had never done before encountering Haleine, but he didn't truly see the point. It was much too late for that sort of reasoning now.

He stopped his wandering when he reached the training field where Ilya divided her attention between two groups. The first was engaged in archery practice. Most were decent shots, and the rest would improve with time. The second group tried out swords and maces and flails and whatever else had been brought back from Trutina.

Dana had taken the sword Varro offered him on the battlefield. Varro would have preferred death, but it was a favor Dana hadn't been willing to grant, so he had claimed Varro's surrender instead. The weapon had gone to his tent upon their return to camp and hadn't moved since. He doubted it ever would again.

"Dana!" Ilya called as she stood amongst the archers. "Come show them how it's done."

He joined them and accepted an offered bow. It was a quality weapon, crafted by the king's finest, but he didn't care for the feel of it. He took an arrow and fitted it. He raised the bow and took aim at the targets set at the far end of the field. He released the arrow and watched it fly. Everyone on the line did the same. As soon as the arrow had left the bow, he knew it would hit its mark and only nodded when it sank into the center of the farthest target. The others cheered. He smiled and shook his head, catching sight of Lucius with Faolan on his shoulder, standing at the field's edge. The smile lessened as Dana handed the bow back to its owner.

"Excuse me," he said.

Ilya looked at Lucius. Her expression didn't change but she barked some orders to those on the line and walked off the field with him.

"Is James on watch?" Dana asked.

"Aye," Ilya answered. "With Bearach."

"Get word to Bearach that we need James here now," he said to Faolan as soon as he was close enough. "Send someone to replace them."

The pegasus nodded and flew away. Lucius handed him Haleine's unopened note. Dana's breath caught as he looked at it.

"Did she look well?" Dana asked.

"Aye."

He nodded. Of course she did. She would never be seen looking otherwise. He closed his hand over the parchment and started for his tent. Lucius and Ilya followed.

"Let's see what the queen has to say," he said.

CHAPTER 8

Aaron awoke at the sound of his mother calling his name. He groaned and stretched and pulled his blanket over his head to drown out the sound, but his mother was persistent, and Aaron eventually relented, throwing back his blanket and rolling off the pallet. He dressed as slowly as he dared and climbed from the loft.

Mahree stood at the table, making porridge. She glanced at him, and he nodded at her as he moved toward the door, grateful to be getting away without a lecture.

"Take those with you," she said before he could escape outside.

"Take what where?"

"Those," she said, gesturing with her chin, as her hands were occupied. "On the table. Take them with you."

He picked up a neatly folded stack of wool garments. He thought they were cloaks, but he couldn't tell.

"You want me to take these to the privy?"

"No, I want you to take those to the cave and leave them for your brother."

"The moths will eat them before he comes for them. He hasn't been back in over a month. Neither of them have."

"Well, of course not. They've been busy, haven't they?"

Mahree stirred the porridge even more vigorously. He knew she was thinking of the gossip that had been coming out of the tavern ever since the strife had started. Most of it was bad. Some was good, but all of it made Mahree nervous and sick. Mostly there were stories of battles in places Aaron had never heard of. He didn't think the crowd in the tavern had heard of them either, but they knew two of their own were a part of it and clamored for whatever information they could get. They wanted to be able to ease Mahree's mind, but Aaron suspected nothing short of James and Dana's safe return at the end of all this would be able to accomplish that.

Mahree looked at him. "Well? What are you waiting for? Take those and go. There's no time to stand around today, what with your grandmother gone to Eluned. It means your help will be needed here as well as in the fields."

He nodded, picked up the stack and went outside. He waited until he was well away from the house before scowling. He was well aware of how much work awaited him. The only thing that had changed since James's departure was that Aaron was now the only son on the farm. Every night, he collapsed onto his pallet, exhausted and cursing his brother's name. Some nights he cursed Dana as well because if it hadn't been for him, James never would have left.

Aaron took his time getting to the cave. He went inside and put the stack on the ground. The absence of light made it difficult to see, even this close to the entrance, but was part of what made the cave such an effective hiding place. No one would venture too far without a light of some kind, so James had left a lantern and some flint and steel with which to light it. Aaron didn't bother to do that now; there was no need. Though, as he straightened, he could tell things were missing. The weapons. The tents his mother and grandmother had taken upon themselves to make from canvas James had brought from the city.

When had they come?

Newly annoyed, Aaron left the cave and stalked through the forest until the scent of smoke filled his nostrils. Something was burning. He stopped and lifted his head to check the direction of the wind. It was coming from the village.

He ran now, abandoning the trail to crash instead through the brush. They always rang the church bell when something like this happened, but the air was silent. Why wasn't the bell ringing?

A woman's scream broke the calm. It was followed by another and another yet. He tripped over a fallen tree and hit the ground, gashing his arm on a rock. He pulled himself up and stood still as he stared at the smoke-filled sky. He knew exactly what was happening.

Another scream broke his trance and Aaron turned for home. He was almost there when the dogs were on him, bringing him down. He cursed at them as he tried to untangle himself from their frenzy.

"Dammit, Liam, Bari," he said. "No!"

Liam took Aaron's boot in his mouth and tugged. Bari took his belt. He pushed her away, leaving a smear of blood across her coat. He slipped his foot out of the boot and got up, threw off his remaining boot, and ran again. The dogs chased after him, barking madly.

The cottage's door was opened, and as he grew closer, he saw it was stained with blood. It almost stopped him, but he kept going, the cry for his mother rising in his throat. His hand slipped on the blood, and the cry died before it could be heard.

Men. Two of them. One, with a knife dripping red, bent over his father, face down on the floor. A pool of blood spread out around him where he lay. The other man held his mother, his arm wrapped around her, holding her tight against him. She fought him but stopped when she saw Aaron. A word formed on her lips, but it was never spoken. She gasped and a crimson spray leapt out at him. It hit his face, his clothing.

Only one thought formed in his head. Run. Aaron ran away from the house, away from his mother and father. He ran through the yard, heading for the forest. He heard the men following him. He heard Liam's growl and a man's yelp of pain, but he didn't stop; he didn't look back. He heard a dog's yip, but he didn't know who it was or what had happened. He didn't look back. He only ran.

He would be safe in the woods. He knew them well. He had spent his whole life in them and around them. These men wouldn't know it like he would. He could hide in the cave, and they wouldn't be able to find him.

As he ran, he wrapped his bleeding arm in his tunic to prevent leaving more of a blood trail. He splashed into the pond and swam to the other side. There was a thicket there, and he ducked into it to catch his breath and listen for his pursuers. He heard nothing at first, but then there was the snap of branches and the rustle of leaves. They were still coming.

Aaron checked the water, but the pond had already settled from his disturbance and wouldn't give him away. He abandoned the thicket and moved silently through the forest. By the time he reached the cave, he couldn't hear his pursuers at all, but still he dropped to his knees and crawled slowly toward the back, using one hand against the side to guide him. When he had gone as deep into the darkness as he dared, he huddled in the black and waited for James and Dana to come.

———✿———

Haleine stood on the balcony and watched a plume of thick smoke rise. The sight itself was not odd. There was more often smoke on the horizon than not anymore. The location, however, was most unexpected. All of Maddox's latest targets had been much farther away than this. She had studied the map enough to know this for certain. Maddox's soldiers had struck a new target, one she hadn't found out about, one Dana didn't know about.

And she had no way of telling him. It was possible he was already aware, perhaps he was even there now, but she doubted it. Her ladies' gossip had last reported him to be days away in Mahile, a western town located at the base of the mountain pass that connected Lira with Feond. When Willem confirmed it, Haleine knew Dana had chosen to hold Mahile and leave her husband to reclaim Trutina. It had been the right decision. Her father would have done the same.

She couldn't tell Dana that either. She had not seen him, nor his messenger, for three weeks now. Even so, she was assured Dana had not come to any true harm. Maddox remained ever agitated and determined to kill the rebel leader and his rebellion.

But in all her husband's ranting and planning there hadn't been any mention of any attacks this close to Eluned. Why hadn't she known? What else didn't she know?

She left the balcony and returned inside where Bronagh was changing the bedding.

"My husband plans to entertain tonight, does he not?" Haleine asked.

"Aye," Bronagh said. She stopped her work and looked at Haleine with suspicion and dread.

"I wish to attend. Please find me something suitable to wear."

Bronagh didn't move.

"Must you fight me on everything?" Haleine asked. "I've asked to attend a party. Nothing more."

"There are others, you know," the maid said. "There are servants throughout the palace who spy for your man. You don't have to—"

"They don't always hear what I do," Haleine said. "Please, Bronagh, I must look my best tonight."

"I don't like this."

Haleine nodded. "I know, but you don't have to."

That evening, the hall was crowded with Maddox's noblemen and their many whores. She stood at the entrance and looked over them all. Omur did not seem to be in attendance, and she was glad for that. It would make talking to Maddox easier.

Her husband sat on his throne, waving a flagon around as he announced his latest plot to destroy the rebel leader. An especially well-endowed and half-dressed woman sat with him. She laughed as she caressed his arm and placed herself in his lap, silencing the king. Haleine was not pleased by that. She couldn't have cared less about his infidelity, but she hated to think she would have to play the jealous wife in order to get Maddox alone.

But she would do what had to be done. Glancing over her shoulder to reassure herself of Willem's presence, she took her first steps into the room.

She had made it only half way when one of the guests ran head-long into her. She hadn't seen him coming and was knocked to the floor. He fell on top of her and kept her from moving.

"Go back to your chambers," he whispered. "He awaits you there."

The last of the words were barely out of the man's mouth before Willem pulled him off. Haleine looked into the dark eyes she had seen before and almost smiled. She caught herself in time and accepted Willem's help in getting back to her feet.

"Are you all right, your majesty?" he asked.

She nodded and watched as Dana's man was removed from the room. "I believe I wish to return to my chambers."

Bronagh tended the fire when Haleine arrived. She stood by the doors and surveyed the room but saw no sign of anyone else. Bronagh didn't turn to bow or even raise her head. Haleine smiled and started toward her.

"You are too familiar," she said. "No other queen would tolerate such insolence."

"You return so soon?" Bronagh asked.

"My husband does not interest me nor do his parties."

"Then I wonder what does interest my lady."

Haleine sat down in her chair. "You have no need to wonder anything. You know what it is I do, and why I do it."

"Why you do it is what I fear. How you do it is even worse."

"I do not answer to you," Haleine said. "I should remind you not to forget your place."

"And I should remind you not to forget yours."

Haleine bristled. "I grow weary and wish to retire. Help me undress, then go."

"Very well, your majesty," Bronagh said, equally brisk.

As soon as Haleine was out of her gown, Bronagh left. Haleine slipped a silk shift over her head and shrugged into a robe. She emerged from behind the dressing screen and returned to her chair. She stared at the servants' entrance, irritated that she was once again at odds with her maid.

"She's angry."

Haleine nodded. "She fears for me."

She turned from the door in time to see Dana, dressed in the garb of one of the kitchen servants, materialize out of one of the darker corners of the room. She was amazed he could be so different each time she saw him. First he was little more than a carefree lad. Then he was the lad grown up too fast, shocked by the brutality of battle. Tonight he was neither of those. He seemed to be at peace, and the sight of him was beautiful. She smiled and gestured to one of the other chairs near hers. He moved slowly closer.

"If I did not know any better, I would think you were a phantom and not a man," she said. "How long have you been here?"

"Longer than you."

"Will you miss anything important?"

"Excuse me?" he asked, coming closer still.

She had to command her heart to stop beating so loud. Was it foolish to worry about him hearing it?

"The party. My husband's babbling," she explained. She was having difficulty forming sentences. "Your man was thrown out after he—and Maddox is—I would think it would be helpful."

Dana laughed. "There are more of my men in that room than you might believe."

"Then I wonder about this palace and its security," Haleine said. "You and your followers seem to move in and out so easily. I question my safety."

Dana moved even closer. "As long as I draw breath, you will never have to worry about your safety."

It was a bold promise to make, and her stomach contracted upon hearing it. Dana stopped and stood on her right, just out of reach. She looked at him and turned away almost immediately because the look in his eyes was unbearable.

"Why do you always keep your distance?" she asked, feeling grateful for it nonetheless.

"Maybe I'm afraid."

"What is there to fear? And why should it matter?"

"I've never been in love before."

Her heart stopped. "And are you in love now?"

"I'm afraid so."

She chanced another look at him. "You say that as though it were a death sentence."

"I don't know what it is," he said. "The longing, the lust. I wanted to ignore it and I've tried; I just don't think I can because no matter what I do, I think of nothing else. God, Haleine, to touch you would be heaven."

Her heart soared. Her head told her to move away, to order him away from her, but she remained seated and silent. She thought perhaps she agreed. Didn't she dream of it every night? To feel his lips on her skin, to be held in his arms? Aye, it would be heaven.

"But I am untouchable," she said, stating that which he had not.

"Aren't you?"

She wanted to kiss him. She wanted him to kiss her. She wanted to know what he tasted like. She held out her hand, palm up, to him.

"No," she said. "I am not."

He backed away. "Don't, Haleine, please. Don't offer me your hand like that."

"Why not?"

"I won't be able to stop."

He hovered near the servants' entrance. She pushed herself out of the chair and crossed the room to stand in front of the balcony doors.

"We've talked about fear before, you and I, and it is that which prevents you from taking what is offered freely. I understand, for it is the same force which drives me to extend to you my hand each time we are together. And I do not know how it is possible that we have spoken but thrice before, and I feel for you what I do, but I do know the terror of becoming untouchable.

"It is an awful feeling to sit in a room full of people—my ladies, the entire court—and know I have not a friend among them. No one touches me, not even Bronagh if it can be avoided. But Maddox is a jealous man. Maddox is a possessive man, and every law in this land says he has the right to keep isolated what is his, and there are few who dare oppose him. It chokes me a little more each day.

"But you? You make me feel as though for the first time since I came here, I am not fighting to stay alive. I simply am alive. So understand, if you will, that when you say you dare not take what is offered for fear that you shall not be able to stop, not after one chaste kiss, that I have only this to offer in response," she paused. "What if I don't want you to?"

The room was silent. Tears filled her eyes, but she held them back as she turned around to face him. He stood so close it made her gasp. She swallowed hard as she looked at him. He touched her hair.

"You frightened me," she said. "You move so quietly I did not hear you approach."

"It has its advantages," he said, his voice low.

Haleine nodded. "I would think—"

Her words were cut short by his kiss. The hand that had touched her hair moved behind her neck. His other arm encircled her waist and pulled her body against his. The kiss itself was sweet, delicate and inviting. It surprised and even shocked her. Despite its fragile nature, it was still overwhelming, this one kiss, even frightening, and she put her hands on his chest, meaning to push him away, only to find herself betrayed by her body as her hands gripped his tunic and held him as tightly as he held her.

The need to breathe forced her to end the kiss, but their heads remained close. His hands slid down her sides to her waist, sending waves of warmth throughout her entire body. He untied the sash holding her robe closed and ran his hands up to her shoulders and pushed the robe clear of her skin. He kissed her neck and the hollow of her throat. She let go of him long enough for Dana to slide the robe to the floor, then she reached for him again, tugging at his tunic's hem and lifting it. He helped her remove it, and she dropped it beside her robe.

He took her hands and kissed them each in turn as he led her across the room to the bed. She followed him willingly, more intoxicated and giddy than she had been since her arrival in Lira, and perhaps in all her life. He lifted her and sat her on the edge of the bed. He kissed her as he raised her silk shift to put his hands on the inside of her thighs. She moaned softly and started to untie the cord around his waist. He stepped back to kick off his boots before sliding out of his leggings and braies. Her shift followed and then they were both naked. He drew close to her, and she closed her eyes and breathed in his scent, her arousal increasing even more with every heartbeat.

He lowered her to the mattress and settled beside her on his side, one leg parting hers. His hand traced a line from her navel to her neck. She saw the slight tremble in his hand and loved him all the more for it.

"If you want to change your mind," he said, brushing her hair away from her face. "Tell me now."

She shook her head. "I want you to make love to me," she whispered. "I want you to show me how."

—◊◊◊—

Bronagh had served Michaela so well for so long that she had been given a most generous gift by the old queen: the privilege of a residence of her own. It was a tiny one-roomed house located against the palace wall, nestled among others belonging to the king's retainers. Michaela's gesture pleased Bronagh greatly, as few people in the royal family's service were granted such a luxury. Having a haven of her own, as small as it was, meant she did not have to fight for space in the maids' quarters. The size was more than enough to meet her needs and was still close enough to the palace for her to be readily available should the current queen have need of her.

But she did not suspect she would be called for this night. She stood in the doorway and looked at the palace. Willem sat on the bed. He stayed here with her frequently. They were both tied to the woman they served, so they suited one another well. There wasn't room for anything else.

"Are you going to stand there all night?" Willem asked. "There's no point to it. She won't be calling for you."

"You know what she's doing right now, don't you?"

"Bronagh, come to bed."

"You know what he'll do to her, don't you?"

"Please, Bronagh?"

"And you. I don't understand you," she said, looking at him. "I thought you were the queen's man."

"I am."

"Then how do you stand there, day after day, and watch the king do those things to her? If she were Michaela—"

147

"She isn't," Willem said. "She is no more Michaela than that man she married is Amatheon."

"And you do not love her like you loved Michaela."

"I said nothing of the sort."

"Then why—?"

"She's not like you and I, Bronagh," he said. "That's why you can't understand it. She doesn't know how to compromise. She's never had to just survive. She doesn't know how."

"What does that have to do with anything?"

"You called me the queen's man then question my honor because I do not act. But neither do you, Bronagh. You see what I see. You know what I know. Are you not wholly devoted to the queen?"

"You know I am."

"Then why don't you act?"

Her hands went to her hips. "If you're going to accuse me of wrongdoing, I think you'd best make your way back to the barracks."

"I don't accuse you of anything, Bronagh," he said. "Listen to me. I'm trying to explain."

She dropped her hands and nodded. "All right, then. Go on."

"We see a lot, Bronagh, a lot of things we don't do anything about. We learn to live with it because that's what people in our class do. We keep our heads down and we ignore it because that's our lot in life. The lowborn don't cause trouble. Not if they want to live. And the queen is anything but lowborn."

"Aye."

"She doesn't know how to ignore it but she doesn't know how to fight it either."

"No."

"You've seen what I've seen. You know what he's done, how he's hurt her," Willem said. "But you don't always call for Rhys to tend to her."

"She won't let me," Bronagh said. "She doesn't want it."

"Aye," Willem said. "She doesn't want it."

Bronagh understood. She looked over her shoulder at the palace, sighed and moved to sit next to Willem on the bed. She leaned against him.

"If she asked you—"

"I would."

"And if he kills her before she asks? What happens then?"

"Then her life and her death would have been of her own choosing, and she will have to be content with that."

"As will you."

"As will I."

"It'll be harder for you."

"Aye."

"But if she asks?"

"Then I would. I am the queen's man after all."

—⁓—

Dana was sleeping. Haleine, wearing only her robe, sat in a chair not far from the bed and watched him. She hadn't dared to sleep, afraid she'd awaken to find it had been another dream. It had only been when she could no longer keep her eyes open that she had forced herself to escape the warmth and security of Dana's arms. She collected her robe and sat in the chair that would offer her the opportunity to gaze upon him as he slept.

Bliss. That's what it was. What she never thought she would find when she left Quatara two months ago. He'd been tender, caring and sensitive to her needs and responses. So much so that when it was over, she cried. She hated herself for doing it but couldn't seem to stop. She raised her hand to wipe the tears away, but her motion brought her the very attention she had been trying to avoid.

"I hurt you," he said upon seeing her tears. "Oh God, love, I'm sorry. I'm so sorry."

"No," she gasped. "You didn't hurt me. Quite the opposite."

Indeed, she felt healed. She felt as though she were once again whole, but she didn't know how to tell him this or even if she should, so she said nothing more. He kissed her and then kissed away her tears. She allowed him to wrap his arms around her, and they stayed like that until Dana fell asleep.

She would have stayed like that the entire night—for the rest of her life—but he would have to leave. It was impossible for him to stay. She was never alone long once the day began, and she suspected neither Bronagh nor Ceallach would react very well to finding the leader of the rebellion in her bed.

So it was the threat of a fast-approaching dawn that propelled her from her chair. She gathered his clothing, laid it on the bed and shook him gently. He moved languidly from sleep and smiled when he saw her.

"Did you sleep?" he asked, kissing her palm and then each fingertip.

"I did not dare," she said. She closed her eyes and shuddered slightly as his lips moved across her skin. "You must go."

"Are you that eager to rid yourself of me?"

"No. No, oh no," she said, looking at him again. "Oh, don't think that. I would have you stay here always, but you can't be—"

He grinned. "I know, love. I was only teasing."

"You should not be so unkind."

"I didn't mean to be," he said, sitting up. "I'll never do it again."

She smiled at his immediate seriousness. "Do you promise?"

"That and more, love. I promise you everything you could ever want."

She shook her head. "If I have you, I want for nothing."

"You'll always have me."

"You spoil me," she said. "I don't know that I am worthy."

"Don't for a moment think you aren't."

He kissed her again before pushing away the coverlets and reaching for his clothing. She stepped back to allow him room to dress but didn't take her eyes off him. It was the first time she had really seen his body. She hadn't quite taken the time to appreciate it earlier.

"You've been fighting for weeks," she said. "And Trutina before that, but you're untouched. No scars, no wounds. I think you must be blessed."

He laughed as he pulled the tunic over his head. "You have no idea. I never thought myself a religious man before last night."

"What are you suggesting? That I am some sort of goddess and not mere royalty?"

He reached for her hand and brought it to his lips. "A fair comparison, I think."

She laughed and blushed. He opened his mouth to say something else, but before he had the chance, they heard the click of opening doors. Haleine looked at Dana in alarm. He raised a finger to his lips and disappeared under the bed.

The doors slammed shut and Haleine jumped. Maddox stalked across the room to where she stood and slapped her across the face. The blow knocked her to the floor.

"Why do you do this?" she asked.

"My whorish little wife," he said.

She sat up. "I don't know what you're talking about."

"Don't you?" he asked, still bearing down on her.

"Stay where you are," she demanded, meaning it more for Dana than Maddox.

Her husband walked past her and sat in a chair. "I was told you came into the hall last night."

"I did."

"I was told of how you let men touch you."

"What? No," she said. "I didn't. I—"

He launched himself at her and grabbed her hair. He twisted it around his hand until she couldn't move away. He pulled her to her feet and dragged her to the mirror. He released her then, twirling her around to face him. He ripped the robe from her body and turned her again so she could see her reflection in the mirror.

"Do you see? All this belongs to me! And you flaunt in a roomful of drunkards what should be for me alone. You are an embarrassment."

Maddox pushed her into the mirror. The glass broke, and she fell in the midst of it, biting her tongue to keep silent and praying Dana would not reveal his presence.

"The engagement of Zoltano Maoilriain to his Feonish slut has been announced," Maddox said next. "We leave for Mairéad today with the evening tide so we may partake in the celebration and nuptials. I will expect you to behave like a dutiful wife and not the slut I see before me now. Fail me, Haleine, and you will not see the outside of this room again."

He left the room without giving her another glance. She watched him go, surprised he had done so. It wasn't like him, and she waited, still lying amongst the remains of her mirror, to see if he might return. When she was sure he had gone, she picked up her robe and used it to wipe some of the blood off her skin.

"You can come out now," she said.

"I'm taking you away from here," Dana said as he emerged. "You're not staying any longer."

She didn't say anything as he helped her to her feet. She walked away from him, retrieved her shift and slipped it over her head. Of course she would stay. She had to. He knew it, too, even if he didn't want to admit it.

"You'd be losing a valuable spy should I leave these walls," she said.

"Hang that," he said. "It doesn't matter. There are others."

She smiled and sat on the bed. If only he knew how much, at the moment, he had in common with her maid.

"They don't hear what I do."

"It doesn't matter. It is too dangerous."

"No more than loving you, I'd say."

He came toward her, and Haleine immediately felt the desire welling inside of her just as it had the night before and every other time they had been in the same room together. When he reached her, he cupped her chin and kissed her. She closed her eyes and put her hands on either side of his face to keep him from pulling away.

"What are you doing?"

Desire was replaced by fear. Haleine's eyes flew open, and she followed Dana's gaze to the servants' entrance. Bronagh stood there, her eyes blazing and her mouth opened in disbelief. Haleine dropped her hands. Dana did the same.

"Close the door," he said.

Bronagh glared at him.

"Please, Bronagh," Haleine said, looking away. "Close the door."

"I think you should leave," Bronagh said as she slammed the door shut.

"And I think you should wait to be summoned before entering the queen's bedchamber," Dana said.

"You are lucky it was I who came through that door!" Bronagh said. "Go now and I will not call the guards."

"Haleine?" Dana asked, still staring at Bronagh. "I will do as you command."

They both knew he had to leave. His unwillingness to back down to the maid almost made her smile.

"It will be best if you go, love," she said.

Dana nodded and leaned in to kiss her ear. "I will not let you go to Tanuba alone," he whispered. "One of my allies will accompany you."

"But how—?"

"Shhh," he warned. "Maddox won't know. No one will."

"But—"

"Do you trust me?" he asked and she nodded. "Maddox won't know. His name is Faolan and he'll arrive today."

Haleine nodded again, and Dana brushed his hand across her cheek before he walked away. He crossed the room and bowed before the still-glaring Bronagh when he reached her.

"Your lady is bleeding, Bronagh," he said. "Maybe you should see to that."

That ended Bronagh's glower. She rushed over to the bed, and Haleine fended off the maid's inquiry long enough to see her lover slip away.

———✿———

James always volunteered for the early morning watch. He was awake anyway, and he liked the sense of purpose it gave him, so he and Bearach spent every morning riding through the forest, guarding their perimeter. They had yet to see anything that could be considered a threat, but it didn't matter that each turn amounted to nothing. He went, he served, he contributed. That was all that mattered.

The scouts set to watch over borders other than their own had reported Maddox's own spies in the south focusing on the Donasien Woods. Few such men had been sighted in their own territory yet, but James knew better than to think that wouldn't change.

But even when the king's scouts did reach these woods in greater number James doubted they would find much. Faolan and the unicorns had seen to that. They had cloaked the entire camp in some sort of spell and disguised it to appear as nothing more than a particularly dense and impassable tangle of trees and other vegetation. James didn't know much about the spell—nor did he want to—but he had faith in its ability. The illusion had managed to fool him more than once.

But it was getting better. Everything was, including himself. He was more comfortable with things now. Faolan's magic didn't faze him as much anymore. Neither did being called 'captain' nor the fact that Rhydwyn and Gair—the brothers from Cinna—were never very far behind him anymore, awaiting his command. Even battles had gotten easier. He fought better. The sword wasn't as much as a mystery as it once had been, and Ilya didn't seem as concerned about him as she used to be. He still hated it; he didn't think that would ever change, but it was better.

Bearach stopped short. James lurched forward but didn't fall. That was improving as well.

"What is it?" he asked, scanning the forest. "Do you see something?"

It was probably more refugees. More appeared every day, coming from the villages and towns Maddox had crushed. For every one the rebellion managed to protect, the king destroyed two. Trutina had been amongst the first to fall, and many of its surviving citizens—Hanah the healer among them—had come while the rebels had been fighting the king's men in Mahile.

"No," Bearach said. "A summons. You're wanted back at camp."

The summons likely meant Dana had come back. The night before, James, Dana, Lucius and some others, had gone to the palace to hear what the king had to say. They had scattered themselves throughout the hall and the kitchens and the rooms in between to gather what information they could. Dana had disappeared early—where to James did not know—and, at the end of the night, all had returned to camp save the rebel leader. It was only Faolan's assurance that Dana was fine that stopped James from going back to find his friend.

James nodded. "Have they sent out our replacement?"

"Yes."

"Then let's go."

When James and Bearach arrived in camp, Dana stood in the very center of it. He was dressed for travel, looking whole but unhappy. James didn't think it to be an encouraging sign.

"There you are," James said, sliding from Bearach's back. "I wondered where you'd gone off to. Did you find the company of some wench to be better amusement than Maddox's slurs? It's too bad, really. Some of them were rather clever."

"She was hardly a wench," Dana said. He looked tired as he ran his hand over his face. "James, something's happened."

CHAPTER 9

Haleine sat in the dining hall, sharing her midday meal with less than desirable company. Maddox sat to her right with his hand clamped firmly on her thigh. Even through the layers of clothing she wore, she could feel his fingers digging into her flesh. Omur sat on Maddox's other side, and although he'd never physically touched her, she still shuddered at the mere thought. She didn't need Dana's warning about the man. He was decidedly more than dangerous.

She forgot about Omur when Ceallach entered the hall, carrying a small cage. When he was close enough, she could see a tiny, smoke-gray pegasus inside, one she thought to be almost small enough to fit in her hand. Ceallach approached the table and held out the cage to her.

"What is this?" Maddox asked.

"A gift for the queen," Ceallach explained. "Your huntsmen came across the animal in the forest. They thought your wife would fancy it for a pet."

"Oh, how delightful," Haleine said, reaching out to touch the cage. "Does he have a name?"

"I was told he will answer to the name Faolan."

Haleine pulled her hand back. This was Dana's ally?

"My lord," Omur said, his voice tight with tension. "I must protest such a gift. Surely it is not proper."

Haleine looked at her husband's advisor. What reason would he have to protest? Did he know about the pegasus and who had sent him here?

"But he's so darling," she said, tugging on Maddox's sleeve. "Please, my lord, I adore him. I would be most grateful should you allow me this."

Maddox nodded and Ceallach surrendered the cage to her. She set it on the table and opened the door. Faolan stepped out and tilted his head as he stared at her. His examination was as potent as Omur's and made her feel almost as uncomfortable. She was glad when her husband raised his voice, for it gave her a reason to look away.

"Don't be tiresome, Omur," Maddox said loudly enough to be heard by the entire court. "Let her keep the damn animal. It is harmless enough."

Haleine smiled at them. Maddox paid her no mind as he returned to his meal, but Omur's angry glower bore into her until she could take no more. She turned back to her own trencher, wondering if her husband was aware of his advisor's true nature.

The pegasus stared at her throughout the rest of the meal. Occasionally he shifted his gaze to Maddox and Omur but kept the majority of his focus on her. He angled his head one way then another as though she would look different from another perspective. Why had Dana sent him here? What purpose would he serve?

When they left the dining hall, Faolan rode on her shoulder. He was slightly too large to do so comfortably, but she wasn't sure what to do about it. She watched him as best she could from the corner of her eye. He examined his surroundings, tilting his head every which way as a bird might. He didn't look at her once.

She entered her chambers to find a still-angry Bronagh ordering about three other maids. Two large trunks were in the center of the room. The scene was so reminiscent of her departure from Parthalan that Haleine was momentarily lost.

"What is that?" Bronagh demanded, bringing Haleine back to the present.

"A gift," Haleine replied. "His name is Faolan."

This only seemed to upset Bronagh more. She obviously had overheard Dana. She looked as though she wanted to say something, but her mouth remained closed, her lips pressed together so tightly they were losing their color.

Haleine appreciated the effort. She left the maids to their work and went to sit on a bench on the balcony so she wouldn't be subjected to Bronagh's ire. It was only a temporary reprieve. Later, when they were alone, Bronagh would do much more than scowl at her. Haleine could only hope they sailed for Tanuba before Bronagh had the chance.

Haleine sat facing the city until Faolan flew off her shoulder and landed on the railing in front of her. She looked at him and sighed.

"I'm afraid Bronagh isn't very fond of your master," she said.

"Dana's not my master, but he did warn me about the maid," the pegasus replied. "Why do you let her do that? You're the queen. Tell her off. She's supposed to fear you. Not the other way around."

Haleine stared. "You can talk?"

"Of course I can. Didn't Dana tell you?"

She shook her head.

Faolan sighed. "He always leaves out what's important."

———∿∿∿———

Lorcan and Bearach carried them to Enimode quicker than Dana could have thought possible, but it was still too slow. An unrelenting sense of urgency had swallowed every other emotion he was capable of feeling. It only grew more intense as they grew nearer to the village.

They'd been chasing the scent of smoke for a while, but now the air reeked of death. Then there were the bodies. The first was a young boy with a crop of dark hair. He'd been shot in the back and died with his face in the dirt. They were moving so quickly Dana almost missed him, Lorcan jumping out of the way just in time. James didn't miss him. He shouted, the first sound he had made since they left camp, and the unicorns stopped. Bearach had barely halted before James was on the ground. He knelt next to the body and turned it over.

"The miller's boy," he said, sitting back.

He sounded almost pleased. Dana could understand it. The boy could have easily been Aaron, and he felt the same relief James did. The feeling was short-lived, as James's face contorted with the shame of his initial reaction.

"We'll make sure he receives a decent burial," Dana said. "He'll not be left here."

James nodded and returned to Bearach. He started to pull himself up but stopped and slid to the ground. He rested against the unicorn and hung his head.

"They shot that boy in the back," he said. "He was running away, and they ran him down and shot him in the back."

"I know."

"I'm scared for them."

"As am I."

James remounted and they continued on until they reached the edge of the family's land. Wafts of smoke blew in their faces. James

157

slid again from Bearach's back and walked away. Dana followed but turned back to look at their mounts.

"Stay close if you would," Dana said. "There may be—"

Lorcan tossed his head. "We'll know if you have need of us. Go."

Dana thanked them and went after James. They emerged together from the forest at the edge of what had once been the wheat field. Most of it had been torched, though none of it still burned. Nothing, it seemed, had been spared. The paddock fences had been broken, the livestock either slaughtered or stolen. Farther on ahead, he could see the remains of the barn and the cottage. Both appeared to have been badly burned. Whether any of it could be salvaged, he didn't know.

Liam and Bari lay dead in the middle of the yard, their breasts split open. There was a still-saddled horse searching for water in the empty trough. Dana recognized it as Sarai's and scanned the yard for a sign of the mare's rider. If the horse lived, it stood to reason that Sarai had somehow escaped the slaughter. Perhaps she had been away and had come home to find everything doused in flame. His eyes settled on the cottage. She would have gone there first.

James apparently had the same thought, as they started for the cottage at the same time. Now that he was closer, Dana could see most of the damage to the house had been done to the roof. The main structure seemed to be in tact. The door still hung but was open and covered with blood. Dana paused and looked at it and the crimson footprints leading out of the house. The king's men had been in a hurry. He held his breath as he stepped inside.

Seoras and Mahree lay on the floor in the common room. Both had had their throats cut. James cried out and fell to his knees beside them, disregarding the blood covering the floor. Dana stayed still and stared at the bodies until his vision blurred and he could see nothing but their tear-distorted shapes. He turned his head and saw Sarai huddled in the corner near the hearth. Her clothing and skin were caked with dirt, ash and blood, but she was alive.

"Sarai?" he said.

James's head came up. He spotted his grandmother and stepped over his father's body to reach her.

"Gran," he said, his voice thick with tears. "Are you hurt?"

"You've come home," she said.

"Aye," James said. "Where's Aaron?"

"I don't know," she said. "I can't find him."

"Dana," James said.

"I'll find him," he promised.

He went outside, stood next to the dogs and examined the ground around them. A man much larger than Aaron had fallen here. A blood trail led into the woods. Whatever had happened, Liam and Bari had tried to stop it.

"Good dogs," he murmured.

He proceeded into the forest. The king's men probably wouldn't have known the area as well as Aaron. He thought he knew where the boy would have gone, but did he get there without getting caught?

He found no sign suggesting otherwise. The blood trail had ended, but there was no sign of struggle. There was no body, and they would have killed him if they had caught him. The miller's boy proved that.

The trail left by the king's men eventually turned back to the village, but Dana abandoned it and went to the cave. If Aaron had hidden here, he had done well to cover his tracks. Dana found no sign of him nor anyone else.

"Aaron?" he called at the cave's entrance. "Aaron? Are you here?"

He took a step inside and tread on something not stone and bent to see what it was.

"Ma made those," Aaron said.

Dana couldn't see him, but it didn't matter just yet. Hearing the boy's voice was enough for now.

"She told me to bring them here for you," Aaron said next.

Dana felt for the flint and lantern. He lit it, and the tiny flicker of light quickly grew into a flame bright enough to illuminate the boy sitting at the back. He couldn't tell how badly hurt Aaron was, so he moved forward.

"Is it over?" Aaron asked when Dana stood in front of him.

"Aye. It's over."

Aaron nodded and dragged his arm across his face. His tears weren't enough to clear the blood splattered across his cheeks. One sleeve of his tunic was ripped. Dana would have to wait until they were in the open air before seeing how bad an injury lay there.

"I ran," Aaron said.

"Anyone would have."

"Da didn't. He was out in the field. He probably heard her scream, and I was there and I watched when they—and I ran."

"There's no shame in that."

"No? The last thing my mother saw was me running away."

"You did the right thing, lad," Dana said. "Are you hurt?"

"No."

"Then the blood—"

"Isn't mine."

"And your arm?"

"I fell."

Dana didn't press for more. "Come on, then. Let's go back."

"What's there to go back to?"

"The rest of your family," he said. "They would very much like to know you're all right."

"Such as it is," Aaron said. He looked at Dana. "Did they come here because of you?"

Dana didn't answer. He didn't know.

The appearance of the pegasus was a surprise, and Omur didn't care much for surprises. With each passing day, he grew more and more convinced that the completion of his goal—his masters' goal—was rapidly approaching, and he could not allow anything to interfere. He hated that he had overlooked something. He despised knowing that Dana had gotten close to the queen, so close as to be able to place a spy in the household. The breach was now obvious; he should have seen it sooner.

She had gone to Maddox. She had left her chambers and bedded him deliberately. She played into him, indulging, coaxing, petting her husband to gain what she wanted. She did it for permission to go to the cathedral and again in defense of that winged vermin. Why hadn't he seen it?

And now that beast was setting up residence in the queen's chambers. The animal would guard it against him first. It would want to protect the room from whatever was said within the queen's walls. Omur had much the same need and returned to his chambers with the intention of performing a similar magic, but when he returned from the dining hall, he found Varro standing by the fireplace. He stopped and looked at the captain. The man did not carry good news.

"My lord," Varro said. "We have returned."

"Obviously. What did you find out?"

"Regrettably, my lord, the whore either lied, or the people of Enimode are unfailingly loyal. We learned nothing."

It would have been easy to blame the whore, but Omur thought it much more likely that Dana inspired their loyalty. The more he learned of Laorans's champion, the more Omur hated him.

"You used all means necessary to try and convince them?"

"Yes," Varro said. "The village burns as we speak, her people within it."

Maybe it would be enough. If loyalty had kept Enimode silent, and Dana did have ties there, maybe learning of its destruction would push the rebel leader to misstep. Omur wouldn't let the man fail entirely—he couldn't—but it would be nice to know Dana was capable of error.

"Go back to the whore," Omur said. "Tell her you were less than pleased, and find out what more she may have for us. Impress upon her your displeasure so mayhap she will do better this time. Whatever she gives you, tell no one but me."

"Yes, my lord," Varro said and bowed as Omur waved him off.

Maybe that would be enough for Dana, but now there was a new threat crossing the ocean with him that very night. The pegasus would require something else.

"One thing more, Varro," Omur said before the man could disappear. "Something to be done before I sail this night."

"Yes, my lord?"

"I need you to gather something for me," he said. "I have a message to send."

—⁂—

They would have to wait until morning to bury Seoras and Mahree. Sarai wanted to make shrouds and no one wanted to convince her otherwise. They found linen in the cottage's cellar, the same fabric they had smuggled out of the city a month earlier, and Sarai set herself to cutting and sewing. Dana and James prepared the bodies as best as they could, washing away the blood and dressing them in clean clothing.

Dana hated to think of them like that, as bodies, as corpses, and not the people who had taken him in and raised him as their own, but he found he couldn't think of them any other way. It was too much, and he couldn't allow himself to become vulnerable. He needed to be aware of what happened around him. The possibility of danger still lingered in the air.

It was this sense that kept his sword strapped to his side. James had left his somewhere between the forest and the fields. Dana hadn't even noticed it was gone at first. When he did, he commented that its recovery would be smart, but James's reaction suggested there would be more loss still to come.

When they ran out of daylight, Dana built a fire to repel the cold and dark. Sarai sat as far away as she could without losing her much needed sewing light. Her stitches were hesitant, and she stopped more than once to wipe tears from her face. Aaron's eyes were dry as he sat close to the fire. His arm hadn't been badly injured, but Sarai had cleaned and stitched it, then bandaged it using some of her linen. As soon as she had finished, he isolated himself on the other side of the fire, ignoring anything that was said to him.

When James came from the house where the bodies were laid out in anticipation of their burial, he sat beside Dana. He folded his arms across his chest and glanced at the sword Dana had laid on the ground but didn't say anything. He looked away and stared at the fire.

"Tell me about the girl," James said.

"What?"

"Tell me about the girl," he repeated. "The one—the one who—just tell me about her."

"You want to hear about that?"

"No. But tell me anyway."

"James," Dana said. "I don't—"

"I can't sit here thinking about—just tell me about the girl. If she got you to stop obsessing over the queen, she must really be something."

"Right," Dana said, not knowing what else to say. He didn't want to lie, but the truth didn't seem appropriate.

"Well?"

"She's beautiful," Dana said. "But of course she's beautiful. She's—I don't know—she's intoxicating. She makes my head swim like I've had too much mead even if I haven't had a drop. And God, the things I say to her, James. I'm really quite an idiot, but she laughs and smiles and says the most remarkable things in response. I don't know how it is she's real, and I don't know how it is she even looked twice at me, but thank God or Goddess that she did."

"It sounds as though you're falling in love."

"Worse than that," Dana said. "I've already fallen."

James laughed. When Dana looked at him, he could see the tears in his friend's eyes.

"God," James said. "The world really is ending, isn't it?"

Dana turned back to the fire. "I don't know."

The conversation ended there, and for some time, the only sound was the crackling of the fire. He lifted his head slightly when he heard someone approaching from behind. Keeping as still as possible, he reached for his sword. He was sliding it from the sheath when Sarai looked over.

"Owain," she said. "Dana, put that away."

James glanced over his shoulder and nodded. Dana put the sword back on the ground and stood. Owain was a scrawny boy, younger than Aaron, whose parents owned the tavern. His sister was Rhiannon, and it was not long ago that Dana had sat at a table there, talking and laughing with all of them. Dana was surprised to see him alive and unharmed.

"Owain," Sarai said again. She left her sewing and came over to him. "Are you hurt? What of your parents and sister? Come by the fire if you want."

He shook his head and looked at Dana. "My parents are dead, and Rhiannon's asking for you."

"She's all right?" Sarai asked.

"No," Owain answered, not taking his eyes off Dana. "Will you come?"

Dana nodded and reached for his sword. "Of course."

He followed Owain into the village. There was nothing to see in the darkness apart from a ring of camp fires around which other survivors now huddled. Rhiannon lay on the ground near one such spot. Her vacant eyes stared at him, and several moments passed before recognition appeared. She beckoned to him, and he caught a glimpse of a mark resembling a rope burn encircling her wrist.

He knelt beside her. "Owain said you asked for me."

She nodded. Even that seemed to hurt her. "They came, six of them. All lords. They stayed in the tavern, took all our rooms. They paid Da in advance, and he never—They wanted to know about you. Where you're from, your family, everything, but we told them nothing. No one here ever would."

"I never thought otherwise," he said. "Did they say how they knew to come here?"

"They were so angry. Said they knew we lied. They knew you came here. Someone had told them. A—a whore," she said, struggling to prop herself up. "In the city, I think. They didn't say her name."

"It doesn't matter," he said. He already knew her name. "Rest now."

Rhiannon nodded and lay back on the ground. He took off his cloak, folded it and tucked it under her head. She smiled at him and held his wrist. He didn't move until she had fallen asleep and her hand dropped off on its own. Then he moved away and sat next to Owain.

"When she dies," Owain said, "I'm coming to fight for you."

Dana nodded. He didn't bother to argue Rhiannon's fate. Owain was fortunate his sister had lived this long. Rhiannon would be fortunate if she didn't make it another night.

"We'd be lucky to have you," he said.

"Luckier than her," Owain said. "I don't know why they didn't just kill her."

Dana knew. It would have been kinder to kill her. But it was kinder not to tell Owain that so he just shook his head.

"I have to go take care of something," he said. "If James comes looking for me—"

"I'll tell him," Owain said.

He left Owain and Rhiannon by their fire and walked straight into the night. He went into the forest where Lorcan was waiting.

"Do you know where I need to go?" Dana asked as he climbed onto the unicorn's back.

"Yes."

Lorcan brought him to Eluned. Dana left both the unicorn and his sword in the forest outside the city walls. He was able to slip past the guards by concealing himself in the midst of a group trying to push their way in before the city's gates closed for the night. It was even easier to make it to the brothel, and once inside, still no one noticed him. The whores were busy entertaining their callers, and the men weren't looking at anything else. He took a couple of flagons of wine off an unguarded table and slipped above stairs to Piala's room.

He sat in the dark and drank wine as he waited for her. He knew her routine well so he didn't wait long. He smelled her perfume first. Cheap, rancid even, but most of her customers were too drunk to notice. She entered the room, humming to herself. He knew the tune. She had had a good night.

She didn't see him at first. He was hidden in shadow, sitting in the room's solitary chair. She draped her shawl across the foot of the bed and moved to light a lantern. She would see him now, just as soon as she turned around. When she did, the song died on her lips.

"Good night?" he asked.

She recovered quickly from her shock and took the money purse hanging from her hip and tossed it on the bed. She looked at the flagon he had discarded on her floor.

"Is there any other kind?" she asked.

"Not for you, I'd wager."

She smiled, sliding back into her languid flirtation. "Gambling and drinking, love? Mayhap you should be out seeking a priest to absolve you of your sins."

"Mayhap later. I may have another sin yet to commit this night."

"Sounds promising," she said. "Do you want to go to Orla's? I'll let you buy me an ale."

"No."

"In a hurry, then? What's wrong, love? Haven't come across any good tumbles on your travels?"

"How did it happen?" he asked. "Did they find you, or did you find them?"

"I don't know what you're talking about."

"The man or men you told about me. Did they find you, or did you find them?"

"I found them."

Her voice slid from careless seduction to matter-of-fact. She sat on the edge of the bed, her eyes daring him to find fault with what she had done. He was always telling her she was too bold for her own good. Even for a whore. She should've known better than to dare him anything. Especially tonight of all nights.

"It wasn't hard. They were around everywhere, asking about you. Asking all the wrong people, of course."

"They destroyed Enimode because of what you told them."

"With that dramatic flair, love, you should have been a player. You would have commanded the stage for sure," she said. "And as for Enimode, they would have destroyed it anyway, sooner or later. It's what they do."

"It was James's family, you know."

It was his family, too, but he didn't tell her that. It wouldn't have made a difference. She still would have sat on her bed, looking at him in that hardened way.

"What else did you tell them?" he asked. "Where else?"

"I gave them some names. Places you go when you leave me."

"I never tell you anything. You only knew about Enimode because of James, so what did you tell them? I know they've been back," he said, looking at her purse. "They would have wanted more because they got nothing in Enimode. The people there are loyal to me and didn't give them anything, so they would have come back to you. What did you tell them?"

"I didn't tell them anything else."

"If that were true, you'd be lying dead in whatever alley you met them in. What did you tell them? Where are they going next?"

"You gonna go stop it, lover? Gonna play the valiant hero? God, those people, you should hear them talk about you. Some of them think of you as a savior. Some sort of pure and righteous savior," she said with a laugh. "Wouldn't they hate to know what you're like in the dark with me?"

"Where are they going next, Piala?"

"You don't really expect me to tell you, do you?" she asked. "If you show up, they'll think I'm playing both sides. What do you think they'd do to me then?"

"I'd hope they'd kill you," he said. "Oh, Piala. Why did you do this?"

"What was I supposed to do? You've not been to my bed, nor I yours, in so long and—"

"Don't lie. You're a whore," he said. "You don't get jealous. There's no profit in it."

"That's right."

"Tell me, then, what is the going rate on betrayal?"

She nodded. "Aye. There's profit in that."

"A village's worth, I hope, because that is what you destroyed."

"No," she said. "I don't care who you think you are. You don't come in here and lecture me."

"I didn't come here to lecture you."

He set the flagon down as he stood and walked the few steps across the room. She didn't move. He stopped in front of her and put his arms on either side of her. She closed her eyes, raised her head and parted her lips.

"Nor did I come here to fuck you," he said.

Her eyes opened as he put his hands on her throat. He kept his thumb under her chin to force her to look at him.

"Tell me where you sent them."

"Culhwch. Then Koulmia."

"Is that all?"

She tried to nod, but he held her too tightly to allow it.

"If you kill me, they'll know," she gasped. "They'll know they hurt you."

"They're going to know it anyway."

"I didn't think I'd ever see you again."

"Nor I you."

"Forget I knew you," she said. "Isn't that what you told me?"

He snapped her neck and she fell limp against him.

"You should have listened," he said softly.

—⁓—

Faolan stood on a table in the shadows and watched the king and queen of Lira as they slept. Maddox had been drunk and now slept heavily. Faolan doubted the king would stir before morning and maybe not even then. Haleine was more restless. He didn't know the cause of her fitfulness. Her husband, probably, or maybe the ship's gentle but constant rocking. Faolan didn't know what was in her mind—he didn't have that power—but he wanted desperately to find out.

He had been annoyed with Dana when the request to accompany Haleine to Tanuba had been made. Traveling with humans across the sea would mean days of standing silent on a ship surrounded by salt water, and he'd never tolerated salt well—none of the goddess's servants did. Sailing to Tanuba would weaken him, sicken him, if only temporarily. He had done it before, and would do it again, he was sure, but this time there seemed to be no reason for it except that Dana had found a new girl to bed.

But the undeniable concern and love in Dana's voice had piqued Faolan's curiosity, so he had gone to the palace and laid eyes on the queen of Lira. Now he wondered about it all because as soon as he had seen Haleine, Faolan knew there was no place more important for him to be.

Although he had acted on Laorans's behalf for centuries, he'd always done so from afar, content to allow the unicorns the care of the land itself. He made only the occasional visit when circumstances created by the dark gods demanded it. It was only in the last eighteen years that he had become a more permanent resident. The balance of power had started to shift, crumble and give way.

Faolan could feel it. There was a darkness eating away at a peace that had been a bulwark for a millennium.

And as the world decayed, so did the goddess. Their deterioration went hand in hand. Faolan had yet to feel the effects, but it would only be a matter of time, for Laorans and the earth were tied together, and Faolan was tied to her. The weakness would trickle down to him, to Luisiúil, to all of them, and eventually would drain them of power, leaving them helpless and vulnerable for the first time in a thousand years.

For a thousand years, they had held the dark gods in check. For a thousand years, they had done this and done this well, but now they were starting to lose it all.

And Faolan was looking at the reason why.

The first thing he had done upon his arrival to Haleine's chambers was seal the room from eavesdropping. It was a simple spell that would prevent Omur from using any magic to hear anything said within her walls. Faolan didn't know if Omur had even paid attention to Haleine before—though he suspected the mage had—but regardless of what had come before, Omur would certainly pay attention now. Faolan's arrival had guaranteed that, so he focused on protecting what he could.

He didn't have to worry about the influx of servants. Most humans were indifferent to magic. They were incapable of feeling it even when carried out in their midst. He didn't know whether Haleine would be included in this majority and had watched her as he cast the spell. She paused mid-sentence, but he couldn't tell with confidence the cause of her hesitation.

He continued to watch her even after the spell was set. He had had no preconceived notions of the queen of Lira except for knowing that Dana loved her, so she had to be extraordinary. He hadn't realized just how extraordinary she was until now.

Pieces of a puzzle long unsolved were dropping all around him, but he still didn't know the key to putting it together. He suspected Omur might. It explained much, starting with why the dark gods and their underlings were acting now. But there was more, more significance of which he was still unaware.

What did they know that he didn't? What did they know that Laorans didn't?

Haleine would lead him to the answers.

Dawn had come and gone, and Dana had yet to return. James sent Aaron to look for him while he and Sarai made the final preparations for his parents' burial. They waited until Aaron came back, saying only that Dana had gone to take care of something. James didn't know what that meant, nor did he care. He didn't want to wait anymore.

So they buried Seoras and Mahree without Dana. Sarai sang one of the traditional songs and sprinkled both graves with flowers she had found in the forest. Eventually the mounds would be covered with grass, but now they were brown, stark and obvious markers of what had happened here. James stared at them, thinking nothing and feeling less. Aaron stood beside him, trying too hard to be the man he almost was. Neither of them spoke.

Sarai finished her song and knelt between the graves to say her final farewell. Aaron left. James knew he should follow him but didn't take the steps. He wouldn't be able to offer his brother any sort of comfort so he left it to Sarai. His grandmother got to her feet and went after Aaron, pressing her remaining flowers into James's hand as she passed.

He stayed and stared. He crouched in front of the graves and dropped the flowers in favor of a handful of soil. He let it slip through his fingers again and again until Dana's approach stopped him.

"I'm sorry I wasn't here," Dana said.

"We couldn't wait anymore."

"It's all right."

He looked over his shoulder at Dana. "Did they come here because of you? Because of us?"

"Aye."

"How did they know?"

"It doesn't matter."

"Doesn't matter?" James asked as he stood. He tried to laugh, but the sound wouldn't come out. "I don't understand that. Those are your parents buried there. How does it not matter?"

"I've taken care of it."

This time he did laugh. "I don't know where you went or what you did, but you haven't taken care of anything. Neither of us have."

"James—"

"We failed them, Dana. Ma, Da, the whole lot of them right down to that boy we found in the woods. We put them in danger, and we left them to die."

"That's not what happened."

"That's exactly what happened," he said. "Where did you go last night?"

"It doesn't matter. Please, James," Dana said. "There isn't much time."

"There never is."

"I know where they plan to strike next."

"You always know. Your spies then, maybe a patrol got lucky, I don't know, but you always know. So why not Enimode? Why didn't you know about that?"

"They wanted us to know about the others. But this?" Dana said. "This is the one they wanted to hurt me."

"Did it?" James asked. "Did it hurt you?"

"I don't even know why you would say that. God, how could you even doubt it?"

He shook his head. "You never lack for energy, do you? It doesn't matter what happens. It never matters because it never touches you, and you never stop."

"It touches me. It would drive me to the ground if I let it. But I can't do that; I *won't* do that. I'm going to fight this war. I'm going to win this war because I don't want this to have been for nothing."

"Aye," James said. "Neither do I."

"Then you know I have to go and stop it."

"You do. And I'm coming with you."

"I thought you'd stay."

"I've been standing here—I don't even know for how long—looking down at my parents' graves and thinking only that I should feel something more than what I do because all I feel is hate. I'm useless here. At least until it's over. What happens then, I don't know."

"And Sarai and Aaron? We'll take them with us, aye?"

"No. This land still belongs to my family. We'll not forfeit that."

"They'll be a target."

"Look around. They already were. No one's going to come here again. There's nothing to come back here for."

"James, they'll starve."

"They won't. This village looks after its own. No one will starve."

"I don't want to leave them unprotected. Not again."

James smiled. "We'll leave Aaron your sword. You've got another after all," he said. "I should very much like to borrow that weapon, though, when we meet the men who did this. I think we'll find the man to whom that sword belongs among them, and I shall like to ram that steel into him. Aye, he'll be the first. Next will be any who follow him. And the very last will be the king and his wife."

Dana was shocked. James knew it wasn't easy to do, and he relished his friend's stunned silence.

"But she didn't—" Dana said finally. "James, she's innocent."

He crouched down once more and picked up the flowers Sarai had left behind. He threw them so they scattered across both graves.

"Aye," he said. "So were they."

CHAPTER 10

Haleine's entourage had swelled considerably since her last trip across the ocean. It now included Faolan, Willem, Ceallach, and a trio of her ladies-in-waiting. None of them were inclined to leave her on her own. It made her long for the privacy of her chambers where it had been possible to have an occasional moment alone.

But she didn't have that luxury aboard the ship. She spent her days walking the deck with Faolan perched on her shoulder, her ladies surrounding her, and Ceallach and Willem trailing close behind. Her ladies prattled on about the latest happenings in her husband's court. Haleine kept an eye on the ship's railing and wondered if Willem might throw the lot of them overboard if she asked.

It was Faolan's company she wanted to keep and conversation with him she wanted to have, but she had learned early on that Faolan would not talk in front of anyone, not even Willem, so it was not until the ship docked in Tanuba, eight days after its departure from Eluned, that she was able to speak to him.

The opportunity came after her ladies finished helping her dress in the cabin she had shared with her husband. She dismissed them in a tone that offered no room for argument, so her attendants curtsied and departed, leaving her alone with the pegasus.

"I am sorry you have been made to listen to naught but my ladies' endless gossip," Haleine said. "I imagine you would've found Maddox's or Omur's company more enlightening."

"It doesn't matter," Faolan said. "I've learned quite a lot already."

"Court scandals interest you?"

"No," Faolan said. "You look pale. Are you all right?"

"It is kind of you to ask, but I am only sea sick and bone weary. I will be grateful to stand on solid land again."

"Me too. I don't enjoy traveling by boat," he said. "I can't say I'm looking forward to the voyage home."

She smiled. "When we arrive at the palace, you will have to go with the servants and the luggage."

"The luggage? Why?"

"Maddox and I will be presented to Nathan and Haraszty. It wouldn't be proper to bring you along to the throne room."

"Oh," Faolan said. "I didn't realize being proper was such a concern for the Liran royal family. Your husband, after all, kills people on a whim, and I know what you've been doing."

"What do you mean you know what I've been doing?"

"I've been with Dana a long time. We don't have secrets from one another."

She felt her cheeks flush. "None?"

Faolan shook his head just as Willem knocked on the door.

"Your majesty?" he said. "They await you on shore."

She hesitated a moment longer, staring at Faolan until he flew from his table to her shoulder. Willem knocked again and she left the room.

She forgot her embarrassment only when she had left the ship and was about to step into the waiting carriage. Maddox and Omur were already seated, one on either side. She accepted Willem's help and sat next to her husband. Willem closed the door, and the carriage started rolling immediately.

"Must you have brought that detestable creature along?" Omur asked.

Haleine turned to Maddox. "Must you have brought your detestable creature along?"

Maddox laughed and glanced at Omur. "Leave the animal be," he said. "And I would prefer it if you did not speak to my wife in such a tone. Do it again and you'll regret it."

Haleine gaped at Maddox in surprise. She was not the only one. Omur also appeared rather astounded. He glared at her and she smiled back, unable to help herself. Omur's glower deepened before he finally looked away. Faolan snorted softly and stamped her shoulder with his hoof. She smiled again and turned her attention to the scenery outside her window. Out of the corner of her eye, she saw Omur do the same.

When they arrived at the palace, Haleine got out of the carriage first and sent Faolan off with the servants, giving him an apologetic glance as she did so. Maddox followed, and Omur was last. He was still reeling from Maddox's reprimand and, as they were escorted to the throne room, skulked behind them. She could feel his eyes on her back, and although she knew she should have been frightened to no end, all she could do as she entered the throne room was grin.

Nathan and his wife, flanked by their sons, were seated side by side on their great chairs of gold. Haleine caught Revelin's eye briefly before dipping into a curtsey.

"Oh, don't bother with that," Haraszty said.

"Your majesty," Haleine said, rising.

"Don't bother with that either, my dear. We need to talk about tonight's party and formalities will only get in our way."

Haleine smiled. She'd always liked Haraszty. The queen of Tanuba truly was in a world of her own. She was a round woman with a face creased by lines of laughter. She was terminally amused but easily bored, so the queen entertained both frequently and elaborately.

"Of course," Haleine said.

She looked at Revelin again. His face was impassive and formal. Only his eyes gave anything away, and she could see he was pleased to see her. She gave him a small smile. He made no indication that he had noticed, but she knew otherwise.

"Haleine?" Haraszty said, tearing her away from her thoughts.

"Yes, excuse me," she said, turning her attention back to the queen. "The traveling—"

She didn't finish the sentence because Haraszty already had lost interest in the answer.

"Your parents will arrive today," Haraszty said. "They'll be here in time for the ball."

Haleine managed a smile but didn't know how else to react. The correct response would be one of joy or gratitude, but since her departure from home, she hadn't thought of her parents in anything other than hatred.

"How wonderful," she said. "It has been months since I saw them last."

Both Nathan and Haraszty smiled at her. Revelin could no doubt see past her words—she was sure of it—although he continued to say and do nothing.

"Well," Nathan said. "Maddox, why don't we withdraw to speak of this troublesome rebellion of yours, and leave these women to gossip as they will."

Maddox nodded his consent and the men exited. Revelin was the last, lingering just long enough that no one but she would realize he was doing it. As she watched him go, she wondered what else he might be able to tell about her.

"Haleine?"

She turned to the queen. "Yes, your majesty."

Haraszty gestured to her husband's seat. "Sit."

"My congratulations on your son's engagement," Haleine said, doing as Haraszty had directed. "You must be proud."

Haraszty waved lazily. "Yes. It will be quite the celebration. God knows I've had long enough to plan for it. We've all waited long enough. You too," Haraszty said with fondness. "I'm sorry you were made to wait, but that does not matter now, does it?"

"Not anymore, no," Haleine agreed.

Haraszty nodded. "I do hope, however, before too long we might be back in Lira to celebrate the birth of your son."

Haleine nearly choked at the thought but recovered and smiled. "We have not been blessed as yet."

"It is always hard in marriages such as yours," Haraszty said, reaching out and pulling her closer. "But Haleine, you do make a lovely queen."

Haleine blushed. Haraszty patted her cheeks and leaned back.

"I apologize," she said. "You're exhausted, and here I am, being as rude as can be. I'll call the servant to bring you to your chambers."

"Thank you," Haleine said.

It was, by far, the shortest conversation she had ever had with Haraszty, as the queen was often given to endless amounts of aimless banter when she had an audience. Haleine didn't want to believe her good fortune and waited for Haraszty to start talking again, but the queen did just as she had said. She summoned the servant and waved Haleine away.

The room she had been allotted was far more richly appointed than those she'd been given on her previous visits to Mairéad. Haraszty saved her best for her royal guests. Haleine examined the room and was assuring the servant she was well pleased by her accommodations when she heard a snort coming from across the room. Turning her head, she saw Faolan standing on the vanity. He let out a sharp whinny and gave her a look of unmistakable impatience. She was as surprised by that as she had been by his ability to speak.

"The pegasus is not very friendly," the servant commented.

"Yes," Haleine said. "I fear he has a terrible disposition."

Faolan whinnied again and stamped his tiny hooves on the vanity's surface. Haleine smiled as she thanked the servant and sent the girl away.

"I do not have a terrible disposition," Faolan said.

Haleine crossed the room and sat on the bench in front of him. "What did you do to make the servants think otherwise?"

"Maybe you should ask what they did to me."

"Mayhap."

"This seems to be like a homecoming for you."

"I suppose it is."

"I thought you hailed from Quatara."

"By birth, I am a native of Tanuba, but I spent most of my life in Quatara. My father has been its seneschal since I was born."

"A hard place to grow up, I'd think, especially when you're not welcome."

"How do you know of Quatara?"

"I hear things," Faolan said.

"Quatara is a source of gossip among Lira's citizens?"

"I didn't say that."

"But you did say you have been with Dana for a long time. All your life?"

"Not remotely."

"All his?"

"Very nearly," he said. "I'm surprised your father would allow you to stay in Quatara. Wouldn't it have been safer to have you grow up in Tanuba?"

"He liked to have us close," she said. "It was not without risk, but he saw we were always well protected."

"We?"

"My sister and I."

"Sister?"

"Sighle," Haleine said. "She is younger than me if you'd care to know."

"Why do you say that?"

"Why are you interested in me and my upbringing?"

"I'm curious about you," Faolan said. "It's not every day Dana professes to being in love. But if you'd rather speak of other things, let's talk about what's going to happen here."

"A wedding's going to happen here. Princess Zaide Romanza will finally wed Prince Zoltano. It will, for certes, be the social event of the year. Did Dana not tell you?"

"He did, but something else is going to happen. Something less festive."

"Why do you think that?"

"Omur wouldn't have made the trip otherwise," Faolan said. "Did Maddox or Omur say anything in the throne room just now that might help me figure out what's been planned?"

"They've hardly said a word except to snipe at each other over you," she said. "But what if they had? What could you do about it? You're so small, and I don't honestly believe you would stand a chance against them."

"You humans need to learn size doesn't always matter," Faolan said. "Do you know from where I came?"

"I don't know. Wherever Dana's from, I suppose."

"No. I don't mean a village, a town, a city or a country even. I should have said it differently. Do you know who sent me to Dana?"

"You say that as though you are some sort of winged messenger from God."

"Even better. Laorans."

"You're making fun of me. Laorans does not exist."

"Neither does your god."

"Dana never mentioned you were a heathen."

"I could say the same to you."

"I am not a heathen."

"It's not your fault. You were raised that way. Your religion has never acknowledged Laorans as anything more than some sort of myth. There are a few who think otherwise. Farmers, sometimes. She is the goddess of the earth after all."

"What of Dana? What does he believe?"

"You'd have to ask him."

"Why don't you know?"

"It's not important."

"How is it not important?"

"He fights for the people. Everything else is secondary."

"And Omur?" she asked. "Is he secondary as well?"

"What do you know about him?"

"I know he's more than just an advisor. Dana warned me against him, saying he was more dangerous than even Maddox, but above all that, I know what I saw. He knew you, and he didn't want you anywhere near him."

"A problem you nicely averted for me," Faolan said. "I don't know how to thank you for that."

"Thank me by telling me who he is."

"I don't think you really want to know."

"Oh, I can say with absolute certainty that I do not," she said, "but it does not change the question. Who is he?"

"He's dangerous. Dana wasn't lying nor exaggerating when he told you that. Omur represents very potent forces, and he will not hesitate to kill you if you stand in the way of what he wants."

"But I have stood in the way. More than once," she said. "If what you say is true, how am I still alive?"

Faolan appeared to consider her question. "Maybe you only think you're standing in the way."

Haleine thought about that. "If you're trying to scare me, you don't have to. I am sufficiently frightened."

Faolan tilted his head to the right. After a moment, he nodded. "I hope so."

—⁓—

When the king and queen of Lira appeared at Haraszty's ball, the guests were already drunk and loud, but the couple silenced them with their commanding presence. The trumpets that announced the arrivals of the other monarchs suddenly seemed cheap and tinny. Nearly every person stared, with dropped jaws, at the striking pair.

Only Revelin kept his head bowed. In all their time together, he had never thought of Haleine as a queen, perhaps because he had never thought of himself as a king, but as she approached him, there was no denying that she carried the crown well. She had been born for it.

She greeted his parents now. Zoltano stood next to them, acting like a dog starved for food, but Revelin stared at the floor, preparing himself for this encounter.

"Your majesty," Zoltano said as he reached for Haleine's hand. "You do honor us with your presence."

"Prince Zoltano," she said.

She used a tone Revelin knew well, as she never had been fond of his brother. She tactfully withdrew her hand and turned to him, but he was still afraid to lift his head.

"Do I look so awful you do not even want to look at me?" she asked.

He breathed deep and looked up. "On the contrary. You are truly a vision," he said. She offered her hand and he kissed it. "Your husband is a fortunate man."

She smiled. "To hear some tell it, the fortune is all mine."

"Haleine?"

It was Darian's voice. Revelin took his eyes off her long enough to see her parents approaching from behind. Haleine stiffened, squared her shoulders and held out her arm to him.

"Walk with me," she said.

"Oh. Well, of course."

Revelin turned away, avoiding Darian's eyes. He didn't know a man hardened by years of battle could look so injured when no weapons were involved.

"I apologize," she said as they walked. "I should not have done that to you or them, but I can't greet them. I am unsure of what would be said if I did, and I am unwilling to find out."

"Your parents did not have a choice."

"Didn't they?" she asked, glancing at the musicians as they began to play. She sighed. "Instead of answering that, why don't you dance with me?"

"It would be a pleasure."

He led her to the center of the room and bowed. She curtsied in return, and they began the dance. He held her close, his hand on her back and his entire body soaking in the feel of her. They had been apart longer than this before, but never had he felt it as keenly as in this moment. God, he was pleased to be near her again.

"You look well," he said as they glided around the floor. "I would even say happy."

She pulled back slightly, looking as though she hadn't even considered the idea of happiness. She smiled. "Happy to be here with you."

"You flatter me. I thought there to be something more to it."

"What else could there be?" she asked. "Where is Zaide Romanza? I haven't seen her yet. Surely she plans to attend a ball thrown in her honor."

"She will come. You know she loves to make an entrance."

"She does at that. Can you imagine her married to your brother? They shall never accomplish anything, for all their energies will be spent trying to outdo the other for attention," Haleine said. "Although, now that I think of it, that may be for the best."

"You do not support their union?"

"Of course I do. I waited for it for so long I shall be glad to see them married. I always thought Zaide Romanza had designs on you. I never liked it very much."

"I would have been a poor match for her."

"No," Haleine said. "She would have been a poor match for you."

"You flatter me again, your majesty," he said. "I am but—"

"Yes, I know. You are but a second son and no good match for anyone."

"Not anymore."

"It's rather tiresome, isn't it?" she said. "That marriages must always be made for the sake of politics or riches."

"What else is there?"

"I don't know," she said, smiling faintly. "Love perhaps?"

"Love is for the lower classes," he said. "It never has and never will be for royalty."

"And what of us?" she asked. "We were to be married once. What would we have been?"

"The exception," he said. "You do look happy, Haleine."

She broke the dance's rhythm. Her eyes flickered to the left, and a smile crossed her face, but it seemed more forced than her previous efforts. She held out her hand.

"Let us get some air," she said. "Please, Revelin?"

"What is wrong?"

"Nothing. Let's just go onto the balcony."

"Your majesty, I know you better than most. Tell me what is wrong."

She shook her head. "I cannot say anything here. There are too many prying eyes and ears about. The balcony might be better; I don't know, but please, Revelin, people are staring."

She still wore that smile on her face. Her eyes darted to the left again, and this time he turned his head to see why. He expected Maddox but standing there instead was Maddox's man, Omur.

"Some air, then," Revelin said.

Her smile became more genuine as they walked out to the deserted balcony. Haleine sat on the bench farthest from the doors and motioned for him to join her.

"What of your guard?" he asked, for the man had followed her and now stood a respectable distance away. "He might overhear."

"Willem is my man through and through," she said. "He may be trusted with any secrets I hold."

"You have secrets?" Revelin asked as he sat beside her. "You never have before."

"Are you so sure?"

"Yes. I would have known."

"Yes, you would have, wouldn't you? But it is different now. You've been here, and I've been half a world away."

"Please, your majesty, tell me—"

"What have you heard about the rebellion in Lira? What did they tell you?"

"Your husband told us rebels murdered Amatheon and Michaela, and now they threaten you."

"It's a lie. All of it."

"Are you suggesting Amatheon and Michaela were not murdered?"

"No, they were indeed murdered but by their own son, not rebels."

"Your majesty—"

"I saw it, Revelin. I saw the blood. He was covered in it, and when I asked him, he called it the blood of the innocent. He murdered his parents on our wedding night before he came to our bed. The rebellion did nothing to Amatheon and Michaela. They fight Maddox and no one else. If they did not oppose him, the entire country would burn and her people would be destroyed."

"If they did not oppose him, there would be no reason—"

"There is never reason enough to justify what Maddox has allowed to happen to his own people. His own parents, Revelin! He does not deserve the title he holds."

"Few men do," he said. "How do you know all this to be true?"

"I told you I have seen it. I told you that I know it," she said. "Once that would have been enough for you."

It was the truth, of course. Once he would have believed whatever she said without question. How had that changed?

"But if you require more," she continued, "know that I have met the leader of the rebellion. I believe him to be trustworthy, and I have promised him my allegiance."

Revelin hadn't expected that. "Oh, your majesty," he breathed. "What have you done?"

"I have found a way. Just as you said I would."

He shook his head. "I did not mean for you to do something so—Oh, your majesty. You must end this."

"I cannot. I will not."

"But you must. If your husband were to discover this betrayal, I fear what he would do to you. I ask only that you look to save yourself."

"That is what I do. Maddox gives me no reason to care whether I live or die. This man does."

He was taken back by her tone and the infusion of passion there. Her happiness. His breath caught.

"You say that as though you might love him."

She hesitated but didn't look away. He knew what her answer would be before she even spoke it.

"I do."

He couldn't breathe. It was sudden and nearly paralyzing as though he had been struck down by a sword rather than her words. He stared at her, their closeness suffocating him even more, and he stood. She turned her head as he did so, and he saw the look in her eyes. Regret. For hurting him? For loving someone else? For letting it be known to him?

"How could you ever—?"

"I know it's nonsensical, Revelin, I do."

"Nonsensical? How could you call *this* nonsensical? Suicidal, perhaps," he spat as his anger grew. "But nonsensical? Please see reason, your majesty—"

"Stop calling me that, Revelin," she said. "You know my name! Why won't you use it? I am still the same."

"You are far from that. The Haleine I knew never would have put herself at risk in this manner."

"The Haleine you knew wouldn't have had to," she said. "You don't know, Revelin. You weren't there. You stood on that balcony and you never looked back."

"You gave to this man what should have been—"

"My husband's. Yes, I did this."

Mine, he thought. *What should have been mine.*

"But I don't love my husband."

"No one thought you would," he said. "Me least of all."

"Revelin, please. I was lost; I was drowning, and you never looked back."

She said it as though it excused her, as though her betrayal were justified.

"Why did you tell me this?" he asked.

"Because you already knew, and I did not want to lie to you."

He nodded. "You were happy."

"Yes."

"I did not expect it."

"I know."

He had never been angry with her before. Never, and he hated it now. He turned and leaned against the balcony's railing. They stayed like that for a while, not moving, not speaking. The anger slowly began to ebb. When he felt calmer, he faced her once more.

"I do not want to see you hurt," he said.

"Aye," she said. "I know."

Her face changed, and he was left wondering what was in her thoughts. He sat next to her, wanting to be near her again, but she slid away from him. He grabbed her arm to stop her from moving any farther. He heard—then saw—her guard as he came forward.

"No, Willem," she said, looking at Revelin's hand encircling her arm. "It's all right."

The guard retreated and Revelin released her.

"You must not see that man again. Not for anything," he said. "Please, Haleine, promise you will do this."

She held his gaze until the trumpets sounded once more. As soon as she turned her head, he knew he had lost her.

"That will be Zaide Romanza," she said. "We should go."

He hung his head. "As you wish, your majesty."

〰

The morning of the wedding, Haleine woke with a sense of dread that only deepened upon her realization that Maddox was already gone from both the bed and the room. It felt so much like the morning after her own wedding that she became nauseated, and she only left her bed when the urge to vomit became too great to ignore.

"Are you all right?" Faolan asked afterward.

"No," she said, moving away from the chamber pot. "Whatever they planned will happen today, won't it?"

She went to the credenza where the wine was laid out. She poured some into a goblet and sat by the fire. Faolan stayed on the vanity, so she couldn't see him when he finally spoke.

"What makes you say that?"

"I don't know," she confessed. "I just feel it, and I know it as well as anything. I don't presume that makes any sense."

"Less and less," Faolan said.

The servants arrived before she could ask what he meant. Faolan withdrew to the bed, lay down and closed his eyes as though he meant to sleep while Haleine was rushed into eating, bathing, and dressing.

When they had finished, she dismissed the servants. Faolan was once again awake and perched on the vanity. And although alone, neither she nor Faolan spoke. Instead they both seemed fixed on her reflection in the mirror.

The gown she wore was beautiful. It was beige in color with tight sleeves that came down to her wrists. The neckline was square and cut across the top of her breasts. Almost every inch of the gown was embroidered with tiny perfect pearls. She wore a necklace with a short chain of gold and a pearl larger than her thumb nestled at the hollow of her throat. Even strands of pearls had been woven into her hair now braided down her back. She hated everything about it, but most of all she loathed the great heavy crown upon her head.

"It is a lovely gown, is it not?" she asked as she removed the crown. She laid it on the vanity and left it there.

"To be honest, I don't care at all about your dress."

She nodded. "Do they plan to murder again?"

"I'd be surprised if they didn't," Faolan said. "Stay as close to Willem as you can today. I don't think you are in danger, but stay close to Willem."

She nodded. "Who is in danger?"

"I don't know, but I would guess Nathan. His death would bring about the most chaos."

"And it is chaos your enemy desires more than anything?"

"At least for now."

She didn't want to think about the implications of Faolan's statement. It was bad enough to think about the possible consequences of Nathan's loss. There would be a struggle for the throne. Zoltano would want what Haraszty would not want to yield. Quatara would want to break free, and her father would want to hold it at all costs. Her mother and sister would be caught in the middle.

"Haleine?"

"This is madness," she said.

Faolan raised his head. Haleine saw her husband's reflection in the mirror. She turned and curtsied.

"My lord," she said.

"My God, but you are beautiful," he said. "It's a shame we have to leave this chamber at all."

Haleine smiled and dipped her head. Maddox stepped in close to her, pressing her against the vanity.

"You spent a good deal of time with Revelin at the ball," he said.

"Yes, my lord."

"Tell me, what did you and the good prince talk about on the balcony last night?"

"He wanted to know if I was happy," she said. "I told him I was."

Maddox was still a moment longer. She stared at him, holding her breath until he reached behind her and picked up her crown.

"You are fortunate I am not a jealous man," he said, looking at the crown in his hands.

"Yes, my lord."

"We wouldn't want to forget this," he said, placing the crown upon her head. "You wear it so well."

Haleine swallowed and lowered her eyes. "My lord."

He offered his arm next. "Shall we go?"

Maddox escorted her into the hall where the wedding would take place. It had always been a favorite room of hers. It was oval-shaped with tall, glass windows overlooking the cliffs of Tanuba and the ocean which met them. Great stone pillars lined the walls and a narrow stone slab ran across them like a shelf. Nathan had lined the slab with guards. He put them there for ceremonial purposes. She doubted any of them even suspected what was to come.

Nathan certainly did not. She watched as he, with Idris Fein at his side, moved among the guests, offering greetings and accepting best wishes. His eyes lit up when he saw her, and the pair immediately came over. Maddox was gracious upon their arrival, offering hearty congratulations to both men. Haleine stayed quiet until Nathan reached for her hand.

"Your majesty," she said. "You must be very pleased."

"Haleine, my dear girl, please dispense with the formalities," he said. "You are a queen now. You're no longer my advisor's daughter."

"Of course."

Nathan kissed her hand, bid her husband farewell and left. Idris Fein repeated the act. When they were both gone, Maddox laughed quietly and moved to take his seat. He motioned for Haleine to sit beside him.

"Splendid morning," he said.

She bit back any response she may have made and sank into her seat, checking on Willem's position before she did so. He stood off to her left side, as close to her as he could possibly be, and still he was much too far away.

When the ceremony started, Haleine divided her attention between the nuptials and her husband. Maddox, she thought, would give away anything he knew. He wouldn't be able to help it. He was far too pleased with himself.

The prince and princess were about to say their vows when Maddox began to squirm. Haleine noticed it immediately and searched the room but didn't know for what she was looking. Haraszty's sudden scream brought her attention back to the front.

Two arrows protruded from Nathan's chest. He stood stunned for a moment before crumpling to the floor. More arrows flew, and Haleine got to her feet. Revelin drew his sword and pulled his mother behind him, but he looked at Haleine and shouted. She couldn't hear what he said; it was too loud. She stumbled toward him, but someone stopped her, dragging her down and away from the confusion. She panicked until she realized it was Willem. She went limp in his arms and allowed him to pull her back.

When it was over, Haleine sat with Haraszty in the throne room, surrounded by guards. Haraszty rocked gently on her throne, her face streaked with tears. Haleine sat at Haraszty's feet, restraining herself from begging the queen for forgiveness. She reached for the queen's hand and pressed it against her cheek.

Haraszty looked at her. "You are very kind, child."

Haleine wanted to argue that she wasn't the least bit kind. She should have done something or said something. Why hadn't she done anything? Why hadn't Faolan? Guilt was on the tip of her tongue, but the queen spoke before Haleine could.

"Where is everyone? My sons, where are my sons?"

Again Haleine was forced to say nothing as she realized she did not know. She searched the room for someone suitable to ask and was pleased when she found Ceallach. She beckoned him forward and he responded immediately.

"The queen wishes to know where her sons are," she said. "Do you know?"

"My lady queen," Ceallach said, bowing to Haraszty. "Prince Zoltano is attending to his bride in her chambers. I'm told the princess is quite distraught. Prince Eamonn is in his chambers, and Prince Revelin, with the help of King Maddox, is interrogating suspects in this tragedy."

"And my husband?" Haraszty asked. "What is being done for him?"

"I assure you, your majesty, his body is being well cared for."

The throne room doors opened then, and Ceallach withdrew. Haraszty maintained her seat, but Haleine rose to see who entered. Maddox appeared first, followed by her father, Revelin and Cathal. Omur came next, and finally two men, bound, gagged and dressed in the armor of the Tanubian army, were led inside. Willem stepped nearer to her.

"Your majesties," Darian said as he bowed before them. He avoided looking at her. "We have found the assassins."

Haleine looked at the two prisoners. Their faces were defiant as they glared at those in the room. She glanced at her husband and his advisor and knew the prisoners had done no wrong. They were the sacrificial lambs.

"Under a close interrogation, your majesty," her father continued, "we discovered these men to be members of the rebellion plaguing the kingdom of Lira."

Haleine held her breath. Omur sneered at her. She looked back at him with hatred and shared the look with her husband. They were all going to believe Dana planned to murder Nathan and had sent these two men to carry out the deed.

"They were sent by their leader," Maddox said, stepping forward. "A man named Dana, the very same man responsible for the murder of my own parents. Now he has come here, wishing to destroy your family as well."

"It's not true," Haleine blurted.

Every pair of eyes in the room was suddenly on her. Omur smiled and made a small gesture with his hand, encouraging her to continue, but she said nothing more.

"Of course it's true," Maddox said. "My queen, we would not bring suspects before you unless we were sure of their guilt."

"I know you wouldn't," Haraszty said. "I wish to send this rebel a message. I wish these men to be put to death immediately, publicly and most painfully. Let their leader know that Tanuba will never fall to the likes of him nor anyone else who may try."

"God willing," Revelin said, "I will destroy him myself."

The hatred in his voice was absolute. It was too much for her, and Haleine felt her body start to slip. It started in her legs and spread quickly to her head. She couldn't stop it; she could only give in. The last thing she saw before she fainted was the satisfied grin on Omur's face.

Faolan stood on the vanity as a gaggle of servants fussed over the newly revived queen of Lira. He wasn't alone. Both Prince Revelin and Haleine's guard stood along the wall, watching as well.

"Please, I'm fine," Haleine insisted. "I don't need—Revelin."

Nearly every head swiveled to look at the prince. Only Faolan and the guard kept their eyes on Haleine. She sat up, seeming much paler than she had been only a moment ago.

"I think you can go now," Revelin said. "She seems quite well to me."

There was no protest. The servants bowed and disappeared. Willem didn't move, and when the others had left, Revelin turned to him.

"You will go as well."

The guard ignored Revelin completely. Faolan hadn't fully formed an opinion on either the guard or the prince of Tanuba but decided in that moment he honestly liked Willem.

"Please, Willem," Haleine said. "It's all right."

Willem bowed and withdrew to the hall. Haleine and Revelin stared at each other. Faolan looked between the two of them and waited to see who would speak first.

"You're hurt," she said.

For the first time, Faolan noticed the stain of blood on the torn sleeve of Revelin's tunic. An arrow must have grazed him.

"Has the physician seen you?" she asked, then shook her head. "Of course he hasn't. You wouldn't be walking around bleeding like that if he had."

Revelin leaned back against the wall but said nothing. Haleine fidgeted slightly. Faolan had to admire her composure.

"I am sorry for what happened," she said.

"Sorry for my father's death or sorry your lover's fiends were caught?"

"I am indeed sorry for your father. He was a good man, and I loved him dearly, but those men who stand to hang for the crime are innocent."

"I will not have you defend them to me," Revelin said. "I keep your secret out of love for you, to keep you safe, but you will not claim those men have done no wrong. Not in my hearing. Not ever."

"Even if it is the truth?" she asked. "You were fed naught but lies today, Revelin. Dana never would have done this. His war is with Maddox and Maddox alone. He has no quarrel with Tanuba."

Revelin pushed off the wall. "He does now," he said as he left. "You tell him that."

Faolan looked at the closed doors for a moment before turning to Haleine. "Are you all right?"

She didn't answer.

"You told him," he said next.

"I didn't want to lie."

"Good plan."

She fell back against the pillows. "We were to be married once, he and I, and we would have been happy. I know it, but now he hates me, and I can't even fault him for it."

"He doesn't hate you," Faolan said. "It would be easier if he did—easier on him, I mean—but he doesn't hate you."

"He was so angry."

"Oh, he's angry all right, but he still loves you," Faolan said. "And for that, we are grateful."

"You said hating me would be easier."

"Easier isn't always better. In fact, it almost never is. As miserable as the prince may be, he'll still keep your secret, and that will keep you alive. If he hated you, he'd have no reason not to tell Maddox what he knows. You were fortunate. You shouldn't have told him anything."

"I didn't want to lie to him."

"You mentioned that."

She sighed. "Do you know what happened today?"

He nodded. He didn't understand it yet, but he had seen everything, more than of which Haleine had been aware. She had been so focused on Maddox and Nathan that she had missed things even more vital. It all brought him back to the reality that the other side was far more prepared than his own.

"Those two men are innocent," Haleine said.

"They are."

"How do we save them?"

They weren't going to save them, but he didn't want to tell her that. He waited for her to come to the realization on her own. When she did, she sat up and looked at him in disbelief.

"I won't just stand by and watch them die."

"You won't convince anyone to let them live either," Faolan said. "Even if you do tell someone what you know and how you know it, those men are still going to die. Staying silent will keep you from joining them on the gallows."

"And you think I am more valuable than they are?"

"I know you're more valuable than they are," he said, "but it doesn't matter because there's no swapping your life for theirs. It's an awful thing to let them die, Haleine, but it's what we have to do. War is about sacrifice. You told Dana that, and it's as true now as it was then. We didn't win this fight, and you have to accept that."

She stared at him for a long moment before nodding. Her concession left Faolan feeling defeated as well. He was surprised by the emotion. He hadn't thought he would care.

"Haleine," he said.

"Stop talking to me," she said. "Maddox will be here soon enough."

"But you're—"

"He's had a great victory this day," she said. "He'll come."

Faolan said no more.

They stayed in Tanuba for another week. Faolan stood by and observed the executions as they were carried out. The funeral for a beloved king followed a day later. Haleine watched as well, no longer showing any sort of emotion. She spoke to no one and forbade any from speaking to her. The only exception was her husband because there was no other choice.

Faolan worried about her. She wasn't well. She was pale and weak. She hardly ate and slept even less, so he wasn't surprised when, before they were to set sail, she collapsed, and the physician was summoned to attend her once again. He reported the queen of Lira was not ill at all but pregnant. Haraszty's court, still deep in their grief and hungry for any small measure of happiness, embraced the announcement and celebrated the good news.

Haleine did not join them, but, Faolan noted, she was not alone. Two others shared in her displeasure. Revelin, the first, was expected. He would have his suspicions, his jealousy, but he would keep silent. Faolan wasn't sure about the other. At the announcement, Omur's face contorted so rapidly and violently that Faolan was amused by his enemy's obvious pain. The feeling changed as the shock melted from Omur's face, leaving in its place a look of murder. For the first time, Faolan was afraid for Haleine. If she hadn't stood in the way of Omur's plans before, she most certainly had now.

chapter 11

Darian took the death of his king harder than most. He had spent his entire life serving Nathan in one way or another, and when he watched his king fall, he was, for a moment, lost.

The moment did not last long. Haraszty wanted to keep her husband's throne, and Darian supported her. Most of the nobles did as well. They feared what would happen to their titles and lands should Zoltano ascend the throne and gladly welcomed the opportunity to hold the prince in check. What they did not realize, and what Darian knew to be true, was that Haraszty, although preferable to Zoltano, was not the ruler her husband was. There would be trouble. Zoltano would not be denied long, and the king's territories, Quatara included, would see Nathan's death as their chance for freedom. It would have been better for all had Revelin been the firstborn.

But Revelin was the second son, and nothing Darian could do would change that, so he did what he could to safeguard his queen. He strengthened her defenses and set men to watch the crown prince. Zoltano left court shortly after his father's funeral and withdrew to Gweneria, a stronghold he held in the north. Darian was pleased to have the distance, but at the same time, he was concerned what the prince might do next.

For this reason, he wanted to stay in Mairéad, at the queen's court, but Quatara demanded his presence, so he commanded Darragh and others in his service to remain behind and assist Haraszty and Revelin in his stead. Then, as soon as Nathan was buried, he instructed Rhoswen to prepare for their departure.

"No," she said. "Please, not yet. When Haleine goes, so shall I."

He agreed because he didn't want to ruin her hope that their daughter might once again look in their direction. He hated the idea that his daughter despised him, but as he could do nothing to change that either, he devoted his energies instead to defending what his king had made.

But Rhoswen had no such purpose and was left pining for her daughter. Haleine had withdrawn from everyone after Nathan's death, refusing any who sought an audience with her, even the woman who gave her life. Rhoswen spent each night sobbing into her pillow. He spent each night staring at the ceiling, wondering if word of the king's demise had reached Quatara yet and what he would find upon his return.

Six days after the king's funeral, he had his opportunity to find out. The king and queen of Lira set sail, and even before their ship had left his view, Darian told Rhoswen of their own imminent departure. Too defeated by Haleine's infallible rebuff, she did not argue with him this time. She only took their remaining daughter by the hand and left. They departed from their city estate before midday.

They spent the night at a soldiers' outpost near the Quatari border and headed out again early the following morning. Darian rode alongside the carriage carrying his wife and daughter. He scanned the woods and hills surrounding them, seeing nothing of note. He spurred his horse to the front of the procession where his captain rode.

"My lord," the man said.

"Anything?" Darian asked.

"The scouts have seen nothing. The roads are clear."

He nodded but did not relax. "Tell them to stay sharp. There may be trouble yet."

There would be trouble. Darian was sure of it. Maybe it wouldn't happen on the road. Maybe there was enough time to get his family safely home, but there would be trouble. There were certain Quataris who would never let an opportunity like this be missed.

Darian reined in his stallion and fell back in the ranks. He checked the landscape again, still saw nothing, and looked into the carriage itself.

Rhoswen slept, her head tilted back against the seat. Sighle had molded herself to her mother's side, her head resting against Rhoswen's chest. She did not sleep though. She looked at him with dark, calm eyes. Darian acknowledged his daughter's glance with a nod. He should have left them in Mairéad. God help him, it would have been safer to leave them behind.

"We wouldn't have stayed," Sighle said.

He wasn't surprised she knew his mind. She missed nothing.

"You'll keep us safe," she said.

"That I will, lass," he said softly.

———❦———

Upon his return to Eluned, Faolan left Haleine in order to journey to the rebel camp. He was reluctant to do it because he didn't want to leave her unprotected. Willem would be nearby, Faolan knew, though if Omur meant Haleine harm, it wouldn't matter how capable or dedicated the guard was.

But as there were matters to which Faolan needed to attend that couldn't be dealt with in Haleine's chambers, a separation was necessary. After promising Haleine he would return as soon as he could, Faolan departed for the seclusion of the Aerona Forest.

He found Dana sparring with James on the training field. Ilya stood to the side, watching along with a group of others, Owain of Enimode among them. Faolan hovered for a moment as he realized what the boy's presence meant, and landed on Ilya's shoulder.

"You're back," she said, not taking her eyes off the mock battle. "For how long?"

"Not long," he said and flinched as James delivered a surprisingly vicious blow. "That's new."

Ilya nodded. "Aye. He hasn't been the same since..."

She didn't finish the sentence, but he knew what she meant to say.

"No reason why he should," Faolan said. "Would you mind stepping in? I need to talk to Dana."

"Is there trouble?"

"Isn't there always?"

She smiled and shrugged him off her shoulder. He hovered while Ilya put herself in the middle of the skirmish. Dana staggered back and looked at Faolan when Ilya jerked her head in his direction. The tension left Dana's body, and he took a moment to catch his breath before coming over. James and Ilya followed.

"Dana," Faolan said. "Hal—"

Dana shook his head imperceptibly. Faolan stopped talking.

"Let's talk in my tent," Dana said. "James, you and Ilya should get these people working."

Faolan landed on Dana's shoulder and didn't speak until they were inside the tent. He left Dana's shoulder in favor of the map-covered table. Dana unbuckled his sword belt and tossed it on his bedroll before sitting in the tent's single chair.

"Did you know what would happen to Enimode?" Dana asked. "Before it happened, I mean."

"No. Why would you think—?"

"He has the stomach for it now," Dana said. "Just as you said he would. I thought maybe—"

"I can't see the future, Dana."

"And your patron lady?"

"She can't see it any more than I can."

Dana nodded, looking more exhausted than he had on the training field. "He blames the king, you know."

"With good reason, I'd say."

"And the queen."

Faolan understood now. "Oh."

"I told him you were with one of the maids."

"He doesn't know?"

"He was so—I couldn't tell him. I didn't want to lie, but I didn't know how I could tell him anything else."

"Does anyone know?"

"Lucius and Ilya, maybe. Nothing's been said directly, but they know I've been in contact with her. Hanah knows. She knows everything. She's one to make you talk, especially if you don't want to. Maddox should put her to work in his dungeon," Dana said. "But not James. He doesn't know anything about it."

"You won't be able to keep it from him forever."

"I don't need forever. Just long enough." Dana sighed. "What brings you here? Something happen in Tanuba?"

"A lot happened in Tanuba," Faolan said. "Missing any followers by any chance?"

Dana stood and went to fetch a flagon from the other side of the tent. He took a drink before responding.

"Aye. There was a pair of men we sent on patrol who never came back. We haven't been able to find them anywhere."

"That's because they were put to death in Tanuba for the assassination of King Nathan."

"What? They were—what?"

"Omur took them, or he had Varro do it, but Omur brought them to Tanuba, and he arranged to have Nathan's death blamed on them. And you."

"He didn't have to take our men for that," Dana said. "He could have used anyone."

"He could have, but he wanted to send me a message."

"That he could get to us if he wanted."

"Yes," Faolan said. "I don't think he's taken too kindly to my appearance at court."

"How did he find us? We're protected by a wall of magic. *Your* magic."

"We are, but magic leaves a trace, a signature," Faolan said. "He must have tracked it and waited for someone to appear."

"We'll have to move," Dana said. "The camp. Everything and everyone."

"Yes."

"We'll need something more for protection," Dana said. "If there is such a thing."

"We're working on it."

Dana nodded and sat back down. "This means Tanuba will be against us."

"They already were against us. Now they're just that much more likely to act."

"That's not reassuring."

"Well, it's about to get worse."

Dana took another drink from the flagon. "How?"

"Omur isn't acting alone."

"Who's helping him?"

"Zaide Romanza."

"The princess of Feond?" Dana asked and Faolan nodded. "How do you know this?"

"I've known about her, her existence, who I thought she was, but I've never been near her," Faolan said. "If I had, I would've known sooner that she belongs to the dark gods."

"Belongs to the dark gods?"

"Humans, all humans, have an aura—a quality that emanates from them like the glow from a lantern. In most people, it's unassuming, unnoticeable really, there but dull enough not to command attention."

"But not Zaide Romanza's."

"No, not Zaide Romanza's," Faolan said. "Her aura is...a hole, Dana. It's a hole so black, I don't know how it is I can still consider her human."

"What does it mean?"

"It means she's tied to Omur," Faolan said. "She's tied to the dark gods. She wants what they want. She may even have magic; I don't know for sure yet, but I suspect she does. Her aura...Oh, Dana, it's evil."

"And what about the crown prince? Zoltano? He had the most to gain from his father's death."

"Zoltano is involved but not the same way. The fact that he didn't gain the throne tells me he's a pawn and nothing more."

"Who did gain the throne?"

"Haraszty held onto it."

"Will that help or harm us?"

"No one but Nathan on Tanuba's throne will help us," Faolan said. "The best we can do is hope Nathan's death causes enough chaos in that country and its territories to keep Haraszty or her sons from coming for us personally."

"The dark gods feed on chaos."

"And now they're feasting."

Dana drank again. "Tell me of Haleine now. Is she well?"

"Well enough. Tanuba was hard on her."

Dana's concern was immediate. "Hard how?"

"She didn't like that you were blamed for the murder."

"I don't like it either."

"She tried very hard to convince the good Prince Revelin of your innocence."

"She did what?" Dana exclaimed. "I don't want her to do things like that."

"Neither do I."

"Then why did you let her do it? If she said something to the wrong person, it'll be her death! How does she know he won't—?"

"He won't."

Dana looked at Faolan. Finally he nodded. "What did she tell him?"

"She told him the men he would see hanged for his father's murder were innocent. She told him you never would have sanctioned an assassination, that your war was with Maddox and Maddox alone."

"Did the prince ask how she knew all this to be true?"

"He did, as a matter of fact. So she told him she had met you, knew you to be trustworthy and had promised you her support. She said it in such a manner that he accused her of being in love with you."

"And she said he was being ridiculous, I hope."

"Oh no. She told him she was in love. She didn't want to lie."

"Good God, Faolan. You know I trust you without question, but please tell me how you know he won't say anything."

"They were to be married once."

"An arranged marriage?" Dana asked, and Faolan shook his head. "A love match?"

"Yes."

Dana closed his eyes and leaned back in the chair. "He must hate me."

"You have no idea," Faolan said. "But—"

"Please don't tell me there's something more."

"Haleine's pregnant."

Dana dropped the flagon and opened his eyes. "How?"

"How? Didn't Mahree ever explain that to you?" Faolan asked. "What do you mean *how*?"

Dana shook his head and stood. He clasped his hands behind his back and started to pace. Faolan waited.

"No, no," Dana said. "I didn't mean that. I meant—she's pregnant?"

"Yes."

"With whose child?"

Faolan didn't answer right away. He had suspicions but nothing he could prove or cared to share with Dana.

"How would I know that?" Faolan said. "It could be either of you, but I have to admit Maddox's odds are better."

Dana nodded and continued to pace. He seemed to be taking the news well. Faolan was glad; he hadn't been sure what to expect. As well as he did know Dana, this was uncharted territory for them both.

"I have to—I have to go," Dana said.

He grabbed a cloak, but not his sword, and was gone from the tent before Faolan could say anything else. Faolan went outside and watched Dana saddle a horse and ride out of camp.

"Where is he going?" James asked as he approached.

"I'm not exactly sure."

"When will he be back?"

"I'm not exactly sure," Faolan said, "but you shouldn't worry about it. You, Lucius and Ilya will have enough to take care of as it is."

"What's wrong?"

"Omur knows where the camp is. We have to move everything and everyone immediately."

"Move where?"

Faolan shook his head. "Get everyone packed and ready to move. The location will be set by the time you are."

"Will Dana be back before then?" James asked. "He won't know where we are otherwise."

"He found you once," Faolan said. "He'll find you again."

"We're in the middle of a war, and he's supposed to be leading these people," James said. "He can't keep running out."

"I know," Faolan said. "Better get people moving, James. We shouldn't waste any more time."

He left James then and flew through the camp until he found Luisiúil and Lorcan in the privacy of the forest.

"Do you know who she is?" he asked. "The queen?"

No, came Luisiúil's answer.

He nodded. "We have to find out. Send whom you can to Quatara. That's where it started. That's where we'll find it."

"Find what?" Lorcan asked.

"What they know that we don't."

—◦◦◦—

Omur thought Haleine was rather fortunate his lords had a use for her because ever since her pregnancy had been announced all he could think of was telling Maddox of his wife's infidelity and watching as the king snapped her neck.

That would be a most satisfying sight, Omur knew, but he did not speak a word. He listened while Maddox crowed with pleasure and glowed with his apparent success. Omur said nothing to the contrary. No matter how he wished it, he could never tell Maddox how he knew the child Haleine carried—the child that could grow to inherit Lira's throne—was, without a doubt, a bastard. His lords had seen to that.

He hadn't yet told them of the infant; there had been no opportunity to do so in Tanuba. He did not know what they would say, but he could not imagine they had use for a child, legitimate or bastard born.

He removed himself from the king's side at the first opportunity and returned to his chambers, not wishing to withhold the news from his lords any longer. Varro, however, was standing outside of his rooms and bowed when Omur approached. His masters would have to wait.

"My lord," the captain said. "I came as soon as I heard of your arrival."

"How fortunate," Omur said, leading the way inside.

"They say the queen is with child," Varro said. "It is good news, isn't it? The king must be pleased."

The king was pleased. It irritated Omur even more. He took comfort in knowing how vulnerable children were. Some did not even make it out of the womb alive. Omur glanced back at Varro, thinking his presence was indeed fortunate.

"Tell me what has happened in my absence," he said.

"You know the whore gave us the villages of Culhwch and Koulmia, so we went, intending to do to them what we had done to Enimode, but Dana was waiting for us at Culhwch."

"And the rebels were not at Enimode?"

"No, my lord. I am certain she was discovered. Upon our return to the city, I sought her out to find she had been murdered, her neck broken."

"How do you know it was not a robbery?"

"Her purse, still full from our payment, was left behind."

Omur smiled. Enimode then. "What happened when you fought the rebels?"

"We engaged the rebels in battle several times, but never once have we come close to defeating them," Varro said. "They have the most unholy luck."

Omur smiled again. "They really don't."

"The unicorns, my lord, when they fight alongside the rebels we cannot defeat them."

Omur nodded. What the captain said was true, but Omur did not hold the same concerns.

"Perhaps my lord," Varro continued, speaking more hesitantly than before. "Perhaps there is something you could do to aid us? I know how important containing the rebel threat is, and someone with your abilities..."

Varro allowed his voice to trail off. Omur was amused that the captain had dared posed the question at all. The captain was of a world that saw magic and those who wielded it as sinners or demons. Men and women accused of witchcraft were summarily drowned or hanged or even burned, so most people did everything they could to avoid the stigma of suspicion. Varro had learned of

Omur's skills only out of Omur's necessity. He needed Dana's men to warn off the pegasus, and he had required Varro to go and fetch them.

"How does my lord know where these rebels will be?" Varro had asked once his task had been explained.

It was only Varro's deep desire for revenge that made the man leave Omur's chambers that day still willing to serve. Varro had gone where Omur had directed and brought the prisoners back, but Omur suspected that the captain had spent the rest of that day, and likely every day since, praying for the salvation of his soul.

"I can do nothing for you," Omur said now. "I cannot touch the unicorns."

The beasts were an integral part of Dana's campaign. Without them, the rebellion would fall. It was still too young to stand on its own. It wouldn't always be true; he would want to crush it eventually, and when he did, he would remove the unicorns. But as Omur still had need of Dana and his rebellion, that time was not now.

"I wouldn't worry. With or without the unicorns, Dana will not last, nor the peasants who follow him. Be patient now and parry his blows. Victory will be yours," Omur said and Varro bowed. "I must say, though, I rather thought you might be elsewhere."

"We have been, my lord, make no mistake. We have pursued the king's cause relentlessly. However, it was necessary to return for supplies, fresh men and horses. A continuous campaign has its demands."

"More likely you found yourself tiring of the camp whores," he said and examined his captain closely. "It's all right. I find I have need of you here before you return to the hunt."

"How may I serve you, my lord?"

"You have a woman, do you not?"

"My lord?"

"A woman," he said. "One here in the palace who isn't one of the queen's ladies? You have one, yes?"

"Aye, my lord."

"Good. Have her go to the whores' district to purchase herbs that will shed a fetus from a woman's womb. When she returns, bring the herbs to me. Recommend to your woman that she keep her mouth shut about it."

Varro started to bow but hesitated. Omur, assured of why the captain had faltered, was unworried and waited for the moment to pass. Varro was a smarter man than Omur usually gave mortals credit for. He was one of the king's captains, after all, and one did not reach that position without a certain amount of intelligence. He knew when discretion was mandatory. Even more vital, he knew how to follow an order without question. If he had any qualms about this, he would swallow them and, as soon as he delivered what his lord wanted, he would pray once again for the salvation of his soul.

The moment passed and Varro completed his bow. "It shall be done, my lord."

—⁓—

Dana surprised himself when he rode through the city gates. He really thought he would have gone in the opposite direction but somehow had steered himself here. It was further proof that his mind was elsewhere.

He watched the guards close the gates for the night before nudging the horse toward Orla's. He'd have to beg her for a room or a pallet in the storeroom or permission to sleep alongside his horse in the stable. He was confident she would at least grant the last if he asked nicely and no one in the barroom had given her too hard a time.

Dana left the horse in the one spare stall and went out to the street to see the palace. He should've gone there. Haleine would be waiting, and getting inside would be easy. He knew when the guards changed posts, and even if he hadn't, he could've just walked past them, announcing his intentions to go to the queen's chambers, and not one of them would stop him. They couldn't. He was still untouchable.

But he didn't go forward. He turned around and went into the stable. There was a back entrance to the tavern that led into the storeroom. He used it and fumbled his way through the dark until he found a barrel on which to sit. He leaned against the wall and waited for Orla to come.

Haleine would be waiting. She'd sit by that fire all night, holding out hope that he would come. He didn't know how it was she could still hope, not with all Maddox had done to her, but he loved her for it. Did he really want to give her reason to doubt?

He didn't want to but knew he would. What would he do if he did see her? Hold her? Kiss her? Make love to her? She would be frightened. How could she not? What would he say to her? Tell her everything would be all right? Tell her she had nothing to fear because he loved her and he was untouchable?

That was exactly what he should have done. But he still didn't move.

The storeroom's door opened and Orla stepped inside. She set a lantern on another barrel and started to look through the supplies. He didn't say anything, waiting until she turned and saw him. When she did, she jumped.

"Dana, damn you!" She crossed the room and hit him. "You scared me."

"I didn't mean to."

She retreated and closed the door. "What are you even doing here?"

He was hiding. He was a coward, the very worst kind.

"Didn't think I should come in through the front," he said.

"No, you couldn't. It's not your crowd tonight."

"Good to know I have a crowd at all," he said. "Although I suppose I should wonder why you're serving the opposing side."

"Their money spends just as well as yours. Better even, I'd say, since they actually have some."

He didn't acknowledge the jibe. "Are they talking?"

"Of course they are. Ain't no whores about, so what else are they going to do?"

"What are they saying?"

"It's all about the queen tonight. Some of the castle folk have been in. They say she's with child."

Dana nodded. "I heard that."

Would it be too much to hope that she carried his child? Would it be selfish to have such a hope? He may have held her heart, but her person belonged to another man, one who would never tolerate adultery. Bearing her lover's child would mean the death of her. The death of them both. And yet, he just couldn't bear the thought that perhaps the baby she carried was her husband's.

"Did you hear then, too, about your girl?" Orla asked. "Someone snapped her neck."

"She's not my girl."

"They thought it a robbery at first, but whoever did it didn't take anything but that girl's life."

He thought of Mahree and Seoras, of Rhiannon and everyone else who died. He thought of Sarai and Aaron and of Owain, lost and alone and seeking revenge.

"Maybe she had it coming."

Orla nodded. "You heard about that too, then. Right. So you want a room, or are you planning to sit on that barrel all night?"

He smiled. "I want a room. If you have it."

"Are you going to sleep?"

"I doubt it."

He was at a loss. When Lorcan approached him about the rebellion, this was never mentioned. Dana didn't know he would love her so. It was something he couldn't fight, not with his dagger, not with his sword, not with the largest army he could muster. He hated the power she had over him.

"Too bad. You look like you need it," Orla said. "Well, stay here for now. I'll come get you when it's safe."

He nodded and leaned back against the wall. "I'll be here."

———∿∿∿———

The sun had long since set before Haleine was able to be alone. Her homecoming had been more of a circus than her initial arrival in Lira, and Haleine was certain she had never been more miserable in her entire life. Still, she knew it would likely get worse. She was only at the start of her pregnancy, and Maddox had made it clear that no chances would be taken with his son.

If it is your son, she wanted to reply every time the words came out of her husband's mouth, but every time she forced herself to back down. There would be no greater mistake than to utter that phrase. The life growing inside of her was innocent in all things, even if his parents were not, and Haleine would not risk that life.

So she suffered in silence as her return was met by the arrival of the king's physician and a score of midwives. They examined every inch of her, poked and prodded and hovered over her as though they expected her to break at any moment. She was about to scream when Rhys announced he thought rest to be the best thing for her. The midwives concurred, and one by one they withdrew until she was alone with Bronagh.

"It is ridiculous," Haleine said then. "Does Maddox not realize for how long a pregnancy lasts?"

"He's not going to take chances," Bronagh said. "Not with his heir."

His heir. It was the first time anyone had said that. It perhaps wouldn't matter whose seed had taken root first. The child could

204

still be raised as Maddox's heir. And she would be his mother in name only.

"I noticed the pegasus is gone," Bronagh said next. "Where did he go?"

"Off spreading his wings, I suppose," Haleine said. "How should I know where the wind carries him?"

"When will he be back?"

"I don't know," Haleine said as she realized she really didn't.

The revelation did nothing to improve her mood. Faolan had said nothing about when he would return. It could be days, or weeks, before she saw the pegasus again. She had no way of knowing where Dana was. She hadn't even heard the latest gossip, nor would she until the morning.

"Will you eat?" Bronagh asked.

Haleine shook her head. "Truly, I am too sick."

It was, oddly, the one thing for which she was grateful. The seas had not been kind, prolonging their eight-day journey to ten days in length, the better part of which she spent bent over a chamber pot, vomiting so severely she was surprised her stomach remained inside of her. But as wretched as she was, her sickness managed to repulse her husband to the point where he avoided her quarters entirely, and she couldn't be upset by that. She wasn't sure what would happen now that they were back in Lira, but she would be thankful for whatever reprieve she received.

"To bed, then," Bronagh said. "You'll feel better in the morning."

More likely she would feel worse, but Haleine didn't say so. She allowed Bronagh to help her out of her gown and into a nightdress.

"Would you like me to braid your hair?" Bronagh asked.

He would like it down. He liked to touch it, run his fingers though it and wrap the curls around his hand.

Haleine knew she shouldn't plan for his appearance. She didn't know where he was nor what he did there. Was he fighting now? Would he be fighting soon? There were so many factors that could keep him away, and she was the only reason he would have to come to the palace that night, or any night to follow. Would he want her enough? Faolan had said Dana had never been in love before. Dana himself had claimed it, too. What if that love had dissipated while she was away? Would he want her at all once he heard of what she had done and how completely she had failed him?

"Your majesty?"

"No," Haleine said. "Leave it down."

She shouldn't expect him to come, not this night at least, but she still wanted it.

Bronagh sighed. "They say he's been in the west. There was a battle at Culhwch and Koulmia, I think, and some other places, not even towns or villages. Fields, I suppose. I don't know exactly, but they say he's done well."

Tears spilled onto Haleine's cheeks. She looked at Bronagh and smiled as she wiped them away.

"Thank you," she said.

Bronagh nodded, looking annoyed with herself. "I'll leave you now."

"Thank you," Haleine repeated as Bronagh walked from the room.

Haleine went to stand on the balcony, telling herself she desired fresh air. She stayed there until the air turned too cold and her legs grew too tired. She left the balcony in favor of her bed, leaving one door slightly open behind her.

—◦◦◦—

Faolan hadn't been lying when he told James he wasn't concerned about Dana. He knew Dana well enough to know the rebel leader was capable of taking care of himself and would be back before long, but Faolan still found himself wanting to know where Dana had taken up refuge. Given Dana's penchant for wanderlust, it was difficult to narrow down the possibilities. Faolan spent as much time as he dared on the search without finding his quarry. Finally resigning himself to not knowing, he returned to the palace and found Dana standing on Haleine's balcony.

"It's always the last place you think to look," Faolan said. "You're a hard man to track down."

Faolan landed on the railing. Dana didn't look at him, rather kept his eyes fixed on Haleine. She looked to be sleeping.

"Isn't that why you chose me for this?" Dana asked.

"I didn't choose anyone for anything."

"Your goddess, then."

"It might have figured in," Faolan said. "I really didn't think you'd come here."

"Neither did I."

"Now that you made it this far, any chance you're going to go farther? Through the door maybe?"

Dana shook his head. "She's sleeping. I don't want to wake her."

"I don't think she'll complain."

"She never does."

"She thinks she let you down, you know."

"Why?"

"If you asked her to, she couldn't even find out what the cooks are planning for dinner."

"I don't want to know what the cooks are planning for dinner."

"Not the point I was making."

Dana didn't hear him. "And even if I did, there are others I could ask. She's not alone in this."

"She thinks she is," Faolan said, "and she thinks she turned a country against you."

"She didn't draw the bow that killed the king. Convince her of that."

"Something tells me it would be more convincing coming from you," Faolan said. "But I think she might be more concerned about Revelin."

"The love match. Does he hold that much influence?"

"Over her or Tanuba?"

Dana looked at him. Faolan could tell he hadn't thought of Revelin's potential hold over Haleine.

"She told him she loves you," Faolan said.

"I wish she didn't."

Faolan didn't know what he meant. Did Dana wish Haleine hadn't told Revelin of her love, or did he wish she didn't love him? Faolan knew he personally wished Haleine hadn't said anything to Revelin, but there were worse things that could have happened and her falling in love with Dana wasn't one of them.

"Revelin has considerable influence in Tanuba," he said, deciding it would be best to move on. "The queen will look to her sons to guide her. Zoltano, thankfully, is absent, and Eamonn is really still too young. It'll fall to Revelin."

"And he hates me."

"That he does," Faolan said. "But worry about that later. Go inside now and wake her. You'll both feel better."

"I shouldn't. I shouldn't have even come this far. Omur will be watching her now because you're there," Dana said. "No, I have to get back. There will be plans to make. I'll have to go to Mahile and make sure we can hold it. If Zaide Romanza's involved, it's more important than ever."

"While that may be true," Faolan said, "you won't be able to do anything about it until morning anyway."

"Still, I don't—I just don't."

"You aren't angry with her, are you?"

"No. Of course not."

"Then what?"

"She's carrying Maddox's heir."

"Yes, she is."

"I'd rather remember her this way."

"That's unfair."

"I know that. God, don't you think I know that?" Dana exclaimed. He turned away from Haleine and sat on the bench. "I think about her with him, and it makes me sick. I know it's not her choice, and I can ignore that because we're alone, but now that she carries his heir? I don't think I can face her knowing she's—I just want to forget. I want to be free of this. Of her."

"She won't like it."

"Don't tell her."

"She's going to ask. I'll have to tell her something."

"I'm fighting a war against her husband. Tell her that. Tell her I'm in the north. Or the south. I don't care where you tell her I've gone. Sooner or later it'll be true."

"Lying to your brother and your lover?"

"He's not my—" Dana sighed. "Aye."

"Just making sure I understand."

"How could you understand when I don't?" Dana asked. He shook his head. "War is easier. Tell her—tell her I'll not forget her."

"No, you'll just abandon her."

"What if I am?" Dana snapped. "Why does it matter to you? You've watched me leave women before. You've even encouraged it a time or two. Why is this different?"

"Because it is, and you know it. If you walk away now, Dana, it may be the last time you see her."

Dana looked over his shoulder. "That may be for the best. I don't have anything to offer her."

"That's not true."

"Isn't it? Look at me. This is the first test, and I'm failing her miserably."

"No, I'd say your failure here is on a spectacular level."

"You've never been angry with me before," Dana said. "Why do you love her so much?"

He didn't know. "Why don't you?"

"I do," Dana said. "I wouldn't have come this far otherwise. Tell her—"

"I'm not telling her anything. If you want something said, you say it."

"Then keep her safe," Dana said. "That's all I ask."

Faolan said nothing more. He flew inside Haleine's rooms and didn't look back to see what Dana did. He passed the bed and landed on a table near the fire. He turned to look at Haleine to find her awake, lying on her side and looking at him.

Part Two:
Shadow's Edge

CHAPTER 12

His daughter hated him.

It was the same thought that had plagued Darian every night since his return from Mairéad. He thought he might escape it, but nothing had driven Haleine's loss from his mind.

Seven months had passed since he had seen his daughter off. Winter was nearing its end, as was her pregnancy. She would soon become a parent herself, and Darian prayed she would not suffer as he did. He didn't want her to know the feeling of having a child who hated its mother. He hoped she would never have to understand why that loathing was justified.

Darian always had hated politics. Now, if it were possible, he hated it more than ever.

In spite of himself, he laughed quietly, being careful not to wake his sleeping wife. He slipped from the sheets and went to the window. He leaned with one hand against the wall as he looked over the darkened city.

He had lost too much in this land. Two daughters so far. Two daughters too many. The first had been lost to war, the second to peace. The irony was not wasted on him. He could not imagine how Sighle would be taken from him, but he had no confidence she would remain. She too would follow the path of her sisters.

Mireille was dead. She had been newly born, not yet through her first year of life, when the monsters had come for her. Darian remembered the creatures' faces. How could he ever forget? He pressed his hand against his chest and felt the scars through his shirt. He wore them like the brand of his king's army upon his arm. Were it not for the quick response of his guards, Darian would have lost Haleine as well.

And yet he had lost her anyway.

Darian looked at the floor. They had done so well to lay those memories to rest. So well, in fact, that Haleine did not know the truth. She would never know. How could she? There was no evidence Mireille had ever been born.

The floor took on an orange tinge, and he raised his head to see the same glow growing and spreading from the center of the city. As soon as he realized what it was, he ran.

"The city's on fire," he said to the guards outside his chamber. "Alert the men."

He closed the doors and went to dress, taking as little time as possible. In his haste, he woke Rhoswen.

"What is it?" she asked through a yawn. "Darian, what's happened?"

"There's a fire in the city," he said as he buckled his sword belt around his waist. "Get dressed and prepare for injuries."

When he arrived in the courtyard, the men were assembled and ready. One of the grooms held his horse, and Darian took the reins and swung himself into the saddle. He motioned for the gates surrounding the castle to be opened and led the men into the city.

Quatara, as he predicted, had embraced Nathan's death. The citizens had been protesting steadily since Darian's return, their violent acts growing in both frequency and intensity. This would not be the first fire deliberately set. It was the perfect ploy for Parthalan's rebels, as Darian could never ignore the alarm.

The fire raged by the time they reached it. He nodded to his captain, and the man barked out orders. Lines were formed, and the battle against the blaze began. Darian stayed atop his stallion and watched the rooftops of the surrounding buildings. The Quatari rebels had become adept snipers over the years, and this could be a perfect opportunity to attack.

His suspicions proved to be accurate. From the corner of his eye, he saw the first glint of a weapon and had just enough time to move as an arrow shot out toward him. He turned the horse quickly and shouted to his captain once more.

"Draw your weapons!"

The soldiers responded, but there was nothing for them to fight, as the snipers were well hidden in the darkness. Darian watched a good number of men succumb to the rebel arrows. Frustrated, he directed his horse to the captain's side.

"Get these men inside our walls," he said. "Let their damn city burn. We'll not fight these cowards."

The captain nodded and screamed for retreat. Darian looked around once more, his anger mounting inside of him. He was desperate to strike back at these rebels. He wanted to show them neither he nor Tanuba were a force with which to reckon, but the desire was lost as he laid eyes upon his castle. The gate was open. They had not closed it after the soldiers had marched. Anyone could have entered and—*Good God.* Darian left his men behind and spurred his horse back home.

He heard Sighle's scream the moment he set foot inside. Darian raced up the stairs that led to the family's private quarters, his sword drawn and ready. At the top, were the bodies of two guardsmen. He paused to examine the wounds. The intruders were human, armed with daggers or perhaps short swords. Sighle screamed again. Darian gripped his sword and continued down the hall to his daughter's bedchamber.

"Darian!"

His head snapped to the side to see Rhoswen stepping out of their own room. He flew at her and pushed her back inside the chamber. He put his hand over her mouth before she could speak again.

"You stay here," he whispered, lowering his hand. "Don't come out, not until I tell you it is safe. Do you understand?"

Tears formed in her eyes. "Sighle," she gasped as their daughter cried out once more.

Darian nodded. "Stay."

He left the room and closed the door behind him. He could hear the soldiers below, their voices loud and frenzied. The attackers would hear it, too. They'd become more desperate now, knowing they were running out of time to make their escape. Darian moved down the hall quickly and quietly.

"Father!" Sighle screamed, her voice wrought with tears.

One door had been left open just enough for him to slip inside. He stood there for a moment to survey the situation and to calm himself. Composure would be the only way he'd get Sighle back safely.

There were two men. One with a short sword strapped to his back stood by the window readying a rope meant for escape. The other man held his arm around Sighle's waist, trying to drag her across the room. She fought him for each and every step.

Darian stepped forward. "You will release my daughter."

Both men looked surprised to see him but did not do as he said. Sighle let out a sob and called to him.

"Let her go." Darian continued taking slow steps toward them. "Let her go—do it now, or I will kill you."

The man holding Sighle pulled a dagger from his belt and held it under her chin. The other drew his sword.

"I think you're outnumbered, old man," he said. "Take another step and my good friend here slits your daughter's throat."

"That would be most unwise," Darian said, but he stopped moving. "You can't escape this, gentlemen. I have men outside these chambers and that window. Release my daughter now, and I will make your deaths quick. I'll make them painless, even, as payment for your courtesy. However, if you have so much as bruised her, I promise I will see you die in the most excruciatingly slow manner possible. I always keep my promises, gentlemen. I think it's important you remember that."

The swordsman seemed prepared to take his chances. His partner, however, hesitated enough that Sighle was able to break free of his hold. She ran head on into Darian's open arms. He watched the two men retreat and slip out the window. For the moment, he didn't care. They wouldn't get far, and Sighle was all that mattered.

She cried. He smoothed her hair and tried to comfort her but found himself failing. He couldn't even convince himself of her safety. If he had been a few moments later, she would have been lost. Quatara was not safe for her, and he could no longer make it so. He knew this. He always had known it, yet he still had made those he loved pay the price for his duty.

"It ends now," he said. "Come."

He took her to Rhoswen. His wife had been crying, and her tears increased when she saw her daughter safe. He relinquished Sighle to her mother's arms.

"Rhoswen," he said. "You are to pack immediately. I am sending both of you away from here."

Rhoswen stared at him, her arms still wrapped around her daughter. "And what of you?"

"I will remain," he said. He did not look at his wife's face. He did not want to see what was there. "Tanuba still has interests here. I have no choice."

"I don't want to leave you."

"I don't care," Darian said. "You'll return to our estates in Mairéad. It'll be safer, and Cathal and Revelin will look after you."

"But—"

"No," he said. "I have decided. Fetch your maids and begin. I want you gone at the first light of day."

Rhoswen untangled herself from Sighle. "If we are to leave you," she said, the resolve in her voice strong, "we will go to Lira."

"Dammit, woman! Are you daft? There is war in Lira."

"Will you break this family farther apart? All in separate corners of the earth? We will leave as you command it, but we will go to Haleine. She is my child. She is *your* child."

"She wouldn't even look at you," he said, "so deep her hatred runs."

"I'll make her see."

He was angry. Not at Rhoswen, but he knew she wouldn't understand. He glared at her another moment before storming from the room. He went back to the courtyard, his desire for revenge renewed. He deflected the requests and questions coming from his men as he moved toward the gates, pausing only long enough to remove a torch from the wall. He continued into the city, a small group of soldiers scrambling behind him.

He used the torch to set fire to the nearest building and the next. He went forward and did the same to other structures. His men protested his actions, but he ignored them as he moved farther into the city. They objected to his distance away from the castle, entreating him to come back for his own safety, but no one shot at him, and there was no sound at all apart from the fire. When he was satisfied, he tossed the torch onto another roof and backed away from the growing wall of flame.

"Now you will feel the true wrath of Tanuba!" he screamed to his unseen foes. "She is merciless, and she will see you destroyed!"

Darian returned to the castle. The gates closed, and Quatara burned.

———⁓⁓———

On a road running south out of Eluned, a settlement of the displaced had developed. They were people who had suffered under the king's brand of justice but not people with whom Dana would find favor, yet Dana stood amongst them, leaning against a lone tree in the center of their camp. He wore a cloak, the hood pulled up to hide his face. He shrugged deeper into the garment, seeking an extra measure of warmth.

He was rubbing his arms and stamping his feet when James came and stood next to him, facing the opposite direction. It was obvious from the man's posture that James was angry. Dana didn't know what had caused the mood and waited to see what James had to say.

"You're sure they're riding out today?" he asked.

Dana nodded. "Faolan said."

"But he didn't know where they were headed?"

"Just south."

"There wasn't much of a reprieve this time."

There it was. It was true Varro and his soldiers hadn't given the rebellion much opportunity to rest. They were trying to take advantage of the scarcity of winter, pushing and pulling the rebellion each and every way, trying to make Dana flinch. Trying to make him break.

Dana knew there were those in camp who were wearing thin. James wasn't alone in his irritation, but Dana didn't consider himself among their number. It would seem the only time he found peace anymore was in the midst of a fight. It was the only time he felt warm.

"No," Dana said. "There wasn't."

"I'd hoped there might be. I'd hoped we might catch our breath if nothing else," James said. "Should've known better than to hope for anything."

"It's been a long winter, I know."

"And growing longer still," James said. "There's no end to it. There's no rhyme, no reason to what they do or where they go. They drag us from one end of the bloody country to the other and back again—"

"To wear us down. To wear us out."

"To see if we'll follow them."

"Do you want us not to follow them?"

"No, I want us to get ahead of them," James said. "I want us to be standing in their way. We knew before. We met them in Trutina; we met them in Culhwch. Why can we not do that now?"

Because Omur knew now. He knew Haleine spied for them, and because of it, he guarded his plans more closely than ever. Dana hadn't yet worked out what do to about it.

"You want to stand in their way?" he asked.

"Aye. I've just said it, haven't I?"

"Then find out where they're going next."

A sharp whistle pierced the air. On the other side of the road, just outside of the trees, stood one of the two men who had taken to following James around since the battle in Trutina. Dana didn't remember his name, but the man gestured to the road and jogged across it.

Varro had arrived.

"Tell Ilya," James said to the man as he passed them. To Dana he added, "It's not too late. One of us can wear that cloak."

The cloak, a brilliant blue, had once belonged to Varro. Dana had stolen it from him in a raid a month earlier. He didn't like it much. He preferred his more utilitarian cloak but taking it had been another slight blow to the king's captain's pride, and that Dana didn't mind at all.

"It's mine to do," Dana said. "You find out where he's going."

James nodded. "Mind they don't catch you."

He held out his hand and Dana took it. They embraced briefly before James pushed the hood off Dana's face.

"See you back at camp," Dana offered.

"Make sure I do," James said.

Dana turned for the road. It didn't take long for the camp's residents to recognize him. Most stared at him for a moment before moving away as fast as they could, but one giant of a man, armed with a hatchet, came straight at him.

"You're not welcome here," the man said.

Dana maneuvered his way around the man so the road was at his back. Having the locals spot him had been a part of the plan, but this man with his weapon hadn't. Dana held up his hands and continued to back away. The man followed.

"Just passing through, friend," Dana said. "I'm not looking for trouble."

"Neither were we, but trouble found us anyway, didn't it?" the man said. "Because of you, because of them"—he gestured to the oncoming regiment—"we live like this. May the devil take you all."

The man shoved him, and Dana fell into the road in front of Varro's advancing group. The lead rider was forced to jerk on his mount's reins to avoid trampling him. The soldier looked down at him while steadying his stallion.

"Watch where you're—" he stopped when he recognized who lay on the ground before him. "Well, what have we here?"

"Very bad timing," Dana said. "Forgive me if I don't stay."

He scrambled to his feet before the stallion could trample him and skittered off the road into the forest. He heard Varro shout the command to pursue and the subsequent sound of horses crashing into the brush.

Dana ran. He made no effort to do so quietly.

He didn't know how many now followed him. He didn't look back. He couldn't, not if he were to keep enough distance between them. As he ran, he worked the cloak's ties. It had served its purpose: drawn the soldiers' attention, piqued Varro's interest and made it easier for them to follow him through the woods. Now it only served to slow him down. When he'd loosened the cords enough, he let them slip through his fingers. The cloak flew off, and Dana kept moving.

He hadn't been free of it very long when a sharp pain hit his left shoulder. It robbed him of breath and threw him to the ground. He pushed himself up, spitting out mud and broken bits of fallen leaves, while fumbling with his right hand to find with what the soldiers had struck him down.

A dagger. It was a dagger. He was glad to see it, glad to hold it in his hand and know it wasn't something worse. He took a moment to breathe and, amongst the thundering of hooves and the pounding of his own heart, he heard the drawing of a bowstring.

"Don't, you fools!" Dana barked.

He understood the intentions behind the one who held the bow, but Dana didn't need cover. He needed the soldiers to move deeper into the forest, farther away from the rest. Dana threw the dagger away and got to his feet to run again. The soldiers were gaining ground now, but maybe it was better that they had drawn first blood. They'd never give up the chase if they believed they were so near to drawing last blood.

His shoulder burned as the hunt continued. Dana dodged and wove his way around trees. The soldiers continued to pursue him, but he still needed them to go a bit farther. He knew he was getting close when he saw Lucius's signal. Dana crashed onto the main trail and heard the soldiers shouting. A log lay across the path before him, and he leapt over it, landing on a pile of damp leaves. He slipped and fell hard on his back, but it didn't matter. One of his own covered him and pulled him clear.

"Sword," Dana said, and it was pressed into his hand. He pulled the weapon from its sheath and left the leather in the leaves. He cocked his head and listened to Varro's men. *He went this way. No, that way. Which way? Where'd he go? He couldn't have disappeared.*

Just a few steps more. That's all he needed them to take.

He heard the whistle, a bird call, and shouted, "Now!"

Men and women burst from their hiding spots and surrounded the soldiers.

"Ambush!" one of them choked out before he was dragged from his horse.

Varro had sent ten men to run him down. It wasn't as great a number as Dana had hoped. He hung back and looked in the direction of the road. Had he left enough fighters with Ilya?

Dana was forced to put Ilya out of his mind when the same rider who had nearly trampled him on the road broke free of the melee and came at him. Dana parried the first strike and the second. The man switched tactics and swung the blade a third time, cutting in a swift arc. Dana jumped back to avoid it. He didn't move quickly enough, and it slashed across his chest. He hadn't worn any sort of armor—no mail, no breast plate—because he hadn't wanted to be weighed down, so just his tunic stood between the sword and his skin. The weapon defeated the tunic easily, and the blade danced across his chest, beginning at his right shoulder and moving down to the ribs on his left.

Dana stood stunned. He wasn't quite breathing. He dropped his sword, and his empty hand hovered over his chest. The soldier smiled and prepared another blow that never fell. Lucius struck first, clubbing the man with a mace.

"Finish this!" Lucius yelled over his shoulder.

Time caught up with Dana then, and he took a step forward, only to collapse in Lucius's waiting arms.

"I've got you," Lucius said. "Come on, let's go."

"No, I'm—I'm all right," Dana said, looking down at himself. "It's not deep."

"It's deeper than you think," Lucius said. "You have to leave. I'll see this through."

"It doesn't hurt," Dana said.

"It will. Get him out of here," Lucius said. "Get him to Hanah as soon as you can."

Dana didn't know to whom Lucius had spoken, but four hands immediately grabbed him from behind and pulled him away from the fighting. He protested at first and tried breaking free of them, but the pain caught up to him, and he found himself slumping into darkness.

He woke up in his tent with Hanah hovering over him.

"Not going to die after all, I see," she said. "How do you feel?"

He wasn't sure. He felt heavy and shapeless. Dead.

"Thirsty," he responded finally.

She nodded. "I'll get you some water. Can you sit?"

He didn't know the answer to that either, but he nodded and she slowly helped him over to the tent's chair. The pain was considerable, but manageable, so he decided he was not dead. He eased himself down and leaned against the table as Hanah fetched his water. He was looking at the bandages wrapped around his chest when she returned.

She handed him a cup. "Maybe next time someone else should act as bait."

"I'm the one they know," Dana said. "I'm the one they'll never stop chasing."

"Anyone could've worn that damn cloak, and Varro would've known them as one of yours."

"It was mine to do."

"I think you're taking too many chances."

Dana laughed, which hurt, and put the cup on the table. "I'm leading a rebellion against the king. Chance is inherent."

"No, it's different," Hanah said. "You're different. You're trying to prove something to someone."

Your failure here is on a spectacular level.

Dana flinched. "Just the king, Hanah."

"Not just that," she said. "I know it's not just the king."

He wanted to tell her she was wrong, but there would be no reason for her to believe the words, not when even he didn't. He was glad when both Lucius and Ilya entered the tent and the conversation ended. Lucius carried Dana's sword and left it to rest against the table. Ilya stopped in front of Dana and leaned in to better examine his bandages.

"You didn't tell me it was that bad," Ilya said, glancing at Lucius.

"It's not that bad," Dana said, eliciting a grunt of protest from Hanah. "Did it work? Did you get the supplies?"

"Of course," Ilya said, backing away. "It was a good plan."

"Any losses?"

"Just theirs."

Dana nodded. "And James? Any sign of him?"

"No. It'll be a while yet." Ilya gestured to his chest. "That was close."

"Not that close," Dana said.

Hanah looked at him and slapped the dagger wound on his back. He yelped.

"Too close," Hanah said.

"Fine," Dana said through gritted teeth. "Next time you can be bait."

Hanah smiled and patted his cheek. "Gladly."

—◦◦◦—

The dream was terrible.

There was a battle in a great open field, the grass trampled and ground into the blood-soaked earth. At the center of it was Dana, clutching a sword and fighting fiercely: screaming, kicking, slashing, hacking through his enemy. There was no end to it, not even a pause for breath, and Dana never stopped his attack. He was wounded, bleeding from a gash in his forehead, the blood running down his face, in and around his eyes, masking him in crimson, but he did not stop.

Instead he screamed at them to come closer, inviting them to their death. The horde parted then, and a dark-hooded man on a dark horse rode to meet the challenge. *Omur*, Haleine thought, and it might have been if not for the sword at the man's hip. He dismounted from his stallion, his black cloak swirling around him like smoke and ash. He drew his sword and held it in salute. Dana raised his own sword and returned the gesture. As soon as he did, the dark man began his attack.

Haleine awoke and stared at the ceiling, painted with its artist's view of heaven. Something was wrong. Even as she thought it, Haleine wanted to laugh. Of course something was wrong. She had carried that feeling now for seven months. She didn't suppose it would ever go away. Not while her country was at war with itself. Not while her husband sat on the throne. Not while her lover fought to end both.

She didn't know why she still thought of him as such. She had not laid eyes upon him since before she'd gone to Mairéad. *You'll always have me,* he had said. The last time she had heard his voice had been seven months earlier. She had been startled, wakened by shouting. *God, don't you think I know that?* She hadn't dared to move, not knowing what was happening. Then she hadn't cared to move. *I just want to forget,* her lover had said. *I just want to be free of this. Of her.*

She didn't cry. She didn't see what she would gain from that, so she listened and lay still, so still that when Faolan came inside, he didn't notice she was watching at first. When he did see her, he came as close to panicking as she had ever seen him come. He wanted to ask if she had heard them talking on the balcony. If she had heard what Dana had said. But Faolan didn't ask, and she didn't tell him. She didn't utter a word.

Dana was gone, Faolan explained in her silence. Because of the war. Because the camp was too far away. Because. The pegasus always had a reason. She never asked him for explanations, but he offered them all the same. She heard him say that night he wouldn't tell her anything, that he wouldn't help Dana justify leaving, but he did it anyway. Faolan's hypocrisy didn't matter, though, because she liked him still.

And God help her, she still loved Dana. She didn't want to love him but couldn't seem to stop. She had lost count of the nights spent crying silent tears, hating him for his absence and hating herself for caring so much about one who would abandon her. She only knew that each night was followed by panic the next morning when rumors of the rebel leader's capture or death spilled from her ladies' mouths. The dread never lasted long, as Faolan was never far away and would refute the rumors with a simple shake of his head.

She would nod and do whatever she could to find out something—*anything*—that could help Dana and the rebellion he had started. Willem brought her information from the barracks. Who had gone where and why, if such a reason existed. She also had found a pair of servant girls who would report what they had overheard in the king's chambers or even in Omur's. Neither of them ever had much to report, but Haleine, not wanting to chance missing something more, kept them at it.

And because Bronagh had refused to do anything that would benefit the rebellion, Haleine set her to aiding Lira's citizens. Haleine knew where the soldiers were going; she knew where they had gone; and, because of Faolan, she knew exactly what transpired there. She knew which villages suffered the most and of what they had the most need. Bronagh was tasked with helping Haleine get those necessary items—food and medicine—into the hands of those who needed them. In order to keep what they did secret from those who would stop them, the work was slow and careful. There was never enough to satisfy every want, but Haleine was determined to do what she could.

Faolan, who acted more and more like her midwives with each passing day, was displeased by her actions, and she made sure to surround herself with others as much as possible so the pegasus could do nothing more than glare at her. It was easy to do, as Ceallach was usually underfoot and her midwives never far behind. They made it harder to get information from her spies, but Haleine managed. In truth, she was pleased by the challenge. It kept her from thinking too much on other things, things that couldn't be avoided once the day had ended.

She was always alone with the pegasus at nightfall. Maddox, as pleased as he was by her pregnancy, was repulsed by her swelling body and had ceased coming to her chambers altogether. When they were alone again, Faolan would sometimes reprimand her for her foolhardiness, but never with much force. She supposed he didn't press harder because he was grateful she had accepted Dana's absence as well as she had.

And she had accepted it. How could she not? There was nothing she could do that would bring him back to her. And mayhap, if he did return on his own, she might refuse him her heart, but she would never wish him ill.

She thought of her dream again and the rivulets of blood streaming down Dana's face. This was not the first she had dreamt of him in battle, nor did she think it would be the last, but it was the first to leave her with such an unsettled feeling. Something was wrong. Something was different than before, and whatever it was, it was keeping her from sleep. She threw back the covers and slid out of bed. She put on her robe as she contemplated sitting by the fire but saw Faolan sleeping on a sofa there and went out on the balcony instead. She wanted to clear her mind, and conversation with Faolan more often than not led to the opposite.

She sat on a bench with her hand on her belly and thought absolutely nothing until the child within her moved. She smiled slightly, but her delight did not last. Her husband's heir was growing well. The midwives were pleased; everyone was. It wouldn't be long before her son was born. Her son. The thought was inadvertent. She'd tried hard not to think of him that way. If she didn't, she imagined it would hurt less when he was taken away.

"What are you doing out here?"

She would have expected Bronagh to be there but knew Faolan had followed her. He flew out in front of her and landed on the railing. Once he was settled, he looked at her, waiting for an answer.

She let her hand fall to her side. "I was not tired."

"You? Not tired?" he asked, sounding genuinely concerned. "You've practically done nothing but sleep. Are you all right? Are you ill? Should I get someone? Bronagh maybe? The midwives?"

She laughed. "I am quite well though I confess I am tempted to lie. It might be amusing to see you fetch Bronagh. What will she think when you speak to her?"

"There are ways," Faolan said. "Ways that don't require me to speak."

His ways were magical ones, or so he claimed. He had referenced his abilities often, but she had yet to see them. Haleine raised an eyebrow at him and said nothing.

"Haleine?" Faolan said.

"I do not wish for you to take offense," she said, "but why are you here?"

"Here on this balcony?"

"Here at all. You've hardly left my side these months. You sit with my ladies and watch us sew. You sit in my chambers with me in silence. You—"

"I don't actually sit."

She smiled. "I am useless to you."

"You really aren't."

"And pray tell how does watching me sew help your cause?"

"It really doesn't."

"Then why are you here?" she asked. "I have not disillusioned myself so much to think that in these last months, I have discovered anything that has made a difference to your cause, and I refuse to believe Dana doesn't have need of you elsewhere."

"He has need of me right here," Faolan said.

"Watching over me or Omur?"

"Both."

"And which one concerns you more?"

"Right now?" Faolan said. "You."

"I tell you I am fine."

"You don't seem fine."

"Bronagh nags me less, you know."

"That's only because you're mean whenever you talk to her now."

It was the truth, and Haleine despised hearing it out loud. Try as she might, she was unable to keep her discontent from bleeding into all aspects of her life. Bronagh never said anything, she never would, but Haleine knew that although they always had been mistress and servant, there was a distant formality between them now that never existed before.

"You said she should fear me."

"I never said you should be mean," Faolan said. "I'm here, Haleine, because I don't think you're safe. Maybe you don't see the way Omur looks at you, or maybe you don't realize how genuine the danger is, but he hates you, and I think he means to do you harm."

"Has he tried?"

"No."

"Has he ever?"

"No."

"From what are you protecting me? His withering stare?"

"Don't make light of this, Haleine. Not even for a moment," Faolan said, his tone so serious it chilled her. "Omur has access to powers: terrible magic you never imagined existed."

"Because it doesn't exist."

"Your religion demands ignorance of you, and that's been all right thus far, but you have to believe now, Haleine. You have to. You can't afford not to anymore. Not if you want to live."

"You said he's done nothing."

"You lived in Quatara nearly all your life, a land that's filled with some of the deadliest vipers anywhere. You know they lay in wait for their prey. They lie, motionless, waiting for that one perfect moment to strike, and when they do, the prey never sees it coming."

She shook her head. "He's laid dormant these seven months. He's laid dormant the better part of a year. Surely he would have struck by now if that were his intention."

"Seven months is nothing to a man like Omur. Neither is seven years or even seven decades."

"I don't understand."

"Omur has been my enemy for seven hundred years now," Faolan said. "And it's entirely possible that he will continue to be for seven hundred more."

"It's not possible."

"There really isn't much that isn't possible."

"How?"

"The dark gods make it so."

She wanted very much to deny what he had said. The dark gods were myth, nothing more, and his telling her they were otherwise was some manner of cruel joke she didn't understand.

"Haleine? What are you thinking?"

"You wouldn't tell me any of this in Tanuba."

"I didn't know you in Tanuba."

"But you know me now?"

"I think so."

She nodded. "Will you tell me more?"

"There are four of them," Faolan said. "One for each direction, like on a compass. The north is named Yelsneh. He is the most potent and acts as their leader. The south belongs to Lamak. The east is Azia and Gargon the west."

"And Omur is to them what you are to your goddess?"

"Yes."

"And you have been fighting each other for seven hundred years?"

"I can't say they've done much until now."

"Why now?"

"I don't know."

He had that look on his face that told her he was thinking something he wasn't going to share with her. She had watched him just as much as he had watched her in the last seven months. He was surprisingly expressive, and she knew even if he claimed the opposite, there was something to tell.

"Something must have changed," she pressed.

"The goddess is weak now," Faolan said. "Vulnerable enough that they feel this is their time to restore the earth to what it was."

"What was it?"

"Your god's hell would seem like a paradise in comparison," Faolan said. "The dark gods love unrest, turmoil, horror. It makes them strong while making the goddess weak. It's why Amatheon and Michaela and Nathan died. It's why the rumor of rebellion was even started. Each battle risks bringing them closer to what they want."

"Their hell," she said and Faolan nodded. "And before, did your goddess wrest the world from their grip?"

"More or less."

"You're always so ambivalent," she said. "Does your goddess tolerate that in her servants?"

"As long as we're not evil."

"Benevolent, is she?"

"As the goddess of the earth should be."

"What if I told you I don't believe she exists?"

"I'd say that's rather naive of you, but your prerogative."

"It is acceptable to deny the existence of the goddess but not the dark gods?"

"You should never underestimate your enemy," Faolan said. "And if you continue to ignore their existence, you are absolutely underestimating them."

"They are my enemy?"

"They are everyone's enemy," Faolan said. "But you in particular, yes."

"Why?"

Faolan shook his head. "I don't know. I really don't."

That felt like the truth. She nodded, and they stopped speaking. Haleine's back ached, and she leaned forward slightly to massage the base of her spine. She should have stayed indoors. Her chair and the fire would have been more comfortable.

"You should go inside," Faolan said. "Try and sleep some."

She almost laughed at him. How would she sleep now with all that had been said? How would she sleep ever again?

"I am not tired," she said.

"Are you sure you're feeling all right?"

"I swear to you I am fine," she said. "Unpleasant dreaming is all."

"What did you dream?"

"It doesn't matter. It's done now."

"Haleine."

"I have very little love for my father anymore, Faolan," she said. "It does you no good to speak to me as he would."

"Did you dream of Dana?"

She sighed. "Aye, I dreamt of Dana. I dreamt of a terrible battle."

"Tell me about it."

"Everything was awash in a sea of blood. It was awful. There were so many of them, but he fought them all. He was wounded, yet he never wavered. Have you ever seen him fight?"

"Yes."

"Of course you have. He fights bravely; no need to tell me that. And he fights well; I know that, too."

"What do you want me to tell you?"

"Is he well?"

Faolan nodded. His tiny body stiffened, and she knew he would offer her another reason why Dana hadn't been to the palace. Would it be something new tonight?

"I'm sorry he hasn't been able to come," Faolan said, "but the war—"

"I know," she said, not wanting to hear the rest.

The war was very convenient. He could leave her; he could stay hidden in the hills or trees or anywhere he liked, and she couldn't fault him for it. He was protected by his war.

"You would tell me if something had happened, wouldn't you?" she asked.

Faolan's hesitation was nearly undetectable, but she saw it was there.

"Of course," he said.

—⁓—

The night Laorans had first summoned Dana to her service had begun no differently than any other. He and Faolan had made camp in the woods outside Labhras. Dana built a fire just large enough to keep the evening's chill at bay and sat on the ground in front of it, his back against a tree. Faolan was off to his left somewhere. The pegasus had been unusually quiet since they had stopped for the day. Dana looked over to check on him and spotted Faolan lying just out of reach, his eyes closed.

"Everything all right?" Dana asked.

Faolan didn't answer nor make any indication he had even heard Dana.

"There's time yet before we're expected in Enimode," Dana said next. "Any particular direction you want to head in?"

Still nothing. Dana shrugged and threw another branch onto the fire. He heard a rustling in the forest and raised his eyes to scan the trees before him. He never had had much trouble with the wolves and boars before, but he still kept a cautious eye out for them. He glanced to his left again. Faolan now stood beside him. The pegasus was absolutely still. Dana's own wariness increased, and he reached for the dagger in his belt. He heard the rustling again, this time coming from the right. He looked, his eyes straining to make out shapes in the darkness. Nothing. He shook his head, released the dagger and went back to the fire.

A unicorn stood across from him. Staring down at him.

"Oh," Dana said.

He had seen unicorns before. When one spent as much time in the forest as he did, a sighting was inevitable, but never had he seen one this close. The beast before him was a huge broad-chested stallion. In the firelight, the animal's eyes looked black. Dana pressed himself flush against the tree and stared. Faolan did nothing.

"Dana ap Seoras," the unicorn said finally. "My name is Lorcan. I would speak with you."

Dana needed a moment for the shock to wear off before he was able to find his voice.

"Your name is Lorcan?" he asked. "And you wish to speak to me?"

"Yes."

"Aye, all right," he said, slowly getting to his feet. "What shall we speak of?"

"The world as you know it, Dana ap Seoras, is going to change," the unicorn said. "And not for the better."

He should have been more concerned with the unicorn's portent—certainly there were no good tidings to be found there—but Dana focused instead on the surname Lorcan had assigned him.

"Why do you call me that?" he asked. "Dana ap Seoras. It's not my name."

"He would not begrudge you the name."

"No, he would not."

"And yet, you lay no claim to it?"

"It is not mine to claim."

From the corner of his eye, Dana saw Faolan nod.

"How did you know to use that name?" Dana asked.

"I told him," Faolan said.

Dana looked at him. "You told him? When would you have—you *know* him? You know a unicorn?"

"I know several," Faolan said.

"And you have secret meetings about me?"

"From time to time, yes," Faolan said. "But, for now, let's focus on the part about the world changing."

"And not for the better," Dana said. "Aye, I heard. What does that mean? And why are you telling me?"

"Because you're going to stop it," Faolan said.

"Stop it?" Dana asked. "Stop the world from changing?"

"Not exactly," Faolan said. "The world will change; we can't stop that, but what we can do—what we *must* do—is prevent it from falling into darkness."

"And you think *I* can do that?"

"Yes."

"Why?"

"Our lady says it's so," Lorcan said.

Dana looked at the stallion again and adjusted his stance against the tree. "Your lady?"

"Laorans," Faolan said. "The goddess. We serve her, and now she wishes for you to do the same."

"Oh." Dana sank to the ground. "Why would she want that?"

"We do not ask questions of her," Lorcan said.

"Maybe you don't," Dana said, "but she's not my goddess."

"This is still your destiny," Faolan said.

The thought of destiny made Dana laugh. He had no name, no land. Everything he owned he could carry either on his back or in a set of saddlebags. Why should someone like him have a destiny?

"Just wait," Faolan had said in response. "This is your destiny, and you will do this. You'll see."

And Dana had seen. For ten months now, he had been on the path of the goddess's choosing, and he had seen the seemingly impossible become reality. He made it happen. He'd walked through the palace as though he owned it. He'd sat in the king's chair, stood face to face with the man before turning his back and walking away. He'd destroyed the king's men and stolen the king's towns.

Stolen the king's wife.

That was something none of them had planned. Not Faolan, not Lorcan, not Laorans. He wasn't supposed to have her. They hadn't arranged it like James. She was not a part of his destiny. Faolan hadn't known she was anything more than another lover. He proved it when he hadn't wanted to go to Tanuba, but now he didn't want to leave Haleine alone. Dana didn't know what had happened to change that. He was only aware of what Faolan had told him, but thought it obvious that there was more the pegasus hadn't said.

Your failure here is on a spectacular level.

He heard Faolan's voice so clearly, he returned immediately to the present. Dana looked to his left. He already knew the pegasus wouldn't be there but expected to see him anyway. Dana sighed and leaned forward, sitting as close to the fire in front of him as he could. He was supposed to be sleeping but had insisted on taking part in the watch. And although he was meant to be guarding the perimeter, he didn't look away from the flames. He tried to shrug even further into his cloak, again searching for—but failing to find—that extra bit of warmth. He wasn't surprised. There was a chill in his bones he suspected had little to do with the lingering winter's cold.

Your failure here is on a spectacular level.

Without wanting to, without meaning to, he glanced again to his left, but still Faolan wasn't there. No, he was in Eluned, in the palace at Haleine's side, and all Dana knew of the two of them was that they were alive. It was enough for now, but how long before it wasn't?

"You know, some of your better watchmen will actually look up from time to time," James said.

Dana didn't move. He didn't even look away from the fire, but something within him relaxed at the sound of his friend's voice.

"Something to aspire to, then," he said.

James sat beside him. "What are you doing out here?"

"Standing watch."

"You're guarding the fire."

"It won't guard itself," Dana said and shrugged when he saw James wouldn't be distracted with a glib answer. "Just lost in thought. Remembering."

"Remembering what?"

"Nothing important," Dana said. "Were you able to track Varro?"

"Aye. He and his men are in Nechtan. At the inn."

"The inn?"

"They ate dinner. They went to bed," James said. "I suppose they'll destroy it in the morning when it's warmer and they're better rested."

"What about their supplies?"

"They either found new ones, or they'll just steal some in the morning," James said. "I don't know, but they're not concerned."

"How many men?"

Now James shrugged. "No less than usual. Are you sure your ambush was worth it?"

That likely meant Hanah or Ilya had told James what had happened in the skirmish. Dana didn't want to talk about it.

"We needed the provisions," he said. "Did you find out where they were headed?"

"They mean to move north. Toward Lanval."

"Lanval," Dana said, running his hand through his hair. "Well, we've not been to the northern peninsula yet. At least we're going somewhere new. Have you told Ilya?"

"Aye," James said. "If we're to get ahead of them, we can't linger."

"We won't linger. We'll be on the move tonight."

"She told me what happened."

"I thought she might have."

"Are you all right?"

"Close enough."

James nodded. "You're staying here."

Dana looked away from the fire. "What?"

"Tonight, when we leave for Lanval," James said, "you're not coming. You're staying in camp."

"To do what?"

James reached over and slapped the dagger wound on his back, just as Hanah had done. And, just as he had before, Dana yelped.

"Heal?" James asked. "Just a thought."

"It's fine. I'm fine," Dana said. "I'm not as fragile as you think."

"Just fragile enough, as it turns out. You're not coming to Lanval."

"That decision is not yours to make."

"It is, and I did. You're not going."

Dana stood and looked down at James. "I'm not staying in camp. I'm not staying behind. If you want to stop Varro, you'll need everyone you can muster. If you want to convince Lanval of what's coming, you'll need me. I'm the one they know, and you need—"

"I need you to stay alive," James said, "because you are the face of this bloody rebellion. I know you think you're untouchable or invincible or whatever, but just because they don't want to kill you doesn't mean you can't be killed. When are you going to understand that? When are you going to realize that it's not your body anymore? It's not your life. You just can't do with it what you will."

"You need all the fighters you can get," Dana said.

"Able-bodied fighters, aye."

"I can still fight."

James looked at him for a moment, nodded and extended his arm. Dana took it and pulled James up. Once on his feet, James didn't let go but instead pulled Dana in closer and used his open palm to hit Dana's chest, hard and fast. The pain was instant and robbed him of breath. Dana let go of James and stumbled back, trying to stay on his feet. Trying to breathe. He bent at the waist, one hand on his chest, the other on his knee. He looked at James who stood looking down at him, arms folded across his chest.

"I can't use you," James said. "Not this time. You're staying here."

Dana nodded.

CHAPTER 13

Maddox did not see the servant girl come into the library. She moved quietly, as not to disturb her king, and in this she was successful. Maddox continued his rant about Dana's rebellion without taking the slightest notice of her arrival. Omur, however, did.

Her name was Sabine. She was a young, tiny wisp of a girl, nondescript in her features. She was the sort of girl men would not look at twice. He only noticed her now and watched every move she made because he knew why she was there and who had sent her.

Sabine was not alone in her deceit. There was one other—Nonna, she was called. She did not come to the library. He often saw her in his own chambers and knew she sometimes visited Maddox's rooms. Neither girl had overheard anything of importance; Omur had taken care to ensure that. It was easy enough to do, and he didn't want to discourage their visits. It kept Haleine from doing something else. She had been harmless thus far, and Omur wanted to make sure she stayed that way.

Again, Omur thought how lucky Haleine was that his lords had some use for her because he found he hated her more and more with each passing day. He was not the sort for wishing but had found himself on more than one occasion doing just that, wishing his lords had given him permission to rid himself of both the queen and the child she carried.

But he had been denied because they did not want the queen harmed. Her child, they claimed, would not matter. They could still control Lira even if Maddox's heir grew into manhood. Omur thought it an unnecessary risk, but if that was what his lords wanted, he would obey.

"We need to divide his forces," Maddox said. "Where are they now?"

"In the northern peninsula. Varro is there or should be soon," Omur said. "If you want to separate his numbers, we could prepare men to go along the southern coast and raid the villages there."

Sabine's head came up. Omur continued, naming the towns he would see attacked. The girl mouthed each name after he spoke it.

Maddox nodded. "Good. See it done."

"Of course, my lord."

"I mean it, Omur. I want this done. I want this over with. I want that man in pieces."

"Yes, my lord."

"I do not understand how he has managed to last this long. I am the stronger side, my army superior. We should have crushed him at the onset. You told me months ago it would be taken care of, and yet, he lives," Maddox said. "He continues to challenge me, and the people—they love him."

He had to redirect the king's train of thought. He did not know what Sabine would report to Haleine, and even if Maddox's words meant nothing to the queen, they would mean something to the pegasus.

"Not all of them, my lord."

"Enough of them, I dare say."

"They won't always," Omur said.

"Really?" Maddox sulked. "You have a plan for that, do you?"

"Yes," Omur said as he watched Sabine leave as quietly as she had entered. "I have a plan for that."

He hadn't intended on putting it into action this soon, but perhaps he would have to do something to appease his king. Maddox was easiest to control when content, and it was important that the king remain under Omur's control. It could also serve to remind Dana that maybe he wasn't as impervious as he thought. There was always Enimode. The village was rebuilding itself and making a modest living again. He could send men there.

But even as the thought entered his mind, he dismissed it. Enimode would be saved for when he really needed it. The first attack hurt the rebel leader. Omur would want the next to do much, much worse.

"You did nothing but stare at that girl from the moment she came in here," Maddox said.

"My lord?"

The king shrugged. "Plain for my tastes, but if you want her, I'll have her sent to you."

"No, my lord," Omur said. "Such a gift is unnecessary."

"I thought you only dressed as a monk, not lived as one."

"And that is true, my lord," Omur said, "but—"

"But nothing. I'll have her sent to you. Do what you want with her."

What would Haleine think if her girl ended up in his bed? Would Sabine remain in the queen's confidence, or would Haleine cast her out? Would the pegasus demand it? Omur had to admit he was curious. It was a sign he'd lived among them for too long.

Omur bowed his head. "You are most generous, my lord."

———

While James and Ilya were off in Lanval awaiting the king's men, Lucius had stayed in camp, presumably to keep an eye on Dana to make sure the rebel leader stayed where he was. He had been shadowing Dana from the moment the others had gone, irritating Dana to the point that he retreated to his tent and stayed there.

But the next morning, Lucius was nowhere to be found, and Dana was restless. He sat through Hanah's ministrations and then, despite her insistence that he rest, made his way to the training field to see what happened there. Most of their fighters had gone to Lanval, but a handful remained. It was a mixture of new recruits— untested, untrained or too young for battle—who populated the space.

Owain was among them. He was the only one Dana knew by name. He worked with a short sword, as he was too slight for anything else. The sword was still a bit large, but the boy was determined to make it work. He'd been involved in a number of the more minor raids throughout the winter but had so far been kept from full battles. Owain had wanted to go to Lanval, but both James and Ilya had denied him. He hadn't been happy about being excluded. He hadn't come to the rebellion to hide in the trees, after all. He'd come—like James, like so many others—to kill the men who had killed his family.

"Dana," Lucius said, appearing on his right.

"I haven't gone anywhere, and I'm not doing anything but sitting and watching," Dana said. "Surely that can be allowed."

"I wanted only to give you this," Lucius said. "Here."

Dana looked to see Lucius holding a folded piece of parchment in his hand. There was no mistaking what it was, but Dana asked anyway.

"What's this?" he said.

"Word from the queen."

"You've been to Eluned."

Lucius nodded, and Dana took the parchment. He held the tiny square in his palm for a moment. It was as close as he'd gotten to her in the last seven months.

"Did you see her?" Dana asked.

"Aye," Lucius said, his tone cautious. "She'll not be delivering messages much longer. Not until—"

Not until the babe was born.

"Aye," Dana said and unfolded Haleine's message.

It was nothing more than a list written in her hand of villages found along the southern coast. He didn't know what he thought he might find—what he hoped he might find—for no letter of hers had ever contained anything different. Dana read the list a second time and looked at the training field.

"What is it?" Lucius asked. "What does the queen say?"

"The king's sending men south. Omur's sending men south."

"Because he knows we're in the north."

"Aye," Dana said and handed the parchment to Lucius. "Gather who and what you can. Anyone who can fight. Anyone who can hold a weapon, anyone who can—anyone. Then make your way south. I'll find you in the Donasien Woods, just outside the village of Labhras."

"You're going to Labhras?"

"Aye."

"There's nothing to be found there but trouble."

"Maybe. Maybe not." Dana stood and nodded toward the training field. "Be sure to bring Owain along with you. He didn't come here to sit any more than I did."

"Dana," Lucius said. "The lord of Labhras is no friend to the rebellion. Why do you think he'll be anything else?"

Dana walked away. "Because once he was my friend."

—⁂—

Lanval was the gateway to the northern peninsula. It was a land that was nothing more than sea cliffs, goat paths and grazing land for sheep and cows. There was no easy access to the sea, and the soil would grow nothing but the sparse grass. The king would gain nothing from attacking here. It was why, James supposed, he hadn't done it before. But now it was part of a cruel plan to see how much the rebellion could take, how far they could stretch.

James was tired of it. He wanted to be done with it. Battle after battle and still no ground gained, only new rules, new stratagems, none of them devised with victory in mind. Survival. That's all they aimed for now. They were just trying to keep their heads above water. He'd meet the king's men here, he'd beat them back, then wait to see where they would go next.

And he'd keep doing it. Over and over again until he could end it. If it could be ended.

He awaited the king's men in Lanval's watchtower. Two of the men from Cinna, Rhydwyn and Gair, waited with him. They were never very far behind him anymore, not since the fight in Trutina. James didn't like it much, but nothing he did discouraged them from doing anything different, so now they watched the road while James leaned against the rail and looked at the sea. He'd seen it before but never like this, so wild and violent. Angry. The waves crashed upon the rocks while the tide threatened to devour everything it touched. Was it always like that? Was it always so imbued with rage? Or did it only appear that way because he had forgotten how to feel anything else?

"Captain?" Rhydwyn said.

"You don't have to call me that," James said.

"Aye, Captain."

They'd had the same exchange before and would have it again, James was sure. Both Rhydwyn and Gair clung to it. It was something they wanted to believe in. Something that might make Cinna's loss worthwhile.

James wanted to believe in the same thing. He wanted something to make Enimode's loss have meaning. Or Cinna or Trutina or anywhere else the king's men had destroyed. He wanted to know they were fighting for something other than the whims of deities he didn't want to believe in.

He didn't know it yet.

"They're coming," Gair said.

Of course they came. They never stopped coming. James turned away from the ocean and looked at the road. The king's men were barely visible as they emerged from the cover of the forest. Somewhere among them was the king's captain, the one man James wanted to kill.

But even then, it wouldn't end.

"Get everyone in position," James said.

"Aye, Captain," Gair said.

Rhydwyn and Gair climbed down from the watchtower. James watched the approaching soldiers a moment longer before following. Once on the ground, he worked his way through the gathering people. Bearach waited for him just outside the village.

"Is Ilya ready?" James asked.

"Waiting for your mark," the unicorn answered.

Ilya, Fáinne and half their fighters waited in the forest to flank the king's men, just as they had done in Trutina. They were there because he had told them to go, and they would wait for his mark because this battle was his to do. The people who died here would do so because he gave the order. How would he make that worthwhile?

Maybe he should have let Dana come after all.

"She knows what to do," James said. "She doesn't need me to tell her."

Nor did he think the people standing with him needed such instruction, so James didn't give a speech. He didn't sit astride Bearach. Instead he stood shoulder to shoulder with Dana's rebels and the people of Lanval to help them form a wall in front of their village. Together they watched the king's men grow closer.

"I've never killed a man," a girl standing to his left said suddenly.

She was a local lass; he didn't know her name. He didn't want to know her name. She was dressed in boys' clothing, probably for the first time in her life. Her brown hair was braided down her back, and her eyes were wide with fear. She held a thick but short staff with a white-knuckled grip. He thought about suggesting she abandon the front line of the fight, or perhaps abandon the fight altogether and instead take shelter along with those villagers who were unable or unwilling to fight, but that was a decision everyone in Lanval had already made. If she were here now, she wouldn't be willing to leave.

"That'll still be true when this is done," James told her. "We may call them men, but that's not what they are. You remember that. You remember that, and you never stop moving. That's how you survive."

She nodded and adjusted the grip on her staff. James continued to look at her, not wanting to care, but feeling himself doing it anyway. He sighed and took the dagger from his boot. He held it out to her.

"Take this," he said. "You may find your staff isn't quite enough."

She looked at the weapon and nodded again. She took it and tucked it into her belt.

"Thank you," she said. "I'll make sure you get it back."

He'd be surprised if she survived the day but didn't say so. James looked away to focus on the approaching soldiers. It wouldn't be much longer.

"When they come, you push them back!" James shouted. "You be the rocks the waves break upon!"

"Aye, Captain," Rhydwyn murmured from somewhere behind him.

The sentiment traveled through the rest of the ranks, and James could feel a wave of nervous energy returning to him. The sounds of swords beating against shields and spears pounding against the ground filled the air. It was enough to cause the king's men to come to a halt. The rebels shouted and screamed insults and jibes at them. James remained silent but indulged in a smile.

He turned to Bearach. "Tell Ilya to go now."

"They're on the move," Bearach said.

James nodded. A man on his right, another resident of Lanval, stepped forward, and James went to stop him, but Gair beat him to it.

"Wait," Gair said.

"For what?" the man asked.

Ilya provided the answer when she started her attack. The unsuspecting men of the king's army screamed.

"That," James said. He drew his sword and shouted, "Forward!"

The battle didn't last long. The soldiers broke like a ship running aground. Ilya flanked them, making escape impossible, and James killed them. He cut his way through one man after the other, never hesitating, never stopping until it was done and the last man had been subdued. No one escaped. A small number of the king's men surrendered before the end. James gave orders to Rhydwyn and Gair to see the captives secured before walking away to search through the dead and wounded for Varro. He started with the wounded, lending his aid where he could, while accounting for his own people and giving others direction where needed. When he was certain Varro was not among the hurt, James turned his attention to the dead. The king's men had sustained the greatest losses, but his own people had not gone untouched. He was on his knees, laying out the body of one of his own, when he was interrupted.

"I lost your dagger."

He glanced up to see the girl who had stood beside him at the battle's beginning. He hadn't expected her to survive, but from the looks of her, she had sustained only minor injuries.

"Did you," he said.

"But not my life."

Her tone was defiant now, as though daring him to find fault with her survival. He nearly smiled. He finished what he was doing and stood.

"Well, that's something," he said.

"Some would say that's everything."

"Aye, some would say that."

The defiance left her face. "But not you?"

He looked at her a moment, contemplating her question and finding himself unwilling to answer it. "Were all the dead brought here?"

"Aye, my lord."

"I'm not a lord," he said.

He walked away and continued his search, but the king's captain remained undiscovered. James eventually found his way back to Rhydwyn, Gair and their prisoners.

"Is he here? Have we Varro?" James asked.

"No, Captain," Gair answered. "There's been no sign of him."

James looked at the captives. "He's neither among the dead nor the wounded, so he must be among the men who surrendered."

Rhydwyn shook his head. "He's not."

"How did we lose him?" James asked, but neither man had an answer.

"I suspect he was never among them," Ilya said, coming up behind them. "For some reason, he left them in Nechtan. I watched all those men ride past me, and I never saw him."

James swore and walked the line of captured men, all bound and kneeling on the ground. None of them lifted their heads to look at him.

"Where is your leader?" James asked. "Scampered off, has he? Left you to die? Or did he send you to die in his place?"

"It doesn't matter, James," Ilya said. "Let's send them off and get back to what needs to be done."

"Send them off?" James said.

"We send them back to Eluned. We send a message to the king," Ilya said.

James shook his head. "Every battle we send what's left of the king's men back to him, in defeat, in shame. And do you know what they do? They get new swords, more swords, and they march again to destroy someplace else. I won't have it anymore," he said, putting his hand on his sword. "This time we send a new message."

Ilya grabbed his wrist. "They surrendered."

He shook free of her grip. "Their mistake."

"Dana wouldn't do this," she said.

James nodded. "Maybe that's the problem."

He drew the sword and swung it in a loose circle before taking it up and driving the blade through the first man's neck.

―⁓―

Jaspaer Emrys became lord of Labhras while still very much a boy after his father died following a fall from a horse. He enjoyed his wealth, enjoyed his privileged state but always remained humane. He worked hard to do right by his people, and in return, they worked hard for him.

Dana first encountered him decades later in a tavern found in Labhras's village. Emrys was on the losing end of a bet made between them concerning the outcome of a brawl between two other men. He handed Dana his money and bought a round of ale to show there was no ill will. Several more rounds had followed through the years, over which a friendship had been formed.

The last time Dana had seen him had been ten months earlier, just before Dana had gone to tell James of their shared destiny. He'd gone to Emrys first, thinking that perhaps this rare benevolent nobleman might be an ally in his cause, but all Emrys had offered him was the assurance that if Dana didn't make trouble for him or the people of Labhras, he wouldn't make trouble for the rebellion.

Dana knew it was as good an offer as he might receive, so he'd left the keep and rode to Enimode. He hadn't been back to Labhras since, but now Omur and the king were planning to attack the south, and Dana was desperate for any way to stop it. Emrys could help.

He had no trouble entering Emrys's keep. He thought at first that it was the goddess's doing, that her protection extended to Labhras as well, but came to decide his own history with Labhras's lord was responsible when one of the guards at the gate spotted him amongst the crowd seeking entrance and waved him through. Dana nodded back as he walked through the gates and into the keep itself. Dinner was being served in the hall, and Dana followed Emrys's retainers inside. He took a tankard off the tray of a passing servant and stood against the wall, sipping ale and watching the scene unfolding around him.

Emrys sat at the center of a table at the far end of the room, picking food off a trencher while listening to the man on his right. Emrys didn't contribute to the conversation, only periodically nodded in agreement. Briefly, Emrys looked away from both his food and his guest to scan the hall. He stared a moment in Dana's direction before shaking his head and turning back to the still-talking man.

Dana left his tankard on a table and exited. He took the stairs to Emrys's solar. The room was empty, but the servants had already prepared it for their lord's use. The candles were lit and a fire roared in the hearth. In front of it sat two chairs, a small table between them. A flagon and a single cup had been placed there. Dana went to the table and lifted the flagon to his nose to smell what was inside. Ale. Dana smiled and poured some into the cup. He replaced the flagon and took the cup instead. He sat in the chair on the right and drank ale as he waited for Emrys to appear.

He didn't wait long. Emrys arrived alone and closed the solar's doors behind him. He didn't seem to notice Dana. He stood there for a moment and looked at the floor. When he moved away, he walked the length of the room and back again, stopping to face the fire.

"My lord Emrys," Dana said.

Emrys turned. "That was you in my hall."

"It was."

"And now you're here. Are you mad?"

"From time to time."

"You certainly are now. What the devil are you doing?"

"At the moment?" Dana raised the cup. "Enjoying your ale."

"You shouldn't be here."

"Why's that?" Dana asked. "You expecting the king?"

"No. But I am his man."

"Are you now," Dana said. "Going to arrest me, then?"

"If that's the last of my ale, I just might."

Dana smiled and took another sip. "I can understand that. It is rather good ale."

Emrys sighed and sat in the other chair. "How did you get in?"

Dana shrugged and set the cup on the table. "The front gates. Then the door."

"Please tell me my sentries didn't see you."

"If it puts your mind at ease."

"Who else is with you?" Emrys asked. "How many traitors now sit within my walls?"

"You'll see none but me."

"That's not an answer."

"It wasn't meant to be."

"Well, you're not alone. I know that."

"Do you?"

"I rather doubt you go anywhere alone anymore. What of your lad? The nervous one—your shadow. He's never far from your side. Where is he?"

"He's not so nervous anymore," Dana said. "Neither is he here. You don't have to worry, Emrys. I'm not—"

"I don't have to worry?" Emrys interrupted. "I'm a man sworn to serve the king, yet the damn rebel leader is sitting at my hearth drinking my ale. Of course I have to worry."

"I'm not here to attack you."

Emrys laughed. "As if you have the forces for that, even with your damned beasts," he said. "No, I know you're not here to attack me, but it does not tell me what you do want."

"I want to know if the king's man has seen reason yet."

"You're not reason, lad. You're folly."

"I'm not."

"You are, and until that changes—"

"Your loyalties won't."

"Yes," Emrys said and hit the arm of the chair. "Dammit, Dana, you shouldn't be here. I told you—I *told* you when you started this how it would go. I said I wouldn't make trouble for you; I wouldn't come after you if you didn't give me a reason to. All you had to do was stay away."

"I know."

"What in the bloody hell are you doing here?"

"I need help. I need provisions. I hoped you might see your way clear to providing some."

"You need provisions?" Emrys asked as though Dana had asked for the deeds to all his lands.

"Aye. Your king has men determined to tear apart the northern peninsula, but he's also preparing to attack the southern coastal villages. I want to stop it, but my resources are already stretched thin."

"My villages."

"Your villages, the king's villages—either way your hands are tied. As the king's man, all you can do is stand back and watch. Help me help those people."

Emrys leaned forward in his chair. "How do you know what the king intends?"

"I have my ways," Dana said. "Ways—I'm sure you'll understand—I'd rather not discuss."

Emrys nodded. "I have my ways, too."

He reached inside his doublet. He extracted a folded piece of parchment and held it out. Dana took it.

"You were in my hall. You saw the man with whom I dined," Emrys continued. "The king bade him to deliver to me that letter."

Dana unfolded the parchment and read the command to join forces with the king's men in an effort to protect the southern coast from a rebel attack.

"You're going," Dana said.

"The king commands it."

"You'll destroy your own people."

"Only if you force it," Emrys said. "Don't go south, lad."

"People will die if I don't."

"Mayhap," Emrys said, "but more will die if you do. I wasn't the only nobleman to receive that summons. It won't be a roaming band of the king's men you'll face this time. It'll be a wall of soldiers, better armed and better trained than any who follow you."

"How many noblemen?"

"More than you can handle," Emrys said. "Do yourself a favor—do those who follow you a favor—and go somewhere else. Just disappear off the face of the earth and let this conflict die."

"He'll never let that happen. He needs it too much."

"What need for such bloodshed does our king have?" Emrys asked.

Dana hadn't been speaking of Maddox, but Dana didn't know if he could tell Emrys the truth about Omur.

"You should know well of your king's need for bloodshed," Dana said. "There are rumors enough."

"And rumors they shall remain."

"Only because none survives what he does to them."

"Be that as it may," Emrys said. "He is still the king."

"For now," Dana said. "I will win this."

"Do you want the throne that badly?"

"I don't want the throne at all," Dana said. "You know that."

"Then let me ask you this: say you win your war. Who do you intend to wear the crown? The king will be dead; there won't be any way around that. Someone will have to take his place. If not you, then who?"

"The queen."

"The queen?" Emrys laughed. "Now I know you're mad. Better you than her. Better some nameless, landless bastard than—"

"Than a woman?"

"Than someone not of this land," Emrys said. "Her only tie to this country is that brat growing in her belly. That does not a ruler make."

"It isn't her only tie," Dana said. "She loves the people more than those who are of this land. You don't know what she's done to protect them. She'll surprise you if you let her."

Emrys shook his head. "I've heard rumors that she's stood against the king, but—"

"They're not rumors."

Emrys sat back in his chair. "Did you somehow involve her in this? In your war?"

Dana didn't answer.

"What did you do? God, what did you do, Dana? How did you convince her to help you? Did you seduce her? Make her fall in love with you?" Emrys asked, but Dana still did not offer an answer. "Well, whatever you've done, however you've done it, you've killed her, lad. No one who stands against our king does so for very long."

Dana looked at Emrys. "She's still standing. *I'm* still standing."

"Not for long," Emrys said. "Not if you go south."

"I'm not going to let those people suffer whatever fate he decides to thrust upon them," Dana said. "I can't—"

"You can. Of course you can. You've done it before," Emrys said. "You let the king burn Trutina to the ground so you could hold Mahile. It was the right decision then, and it's the right decision now. If you asked whoever it was who convinced you of that the last time, they would tell you the same."

"You won't help."

"I am helping," Emrys said. "You just can't see it."

Dana picked up the cup and drained it. "You're backing the wrong man."

"I have to do it, lad," Emrys said. "It's what's best for my people. They're protected this way."

"I'll—"

"Don't tell me you'll protect my people because you can't. Not the way I can," Emrys said, "and you know it."

"It's the wrong decision."

"It's the only decision," Emrys said in a tone that indicated the lord of Labhras was finished with the conversation. "You showed yourself in. You can show yourself out."

Dana nodded and rose from his chair. He left the cup on the table and walked to the doors. He had his hand on the latch when Emrys called out.

"It was good to see you, lad," Emrys said. "Truly, it was. But I hope never to see you again."

"You shouldn't follow him, Jaspaer," Dana said. "He's an evil man."

Emrys didn't look at him. "Aren't we all?"

—⁓—

Dana's decision was made when he returned to the Donasien Woods and found his people waiting there for him. Lucius stood at their head. Lorcan and Kynon—the unicorn Lucius had ridden into past battles—stood on Lucius's right. Owain stood on the left. Dana looked at them—the untested, untrained and the too young. It was a force that would barely stand a chance against Varro's men, and if Emrys was to be believed, the men waiting for them in the south would be much worse.

"Did you find what you were looking for?" Lucius asked.

"No."

"Well, at least you've come out of there alive," Lucius said. "Shall we go?"

Dana shook his head. "Change of plan."

"What happened?"

Dana jerked his head over his shoulder and walked away. Lucius followed.

"Emrys and some of the other noblemen are marching south to protect their villages against rebel attack," Dana said, pitching his voice low to keep anyone else from hearing.

"And you believe him?"

"If he wanted to harm me, he wouldn't have let me leave his keep alive," Dana said, leaning against a tree. His strength was waning faster than he thought it would. "I saw the king's letter myself, Lucius. It's true. If we continue south, it'll be a hornets' nest."

"What will happen if we don't go?"

Dana shrugged and winced as his body protested the simple movement. "Maybe nothing. I don't know. But Omur's mobilized the noblemen where he's ignored them thus far. I can't imagine he'll be satisfied letting that strength go to waste."

"If we don't meet them on the battlefield, they'll tear those villages apart looking for us. It's what they did in Cinna. It's how this whole thing began."

"Emrys will know we're not there."

"How will he explain that to the others who don't know it?"

"He'll find a way. He doesn't want harm to come to his people. He'll protect them, and he'll lose fewer men in the process. He's a good man, Lucius."

"Good men do not serve our king."

"Good men do what they must to protect their people."

"Then why is it you are preparing us to return to camp when we should be moving south to do what we can?"

Dana looked again at the people Lucius had gathered. "What can we do?"

"They didn't come to us to just sit," Lucius said.

"No, but neither do I want to sacrifice them in a fight we can't possibly win."

"Is that what we do now?" Lucius asked. "Fight only the fights we can win?"

"That's not what we do," Dana said. "We've done this before, Lucius. We let Trutina slip away because we had to, because we wanted to keep fighting. If we go south, we will lose and losing there could cost us the war as well. If we stay away, we still have hope."

"But the southerners don't."

"We don't know that. Not for sure."

"Don't we?"

"Emrys will do what he can for them," Dana said. "We're going back to camp."

"Where we'll hope for the best."

"We always do."

Lucius nodded. "It's not working as well as it used to."

Dana felt himself starting to slip and pressed his hand against his chest in an attempt to shock himself back to awareness. "I know."

Would this be another failure? Lucius thought so, and Dana would hear it in the man's voice when the others were told they had come all this way just to run away and—

Run away.

"Wait," Dana said. "There might be something we can do. Something *you* can do."

"What?"

"We run away."

"Run away?"

"Go south, aye? All of you, go south to meet this army Omur's assembled. We don't have the numbers to face them head on, but if you time it right, you don't have to. Give them something to chase, and they'll have to follow you," Dana said. "You draw them away from the villages, you lose them in the forests, and they'll have no reason to destroy anything."

Lucius nodded slowly. "They may decide they don't need a reason."

"We will have done what we can," Dana said. "Emrys will see to the rest."

"You have a lot of faith in that man."

"All of it's deserved," Dana said. "I promise you that."

"All right then," Lucius said. "We go south."

"I look forward to hearing the tales of your success."

"You don't mean to join us?"

"Not this time. I mean to crawl my way back to camp, back to my bed, and hope Hanah doesn't tell James I left it at all."

Lucius's eyes slid down to Dana's chest. "I think that would be wise."

—◦◦◦—

When he arrived back in camp, Dana went straight to his tent. He removed his sword belt, his vest and his shirt. The bandages around his chest were soaked through with blood and sweat. He was picking at them when Hanah came in.

"This is why you were meant to stay behind and rest," she said. "Not ride all over the countryside."

"To be fair, I did walk a great deal."

Hanah made a noise that indicated she didn't think him clever. "Sit down and let me have a look."

He did as she commanded. She cleaned the wound and bandaged it once more, all the while not speaking. She did not interrogate him nor harangue him. She didn't even offer him promises that he was healing nicely and would assuredly survive this injury.

"Will you rest now?" she asked when she finished.

When he nodded, she called him a good lad and left the tent. He sat a moment longer before retiring to his bedroll. He fell quickly into sleep and dreamt of Haleine. When he woke, night had fallen, and his tent was illuminated by lantern light. James sat in the chair by the table, leaning forward and looking at the ground.

"You're back, then," Dana said. "Everything all right in Lanval?"

James didn't respond. Dana pushed himself up on his elbow. James held a bottle in his hand. Dana didn't know what was in it but thought he could guess.

"James?" Dana said. "Are you all right?"

James took a drink from his bottle. "I should be asking you that."

"I'm fine. What happened in Lanval?"

James shrugged. "They came. They died."

"Better than the other way around."

James nodded and had another drink. Dana got to his feet and went to stand in front of his friend.

"Are you drunk?" he asked.

"Not yet."

"Is that your plan, then?"

"It is tonight."

Dana took the bottle and held it beneath his nose. Ale.

"What else happened in Lanval?" he asked. "Did Ilya—?"

"Ilya," James laughed. "Ilya decided to go south once Hanah told us what happened there. She requested I stay behind."

"To watch me?"

"No." James stole back the ale and had another drink. "You know, it's ridiculous of you to ask if everything was all right in Lanval. You don't have any idea how many graves were dug."

"You're right. I don't."

"Varro wasn't there," James said. "He left his men in Nechtan to go somewhere else—south, I suppose—and he wasn't there. So I killed his men instead. The ones I came across in battle, the ones who surrendered afterward. I killed them all."

"You didn't do it alone."

"It was done either at my hand or my command. There's no difference."

"That's what it is," Dana said, "to do what we do."

"To do what we do," James echoed. He looked at Dana, grunted with annoyance and stood up. "Sit down before you fall over."

Dana sank into the chair. "Maybe you should take some time and go home. Go back to Enimode and—"

"And what?"

"And remind yourself why you're doing this."

"I know why I'm doing this," James said. "Don't ever think I've forgotten that."

"I think you've forgotten there's more than what you buried that day," Dana said. "Sarai, Aaron—they survived, James, and you need to remember that. You need them to anchor you to the living. You have one foot in a grave and—"

"*I* have a foot in a grave? What about you? You and Varro are racing to see which one of you can put you in the ground first, and I honestly can't say which will succeed," James said. "Where's your anchor? *Who's* your anchor? Is it my family? Your lady's maid? You haven't been near Enimode nor Eluned for months now, so tell me who is it? What keeps you tied to the living?"

Dana gestured to the tent's entrance. "Them? You?"

"And aren't we performing admirably," James said. "If you want me to believe that, you'll need to stop trying to kill yourself."

"I'm not trying to kill myself."

"The hell you aren't." James moved in a drunken circle. "You should really get a second bloody chair in here, you know."

"I'll do that," Dana said. "Just as soon as we finish beating back the forces of darkness."

James finally sat on the ground, his elbows resting on his knees. "We'll never be finished with that. We could kill Varro, Maddox, Omur—all of them—tomorrow, and still it won't be done. Their gods would only find someone else to do their bidding."

"True," Dana said. "Still, I wouldn't mind seeing those three dead."

"No one would," James said. "Why did we ever think it wouldn't matter? That *they* wouldn't matter? Four bloody *gods* want us dead, and we didn't think it changed anything."

"*I* didn't think it changed anything," Dana said. "And, at the time, I don't think it did."

"Well, we can't say that anymore, can we?"

"No."

"How do you suppose one kills a god?"

"I don't know."

"We'll have to work it through if we're to truly end this, but I can't imagine it's easily done."

"I can't imagine that's something a person comes back from."

"Do you really think either of us will come back from this?"

"No."

James held out the bottle. "Well, at least you didn't lie about that."

Dana suddenly felt as if he'd been stabbed all over again. He forced himself to take the ale. "Lie? What lie have I told?"

"You keep claiming you're fine," James said, pointing at him. "You're not."

The rush of relief robbed him of breath, and it was some time before Dana could respond. He had some ale to calm him.

"I'm not dead," he offered.

James laughed. "It's a start."

CHAPTER 14

Before Haleine was due to deliver, her mother and sister came to Lira. The news surprised her, as she had not been aware her mother was planning a visit. There had been no letter detailing her mother's plans. The only notice came from an advance rider charged by Rhoswen to come from Eoten ahead of the carriage which carried her family. He informed Ceallach of her mother and sister's imminent arrival but had made no mention of her father. Haleine had never known her mother to travel anywhere—particularly the other side of the sea—without him.

But as curious as she was about the circumstances surrounding her mother's journey, Haleine still had little desire to see her, though that did not seem to matter to anyone other than herself, as the servants prepared the room for Lady Rhoswen's appearance. Only Haleine remained motionless as she sat by the fire considering the possibilities.

Her first instinct told her something was wrong. It was a feeling she had so often now she couldn't be sure it was connected to Rhoswen. Her second instinct chastised the first. Of course something was wrong. Nathan was dead and his empire crumbling. She'd known that would happen even before the king had died, just as she'd known her father would try to hold on to whatever he could, no matter the cost. But if her father did send Rhoswen and Sighle away because of the danger, why would he ever send them to Lira?

"Well, look at you," Rhoswen said. "I thought I would have missed it."

Haleine leaned forward as Bronagh offered a pillow to put behind her back. She could see her mother standing just inside the room. Sighle was not with her.

"Mother," Haleine said. "I did not hear you come in."

Her mother's face fell slightly at her tone. "I thank you for agreeing to see me."

"Thank the servants," Haleine said. "Had the choice been given to me, you'd still be out in the hall."

Rhoswen looked for a moment as though she meant to leave. Haleine waited, keeping her stare as flat as her greeting. Her mother finally squared her shoulders and stepped forward.

"Is it not your decision?" she asked. "You are, after all, the queen."

"That does not appear to matter today."

Rhoswen nodded. "Is it always this busy in your private chambers?"

Haleine looked at Bronagh. The maid bowed and called for the others to depart. Rhoswen waited for the room to clear before coming to sit across from her daughter.

"They prepare for your visit," Haleine said. "They are nervous in the face of such nobility. It is, after all, not often we receive such esteemed guests on such short notice."

"I know. I do apologize for that."

Haleine laughed. "You apologize for that?"

"Haleine—"

"Where is Sighle? Ceallach said she arrived with you."

"She did. She wanted to see the castle. She is anxious to see this place her sister calls home," Rhoswen said. "I let her go, thinking it best that I first see you alone."

"And Father? Where is he?"

"He could not come."

"You have taken to traveling alone?"

Rhoswen looked down at the floor. "I wanted to see my grand-child, regardless of your father's impossible commitments."

"But you did not want to see your daughter married."

"You have changed, Haleine," her mother said. "I have never heard cynicism from your lips before."

"My marriage to Maddox has made me many things I never was. Cynical is the least of them."

Rhoswen rose to pour herself some wine. Haleine watched her and didn't speak until her mother had returned to her chair.

"What is wrong?" she asked. "Why are you here?"

Rhoswen set down her goblet and smiled. "I think you have made me a grandmother twice over. I swear you carry twins."

Haleine grimaced and shifted her position. "The midwives believe it to be a strong, healthy son, a fitting heir for my husband."

"Oh, there will be a son, but he won't be alone."

"Mother, I am tired, and I do not wish to play this game with you. Tell me what is wrong."

"Why do you think something is wrong?"

"I know the consequences of Nathan's death as well as any," Haleine said, checking Faolan's whereabouts. He was asleep on her bed. "Tell me what has happened. How bad is it?"

"Quatara is in a terrible state. It is why your father sent us here. Haraszty is a good queen, but still Tanuba's hold is slipping more each day."

"Father has not changed."

"No, but other things have. Haraszty is not her husband, and there are those, both within her court and out of it, who seek to challenge her. Your father, Prince Revelin and Lord Cathal are doing all they can to keep her on the throne, but there is still resistance. Prince Zoltano has retreated to his fortress in the north, and no one knows what he does there—"

"Scheming against his mother, no doubt."

"Haleine!"

"If you think he will not seek to undermine her, you are a fool," Haleine said. "She sits on the throne that should be his, and Zoltano does not stand for others to have what belongs to him."

"You speak of his mother."

"Yes, such a sacred bond," Haleine said. "Why did Father send you and Sighle here? Did he forget Lira is in the midst of her own war?"

"He did not forget. He didn't want to send us here. I demanded it."

"Why would you ever demand such a thing?"

"Because you are my daughter," Rhoswen said. "No matter what you may feel for me, that will not change. I have always tried to hold this family together as best I can, and that meant coming here to you. You may refuse any further audience with me if it is your wish. I ask only that you do not do the same to your sister."

Haleine shifted her position again. The pillow was not helping. "I have no reason to do the same to her."

"I know you don't," Rhoswen said. "You're uncomfortable. I can see that, and I will leave you to rest. Should I help you to the bed? Or call your maids?"

"Neither," Haleine said. "Just go."

As soon as Rhoswen had left, Haleine reached behind her and removed the pillow. She turned as best she could and threw the pillow at Faolan. She didn't hit him, but she came close. It was enough to startle him awake. He looked first at the pillow and then at her.

"What are you doing?" he asked.

"Trying to wake you."

"I wasn't sleeping," he said as he flew over to her.

"Then you heard what she said?"

He landed on the arm of the chair across from her. "You're probably right about Zoltano."

"Probably?" she asked. It seemed more likely than that. "Why do you still hide things from me?"

"What are you talking about?"

"You do it all the time. You know I'm right about Zoltano, yet you won't say it. You—"

"How can you think I hide things from you? You know more about the causes of this war than most of the people fighting at Dana's side."

"Why don't they know?"

"They don't need to know. They don't want to know. They're fighting Maddox for what's been done to their families and homes. Laorans and the dark gods are meaningless to them."

"I envy them that," she said. "What do you suppose will happen in Quatara?"

"Nothing good."

"And Tanuba? Will she fall as well?"

"I imagine so."

"Why is there no help there?" Haleine asked. "You, your goddess, your unicorns, you fight to save Lira, you fight to stop the chaos, yet across the ocean it reigns unchecked. Why?"

"Because it doesn't matter," Faolan said. "Lira's the center of it all. Tanuba, Quatara—they're just distractions. We let them burn because we must."

"Revelin could save Tanuba."

"Revelin probably could."

"You don't think he will?"

"I don't know. Last time I saw him, he seemed more concerned with saving you."

"I don't need saving," she said. "Even if I did, that's why you're here, isn't it?"

"It is. But I don't think he knows that."

She nodded. "And I can't tell him."

"Well, you could, but he wouldn't believe it any more than he believed anything else you told him."

She sighed. "I am right about Zoltano though, aren't I?"

"Why don't you let me worry about that," Faolan said. "And while we're at it, let me worry about everything else, too. I can't imagine it's doing you any good. You should rest. You look exhausted."

She imagined she looked much worse than that, but there was no help for it. It would be a good long while before she felt otherwise. She didn't want to sleep. If she did, she would dream. And if she dreamt, there would be Dana.

There were still visions of him in battle, in some he was wounded, in others not. The man in his black cloak was there, fighting Dana as he had before. Their duel never finished before she woke, but even so, that was not the cruelest vision.

No, her most malicious dream didn't involve a battle of any sort. There were no weapons, no blood, just her and Dana and their son on a perfect summer's day. The boy was young and beautiful, blond and blue-eyed like his father. Dana had placed the child upon a pony and was teaching the boy to ride. She sat under a canopy protecting her from the sun and watched the lesson. The pony broke into a trot, and the child swayed but kept his seat. She called for them to be careful. Dana laughed and glanced at her over his shoulder, his grin as wide as the ocean.

"Haleine? Are you all right?"

She jerked out of the memory and brushed the tears off her cheeks. Faolan looked at her, his concern obvious. She hated him in that moment.

"I am fine."

"Do you need—something? Someone?"

How could he even ask the question? She needed Dana. She needed him to stand in front of her so she could rail at him—*scream* at him—for making her love him. She found it agonizing to love someone she hated. It was just as unbearable as hating someone she loved.

"Do you speak often with Dana?" she asked.

"He's all right."

"That's not what I asked. Do you speak with him?"

"Not directly. I contact one of the unicorns who gets a message to him."

She nodded. "Then tell him of how much I hate him."

As he was too great a coward to face her, it would have to do.

"Haleine? Are you sure you—?"

"Aye," she said. "Tell him that."

—◊◊◊—

The first time Dana had found his way to Enimode, he was five years old. He was hardly a green lad—or so he thought—because he had taken care of himself so well. He and Faolan had spent the day exploring the village, taking care to avoid attracting attention. That night, a storm drove them to seek shelter in a barn on the very outskirts of town. Dana slept in the loft, submerged in a pile of loose hay to keep hidden and warm.

Normally, Faolan would make sure he was awake well before the sun rose, but that morning after the rain, Dana was still asleep when Seoras found him.

"What have we here?" Seoras asked.

"So sorry, sir," Dana said. "The storm—"

"Have you a name, lad?"

"I am called Dana, sir."

"And to whom do you belong, Dana?"

"None but myself, sir."

"Your father? Mother?"

"My mother is dead," Dana said.

"And your father?"

Dana shrugged. If he had a living father, it was unknown to him.

Seoras nodded. "You're on your own, then."

"No," Dana said. "I've got Faolan."

"And who is that?"

Dana looked around the loft and spotted the pegasus perched on one of the barn's beams. He pointed and Seoras turned.

"That's Faolan," Dana said.

Seoras looked at the pegasus a long time. Dana fidgeted.

"I'll just go, sir," he said finally. "Sorry for—"

"Go where?" Seoras asked, looking at him again.

Dana shrugged a second time. "Don't know. Won't know until I get there."

"I see," Seoras said. "Well, why don't you come inside the house and let my wife feed you before you go."

"I can feed myself."

"I don't doubt it, lad," Seoras said. "Still, come and eat."

"Aye, all right," Dana said. "But then I'm going."

Seoras nodded again and put his hands on Dana's shoulders to guide him to the loft's ladder.

"As you like," Seoras said.

But Dana hadn't left after breakfast. Instead he allowed Sarai and Mahree to fuss over him, helped James with chores and spent some time playing with an infant Aaron in his cradle. He stayed so long that Seoras suggested he stay the night and set out in the morning. Dana agreed, but he didn't leave the next day either. He didn't leave the homestead for months, and when he finally did return to the woods, he left with an unmistakable pull that guaranteed he wouldn't be gone for long.

Each time he returned, he used the main road, greeting, and being greeted by, Enimode's residents as though he lived each day among them. The very last time was the day he came to steal James for the goddess's cause. Mahree had welcomed him with a wide smile and open arms. Would she still have done so if she'd known what hell her foundling lad would bring to her family? Would she still have smiled to see him approaching on the road?

It didn't matter now. Those days were gone. Now Dana stood in the woods and watched the house as he waited for the sunset. He didn't know how closely Omur watched the village and couldn't risk being seen. When it was dark enough, he left the trees and crossed the yard. As he passed the barn, a light caught his eye and he changed direction to see who was there.

Upon entering, he had just enough time to register the sight of Aaron working with a sword by lantern light. The boy whirled around, swinging his weapon in a wide, uncontrolled arc. Dana drew the dagger on his belt and met the blow. Sparks flew as the blades clashed and Aaron froze, his face a study in shocked surprise. They studied each other while Aaron regained his composure. Eventually, Aaron lowered his blade, and Dana followed his lead.

"How did you know I wasn't Sarai?" Dana asked, returning the dagger to his belt.

Aaron shrugged and returned to his practicing. "Her step is different. Lighter."

Dana nodded. "Where did you get the sword?"

"Not all of those bastards lived," Aaron said. "Are you alone?"

"Aye."

The answer angered Aaron. He swung his sword at the post with such force, it stuck in the wood. Aaron lost his grip on the weapon and staggered back.

"He's not been back since..."

Aaron's voice trailed off, but Dana knew how the sentence would have finished. James hadn't been back since Seoras and Mahree had been laid to rest. Dana knew.

"Aye," he said.

Neither of them had anything to say after that. Aaron removed the sword from the post and continued to practice his strokes and placement. They were clumsy and unrefined attempts, but the determination was there. It would seem both of Seoras's sons had talent.

"What are you doing here?" Aaron asked as he worked.

"Came to see that you and Sarai were all right."

"We'd be better if you'd just stay away," Aaron said. "Why do you keep coming here? Why did you ever come here?"

"A storm," Dana answered. "There was a storm."

Dana glanced up at the loft and found himself looking at the stars.

"Do you not have what you need?" he asked.

Aaron jerked to a halt and gave him a hard look. Dana pointed to the damage above their heads. Aaron relaxed then, but only marginally, and lowered the sword. He wiped his arm across his forehead and shrugged.

"We've been working in town mostly where the worst damage was done," he said. "All things considered, this is nothing. We were—we were lucky."

It killed Aaron to utter that sentence. Who wanted to believe a day that had brought such loss could ever be thought of as fortunate? Certainly Dana did not.

"You've got some natural talent with that blade," he said. "And the motivation to harness it."

"Strange how watching your parents die on a blade motivates you to learn to use one."

"Maybe not so strange," Dana said. "Are there others like you? Others trying to learn?"

"We won't be defenseless again," Aaron said. "We won't be unaware again. Those men came here because of you once. They'll do it again."

"I'll stay away," Dana said immediately. "If that's what you want, I'll leave, and I'll not come back."

Aaron considered this. "It's not what I want. Besides, Gran would miss you. Have you seen her yet?"

Dana shook his head. "Got distracted by the light."

"Well, come on. She'll be glad to see you."

"Will she?" Dana asked. "I'm the reason why—"

"We don't abandon the ones we love," Aaron said. "That's what she says. You can have every reason to do just that, but you don't. You stay and you—"

"He didn't abandon you," Dana said.

"Aye," Aaron said. "That's why you're standing here and he's not."

"You shouldn't be so quick to pass judgment," Dana said. "I've done my share of abandoning."

"Someone you love?"

"Aye."

"Then fix it."

"Is it that simple?"

"I don't know," Aaron said, "but there's only one way to know for sure."

"And if your brother were standing here in my place," Dana said, "would you still be speaking calmly? Would you open your arms to him? Would you forgive him? Or would you not be standing here at all?"

Aaron looked at the ground and Dana nodded.

"That's what I thought," he said. "James will come back, Aaron. When he can, he'll come back. It's unfair, I know, to ask you to wait and to give him more time, but if you can do it, you should."

Aaron laughed quietly and lifted his head. "Who tells that to the one you abandoned?"

"I can't imagine anyone does any more," Dana said. "If they ever did."

"Maybe it should be you saying it."

"Maybe," Dana said. He knew Aaron was right, but he didn't want to imagine what Haleine might do should he show himself again. "Well, shall we go to the house? We're keeping Sarai waiting and, if I remember correctly, she hates it when we do that."

Aaron nodded and walked past Dana. He leaned his sword against the wall and continued on to the door.

"You're not bringing the sword with you?" Dana asked.

Aaron shook his head. "She doesn't like it in the house."

"No, I guess she wouldn't," Dana said. "But if you don't wish to be caught unaware—"

"There's always someone in the church now," Aaron said, "in the steeple, keeping watch. If they see anything, they'll ring the bells, and we'll know. We'll be ready."

"Good lad," Dana said although Aaron was far from being a child now.

Aaron looked Dana in the eye. "I won't run away the next time."

"Are you so sure there will be a next time?"

"Aren't you?"

Dana glanced at the stars again. "As anything."

⁓

The night her labor began, Haleine sat beside her husband in the dining hall. She had come against the advice of her midwives, but at the request of her husband who wanted all to see his wife's enormous belly. She had been uncomfortable and miserable all day and now had little appetite of which to speak. She pushed the food on her trencher around to pass the time until she received permission to retire.

Faolan stood on the table at her right side, and she stopped toying with the food when she realized he wasn't paying attention to either her or Omur. Instead he gazed out into the crowd in front of them, his head tilted slightly. He saw something unexpected. She looked up but saw nothing. Then she glanced quickly at Omur to see if he had taken notice of Faolan's interest.

She barely had laid eyes upon him when the pain started. It was so sharp and sudden that she lurched forward, clutching her stomach with one hand and grabbing hold of Maddox's arm with the other. Her husband broke off in mid-sentence and looked at her.

"The babe?" he asked.

She couldn't speak, so she nodded and released his arm, hating the impulse that had made her reach for him at all. Faolan looked at her now, as did everyone in the hall. Maddox motioned to the midwives, and they, followed by her mother, came forth.

She felt a hand under her elbow and knew it belonged to Willem. When the contraction had passed, she nodded, and he lifted her gently and helped her out of the hall. Maddox stayed behind, calling for a toast.

The midwives and her mother shooed both Willem and Faolan away at the entrance of the birthing chamber. Haleine wanted to protest Rhoswen's presence but lacked the strength to argue and let her mother stand close to whisper whatever encouragement she wanted.

The midwives stripped Haleine of her gown and dressed her in a simple linen shift. Bronagh came with Sabine and Nonna, carrying swaddling cloths and other supplies. Bronagh put down her basket and came to Haleine's side to help her onto the bed. As soon as she was down, Bronagh twisted her hand free from Haleine's grip and walked away.

"Stay," Haleine gasped when she saw her maid meant to go.

Bronagh froze.

"My daughter, your queen, has asked you to stay," Rhoswen said. "Will you deny her?"

Bronagh shook her head and curtsied. She dismissed Sabine and Nonna, returned to the bed and stood opposite Rhoswen. She held out her hand and Haleine gripped it gratefully.

"Thank you," she mouthed and Bronagh nodded.

The labor continued throughout the night and into the next day. Haleine walked when she was directed to, rested when permission was granted, drank when a cup was held to her lips and screamed when a contraction's intensity demanded it. Rhoswen never left her side, never rested, simply held her daughter's hand and kept up a continuous stream of encouragement. Bronagh said very little, but Haleine didn't mind. It was enough that the maid remained.

It was well past midday when her mother's prophecy proved correct and the first of her sons was born. His lusty cries broke the tension in the air. Haleine cried and fell back against her pillows. Her mother kissed the top of her head. Bronagh wiped the perspiration from her face.

"My lady," the midwife said. "You have a son, a beautiful son."

Haleine only caught a glimpse of the child as he was passed off to the second midwife to be cleaned. She was about to demand he be passed to her when the pains began again as his brother pushed his own way into the world.

When it was done, Haleine was beyond exhausted, but her exhilaration kept her awake, and, as soon as she had been cleaned and dressed in fresh clothing, she beckoned to the servants standing over the cradle where her sons lay.

"I will see my sons," she said. "Bring them here."

Her eyes welled at the sight of them. They were tiny and perfect, each with a promising sprout of flaxen hair. It would darken as they grew older, the midwife said, but Haleine was not so sure.

She asked to hold them, and carefully the children were transferred to her arms.

It was a mistake to hold them, she knew, and she hadn't intended on it. They'd be brought to the wet nurse soon, as soon as Maddox had made his inspection, and her role in their life would be done. Everything then would be a formality. She would be a stranger to them, so she hadn't planned to hold them, hadn't wanted to give herself a chance to love them. It was too late now, she realized as she lowered her head to be even closer to them. She'd already lost her heart.

"What will you name them?" the midwife asked.

Haleine shook her head. The first born would be called Alain, she knew, as Maddox had decided his son's name months ago. She didn't know what the other would be called but would have no say in the decision. Maddox would never grant her such a gift as the naming of his heir, even a second son.

The first, Alain, opened his eyes, and the women surrounding the bed cooed and sighed. Haleine's breath caught at the sight of the blue eyes looking back at her. She had only ever seen those eyes, those azure eyes, in one man.

And that man was not her husband. She tore her eyes away from her sons as Maddox entered the chamber. He swaggered in his usual drunken manner, demanding to see his boys. The midwives took them from her arms. Haleine watched as Dana's children were presented to the man she could only hope would claim them as his own. He asked for the firstborn, and Alain was offered to him. Maddox held the infant and looked the boy over.

"Alain, my son. Such golden hair," he muttered, and Haleine closed her eyes. "I wouldn't have thought—"

"Oh, it will darken, my lord king," Rhoswen interrupted.

Haleine opened her eyes to look at her mother.

"I remember when your lady wife was born," Rhoswen continued. "She was so blond one would have thought she was a changeling. It did not last, and neither will theirs, my lord."

Maddox seemed to consider this. Haleine did not know if the story was true, and judging by the look her mother wore, she thought it a falsehood but did not question it, as Maddox merely nodded and handed Alain back to the waiting midwife. Haleine gasped in relief and was not the only one who did so. She looked at Bronagh still standing to her right, but the maid refused to return her look.

"Would your majesty like to see the other?" the midwife holding her second-born ventured. "This son still requires a name."

Maddox looked at the swaddled infant in her arms and waved a dismissive hand. "Auryn," he said. "Take them to the nurse."

The midwives bowed as Maddox, strutting worse than before, left the chamber. Haleine paid him little mind, focusing more on her sons as they were carried out behind him. She cried out and leaned forward, reaching for them. Bronagh's hand clapped onto her wrist and pushed her arm back down.

"You must rest now, your majesty," she said. "You'll need your strength for what's to come."

Haleine looked at Bronagh's hand for a moment before raising her eyes. She saw what was there and nodded.

———

When Haleine's labor began, Faolan had been staring at Dana. The rebel leader had placed himself at a far table in the dining hall and was cavorting and eating and drinking with the king's retainers. Periodically he cast a glance to the head table, and the merriment faded for the shortest of moments. Faolan was certain Dana saw nothing but Haleine and had no idea just how irritated Faolan was.

But then Haleine bent over in pain, and Faolan thought no more about it. He followed the slow-moving procession to the birthing chamber, and, when Willem was left out in the hall, he perched on the guard's shoulder to wait.

They remained there throughout the night. Faolan thought Willem remained out of habit, but when his replacements arrived, Willem sent them away. He never moved from his spot, never moved at all except to tense whenever Haleine screamed. Faolan never expected much from humans, really liking only a select few, but had to admit that Willem was one of the good ones.

Faolan was pleased Willem was among Haleine's first line of defense. He'd hate to lose the guard for any reason. Omur remained the most immediate threat. To make a run at Haleine, Omur would have to dispatch the guard one way or another, but the truth remained that the mage had never given Willem even the smallest of glances.

Faolan considered the possibility that he had been wrong, that Omur wasn't interested in harming Haleine, but as well as he could accept his mistake, Faolan couldn't dismiss Omur's face. Haleine had done something to infuriate Omur. What kept him from acting?

Even as he thought it, Faolan knew it was a question easily answered. The dark gods kept Omur from acting. The mage would only take action upon their bidding. His own desires were non-existent, as he would want to carry out the wishes of his lords at all costs. If Faolan was right and they prevented their servant from touching Haleine, that would mean they had some use for her.

He couldn't even guess what that use might be. At Laorans's request, he had spies everywhere, in this world and others, searching for information. He thought searching the other worlds was a waste of time and resources because he was certain there was only one thing of value in only one other world, and they already knew where that was. But he followed his mistress's orders anyway, making him in that way the same as Omur.

The most promising lead yet came out of Quatara, just as he thought it might. There was rumor of an ancient prophecy there. Faolan did not know what the prophecy foretold, but he pushed the goddess's agents to discover more. Nothing had been found yet, so Faolan waited and stood guard alongside Willem.

Faolan was still perched on the man's shoulder when Bronagh came out to tell Willem all was well. She glared at the pegasus and chided Willem for having stayed in the hall the entire time.

"And what would you have me do?" Willem asked softly.

She sighed and frowned at Faolan again. "Nothing different," she said. "I have to get back. When your replacements arrive next time, don't send them away."

Willem nodded and Bronagh left. Maddox arrived shortly after she had done so, Omur skulking behind him. Both Faolan and Willem tensed at their approach, and only Faolan relaxed slightly when Maddox entered the chamber alone. Omur stood a good distance away, but Faolan didn't take his eyes off him.

"Two sons!" Maddox crowed as he reemerged. "Two excellent sons!"

"That is most fortunate, my lord," Omur said, shooting Faolan a lethal look before following Maddox away.

As soon as Omur's back was turned, Faolan set to work creating a barrier to protect Haleine's chamber. Omur's step hesitated as the mage undoubtedly felt the spell he wove, but he didn't challenge it, and Faolan didn't stop. The shield wasn't much and wouldn't hold up to a serious attack, but it would alert him if any attempts were made.

Once Faolan was convinced his shield would hold, he returned to the hall. The room was darkened, lit only by a few torches and the fire pit in the center of the room. The atmosphere was loud, ringing with music, both sung and strummed. Faolan wondered if there had been any break at all in the revelry. People danced and shouted and laughed and celebrated the king's good fortune. Men coupled with women against shadowed walls. Dana was not among any of them. Faolan finally found him in a window alcove half-hidden by a banner knocked askew.

"Shouldn't you be elsewhere?" Faolan asked.

"No," Dana said. "Is she all right?"

Faolan glanced at the commotion. "You didn't hear the news?"

"They said the king has two sons. Two excellent sons. They said nothing about her."

"Well, she's fine. She's resting now," Faolan said. "What are you doing here?"

"I would have thought it obvious."

"It would have been obvious nine months ago."

Dana sighed. "I had to see her again."

"I'm not sure she wants to be seen," Faolan said, remembering the message Haleine had asked him to deliver. He hadn't done it. "At least not by you."

"She's angry with me."

"Yes."

"I saw her reach for him," Dana said. "She didn't—she's not—"

"Don't be tiresome. She was in labor. It was involuntary," Faolan said. "What are you doing here? Shouldn't you be out fighting a war?"

"Not tonight."

"I want you to leave now. You shouldn't be here in this hall. It's too much of a risk."

Dana shook his head. "Do you forget I am untouchable?"

"You won't always be."

"No," Dana agreed, "but I am tonight."

"I'm not sure about that."

"I'm still here, aren't I?"

"Yes, and herein lies the problem. I can forgive some of it. You weren't in Mairéad and you didn't see what I saw there."

"And neither did you tell me what you saw there."

"I'm telling you now. You didn't see Omur's face when Haleine's pregnancy was announced," Faolan said. "The birth of those boys has changed everything."

"Has Omur tried to hurt her?"

"No."

"But you think he will?"

"I do. I expected him to try sooner," Faolan said. "I was wrong, but I won't always be. He'll try. Sooner or later, he'll try. I know it."

"You know it, and you left her unprotected?"

"No," Faolan said. "You should leave now. You can't see her tonight. She's exhausted, and she needs to rest."

"And what are you? Her nurse?"

"Now you're being churlish," Faolan said. "Don't."

"I have as much right to be here as Maddox," Dana said. "Those children could be mine."

Faolan had yet to see Haleine's sons but didn't think he needed to in order to guess who had fathered them. Still, he didn't hesitate.

"They're not."

Dana was so absolutely still that, for a moment, Faolan wasn't sure he had been heard. Then Dana's eyes started to glisten, and he looked away.

"I'm sorry," Faolan said.

Dana nodded and even smiled. "We knew they weren't likely to be," he said. "I should go."

"Yes, you should."

"Will she ever speak to me again?"

"I don't know," Faolan said. "I really don't."

"I shall have to ask her."

"But not tonight."

Dana nodded again. "No. Not tonight."

―⁓―

He waited nearly three weeks.

Dana did not move from the shadows of her room as he watched her. She was restless, pacing as though she were missing something. She finally settled at her vanity and unraveled the braids wrapped around her head.

He wanted to do that for her. He wanted to feel her hair in his hands. He wanted to be close to her again, the urge as strong as it ever had been, but still he stayed hidden. They were not alone yet. Faolan had known of Dana's intention to come and was now scarce, but Bronagh was still there, attending her queen as always, and Dana did not wish to reveal himself while the maid remained.

Haleine finished with her hair, content to leave it loose and about her face like a lion's mane. She called to Bronagh and asked for help undressing. He looked at the gown she wore and wondered what event she had attended. The ceremonies for her sons had been numerous, as there was much to celebrate. He had spent what time he could standing among the crowds waiting to catch a glimpse of her as she moved between the palace and the cathedral. Everyone wanted to honor the princes. Dana wanted only to win back their mother.

His opportunity came when Bronagh finally departed, leaving him alone with Haleine. He waited until she was walking toward the fire before stepping out of the shadows. His throat was raw as he went to speak to her.

"I had almost forgotten how beautiful you are," he said.

She whirled around and stared. When he stepped forward, she immediately moved away. He stopped and waited.

"I must say I was not expecting to see you," she said.

She could have been conversing with a servant for all the emotion there was in her voice.

"I know I've been gone a long time," he said.

"Yes," she said. "What has kept you away?"

Her question caught him by surprise. She was well aware of the war. She would have heard of each and every battle, and he knew Faolan had said nothing of their conversation on the balcony. He managed a smile and walked forward. This time she didn't move.

"Your husband," he answered. "You are well?"

"Well enough. Your followers?"

"Still alive," he said. "Your maid? Is she still as enamored with me as before?"

She nodded. "Bronagh's mood has improved dramatically with your absence."

"And which would you prefer? Me or a cheerful maid?"

"There is no contest."

She couldn't decide if she wanted to be angry. Her face might have given nothing away, but her voice betrayed her. Faolan had warned him.

"I live with Bronagh day in and day out," Haleine continued, "while you, sir, only come when you see fit. I found her change of mood most welcome."

So anger won out. He couldn't begrudge her that. All he could do was ride out the storm and see what damage was done, then hope to find something in the wreckage to salvage.

"I was fighting your husband."

"Oh yes, I am aware of that. I live that every day of my life. Do not dismiss me as a fool."

"I don't," he said. "I'm sorry. I meant—"

"Don't tell me what you meant," she said as she moved to sit by the fire. "It is a waste of breath, for I already know the truth."

"And what truth is that?"

"If I had not become pregnant, you would not have stayed away so long."

"No," he said. "No, that's not true. The war—"

"Yes," she interrupted. "The war was most convenient, wasn't it?"

"I don't always have a choice, Haleine."

"No, I suppose not," she said. "But you did that night."

"What night?" He feared the answer.

"Why do you ask when you already know? What other night could there be?" she asked. "You stood on my balcony. You thought I was asleep and, for a time, I was. But you shouted, you see, and I awoke. You said you wished to be free of me."

He didn't offer a response right away. He didn't know what to say. How could he ask her to try and understand what he had done? He crossed the room and sat across from her. They had sat like this before, but never had he been afraid to look at her.

"I couldn't bear it," he said at last.

She looked at him now. The expression she wore was terrible.

"The children," she said.

"Aye, the children. *His* children. He'll raise them to hunt and hate me. They'll spend their lives trying to kill me if I should live that long," he said. "And you are their mother."

She took her time answering. He didn't know what she was thinking, for her face still revealed nothing.

"Aye," she said. "You punish me for that which is not my fault."

Again, he was speechless. He looked at the floor instead of her eyes. She stood and walked away to stand in front of the balcony doors.

"I've failed you, I know," he said.

"Do you think that is the proper word?"

"That is what I did," he said. "And I am sorry for it."

He thought he heard her laugh, but the sound was so faint he couldn't be sure.

"So long as you're sorry," she said. "Why did you come here?"

"I came for you."

"I thought you wanted to be free of me."

"I was wrong."

She nodded. "I see."

He stood. "I don't know what Faolan might have told you but—"

"Faolan said nothing of the truth behind your absence. He defended you always, even though he claimed he wouldn't. You should thank him when you see him again."

"Should I?"

"He didn't know I overheard you. I didn't tell him."

"Haleine—"

"Release me."

Her voice was so soft he almost didn't hear her. He took a step forward.

"What?" he breathed.

"Release me."

Her voice was stronger now. She turned to face him, and he stopped, suddenly stunned.

"I am married, and you are my husband's enemy," she said. "We can do this no longer. We were fools to do what we have done. You must release me."

"No," he said. "No, I won't."

"You must."

"I will do anything," he said. "I'll do anything you want, but please, Haleine, just don't ask me to—"

"Leave," she said. "Faolan may stay or go as he pleases. If he remains, I shall continue to do what I can to aid your cause, but I shall have no more contact with you."

Each word was said so carefully. She must have rehearsed it, repeating each word over and over again until it was perfect.

"You wanted to be free of me," she continued, "and I need to be free of you. So please, I ask that if you ever cared for me, release me now."

There was nothing for him to do but leave. Not when she put it like that. If he ever cared for her, he would leave. What else could he do? He began backing away.

"I'll—I'll go, then."

She watched him. He thought he saw tears forming in her eyes, but she blinked and they were gone. He hesitated in front of the servants' passage, hoping that she would call out, praying she would ask him to stop.

But she said nothing. Dana closed his eyes in anguish and left.

CHAPTER 15

The final celebration of the birth of Prince Alain and Prince Auryn was a feast, followed by a ball, held when the twins were two months of age to allow Lira's most valued allies—the royal families of both Tanuba and Feond—to attend. The event itself was the most elaborate gala thrown in Lira since Haleine's wedding. It rivaled even those hosted by the queen of Tanuba. Haleine knew this because a joyful Haraszty was in attendance and had told her so.

Haleine sat on her throne on its raised dais as the festivities played out before her. Dancing, feasting, singing, laughing—she had no interest in any of it, so instead she watched Haraszty, with Rhoswen at her heels, weave her way through the throngs of people. Haleine sat straighter when the queen of Tanuba stopped to greet Zaide Romanza who, Haleine realized, was talking with Omur. What business would Feond's princess have with the king of Lira's advisor?

"Your majesty."

Haleine reluctantly looked away to see Revelin standing in front of her. He had come along with his mother though Haleine doubted the trip had been made willingly. They had avoided each other thus far, but what else were they to do? His appearance now was a surprise, but she offered first a smile and then her hand. He took it.

"All this fuss for the birth of two boys and yet," he said, "nothing have I seen to celebrate the birth of their mother."

She had forgotten she was now in her nineteenth year. How strange that he should remember.

"Do you celebrate the birth of a broodmare?" she asked. "I hadn't been aware."

Her smile faltered as he brought her hand to his mouth.

"It is done," she whispered as he brushed his lips across her skin. "What you asked of me. I told him I'd not see him again."

Revelin kissed her hand again and squeezed it slightly before he released it.

"Do you not dance, your majesty?"

She shook her head. "I have not been asked."

Nor did she imagine she would. She had no one with which to dance. At court, she was viewed as Maddox's and Maddox's alone. No one but him would ever ask, and Maddox was no longer in attendance. Her husband had made a brief appearance earlier in the evening but had disappeared quickly. She had not yet discerned which of her ladies or maids had disappeared with him.

"With all due respect, your majesty, I doubt any have dared to ask," Revelin said. "You have not appeared at all approachable this evening."

Her smile disappeared. It had been more than a month since she had seen Dana last. He had done as she asked and stayed away, allowing Faolan and his messenger to be her only links to the rebellion. Sending Dana away had been necessary—she *knew* it was—but the wound was still fresh. Despite everything, she still found herself questioning if she truly wanted to be apart from him. She was thankful he had not fought her when she asked him to go. She didn't know if she would have been able to resist him.

"You dare," she said.

"I do," Revelin said. "A dance, then?"

She placed her hand in his once more. He led her to the floor where everything—the dancers and musicians included—stopped. Apparently Revelin had not been the only one to sense her melancholy. Haleine waited, but no one moved.

"Perhaps, my lord prince, we shall have to provide our own music if we wish to dance," she said.

He smiled. "I do not think that will be necessary."

Revelin gestured to the musicians and they immediately began to play. Their chosen tune belonged to a dance that had been her favorite before her marriage, before she had ever come to Lira. It had always been popular in Haraszty's court, and Haleine couldn't count the number of times she had partnered with Revelin for it. They would start out together and when their pattern was complete, Haleine would move to her right and perform the next sequence with the next partner. The dance continued until each woman was returned to the arms of the man with which she had begun.

It was a boisterous dance, loud and joyful, and it was a reminder of all things past and lost. It was something of which Haleine wanted no part, but when Revelin bowed to her, she curtsied in return.

She had gone through three partners and was moving on to the fourth when she came face to face with Dana. She stopped short and stared. His hair had changed from blond to brown. He had not shaved in several days, and his commoner's clothing had been replaced by the attire of a nobleman. He didn't look much like himself. He looked as though he belonged here in this room full of nobility, but she knew it was him.

He grabbed her arms and started the dance. She fell into place readily and completed the steps without thinking, unable to take her eyes off him. What was he doing here?

"I have thought on your terms," he murmured, "and found them unacceptable."

Terms? She had offered him terms? She couldn't breathe. Why did he always do this to her? Leave her breathless, burning, yearning like this? Why did she let him? What was wrong with her?

"I'll not release you," he continued, taking her hand and kissing her palm. "Do you understand? Ask of me what you will. Call for my life if you want it, my soul is yours, but I'll not release you. You are mine."

She closed her eyes and shook her head. She opened her mouth to tell him that despite her treacherous body, she wasn't his and she didn't want him, but the lies would not form before their moment ended. Her eyes opened as Dana passed her on to the next man. She watched him spin another woman in his arms, doing so for as long as the dance allowed. He showed none of his gravity now. He laughed and smiled at his new partner. His grin was dazzling. It always was.

She didn't know how she made it through the remainder of the dance. She had stepped on more than one foot, and it was with relief that she was returned to Revelin. The music came to its end, and she curtsied to him once more. Spectators and participants broke into applause and cheered for more. Haleine did neither. She searched the room for Dana.

"Are you all right?" Revelin asked.

Dana was working his way through the crowd. He was leaving.

"Your majesty?"

"What?" Haleine asked.

"Are you all right?" Revelin repeated. "You seem flushed."

"Do I?" she asked, feeling her cheeks. "Perhaps I should retire for the evening. The night has been most—most exhilarating after all."

"Are you sure you are all right?"

She smiled at him. "I am."

Revelin pursed his lips and nodded. "I shall escort you to your chambers."

"No," she said.

Her protest was too abrupt, and Revelin's face creased with the affront. She placed her hand on his cheek and continued with a softer tone.

"There's really no need for you to bother with it. I have my guards. They'll see me safely there."

"It is no bother."

"I didn't mean that," she said. "Thank you for the dance, my lord prince."

"Always," Revelin said, taking her hand so he could kiss it again. "You know this."

She squeezed his hand before letting him go and walking out of the ballroom. When she reached her chambers, she dismissed Willem and the other guard at the entrance and slipped inside.

Dana waited across the room, but she lingered by the doors. Her fingertips rested on the wood, anchoring her there though she knew full well she should leave, that she should go and find a place where he could not follow. She looked at him, loving and hating him at the same time, while her damn heart thudded against her chest.

"You shouldn't be here," she said, her voice scarcely more than a whisper.

"I came anyway."

She nodded and moved forward. He met her in the center of the room and pulled her close. She leaned into him, her fingers curling around his clothing, and closed her eyes.

"I'm sorry," he said, his lips against her forehead. "I'm sorry. I'm sorry."

Tears pricked at her eyes as her skin absorbed his words.

"I'm sorry," he said. "I never should have—"

She brought her head up and kissed him. She didn't need to hear more. She didn't want to hear more. She already knew what he never should have done, just as she knew what she never should have done. His words didn't matter. She was already damned, her fate determined by his eyes and sealed with his kiss.

But she didn't care.

That one kiss led to a second and a third and then more, each one more ardent than the last. It was her reawakening; it was her swan song. In his arms she was healed; in his arms she was poisoned. She was—

"What is this? Haleine, what are you doing?"

Revelin. She broke away from Dana and spun to see the prince standing before opened doors.

"Revelin," she said. "What are you—what are you doing here?"

He did not answer. He looked only at Dana as he closed the doors. He drew his sword and started forward. She shook her head and spread her arms out to either side.

"No," she said. "You're not going to do this."

"Haleine, move out of the way," Dana said.

She looked at her lover to see he held his own sword in readiness.

"Dana, please," she said. "You can't do this."

"Move out of the way," he said.

The tone of his voice chilled her, and she backed away as the two men circled each other. This wasn't happening. It couldn't be happening. It was a dream, nothing but a dream, and soon she would wake and neither man would be in her chambers determined to kill the other.

She stopped waiting for the dream to end when Revelin lashed out. Dana blocked the attempt easily, and they returned to circling and staring.

"You can't do this," she repeated. "Either of you—both of you—please, listen to me and stop this now!"

The only response she received was Revelin's second attack. This time when they pushed away from each other, Revelin fell against a chair, knocking both it and himself to the floor. Dana took advantage of that and brought his sword down upon his rival. Revelin rolled away from the attack, and Dana's sword struck nothing but the floor.

"Dana!" she screamed. "You can't do this! You can't kill him! Stop this now!"

But he didn't stop. He didn't even acknowledge that she had spoken. The fight continued, swords clashing as they parried each blow. They fought faster and more furious now. She had to find a way to end it before one of them cut down the other. Neither would stop on his own before then.

But what could she do? There were obviously no guards in the hall outside her room to call upon. She looked next at the servants' entrance, suddenly furious that for the first time in months, Bronagh was not lurking underfoot.

She returned to the duel when she heard another crash. She turned in time to see Dana's sword spinning away from him. Dana was on his back on the floor, and Revelin's sword was at his throat.

"Revelin, no!" she cried.

She ran across the room and threw herself against him, knocking him off balance. His sword wavered, and she fell to her knees and placed herself in front of her lover.

"Haleine, don't," Dana said.

She ignored him. By the time he had even uttered his protest, Revelin had recovered, and when he did, she found herself facing the tip of his sword. She looked at him and didn't flinch.

"Move out of the way, Haleine, and let me finish this," Revelin commanded through tightly clenched teeth.

"No," she said. "I will not. I cannot allow you to hurt this man."

"Do you know what it is you do?"

"I do," she said. "Can you say the same?"

Revelin looked at her a moment longer before breaking his stance. He threw down his sword and stalked out of the room. Haleine didn't move until the doors had closed and she felt Dana stir behind her. Her shoulders sagged and she hung her head in sudden exhaustion.

"That's the prince of Tanuba?" Dana said. "He's a remarkable swordsman. Do you think he'd be interested in giving up his birthright to join me?"

She looked at Dana. He couldn't have been serious, but how could he make light of their situation?

"Somehow I doubt it," she said.

He nodded. "Haraszty probably wouldn't approve anyhow."

He stood and went to retrieve his sword. She watched him and saw for the first time the damage to her chambers the skirmish had caused. Considering the event's brevity, they had created quite a disaster. Bronagh would be far from pleased.

"Are you all right?" Dana asked.

She should have told him the truth. How could she possibly be all right? But she did the same as she always did and nodded.

He came back to her side and held out his hand for her. She didn't move to take it. Instead she raised her eyes to look at him.

"How did you change your hair?" she said, asking the first thing that came to mind.

"I believe herbs were used. Maybe berries. I don't know; I didn't ask."

"Why?"

"I wanted to be close to you, and I didn't want to be recognized. I wasn't sure you would know me."

"I would know you anywhere," she said. "Will it be like that always?"

"I'm told it will fade eventually. Do you not like it?"

What did the color of his hair matter? She wanted to laugh at him and nearly did, but Revelin's sword caught her eye, and she cried instead. Dana's sword clattered as it hit the floor. He knelt beside her, and she leaned into his shoulder and cried.

"I'm sorry," he whispered. "I'm so sorry, love, but it had to happen. It couldn't be helped."

She didn't know about that. If she hadn't sent Willem away, Revelin never would have gained entrance to her chambers unannounced. He could have been spared this hurt. He had been angry before, but it would be nothing compared to what he would feel now.

Dana smoothed her hair. "Haleine?"

She pulled back and wiped the tears from her eyes. Then she held his face between her hands and kissed him.

"You have to go," she said, kissing him again. "Now. You have to leave. We don't know where he's gone, what he might be doing, who he will tell."

"He won't tell anyone."

"You don't know that. Why do you and Faolan both talk like that? How can you be so sure what a man you hardly know will do?" she asked, letting her hands fall away. "He hates you. More than Omur. More than Maddox. He thinks you killed his father who he loved well. He thinks you stole—"

Dana stopped her with a kiss. "You."

"Aye. He thinks that."

"He thinks I stole you who he loves well."

She nodded. "He did love me well. I doubt he does still. Surely I've destroyed that tonight."

"He loves you still," Dana said. "Even if he wanted to, he wouldn't know how to stop."

He meant to comfort her, but it made her feel even worse. She looked again at Revelin's sword, her betrayal so obvious. She was supposed to love him.

"We shall see," she said.

"Does it matter?"

"Of course it matters. If he tells my husband what he saw tonight, what will be believed? His jealousy or my lies? Would you please go? Someone could come and—"

"Someone could always come."

"Yes, as has been well proven this night. Go, Dana. Please do not make me ask again."

Dana stood. "Do you love him?"

"Does it matter? I chose you."

"It does matter. If you—"

"Don't be jealous. Not tonight. Not ever," she said. "I destroyed him to save you. If I had to do it again, I would do the same. Be content with that."

"I am," Dana said, backing away. "Are you?"

She stared at the sword. She was supposed to love him.

"I chose you," she said finally, looking up.

Dana was gone.

———❦———

When the sunrise came, Revelin watched it from the windows of his borrowed chambers. And while the sky changed from the blacks and blues of the night to the pinks and oranges of the dawn, his soul remained dark.

Revelin decided long ago that anger was a useless emotion. Zoltano was all too often ruled by it, and never had Revelin desired to emulate his brother in any way. He learned early to control it, to suppress it, mastering the emotion to the point where some believed it did not exist within him at all.

It reigned unchecked now.

He could feel it working its way through him, roiling, twisting and turning inside him. It threatened to burn through him like a wildfire in a too dry forest. When his father died, he was angry, he was grieved, but he wasn't *this*. It was anger, but it was more than that. He couldn't name it nor did he know what to do with it. He didn't know how to purge it from his skin.

She protected that—that man. That vagabond. She placed herself in front of him, and she protected him. That man was the reason his father lay dead, and she protected him. She *loved* him. She loved *him*.

And she had lied.

Revelin lashed out, and his fist hit the wall closest to him. The pain did not register with him. Instead it was swallowed and lost inside him.

When the sun was firmly ensconced in the sky, he left his chambers in search of Haleine. He did not know what he would do when he saw her. Rail against her? Beg her? However he went about it, she had to be made to understand her folly. Her betrayal.

There were still no guards outside her doors, so he opened them as he had last night. Three maids froze upon his entrance and stared at him. One of the king's advisors—Ceallach, Revelin thought his name to be—was also there. He came forward and made his bow.

Revelin looked at him. "Where is your mistress?"

"The garden, your highness," the man said. "The queen has gone to the south garden, but if you seek an audience with her, you will have to wait. She has requested she be left alone. I can appeal to her on your behalf if you'd—"

"Alone?"

"Yes, your highness."

Revelin left the room and made his way to the south garden. Two guards blocked the entrance. One of them was the man who was always with her, the man who had ignored him in Mairéad.

"Move aside and let me pass," Revelin said.

Neither man moved, showing little interest in his demand or even his presence. He repeated himself, and when they still did not move, he went for his sword. When he realized it wasn't there, he prepared to force his way past them. Haleine's voice stopped him.

"It's all right, Willem," she called. "Let him pass."

Willem hesitated but gestured to his companion and opened the way for Revelin. He walked outside and saw Haleine seated on a stone bench. She did not look at him. Her pegasus was next to her but flew away as Revelin approached, perching on top of one of the walls.

"Your man said you wished to be alone, but I did not care," Revelin said.

"I did not think you would."

"I went first to your chambers. I was surprised to find you were not there."

"It is true I do not get out-of-doors very often, but there are times when I grow weary of my prison. The walls here are much more pleasant, I find, even though they are still a cage. It is lovely out here, do you not agree?"

"I had not thought of it. I only thought perhaps your lover had not yet vacated your bed."

She looked at him now. "If you have been to my chambers and have spoken with Ceallach, you know very well that is not true. I understand you are upset, Revelin, but I will not have you speak to me that way."

"You lied to me."

"It was not my intention."

"You told me it was done. You told me you would not see him again."

"It is what I told him," she said, smiling gently. "He came anyway."

Her smile revolted him. "And you love him the more for it."

"God help me, I do."

"You do not think, Haleine."

"Perhaps my problem is I think too much."

"I do not know how to make this any clearer to you. You cannot pursue this any longer. It is too dangerous, and I fear for your life."

"Do you?" she asked, looking angry for the first time. "Well, there is no need for you to fear for me. I am well protected."

"You are a fool to think that. Who protects you? Your guards?" Revelin asked, gesturing toward the two men. "What match are they for your husband's fury?"

"His fury? He knows nothing of this, and even if he did, I would not care."

"You should care. It is your life at stake."

She walked away from him. "You do not understand, Revelin, and I do not expect you to. Just know that I love him. Even though I shouldn't, I do. He is all I see."

"And what of your lover? Does he return your sentiment?"

"God help him, he does."

"No. This is not you. You are not—you would not—Haleine," he begged. "Hear me. You throw your life away with this man."

She spun around. "Your father threw my life away when he condemned me to come here. I had nothing to do with that."

284

"He did not make you a whore," Revelin said. "You did that on your own."

She looked stunned. She looked as though he had struck her. He pulled away.

"I did not mean—"

"I suspect otherwise," she said. "I must ask that you leave me now."

"Haleine—"

"No. You have said what you wanted. Now go."

"But you have not heard me. I wanted to say—"

She turned her back. "You have called me foolish, and you have called me a whore. Forgive me if I care not to hear any more of what you have to say."

He stayed.

"I have asked you politely to go," she said. "If you continue to refuse me this, I will call my guard and ask him to remove you from my presence."

"Haleine, I—"

"Be gone from my sight, and do not show yourself again."

Now he was bewildered. She sat on a bench and put her head in her hands. Revelin stared at her until the pegasus entered his line of vision as it returned to Haleine's side. Revelin looked at the animal for a moment before shaking his head and looking at Haleine again.

"I am"—he couldn't finish the thought—"Haleine, please."

She would not look at him. "May you fall in love so desperately you are blind to all else," she said. "And may that love forever be unrequited."

Her words made his blood run cold. He stared at her until she raised her head and called for her guards. The two men came forth immediately. Revelin took one last look at her and left the garden.

He wandered through corridors only stopping when he found one empty of people. He felt weak; he felt ill and leaned against the wall. He thought he might slide right to the floor.

"Leaning?" a woman behind him teased. "How inappropriate for a man of your stature. What would your mother say?"

It was not Haleine. He didn't know why he should think of her. He straightened without comment and turned to bow to his unwanted companion. His heart sank further when he saw his brother's betrothed and her four guards standing there.

"She would share your sentiment," he said. "Of that I am certain."

But nothing else. Not anymore.

"Revelin," Zaide Romanza said. "I've been looking for you."

She waved her guards away, and they split into two pairs, taking posts at either end of the hall.

"I am at your service, your highness," he said.

She ran her fingers up and down his arm. "Please, Revelin, use my name. After all, we are practically family."

He stepped back. "Did you say you were looking for me?"

"I did. I missed you this morning in the dining hall. You left me alone to breakfast with the most dreadful company."

"I do apologize," he said. "There was a matter to which I had to attend."

"Of course there was. There always is with you," she said. "Whatever it was, though, it can't have gone well. You look dreadful."

He didn't know why he should look otherwise. Had Haleine really said those things to him? Had he really said those things to her?

"Revelin?"

He looked again at Zaide Romanza. "Yes?"

"That was an invitation for you to tell me what the matter was."

He shook his head. "It is done."

"Revelin—"

"I am afraid all I may offer you are further apologies," he said. "I cannot stay here any longer. I must go."

"Go where?"

"Do you know where my mother is this morning?"

"I believe she is in the solarium surrounded by Haleine's witless ladies, and likely her mother, too. The woman hasn't left your mother alone since you arrived."

"Lady Rhoswen?"

"Why would I know her name? It was luck that made Haleine important. Not her birth."

He stared at her. "The solarium, you said?"

She nodded. "Where do you go?"

"Home," he said. "To start."

"And then?"

He looked down the corridor that would lead to the south garden. He couldn't see it nor her, but it didn't matter. It was as she requested.

"Parthalan," he said.

—⁓—

Long after Revelin left, Haleine stayed. Her guards returned to their positions, and Faolan stood beside her on the bench. He had been gone the entire night, because of Dana, she supposed, and hadn't returned until after dawn. It had been strange to spend a night alone, and she had missed him. She raised her head to tell him this, but the urge to cry was so strong, she immediately put her head back down to stave off the tears. She didn't want to cry here. She didn't want to cry anywhere. She was tired of it, all of it, but she would not cry here where someone might see her.

"Are you—?" Faolan started.

"Don't ask if I'm all right," she said.

"Tired. I was going to say tired."

She smiled and chanced looking at him again. "Exhausted, actually," she said. "You never told him, did you?"

"What?"

"Dana. You never told him what I asked you to."

"Oh. No."

She nodded. "Thank you."

"I wasn't sure you would thank me."

"Neither was I."

"Wouldn't you rather go back to your chambers and have this conversation there?"

"No. Here is better."

"You're avoiding Bronagh."

"Wouldn't you?"

"Why do you think I'm here and not there?"

"I thought it to be because I am here, and you loathe to leave me alone and unguarded, for fear of my life."

"Yes, there is that, too."

She smiled again. "Why does it matter where we have this conversation? Willem can't hear us unless we raise our voices. Neither can the other."

"You mean the other whose name you do not know?"

"Do you know it?"

"He's not my guard."

"No, he isn't," she said. "But he doesn't matter. Not to you. Not to me. Tell me what does worry you."

Faolan looked up. "She does."

Haleine lifted her head to see Zaide Romanza, surrounded by guards, walking along one of the open air corridors that overlooked the gardens.

"We're being watched," Faolan said.

"Watched, perhaps," Haleine said, "though I do not know why. She certainly cannot hear what we say. Not from that distance."

"Why do you always talk like that? How can you be so sure what a woman you hardly know can hear or not hear?"

She stared now at Faolan. "How do you know what I said? Did Dana tell you?"

"No. I haven't seen Dana in days, actually."

"Then how do you know?"

"How do you think?"

Haleine looked again at the princess. "You really think she can hear us?"

"It's possible."

"I saw her last night at the ball," Haleine said. "She was talking to Omur."

"Not surprising," Faolan said. "They're working together."

"How long have you known that?"

"Since Mairéad."

"Since Mairéad? I was in Mairéad, and I didn't see anything to suggest that."

"You were preoccupied in Mairéad. If it wasn't on Revelin's face, you didn't see it."

"That's not true."

"It is," Faolan said. "Do they know you saw them last night?"

"I don't know. I don't think so," she said, glancing at Zaide Romanza once more. "Why? Do you think that is why she watches us now?"

"I think we should go back to your chambers."

It was nearly the last thing she wanted to do, but she couldn't dismiss Faolan's concerns, so Haleine relented and returned to her chambers where Bronagh, Sabine and Nonna were still restoring the room to rights. All three stopped upon Haleine's arrival. Sabine and Nonna curtsied. Bronagh saw the others and made an attempt to curtsey but crossed the room in such a way that made Haleine consider leaving again.

"Perhaps you can tell me now what happened here," the maid said, "since you were in such a rush to leave this morning."

Haleine looked past Bronagh to see the other two. Her eyes lingered particularly long on Sabine. The girl had been to Omur's bed more than once. She was starting to spend more time in his bed than out of it. Haleine heard the rumors, and Bronagh confirmed them as truth. Faolan, not knowing if Omur had turned their own spy against them, encouraged her to dismiss Sabine, but Haleine had kept the girl on. Faolan was probably right, but Haleine was reluctant to let Omur know she suspected anything had changed. Sabine continued to bring information when she had it, and even though Haleine knew it was likely tainted and not to be trusted, she thought it was still purposeful to hear it. She wanted to know about what Omur would lie.

And now he would know that she lied. He would never think what she was about to say was the truth. He and Bronagh would have that in common.

"I threw a tantrum," she said.

"You threw a tantrum?" Bronagh asked.

"They didn't have my favorite dish at the feast," Haleine said. "The musicians at the ball were terrible, and the dancing—"

She stopped as she thought of the dancing. She would have smiled had the aftermath not so recently been so horrifying.

"What of the dancing?"

"I threw a tantrum, Bronagh," Haleine said. "I'm the queen, lest you forget. I can throw a tantrum if I so desire."

"Yes, your majesty."

"I may throw one now."

"Of course, your majesty," Bronagh said, "but before you do, might I inquire about this?"

Haleine looked. Bronagh pointed to Revelin's sword.

"It's a sword," Haleine said.

"I know that. Whose?"

"It belongs to the prince," she said. "It belongs to Revelin. I would have you take it to him now. He shouldn't be without it."

"Your majesty?"

"Bronagh, please, just take it," she said and nodded to the other maids. "Them as well. I would like to be alone now, and the room can wait."

"My lord Ceallach saw this," Bronagh warned as she motioned to the girls to go. "He may be gone now, but he will not be distracted for long. He will want answers."

"He will get none," Haleine said.

"He will insist."

"He may insist all he likes. He will find it futile."

"Because you will throw a tantrum?"

"If I must," Haleine said. "The sword, Bronagh."

Bronagh bowed her head. "Very well, your majesty."

When her maids had gone, Haleine stood in the center of the room and looked at the damage that had yet to be repaired. She thought she might start crying anew when Faolan spoke.

"You threw a tantrum?" he asked.

"What would you have had me tell her?" Haleine returned. "And in front of Sabine? Should I have said how my lover and former betrothed fought here for my honor, or for the loss of it?"

"Bronagh's fairly observant. You don't think she suspects that much already? You don't think she'll confirm that much when she returns Revelin's sword?"

"Must you ever mock me?" Haleine asked and sighed as exhaustion overtook her. "I feel as though I could sleep for a week."

"Not the worst idea you've had."

"But an impossible one."

"Why impossible?"

She shook her head. He didn't know about her dreams, and she didn't want to tell him.

"There's bound to be something," she said. "There always is."

"But not just now," Faolan said. "Maybe you should rest while you can."

"And here I thought myself to be free of nursemaids."

"I only meant—"

"I know what you meant," she said. "Still, I think I will sit on the balcony."

Faolan sighed but didn't pursue the matter further. He followed her onto the balcony and stood in silence while she sat and looked at the city. She couldn't see the harbor. She would have to go to another part of the palace for that. Would there be activity on Revelin's ship? She didn't know how long she had sat in the garden. Would he have had time to send word to the ship's captain? Would he have sent word at all? What if he didn't leave?

"Where is Dana?" she asked. "Do you know?"

"Gone back to camp, I imagine. How long he'll stay there, though, I don't know. Why?"

"Would you believe I am worried? Until Revelin sails, I will be much relieved to know Dana is far from here."

"Dana won't be brought down by Revelin."

Haleine stood and turned her back to the city. "Do you know the future, Faolan?"

"No."

"Your goddess?" Haleine asked. "Does she?"

"No."

"I thought gods and goddesses to be all-knowing."

"A common misconception."

She smiled. It faded quickly when she spotted Ceallach coming toward her.

"We have a visitor," she murmured.

"We do?"

"Ceallach," she said and frowned as she saw Rhoswen. "And my mother."

Faolan flew to the opposite end of the balcony. He lay on the railing, folding his legs beneath him, and closed his eyes. It was unlikely he slept. Was that instead how he communicated with the rebellion?

She had no more time to think about it when Ceallach and Rhoswen walked out onto the balcony. Ceallach bowed. Rhoswen did not.

"Your majesty," he said. "Your mother wanted an audience with you, but your guard refused her entrance."

Haleine looked at Rhoswen. "She seems to have found her way anyhow."

"Yes, your majesty," Ceallach said. "Would you like me to speak with him on your behalf?"

"My guard? No. I can thank him on my own."

"Thank him? I think you misunderstand—"

"I misunderstand nothing, Ceallach. Now," she said, sitting once again. "My mother would like an audience with me. Perhaps you shall be kind enough to allow us the privacy with which to proceed."

Ceallach bowed again. "I shall not go far."

"I did not think you would," she said as he left. Then she looked to her mother. "What are you doing here?"

"Your chambers are in a terrible disarray."

"I threw a tantrum."

Faolan snorted. Both she and her mother looked at him. The pegasus hadn't moved, and Haleine smiled.

"You threw a tantrum?" Rhoswen asked.

"What do you want?"

"I came to see that you were well," Rhoswen said. "You weren't at breakfast."

"I wasn't hungry."

"But your guests—"

"I didn't care about that."

"I think I would be hard-pressed to find something you did care about."

Haleine cocked her head. "Did they withhold your breakfast because I was not there?"

"No."

"Then I suppose my absence cannot be counted as one of the world's great tragedies."

Rhoswen sighed and sat so she was situated between her daughter and the pegasus. "I do despise seeing you like this, Haleine," she said. "So hateful, so cruel."

"You did not have to come here. You do not have to stay."

"Indeed not. Prince Revelin came to tell me of his intention to sail home today, as soon as possible actually. I am sure he would gladly welcome me and your sister along."

Haleine felt an ounce of relief at the prospect of her mother's departure. The feeling would have been even greater had it not been for the mention of Revelin.

"Why would he tell you?" she asked.

"He travels to Parthalan next. He means to bring your father home."

Haleine shook her head. "He won't do it. It will mean losing Quatara."

"Believe me, daughter, when I tell you it is already lost."

"I do not doubt that truth. I only question Revelin's ability to see it."

"Of course he sees it. Why else would he go?"

Because he had called her a whore.

"I don't know," she told her mother. "You must be pleased by his intentions."

"Are you not?"

It didn't matter to her what Revelin did any more than it mattered what her father did.

"If Father does not serve in Quatara, he will serve elsewhere."

"You don't know that."

"He doesn't know anything else."

"He knows us."

He didn't know her. Not anymore.

"Then I suppose you will leave anyway," she said. "Wherever Father goes, you do follow."

"This time I hope he will follow me."

"I don't know why. Alliance or not, Tanuba has no true interests here."

"Your father does."

"Father's interests are where the Maoilriains tell him they lie."

Rhoswen nodded. "Which is why you must go to Revelin and ask him—"

"No."

"Haleine! You must!"

"No."

"If you ask him, he will see it done."

And he would. He would never hesitate to grant her whatever she asked.

"No," she said. "I'll ask him nothing."

"Why? Why will you not do this?"

"I want nothing from him."

"Well, I do!"

"Then go and ask him yourself," Haleine snapped. "And might I suggest you make haste, for I am certain he intends to sail with the tide. He's not accustomed to waiting."

"Only for you."

Tears welled up in Haleine's eyes so quickly she never had a chance to stop them. She turned away, not wanting her mother or Faolan to see, but failed on both accounts. Rhoswen fell to her knees in front of her. Faolan stared openly at her.

"What is it?" Rhoswen asked. "What is wrong?"

"Nothing. I am tired," she said. "I am exhausted. Surely you must have felt the same when I was born, when Sighle came?"

Rhoswen smiled. "You forget seneschals' daughters would never receive the same welcome as the sons of kings. Even when the seneschal is one so favored by the king as your father was."

"And yet, this seneschal's daughter just gave birth to two king's sons."

Rhoswen nodded. "Yes. Your father gave up so much. His daughters—"

"Daughters?" Haleine interrupted. "What have you planned for Sighle? To whom will you marry her? The devil himself perhaps?"

Now tears formed in her mother's eyes. "No. No, Sighle is unclaimed, but the truth remains that your father sacrificed more than you know."

"Don't talk to me of Father's sacrifice. From where I sit, the forfeit was of his choosing."

"From where you sit? You sit upon a throne."

"Of the wrong country."

"You never would have been queen."

"I would have been happy."

No one said anything then. She didn't look at Faolan, but she could feel his stare. She nearly apologized. She opened her mouth to say the words but kept them from tumbling out. Her mother would think they were meant for her. She wouldn't know Haleine offered them to the pegasus and his unseen ally.

"You're overwrought," Rhoswen said quietly. "You're exhausted, and it's no wonder. You haven't been given a moment's peace in weeks. Months, even. But it's done now. He's gone, and you can look to yourself again. You must regain your strength, Haleine. You must. It will be vital to do so before you travel."

"Travel?" Haleine asked. She glanced at Faolan. He looked as surprised as she. "What are you talking about? Where am I to go? I know nothing of this."

"Oh?" her mother said. "And because you know nothing about it, it cannot be true?"

"I do not suggest that, Mother. I say only it is news to my ears."

"Mayhap such news would not surprise you if you would leave your chambers from time to time."

"Mayhap. Now will you tell me of this journey?"

"You and your husband will go to Feond to form a truce between your countries. He means to go when all your guests have gone."

"But Idris Fein is here now. Why travel to Feond when all persons needed for such an event are already together?"

"You truly have been in a daze these past weeks if you think that," Rhoswen said. "The king was too ill to come. The princess came alone."

Faolan's head tilted.

"Ill?" Haleine asked. "It is nothing serious, I hope."

"Do you?"

"However malicious you think I have become, I still have no cause to wish an innocent man harm."

"I am glad to hear that," Rhoswen said. "I had wondered."

Faolan was growing restless. He wanted her mother to leave. Haleine offered him a small nod to show she understood.

"I am glad to have put your mind at ease," she said. "Well, I should not keep you from your errand any longer."

"Errand?"

"Begging for the favor of your prince," she said. "I'd suggest groveling at his feet. He'd like that."

"And you? What must I do to gain your favor?"

"Nothing." Haleine stood. "Sometimes things are lost at sea, Mother, and cannot be recovered."

"There must be something. What do you want me to do?"

"I want you to go."

Rhoswen sat still for a moment longer then rose to her feet. She looked as though she meant to say something more. Haleine prepared herself for it, but Rhoswen only bit her lip and walked away.

Haleine folded her arms across her chest and watched her mother depart. Faolan flew over and settled on her shoulder.

"What need is there for a truce between two countries not at war?" she asked.

"None," Faolan replied.

"Then what need is there for a journey to create such a truce?"

"None."

"What does Omur mean to do?"

"Let's find out."

❧

Omur stood on a balcony overlooking the harbor where Revelin's ship made its way into the open sea. He wondered for a brief moment whether Haleine did the same. He was still watching when Zaide Romanza joined him.

"Revelin knows," she said.

"You should not be here. We should not be seen together in such a manner."

295

"As if it matters. Haleine is already aware of our situation. The pegasus told her."

What else might the pegasus have told her? What had he kept from her? They were questions to which Omur was anxious for answers.

"What does Revelin know?" he asked.

"The name of Haleine's paramour. They discussed him in the garden this morning, but they never mentioned him by name. I had hoped they would. I admit I am curious. I'd like to know the man who convinced Haleine to part with her morals. She always guarded them so well. If I had to guess—"

"You don't," he said, but she carried on as though he had said nothing.

"I would say Dana himself. Those boys are fair enough to be his."

"You say they were discussing it in the garden?" Omur asked.

"Yes. They barely raised their voices. They're nobility, after all, and are much too civilized for that sort of thing," Zaide Romanza said. "Even when talking about how one of them is a whore."

"How did Revelin respond?"

"I'd say he's more upset she's not fucking him than anything else," Zaide Romanza said and smiled when Omur raised an eyebrow. "Oh. Did I make you blush?"

"It is always a surprise to hear how crass the nobility can be."

"After all these years spent wiping Maddox's ass, I would have thought you'd be immune to such shock. He is, after all, particularly obtuse, second only to my betrothed."

"You say Revelin is jealous?"

"Revelin is beyond jealous. He's obsessed. He thinks he'll be able to win back her adoration."

"How?"

"He's going to take Darian out of Quatara. He thinks it will make her love him again, but I doubt Haleine's spared a kind thought for her father since she boarded the ship that brought her here. But Revelin doesn't know and doesn't care, so he'll take Darian from Quatara and leave it to its own defenses. He's going to let it go."

"That does not matter. We have gotten what we wanted from it."

"The same can be said about my betrothed, yet we don't seem to be rushing to cut him free."

"Why so concerned?"

"If we don't kill him soon, I may have to marry him."

"So you may. I'm told he has purpose yet."

"What purpose is that?"

"That I have not been told, but each of Nathan's sons has his part to play."

"Is Revelin's role to destroy an empire for the love of a whore?"

Omur raised his eyebrow again. "If I did not know better, I would think you jealous," he said. "As for Revelin, you know what we need from him, and you will make sure we get it when the time comes. But for now, our attentions shift to Feond. Will we get what we want from that?"

"It will be done," she said. "I do live to serve you, my lord."

Her tone was sarcastic, but he didn't mind. Were they anywhere else, any place with witnesses, their roles would be reversed.

"Then get thee gone," he said. "Now. We will follow when opportunity presents itself."

"I do not understand why you come at all."

"I know, but you don't have to," Omur said. He took an amulet from his cloak and dropped it into her hands. "You only need to do as you're told."

She examined the necklace, tilting her hand from side to side to see the red stone react to the sun. "And this?"

"Upon his arrival, get Maddox alone. Give him this to give to his wife."

"Why go through me? Surely you could—"

"Just do it."

"The pegasus will know what it truly is. He won't allow it in her chamber."

"Not if he doesn't know it's there," Omur said.

"How will you manage that? He never leaves the queen's side."

"He'll leave," Omur said. "I'll make sure of it. You worry about getting that jewel into Maddox's hands."

Zaide Romanza bowed her head. "As you wish."

chapter 16

Dana left Eluned in the morning after Orla rousted him from the stall in which he had spent a nearly sleepless night with a bottle of ale he'd stolen from her stores. She sent him off with a change of clothing and a lecture on how he shouldn't be so reckless. It was far too late for advice such as that, but he thanked her anyway and took his leave.

The day was more than half over when he arrived at the rebel camp, and his absence had not gone unnoticed. The moment he set foot within its boundaries, he was swarmed by one person after another, each with a request to make of him. For the first time, he had neither the patience nor the interest in any of them and directed them instead to Ilya, Lucius and Hanah while he went in search of James.

James was on the training field in the middle of a swordplay lesson with Owain. James demonstrated a series of parries and Owain copied him. They ran through the sequence three times before James took the position of attacker and left Owain to defend himself. The lesson came to an end midway through the exercise when James delivered a blow that sent Owain sprawling back at Dana's feet. Owain gazed at him, looking dazed, and Dana held out his hand to help the boy up.

"All right?" he asked and Owain nodded.

"Dana," James said as he approached. "What are you—what did you do to your hair?"

"Hanah did it."

"Did you make her angry?"

"No," Dana said. "I needed to go to Eluned and didn't want to be recognized."

James nodded. "And how did you find our king? In good spirits, I hope."

"I didn't go to see him."

"Oh, aye. Your lady's maid," James said. "And how did you find her? Still in love with you?"

Does it matter? she'd said. *I chose you.*

She'd told him not to be jealous. Nor did he want to be, but how could he be anything else? Revelin was her match, her love match. The prince could have been with her now, urging her to turn away from Dana. If Revelin did, would she listen?

"You know, Owain," Dana said, "you'll never put James, nor anyone else, on the ground fighting like that. Let me show you how it's done, lad."

James grinned. "It's been a while since we've done this. Are you sure you can keep up?"

It was true that in such a short time James had become more than competent with a blade. The fact that he was still alive proved that. He'd not be easy to take down, but Revelin had been at it longer, probably from the moment he could hold a sword. And though their fight had been interrupted by Haleine, one truth remained clear: the prince had swung to kill.

"Aye," Dana said, drawing his sword. "I think I can manage."

"Well, let's have at it, then."

Owain scrambled out of the way as they raised their weapons in salute and began. James's first few parries and thrusts were surprisingly half-hearted. Dana answered with everything he had. James staggered back and smiled.

"You seem angry about something," he said. "Your girl giving you trouble?"

Dana swung again, not thinking, not aiming. James blocked the attack and laughed.

"Well," he said, "this is new. Has a woman ever given you trouble before?"

"Do you want to fight, or do you want to chat?" Dana spat.

"Oh, I want to fight."

"I wasn't sure, what with the way you've been swatting at me. I'd get more fight from Owain. Maybe we should send him to avenge your parents."

It was the right thing to say. James grinned again but gone was his easiness and amusement. He adjusted his grip on his sword and attacked. This time James swung for real, and they didn't talk again.

It felt good to be fighting. It felt good to be doing something. Dana hated the resentment he felt and despised that she could see it, too. He wanted to hit hard and be hit hard in return until it was out of his blood.

Don't be jealous, she said. *I destroyed him to save you.*

And she had. Dana had seen it in the prince's face as she'd shielded his body with her own. Haleine was all Revelin knew or cared to know of love. He and Dana had that in common.

"Stop it!" Ilya yelled. "That's enough, both of you!"

Suddenly, she was between him and James, ducking to avoid steel. She put her hands on James's chest and pushed him back. Dana lunged forward, to stop her, to keep his momentum. He didn't get far. Lucius was on him, pulling him back and holding him so tightly, he was forced to drop his sword.

"All right," he said to Lucius. "It's done. Let me go."

Lucius held him a moment longer. "Make things right with the queen," he said quietly before letting go. "Don't do this."

Dana turned to tell Lucius he didn't know what he was talking about but said nothing more and did nothing more than pick up his sword and walk away. He returned to his tent and saw Faolan standing on the table.

Dana threw down his sword. "What are you doing here?"

"It's always a pleasure to see you, too."

"Is Haleine all right?"

"Haleine's fine."

"But something happened. You wouldn't be here otherwise," Dana said. "Tell me what Revelin did."

"It doesn't matter what Revelin did or did not do."

"What did he do?"

"I'm not going to tell you," Faolan said. "I'm not going to tell you because if I did, I would likely then have to waste precious time preventing you from tracking him down and doing something stupid such as challenging him to another duel."

Dana sat. "He started it."

"I don't care who started what," Faolan said. "There's something much more urgent we have to deal with."

"And what's that?"

"Maddox is planning a visit to Feond. They'll be leaving within the week."

"Will Haleine accompany him?"

"No. She feigned ill and begged to be excused. Maddox agreed, and Omur let the decision stand without a protest, so the king and Omur will travel alone."

"Did you think he would protest?"

"Yes. I didn't think he'd want that much distance between us."

"What does that mean?"

"It means she's not his target," Faolan said. "Not this time."

"Who is the target? Why go to Feond at all?"

"The official story is to form a truce."

"They're not at war with each other."

"I know."

"Oh," Dana said as Faolan's meaning became clear. "You think he's going to kill Idris Fein. And blame me."

"It's only a guess but a fair one, I'd say. It worked so well in Tanuba," Faolan said. "Why not try it again?"

"It'll put Zaide Romanza on the throne. You had concerns about her before. Do you still?"

"Yes."

"If her father dies, she'll have command of an army that wants to kill me."

"Another one that wants to kill you," Faolan said and took note of Dana's expression. "But it's possible I didn't need to point that out."

"We'll go to Mahile," Dana said, standing and pacing. "They have to go through Mahile. It's the only road the king's entourage could travel. We go and we meet them. We go and we stop them. We'll kill Maddox. I'll kill Maddox and—"

"You can't kill Maddox."

Dana stopped. "I can't kill Maddox?"

"No."

"Then I'd like to know what the hell it is we've been trying to do all this time."

"Save the world. I know you like to think it, but the two aren't one and the same."

"This is what you asked me to do, isn't it? Dammit, Faolan, we can't keep doing this. We can't keep fighting these battles when we're not gaining any ground. I don't want to keep running into the same wall over and over again. And I don't want—"

"When did we stop talking about Maddox and start talking about Haleine?"

"I wasn't talking about Haleine."

"Yes, you were."

Yes, he was. He knew it; Faolan obviously knew it. There was no point in trying to argue otherwise.

"Killing him would save her," Dana said.

"I don't know about that, but I do know that killing him would destroy everything else, so hold your sword in check."

Dana sat and stared at Faolan. He was still sitting and still staring when James arrived.

"Dana?" he said. "Ilya seems to think we have some sort of problem to work out that she'd rather we take care of without weapons in our hands. Can you—Oh. Faolan. I didn't know you were here."

"Come in, James," Dana said. "Faolan just finished telling me how we can't kill Maddox."

"We can't kill Maddox?" James echoed.

"You can't kill the queen either," Faolan said.

"Why can't we kill Maddox?" James asked. "Isn't that what we've been trying to do all this time?"

"No, it really isn't," Faolan said. "We have to be able to control who gets the crown, and right now we can't do that. So Maddox gets to live. You can kill him, and you will kill him, but you can't do it now."

There was a long period of silence before Dana spoke again.

"What about maiming?"

—⁂—

The people of Feond, her father's subjects, liked to say the queen of their country—whoever she may be—was doomed to an early death, so praise God their princess remained a princess. It had started with the death of Idris Fein's first wife, her mother. She was four and twenty when she died. Zaide Romanza was seven and remembered it well. Her mother died beautifully.

Her father remarried, only to lose his second and third wives as well. His fourth wife came, and she, Zaide Romanza also remembered, did not die beautifully. She died screaming and crying for her god to deliver her. Zaide Romanza had hesitated then, curious to see her stepmother's god, wanting to see this dying woman delivered. But no god came, and her third stepmother slowly bled to death, still chanting to her god, still convinced of his mercy.

Zaide Romanza had been disappointed.

"How stupid," she said to her stepmother's corpse. "Your god didn't even spare your pain. I would have done that."

Yes, she would have done that a decade ago. Then she didn't know. Kill for the sake of killing. Kill because she was so moved.

It was only later she learned what pleasure there could be. She was thirteen when one of her father's grooms had caught her unaware and unguarded and held her against the wall of a vacant stall smelling of soiled hay and horseflesh. He tore at her bodice to reveal her still-small breasts and lifted her skirts and used her and ravished her like she was a milkmaid and not a princess. He bruised her skin with his grip. He raked his teeth across her breasts and her throat. He groaned and growled like a mongrel as he worked inside of her. She did not fight him. She watched him instead, relishing his transgression, appreciating his malice. He took pleasure in it, in hurting her. She wanted to do the same.

When he finished with her, he dropped her in the hay and set about putting himself to rights. She didn't move except to slide from its sheath the small knife she always carried on her hip. She concealed it in her palm. He came back and bent over her, presumably to threaten her. Don't tell or I'll kill you, he would have said had she not gutted him first. Blood spurted, and he fell forward on top of her, pawing at her once again, but this time out of panic and desperation. She smiled and laughed as she pushed him off her. She straightened the remains of her clothing as she watched the life seep out of him, the life she had held within her. The life she now wore.

"Where is your hardness now?" she asked as she stood over his dying form.

No god came to deliver him either. What god would want him? Certainly not her father's deity, and not a goddess of the earth. Even her own dark gods would not have him. Not because of his cruelty—they would have celebrated that—but because he had dared lay hands on their daughter. Their one and their only.

She had known for quite some time that Idris Fein may have contributed to her birth, but it was her lords, her dark gods, which gave her life. They were terrible in their fury but more ferocious in their love of her. She was precious to them. Second only to Haleine's second born.

She had hated that truth at first. She'd never liked the redheaded mouse that completely held Revelin's interest, and had found it infuriating that someone as utterly unworthy as Haleine was the vessel through which her dark lords might be restored. But who was she to question prophecy and fate? She took pleasure instead in knowing Haleine would remain ignorant of her son's destiny until it was too late.

So she had gone to the princes' welcoming and met both her lord and her enemy. She stood over the matching bassinets and looked down at the infants. She smiled.

Two from one, they'll come, they'll come.

The first, the crown prince. Alain.

The first from moon. The next from dark.

She leaned over the other's cradle. Auryn. The second by birth. The first by prophecy. She stroked the child's cheek and placed her fingertips lightly on his forehead. She smiled again.

"You wait, lad," she whispered. "My little dark lord, my high prince. They don't know how great you'll become."

No one would. The secret would not be revealed for nearly a score of years. And maybe she would never know. She doubted she would live that long. She was about to become the queen of Feond, and as her subjects would tell anyone who would listen, the queen of Feond was doomed to an early death.

When death did come for her, she would die beautifully as her mother had. She would not scream; she would not cry. She would not call out for a deliverance that would never come. She would laugh, and she would die knowing she had served her lords, having done all they required of her, and that her death was their last request.

But for now they called only for the death of her father. It was not much, a simple spell, an even simpler potion, and her father would be gone. He would drift off during the night when she was far from his chambers and free from the taint of suspicion.

Omur wanted to think she would fail her lords in this. He wanted her so polluted by love for her father that she would be unable to do their bidding. She wasn't. If they had asked her to slit the man's throat and drink his blood, she would have done that. If they had wanted her to walk through the halls of his home drenched in his death and her guilt, she would have done that. But they hadn't. They just wanted Idris Fein to die. They didn't want to blame anyone; they only wanted to place their true daughter on the throne. She was more than happy to oblige.

When her carriage arrived at her father's palace in Eacha Donn, she wasted no time in going to his side. She walked into his chambers, giving the servants within no opportunity to hide their laziness. She removed her traveling cloak and dropped it, not waiting for someone to take it from her. She strode across the room and stood in front of her father's physician, who had slowly drawn himself out of his chair at her arrival.

"How is he?" she asked. "Do you expect him to live?"

The healer didn't answer, not knowing what to say. He didn't expect the king to live, but he could never say it. To suggest that the king might die, that he was vulnerable, was treason and death. To suggest that he would live would be a lie, which could also lead to the chopping block or the noose when the king did perish. She ducked her head as she studied her father's inert form to keep the healer from seeing her smile. She enjoyed his dilemma. She was the only one in the room who did.

"I see," she said in response to his silence.

He made some noise of complaint, but no actual words formed.

"I wish to be alone with my father," she said. "Go wait in the hall."

The protest ended, and the healer and all the rest who attended the king walked out. She sat on the edge of the bed and looked at the frail and sick man beneath the blankets.

This was what it came to, life. Her father was not terribly old, but any youth he held would not save him. It would not save her, either, when the time came, and she would never live as long as her father had. Her path was far more violent than the one he had chosen, and the people's curse would hold true. It was very possible she would be the end of her father's line. The king had no other heirs; she had seen to that. What would happen when she was gone?

But now was not the time to be concerned with that. She reached into the bodice of her gown and drew out the small vial concealed there. She removed the cork that sealed the bottle and tossed it away. She began the chant. She opened her father's mouth and poured the vial's contents down his throat. When empty, she put the vial back and stroked her father's throat.

He awoke then, choking and sputtering. His eyes opened and he saw her. He grabbed her arm, and with wild eyes, he looked at her.

"Daughter," he gasped. "What is this?"

"They want you dead," she said, "which means I want you dead."

"Why?"

"I didn't think to ask."

His grip became slack and his hand fell away. His eyes widened and disappeared as his eyelids settled over them. It was done. Nothing would save him now. She smiled and leaned over to kiss his forehead.

"Pleasant dreaming," she said.

—◊◊◊—

The better part of a year had passed since Darian had left his man, Darragh, in place at Haraszty's court. Before then Revelin had had very little contact with the man, dealing more with Darian himself than his servant. Now Revelin saw just how alike the two men were. It was not unexpected, as Darian would have chosen a man much like himself to be assured his will would be carried out in his absence. The arrangement had worked well, however Revelin hoped now to find Darragh more easily broken than his master would have been.

"You want me to do what, your highness?" Darragh asked.

"I want you to prepare a small group of men to accompany me to Parthalan. No more than five," Revelin said. "Is there a problem?"

He knew there would be a problem the very moment he first thought to confront Darragh with this request. Darian would have flat out refused from the start. Revelin waited to hear Darragh's response.

"I—I cannot," Darragh said. "Your highness, it is far too dangerous for you to travel to Quatara with so little protection. Might I not go in your place?"

"I have need of you here," Revelin said.

"Send one of your mother's messengers," Darragh said. "More than one if you think it necessary."

"I think it necessary I make this journey myself."

"I cannot allow you to go, my lord."

"I do not see where it is your place to allow me anything," Revelin said. "Make the arrangements. I wish to leave immediately."

Darragh still didn't move. "My prince, if you remove Lord Coileáin from Quatara, Tanuba's rule there will be ended."

"It was ended well before now."

"There will be no going back."

"I know," Revelin said. "Make the arrangements."

Darragh hesitated a moment longer, then nodded and bowed away.

Revelin next went in search of his mother. He found her in her solarium, surrounded by her ladies. They weren't aware of his presence, and he stood in the back and listened to their chatter. They were planning another gala; he didn't know why.

"Oh, Revelin!" Haraszty said when she did notice him. "I didn't see you there. Come in, come here! We are preparing for a party."

"Are you?" he asked, doing as she requested. His mother's ladies all rose to their feet only to drop into deep bows. "What do you celebrate?"

"Anything, everything," Haraszty said, patting his cheek as he bent to kiss hers. "It doesn't matter."

"It never does," he said. "I came to tell you I must leave for Parthalan today."

"Can't someone else go?"

"No."

Haraszty nodded. "You'll miss the party, you know."

"There will be another," he said. "I will be gone four or five days maybe, a week at the most. I hope it will not be longer, but Darragh will attend to your needs in my absence."

"Fine, fine." Haraszty looked at him and sighed. "Are you all right, my boy? You seem different."

"I am the same."

"Ever since we left Lira, you've seemed different. Did you quarrel with Haleine?"

He bent down and kissed his mother's cheek once more. "I must go."

"Oh. Well, fine. Travel safe," Haraszty said as she waved him off.

Revelin pushed the five men Darragh had selected as hard as he could. They stopped only when darkness forced it and started again as soon as there was light enough to do so. When the border between the two countries came into sight, they paused only long enough to unfurl the white banners that would announce their intentions to those guarding the Quatari side of the border.

"I see no one," one of the soldiers said.

"They're there," the captain said.

His name was Idwal Kai. He was one of Darian's men, selected by Darragh because of his familiarity with Quatara and her rebels.

"Are you sure you will not reconsider, my prince?" Idwal asked.

Revelin shook his head and nudged his horse forward. "We go on."

They did not get far before groups of Quatari patrols blocked their path. Revelin stopped and held out his hands. The soldiers surrounding him reached for their weapons.

Revelin looked at Idwal. "No."

"Your life will be forfeit, my prince."

"Allow these men to draw their weapons, and you will be right," he said. "The Quatari chieftain will be among these men. I will ask for safe passage, and he will grant it."

The captain nodded and gave the order. Revelin waited. He hadn't worn a helmet or even a hood, wanting his identity to be unmistakable for that purpose alone.

"What do you want here?" one of the Quataris shouted.

"I want to talk to your chieftain," Revelin answered. "Tell him the son of Nathan has a request to make of him."

"Nathan's second son has a request to make of me?" A voice came from the back of the group. "How bold."

The Quataris parted, and their chieftain, Reamann Einar, strolled to the front. He was a short man with a shaved head and a reputation for being as fearless as he was fearsome. Revelin dismounted and went to meet him. Idwal and one other followed just behind. Revelin bowed. Einar did not.

"What is this request?" Einar asked.

"You have won," Revelin said. "I do not wish to fight you any longer, and I have come to remove all evidence of our rule from your land."

"Not all evidence," Einar said. "My cities have burned. My people have died."

"They did not have to," Revelin said. "Lord Coileáin was ultimately good to your people. My father could have left you with much worse."

"The crown prince?" Einar asked.

Revelin nodded. "My father did not wish to destroy this land. My brother would have done that and more."

He still might. Zoltano would try for Quatara once he heard what Revelin had done, but he didn't tell Einar of his suspicions. What happened after Revelin retrieved Darian was none of his concern.

"You wish me to be grateful that your father's man isn't as evil as your brother?"

"I do."

The chieftain laughed and drew his sword. Revelin's guards responded in kind. Einar's men raised their bows.

Revelin didn't flinch. "Tell your men to lower their weapons."

"Tell your men to lower theirs."

Revelin looked to Idwal and nodded. The man looked as though he wanted to disobey but returned his sword to its sheath. The rest followed. The Quataris' weapons remained drawn.

"I have come to take Lord Coileáin away, nothing more," Revelin said. "Allow me to do this, and I swear you will never hear from me again."

"Why should I believe the promise of the second son of a dead king?"

"Because you know it would be unwise not to," Revelin said. "You see me here now with five men. If I had wanted to continue our occupation of your country, I could have, and would have, brought five thousand. I want my man and I will have him."

"You ask to retrieve the man who led your father to victory. I think I'd rather he stay here where I can watch him."

"I will have him," Revelin repeated. "If you refuse, if you kill him, I will drown this country in my army, and I will have instead your head."

Einar smiled. "Perhaps Nathan's son after all," he said. He motioned to one of his men, who immediately sprang forward. "Escort them where they want to go, and escort them back. You will have three days, son of Nathan, before your safe passage ends. I suggest you make haste."

Revelin bowed. "Haste will be made. I thank you."

"Don't waste time thanking me," the chieftain said, disappearing back within the ranks of his men.

Revelin waited for the Quatari ranks to close and withdraw. When none were left but their escorts, Revelin returned to his horse and pulled himself into the saddle.

"My prince, please," Idwal begged. "You must stay here. This is a trap. There will never be enough time to fetch Lord Coileáin and make it safely back. You don't know what we will find there. You don't know—"

Revelin spurred his horse forward. Einar's men rode with him while his own scrambled to catch up. They covered the distance to Parthalan quickly to find the city very much ruined, though the castle where Darian had made his home appeared to be intact. Guards were posted at the gates, and they raised their weapons as they saw the party riding toward them. The Quataris dropped back, but Idwal rode forward.

"Open the gates for your prince, you dogs!" he shouted.

The guards looked at Revelin, and orders were immediately given for the gates to be opened. While they waited, Revelin rode aside his captain.

"Gather the men, horses, weapons, anything we do not want to leave behind. Torch the rest, and do it quickly," he said. "I will fetch Darian."

When the gates were parted wide enough, Revelin rode through. He dismounted in the courtyard and handed his mount to one of the grooms.

"Where will I find Darian?" Revelin asked.

The groom bowed. "Likely the library, your highness."

Revelin thanked the man and entered the castle. He pushed past the men and ignored those who bowed before him or called his name. Idwal would deal with them. He had his own problem to which to attend.

Darian was indeed in his library, standing in front of his desk with a stack of papers in his hand. He leafed through them, his frown deepening with each passing moment.

"I would ask why you are still here," Revelin said from the doorway, "but I already know what you would answer."

Darian looked up and dropped his papers. "My prince! Why—why have you come?"

Revelin looked away. "It has gotten away from you. From us."

"My lord?"

He crossed the room and stood by the window. "We are done here."

"And what of your brother, my lord? Does he know of this decision?"

"No. Not yet."

"He will not share your view, I fear."

"Then perhaps this will draw him out."

"It will, most assuredly. When he hears of this, he will not hesitate to reemerge. He will not like losing such a large portion of his father's kingdom."

"He may attempt to win it back with his own men if he so desires," Revelin said. "But he will not use mine—the crown's—any longer."

Darian nodded. "We will prepare for his coming."

"Darragh is already seeing it done. He has proven his mettle thus far. I have no reason to think he will fail me on this."

"Is it the crown's desire that I no longer serve?"

Revelin looked at Darian, surprised. "No. Of course not. Why do you ask that?"

"You've asked Darragh to do what I would—"

"But not because we do not wish to continue your service. Good God, Darian! You are the most loyal, capable man the crown has. We would never let you go."

"Then why—?"

"Do you not wish to go to Lira?"

"Tanuba has no true interests there."

"You do."

Darian seemed to consider this. "Forgive the question, my lord, but why are you here? These orders could have been brought by any of the queen's messengers. Knowing the status of this territory as you do, why would you risk coming here yourself?"

"Perhaps you are not the only one with interests in Lira."

Darian nodded his understanding. "You saw my daughter."

"I did."

"Is she well?"

"She is—" Revelin hesitated. "I do not know what she is."

"She is angry."

Revelin almost laughed at the simplicity of the truth. "She is that."

"What would you have me do, my lord? Go and grovel before her? To beg her forgiveness for what I have done?"

"I do not know."

"Your father requested I send her," Darian said. "I could not refuse him."

"He was not a man who was refused anything."

"And I failed him."

"No. If anything, he failed you. *I* failed you."

"My lord?"

"My father died, and I left you here to do the same."

"That was not your decision."

Revelin smiled. "It was, and we both know it. The only reason any of my mother's court backed her instead of my brother was me."

"Yes, my lord, but still—"

"You make it very difficult for a man to offer you an apology."

"You owe me nothing, my lord," Darian said. "Please."

Revelin looked to the floor. "Rhoswen is in Lira. Do you not wish to go to her?"

"She has followed me thus far. She will come to me," Darian said. "Unless you wish me to go to Lira on the crown's behalf. Then of course I shall go."

"I wish you to leave here," Revelin said. "Beyond that, I do not know. I shall have to confer with my advisor."

Darian was motionless for a moment. "My lord, your brother first. And then—"

Revelin nodded. "And then."

Darian still didn't move. His eyes darted in every direction before he dropped to his knees to gather the fallen papers.

"It is good I return," Darian said as he worked. "I need to speak with Darragh. He should not have let you come here."

"Rest assured he did not want me to do so."

Darian stood, his papers in his hands. "And yet here you are. I will speak with him. It will not happen again. You have my word."

"The decision was not his to make," Revelin said. "It was mine, and I did this of my own free will."

"I don't think that is exactly true, my lord," Darian said, "but in any case, you have proven why we do not let the royal family make decisions of their own free will. It tends to place them in dubious circumstances."

"Einar knows I am here. I spoke him with at the border and he granted me safe passage."

"You spoke with Einar? He allowed you to come here? To my aid?"

"He gave me three days. After that..." Revelin shrugged.

Darian stared. "Oh my lord," he said. He sprung into action, gathering whatever he could reach. "We must leave immediately. *You* must leave immediately. There will not be enough time, not with all that must be done, and he knew there would not be. Damn that man! We must cover whatever ground we can."

Revelin wasn't concerned. He didn't believe Einar would truly bring harm to him. There would be too much risk in that. But it was better not to argue, so he backed away while Darian prepared to leave this place he had lived for nineteen years.

"What if my father had wanted to come here?" Revelin asked. "What would you have done?"

Darian sighed. "That, my lord, I would have denied him."

Dana sat atop Lorcan's back and watched the king's procession make its way along the road to Mahile. It was flat here and open, the only cover coming from the small grove of trees in which he and those who followed him were now hiding.

The king—and Omur too, Dana suspected—rode in a gilded carriage surrounded by a large number of both mounted knights and foot soldiers. Dana had counted three hundred in all. It was to be expected. Mahile had belonged fiercely to the rebellion since Dana's first appearance there, and it would inherently be a risk for the king and any of his confederates—especially a band of soldiers—to ride through it.

But Dana had given orders that the king not make it to Mahile's borders. He didn't want the fight to touch the people there.

"Are we going to do this?" James asked. "Or are we just going to watch?"

Dana looked toward Faolan, perched on his left shoulder. "Are you sure she's not with him?" he murmured so James would not hear.

"Yes."

Dana nodded and twisted around to see the seventy people who waited behind him. They expected a speech; they expected something he feared was no longer within him.

"The king lives," he said. "Do as you will with the rest."

"Uplifting," Faolan said as Dana turned back.

Dana said nothing as he shrugged the pegasus from his shoulder. The time for games was done. He would end it. For her. For them both. He drew his sword. On his right, James did the same.

"Attack!" Dana shouted.

Lorcan sprang forward. He was the first to emerge from the grove, James and Bearach close behind. The others followed, all screaming a war cry that shook the earth more than the pounding of the unicorns' hooves. The king's caravan stopped. Knights shouted orders and soldiers took action. The carriage broke away with a small group of mounted men for protection.

"Dana!" James shouted.

"Let him go!" Dana yelled back.

His head was turned, so he didn't see what happened. He didn't even realize at first that Lorcan had stumbled. He only knew the unicorn fell forward. Dana fell as well, flying over the unicorn's head and landing on his face in the grass. He wasn't hurt, simply stunned, and shook his head as he pushed himself back up. He recovered his sword, only then noticing the silence.

There was no noise. No battle cries, no wounded men screaming. No hooves grinding into earth. No clashing of metal. Nothing. He stood and looked around, finding himself surrounded by a milky-white barrier, a cage made of something like stained glass. He could see the battle surrounding him, but individual faces were impossible to make out. The best he could do was distinguishing his own men from Maddox's. He stepped closer to the wall and reached out to touch it, only to draw his hand immediately away as a surge of white-hot heat seared his palm. He looked at his hand for a moment before taking up his sword.

"I wouldn't do that if I were you."

The warning came too late, as Dana was committed to completing the swing. The blade struck the wall, and he was lifted off his feet and thrown back. He landed hard on the ground, looking up at the distorted sky.

"I did try to tell you."

Dana stood. "What is this?"

"Magic."

The voice finally registered with him. He tightened his grip on his sword and whirled around, ready to strike. Omur caught the blade and held it as though its steel wasn't cutting into his flesh.

"You're not using Varro's sword," Omur said, twisting his wrist and disarming Dana. "I think he'd be rather hurt by that."

"Ask me if I care."

"Do you care?"

"Do you really not know?"

"Of course I know. I was trying to be accommodating. You're my guest, such as it is, and you made a request of me. It would have been rude otherwise."

"The very picture of manners," Dana said. "How fortunate for me."

Omur smiled. "Yes. How fortunate."

"Then might I request that you take my sword and run yourself through with it?"

"You could, and I would, but no good would come from it," Omur said, throwing Dana's sword back to him. "I can't be killed. At least not by you."

Dana caught the sword. "Let's find out."

He swung the weapon and embedded it in Omur's chest. His enemy looked at what he had done. Dana staggered back. There was no blood. Why was there no blood?

"Well," Omur said. "That was uncalled for."

Omur pulled the sword from his chest and dropped the weapon on the ground. Dana looked at the blade and then at Omur. He couldn't even tell where the sword had gone through. If it hadn't been for the tear in Omur's robes, there would be no evidence of his attempt at all.

"I had to try," Dana said. "You understand."

"You humans always have to try," Omur said. "Yes, this I understand."

"If not human, what are you?"

"Is that what you really want to know?"

"I must admit I am curious."

"I'm sure you are."

Dana nodded. "I'm surprised to find you here on the battlefield. I thought you'd be with the king."

"You thought wrong," Omur said. "If I were with him, I wouldn't be able to be here with you. Besides, the king brought a guest along to entertain him in the absence of his wife, and, while I must admit I can be a bit of a voyeur, there are still things I do not wish to see. I think you know what I mean."

"What do you want with me?"

"Does it bother you?" Omur asked. "Does it make your blood boil to think of how unfaithful he is to her? Does it bother you how unfaithful she is to you?"

"That is not of her doing," Dana said. "She is faithful in every way that matters."

Omur smiled. "I am sure Revelin thought the same."

Dana pulled the knife hanging from his belt before he could think. He brought it up as though he meant to attack. He didn't know what stopped him.

"What purpose stabbing me a second time will have, I do not know, but have at it, if you must." Omur spread out his arms to his sides. "My heart is found in the usual place."

Dana put the knife back in his belt. "What heart?"

"Still so rude," Omur said, "and after I've been nothing but infinitely polite. I should snap you in half for your insolence."

"What's stopping you?"

"It's not what you're here for."

"What am I here for?"

"I wanted to talk to you, and you never stop by the palace anymore," Omur said. "At least not to see me."

"Talk to me? Why?"

Omur sighed. "You're annoyingly good at this."

"Conversation?"

"No. You're appallingly bad at that. I meant this," Omur said, waving at the scene surrounding them. "Your success on the battlefield. The success of your rebellion. It angers my king which, in turn, annoys me."

"Your king?"

"I thought perhaps I would offer you a chance to surrender."

"Surrender to you? Surrender to your king?" Dana asked and Omur nodded. "Why would I ever do that when I am, as you said, annoyingly good at this?"

"It might save your life."

"This coming from a man who can't hurt me."

"Can't I?"

"You can't," Dana said. "Or you won't. You need me to do exactly what I've been doing."

"I didn't need you to swive the queen as though she were one of your whores."

Dana clutched the knife once more. "Do you threaten her?"

Omur almost smiled again and turned his head toward the battle. "You do spill their blood too lightly."

"You murder for no reason at all, and you say I spill blood lightly?"

"Only one here has committed murder. And it wasn't me."

"Wasn't it? Amatheon? Michaela? Enimode? Upon whose hands is that blood?"

"Maddox killed his family. His soldiers murdered yours. You snapped the neck of a whore."

"A casualty of war."

"And so aren't they all. But here's what I'm very curious to know," Omur said, turning back to him. "Will Haleine share the same fate?"

"Don't threaten her."

"Don't be irksome. I'm not the threat. You are," Omur said. "You like to think your passion and your quest are the same, that

Haleine and your rebellion are intertwined. They're not. You'll have to choose, one day soon. Her or them."

"If you harm her, I will—"

"You'll what? Run me through with your sword? Or better yet, your dagger?"

"I'll think of something," Dana said. "I won't let you hurt her."

"Noble, perhaps, but if I wish her harm, you won't be able to stop me."

"I can. I will."

"Tell me, do you think loving her will save her?"

Dana offered no answer.

"It won't," Omur continued, "in case you wondered. It will bring her nothing but harm. It'll bring those who follow you much worse. You do spill their blood too lightly. You have proven that this day."

"I don't do anything lightly. This least of all."

"Then what are you doing here?"

Dana glanced to either side. "Winning, by the looks of it," he said. "I came here to stop you. I came here to keep you from killing Idris Fein and putting your whore on the throne."

"While it cannot be denied that the heir to Feond's throne is an inexhaustible slut, I am one of the few who cannot lay claim to her."

"But you still want her on the throne."

"Of course I want her on the throne," Omur said. "Do you really think your presence here today will prevent that from coming about?"

"Aye."

"What makes you think it's not already done?"

"You're planning to go there, kill him and blame me, aren't you?" Dana asked. "It's what you did in Tanuba."

"And I do hate to repeat myself, so no, that isn't the plan at all."

"What is your plan?"

"Would you also like to know the key to destroying me?"

"If it's not too much trouble."

Omur laughed. "I almost like you."

Dana didn't laugh. "Make no mistake when I say I do not feel the same."

"How disappointing," Omur said. "Idris Fein is dead, and his daughter sits upon his throne. You will find no blame will befall you for this tragedy. Maddox will go to Feond, as planned, and will take the first steps toward aligning himself with Zaide Romanza, thinking she will be as easily controlled as his own queen. She won't be."

"Why make the trip at all?"

"Curiosity. You followed me. You and your pegasus. I wasn't sure if you would. I did not know if you would leave her unguarded, and I wanted to find out. Thank you for obliging me."

"I swear if you touch her—"

"Maybe you have already chosen," Omur said, looking skyward for a moment. "Your pegasus is growing restless, and given enough time, he will find the way to free you from this spell. Since I do not relish the idea of his interruption, at least not this soon, let me say one thing more. You are not infallible. You will not win this."

"I think I just might."

"You won't as long as you love her," Omur said. "She will be the end of them. The end of you as well."

"You shouldn't make threats," Dana said. "It's a waste of time when we both know you can't kill me."

"Can't I?" Omur smiled and raised his hands. "Let's find out."

CHAPTER 17

For generations, the Brollachan standard had been a black wolf's head on a yellow background. Idris Fein had draped it everywhere possible in his palace, but after his death, Zaide Romanza had wasted no time in removing all signs of her father's rule.

The new standard of Feond's ruling house was a silver, two-headed dragon, its necks intertwining and its mouths holding a crimson stone. It had been placed in the center of a sea of black and was displayed in even more places than the Brollachan wolf had been, including two great banners swathed on either side of Eacha Donn's entrance gate.

Omur had sat in Maddox's carriage and looked at them as they rode into the city. Next he saw the flags flying from the turrets and the wall of the outer bailey, and inside the palace itself were painted shields and tapestries hanging on the walls. More banners were suspended from the ceiling in the great hall. Each sighting irritated him further, but there was no place they were not found.

The newly crowned queen of Feond knew he would not react well to seeing the change in crests and had, since his arrival, kept herself surrounded with the people of her court to keep Omur at bay, so as badly as he wanted to confront her about this impertinence, it took five days for an opportunity to arise. He approached her in her throne room. She sprawled across her great chair, her crown on her head, a goblet in her hand and the amulet he had given her around her neck. When he stood before her, he bowed. The action delighted her greatly.

"And what might I do for you?" she asked.

"That standard does not belong to you," he said, indicating the banner behind her.

"Of course it does," Zaide Romanza said. "To whom else would it belong? You? I'm their true-born daughter. You're their errand boy."

"You'll not play the queen with me."

"But I am the queen."

"That crown is meaningless," Omur said. "It'll get you nothing."

Zaide Romanza smiled. "Nothing but your bow in polite society."

"How easily you are amused."

"How easily are you irritated," she replied. "You'd wear the crown had you the chance."

"Not of this—"

"Hell?" Zaide Romanza volunteered.

She may have been pleased, but he was not. "I gave you that necklace to give to Maddox. Not to accentuate your...assets."

Zaide Romanza laughed and ran her fingers over the jewel. "You always think me incapable. I don't know why. Haven't I done everything you've asked?"

"I can think of one thing you've failed to do."

"I will give it to him. Our lords want it, so it will be done."

"It best be done soon," Omur said. "I wish to depart in the morning. We would have gone already had you only done your duty."

"Why the rush?" Zaide Romanza asked, signaling to a servant for more wine. "You left your rebellion for dead, didn't you?"

"You know very well I did not," Omur said.

"Such an elaborate ruse," she said. "Will it be worth it?"

"Necessary, my queen," he said as the servant approached and refilled the empty goblet. "And yes, it will be worth it."

The servant bowed and backed away. Zaide Romanza raised the goblet to her lips and took a small sip. "For your sake, you should hope so."

"Worried?"

"Not about you," she said. "If Dana knows what's good for him, he'll take advantage of your gift."

"He won't," Omur said. "He won't be able to keep away from the queen."

"You're counting on it."

"Yes. That is why it is imperative you get that necklace into Maddox's hands. I need it placed in her chambers before either her lover or the pegasus return there."

"You worry too much," Zaide Romanza said. "It can't be good for you."

Omur's temper flared, but their conversation was delayed when Maddox entered the room. Omur stepped back from Zaide Romanza and offered the king a bow he did not notice.

"I was just asking your man where you were," Zaide Romanza said to the king of Lira. She offered her hand, and he took it. "I was starting to think you would slip away without saying a proper farewell."

"Would I be so cruel?" Maddox asked, kissing her hand.

"Crueler," Zaide Romanza said.

"You know me too well."

"Too right I do."

Maddox took the goblet from her and drained it of wine. He set the cup on the floor and offered Zaide Romanza a shallow bow.

"I await your presence," he said and walked away.

"Your puppet will be most unmanageable when he finds out," Zaide Romanza said to Omur. "He's been so gleeful these past few days. To discover the truth—"

"I can manage him."

"I don't doubt it." Zaide Romanza rose from her chair. "Haleine however...I do wonder when the time comes if you'll be able to destroy her."

"If all goes well, I won't have to," Omur said. "If all goes well, she'll do it for me."

———⁓⁓⁓———

Somehow, when the dream ended and Haleine woke, she did not scream. She lay on her back with her hands over her mouth to prevent any noise from escaping while she worked to control both her breathing and her tears. Feeling as though she would fail on the latter, she very cautiously turned over and buried her face in a pillow. She didn't want Bronagh to hear.

Haleine's dreams had become so bad that the maid had taken to sleeping on a pallet near the fire so she could rouse her mistress when the need arose. Haleine hated it but did not order Bronagh away. The need was there and would be there, she feared, until Faolan returned to tell her her worries had been for naught.

She'd known when Faolan left that a battle would be inevitable. Now she dreamt of nothing else. Fighting, killing and worse. Dana dead and herself lost and alone.

She lifted her head and looked toward the fire. She couldn't see Bronagh, but she could hear the maid's steady breathing and knew Bronagh had not heard her wake.

Haleine slid from the bed and looked for her robe. She found it carefully draped over the top of a chair. She wanted the robe; she didn't want to leave the room without it but thought it too near her sleeping maid to risk fetching, so Haleine left it behind.

"Your majesty?" the guard in the hall said, falling hastily into his bow. "Is all not well?"

All was not well, and she was tired of saying otherwise.

"I am going to see my sons," she said.

With both her husband and Omur gone, Haleine had free reign of the palace. There was no place she was not allowed to go, yet the nursery was the only place she wanted to be.

"Now?" he asked.

"Yes, now," she said. "Stay or come as you wish. It matters to me not."

He would come because both Bronagh and Willem would have the man's hide if he allowed her for a moment to wander around unescorted. Each of her guards prayed that should any harm come to her under their watch that Willem would find them first because the hell Bronagh would bring onto them was too terrifying to imagine. Haleine was always amused by how much the men of her husband's army feared her maid. It was the only thing that amused her anymore.

The nursery was dimly lit, as all its occupants were sleeping. The nurses lay upon their pallets by the fire. Neither of them had heard her enter. She didn't mind; it was better that way. She motioned to her escort to wait in the hall and sat in the simple chair that stood between the two cradles. She hadn't been sitting long when Bronagh came in.

"Why is your guard standing out in the hall?" the maid asked.

"I told him to."

Bronagh sighed. "You forgot your robe."

"No, I didn't."

"You frightened the life out of me, you know," Bronagh said. "The next time you decide to stroll around the palace in the middle of the night, tell me first. That way, when I wake and find your bed empty, I will not think you've been kidnapped."

"And who do you suppose would have done the kidnapping?" Haleine asked. "And done so so quietly as to not disturb the overly light sleeper by the fire?"

"How did you manage it?"

"I left my robe."

Bronagh held out the garment. Haleine smiled upon seeing it and shook her head. Bronagh folded the robe over her arm.

"Did you dream?" the maid asked.

"Yes."

"Will you tell me what you dreamt about?"

She always asked. Haleine couldn't blame the curiosity and concern. It would be hard to ignore the tears and screams that now so often accompanied Haleine's dreams, especially for someone trained to do anything but ignore her.

"No," Haleine said.

She could ignore whatever she wanted. Apart from her dreams. They were not the sort to be disregarded. Fighting, killing, dying. Dana dead.

There was a wide-open field with two opposing sides charging toward each other. Death crept close behind, awaiting his offering. There would be much from which to choose. She stood in the center of the tall grass, aware of the two sides enclosing upon her but seeing only the corpses littering the ground. Rebels, the king's men, all of them intertwined and covered with a blanket of blood.

She was only able to look away from the carnage when she heard the screams. Dana's screams. Any part of her not previously frozen by the horror already witnessed died in that moment. She turned to see her lover lying prone on the ground, his screams filling her ears, and Omur, draped in black, hovering over him.

"There's been no word," Haleine said, pushing the image from her mind.

"Your majesty?"

"Mahile is not so very far away."

"What about Mahile?"

"That is where they would have fought. There or before it. He would have made sure of it. He wouldn't want the war to cross to Feond. It's why he went."

"How do you know there even was a battle?"

"None who left this palace had peace in mind, and you truly do not think otherwise."

"I don't; that's true," Bronagh said, "but you are worrying yourself to death. I would say anything if it would ease your mind for even a moment."

"Then tell me what has happened, for I need desperately to know why there has been no word, why we have heard nothing—not even rumor—from any of them. It would have happened by now."

"I don't know."

"I will want to go to the cathedral in the morning," Haleine said. "Will you be sure Willem knows it?"

"He already does."

Haleine nodded. Of course he did. It had become her habit to visit the cathedral at least once a day. Each time she hoped to see Dana's messenger. She hadn't yet.

"Will you come back to bed, your majesty?" Bronagh asked next.

Haleine looked at her sleeping sons and felt the smallest measure of peace stir within her.

"No," she said. "Not yet."

She stayed there the night, eventually falling asleep in her chair and snapping awake when Auryn started to cry. She went to his cradle and hovered over her son. She caught his tiny, flailing fist. When he wrapped his fingers around her thumb the strength of his grip surprised her.

"Oh my boy," she whispered. "So strong. Just like your father."

Alain took up his brother's cry and Haleine turned her head toward him, but his nurse was already there, lifting the child and cooing to him softly.

"I beg your pardon, your majesty."

Now Auryn's nurse stood at her side. Haleine looked at her son once more before untangling his fingers from her thumb and backing away to relinquish her position.

"I'll have a more comfortable chair brought in here for you," Bronagh said.

Bronagh's presence startled her, but only momentarily. She didn't know why she thought Bronagh would be elsewhere.

"A more comfortable chair?" she asked.

"You slept more here last night than you have in a long time. No dreams," Bronagh said. "At least not unpleasant ones."

Haleine watched the nurses care for her sons. "No dreams."

His head hurt. It hurt as though he had had entirely too much ale, but Dana knew there hadn't been even the smallest drop involved in making his head hurt like it did. There had only been Omur. The mage had threatened to kill him. He had threatened to kill Haleine.

That thought made Dana open his eyes. He didn't know where he had been or how long he may have toiled there, but he was back now in a tent at camp by the looks of it.

"Oh, thank the goddess," someone—female, but not Haleine—said. "You're awake."

"Where's Haleine?" he asked, starting to rise. His head pounded its protest. "Is she all right?"

"Dana," another voice—Faolan this time—said. "What's the last thing you remember?"

Hanah appeared over him, pushing him back down. She tried to mop his forehead with a damp cloth. He fought her off, but just barely.

"He said he was going to hurt her," Dana said. "Where is she?"

"She's safe. He didn't touch her."

"How do you know?" he asked, fending off Hanah a second time. "Have you seen her?"

"No, I haven't seen her, but I know because I know," Faolan said. "Now tell me—"

"Tell you what? I can't sit here and talk to you, Faolan. Why do you always insist on just sitting and talking? I can't do this now." Dana threw his legs over the side of the cot. "I have to go."

Faolan sighed. "Catch him."

"What are you talking about now?" Dana asked as he stood.

Almost as soon as he did, his knees gave out. Hanah caught him, preventing him from falling outright. He stood still for a moment, leaning on Hanah and staring at the ground before lifting his head to look at Faolan.

"You swear Haleine's safe?"

"Do I have to swear it?"

"Aye."

"Then yes, she's safe. I swear it."

Dana nodded as Hanah helped him back down. "What happened?"

"Omur attacked you," Faolan said. "He locked you inside a spell complicated enough that I couldn't break it before now. Everyone saw you fall on the battlefield and thought you were dead. I convinced your people otherwise, so they brought you to camp instead of burying you in Mahile. I started work on the counter spell, and you spent a good deal of time shrieking and writhing in pain. You've been quiet the last few days, though, and Hanah was worried I might have lost you."

Hanah shot the pegasus a look. "Everyone was. Including your friend here."

Faolan nodded. "*We* thought you were lost and, in a way, you were. I imagine, though, that's not what you experienced. Tell me what you remember."

"How many days?"

"Seven," Faolan said.

"Seven? Seven *days*?" Dana said. "I've been lying here for seven bloody days? How in the hell—How can I even—?"

"There are some benefits to a magical coma," Faolan said. "Now, please, tell me what you remember."

Dana closed his eyes and rubbed his temples. "Omur. Claiming he would kill me. I take it he failed."

"Not by much," Hanah murmured.

"Omur talked to you?" Faolan said.

"Patronized mostly," Dana said. "He wants to hurt Haleine."

"He wants to hurt everyone. What did he say to you?"

Dana thought about it. He remembered every word Omur had spoken, but he didn't know if he wanted to share that knowledge with Faolan.

"Does Omur know the future?" he asked instead.

"He thinks he does."

"Why does he think that?"

"There's a prophecy," Faolan said. "One that foretells the downfall of the goddess and the return of the dark gods."

Dana sat up again. He was still dizzy but as long as he didn't try to stand, he thought he could manage it.

"You've never mentioned a prophecy before."

"We didn't know about it before."

"How did you find out? *When* did you find out?"

"We placed spies—some human, some not—in different places, trying to glean whatever we could from whatever was available.

And the same night you met the prince of Tanuba, I thought we finally got lucky," Faolan said, "but now I can't be sure."

"Because of Omur."

"Yes. Now I need time to work out what's truth and what's lies," Faolan said. "What did Omur say to you?"

"Tell me about the battle. Tell me about our losses."

"Dana," Faolan said. "What did he say?"

"He said I spill their blood too lightly. I'd like to know if he was right."

"The losses were considerable. They always are," Faolan said. "Whether we lose one or one hundred."

"Which was it? One or one hundred?"

"You know which."

The fact that Faolan was unwilling to be more precise was an answer in itself. Dana glanced at Hanah and saw the terrible truth reflected in her eyes.

"And Mahile?" Dana asked. "What happened there?"

"We lost."

"We lost?"

"Yes. Maddox and his army came through and destroyed everything in their path. We didn't have enough people to hold it, and we lost."

"He was right. Omur was right. I took them to that place and asked them to die for me so that the king of a country none of them have ever seen might live. And he died anyway."

"How do you know about that?"

"Omur told me. Told me the deed had been done even before Maddox had left the palace."

"He was testing you?"

"Aye. He wanted to see if I would follow him. He wanted to see if we would leave Haleine unguarded. And we did."

"She's all right, Dana. I swear it."

He nodded. "Does she know I'm all right? You said they thought me dead in Mahile. What do they say now?"

"There are rumors you are dead. There are rumors claiming the opposite. I know both are circulating around the city, but I don't know what they're saying in the palace itself. Maddox and Omur are returning from Feond now. If they never sent word, I suppose it's quite possible Haleine knows nothing."

"But what if—"

"I sent Lucius to take care of it."

"Just now?" Dana asked and Faolan nodded. "Why did you wait so long? If she thinks I'm dead—"

"I wanted to be sure he wouldn't be lying," Faolan said. "That was a legitimate attack Omur made against you. He almost did kill you."

"Do you think he failed on purpose?"

"I don't know."

"I tried to kill him, you know. I put my sword through his heart."

"Oh. How'd that go?"

"Not as well as I'd have hoped. What is he?"

"He was human. I'm not sure there's a word for what he is now."

"How did that change?"

"When he proved himself worthy, the dark gods imbued him with an unnaturally long life."

"And the inability to be killed."

"At least by mortal means."

"Do I even want to know how such a thing is possible?"

"I can't imagine you would."

"Do I need to know?"

Faolan considered this. "I don't think so."

"And what of Zaide Romanza? Is the same true for her? Does she also have this...protection?"

"I don't know. You'll have to knife her and see what happens."

Dana almost smiled. "Do you think she'll let me get that close?"

"No."

"Something to worry about later, then," Dana said. "But first, we're going to see Haleine."

"Are you sure that's wise?" Faolan asked. "You're not untouchable anymore."

Dana tried to stand and, once more, he failed. "Wise or not," he said, preparing for another try. "I've still got to go."

—⁂—

The air in the cathedral was stifling. Haleine sat on a bench and stared at the altar built to honor a god she no longer was sure existed. How had she lost that? Something she had believed in all her life suddenly gone and replaced by what? She didn't believe in Faolan's goddess. All she seemed to have was fear for figments Faolan called her enemy.

It hadn't mattered to her before now. It was easy to ignore something for which there was no need. But now she wanted to offer a prayer, she wanted to beg a higher power—any higher power—to grant the safe return of her lover. But to whom would she direct such a plea? What ears would hear it? What ears would care?

"Please send him back to me," she whispered. "Please, I beg you."

She caught the movement of the Archbishop as he roamed the choir loft above. He had been eager to see her, wanting very much to talk to her but, at her wordless request and Willem's insistence, he had found himself relegated to the background. She did not come there to talk to him.

"Your majesty," a quiet voice said.

One of the monks, his face obscured by his hood, now knelt before her. She started to speak when he held up his hand to stop her. He pulled down the neck of his habit to give her a glimpse of the embroidered silver unicorn underneath.

"You have to know," he started.

There was a disturbance at the far end of the sanctuary. Haleine jumped and looked to see her mother and Ceallach arguing with Willem. She sighed and turned back, but the monk was gone. She scanned the sanctuary for a sign of him, but there was none.

"Willem," she said, her frustration heavy in her tone. "Allow my mother to pass. Clear everyone else."

There were protests, this time by Ceallach, but Willem silenced them and saw the man removed. Haleine stayed still while her wishes were carried out, preoccupied with Dana's messenger. What did she have to know? What had happened? It could not possibly have been good news he carried. That much had been in his voice.

Her mother sat beside her, and Haleine stared at the altar. "This is not an attractive quality."

"Caring for my daughter?"

"Stalking your daughter."

"That is a hateful thing to say."

"Aye, and I am the hateful sort now," Haleine said. "I thought you knew."

"Aye?" Rhoswen asked. "I didn't raise you to speak like a commoner."

Haleine laughed. She couldn't help it. The sound was loud and echoed throughout the chamber. The Archbishop glared at her.

"That is truly a ridiculous thing to say, Mother," she said. "Do you know that?"

"Haleine, I—"

"Oh, stop," Haleine sighed. "I don't wish to fight with you."

"Nor I with you."

"Why keep coming to me? I have dismissed you time and time again since you arrived, but you never stop coming."

"You will know this soon enough but without, I do hope, the pain I now feel," Rhoswen said. "A mother will never give up on her child."

"And if the child has given up on its mother?"

"Then she works twice as hard."

"Well, I don't think I shall ever have to worry about that, for I shall never do to my children what was done to me."

"No, what you have done to them could prove to be worse," Rhoswen said in a harsh whisper.

"What I have done? I don't know what you're talking about, but I have done nothing."

"Have you seen how very blond your sons are?" Rhoswen asked. "Their coloring never would have come from your husband's seed."

"You said so yourself," Haleine said. "You said my hair was such a color when I was born. So my sons will grow to resemble their mother instead of inheriting their father's abhorred darkness. I see no fault in that."

"Your hair was not so. I lied to your husband and claimed the opposite to be true to save you from his wrath. The fact his sons are blond cherubs did not escape him. It did not escape anyone."

"You're wrong."

"I'm not. Who is the father? I thought perhaps it was your man there," Rhoswen said, gesturing to Willem. "He is certainly protective enough to have—"

"Willem?" Haleine hissed. She stole a glance at her guard. He didn't appear to be paying attention to them, but she knew he heard every word. "He protects me as it is his duty to do so!"

"Then who?" Rhoswen asked. "Oh Haleine, why did you do this?"

Haleine sniffed in an attempt to keep from crying. Her shoulders sagged. "Why did you send me here? Did you not wish to protect me then?"

"Of course I did, your father too, but we had no choice, Haleine."

"Yes, you did. You had a choice. You could have said no. You could have refused."

"You don't understand."

"Of course I understand. What is there to misunderstand? Nathan demanded, and you said yes because you were too weak to say otherwise."

"He was our king. We were bound by duty."

"He was a man," Haleine said. "He was a man, not a god, and yet your loyalty to him outweighed the love you had for your own daughter."

"Haleine—"

"You didn't even fight for me, did you?"

"Haleine, please—"

"I would have rather died than come here."

"Don't speak that way," Rhoswen said. "Please, Haleine, don't."

"You do not know," Haleine said. "You do not know this life to which you have condemned me, all for the sake of your duty. I have done what I deemed necessary to survive, and I do not need your judgment."

"I do not judge."

"You do. You judge me as Revelin did, dismissing my actions as immoral, completely blind to the evil my husband does. Because he is a man, he has the right but because I am a woman, I have none."

"Tell me please."

Haleine shook her head and looked up when Willem approached. "What is it?"

"The king has returned," Willem said. "You are summoned to the palace to greet him."

Haleine nodded and dragged the back of her hand across her face to help rid it of tears. She walked out of the cathedral, her mother and guard following. Outside, a group of Eluned's citizens waited for her, just as they always did, and she still did not know what she had done to deserve their continued devotion. She scanned them all, but did not see the one face in which she was most interested. Rhoswen followed her into the carriage and sat beside her, taking her hand and holding it tightly in her own. Haleine let her, looking over her admirers until the carriage pulled away and left them in a cloud of dust.

Haleine's heart sank when she saw the scene in the palace's courtyard. There were soldiers everywhere, and they turned and cheered when they realized who had arrived. It made her ill. She gripped her mother's arm tightly.

Willem opened the door and offered his hand. Haleine shook her head minutely. The carriage was safe. As soon as she stepped out, she wouldn't be able to hide from what had happened. Things had gone wrong, terribly wrong. She didn't want to know more.

"Haleine?" Rhoswen said.

"Your majesty?" Willem said.

"Get me inside, Willem," she said, putting her hand in his. "Do it quickly. I wish to see no one."

"What is wrong?" Rhoswen asked.

"Go to your chambers and stay there," Haleine said. "Keep Sighle close."

"Haleine—"

"Go," she said and launched herself into the crowd.

Maddox waited in her chambers. He sat in her chair with one leg hooked over the arm. He was whole. Whatever had happened, he hadn't been harmed. Her eyes flickered to the fireplace where Bronagh was standing. The maid looked unusually frightened. Haleine untied her cloak and slipped it off her shoulders.

"Bronagh," she said. "Take this and go. See that my mother is comfortable. I fear she is not well."

Bronagh came forward and accepted the cloak. She backed away to the servants' passage, not taking her eyes off Haleine until she had to. When she was gone, Haleine scanned the rest of the room for Faolan but saw no evidence the pegasus had returned.

"Hello, my wife," Maddox said. "Did you miss me?"

The sight of him was replaced by a flash of him twisted in bedding and tangled in another woman's arms. Haleine shook her head slightly and the image disappeared. She leaned against the back of a chair. What had she just seen, and how had she seen it?

"Problem, love?"

She looked at Maddox and continued forward. "Your men in the courtyard seem to be in high spirits."

He smiled. "The rebellion has been crushed. What else would you expect?"

"Crushed?" She couldn't breathe.

"On Mahile's plains. I wish you had been there. It was truly a sight."

"I am sure." She slowly sat across from him. "Are you certain they have been destroyed? Will they not regroup and attack again? They have done this before."

"They won't this time. Not with their leader fallen," Maddox said. "They destroyed themselves once they saw him gone. It was an easy victory."

You have to know, the man had said.

"Dana—Dana is dead?"

She was suddenly and thankfully numb. It kept her from crying. It kept her from feeling. She didn't know what would happen when that faded.

"Very."

"You should—you should have sent word."

"I wanted to tell you myself," he said. "I wanted to see the look upon your face."

More like than not, Omur had wanted to see the look upon her face. He would be disappointed to have missed it.

"Surely you deserved a much grander homecoming than this," she forced herself to say.

"Indeed. We'll celebrate tonight and tomorrow and for weeks to come, I am sure, but tell me now, where have you been? I returned home to find my wife missing, and it pleased me not. I brought a gift for you from Feond, but you were not here to receive it. I do not know if I want to give it to you now."

He held an amulet, the chain hanging from his fingers. Her eyes slid down to the necklace's stone, a great red gem secure in a bed of gold. She wondered from where it had come and what had possessed him to give her a gift of any kind.

"I was at the cathedral," she said.

"Praying for my safe return?"

He shifted his position and held out the necklace. She hesitated but reached for it. It was heavy in her hand.

"Praying for your death." She dropped the amulet on the floor.

Maddox frowned and stood. He covered the distance between them and stopped when he towered over her. Haleine sat calmly as he placed his hands on top of hers and leaned in. She couldn't free herself, but neither did she want to.

"As you can see," he said, "your prayers have failed."

Haleine nodded. "I noticed. Next time I shall pray harder."

He hit her across the face hard enough to knock her from the chair. She lay on her stomach and waited for the riot of color flooding her field of sight to dissipate. He pulled her up by her elbow before it could and pushed her away. She stumbled a few steps before recovering both her balance and her vision. When she turned, he was bearing down upon her, seeking to grab her again. She tried to swat his hands away, and he grinned and laughed.

She lunged at him, arms outstretched in her determination to hurt him. He caught her, still laughing until she clawed at his neck. When she drew blood, he hissed and shoved her away. She made to attack him again, but he kicked her stomach and sent her back against the wall. He was pressed against her before she could move and held her in place with one arm across her throat. The other worked the fastenings of his breeches.

"Come, Haleine," he said, lifting her skirts. "Won't you fight me now? Won't you beg me to stop? I always enjoy it whether it is my enemies or you. I find it always has the same effect."

"The rebels beg you, then?" she asked as he forced her legs apart. "Beg you for their lives?"

"The one who mattered did. What concern is it of yours?"

She shook her head. "You're lying. He wouldn't have begged you. Not for anything."

"On intimate terms with a dead rebel, are you?" he asked, thrusting into her. "Be careful what you say, dear. I'd hate to have to kill you, too."

She closed her eyes. It would be the most for which she could hope.

Maddox held a lavish celebration that evening. Haleine attended because she was expected to do so, but she did not—would not—raise her cup in acknowledgement of her husband's gain and the rebellion's loss. She merely sat at his side, looking at everything while seeing nothing.

She left the hall when Maddox was drunk enough not to notice her absence. She went next to the nursery and sat in the chair Bronagh had placed there for her. The nurses tried speaking to her, but she had no interest in conversation and ignored the two women.

"Would you like to hold your sons?" one of them asked.

Her sons. Dana's sons. No, she couldn't hold them. Not this night. Just looking at them made her heart ache, and she realized she would find no peace there, nor anywhere else, and rose abruptly to leave the room.

But she had nowhere else to go but her chambers. Bronagh waited there and would not be ignored like the nurses. The maid swooped down upon her, instantly smothering her with care and worry.

"Where have you been?" Bronagh asked.

"The hall with my husband and the nursery with my sons," Haleine said, looking at Sabine tending the fire. "Willem will verify it as truth if you'd like."

"I didn't mean—I was only worried," Bronagh said.

She didn't say any more. She couldn't. She glanced over her shoulder at the other maid. Haleine stared at Sabine. Had Omur sent her, curious to know the queen's state? Would he want to hear of how she wept?

"Help me out of this gown; then you both may go," Haleine said. "I find I am rather weary and want nothing more than to sleep."

She looked at Sabine when she said this. Let that be all the girl carried back to her master. Bronagh barked at Sabine, calling for the girl's departure, but did not go herself.

"I shall stay with you," Bronagh said.

She couldn't breathe. If Bronagh stayed much longer, Haleine would faint outright.

"No," Haleine said. "I wish to be alone."

"What of your dreams?"

She shook her head. "There will be no dreams tonight."

When Bronagh finally left, Haleine stood in the center of the room, not knowing in which direction to move. She didn't want to sit by the fire where his ghost would be staring back at her. She didn't want to lie down and feel his hands on her skin. There were too many memories of him, of her. They were everywhere. She couldn't escape them.

She had dreamt this, too. This sense of hollowness. She wasn't dead, but neither was she alive. How long would she stay like this? How long could she? Certainly not forever. No one could. She was nineteen, just newly nineteen, and done with life.

And she didn't even care.

So she did what she had in her dream and sat on the floor in the darkest corner, hugging her knees to her chest. She would wake soon and find herself in her bed with Bronagh hovering over her. Then it would start again.

"Haleine?"

She didn't move when she heard his voice. She would wake soon. This was always when it happened. He spoke her name and it was done. He would be gone, but she would still have hope. At least for another day.

"Haleine?"

She heard his step. Her eyes watered, but she didn't move.

"Are you real?" she asked. "For I have dreamt this before, this, and the battle that took you from me. Is this real? Are you? Or do I dream again?"

He knelt in front of her and lifted her chin. "I am real," he said. "This is no dream."

She touched his face. He hadn't shaved; the line of his jaw was roughened by the growth of beard. She ran her hand over his lips before letting it drop away.

"They said you were gone," she said.

"Lucius was supposed to tell you." He took her hand and kissed it. "Faolan, you said he would—"

Haleine's eyes flickered to the right long enough to see the pegasus hovering there.

"He tried," she said. "He did. He was interrupted before he could tell me anything. Don't be angry."

"I'm not." Dana blew out a frustrated breath. "I'm not. I hate that even for a moment you thought me gone."

He reached for her. She was slow to see it coming and didn't pull away quickly enough or prepare herself for his touch. She winced. He noticed, even in the dark, and frowned. He took her hands and drew her into the light.

"Dana, no, it's all right," she said. "Maddox was—he was celebrating."

He touched her again, this time carefully. "I see."

"Bronagh covers them," she said. "If you had come sooner—"

"I would have seen them anyway."

"It's my own fault," she said. Immediately, both Dana and Faolan started to protest, and she shook her head. "No, it is. I provoked him. I told him I prayed for his death, and he did not find it at all amusing."

"Why would you ever—?" Dana stopped when he realized the answer to his question and looked at the ceiling, his own eyes now bright with tears. "I am sorry."

"I do not need you to be sorry."

He looked at her again. "Then what do you need?"

"You, here and now, are enough. I would never presume to ask for more."

"You never presume to ask for anything."

"I asked that you be returned to me. I sat in that cathedral today and I prayed for it. I don't even know to whom I prayed—your goddess maybe, I don't know—but pray I did. For you to come back to me," she said. "Selfish, I know, and I should not have done it, but I don't know how I could have done anything else."

Dana put his hand behind her neck and pulled her close. "Oh, Haleine. Oh, love."

"When he told me you were gone, there was nothing. Just nothing," she said. "I don't wish to feel that way again. So, please, stay with me tonight. As long as you can. It will be enough. Please? Just...stay."

He looked at her for a long time. "Faolan," he said finally and glanced around the room when the pegasus failed to answer. He was nowhere to be seen. "Where do you suppose he went?"

She had yet to take her eyes off Dana. "I don't care."

He nodded and went to kiss her. "Neither do I."

———◆———

Rhoswen had not closed the balcony doors when she had retired for the night, so Faolan was able to slip inside her chamber easily. Haleine's mother was asleep on the bed, and her youngest daughter slept on a pallet by the fire. Faolan landed on the small table that sat at Rhoswen's bedside and contemplated his options.

The safest thing to do would be to leave Rhoswen just as she was and return to Haleine's balcony. It would have been the smartest thing, too. He could guard Dana and Haleine better that way. Neither of them was as untouchable as he once thought. Omur knew too much and posed too much of a threat, and Faolan didn't yet understand why the mage—and the gods he served—hadn't acted. Omur knew Maddox wasn't the father of Haleine's sons and that Dana was. And he hadn't wanted Haleine's sons to be born at all.

Two from one. Those words were what brought him here, and they were the reason why he wasn't going to do the safest or smartest thing. Instead, he was going to wake Haleine's mother and try to change the game.

He had to rely on the hope that Rhoswen was a light sleeper. He could have used magic to wake her or even to speak to her while she slept, but he didn't dare. He could sense a darker magic, Omur's sort of magic, lurking nearby. He didn't want to risk alerting the mage to his presence here.

"Rhoswen," he said in a normal tone.

Nothing happened.

"Rhoswen," he said louder. "I need you to wake up now."

This time she jerked awake. She was groggy and disoriented, and when she rolled over and saw him, she jumped and screamed. He stood quiet.

"Mother?" Sighle sat up. "What's the matter?"

"Nothing, love, nothing," Rhoswen said, glaring at him. "It's your sister's wretched beast. He's found his way here and startled me. It's all right; go back to sleep."

Sighle looked at him for a moment before lying down again. Rhoswen watched her daughter until she was satisfied of the girl's well-being before turning to him.

"Still here?" she asked and waved her hand at him. "Go away now. Be gone with you. Shoo."

"Shoo?" he asked. "Oh, and if you wondered, the wretched beast comment wasn't well received either."

Rhoswen stared.

"We should go outside," Faolan continued. "I came to talk to you. Not Sighle."

"Oh God," Rhoswen said. "You talk."

"You noticed."

"And you wish to talk to me?"

"Yes. Outside."

"Is my daughter in danger?"

"No more than usual," Faolan said. "Let's go outside."

Rhoswen still didn't move. "I don't understand."

"I know what you haven't told Haleine. Or Sighle."

"I don't know what you're—"

"Mireille."

Rhoswen immediately shrank back and looked over her shoulder to assure herself that Sighle hadn't heard. The girl was asleep and was aware of nothing, but Rhoswen nearly fell out of bed in her haste to get out of the room. Faolan followed.

"How do you—how could you possibly know about her?" Rhoswen asked, closing the doors behind them.

"I know the creatures who took her. I was there."

This seemed to hit her harder than anything else he had said. It did not bode well for the remainder of the conversation.

"You were there?" she asked.

"I make it a point to be there whenever and wherever they appear in this dimension."

"Dimension?"

"Too much too soon," Faolan said. "Let's go back."

Rhoswen shook her head. "I don't want to talk about this. I don't want to talk to you."

"Too late," Faolan said. "They're called neruals, a particularly nasty breed of lycanthrope. An entirely evil breed of lycanthrope. They're one of the few living creatures that can truly make such a claim. They kill to feed; they kill because they want to. They're good at it. It's really the only thing they're good at. Or for. Part of the reason they're such effective killers is that their bite and claws are laden with poison. If they break skin, you're dead. A mere scratch would kill even the strongest of men. An infant, you can understand, wouldn't have stood a chance."

"They stole entrance to our home and went after my daughters. They took Mireille. They would have taken Haleine as well had my husband not stopped them. Those creatures, whatever you called them," Rhoswen said, "why did they want my girls?"

"They didn't want your girls," Faolan said. "They wanted Mireille."

"Why?"

"I'm not sure I know," Faolan admitted. "But trying to explain what I think would be like trying to explain dimensions, so I won't."

"Then why are you telling me any of this?"

"Because I'm afraid if we don't do something, you stand to lose Haleine the same way you lost Mireille."

"You said they didn't want Haleine."

"They didn't then. They might now."

"Why?"

"Who was the first born?"

His question confused her, and he could see the answer saddened her. Her eyebrows furrowed, and she sat on a bench and looked at her hands for a moment before responding.

"Haleine came first. Mireille was so close behind," Rhoswen said, smiling through her tears. "I remember the night they were born. Of course I remember; it's not something a woman forgets. My husband was away, battling for control of Quatara, so I had instead his steward pacing the halls, waiting to send the letter to my lord at the very announcement of the birth. Darragh was the only one who thought I might carry twins. I don't know why; the midwives thought him foolish, too, but he was right. I remember the moon was so bright when Haleine was born. It lit that chamber almost as well as daylight would have. It didn't last though. The clouds swallowed it when Mireille came. The servants had to scramble for more light."

Two from one. The first from moon, the next from dark. It couldn't have been right. So blatant? It wasn't how prophecy normally worked. Of course it didn't mean it wasn't how this one would work. That was the problem with prophecy. Faolan couldn't even be sure if this one was to be believed at all. It could have been planted. Was Omur trying to force him into revealing something?

"What about the night the neruals came?" he asked next.

"Yes, I recall that as well. It was dark, the darkest night I could remember, and I was uneasy. I wanted to see them, my girls. I wanted to know they were safe. Darian came with me. And I saw those—those things and—"

Rhoswen clapped her hands over her mouth.

"It's all right. You don't need to say any more," Faolan said.

"Why did I have to say anything at all?" she asked when she was able.

"Trying to make a point, in my own crude manner," Faolan said. "Losing Mireille hurt. It still hurts. That's plain to see. But you didn't know, you couldn't have known, what would happen. And I've already told you what they are, so now you know you couldn't have stopped them, even if you had known."

"I don't understand."

"I fully expect the neruals to come for Haleine. I don't know when it might happen—I don't know how—but they're coming. And this time, when they take your daughter, you won't have the luxury of ignorance to help comfort you."

"But you said I couldn't have stopped them."

"It's true. You can't stop them, but I can," Faolan said. "With your help."

"What do you need me to do?"

"I need you to convince the Tanubian army to come here," Faolan said. "And fight against Maddox."

Rhoswen laughed. "What makes you think I have any influence over what the Tanubian army does?"

"I think you have influence over your husband," Faolan said, "and I think your husband has enormous influence over what the Tanubian army does."

"You want me to convince my husband to convince the prince to convince the queen to renounce an alliance in order to join forces with a dying rebellion, all on the word of a—of a—what are you?"

"You shouldn't trust the court gossip, Rhoswen. The rebellion isn't dying," Faolan said. "And Revelin won't have to convince Haraszty of anything. We both know that."

Rhoswen nodded. "Even if I could convince my husband, Revelin will not be moved to break an alliance his father formed."

"He might if you use the correct bait."

"You mean my daughter," Rhoswen said. "You mean Haleine."

"Yes."

Rhoswen looked at her hands again. "You are willing to exploit love?"

"When it suits my needs."

"You exploit me as well. You've seen how desperate I am, how pathetic I've become. You think maybe I will be easily bent to your purposes, that I will act without having questioned whether I should believe anything you say. Tell me this," Rhoswen said. "You were there when those creatures came for my child?"

"Yes."

"Why did you not stop them?"

"I tried," Faolan said. "I failed."

"You failed," Rhoswen whispered.

"I did. It's not something I like to admit about anything, but that's the truth of the matter," Faolan said. "It still won't quell your suspicions though, so in the morning, ask Haleine what you should believe. She'll tell you."

"She'll tell me nothing."

"She'll tell you everything."

Rhoswen's eyes filled with tears. "Do you know the one my daughter fancies herself to love?"

"It's more than that. More than fancy."

"It isn't Revelin."

"No. Tomorrow, come early," Faolan said. "That way Bronagh won't have a chance to hide it."

"Hide what?"

"What you need to see," he said. "What Haleine needs to show you."

Rhoswen nodded. She wasn't looking at him anymore. Faolan was preparing to leave when she spoke again.

"You were wrong," she said. "About the neruals."

"I doubt that."

"You said a nerual's scratch would be enough to kill a man," she said. "Yet my husband endured far more injury than that at their doing, and he lives."

Faolan thought about that. He hadn't expected it but found he wasn't surprised by it. Especially not after everything else she had told him. It was just another piece of a puzzle he was starting to think might never be complete.

"I wasn't wrong," he said and flew away.

CHAPTER 18

They stayed close the entire night. Haleine laid her head on his chest. Her hand was on his shoulder, near his neck, and her fingers wrapped around the wisps of hair there. It felt as though she feared he would disappear if she didn't have some hold on him, however small. And even more than that, it felt as if she feared him knowing. Dana kept his arm around her, to reassure her but also to reassure himself. As if maybe he was afraid of losing her. As if he was afraid of her knowing.

"You'll be gone when I wake," Haleine said, drawing away suddenly. "Won't you?"

Dana gazed at her. She lay beside him, looking impossibly beautiful and serene despite her tone. He rolled on his side and put his hand on her cheek. "This is not a dream."

She covered his hand with hers. "It might be a dream."

"It isn't."

"Either way, you will be gone when I wake."

"You know I can't stay."

"That never seems to stop me from wanting it."

"Nor I," he said. He took her hand and kissed her palm. "Have you any idea how much I love you?"

"I do, but it is still lovely to hear."

"Then I shall tell you every time I see you. Every moment we are together, you shall hear it."

She laughed and leaned in to kiss him. "I look forward to it. Will you stay until I fall asleep?"

He nodded and rolled onto his back. She slid against him and laid her head once again on his chest. He put his arm around her and kissed the top of her head.

"I will stay as long as I can," he said. "I promise."

It did not take long for her to fall asleep. With what Faolan had told him about Haleine's state, he was surprised she hadn't done so sooner. But it didn't matter. He was content to hold her.

She will be the end of them. The end of you as well.

The thought entered his mind so suddenly and unexpectedly that he tightened his grip on Haleine's arm with enough force to rouse her from sleep.

"What is wrong?" she asked.

"Nothing, love," he answered. "Nothing. I'm sorry for waking you."

She looked as though she thought him a liar, but she didn't press him further, probably afraid to know. She nodded and drifted off again. He stared at the ceiling and the angels painted over the whole of it. In the firelight, they looked to be more like demons. Everything was a lie.

When he heard the servants' passage open, he immediately separated himself from Haleine and prepared to roll from the bed, but Bronagh entered before he could. She wouldn't be pleased by his presence, but he settled back against the pillows and waited for her to see him. She walked toward the bed, her eyes sweeping the room before resting on the bed. On him. She hissed as though she were a cat. He didn't move, waiting to see what she would do.

Her eyes flickered between Haleine and him. She set her lantern down and put her hands on her hips so she could glare at him properly. He bit back an urge to smile, doubting she would find it the least bit charming.

When she sighed and broke her stance, Dana knew he had won. She moved to the fire and threw logs into it with more force than Dana felt necessary. When she finished, she glanced in their direction, looking, Dana thought, slightly guilty. He smiled and was rewarded with another hiss. He ducked his head so she wouldn't see his continued amusement. She would think he was laughing at her, but he wasn't. He laughed because he was very much like her.

He shouldn't have been there; he never should have been there. They both knew it, but neither did anything about it. She never did anything out of fear of what Maddox would do to Haleine. If she could find a way around it, if she could be assured of Haleine's safety, she would turn him in without hesitation. And Dana suspected that as soon as Omur no longer had need of him, Bronagh's opportunity would be found.

But even knowing that and expecting it was closer than he wanted to believe, he still didn't go. His place with Haleine was too intoxicating. When she dismissed him after the birth of her sons, he should have stayed away. She hadn't said one false word. They were fools to do what they had done. They were larger fools to continue on. But still, he had come back, unable to stay away, and she had welcomed him back, unable to turn him away a second time. He should have been strong enough for the both of them. Instead he made it worse.

How did he ever let her do anything for him? Asking her to spy for him, to go to Maddox for him? He only put her at greater risk. He put her in Omur's path and made her vulnerable to him. Omur would kill her the very moment he thought he would profit from it most.

His delight gone, he checked to see if Bronagh remained. She had picked up her lantern and was now on her way out. She opened the door and looked at him over her shoulder.

"If you loved her, you wouldn't be here," she said.

He didn't respond. He couldn't argue with her because she was right. Omur had it wrong. Haleine wouldn't be the end of him. He'd be the death of her.

He had to end it before it got that far. There had to be a way to defeat the mage. He didn't know why Faolan hadn't told him before—maybe the pegasus didn't know how—but there had to be a way. He refused to believe he was powerless to end this, to save her.

Suddenly energized and restless, he left the sanctuary of Haleine's bed and sat by the fire while he waited for Faolan to return. He didn't know to where the pegasus had disappeared, but Dana found himself irritated by the extended absence.

"What are you still doing here?" Faolan asked when he did arrive.

"Where have you been?" Dana demanded.

"Taking care of some things," Faolan said. "What are you still doing here? The sun will be up soon, and Bronagh will be far from thrilled if you're here when she comes."

"She already came and is already displeased, but I couldn't very well leave. Haleine needs to be taken care of. She needs to be guarded, and I want you to protect her. I don't want her to be left alone any longer. Ever."

"You know I only go when necessary."

"We'll find a way around that. You're not the only magical being in that camp," Dana said. "You have to watch over her. Mahile was a warning. Omur's going to come after her, and we can't let him succeed."

"You'll have to come up with something else because me tethering myself to her side isn't going to solve the problem."

"I'm going to bring the fight to Omur. He's going to learn what it is to have me as an enemy."

"Dana," Faolan said. "You can't—"

"Don't tell me I can't. Help me to figure out how."

Faolan was quiet for a moment. "All right. Go back to camp. Stay there. Talk to Lucius and Ilya and James. Make plans if you'd like, but don't act until I tell you."

Dana looked up, ready to protest. Faolan didn't offer him the opportunity.

"Don't act until I tell you," Faolan repeated. "If you want to do this—and you want to survive it—you'll listen to me."

"How long?"

"As long as it takes."

"As long as what takes?"

"A sea voyage, I hope," Faolan said. "We're going to need Tanuba."

"Tanuba?" Dana asked. "Has something happened to Revelin?"

"No."

"Then what do you suppose Tanuba will be willing to do for us?"

"That's what I intend to find out," Faolan said. "Now get out of here. I'll send word."

"On Tanuba?"

"Yes. Now go away."

"What makes you think Revelin will be interested in doing anything other than putting a noose around my neck?"

"The same reason you think he'll only be interested in putting a noose around your neck."

Dana sighed. He had no more time to argue with the pegasus. Was that why Faolan had delayed so long in his return? He looked at the floor for a moment before reaching into his boot to remove his dagger.

"What are you doing with that?" Faolan asked.

Dana didn't answer. He stood and went over to the bed. He kissed Haleine's forehead before leaving the dagger at the foot of the bed.

"Make sure she gets that," he said as he walked away. "Make sure she keeps that."

"Dana, what do you—?"

346

"Just in case, Faolan," Dana said. "Please. I can't lose her."
Faolan looked at the dagger and nodded.

———◦◦◦———

Coming awake, Haleine was first aware of the pain. Arms and legs stiff, bruises she hadn't been aware of before now. She stretched carefully and turned her head to see if Dana remained.

"He's gone," Faolan said.

The pegasus stood near the foot of the bed. She nodded and smiled at him as she sat up.

"I knew he would be," she said. "It's never safe to linger here for long, especially not with Bronagh lurking around the way she does."

"Dana left you something."

Faolan glanced down, and she followed his gaze to see a glint of steel obscured by coverlets. She pulled them back to reveal a dagger. She looked to Faolan for an explanation.

"Just in case," he said.

"In case of what?"

"You know what."

"But I barely know what to do with it."

"Do you know which end to hold?" he asked and she nodded. "I'd say you've mastered the most important lesson."

"Aren't you amusing."

"Maybe on occasion, but not just then," Faolan said. "He wants you to have it, and I want you to have it. Just in case."

She nodded again and sank back against the pillows, leaving the dagger where it was. She'd have to hide it later. Where, however, she did not know. Where could she conceal it that Bronagh or one of the others would not find it?

"Where is Bronagh?" Haleine asked. "It's late. I'm surprised she is not here. Nor anyone else."

"She was here earlier," Faolan said. "You were sleeping, and she didn't want to wake you. She's been terrorizing just about everyone who's tried to get in here."

"Just about?"

"Your mother came by."

Haleine groaned. "I should not be surprised I am again made to suffer a visit from her. I have spent too much time worrying about my lover and his pegasus, and it has made her concerned. She thinks I live in sin."

"She does more than think it."

It was not Faolan who had spoken but instead her mother. Haleine sat up again and saw Rhoswen rising out of a chair near the fire.

"Faolan," Haleine said, not looking away from her mother. "What did you do?"

"What I had to," he answered.

She heard him, but his words didn't register with her. She threw aside the coverlets and slid out of bed. Dana's dagger clattered to the floor and landed at her feet. She looked at it as though it were a serpent waiting to strike. She snatched her chemise off the floor and turned away from the weapon. Rhoswen stood in front of her.

"Go," Haleine said. "Get away from here. From me."

"Dana," Rhoswen said. "The man who leads the rebellion? This is who—"

She stopped as she examined her daughter. Her expression tightened, and Haleine threw the shift over her head.

"He did this?" Rhoswen asked. "He hurt you?"

"Dana didn't do that, Rhoswen," Faolan said. "You know he didn't."

"Don't you talk to her," Haleine said, whirling around.

"Yes, I will second that request," Rhoswen said. "You have said quite enough to me."

"What have you told her?" Haleine demanded. "What do you want with her?"

"He wants Tanuba."

Her mother again. Rhoswen stood close but stayed behind her. Haleine stared at Faolan.

"And what," she asked, "does he want with Tanuba?"

Faolan stared back at her, calm and waiting. He would let her rail against him. He would listen to every hateful thing she could think to say. Then, when she was done, he would tell her what he wanted. He would tell her why he now had use for Tanuba, and she would see it delivered to him. As long as he had use for her, he would never leave. But what was worse was that she depended upon it.

"Well?" she said. "What use have you found for Tanuba?"

"Stopping Maddox, stopping Omur," Faolan said. "Saving the rebellion, saving Dana."

"Don't," Haleine said. "Don't make this about him."

"I can't make this about anything else," Faolan said. "Without Dana to lead it, the rebellion will fail."

"Let it fail," she said. "If Dana doesn't fight, Maddox will have no reason to continue his attacks. The chaos will die, as will your enemy."

"If Dana doesn't fight, it'll only be because he's dead." Faolan used a patient tone, one similar to a tutor instructing a pupil. "And when the rebellion dies with him, Maddox won't stop because Omur won't let him. He's worked for this for seven hundred years. He won't let it slip away now."

"And neither will you," Haleine said.

"Seven hundred years?" Rhoswen asked.

"And neither will I," Faolan confirmed.

"No, you won't," Haleine said. "You'll sacrifice Dana; you'll use me, my mother, any who further your purpose."

"All true," Faolan said, "but it still doesn't change the fact that we need Tanuba. We need Revelin."

She shook her head. "I don't want him here."

"I know," Faolan said, now sounding tired. "Haleine, if it was a choice between saving Dana and saving the world, I would, without hesitation, choose the world."

"I wouldn't."

"I know that, too. As does Omur."

"What does that matter? Why should he care what choice I would make? What have I to do with the saving of the world?"

"Probably more than any of us in this room realize," Faolan said.

"What are you talking about?"

"I mean saving Dana and saving the world is the same thing right now. And you have the key to doing both. You *are* the key to doing both."

"There must be another way."

"No. We need Tanuba. We need Revelin."

"No. No, I don't want him here," Haleine said. "I won't do it."

"You will," Faolan said. "If you want to save Dana, you will."

"You don't mean it," Haleine said. "You're only saying it so I'll do what you want."

"I wish that were true. I really do, but it's not," Faolan said. "Things are changing, Haleine. Dana's dagger there on the floor proves that. We can't be sure now of what we were before. That battle on Mahile's plains was a direct attack on Dana. Omur went after him. I didn't think he would, but he did and he didn't miss by much. We were lucky. We might not be again. The rebellion needs help. As much as you don't want it to be true, it is. We need Tanuba. We need them on our side, and I think you might be instrumental in convincing Revelin of that."

She looked at Faolan and glanced at her mother before walking away from them both. She stood in front of the fire. "Why did you do it like this? You knew I would give in eventually and do whatever you asked. Why did you involve my mother? Why did you bring her here?"

"He did it for me," Rhoswen said. "So I would agree to help where I wouldn't before. He wanted me to see what you had hidden and bade me to come and hear for myself what you did not want to tell me. He exploits love, you see."

Haleine smiled and sat in her chair. Rhoswen came and sat across from her.

"Aye, so do we all. And why wouldn't we?" Haleine said. "I am in love with the leader of the rebellion. It is he who fathered my children. I am whole when he is near, and every time he is gone, whatever the reason, there is a hole within me that grows larger with each passing day. Only he can fill it and only he can staunch its growth. One day he will leave for the last time and will never come again. And that day, I know, will be the end of me."

Faolan joined them now. He stood on the arm of her chair and looked at her. For a moment, she thought he seemed sad.

"Faolan is wise to use another's love to get what he needs," Haleine said. "He knows I could never say no. What love did he exploit to get you to come and listen? Father?"

"You."

"Well, it is a rare mistake you have made, Faolan," Haleine said. "For there is no love to be found there."

"Haleine," Faolan said. "Stop it."

Both she and her mother gawked at the pegasus.

"Your mother made a choice. For better or worse, it's done and it can't be changed," he said. "All you can do is move forward. You either forgive her or you don't. And since we both want something from her, I'd suggest forgiveness."

She felt her mother's eyes on her, but she stared at Faolan as she tried to think of something to say in response.

"Tell me, Haleine," Rhoswen pleaded. "For the love of God, tell me."

"What god?" Haleine asked.

"What god?" Rhoswen echoed. "Haleine, what do you—?"

"We need Tanuba. We need Revelin and Father to bring their men here and fight against my husband at the cost of their alliance, so that the people of this land might live. So that I might live in something other than fear. Will you help, Mother?" Haleine looked at her. "Will you help me to save my lover? To save myself?"

"Why did Maddox hurt you?" Rhoswen asked.

"Because he could. Because he was pleased."

"Because he thought Dana was dead," Rhoswen said. "He thinks it still."

"Aye," Haleine said. "And you won't tell him otherwise. Him, nor anyone else."

"I will return to Tanuba if you want it," Rhoswen said. "As soon as I can find passage, I will go."

"I will get your passage," Haleine said. "Maddox will grant me that. You must take Sighle with you, to keep her safe."

"Of course."

Haleine looked at Faolan. "Where do you want the army to go when they arrive? You cannot want them sailing into the city's main port."

"No," Faolan said. "I'd rather they didn't. I'll have you write instructions for them. Will Revelin know your writing?"

"Yes."

"Good. That will help convince him. Rhoswen, prepare to leave. With the armada the king has, you should be able to sail before nightfall. Haleine will have letters for you by then. It's important, Rhoswen, that no one see these except for Revelin and your husband, but only if they agree to help. If they say no—"

"They won't," Rhoswen said.

"If they do," Faolan said, "burn them."

Rhoswen stood. "I will do as you ask, but they won't say no. I will make your father hear me, Haleine. I will make the prince hear me. We will change this."

Haleine nodded and looked at the floor so her mother wouldn't see her cry. Rhoswen put her hand over Haleine's and squeezed it slightly before she walked away.

"You'll need to go to Maddox and secure your mother's passage," Faolan said.

Haleine cleared the tears from her eyes. "You should not have involved her."

"I had to."

"Why?"

"Things are changing," he said. "And on that note, when you come back and the letters are written, I want you to tell me about your dreams."

She bit her lip. "My dreams?" She shook her head. "I don't remember them."

"You're lying."

"Faolan!"

"Ever since I met you, you've been plagued by dreams. They keep you awake more nights than not, and I doubt very much you've forgotten any of them. I want you to tell me about your dreams. Everything involving Dana."

She blushed.

"All right," Faolan amended. "Almost everything involving Dana."

—*ww*—

Omur's timing could not have been better, and his plan was playing out perfectly. He smiled as he ended the spell allowing him to hear anything said within the queen's chambers. No doubt there would be further conversation between Haleine and the pegasus; she was angry with him for involving her mother and would not let the offense pass easily. Indeed, Omur himself was irritated with the pegasus for the very same reason, but he did not need care what the queen would say on the matter. He had heard enough already.

Back from the dead, and the first thing the rebel leader did was not to see to his followers but rather run straight into the arms of his lover. But what had proven to be even more interesting was Dana's conversation with the pegasus.

I'm going to bring the fight to Omur, the rebel leader had said. *He's going to learn what it is to have me as an enemy.*

Within the walls of his own chamber, far from the queen's rooms, Omur laughed loudly. The rebel leader meant to school him in the art of war, did he? Well, Omur would certainly welcome the entertainment.

He laughed to himself all the way to the soldiers' barracks, where he dispatched two men with orders for Varro to return at once. He would recall all troops and wait. That was first. Dana would plan his attack, the pegasus would tell the queen, and Omur would know everything.

There were other arrangements to be made, but he would have to see to them himself once Haleine did as the pegasus had instructed. He did not suspect he would have to wait long, for she was always prompt about delivering to the vermin what he wanted. Omur climbed the stairs back to his chambers, wondering where she was and what she was doing. Had she already gone to her husband? Was she already back in her quarters? There was still the promise of a very interesting conversation concerning the queen and her dreams. If the pegasus wanted to know about them, Omur did as well.

He looked up when he heard someone approaching from the opposite direction. It was the queen. Maddox's stench surrounded her. She begged him for a ship to carry her mother safely home to Tanuba so she might rally an army against him. She used her sex to purchase from him his own end. Omur never understood why the majority of mortal men considered women the weaker sex when so many of them were led by the promise of a woman's snatch.

As she grew closer, she glanced at him, fearless and daring. Then she ignored him as though he were someone of no consequence. The guard did not share her view. He locked eyes with Omur and stepped nearer to his charge.

The guard's reaction angered him, but it was Haleine's lack of concern that sparked the rage within him. Without thinking, Omur released the spell to stop the guard where he stood. Haleine, sensing her guard's sudden withdrawal, turned her head. Her eyes widened, and Omur pounced.

He flew at her, grabbed her by the throat and slammed her against the wall. She gasped for air and looked at him in complete and utter terror.

"Your highness does know fear," he said. "I had wondered."

He didn't think he had ever felt this much pleasure all at once before. Her eyes flickered to the left where her guard stood frozen in mid-stride, hand on the hilt of his sword. Omur applied more pressure to her throat.

"Don't look at him. Look at me," he said and smiled when Haleine obeyed. "You may think—you may believe yourself to be smarter than your husband, and it may well be true, but I warn you to take caution with me, my lady, for you are far outmatched here."

She started to whimper. He should have let her go. His lords didn't want her harmed. He should have loosened his grip on her, but he didn't.

"You are not so brave without your man, are you?" he asked. "Without your guard, you are no better than those whores you call your ladies-in-waiting, are you?"

She didn't answer him. Of course she didn't. The woman could hardly breathe.

"What does your rebel lover call you?" Omur asked. "His mistress? His whore?"

The terror grew in her eyes. He smiled. "Oh yes, I know, your highness. I know who you are. What you are."

He needed to let her go and release the guard from the spell. Someone would come before too long, and it would do him no good for anyone to see what he did there.

"He'll leave you," Omur said next. "He and the pegasus. They will both leave you. Have you dreamt that yet?"

The look in her eyes changed. Fear was still there, but it was a different sort. He smiled once more and dropped her as suddenly as he had grabbed her. She fell to the floor, rubbing her throat and gasping for air. When she had recovered enough, she looked at him.

"Let's talk about your husband," he said. "It would be in your best interest should this encounter not be made known to him. It would be most unfortunate for you were the king to discover your infidelity."

She remained silent. Was she calculating how much weight his threat carried?

"How do you suppose Maddox would react to finding out his wife was impregnated by his enemy's seed?" he asked. "How long do you think it would take for him to drown those bastard boys of yours?"

Her face paled. She carefully got to her feet and slapped him across the face. He laughed at her gesture until he felt the heat from her fingers searing his flesh. Stunned and in pain, he pulled away from her and rescinded the spell that bound her guard. The man stepped forward as if no time had been lost, but he was smart enough to realize something had happened. It was enough to distract Haleine and allow Omur the chance to escape.

He went to his chambers and locked the doors behind him both physically and magically. Haleine would report to the pegasus who would be sure to be interested in what was said both then and now. Omur wouldn't be able to keep the beast ignorant about what he had done, but he couldn't allow him access to this.

With a wave of his hand, a fire sprung to life. He took a handful of powder made of elements not found on this earth from a vase resting on the mantel and cast it into the flames. He fell to his knees and lowered his head as he began the chant.

"My lord!" he cried. "Yelsneh, god of the north and commander of my will, I beseech you to appear before me now!"

When the air thickened, Omur knew his lord had arrived and rested his head on the floor.

Why have you called me?

"My lord, I seek your wisdom and guidance."

On what matter?

"My lord, who is she? The queen, my lord, what is she?"

What has happened to make you ask this question?

Her touch still burned. He covered his cheek with his hand. The pain of it made him pull away almost immediately.

"She touched me, my lord. She burned me."

She touched you? How did she ever get that close?

"I am at fault, my lord," Omur said. There was nothing to say but truth. "Punish me, please, I beg you, for I have defied your orders and put hands to her."

Why did you do this?

"I do not know," Omur said. "I acted without thought, my lord."

We are displeased.

"As well you should be. I do not argue that."

And yet, you beseech us for favor.

"Please, what is she?" Omur begged. "Please, I must know."

There was another long pause. Omur held his breath while he awaited the decision.

She is a means to an end. Yelsneh's voice came. *Kill her.*

Faolan lay in the center of Haleine's bed when she came in. He broke off his exchange with Luisiúil but didn't open his eyes.

"Clear this room," the queen said, sounding almost shrill. "And yes, Bronagh, I do mean both you and Ceallach. I want all of you gone now."

Something had happened. Was it Maddox? Haleine had planned to go there first to see about securing Rhoswen's passage to Tanuba, but she would've gone to her mother afterward. Had Rhoswen said something to her daughter? Something about Mireille? He had to hope not. He wasn't ready to answer questions about her.

He opened his eyes and watched Haleine. He couldn't remember ever seeing her so distraught before. It was apparent in everything about her: her voice, her movements, her face. Faolan knew that was why both Bronagh and Ceallach fought so hard to stay.

But Haleine won out in the end, and her maid and chaperone were banished to the hall. Willem closed the doors behind him and left Faolan alone with Haleine. She stood near the doors with her back to him.

"Haleine," he said. "What happened?"

"You can't tell Dana."

"What happened?"

She turned around, massaging her throat gently. "I want you to promise not to tell Dana."

"What did Maddox do?"

"It wasn't Maddox," she said. "Faolan, please, I need you to promise."

"I promise."

The words were easy to say. Judging by her actions, how unsettled she was, he was already convinced telling Dana would be a bad idea.

"It was Omur," she said.

"Did he hurt you?"

"He tried to choke the life from me."

"He laid hands on you?"

There wasn't a mark upon her. He had no doubt she spoke the truth. He could feel her terror, but there wasn't a mark on her.

"Tell me everything," he said. "Please."

She walked toward him. "You can't tell Dana."

"I already promised I wouldn't."

She sat in her usual chair. He flew over and landed on the table in front of her. She glanced at both entrances to the room.

"I met him on the stairs," she said, keeping her eyes on the doors. "I was going to see my mother, and there he was, coming toward me. I ignored him. He had nearly passed by when I saw his hand rise up, just so."

Faolan watched her raise her hand barely off her lap. Her palm faced him and he knew. Omur had cast a spell. But not against her.

"What happened to Willem?"

"He just...stopped. He was frozen, as still as a statue. Omur did something, magic, I know. I felt it. I felt the malice behind it."

"You felt it?" Faolan said and she nodded. "What happened then?"

"I was looking at Willem. I didn't see Omur. He grabbed me and held me against the wall."

She stopped. She still didn't take her eyes off the doors. He waited a moment.

"Haleine?"

"He knows," she said. "He knows about the boys. He threatened them. And Dana."

Omur had become very fond of threats of late. Maybe it meant nothing and perhaps Faolan was just seeing conspiracy where there was nothing more than general spite. How could he know for sure?

"But not you," Faolan said. "He didn't threaten you."

"Apart from choking me, no." Haleine slumped in her chair. "I am afraid of him. I wasn't before, even with all your warning, I wasn't. Not really. But I am now."

"I will keep you safe. I will always keep you safe."

"And what if there was a choice between saving me and saving the world?"

He looked again at her unblemished neck. Two from one.

"I don't expect to ever have to make that choice," he said. "I'll keep you safe. I promise that, too."

She scanned the room again. "He told me you would leave me. That you, and Dana too, would leave. He asked if I had dreamt it yet."

So Omur also suspected her dreams. Faolan was more disconcerted than ever. He took some comfort in knowing it wouldn't be long before something else came along and unsettled him even more.

"Have you?" he forced himself to ask.

"Why would he ask that? Why would you?"

"Haleine—"

"And I don't want riddles either. I ask you a question, and you answer with some comment that makes no sense, and I never say anything. I never question it, but I won't have it anymore. Truth and truth only."

"I won't lie to you."

"You may well be lying now," Haleine said. "How am I to know?"

"There is a prophecy," Faolan said. "Well, more than one, truth be told, but one in particular that deals with the downfall of the goddess and the rise of the dark gods."

"I don't believe in prophecy."

"Omur does," Faolan said. "And he believes you have a part to play in this one."

"But why would he think that? Why would he ever—how could I—Faolan, that is madness."

"Listen to me, Haleine," he said. "I know you're frightened and you need to ask questions, but I don't have the answers. Not yet. But I will get them, and I will keep you safe. I won't let him touch you again."

She stared at him a moment. "This prophecy...is this why he asked about my dreams? Why you asked the same?"

"Maybe," he said. "I might know better when you tell me about them."

She nodded and began talking. Faolan listened as she described battles Dana had fought in Trutina and Culhwch. He stopped breathing when she told him, in near perfect detail, the battle that had taken place outside of Mahile. He took heart from her portrayal of Dana teaching his son to ride but lost some of it when she told him of the mysterious man in black and the duel the two men fought, the end of which she had never seen.

"What say you, Faolan," she said when she had finished. "Do you think you can help me? Can you bar these visions from my mind?"

"No," he said without hesitation. He didn't want to offer her false hope. "I can't."

Sighle sat on the bed and watched with detached interest as her mother ordered the maids about. They were packing. They were leaving. Going home, her mother had said, to be with her father. But that was a lie. They were going home, Sighle knew, to start a war.

Anyone in the palace would say a war had been raging for almost a year now. But the people who would say that would be wrong. When Tanuba washed up on Lira's shore, the war would begin.

But only if Revelin was handled correctly. He was an emotional being, that prince, for all his claim to the opposite. It would have been better, safer, if Zoltano was the needed son.

358

His desires and actions were always intertwined around the female form. And though Revelin's motivation was always Haleine, it was difficult to know if there would be love or hate, or hate of his love for her, or love of his hate driving him from one day to the next. But it had to be Revelin because it had to be Haleine. And Mireille.

Mireille. The air crackled whenever her name was uttered. Little bursts of color exploding in the air. She was the child lost, the sister about whom she wasn't supposed to know. They always whispered it in almost-reverent tones. Except the pegasus. He spoke it as a being who knew something more than anyone around him.

Almost anyone around him.

"Sighle!" Rhoswen said. "What are you doing? I told you we are leaving as soon as the ship is made ready."

Sighle slid off the edge of the bed and tilted her head as she looked at the parchment in her mother's hand. No one else could see the blood.

"I'll be ready."

They sailed before nightfall, just as the pegasus said they would. Four days passed. Her mother was nervous, more nervous now than she had been before they sailed. Each day she clutched Haleine's letter close to her heart. She didn't set it down until they had retired to their cabin for the evening. Then it was tucked into her belt while Rhoswen circled the room, gathering her courage. Sighle sat on what passed for a bed and watched the blood drip from it.

"They're here," she said at the end of the fourth day. She hadn't meant to speak the words out loud.

Rhoswen turned, looking curious. "What do you mean, love? Who's here?"

The door was kicked in, then, splintering in some places. Rhoswen screamed. She whirled around to see two burly men, carrying slender knives already wet with blood, coming toward them. She threw her arms out to her sides and backed up, meaning to shield her daughter.

They were early. If they were too close to Lira, Sighle would be sent there. She needed to go to Tanuba. It was the only way Haleine would leave. Omur should have known better than to leave it in the hands of imbeciles. She didn't understand why he did what he did, but she supposed he didn't see what she did.

How or why she saw, she did not know, but see she did. She saw everything meant to happen laid out before her. The end of all things, some would call it. A new dawn, the others would say. Sighle didn't know what to call it yet. She only followed the path in front of her, guided down it by something akin to fireflies in the darkness. Where it would lead was a mystery, but she understood she was meant to follow. For now, that was enough.

Rhoswen's screams pierced her vision and she looked sharply at the men mauling her mother. They were cruel, to be certain, but not inventive. They weren't interested in prolonging the torture, and after they had taken their pleasure, they killed her. Sighle waited for them to notice her.

"Well, look at what we have here," one of them said.

The other grinned when he saw her. "Hello, little girl."

They abandoned her mother dead on the floor and came toward her.

"Stop," she said, and they did. "You're done here. Go back and report there was no one else."

The men turned and started to leave.

"Wait," she commanded and pointed to the parchment that lay soaking in her mother's blood. "Take that with you. Your master will be wanting it."

—⁓—

"Your highness?"

Revelin groaned and turned in his bed. He did not speak, hoping whoever stood in his chambers would understand he did not wish to be disturbed. He hadn't wanted to be bothered with anything since his return from Parthalan. Darian had performed this task well, only involving Revelin when it became absolutely necessary.

"I regret I must wake you," the voice continued, "but I am told the situation is most urgent."

"It always is," Revelin muttered as he sat up and looked at the servant hovering at the foot of the bed. "What has happened?"

"I'm sorry, my prince, but I do not know. Lord Darragh did not say. He asked only that I fetch you immediately."

Darragh. Not Darian.

"Where is Lord Coileáin?" Revelin asked, throwing back the coverlets.

"I do not know," the servant said. "I was instructed to find you and only you."

Revelin nodded. If Darragh, not Darian, was sending servants to rouse him from sleep, whatever had happened involved Darian. It involved Haleine. Revelin dressed quickly and went to the library to find Darragh. The man leaned against the wall, looking over some papers, but he straightened and bowed as Revelin entered.

"What happened?" Revelin asked. "Has he finally killed her?"

"Sire?"

"Maddox. Has he finally killed his wife?"

"To my knowledge, the queen remains unharmed. It is the Lady Rhoswen—"

"Rhoswen? What happened?"

"I am told she was coming here, coming home to Lord Darian, when her ship was attacked. There were few survivors. The Lady Rhoswen was not among them."

"Are the survivors here?"

"They are in the great hall. The court physician has been summoned to tend to them. My lord, Darian's daughter, Sighle, is among their number."

Revelin immediately walked out of the library. Darragh trailed behind.

"She is in the hall?" Revelin asked. "Is she hurt?"

"I am told she sustained no injury."

"You are told? You have not seen her?"

"No, my lord, I have not."

Revelin turned, grabbed Darragh by the neck of his tunic and slammed him against the wall.

"She is Darian's daughter," Revelin hissed. "She deserves more than your indifference."

"It is hardly indifference, my prince," Darragh gasped.

Revelin released him. "Take me to her."

The hall was nothing short of chaos, despite the small number of them. Judging by their uniforms, they were all crew members, none of them officers. Sighle sat apart from them, perched nervously on a bench and rocking back and forth. One of the palace maids sat with her, holding the girl's hands and talking quietly. Revelin saw no indication that Sighle heard anything.

"Shall I fetch Lord Darian?" Darragh asked.

Revelin shook his head. "I will do it myself once we have the answers he will need. Find out from the crew exactly what happened. I will talk to Sighle."

He crossed the room swiftly in his determination to reach her but slowed when he was close enough to see the blood covering Sighle's clothing, skin and hair. What had they done to her?

Sighle's companion eventually noticed his approach and slid off the bench to make her curtsey. She nudged Sighle and whispered for the girl to do the same, but Sighle did nothing.

"Do not bother with that," Revelin said to the maid. "See that a chamber and a bath are prepared for her, and tell the physician to make a potion to aid her sleeping."

"He has already said he would, my lord," the girl said.

"Then see to the rest."

She curtsied again and scurried away. He looked at Sighle. She still didn't seem to notice him. He said her name and received no response.

"Sighle," he said again.

She jumped and looked from side to side with her eyes wide with fear. When she saw him, she gasped and dropped to the floor. "My lord! Oh, forgive me."

"Surely there can be nothing to forgive," he said.

He knelt in front of her and held out his hands. She jerked away in what could only have been fright then looked mortified to have done so. She collapsed into his arms and began to cry.

"M-my m-mother," Sighle sobbed. "Oh my lord, they k-k-killed my mother."

"I know." He stroked her hair. "I am sorry for it."

"Why would they do that? Who was she to them?"

"Do you know who did this, Sighle?"

"There—there were two men. There were others above deck but two who came and—Rebels. They were rebels. Dana's men. I heard them say it. They—they didn't know I was there; I—I hid. They didn't know I saw everything. Everything they did to her."

"Revenge for their leader's death?"

"No," Sighle said. "He is alive. Dana is alive. Those who say otherwise are wrong. I hate them—the rebels. Why would they come for us? What are we to them? We weren't part of their war. We were just going home."

"I know," he said. "I will put this right, Sighle, I promise. Your father and I will see it done."

She tilted her face toward him, her brown eyes still glistening. "I hope so."

They didn't speak further. He sat on the floor with the girl crying softly in his arms. They stayed like that until the maid came back to say everything was as Revelin had requested. He gave Sighle over to her and watched the two girls depart. As soon as they were out of sight, Darragh advanced.

Revelin sat on the bench. "Did you find out what happened?"

"They report that shortly after sunset on the fourth day, they were boarded by Liran rebels sent by Dana with orders to claim all souls on board."

"They seem to have a rather high level of incompetence," Revelin commented. "Go on."

"After leaving the men for dead, the rebels set a fire and sailed off on their own vessel. The surviving crew was able to stop the flames, but their injuries and losses were severe enough to be unable to sail with any great efficiency. By their account, they spent two days adrift until they were discovered by one of the queen's ships."

"And Sighle?"

"The men maintain they thought her dead. They did not know she was alive until after their rescue. It was then she was found in the cabin where her mother had been—"

"They did not look before? Knowing who their passengers were, they did not look?"

"They did, my prince," Darragh said. "The girl, I am told, had hidden herself well. She was probably too frightened to respond to anyone searching for her."

Revelin nodded. "Did they bring Rhoswen's body back with them?"

"Yes, my lord, but it is in a most grievous state. Had it not been for the lady Sighle, I doubt any would have been able to identify it."

Revelin didn't want to think about that. "You will see she is properly prepared for burial?"

"Of course, my lord. It is already being done. I did not wish for Lord Darian to see his wife that way."

"We will need to send word to Lira on the very first ship available," Revelin said. "Haleine will not—the queen will need to know what has happened."

Darragh bowed. "I shall see it done immediately, my lord."

His advisor started to walk off, but Revelin reached out and caught the sleeve of the man's tunic. "No. I will write the letter," he said. "She should—I will tell her."

"As you wish, my lord. Will there be anything else?"

Revelin stood. "Keep things in hand here. I will go to Darian now."

He left the hall and walked through the corridors that would lead to Darian's chamber. With each step, he wondered how he would tell Darian, what he would say. What was the best way to inform a man his wife was dead? How did one explain to a man that she'd been coming home to him, but if he had only gone to her, she would still be alive?

Revelin was no closer to an answer when he arrived at Darian's door. He knocked on it and pushed his way inside without waiting for a response.

"Darian," Revelin said.

"My lord?" Darian asked, struggling to wake fully. "What is it? Has something happened?"

Revelin sighed. "Yes."

Part Three:
Sacrifice

CHAPTER 19

Haleine sat in the solarium, surrounded by her ladies while half-heartedly sewing a banner, when Ceallach arrived. She watched him from the corner of her eye as he wove his way through the room. When he reached her, he bowed.

"Your majesty," Ceallach said. "I must speak with you immediately."

She didn't look up. "Then do so, if you must."

"Really, your majesty, this is quite a private matter. It would be best if your ladies were elsewhere."

Haleine glanced at her attendants. They stared at Ceallach, their eyes revealing their eagerness for the potential gossip. Next she looked at Faolan. He stood on a window sill, watching Ceallach with marked interest.

"Send them away," she said. "Surely you don't need me to do that. If you do require aid, Willem can be found in the hall."

Faolan whinnied sharply. Everyone looked at him, but only Haleine recognized the interruption as the chastisement it was. She smiled at him and bowed her head in deference.

"Ladies, you are all dismissed," she said. "Thank you."

The women rose from their chairs, their disappointment poorly concealed. As soon as they were gone and the doors had closed behind them, Ceallach spoke again.

"I am sorry to bring your majesty such grave news," he said, "but your lady mother is dead."

Haleine stared at Ceallach for a moment before returning to her sewing. She attacked the cloth.

"No. You are mistaken," she said. "She is on her way home to my father."

"There is no mistake. I am sorry, my queen, but your mother is dead."

She put the needle through the fabric so hard it ripped, and she tossed the banner aside. "How do you know this?"

Ceallach held out a letter. As he offered it to her, she could see the already broken seal. It was Revelin's crest.

"The prince of Tanuba has written to tell you," Ceallach said.

Above the seal was her name. *Her* name.

"If he has written to me, as I can plainly see he has," she said, "why is the seal on that letter broken? Who else has read this? You?"

"No, your majesty," Ceallach said. "I have not. Lord Omur handed me the parchment as proof of what he asked me to tell you. I do not know who else may have been privy to its contents."

She took the letter and opened it. Revelin's words leapt out at her.

Your lover has slaughtered your mother. Your sister was spared. She is safe now with her father.

She tore the parchment into pieces. Afterward, she gathered every last scrap and carried them to the fire. She threw them inside and did not look away until it all had been reduced to ash.

"Where is my husband?" she asked. "The library?"

"To my knowledge."

"And his snake of an advisor? He is there as well?"

"I would presume so."

"You would presume," she mocked. "Get out."

"Your majesty—"

"Get out."

Ceallach nearly tripped over himself in his haste to leave. Haleine sat down and put her head in her hands to steady herself.

"What did the letter say?" Faolan asked.

"It said my mother is dead."

"Did it say how?"

"He said it was Dana."

"It wasn't."

She looked at the pegasus, more annoyed with him than ever. How could he think she would believe otherwise? She pushed herself out of her chair and started for the doors.

"I know it wasn't. I know where the fault here lies."

"Where are you going?" Faolan asked.

"I have to see Maddox. I have to see him now."

"What do you want with Maddox, Haleine? He didn't do this; you know he didn't."

"I know he didn't. I want to go to Mairéad and I need his permission to go."

"You can't go to Mairéad."

She spun to confront him. He hadn't moved from the window sill.

"Don't tell me I can't. I will go to Mairéad, Faolan. I will convince Revelin to help you," she said. "And, above all, I will bury my mother."

"That, I fear, would be a wasted trip," a new voice said from behind her.

It was Omur. She turned to face him, her anger overriding any other emotion.

"From my understanding," Omur continued, "there is not much left to bury."

"What are you doing here?" she asked. "What do you want from me? Gratitude, perhaps, for having spared my sister?"

Omur smiled. "No. It would be dishonest of me to expect that. Your sister's survival, you should understand, was unintentional. They were supposed to claim all souls found on board. My mistake. I'll send more thorough men the next time."

"No survivors? However would you have blamed the rebels for your evil if all your witnesses had been slaughtered?"

"Do you think I need witnesses to blame this on your lover? The only place he finds favor within these walls is in your bed."

"They think him dead."

"Not for long. I killed him, after all. I can bring him back."

"What do you want?" Faolan asked, a deadly edge to his voice.

Omur reached inside his robes and removed a blood-soaked parchment bearing Haleine's seal. "I thought I should return this to you. Perhaps you would like to bring it to Mairéad when you go."

"Haleine," Faolan said, "you can't go to Mairéad."

"I don't need your permission," she snapped as she snatched the parchment from Omur's hand.

"You will need your husband's permission though," Omur said, "and given how unsafe sea travel has just been proven to be, I think he will be most reluctant to grant it. I could help persuade him if you'd like."

"I will never want your help."

Omur nodded. "I suppose you could always explain to him how you know yourself to be impervious to rebel attack. But do allow me to be there when you do it. I'd love to see the look upon his face at that moment."

"It doesn't matter," Faolan said. "She's not going anywhere."

Haleine looked at the parchment. The blood likely belonged to her mother. What had they done to put it there? Her anger crumbled, and horror arrived in its place. Indeed, she knew who was responsible here.

"Haleine—" Faolan said.

"He's going to tell you you can't go," Omur interrupted. "That it isn't safe. He's going to tell you that should you leave these walls, I'm going to kill you."

Her hand closed around the parchment. She looked at Omur. "You want to kill me?"

He smiled again. It made her sick.

"I might," he said.

"Then do it," she said. "Make the arrangements."

When she left the solarium, only Willem trailed after her. Faolan stayed behind to contend with his enemy, she supposed, but she did not care. As he told it, he had faced Omur for seven hundred years. He would surely survive another day.

Both Bronagh and Ceallach waited in her chambers. Bronagh looked afraid as she came forth, and Haleine pressed the parchment into the maid's hands.

"Keep this safe," she said.

Ceallach spoke next. She didn't know what Ceallach was saying nor did she care. She held up her hand to silence him and walked past. She went to the balcony doors and threw them open. It was raining outside, but she didn't care about that either as she stepped out.

She stood in the center of the balcony, first looking at the sky as the rain fell over her. She started to ask why this had happened but stopped herself. There was no one there to hear her, nor did she need anyone to tell her the answer. Next she went to her knees and dropped her head. Her arms hung limp at her sides. After a while even that was too much effort and she fell forward, resting her forehead on the cool, wet stone.

She didn't know how long she stayed like that, not moving, not crying, hardly thinking, and only for sure breathing. She didn't move even though the water streamed down her face and into her nose and mouth. Were she to drown there, where would she go?

"Haleine?"

She heard her name. The sound cut through the fog wrapped around her brain. She ignored it and went on breathing.

She felt hands on her body and jerked away from them, coming up against the balcony's railing. She pinned her back against it and looked to see who had touched her.

Dana.

He came forward, and she relinquished herself to him.

—⁓—

Haleine lay on her stomach, her head turned to the side. Her eyes were closed, but Dana could not tell if she slept. He stayed close to her, stroking her hair gently. If she were awake, she didn't seem to want to speak or be spoken to, and if she slept, he did not wish to wake her, so he listened to the rain and waited.

Faolan had sent word to Luisiúil. Luisiúil had told him, and he hadn't wasted any time in going to the palace. He used the servants' passage and entered a darkened, strangely still room. Bronagh stood near the fire and looked at him when he arrived.

"Where is she?" he asked, prepared to fight his way through her usual onslaught of threats and slurs.

"On the balcony," Bronagh replied, surprising him greatly. "She'll not come in."

He had gone out there for her. She had been there for quite some time. Her clothing was soaked through, and she was shaking violently. Whether it was the cold making her shiver or something else, he didn't know.

Bronagh helped him to strip Haleine of her sodden gown. It clung to her skin, making it difficult to remove. They dressed her in a nightgown and dried her hair as well as they could before laying her on the bed. She hadn't moved since.

He kissed her head and slid off the bed. With the exception of Faolan perched near the fireplace, they were alone. Bronagh had left after Haleine was dressed and hadn't returned. He didn't know for how long she would stay away.

He joined Faolan and sat in the chair that offered him a view of Haleine. He glanced at the pegasus, the fire and finally the table in front of him. On it laid a letter. He recognized Haleine's crest and her handwriting.

"What is this?" he asked, picking it up. It was addressed to Revelin, but the prince's name was mostly obscured by blood.

"It was supposed to be how we convinced Revelin to fight on our side," Faolan said. "It ended up being what killed Rhoswen."

Dana glanced at Haleine, still motionless, and broke the seal. He opened the letter and read the plans she had written there.

"How did Omur know she carried this?" he asked.

"I don't know."

"He didn't read it."

"I don't think he had to."

There were too many possibilities, none of them good. Dana nodded and tossed the letter back onto the table.

"Dana?"

Haleine's faint voice floated across the room and he lifted his head. She still had not moved, so he returned to her side and knelt on the floor in front of her. She pressed her hand against his cheek.

"Ah, you are here," she whispered. "I thought perhaps you were a dream."

"No," he said and kissed her palm. "I am most real."

She let her hand fall. "I want you to do something for me."

Dana fought the urge to pull away as a dread feeling grew inside him. He smoothed the hair out of her face and waited to hear her request.

"I want you to kill Maddox."

He looked away. "Maddox didn't do this."

"You say that as though it matters, but it doesn't," she said. "I want you to kill him."

"I can't."

The words hung uncomfortably in the air. He stood and backed a few steps away.

She sat up. "You can. You must."

"No. I can't."

"Why?" she asked. "I will take you to his chambers. I will show you where he sleeps. You can murder him and the whore who sleeps with him. I care nothing for her."

He walked around the bed. "Please listen to me. I cannot do this. Ask me for anything else, and I will do it gladly, but do not ask me this."

"You have no sword," she said. "Is this why? I will find you a sword. There is an entire army inside these walls. Somewhere is a sword you can use."

He turned to face her. "I can't do this. I can't kill Maddox. Sword or not, I just can't do it."

She sat back. "Why?"

"If I killed Maddox, Omur could control the throne, and I can't let that happen."

"Kill him, too."

"I can't."

"Why?"

"I tried. Know that," he said. "I tried. I ran him through with my sword. It didn't leave so much as a scratch."

She seemed to grow smaller. "My mother is dead."

"I know."

"They deserve to die."

"I know."

"You know this, yet you do nothing."

"Because I can do nothing."

She shook her head. "How do you expect to win this war without ridding yourself of your enemies?"

"I've already explained why—"

"Yes. Yes, you have. This is not my husband's sin therefore he does not deserve to have his own throat slit," she said, her voice growing in volume and intensity. "But what of his past sins? How many people need he kill or order killed before you will consent to stop him? He murders kings and you do not act; he murders children and you do not act. If that holds no meaning for you, what does?"

"Haleine, it's not—"

"I will be next. Did you know that?" she asked. "What will happen then? Will you again spare him, or will that be an appropriate time to end your war?"

"Maddox will not kill you."

"Would you mind terribly if I ask from where this knowledge came? Was it your goddess, your useless goddess? I curse the day I ever heard her name!"

She screamed the last of it at him, lost her balance and fell to the floor. Dana started forward but stopped as he realized she wouldn't want his help. She sat up and leaned against the bed, her knees drawn to her chest and her face pressed against them. Her entire body shook as she cried.

"I'm sorry, love," he said. "I'm so sorry."

It seemed he offered her those words every time he came, but never had they been so empty. He went to her side and took her in his arms, ignoring her protests and her fists beating against his chest. Eventually her fists unclenched and her fingers ensnared his tunic instead, pulling him closer. She buried her face in his neck, and he held her until her tears lessened. When they did, she moved her head to speak.

"It is my fault she is dead."

"No, Haleine, no. Omur—"

"Aye, it was Omur who ordered the murder done. But the order never would have been given if not for me."

"You're not to blame," Faolan said.

"I asked her to go. I asked her to carry that wretched letter. Save my life, I said to her. How could she say no when I had accused her of such indifference?"

"This is not your fault," Dana said. "I don't know how it happened, how Omur discovered your letter, but it is not your fault."

"Revelin thinks you are responsible."

Dana shook his head. "I don't care."

"He'll bring his army here to hunt you."

"I don't care."

"You cannot fight two armies."

"I can if I must."

"You cannot fight two armies," she repeated. "I will convince both Revelin and my father of your innocence."

"And how will you do that?" Dana asked, already fearing the answer.

"I will go to Mairéad," she said. "I will see it done."

"You can't go."

"I don't need your permission either," she said, breaking free of his hold. "Please don't act as if I do."

"No, it's not that," he said. He tried to catch her but she was on her feet and walking away before he could. "Haleine, it's too dangerous. Omur will—"

"Try to kill me," she said. "Yes, he has already told me so."

Dana bolted to his feet and sought out Faolan. The pegasus was conveniently not looking in his direction.

"He already told you?" Dana asked, trying to control a sudden onset of anger.

"Yes." She sat by the fire. "I asked if he wanted to kill me. He said he might."

"You spoke to him?"

"It is not the first time."

"Not the first time?"

"The time before, he tried to choke me. He was unsuccessful," Haleine said. "Faolan thinks the next attempt will be made should I leave these walls."

"Then why on earth would you ever consider leaving these walls?"

He rounded the bed to confront her where she sat. He slowed down when he saw the letter in her hands. Faolan stood on the table, staring into the fire.

"Because you cannot fight two armies," she said. "And I cannot lose you."

He knew he had lost. He would have to find another way to protect her now.

"You'll take Willem with you, won't you?" he asked.

She shook her head. "He will stay here. He will guard my sons."

Faolan looked away from the flames. "Willem won't like leaving you unguarded."

"Willem will do as he is told," she said.

"If you must do this, bring the man with you," Dana said. "Your sons will be in no danger. Neither Maddox nor Omur have any cause to harm them."

She looked at Faolan, not him. "I'll not take the risk. Willem will remain behind."

Faolan nodded and turned back to the fire. Dana fell on his knees in front of her and took her hands in his.

"Please don't do this," he said. "It could be suicide."

"Omur will be sorry to hear that," she said, a strange smile on her face. "I suspect he has his heart set on murder."

—⁓—

It was early morning, and James and Bearach were on their way back to camp, having completed their patrol. There'd been nothing to see except the sunrise. James appreciated that he was still alive to see sunrises but wanted to be doing something other than watching them.

The rebellion had spent the last fortnight in a holding pattern. James didn't understand it and had received very little in the way of explanation. After the first few days of inactivity, he went in search of answers and tracked down Dana studying maps in his tent.

"What's going on?" James asked.

Dana kept his eyes on the maps. "What do you mean?"

"We're not doing anything," James said. "We're not fighting, we're not preparing to fight, and we don't seem to be spying. We're just sitting here not *doing* anything, and I don't understand why."

"You wanted a reprieve."

"This isn't a reprieve," James said. "This is something else entirely. What's going on?"

Dana shrugged. "We're waiting."

"For what?"

"Faolan. He's going to get us Tanuba as an ally."

James thought about that. "How is he going to do that?"

Dana shrugged again. "I don't know."

"Don't they hate you in Tanuba?"

"You have no idea how much they hate me in Tanuba."

"Then how—?"

"I really don't know."

"We're just going to sit here?"

"Aye."

"For how long?"

Dana shrugged a third time. "As long as it takes."

Their conversation ended then, and there had been no word of Tanuba nor anything else since. The conflict had stopped as both sides waited to see with whom Tanuba would join. James didn't know very much at all about the country, but he found it hard to believe its support was suddenly pivotal to their mission. Neither did he understand why Faolan thought Tanuba would ever choose the rebellion.

For two weeks he had waited to find out. Every morning he patrolled with Bearach for an enemy that wasn't coming. Every afternoon he trained for a fight that wasn't happening, and every night he sat by a fire and waited for word on a country that wasn't his ally.

But now as James returned to camp and found it to be a hive of activity, it became obvious that word had come at last. Men and women gathered weapons and armor. Horses were being saddled, and the unicorns were congregating. They were preparing for a fight, and James smiled at the sight as he slid from Bearach's back.

"There's been word," he said.

James pushed his way into Dana's tent. It was crowded with men and women preparing supplies. James worked his way to the table where Dana and Ilya were making plans.

"What's happened?" he asked.

"They're going to kill the queen," Dana said.

"And blame us," Ilya added.

"And you mean to stop it?" James said.

Dana looked at him. "Of course I mean to stop it. We can't just let it happen."

"We can let it happen," James said. "And we should."

All commotion in the tent stopped as every pair of eyes focused on him. Dana turned to face him. Ilya moved to stand at Dana's side.

"They're going to kill her, James," she said.

"Good. Let them," he said. "I'd even help if I could. She's nothing to us. She's certainly not worth risking our necks over."

Dana took a step forward, but Ilya placed herself in between them, her hand on Dana's chest.

"Out," Ilya said to the others. "All of you out now."

Everyone immediately did as she asked. When the three of them were all that remained, Ilya turned to Dana and quietly said, "You need to tell him."

"Tell me what?" James asked.

Dana looked at the table and said nothing.

Ilya sighed. "The queen. She's—"

"She's what? She's innocent? She's a victim of this war?" James asked. "Well, who the hell isn't?"

"James," Ilya said.

"We have let villages burn. We have let entire populations be eradicated because the risk to this cause was too great," James said. "And now you mean for us to chance everything for one woman?"

Dana looked at him. "Aye."

"Well, I won't do it. I won't do anything to save her."

"James," Ilya said. "She's—"

Dana moved around Ilya and put his hand out to stop her from continuing. "We're doing this."

"Why?"

"Not every soul is as black as yours, James," Dana said. "The people of this land love the queen, and if Omur were to kill her and convince them we were responsible, what do you think will happen to us? What will become of the rebellion? Saving that one woman may save us, so aye, we are doing this. If you're not with us, you're against us, and I have no use for that. For you. If you're not going to help, get out."

"When have I ever been against you?" James asked.

Dana didn't answer. He turned back to the table and the maps. Ilya waited, hands poised to stop either man should a move be made. She didn't break her stance until Dana said her name and held out one of the parchment pieces. She took it and returned to planning. James watched them briefly before rolling his eyes and stepping up to the table.

"What do we know?" James said. "When will it happen? How will it happen?"

"The queen intends to sail to Tanuba," Ilya said when she saw Dana wasn't going to reply. "Her ship will likely sail with the afternoon tide."

"Will this attack happen on land or at sea?" James asked.

"On land," Dana murmured. "At sea won't grant Omur the audience he desires for this."

James looked at the map of the city and frowned. "Will she sail from the main harbor?"

"We can assume so," Ilya said. "Faolan hasn't said otherwise."

"Of course, Faolan didn't tell us Omur was threatening her in the first place," Dana said.

"Maybe he didn't know before," Ilya offered. "I'm sure his palace benefactor has limits to what she hears."

"There is more truth to that than you know," Dana said. He pointed down at the map. "If she goes this route, the carriage will depart here and take this road straight to the harbor, by-passing just about everything. It doesn't make sense."

"No, it doesn't," James said. "If he wants the people to see it, he'll send her another way."

They traded the map of the city for one of the country.

"Here," James said, pointing. "Eoten. It's where she arrived before, isn't it?"

"But she sailed from Quatara," Ilya said.

"Aye, but look at the towns she'll pass. Look at the forest she'll pass through. It would lend itself well to an ambush. That's where he'll do it. It's what I would do. Invent a reason why she can't sail from the city and—"

"He won't need to invent anything," Dana said. "She wants to go badly enough; she won't question it. She would travel to Feond first if she was told she had to."

Dana's tone was bitter. James glanced at Ilya, but if she noticed, she wasn't concerned.

"I think James is right," she said. "That is what Faolan will report to us. Send people to watch the city port if you want, but Eoten is where they will likely go."

"She won't have a guard with her," Dana said. "At least not one I trust. If we lose that carriage—"

"We won't," James said.

"We have to protect her," Dana said.

James nodded. "We will."

———ᴠᴠᴠ———

When the carriage left the palace gates the next day, Haleine was alone inside. As expected, Willem was displeased when she called for him to stay behind but had done as she asked. Bronagh glared and muttered and did everything she could think of to shame her mistress into changing her mind, but Haleine held firm. Even Ceallach attempted a similar tactic but with no better results. Faolan stood silently by, everything he would have said in his eyes. Only Omur didn't argue. He came to the courtyard to see her off, bowing and bidding her luck on her journey.

When the carriage next left the city gates, she was not surprised. The city port would not offer Omur what he was after. What good was killing a beloved monarch if no one was around to witness it? He was mad to attempt this assassination, but she was even more so for allowing him the opportunity.

They had been on the road a considerable length of time when Faolan flew in through the window. She was surprised to see him.

"What are you doing here?" she asked.

"Not letting you go by yourself."

She sighed. "Where is Dana?"

"Skulking in the forest, I imagine."

She leaned forward to look out the window.

"You won't be able to see him," Faolan said. "He's good about that. If nothing should happen, you won't even get a glimpse of him."

"But you think something will happen."

"As do you," Faolan countered. "Why did you ask for this?"

She looked at her skirts and picked at imaginary threads. "I told you."

"This is quite an elaborate punishment."

"Dana cannot fight two armies; you know he can't. Someone needs to go to Mairéad to speak with Revelin, and I am the one to whom he will listen."

"How can you be sure you'll get there in time? That you won't pass each other on the sea?"

"They will not have done anything the first week. My mother was loved at court, thick as thieves with the queen; they will mourn her. That will have given Revelin's letter time to reach me."

"And the next week it'll take for you to sail there?"

"To prepare an army of Tanuba's stature is no quick task. If my luck holds today, I should arrive in time to convince Revelin to use the men he's gathered to fight with you and not against you. If it does not"—she paused—"If it does not, it is no more than I deserve."

"What happened to your mother wasn't your fault."

"Nothing ever is," she said as the carriage came to a stop.

"Oh no," Faolan said. "Whatever happens here today is, without a doubt, your fault."

Haleine smiled and leaned forward to glance out the window again. They couldn't be there yet. They hadn't been on the road nearly long enough. At first there was nothing. Then an arrow came screaming toward her. She ducked, not knowing how it missed her. Haleine remained perfectly still in her crouch as she stared at the arrow that was now embedded in the carriage's wall.

"Get on the floor," Faolan said.

She let her breath out slowly and slipped off the seat.

"I'm going to see what's happening," Faolan said, flying toward the window. "Don't get out of the carriage."

The urge to laugh rose within her but not for long. The sounds of battle forced it out of her. She listened to the clash of swords surrounding her. She threw herself flat on the floor as another arrow flew inside, swallowing a scream as she did so.

There was a thud on top of the carriage. Her head snapped up at the sound, and her breath caught in her throat. She heard someone walk along the length, and the sound disappeared. A moment later, the carriage sprang into motion, moving far faster than before. Haleine braced herself between the seats and waited for it to end. When the carriage finally stopped, she stayed on the floor, listening to her heart beat more rapidly than she ever thought possible. What would happen now?

The door to her left opened, and she turned her head to see a large man, flanked by two others, standing outside the carriage.

They wore the clothing of peasants though she knew it to be little more than a costume. The garments were far too fine to belong to commoners. She didn't know what weapons the men in back carried, but the first man wore a sword on his hip and a dagger in his belt.

"Get out," he said.

She shook her head and slid as far away from them as she could. She pressed her back against the opposite door. She fumbled behind her for the latch. When she found it, she curled her fingers around it and forced it down, but the door didn't open. Her hand formed a fist, and she pounded the door, but it stayed shut.

"That door ain't gonna open," the man said next. "If you're finished, you best come here. Otherwise, I'll come in and get you."

She didn't move. He waited another moment before climbing in. He grabbed her ankle and dragged her to him. She kicked at him with her free leg, but he did nothing but laugh at her. When she was close enough, he picked her up by the front of her gown and pushed her out of the carriage. The two other men stepped aside and let her fall. She landed on the ground and immediately pushed herself up. She meant to run, to hide, to do something other than sit and let this happen. She'd only gone a few steps when she tripped on her gown and fell to the ground again.

Her assailants were even more amused by this and laughed heartily. The first man picked her up again, this time by her elbow, and dragged her into a small clearing. This time, when he released her, he kept his foot on the hem of her gown. She tugged at it to no avail.

"Don't do this," she said. "Please don't do this."

"Oh, hear the lass beg," one of the others said, using his sword to lift her skirts. She whirled around to stop him, lost her balance and hit the ground yet again. The third man crouched down in front of her.

"Wonder what else she'd beg for," he said, grabbing her exposed ankle. "What say you, miss?"

She tried to kick at him but had no more success than before. He pushed up her skirts and ran his hand up her leg. She lashed out at him, scratching his face with her nails. He yelled in pain and raised his hand to strike her. The second man dove for her and held her down. She screamed.

"That's enough," the first man said. "He said no delays. He wants it done."

The man she had scratched snarled at her, a lion deprived of his prey. He lowered his hand and backed away. The man who held her let her go. She lay in the center of the circle they formed around her. She was terribly afraid; she couldn't get enough air. The first man nudged her with his boot.

"On your knees," he said.

She looked at him. Was this it? Was she to die here by this man's blade? His eyes told her he was resolved to his task. Should she fight him? *Could* she fight him? He shook his head as though she had asked the questions aloud.

"It'll only make it worse," he said. "On your knees."

She closed her eyes and did as he had directed. He moved closer and pushed her head down. He swept her hair all to one side, off her neck. She heard him draw his sword, and her stomach lurched. She braced herself for his killing blow, but instead of feeling steel cutting into her flesh, the man fell forward on top of her.

She stifled a scream and struggled to get away from him. There was blood, but from where had it come? She was uninjured; he had not cut her. She wriggled free of him and rolled into the grass beside him.

There was an arrow lodged in the center of his back. The other two were dead as well, killed in a similar fashion. She inhaled sharply, knowing this did not mean the danger was over, and scanned the forest for those responsible.

Men and women slowly came out of the forest, materializing as though they had been a part of the trees themselves. They were armed with bows and swords and cudgels. Some wore mismatched pieces of armor, but the clothing underneath marked them as true commoners and not imposters. Were they Dana's people, or was this another trick of Omur's? Let her think she was about to be rescued, only to slit her throat? She pulled the dagger from the fallen man's belt and held it close to her chest. It was a meager weapon when compared to with what she was now faced, but still she clung to it. It was all she had.

Before they reached her, a young man wearing a worn leather breastplate spoke a word and stopped their progress. He was their leader, then. He handed off his bow and continued toward her alone, murder flashing in his eyes and anger fueling his step. His hand remained on the hilt of his sword. She adjusted her grip on the dagger and stood.

"Who are you?" she asked.

He did not answer her. If he was Dana's man, why would he not offer her some sort of assurance? Why did he approach her in such a menacing manner? His face showed he was unconcerned with her and her weapon. She gripped the handle tighter and held it out.

"Should you come any closer without identifying yourself," she said. "I will kill you."

The man smiled but did not stop. "Is that so?"

She lowered the dagger to her side. The breastplate took away the largest and easiest target; she would have to aim lower, but there was plenty of damage to do there. She rushed him and thrust the dagger forward, but he caught her wrist and twisted it. She nearly shrieked in pain and her weapon landed in the grass. She looked at it, then at the man holding her. He let her go, shoved her back a little and bent to retrieve the fallen dagger.

"Would you like to try my sword?" he asked. "You might have a better chance of killing me with that, provided you could lift it. I'll even stand still if you want."

She rubbed her wrist. "Who are you?"

"My name is James ap Seoras. Your husband murdered my family," he said and gestured to the people behind him. "And most of theirs as well."

"Mayhap that is why he has now started on my own," she said. "Where is Dana?"

"Dana?"

"Yes, Dana. You are one of his followers, are you not? I assume you are, for you have come to my aid though you plainly do not like me. Was I mistaken?"

James tucked her dagger in his belt. "No."

"Will you take me to him? Or Faolan, perhaps, if he is nearby?"

"How do you know Faolan?"

"He has been living with me for quite some time now. Where are they? Do you know?"

Something in James's eyes flickered, but Haleine did not know what it was. He looked her up and down, his already-unfriendly face becoming even more so. He glanced over his shoulder and called his people to action before resuming his silent study of her. She lifted her chin, squared her shoulders and returned his look. She didn't know what she might have done to offend him, but she would not cower before him.

"Captain," one of James's men said.

James walked away to confer with him, and Haleine watched the others work. They stripped the dead men of anything valuable and dragged their corpses from her view. They unhitched the horses from the carriage and disappeared with two of them. They moved efficiently, obviously having performed this sort of task before. When they finished, James took possession of the other two horses before sending off the rest of his people. One by one, they evaporated back into the trees until none were left but James and herself.

"Can you ride?" he asked.

"Yes, but I have never done so without a saddle or a proper bridle."

James nodded. "Don't fall off and you'll be fine."

She wasn't as confidant as James sounded but allowed him to help her onto the horse's back and show her how to use the harness as a bridle. She took control of the animal and looked at James.

"I have not yet thanked you for saving my life," she said.

"No, you haven't."

"I will not take your rudeness personally, for I can see how easy it would be for you to blame me for the actions of my husband," she said. "But no matter your opinion of me, I am sincerely grateful to you—to all of you—for your help here today. Thank you."

James stared at her for a moment and walked away without comment. He mounted the other horse and rode off. Haleine dug her heels into her horse's side and followed. They rode in silence on a trail running in the opposite direction from which she thought she had come.

"Where are we going?" she asked finally.

"You wanted to find Dana, didn't you?"

"I did," she said. "Where might he be found?"

"That doesn't seem to matter now," James said, his posture becoming even more rigid. "Dana appears to have found you."

He pointed, and Haleine saw Dana on the trail coming toward them. She urged her horse into a faster gait and stopped the animal alongside him. He lifted her from the horse's back and she wrapped her arms around him and kissed him.

"Are you all right?" he asked when he at last set her down.

"I am," she said, indicating James with a nod of her head. "Your man there, he saved me."

Dana nodded and tightened his grip on Haleine's shoulders. "James—"

384

James's face was expressionless as he rode past. "I've brought your whore back to you. Just as you asked."

"James, wait—"

"It's not acceptable, Dana," James said before urging his horse into a faster gait. "Take her back."

Dana swore softly and looked at the ground. His hands dropped to his side, forming white-knuckled fists. Haleine glanced at James's retreating figure.

"Dana," she said. "What is—?"

"Come on," he said.

He mounted the horse and held out his hand for her. She didn't move.

"Do any of them know?" she asked.

"They do now," he replied. "Come on."

She took his hand and he pulled her up behind him. "Where are we going?"

"You'll see," was his answer.

Chapter 20

Dana brought her to the rebel camp. It arrived out of nowhere. One moment they were in the thick of the forest and the next in the midst of a throng of people. Haleine tightened her grip on Dana's belt as she took in this sudden change to her surroundings.

It was a village of tents in various degrees of size and disrepair. The number of them surprised her. She saw horses and stockpiles of weapons. People were everywhere. Men, women and children all had been forced into this life of exile because of her husband. Would they harbor the same resentment toward her that James did?

Some bowed or curtsied as she rode past. Others did not, but they all spared her little more than a glance as they stripped off their worn armor and bloodied weapons. Their hatred was obvious, yet they had still fought to save her life.

"They fought because you asked them," she said. "James fought because you asked him."

Dana nodded and pulled the horse to a stop and dismounted. "Stay with Hanah while I'm gone."

"What?" she asked. "Dana, wait!"

But he did not wait. He walked away and disappeared into the crush of people, leaving her in the middle of a camp filled with those who hated her. She shouldn't fear. Their loyalty to Dana had been proven, and she would go unharmed here. She would.

"Really, that man has no sense at all."

Haleine looked to see who had spoken. An older woman, gray-haired, simply dressed and barefoot, stood on her left.

"I beg your pardon?" Haleine said.

The woman smiled at her. "He apparently also has no manners. No gentleman would have gone off and left you so precariously stranded. I'm afraid he forgets. Lucius!" she called. "Come help us. Your fearless leader has failed this lady."

"Oh no," Haleine protested. "I am quite able to—"

The tall, dark-haired man who lifted her from the horse's back did not care. He set her on the ground, and she looked into the eyes she had seen so often before. She was pleased to see a familiar face, even if she had never been properly introduced to the man.

"Well," she said. "We meet again."

He bowed. "Your majesty."

"No," she said, catching his arm. "You and your companions saved my life. I'll not have any of you bowing before me."

"As you wish," Lucius said. "Shall we also allow you to find your own way back to the palace?"

He was teasing her. She managed a small smile in return.

"Perhaps we can negotiate on that," she said. "I do, after all, owe you for serving me so well in the past."

"There will be no need for negotiating," Dana said as he returned to her side. "She's not leaving."

"Dana," she said, "I can't—"

"Lucius, James seems to have gone missing," Dana said. "See if you can find him, would you?"

Dana took Haleine's elbow and led her toward a nearby tent. The gray-haired woman followed them. Just before entering, Haleine looked over her shoulder briefly at Lucius, who nodded in acknowledgement before leading the horse away.

"Sit down, child," the woman said, nudging Haleine in the direction of a chair. "You have been through hell this day. It will catch up with you momentarily, and I'll not have you fainting."

Haleine didn't argue. She sat in the chair the woman had indicated, the only chair to be found. The woman started to check her over for injuries. Haleine knew she had sustained no harm but allowed the woman to perform her examination. She took advantage of the time to examine her surroundings. There wasn't much. A table covered with parchment and a single lantern sat to her right. On her left was a bedroll and a small store of weapons.

And there was Dana. He had shed himself of his weapons and armor and now paced in as large a circle as the small tent would allow.

"Oh, for Laorans's sake, Dana," her caregiver snapped when she was satisfied of Haleine's well-being. "Stop that. You're scaring the wits out of this poor girl. And this talk of keeping her here! It's foolishness, Dana."

He stopped. "Don't be so rough, Hanah."

"I have to be. It's the only way to get you to mind what I say. You know Faolan would say nothing different were he here. She must go back," Hanah said. "And the sooner the better."

"They tried to kill her," Dana said. "What will stop them from trying again?"

"The palace walls," Hanah replied. "As long as she is there, she will be safe. You know I speak the truth. Look at her. She knows it as well."

"I know you do not want to hear it, Dana," Haleine said, "but I cannot argue with her. I must return. I would cause nothing but anguish for you and your followers were I to remain, and I do not wish to further their misery."

"Their misery did not concern you when you decided to leave for Tanuba in the first place," he said.

The comment had been made quietly. Dana focused on the ground. Hanah pursed her lips and walked out. Haleine heard her driving away the audience that had no doubt grown outside the tent.

"No, it did not," she said. "You are right to remind me. The last self-serving decision I made also caused someone their life, and I would not want to do that again. Nor would I want you to make the same mistake."

He turned his head to the side and looked at her.

"Tell me," she continued. "If Maddox's men were to attack now, would your loyalties be with these people who have given their lives to follow you and to serve your cause? Or would you give all to protect me?"

"If they attacked now, their purpose would be to kill you."

"But only because I have left the palace," she said. "You were right that I should not have gone at all, and the problem will not be corrected should I stay here. I must return."

Dana shook his head. "Let him come. Let him try to take you from me."

"You don't mean it."

"I damn well do."

"Then you sentence all those who follow you to death," she spat as she stood. "And I'll not be a part of that."

She started to leave. Dana caught her arm before she could make it outside and pulled her back.

"What are you doing?" he asked.

She pushed him away. "I don't want to fight with you."

"Then we won't fight."

"Then listen to reason. Maddox and Omur will have men searching for me. It does not matter that they want to kill me. What does matter is that they'll kill any who are found with me."

Dana smiled, but it was not in amusement. "They've been living with the threat of death since this war began, your majesty. We are all outlaws here."

"Aye," she said, "and you have brought the enemy into their very midst."

"Not their enemy. You."

"They don't know the difference. They don't know what I am to you, what you are to me."

"Fools in love," Dana murmured, coming closer to her.

"Aye, we are that," she said. "But they don't know it."

"What we are," he said. "It is none of their concern."

She smiled and put her hand on his cheek. "You are their leader. Everything you do is their concern."

He took her hand and kissed her palm. "It hardly seems fair."

"You are acting as a man," she said. "A fool in love."

"I am a man. I am a fool in love."

She freed her hand from his. "You are a man second. You are a leader, *their* leader, first and foremost. Keeping me here is the decision the man, the fool, would make. Sending me back is what—"

"I'm not letting you go."

"You can't keep me here. I'm not your prisoner," she said. "If you won't take me back, I'll ask James. He does not want me here. He will be more than obliging, I am sure."

"He'll be obliging enough to slit your throat once you're away from here. He wants you dead."

"They all want it, Dana," she said. "Every last soul out there would like nothing more than to slit my throat as retribution for what they've lost."

Dana was momentarily stunned. He reached for her, but she moved back and his hand caught nothing more than air.

"No one here will lay a hand upon you," he said.

"Because you've asked them not to," she said. "Don't betray their trust. Let me go back."

He was quiet for a long while. "In the morning," he said finally. "I will take you back then."

She searched his face. It wasn't soon enough, but she didn't want to argue any more. She nodded.

"I am trying to save you," he said.

"And I you."

He smiled again. "Fools in love."

She did not smile. "Fools in love."

———⌇∿⌇———

Revelin sat in the library, looking over the latest batch of papers Darragh had handed him. They never stopped coming. Border reports from Quatara, spy reports on his brother's doings in Gweneria, farming reports, trading reports, criminal reports. There were reports on everything under the sun, but there were considerably more when an army was preparing to be on the move, as Tanuba's now was.

"Your highness?"

Revelin set the reports down, relieved to have a reason to do so, and saw Darragh approaching. When Darian's steward sent away the servants and the guards, Revelin knew this would lead to nothing good and wished for the man's immediate departure.

"Who has died now?" he asked when they were alone.

Darragh smiled. "No one, your highness. There is, however, a situation I feel requires your attention. It is Lord Coileáin."

"Where is he?"

"A tavern, sire."

"And what is he doing there?"

"What most men tend to do at taverns, my lord," Darragh said. "But I have been told Lord Coileáin has become most out of hand."

"The man's grieving," Revelin said. "Send some men to bring him back."

"They have tried," Darragh said.

"What do you wish me to do?"

"He will listen to you."

Revelin was doubtful. More likely Darian would take a sword to him for what had happened to his family.

"He will listen to you," Darragh repeated, perhaps sensing Revelin's hesitation.

"Very well," Revelin said. "I will go."

As soon as he set foot in the tavern, Revelin saw why he had been summoned. Darian stood on a table in the center of the building, a tankard in one hand and his sword in the other. He waved the sword in the air as he ranted about the Maoilriain monarchy and the Liran rebels.

Revelin scanned the rest of the room. The other patrons were oddly silent as they listened to Darian's speech. It was a monologue Revelin thought they needed not hear.

"Clear this room down to the last man," he said to Darragh. "Then wait for us outside."

Darragh carried out his orders without delay. The patrons seemed only too glad to leave. The tavern's owner was more reluctant but stopped his complaint upon seeing Revelin standing just inside the entrance. Darian, noticing his audience dissipating, ceased his tirade. He lowered his sword, drained the ale from his tankard and threw the cup to the floor.

"Darian," Revelin said once the last man had left the building. "Get down from there."

"My prince!" Darian laughed. "To what do I owe this unexpected visit? Come to tell me I've lost another daughter? I think it must be her; she's all that's left."

Revelin never had seen his advisor in such a drunk and disheveled state. Darian stumbled back and slipped off the table. He hit his head on its edge before landing on the floor. When he pushed himself up again, a bright red stain was smeared across his forehead. Darian didn't notice. Revelin went in search of something to staunch the blood.

"Forgive me if I do not bow," Darian said. He fell into a chair and threw his sword upon the floor. "But lately I find myself questioning my loyalty to this monarchy."

"Do you?" Revelin asked as he stepped behind the bar. "I could not tell."

Darian didn't hear him. He had just become aware of the cut on his forehead and the blood trickling down his face.

"For God's sake, Revelin!" he exclaimed. "Get me a damn towel for this infernal cut!"

Revelin found a towel behind the tavern's bar and brought it to Darian. He sat and watched his advisor dab at the wound.

"I did not question it so many times," Darian said. "Even with what happened to Haleine's sister, I never doubted. Maybe if I had known it was only the beginning."

"Sighle is unharmed," Revelin said.

"Not Sighle. Haleine's sister."

"I do not understand."

Darian nodded. "No, of course you don't. You were too young when it happened, and by the time you were old enough, no one spoke of it. Haleine doesn't even know."

"Know what?"

"Haleine had a twin. When they were born, your father and I were off claiming Quatara. I never left. Rhoswen and the girls came to me because I wanted to know my daughters."

Darian picked up a tankard and looked inside of it. He frowned, tossed it to the floor and tried a second mug. It, too, was empty.

"Why is there no ale in here?" he asked. "This is a tavern. There should be ale, yet all these tankards are empty."

Revelin rose to fetch Darian more ale. When he returned, he sat in his chair and waited for Darian to continue with his story, but the man seemed to have forgotten he had been telling it.

"Perhaps I shall die," Darian said into his tankard.

"No one truly dies of grief," Revelin said.

"I was more thinking of using my sword or my dagger," Darian said. "It'll be quicker that way."

"And what of Sighle?"

Darian shook his head. "I have done no daughter of mine any favors. She will be better off without me. You'll look after her when I am gone. You'll make sure she's safe."

Darian tipped his head back to empty his tankard. Revelin took the opportunity to kick Darian's sword out of the man's reach. The dagger would have to come later. Revelin looked at the weapon strapped to Darian's side. Maybe one of the maids—

"Well, shall we go?" Darian asked, interrupting Revelin's thoughts. "I doubt you came here for the ambiance or the ale."

"Indeed not," Revelin said. "Are you sure you are finished?"

"Quite finished," Darian said. "Mayhap with the whole damn country."

Revelin allowed that to pass without comment and followed his advisor out of the tavern. Darian climbed into the carriage and leaned into the far corner. Revelin sat on the opposite side.

"Why did you not send Rhoswen and Sighle to Mairéad?" he asked as the carriage started to move. "You have an estate here. They would have been welcomed and looked after. You know that."

"I should have," Darian replied after a moment. "God have mercy on me, I should have. I should have stopped her from going. I knew about the rebels, about the war. Why didn't I stop her? I don't know. She just wanted to be with Haleine, and I didn't want to refuse her. I have so many times before. After Mireille—and she *begged* me—When Sighle came—I couldn't bring myself to do it again."

Mireille was a name Revelin didn't recognize. He thought she was likely Haleine's twin, but he didn't want to ask and Darian said nothing more.

The remainder of the ride was in silence. Darian stretched out across the seat and fell asleep. He mumbled occasionally, calling out Rhoswen's name and then Haleine's. Mireille was the third name to escape from his lips.

When they arrived at the palace, Revelin left Darragh to see Darian safely back to his chambers and returned to the library. He stopped just outside of it when he saw his mother's guards standing in front of the doors. They moved to allow him to enter, but he was hesitant. If his mother was here in the middle of the night, something else had gone wrong.

Haraszty sat at the desk, still dressed in her bedclothes. She looked up at his arrival and held out a piece of parchment.

"This came from Lira," she said. "The servants had to fetch me because you and Darian were nowhere to be found! Where did you go?"

"A tavern," he said. "What exactly came from Lira?"

"This! This letter!" she said, thrusting it into his hands. "It's from Maddox's advisor about Haleine. Those damned rebels have made an attempt on her life."

"An attempt?" Revelin asked, his stomach tightening.

"He says she is injured but still alive," Haraszty said. "What were you doing in a tavern?"

Revelin looked over Omur's note. It was as his mother had said. Haleine was hurt. The rebels were responsible. He crumpled the letter.

"Your father used to take you boys when you were younger, but I thought that foolishness would have died out by now. I hope Darian managed to keep you out of trouble. I'd rather not hear any tales of your public drunkenness."

"I have never been publicly drunk in my life," he said. "I do not intend to start now."

"Why go at all?" she asked. "I don't understand it. Even after all those years with your father, the mysteries of men are still lost to me."

"I am sending men to Eluned on the morrow," he said. "Whatever men we have ready. More will follow if necessary."

That ended Haraszty's interest in the tavern visit. "You can't go to Lira."

"Nor do I intend to," he said. "I will send Darian in my stead. I am certain he will be most eager to hunt these men who have hunted his family."

"Yes, well, fine, whatever you think is best," Haraszty said, rising from the chair. "I am returning to my chambers now, unless you have further need of me."

"Who is Mireille?"

His mother gave him a strange look. "Where did you hear that name?"

"Darian mentioned her, but he did not say who she was," Revelin said. "Do you know her? Was she Darian's daughter? Haleine's twin?"

Haraszty sighed. "Yes."

"What happened to her?"

"She died, the poor thing. I don't think she was even a year old."

"How?"

"Murdered, I suppose. Men broke into the castle in Parthalan and went after the girls. He almost lost his life doing it, but Darian managed to save Haleine. But not Mireille. They took her, whoever they were. Darian looked everywhere for that little girl. He tore that city apart. Tore the entire land apart, but she was gone and so were her abductors."

"And Darian agreed to stay in Quatara? Even after a loss such as that?" Revelin asked.

Haraszty shrugged. "It's what your father wanted," she said as though it answered everything.

Revelin frowned as he realized it truly did.

———∿∿∿———

That night Haleine lay on a bedroll in the grass. Someone outside had built a fire, and now she watched the shadows on the tent wall. Dana lay beside her. They didn't speak. They hadn't spoken since he had said he would return her to the palace and she had agreed. It was awful. They finally had gotten what they'd both wanted for so long. They had a night together to do as they would. From dusk until dawn they could lie together, wrapped in the other's arms without fear of discovery, and she couldn't bring herself to touch him.

Neither did he reach for her. They hadn't touched since he had helped her undress so she would not have to sleep in her gown. Now they lay side by side as though they were not lovers but rather two strangers thrown together by chance.

That had been true once. He'd fallen into her world, and she'd clung to him as a drowning person would cling to a lifeline, but he wasn't a stranger anymore. He was the standard by which all else was measured. He was the reason behind any decision she made. Even forgiving her mother.

Especially forgiving her mother.

She cried large, silent tears that ran down both cheeks. She didn't want the man beside her to know of her grief. He would try to comfort her then, and maybe he would succeed, but she did not want it. She did not deserve it.

She thought of the three men who had sought to end her life that day. Their laughter, their jibes, their hands, dragging her from one place to the next, wanting her to beg, their hands on her skin, lifting her skirts, holding her down, bellowing like the animals they were, her cowering like the prey she was. And then. Asking for her death. On her knees. Moving her hair for a swifter stroke and a cleaner cut. He didn't want delays. He wanted it done.

Was that how Rhoswen died? Was that how she passed her final moments? Terrified, ashamed, unable to breathe? Did Omur want delays then? He would have wanted it to be as horrible as possible. How many had he sent to see it done? One? Two? Three? More? What might they have done to her? Teased her? Made her beg? Had they raped her before finally robbing an innocent woman of her life?

Her breath caught, and she cried out loud. She clapped her hand over her mouth, but it was too late. He stirred and turned his head toward her.

"Haleine?"

She didn't want to talk. She didn't want him to talk, so she rolled on top of him before he could move and pressed her lips against his to keep him from saying anything else. He was surprised, and she could not blame him. She shared the emotion, but she didn't back down. She kissed him as hard as she ever had and stopped only when she needed to breathe. She laid her head on his chest to listen to his heart.

"Tell me you love me," she said against his skin.

She asked her mother to carry a letter to save her daughter. To save her daughter's lover.

His hands were in her hair. "I love you."

The feel of him beneath her was intoxicating. She nuzzled his throat, kissing and nipping at his warm skin. He smelled of earth, tasted of salt, and he would ground her. She moved her hips slowly, deliberately, and heard his breath catch.

"Haleine—"

"Tell me you love me," she said.

"I love you."

She didn't know what she was doing anymore. She didn't want to know. She didn't want to think. She wanted to be lost. She wanted to be lost in him. It was where she belonged.

She sat up to pull her slip over her head. She felt his response, felt him grow hard. His hands were on the inside of her thighs and slid up across her stomach and over her breasts. He helped with her slip, taking it from her and tossing it aside. He put his hand behind her neck and pulled her down to him.

"I love you," he said again.

A sob rose in her throat, but she refused to allow it to escape. She kissed his throat and worked her way to his navel. He reached for her, stroking any part he could. She pleased him. She could feel it in his touch. She could hear it in the breaths he took.

She had heard him before, the other times they'd made love. He moaned, panted and called her name. He loved her. She was more to him than the others. She was his whore; she was his only whore because he loved her. Above all else.

If he loved her, it was worth it. If he loved her, it wasn't for nothing.

She tugged at his braies, searching for the cord that would allow his skin to mesh with hers. He started to rise—to stop her, she thought. "No," she begged. "Dana, please—"

There could be nothing between them. She'd given all for him; she wouldn't allow anything to separate them now.

"Shhh." His lips were against her forehead. "Shhh."

He took her hand and guided it to what she sought. She fumbled with the cord, unable to loosen it. A sound of frustration escaped from her throat. Her hands shook too badly to try again.

He untied the cord himself. "Shhh."

His braies soon joined her slip in the black void. She watched them disappear, wanting her own oblivion. She fell forward and sobbed into his shoulder. He held her until she pulled him to the ground where she lay on her back, and he lay on his side next to her. It was so much like the first time when pleasure was all, right and wrong meant nothing, and she panted just as hard for him as he had for her. It was simple then—she knew that now—though it seemed to be anything but at the time. A stolen look, a touch, a moment of playing at being alive. What it was now, what it had turned into, she did not know. Desire, lust, passion did not begin to describe it. Simple, it wasn't.

But it was everything.

"I love you," he said, covering her with his body.

She clung to him as they made love, her nails digging into his flesh more with each stroke. She was exhausted, drenched with her passion, her love, her need. He murmured in her ear. *I love you* over and over again. As she neared the height of her much needed, yet unwanted ecstasy, she opened her eyes.

His eyes were closed and his head thrown back. He was losing himself in her. He moaned for her. He did it because he wanted it, wanted her. He did it because she wanted it, wanted him. Because he loved her. She tightened her grip.

"Tell me you—" she started, but the storm within her broke and she said no more.

She cried out, in pleasure, in pain, in grief, in joy. It was all the same.

I am whole when he is near, she had told Rhoswen.

She was whole now.

It would have to be enough. It was all she had.

James hadn't slept. He'd spent most of the night standing in front of the fire in the center of camp, keeping company with the others awake. While they patrolled the camp borders, he guarded Dana's tent. He was still watching when the queen of Lira, barefoot and dressed in naught but her silk shift, came out.

For a moment, he was back in the woods, witnessing her contend with her captors. His bow was readied and the arrow trained on one of the men in Omur's service, but his eyes were on her. A few inches to the left. That's all it would have taken for the arrow to kill her instead. Had he known then what he knew now, he would have let that arrow fly wide.

Now the queen walked away. She didn't see him, nor anyone else, as her head was turned toward Dana's tent. When she ran head-on into James, she started to fall. He caught her elbow and helped her regain her balance.

"You've come back," she said.

He released her and looked at the fire. "I never left. But what of you? You've only just arrived. You can't be thinking about leaving us so soon."

"You know I can't stay."

He did know it.

"I need to return to the palace," she said next.

"And to your husband?"

"I do expect him to be there."

"Because of your undying love for one another?"

"Maddox loves none but himself, and the only undying love I have is for the man in that tent behind me."

Her tone was sad. If he saw her face, it would have been etched on her skin. No one could hide a sorrow like hers sounded. But he didn't look. He wasn't interested in her grief.

"If that is true," James said, "why is he in there and you out here?"

She didn't answer right away. It was enough for James to know Dana had no idea his lover was abandoning him. He almost smiled.

"It is the only way to save him," the queen said. "To save you all."

James looked at her over his shoulder. "How fortunate you hold us in such high regard."

He had annoyed her. He saw a flash of it in her eyes before she swallowed it and went on.

"I am very sorry for any loss you may have experienced at my husband's doing," she said. "I only ask that you set it aside long enough to help me back to where I should be."

He turned around. "You want my help?"

"I cannot ask Dana. I fear he would only seek out one reason after another why I cannot leave."

He examined her now. The unhappiness wasn't only in her face. He glanced at Dana's tent.

"Fine," he said. "Wait here."

He went to his tent first to fetch his weapons and a cloak for her. Faolan was there. He'd been there since the attack had ended. It was another reason why James had chosen to spend the night elsewhere. He wasn't any more willing to talk to Faolan than he was Dana. James took his sword belt and buckled it around his waist.

"The queen wants to go back," James said, picking up his bow and quiver.

"I'll come with you."

"Suit yourself," he said, tucking a dagger into his belt before walking away.

He found horses next, selecting a mare for the queen. He slipped bridles on both beasts and put a man's saddle on the mare's back. The queen would have to make do.

When James returned to the fire, he saw Faolan balanced on the queen's shoulder. James didn't know what might have been said between them, but there was a marked difference in the queen's posture. She was more secure with the pegasus at her side.

"Here." James held out the cloak. "Put this on."

She thanked him, took the garment and threw it over her shoulders as soon as Faolan gave up his perch. After she secured the ties, James helped her into the saddle.

"It was kind of you to remember a saddle," she said. "Thank you."

He found her manners irritating but didn't say so. He mounted his own horse and started out of camp. Faolan muttered something, and James heard the mare scramble to catch up to him.

He didn't speak to the queen as they rode. She stayed behind him, occasionally speaking to Faolan. Faolan urged her to stay close, to not let James get too far ahead, and James smiled. Faolan didn't trust him.

"He's not inclined to take you into the tunnels," the pegasus said. "He could lose you easily along these paths if he wanted."

"What tunnels?" the queen asked.

James turned around—first his head, followed by his mount. He pulled the animal to a stop and stared hard at Faolan. What the hell did he think he was doing?

"There is a series of interconnecting tunnels beneath your feet," Faolan said. "They run from one corner of the country to the next. It makes it easier for us to avoid the soldiers."

"Faolan," James warned.

Both Faolan and the queen looked at him then, noticing for the first time that he had stopped moving. He shook his head, intending to admonish the pegasus when something in the forest caught his eye. He dropped the reins and reached for his bow.

"What is it?" the queen asked, stopping her horse. "Faolan?"

Faolan didn't say anything as he stared into the forest.

James took an arrow from the quiver and readied it. They were on his left and his right. He thought there were just the two, but he couldn't be sure. Why they waited, he didn't know. Were they hesitating as he had the day before, or did they not realize they'd been seen?

"Get her out of here," he whispered, knowing Faolan could hear him. "Get her somewhere safe."

Neither the queen nor Faolan moved. The queen stared at him. The pegasus still watched the forest.

"Faolan," James said again. "Get her out of here."

"There are three of them," Faolan said.

One of the hidden men flinched. James saw it and immediately raised his bow and released his arrow to the right. His shot went wide, and the attack began. Arrows flew out from all directions. Two bolts found their way into the queen's mare. The horse crumpled, and the queen let out a cry as she fell to the ground.

James slid from his horse as an arrow grazed his arm. He grimaced but readied another arrow. He saw the man on the right, aimed and released. This time he knew it was a killing blow even before the arrow struck and turned to contend with the other attacker. The man showed himself briefly before turning to run. James followed, dropping his bow at the edge of the forest.

"Protect her!" he shouted to Faolan.

He was stupid to be chasing down a man running away. He should have stayed with the queen. He should have protected the horse. He should have gotten the both of them away from there before any more of Omur's men came along, but he didn't. He continued to crash through the brush. He didn't know what they might have overheard or what they would carry back to their master. He couldn't risk letting any of them survive. He had to protect the rebellion. Faolan could defend the queen.

"James!"

He stopped short as he realized the voice belonged to Faolan. The pegasus wouldn't speak in front of certain people, Omur's men among them. James looked over his shoulder and saw nothing but the path he had created. He turned back in time to see a man wielding a dagger aimed at his neck. He threw his arm up so the weapon struck that instead.

The blade slit his skin from his wrist nearly to his elbow, and the pain forced him to his knees. He ducked to avoid another wild swing from his opponent. While the man was regaining his balance,

James took his own dagger from his belt and drove it into the man's side. James withdrew the blade and staggered to his feet as the other man fell screaming. James grabbed the man by his hair and yanked his head back. He dragged the dagger across the man's throat and threw the body to the ground.

"James!" Faolan shouted again.

Faolan's last words before the attack came rushing back to him. *There are three of them.* James swore. He replaced his dagger, drew his sword and ran. He stopped just short of the trail and crouched down in order to survey the situation. He saw the queen lying face-down next to her fallen mare. Faolan hovered over her, and a man holding a slender knife in each hand slowly circled them. The man lunged forward, but a blue-gray barrier appeared out of nowhere and threw him back. The shield dissipated as the attacker steadied himself and started circling once more.

James looked next at his mount, still alive and somehow still standing in the middle of the road. His bow lay on the ground where he had abandoned it. He glanced back at Faolan and saw the shield reappear as the man tried another attack. The result was the same. James set down his sword and waited until the man's back was to him before stepping onto the road. He recovered his bow and took an arrow from the quiver. Faolan now faced him but watched his assailant so intently that James didn't know if he had been seen. As he nocked the arrow, his arm throbbed its protest. Blood ran down to his fingers and threatened his grip on the weapon. He'd only get one chance to make his shot, and if he delayed much longer, he wouldn't even get that. He raised the bow and took aim.

"Faolan, down!" he shouted before releasing the arrow.

The shield dissolved, the pegasus disappeared from view, and the man spun around in time to see the arrow as it struck. James's shot had been a good one, sinking deep into the man's chest. The would-be assassin's eyes widened as he gasped and fell to the ground.

James readied another arrow immediately and waited. When no one emerged to continue the fight, he blew out a relieved breath and lowered his weapon.

"What took you so long?" Faolan said, reemerging in the air. He looked at James and the blood dripping from his arm. "Oh."

"What happened here?" James asked, dropping his bow.

"I told you there were three of them. Are you all right?"

"I'm fine."

"You don't look fine."

"Be grateful it was the left arm. I'd never have made that shot if it were the right," James said, moving to the queen's side. "I told you to protect her."

"I was."

"Not very effectively."

"I tried to shield her, but she's impervious to my magic," Faolan said. "I—I forgot. I had to settle for shielding myself."

"And the king's men? Were they impervious?"

"I don't kill people, James."

"You're fighting a war, Faolan," he muttered, kneeling beside the queen. "You might want to reconsider."

Apprehension rose inside him as he rolled her over. He relaxed when he saw she was still breathing and was only unconscious. Quickly, he took stock of her injuries. Her right wrist was twisted unnaturally, but her most serious injury was the arrow that had been shot into her left shoulder. She was fortunate the man had missed her heart.

"James?" Faolan said. "We need to leave. There could be others coming."

"Aye, I know," he said. "I need something to slow the bleeding first."

"I'm glad to hear you aren't planning on letting her bleed to death."

"Don't misunderstand me. I do want her to die." James went to the fallen mare and stripped her of the saddle to get the blanket underneath it. "But it will have to happen within the palace walls. Not here."

He cut the blanket into four strips. He used the first to fashion a sling for the queen's injured shoulder. The arrow would have to stay where it was for the time being, and the less it moved, the better. The second strip he used to staunch the flow of blood. A third strip went around her wrist to offer it better protection until a physician could set the bones properly. The final strip he wrapped around his own arm.

"It will have to do," James said. "I can't do anything else here."

He stood, looked at the unconscious queen, then his horse. How was he going to do this?

"I suppose I have you to thank for the horse still being here," he said.

Faolan nodded. "I thought he might be useful."

"Aye," James said, scanning the area around him.

He spotted a boulder just off the path on the right side. He knelt again, picked up the queen and carried her over to it. He laid her on top and went back for the horse.

"Can you make sure the horse won't move until I tell him?" he asked Faolan as he positioned the horse alongside the boulder. "I don't want to jostle her more than I have to."

Faolan nodded and James climbed into the saddle. The horse's back was nearly level with the top of the rock. It took some maneuvering, but James got the queen onto the horse. He kept one arm around her to hold her in place and held the reins with his other hand.

"Let's get out of here," James said, nudging the horse forward.

Faolan followed. "We've lost a lot of time, James. And now you're injured, she's injured, and there's an excellent chance that more of Omur's men are out there. We should—"

"Aye, I know," James said. "We'll have to use the tunnels now."

"We should have used them from the start."

"I wasn't about to show them to her. It's bad enough she knows they exist at all," James said. "We'll use them now, and we'll get her back to the damn palace before anything else can happen."

"Good idea," Faolan said. "Do you happen to have an equally good plan to get her into the city unnoticed?"

James nodded. "It's market day."

CHAPTER 21

Word of the queen's disappearance traveled quickly to the palace.

Bronagh retreated to Haleine's chambers to escape the chaos and wait out the storm. She paced and tended the fire while she worried and waited. After a while, pacing took too much energy—energy she needed to worry—and she sat on the floor in front of the fire.

Dana had her. Bronagh knew it. So did the soldiers. Dana may not have wanted to cause the queen harm, but the soldiers wouldn't care about that.

She was so afraid. She had been for so long that it was difficult to remember the last time she hadn't felt that way. Only now that she thought about it, it wasn't difficult at all. It was before Haleine had come to Lira, back when Bronagh still served only Michaela and lived in ignorance of Haleine's existence.

The day that changed, she and Michaela were alone in the queen's chambers. Bronagh was setting the other woman's hair for a ball celebrating the prince's birthday. They had been chatting easily about whatever crossed their minds when Michaela shifted in her seat. The queen's posture became rigid, and Bronagh knew something more serious was to follow.

"Did I tell you," Michaela said. "Tanuba has agreed to a bride for my son."

"King Nathan only has sons, doesn't he?" Bronagh asked and the queen nodded. "Who will they choose?"

"Her name is Haleine Coileáin. She is Nathan's seneschal's daughter."

Bronagh was unable to disguise her surprise and met her queen's eyes in the mirror's reflection.

Michaela laughed. "It would not happen here, I know, but Nathan holds the man in the highest regard. The girl was betrothed to one of his own sons."

"Do you know her, your majesty?"

"I made her acquaintance once at Nathan's court," Michaela said. "I doubt very much she would remember the encounter. She was very young then, a very intelligent little girl. I do not imagine she has changed. Her father would not be the sort to brook insolence."

"Will she understand what is expected of her?"

"She will have been well-versed in that," Michaela said. "But as intelligent as she is, as well-prepared as she thinks she may be, she will still be alone. She will be frightened. You will have to help her. You and Willem, too, I think. You will have to take care of her. Protect her."

Bronagh stared at the queen. "Protect her?"

"It will not be easy, I know. My son is—" Michaela paused and looked away. "Well, you know what he is. She will not."

No, Haleine hadn't known what she was marrying but, Bronagh remembered, it did not take long for the girl to learn. Michaela had said she was smart, and Bronagh knew that was true, but despite all her intelligence, Haleine still had fallen into folly.

What was it Willem had said? Haleine didn't know how to compromise, how to just survive.

"Why couldn't she have asked?" Bronagh whispered.

She couldn't put the blame on Haleine. She couldn't. She herself would have to wear that badge. Why hadn't she done something? Michaela had charged her with Haleine's protection, and what had happened?

It was the first time she had ever failed her mistress.

A persistent and desperate knocking caught Bronagh's attention. She searched the room for its source and saw a man in a blood-stained tunic standing on the balcony, pounding on the doors with both hands. She almost called for guards, but the sight of Haleine's pegasus hovering in the air beside him stopped her. He was one of the rebels. She got to her feet and ran toward him.

Bronagh threw open the doors. "Where is she? Who are you? What have you done with her?"

"My name is James, and your queen is in the city," he said, stepping into the room. "She is injured."

Bronagh's heart all but stopped, and her eyes slipped to his tunic. "What did you do to her?"

"I saved her," James said, disgust dripping from his voice. "Twice now, actually. But she's badly hurt and she needs care. I need you to help me get her in the palace."

"Come with me," Bronagh said.

Together they went into the servants' passage. She looked at him more than once, not quite sure what to make of him. Why hadn't Dana come?

"Where is she?" Bronagh asked. "Where in the city?"

"She's nearby," James said. "She's being looked after by—she's being looked after. How can we get her inside the palace without raising suspicion?"

"How did you get her into the city without raising suspicion?"

James offered no answer. She glanced at him again.

"Why don't you just tell me where she is, and I'll send men to fetch her," she suggested.

"No."

"No?"

"No," James said. "I won't be able to trust the men you'd send not to hurt the queen nor the people who help me. God knows you'd do well not to trust any of them either. Twice I've saved her, and twice it was members of this country's army masquerading as rebels. If she dies, and she may, it'll be here, within these walls, under the care of her physician and you. I won't have the blame fall on me—on us."

"Idiot. The blame will fall on you anyway. It already has," Bronagh said but relented, as it was the only way to get Haleine back. "There is a passage, one most soldiers don't know about. It leads from the kitchens outside. There is good cover there. No one will see."

"What is it used for?"

"The protection of the king and queen."

"Why don't the soldiers know about it?"

"Only their personal guards know," Bronagh said, leading him into the kitchens.

"How do you know?"

This time she offered no answer. "I'll open the passage for you, and I'll wait here while you fetch her."

James looked at the pegasus who had followed them this far and now settled on her shoulder.

"Keep an eye on her," he said to the beast.

"What do you expect him to do?" Bronagh asked.

"Watch my back," James answered. "I'll go and get the queen and bring her here, but I warn you, if I see anyone I shouldn't, or if anything at all feels suspicious, I'll finish her and make sure you never find the body."

She never thought she'd wish for Dana to be there. "You won't. I only care for her."

James nodded and disappeared into the black. "I'm counting on it."

—◦◦◦—

Haleine was floating.

When she was a girl of ten, her father taught her to swim. There was a lake not far from their home, and one impossibly hot day, Darian had taken her and her sister there. Sighle refused to get wet, refused to put in so much as a toe no matter how Darian coaxed.

"Mama will be mad," Sighle said, a child of four speaking with the gravity of a woman grown. "She doesn't want us here."

Haleine, stripped down to her linen shift, didn't hesitate and plunged into the water. She gasped as the cold bit into her skin. She laughed at everything else. Her father's men surrounded them, watching the trees and the road and everything around them for enemies seeking to ruin the day. But none appeared, and so Haleine played and swam and, before the day had ended, Darian taught her to float.

After that, she lay on her back, floating in the water and staring at the sky. She stayed like that until she shivered too badly to float anymore. Darian carried her from the water then and wrapped her in a thick towel. When they returned home, Sighle sat in front of her father, and Haleine sat behind him, holding his belt, still exhilarated from the day.

When they rode through the castle's gates, Rhoswen waited for them in the courtyard. Her mother looked both furious and relieved at the sight of them. Darian pulled the horse to a stop as Rhoswen rushed up. She took Sighle from him and gave her over to the waiting nurse. Next, her mother reached for Haleine and stopped when she saw the state of her daughter's clothing. The relief disappeared, completely swallowed by anger.

"Where is her dress? Where did you go?" Rhoswen demanded. "Have you taken leave of your senses?"

Rhoswen pulled her from the horse's back. She was too rough and it hurt, but Haleine didn't say so. Her mother's expression was one to inspire silence. Indeed her father must have felt the same, as he offered her mother no explanation.

"He taught us to swim," Haleine ventured later when she and her mother were alone in a room, rolling bandages for Parthalan's hospital. "He taught me to swim. Sighle wouldn't go in. She was afraid you'd be angry."

"Was she?" Rhoswen said.

Her mother wasn't listening. Not really. She was focused on her task, rolling linen with a precision that indicated Sighle was the wisest of them all.

"Are you?" Haleine asked.

"Yes. No." Rhoswen looked at her daughter and sighed. "No, love, I'm not angry with you. Nor your sister."

"Are you angry with Father?"

"That doesn't matter," her mother said. "Why don't you tell me about the lake? What was the water like?"

"It was cold," Haleine said. "Cold like snow."

"Snow?" Rhoswen said. "What do you know about snow?"

"My tutors told me about it."

"It doesn't snow here."

"Only in the north, in the mountains," Haleine said. "I know that, but I'll see it someday."

Someday came six years later, when she stood in the snow and shared a stolen moment with her betrothed. It was rather strange that she had Zoltano to thank for it.

Whenever the crown prince did not get his way at his father's court, he would withdraw to Gweneria. It happened all too often, and eventually, Nathan started sending his second son to deal with the first. One such occasion arose during one of Haleine's visits to court, and Nathan ordered Revelin to depart for Gweneria the following morning.

"Come with me," he entreated as they sat together in a window seat. He took her palm and kissed it. "Make this chore a bearable one."

"I shall have to ask your mother for permission to leave," she said. She drew her hand away and looked to see if any watched. "I am supposed to be attending her after all."

"I thought you were here to visit with me."

"I am here to attend her," Haleine said. "Like the dutiful daughter-in-law I hope to someday be."

"Soon," Revelin said. "It will happen soon. Father is negotiating with Idris Fein for Zaide Romanza. They will reach an agreement before we know it."

"I think you told me that last year."

"I mean it this year," he said. "Go ask my mother for permission."

"If my father were here at court, would you still have asked me to come?"

"I would have known better."

Haleine smiled. "You sound afraid of him. I don't know why. He likes you."

"Not enough to allow his daughter to accompany me so far north without an escort."

"Won't your mother insist upon one?"

"Yes," Revelin said. "But better my mother's choice than your father's."

It was true enough, and the next morning, when the carriage carrying her and her betrothed left the palace, her chaperone, one of the queen's more elderly maids, rode with the driver. Had her father selected the woman, she would have been in the carriage with them, sitting next to Haleine while providing Revelin with one suspicious glance after another.

But now they were alone and free of anyone's eyes. They sat together, their hands intertwined. She laid her head on his shoulder.

"What has your brother done now?" she asked. "Or rather, what has he refused to do?"

"I am not supposed to say."

"You never are," she said, "but you always do."

He never hid anything from her. He never lied to her. She never gave him a reason to.

"My brother wants control of Quatara," Revelin said. "He thinks he should have been given its command years ago and demands it now. My father refused him, and now Zoltano means to take it by force."

Haleine sat up and stared at her betrothed. "He'll have to fight not only Einar but also my father," she said. "Does he not realize that? What makes him think—?"

"Zoltano does not think. He never does."

"He doesn't have to," she said. "Not so long as he has you to save him from himself."

"That is my father's hope."

"His hope is well-founded," she said, settling back against Revelin. "It is certainly no grand task, but you'll convince your brother to stand down."

"You sound quite confident."

"I am quite confident. You've never failed before. Why would you begin now?"

Revelin kissed the top of her head. "You always know just what to say. What would I ever do without you?"

"Fortunately, you shall never have to find out."

When they arrived at Gweneria, Revelin went in search of his brother. Haleine was left to wander with no company but that of her chaperone. At the end of a hall, she found a door that opened onto a small garden. It was evidence that Zoltano hadn't always been the master here.

The garden was dormant now, slumbering through the winter cold. Haleine walked into the middle of it, examining the brittle, brown vines still clinging to the walls. She wondered if any cared for them during the growing season.

She hadn't been outside very long when the snow began to fall. One flake, then another, and a third. She looked up in delight as she realized what she was seeing. The sky was suddenly filled with it, and she laughed.

"My lady, please," her escort said from the doorway. "Come inside."

"Yes, in a moment," Haleine said, having no true intent of doing anything of the sort.

She stood there, delaying her moment long past the appreciation of her chaperone. She was cold, nearly frozen and shivering madly even in her fur-lined mantle. Her hands were growing numb, but she didn't care. She watched the snow pile on the benches and walls. She held out her hand and watched the snow melt upon contact.

"What are you doing out here?" Revelin asked.

She turned around and smiled. "It's snowing."

"I can see that," he said. He came forward and took her hands in his. "You should not be out here. It is too cold. Your hands are ice."

"Do you want to go inside?"

He glanced over his shoulder to see if they were alone. They were. Her chaperone was, for the moment, gone, too cold to remain, so Revelin pulled Haleine into a corner, out of sight. He backed her against the wall and kissed her. She put her arms around his neck.

"Did you stop him?" she asked.

"Do I ever?"

"Every time."

He nodded. "There will be a day when I cannot."

"But it is not this day."

"No," he said, bending to kiss her again. "Not this day."

Their next kiss was rougher than the first. It was not unexpected. It was always like this after a confrontation with the crown prince. Revelin hated his brother and the responsibility he held for Zoltano's actions but was still a slave to both that and his father's will. He could never say so, but with her he never had to.

He pushed aside her cloak and placed his hands on her waist. He kissed her neck, moving from one side to the next. She let him, knowing he wouldn't press for more. Above everything, he was honorable.

"Revelin, love," she said in his ear. "Someone will come."

His hands slipped to her hips, one clutching her skirts and pulling them up. She felt the cold biting at her ankles and panic building in her stomach. She put her hands on his chest and tried to push him away. He grabbed her hands and forced them down. She cried out.

"You're hurting me," she said.

He looked at her. But it wasn't Revelin anymore. It was Maddox.

"Don't tell me you're complaining," he said.

"Of course not. Just thought you'd like to know," she said. "It's the sort of thing you take pleasure in."

She wasn't herself. She wasn't Haleine. She lay naked on her back on a feather bed. Maddox hovered over her, naked and grinning.

"And you don't?" he asked.

She smiled. "I take pleasure in everything."

She had to get away. She didn't know what this was, but it wasn't her. She wasn't saying these things. She would never say those things.

She rolled to her left, finding the edge of the bed and falling. She got to her feet and ran to the other side of the room, tripping on her skirts before she realized she even wore them. What was this? What was happening to her? She stood against the wall and looked at her husband.

He hadn't noticed her departure. He remained in the bed, making love to Zaide Romanza. The queen of Feond wore naught but a necklace, a great red stone set in gold. It was the amulet Maddox had given her.

"Marry me," Maddox said when they were done.

"Marry you?" Zaide Romanza asked. "And how would we do that? You, as I recall, already have a wife, and I already have a betrothed."

"You don't love him."

"I don't love you either."

"I should hope not," Maddox said. "However, you do love power quite a lot, and I happen to have quite a lot of power."

"You also happen to have quite a lot of rebels."

"Had," Maddox corrected. "The rebellion, like your unfortunate father, is dead."

Zaide Romanza turned her head to the side and smiled. Haleine could have sworn the woman was smiling at her.

"Not quite like my father," Zaide Romanza said. "Is it, your majesty?"

"No," Haleine whispered, knowing she was being addressed. She didn't know how it was possible, but it didn't make it any less true. "It isn't."

"Still, I think I shall decline your offer," Zaide Romanza said next. "Surely it would only be a matter of time before I bore you as much as your current wife does."

"I doubt that."

"The novelty of her purity has already worn off, and you've not yet been married a year," Zaide Romanza said.

"You wouldn't have to worry about your purity," Maddox said.

"I haven't for years," she replied. "I think I'd have to worry about my neck though."

"You have no faith in me."

Zaide Romanza grinned. "That is very true. But in order to marry me, you'd have to rid yourself of your current wife. I'd say you'd have to kill her since she gave you two sons, and you can't set the woman aside. And then, should you marry me, you'll lose interest because you have me, and I shall spend all my life waiting for the day some other woman with a small country of her own catches your eye. If I wasn't so fond of my neck, I'd consider it. But I am fond of my neck, so it looks as though you'll have to be satisfied with this tryst."

"I've not been satisfied yet," he said.

Zaide Romanza smiled. She licked her lips and placed her hand between his legs. Haleine was turning away when Zaide Romanza spoke to her again.

"Oh, don't be such a prude," Zaide Romanza scolded.

"Who are you talking to?" Maddox asked. He looked over, and his mouth twisted into a lopsided grin. "Oh. You. See anything you like?"

She was going mad. It was the only explanation.

"Really, Haleine. Do you mind?" Zaide Romanza said. "You're making a mess, love."

Haleine looked and saw blood running down her arms and legs. She saw the blood smeared across her chest. There was a hole there, not far from her heart. She searched for something to stop the bleeding.

"Let it bleed," Maddox said, suddenly in front of her. "Perhaps then you will remember who is master here."

She put her hands on his chest and pushed him away. He stumbled back.

"Haleine?"

It wasn't Maddox anymore. It was Revelin. She was a girl again, a girl in a snow-hushed garden, with her betrothed standing in front of her, hurt and stunned.

She didn't love him. She hadn't known it when she was sixteen, but she knew it now. How was she both the girl in love and the woman out of it? She looked at him, feeling as bewildered as he appeared.

"Someone will come," she said finally, knowing it was what she had told him then.

Revelin nodded and studied the ground as he composed himself. She shivered and pulled her cloak tighter around herself as she waited.

"You are cold," Revelin said.

She was cold. She couldn't stop shaking. Her fingers hurt. She had spent too much time floating and too much time trying to catch snowflakes that couldn't be caught. It hurt, and she was growing tired of the pain.

But there was always pain. There was no end to it. She longed to be a garden in winter. She wanted to slumber in a deep, oblivious sleep until the warmth of spring offered her rebirth.

"Haleine?" Revelin asked.

"I don't love you," she said. "I'm sorry. I wish I did."

Revelin turned his back on her. He had done that before, she remembered now. They stood together on a balcony. She was newly married, and he never looked back. She searched a sea of faces for him, but he was not to be found.

She found Dana instead. Would she still have loved him if Revelin had followed her inside that night? If it were the prince's eyes in which she had taken comfort as the doors closed upon her, would she still have loved the rebel leader?

"I still would have left," Revelin said. "You still would have called him."

"Called him?" she asked. "I don't understand."

Revelin nodded. "You will. Before long."

"What is this? Is this real?"

"You know better."

"What is this, then?" she asked. "Do you know?"

"Little more than a fever dream."

She put her hand over her heart and Revelin nodded.

"You do not belong here," he said. "You need to go back."

"I do not belong there. I do not belong anywhere. I'm so tired, Revelin. I do not think I can do it anymore. It's too hard."

"What is right is never meant to be easy. You should go. You should not tarry."

"What if I cannot find the way?"

"The way will find you. It has before," Revelin said.

He wasn't looking at her anymore. He looked beyond her. She turned now, finding herself on the balcony at the palace in Eluned. It was her wedding night, and Dana stood out among the guests. She had no sooner laid eyes upon him when he turned and walked away.

"Where is he—why is he—?" She looked at Revelin. "I have to go. I have to follow him."

"Yes," Revelin said. "So you have said."

"I'm sorry," she said again. "I wanted to love you. And I did once. We would have been happy."

"Yes," Revelin said. "We would have been that."

She nodded as she left the balcony. She worked her way through the guests, never taking her eyes off Dana. She wanted to call out to him but was afraid to do so. The guests grew closer together, and it became impossible for her to move past them. She pushed at them—begging them to move out of the way—but they did not move. They didn't acknowledge her.

Ceallach put his hand on her arm. "My lady, it is time for you to be conducted to bed."

"No." She shook her head and continued her search for Dana, but she couldn't see him anywhere. "I need a moment. He's here; I know he's here."

"No, my lady," Ceallach said. "There is no time. You must come now."

There were hands on her, hands she couldn't see, grabbing her arms and waist. They pulled her back, and the harder she fought, the harder they pulled, but she struggled against them, screaming Dana's name. She lost the fight and was thrown back into her chambers. The doors started to close, and she scanned the sea of faces staring at her, but Dana was not among them.

Where had he gone?

He'll leave you.

The doors closed, and she threw herself against them, pounding on them and screaming Dana's name again and again. She couldn't stay here. She knew what was coming next, and she wouldn't do it again.

"You're trembling," her husband noted. "Afraid I won't be gentle?"

She stopped screaming. She stopped pounding but didn't drop her hands. She sank to her knees and pressed her forehead to the door. She felt his hand on the small of her back and the warmth of his breath on her neck. His other hand caressed her hip.

"I won't do this again," she said. "I won't."

"And how do you propose to stop me?"

"He's here."

"He walked away from you."

"He'll come for me."

"He's already gone. You saw him walking away."

"No," she said. "It was a trick. It was some sort of evil on your part. You want me to think it. You want me to think I am helpless and alone."

"Aren't you?"

Wasn't she?

"No," she said.

"Then prove it."

He forced her to stand, turned her around and pinned her against the door. The breath was knocked out of her, and she stood there, unresisting.

"Come on," he said, grinding his hips against her. "Show me. Fight me. Stop me. Tell me you don't want it."

"I don't want it."

"Liar. You've made a career of whoring yourself out to me."

"For him. For him only. Never did I want you. I touched you only to help him."

"And now he's left you. Walked away without even a glance."

"No."

"Yes." He grinned. "Call it what you want, love, but a whore is a whore no matter how she may dress. Revelin knew that, didn't he?"

He was losing interest in her physical rape. She glanced around, her eyes falling to her vanity. Inside it was the dagger Dana had given her. Haleine had pressed Bronagh to find a place to hide it, where it would be safe, where it would be secret. The maid, Haleine remembered, didn't protest.

"What's wrong, Haleine? Why won't you fight me? You used to fight me all the time. I would lie in bed each morning, fondling some pretty, young wench and imagine what gauntlet you might throw down that day. But you don't do that anymore, do you?" her husband said. "Have I done it? Have I at last beaten the spirit from you?"

Had he?

"Revelin thought you wouldn't be easily defeated, didn't he? He told you that on our wedding night," Maddox continued. "Poor sop. Wrong about you again, wasn't he?"

She looked at Maddox. "No. He wasn't."

Was he?

"Prove it. Fight me now."

"I don't have to. This isn't real," she said. "Any of it."

"It's all real. You've lived it. You should know."

She shook her head. "He never walked away."

"He did," Maddox said. "When he thought you carried my brats in your belly, he abandoned you. And he will again."

Would he?

She shook her head again and walked past her husband. Through him. She turned back to face him, but he was gone, and she now stood alone in the center of the cathedral. She wore her coronation gown and robe with the great, heavy crown on her head. The room was silent and still. She stared at the altar.

On her judgment day, she would stand alone. She had been taught that as a small child and had the lesson reinforced her entire life.

Was she dead? She pressed her hand against her heart. What was before bloodied and raw was now repaired and smooth, as if it had never been.

Dead, then. Or dying. She smiled and let her hand fall to her side.

There was the sound of rushing water, like a river, and she turned from the altar to see beautiful, pristine water rushing at her from all sides.

From above her, glass started to crack. She looked at the great window above the altar. The colors were as bright and beautiful as ever, vibrant reds and blues and yellows seeping together. It made her eyes hurt to look at it.

One crack appeared, then another. Water trickled through them. The glass continued to splinter. She knew what was coming. How strange it should happen there. And stranger still to find she didn't care.

She didn't belong here. There were other places to go and things to do there, a battle to be fought, a war to be won, but there was beauty here in this sanctuary, and peace. She had missed them, and she didn't want to leave.

When the window exploded, she spread her arms out to the sides and closed her eyes. Water and glass showered her. She raised her head to meet it, and her crown fell away. The water rushed to meet her. It was rising faster now. It was at her waist. Soon it would consume her.

She fell into the water and, for a moment, she floated. She was a girl of ten again, reveling in the sun and its warmth. Her mother would be angry when she found out, but Haleine delighted in that, too.

It lasted only a moment. Then her garments, soaked through and heavy, pulled her under. She couldn't fight it, and she didn't try.

She was sinking. She was drowning. She was dying.

It was beautiful.

Orla's tavern was full when James arrived. He didn't look at any of the patrons as he walked through the crowd. Orla was behind the bar and nodded briefly at him. He acknowledged her and entered the storeroom.

The queen lay in the far corner of the room on a pallet made of empty grain sacks. He knelt to check on her. Orla had given him some old towels which he had stuffed around the chest wound, but it still bled. The queen's skin looked more pallid, but he wasn't sure if it was her condition or the poor light. He laid the back on his hand on her forehead. She was warm to the touch, too warm, but the woman shook as though she lay in a bath of ice.

"I don't thank you for this," Orla said, joining him.

"I don't expect you to."

"She's been talking, you know."

"She woke up?"

"No, God, no," Orla said. "With the pain she'd be in, the lass is fortunate she hasn't. She's been talking in her sleep."

"Saying what?"

Orla shrugged. "There was some talk about snow. Someone she doesn't love."

Snow? He wondered briefly where her mind was but decided he didn't care. As long as she wasn't talking about Dana, she could say what she wanted.

"Did she say who she didn't love?" he asked.

"No," Orla said. "She did scream Dana's name later, though, and that was before she started screaming nothing at all. Just screaming. I had to have the lads give out free ale to distract everyone until she stopped. When are you taking her away from here?"

He looked at the queen. Her lips moved now, but no sound escaped.

"As soon as you provide me with a cart and someone to drive it," he said.

Orla pursed her lips. She was mad about the further imposition on her good will, but James was certain her desire to rid herself of both him and the queen would override her objections.

"Why was she shouting Dana's name?" Orla asked.

"Does it matter?"

"Does he love her?"

"He thinks he does."

"Damn fool," she said, shaking her head. "I'm not doing this for you."

"Neither am I."

"Take the lass out to the stable," Orla said. "I'll send one of the lads along to help you, but if any harm comes to him, I swear I will geld you with a spoon."

James nodded. "I'll keep that in mind."

When Orla went back to the bar, James picked up the queen and carried her to the stable. He put her down, this time in an empty stall, so he could prepare the cart. He hitched one of Orla's ponies to it and laid the queen in the back. He returned to the storeroom to gather some of the grain sacks and a couple of small barrels of ale and wine. He covered the queen with the sacks and arranged the barrels in front of her. Orla's boy appeared just as he finished.

"Orla sent me to help you." The boy shrugged. "Said I should take you where you want to go, and be quick about it."

"Aye," James said. "We'll be quick."

James sat next to the boy as they rode through the streets. He sat at an angle in order to better keep an eye on what came behind and before them. He saw nothing to raise even his suspicions and finally accepted the maid's word as truth. He stopped the boy before they could be seen by the maid and jumped out of the cart. He took the queen and sent the boy back to Orla's. When the cart was out of sight, he walked the rest of the way to the passage. Both Bronagh and Faolan met him outside of it.

Bronagh gasped when she saw the queen. "You've killed her!"

"No," James said. "I haven't."

Bronagh beckoned him inside and led him to the queen's chambers. He laid the queen on the bed. As he eased his arms out from under her, he took notice of an abundant supply of salves and bandages sitting on a small table. He straightened and looked at the maid.

"How did those get there?" he asked, putting his hand on his dagger.

"While I waited, I sent one of the kitchen girls up with them," the maid answered. "I didn't want to waste any more time. She'll tell no one. She has nothing to tell."

James cast a glance at Faolan who gave a curt nod. He released the dagger as Bronagh came toward him. He had pushed the maid about as far as he could. He saw it in her face and in her walk. When she reached him, she forced him aside and set to attending her queen.

"You can leave now," she snapped.

"You'll need help yet."

"If you leave, I can call for the physician."

"If you call for the physician now, you'll have to explain why you need the man, and I imagine that will lead to a sort of chaos you'd rather avoid at the moment. Let me help you."

Bronagh didn't disagree. She took a small knife off the table and cut away the material wrapped around the queen's shoulder.

"What is this?" she asked once it was free.

"It was a horse blanket and some old towels."

"You put those filthy things on the queen?"

"I used what I had. You would rather I let her bleed to death?"

She glowered at him and threw it all to the floor. She took the cloak off next and tossed it aside as well. She examined the queen's shoulder.

"What can I do?" James asked.

"Haven't you done enough already?"

"That arrow needs to come out," James said. "Do you want to do it alone, or shall I help you? Every moment you waste sniping at me brings her closer to death."

She glared. "I'll hold her. You pull it out."

Bronagh climbed on the bed and he helped her shift the queen to a more manageable position. He put one hand on the queen's shoulder and the other on the tip of the arrow. It didn't break easily, but he snapped it off and dropped it to the floor.

"Are you ready?" he asked, glancing at Bronagh.

She nodded and tightened her hold on the queen. James adjusted his position and slowly pulled the arrow's shaft from the queen's shoulder, taking great care not to break it. It was followed by a gush of blood. He cast the shaft behind him and fumbled for something to use against the bleeding.

"The bandages! The bandages, you idiot!" Bronagh shouted. "They're right beside you!"

He found them and pressed them against the wound. He took a deep breath and looked at the maid. She stared at him, her anger unmistakable.

"Perhaps I was wrong about just who Dana's greatest enemy is," he said.

"Don't forget it either," she hissed.

He offered her a mock salute and helped her lower the queen back onto the bed. She pushed him away again and placed her hands on the bandages.

"Now get out of here," Bronagh said. "And tell your leader should I see him here again, I'll have him arrested."

"I shall be certain to pass on your most generous warning," he said.

He looked at Faolan and the pegasus jerked his head toward the servants' passage. James nodded and followed him into the hall.

"I've sent word to camp," Faolan said. "Dana knows what's happened. He's not happy."

"Brilliant," James said. "Neither am I."

James left the palace without anyone giving him a second glance and returned to Orla's. He refused her offer of a physician, borrowed a clean tunic and cloak from her and took his horse from the stable. He passed through the city gates without trouble and rode into the forest. He had left his weapons within the tunnel's entrance and stopped just long enough to recover them before riding back to the rebel camp.

His eyes burned and his arm throbbed. He'd nearly forgotten about it, so focused he'd been on the queen, but there was nothing to distract him from it now. The injury was bad enough he thought Hanah would likely have to cauterize it. He did not look forward to that but still thought it to be more inviting than Dana's welcome was sure to be.

When he got closer to camp, two of the men on patrol showed themselves. He acknowledged them and they nodded back. They watched him ride past as though he were a man heading to his own execution. Irritated, James spurred his horse to move quicker.

Hanah waited for him inside the camp borders. Rhydwyn and Gair stood just behind her. As soon as he appeared, the three approached him. They were the only ones to do so. Rhydwyn held his horse as James dismounted. He was barely on the ground before Hanah took his arm.

"How did you know?" he asked.

"Word got to me, just as it always does," she said. "Is it bad?"

"Aye."

"Well, come on," she said. "Let the lads care for your horse."

She led James to her tent. He was worn out enough to let her. She had a stool near a lantern and he sank onto it. Hanah picked up a small knife and gestured that he should lift his arm. He did, supporting it under the elbow with his good arm.

"Dana's angry, lad," she warned as she removed his makeshift bandage.

"So am I," James replied.

She nodded and prodded his wound. The pain was excruciating. He closed his eyes and gritted his teeth.

"I know he didn't tell you, but—"

"I'm not looking to talk about it," James said. "Just cauterize my damn arm already and let me sleep."

"Well, it needs to be cleaned before I do anything else," she said, "but I'm not sure it's bad enough for cauterizing."

James thought about the blow that had resulted in his injury. "How is that possible?"

"I don't know, but let's thank the goddess that it is," she said. "If I can stitch it, both the pain and the scar will be less."

"Thought you said women loved scars."

She smiled and sorted through her supplies. Her response was interrupted by Dana's arrival.

"What the hell were you thinking?" Dana demanded.

Hanah looked at the two of them. "I think I'll go get some water."

"She didn't belong here," James said as Hanah left.

"I was going to take her back."

"You never were going to take her back. She knew it, so she asked me."

"And you paraded her through the forest when you knew they'd be after her," Dana said. "Why didn't you use the tunnels?"

"I thought they'd be better left a secret. I didn't want word of that getting to Omur or her husband."

Dana shook his head. "She wouldn't have done that. She never would have done that. Why do you insist upon seeing her as an enemy?"

"She is an enemy."

"She's loyal to me, James. You should never question that."

"That is exactly what I should do. It's exactly what you should do. She'll be the end of you. The end of us."

Dana took a step back, looking shaken. It was the first encouraging sign James had seen. He stood.

"She'll betray you, Dana. If she lives."

"If she lives," Dana echoed. He lunged forward and pushed James. "If she lives? Damn you, how could you do that!"

James rocked on his heels and pushed back. "How could *you* do this? You lied to me, Dana."

"I don't answer to you."

"The hell you don't. Who the hell do you think you are that you're above that?"

"I am the leader of these people. I have brought them this far and I will—"

"You'll what? Throw their lives away for a woman?" James said. "These people trusted you."

"They still trust me."

"Aye, maybe they do for now, but how long will that last? Do you know how many men heard you in your tent, a rutting stag sobbing the name of that wench? Word travels in a place like this, Dana. It won't be long before they all know you're risking everything for the favor of the woman married to their enemy. What happens then? Will they trust you then?"

"Haleine is innocent. She's done nothing but help us at every turn."

"She didn't tell you about Enimode, did she?"

"No," Dana said. "She didn't know about Enimode. If she had, she would have told me. I know it."

"You know nothing. She'll betray you, if she hasn't already. She'll tell her husband everything."

"She won't."

"How can you be sure? You make a girl squeal and she's bound to you forever? I'm not sure that's how it works."

"Faolan would have said—"

"Faolan?" James said. "Faolan is half in love with that bitch himself."

"Don't call her that," Dana said. "She won't betray me. You don't know anything."

James smiled. "I know enough. Forget her, Dana."

"I can't."

"Mark my words. She will be the end of you."

"You're wrong."

"Am I?" James asked. "She doesn't love you. Did you know that? Orla heard her say it."

"You're lying."

"You don't trust me? I can't understand why not. Out of the two of us here, after all, which is the one who hasn't spent months now lying to the other?"

"James, I—"

"You know what? I don't even care anymore. You do what you want." James pushed past Dana on his way out of the tent. "You always do."

—◊—

We are displeased.

Omur was once again on his knees. This time he had been called upon. Most feared a summoning from his lords. He might have as well had he not already known the source of their displeasure and how he meant to counter it. He looked up at this proclamation.

"My lords?"

We told you to kill her, yet she lives. You appear to have failed us yet again. This displeases us.

"Yes, my lords, live she does," Omur said. "But not for much longer, I am certain."

It is not what we wanted.

"Perhaps not, but I beg you to trust me," he said. "For when she dies, I shall be able to deliver to you that which you have longed desired."

He paused to see if his lords would speak. They didn't, waiting for him to continue. He sat up and smiled.

"The world," he said. "I shall deliver to you the world."

chapter 22

Bronagh stood along the wall in the queen's chamber, near the servants' passage. Her hands were clasped together behind her back and her head angled toward the floor, but she could see Haleine.

Lord Coileáin sat with Haleine now, not speaking, not moving, just cradling his daughter's hand as he gazed upon her. The Lady Sighle was also there, waiting near the balcony. She stood sideways and watched both her sister and the sky.

It was not their first visit, nor did Bronagh think it would be their last. They were the latest in a steady stream of callers. The king, Lord Omur, Ceallach and a number of the queen's ladies came, looked and left. Rhys came repeatedly, his face now a permanent frown. Haleine was oblivious to them all as she continued to drift in and out of her feverish sleep.

Bronagh was not oblivious. She watched them all, wary of their attendance, suspicious of their motives, even Rhys. The king and his advisor worried her the most. In their presence, she was relegated to the farthest corners of the room, so far away that should they decide to finish what they started in the forest, they could have put a pillow over the queen's face and done it before Bronagh would realize what was happening.

It was for this reason she was relieved when Willem arrived. He walked into the room on the second day and resumed his position near the door as though he had never left it. Bronagh was so pleased to see him and opened her mouth to tell him but instead out tumbled Haleine's request.

"She doesn't want you here," Bronagh said. "She wants you with her sons."

"They're safe," Willem said.

She pressed him for more, but he wouldn't say anything else. It wasn't until later, when the first page appeared, that she started to understand the lengths to which Willem had gone to protect the princes.

Two men were in the nursery at all times. Two more stood watch at the nursery door and two others were set in the servants' passage. Pages had been given the task of moving constantly back and forth between Willem and the nursery so he could be assured of their continued well-being.

That left him free to stand, wait and worry alongside her. Rhys was certain Haleine would recover, but as one day passed into the next and Haleine remained lost, Bronagh became less and less convinced of Rhys's assessment.

But the physician clung to it and repeated it to anyone who asked or would listen, most recently Lord Coileáin and his youngest daughter. Lord Coileáin had had no more of a response to this than anyone else had, just nodding before sending Rhys away and taking a seat at Haleine's bedside. Lady Sighle watched Rhys depart, touched her father's shoulder and said, "He's right," before she drifted away to the balcony. And so they were, a family of three, a study in silent suffering.

A knock at the door roused all occupants from their ruminations. Willem opened the door, spoke to whoever stood outside of it and carried a message to Lord Coileáin. He read it and stood. He leaned in to kiss Haleine's forehead, called to his other daughter and left the room.

"Has something happened?" Bronagh asked when they had gone.

"I didn't read it," Willem said. "He shouldn't be here."

"Lord Coileáin?" Bronagh said as she went to Haleine's side. "He's her father. Where else should he be?"

"How did he know she was injured?"

Bronagh examined Haleine. The queen was unchanged.

"There was a letter, I think." Bronagh sat in the chair Lord Coileáin had vacated.

"He received it too soon," Willem said.

Bronagh started to look at him when Haleine began to writhe. Bronagh slid to the edge of the chair and Willem stepped closer as they waited to see what, if anything, would follow. Haleine surprised them when she jerked awake. She was motionless for a moment then struggled to sit up. Bronagh jumped to her feet.

"You're hurt. You need to stay still," Bronagh said, but Haleine didn't seem to hear her. "You're all right. You're safe. Please, your majesty—Haleine, you need to calm down. You need to stay still."

Eventually Haleine stopped fighting. She stared at Bronagh and gasped for breath.

"I was drowning," Haleine said when she was able.

"No," Bronagh soothed. "No. It was a dream."

"It was no dream," Haleine said. "I was drowning. I-I couldn't swim; everything was so heavy. I was dying."

"It was a dream. You've not been near the water."

"It was not a dream," Haleine said. "I do not know what it was, but it was not a dream. Oh, it was beautiful."

"Your majesty?" Bronagh asked, frightened by Haleine's tone as much as the words.

"I think I've gone quite mad," Haleine whispered.

"No, of course you haven't," Bronagh said. "You've been injured and ill. That's all."

"Where is Faolan?" Haleine asked. "Is he here?"

"He's flown off somewhere. I don't know where," Bronagh said. "Do you remember anything? Do you remember what happened?"

"We were talking about tunnels."

"Tunnels? What tunnels?"

"They move in tunnels," she said. "It's why you never see them."

"I don't understand."

Haleine smiled, her drowsiness apparent. "Neither do I."

Her eyes started to close again. Willem shifted his weight, and the queen was awake once more. Bronagh held her breath.

"What was that? Who?" Haleine asked. "Was it Willem?"

Bronagh considered lying. She glanced at him and he shook his head. *Truth*, he mouthed. She nodded. "Aye, that's Willem."

"Why is he here?" Haleine asked. "He's supposed to be watching my sons. I told him he needs—"

"He needs to be here watching you."

"I don't need protection."

"Says the woman with a hole in her shoulder."

"I don't need protection *here*."

"I think we're going to let Willem make those decisions from now on."

"But my sons," Haleine said, nearly crying. "My boys."

"They're safe," Bronagh said. "Willem didn't abandon them. He's set men to watch them. Men he trusts. They're safe. I swear it."

Willem stepped forward to allow Haleine to see him. When she turned her gaze to him, he nodded and some of the tension left the girl's face. Haleine lifted her hands in an attempt to wipe the tears from her face and noticed for the first time the bindings covering both. Her agitation returned.

"It's all right," Bronagh said, taking a cloth to clear away the tears.

Haleine pulled away from her. "What happened?"

"I don't know. You were unconscious when he brought you back. He didn't say and I didn't ask."

"He?"

"That man. That odious man," Bronagh said. "I think he called himself James."

"Faolan isn't here?"

"No, but he'll come back soon, I'm sure."

Haleine looked away. "Why did he leave?"

"I don't know."

"He'll come back," she said. "He will."

"I'm sure you're right."

But Haleine wasn't talking to her anymore. She wasn't talking to anyone other than herself. She continued to utter *he'll come back* over and over again, her voice a little more quiet each time until eventually she drifted back to sleep. Bronagh stood frozen for a moment longer to be sure Haleine wouldn't awaken before sinking into her chair, feeling drained of all energy.

Willem, however, suddenly seemed to have it in spades. She watched him out of the corner of her eye as he fidgeted as much as he could without actually taking a step. He'd always been the most stoic, unflappable man she'd ever known. To see him like this was utterly disturbing.

"What's wrong?" she asked finally.

"It's past time."

Her eyes widened with realization. She looked around the room, searching for the boy she already knew wasn't there.

"You have to go," she said. "You have to make sure they're all right."

"Don't leave her," he warned as he left.

"I haven't yet," she said to the silent room.

It couldn't have been coincidence. Those boys hadn't been lax once in their duties. Willem had instilled so much fear in them—fear of what would happen should they disregard their responsibility— that they had been unfailingly dedicated. But for one of them to turn up missing now, now that the queen was reawakening? It wasn't chance. Again Bronagh found herself wishing for Dana's presence. He would have answers. He would understand what was happening. He wouldn't have wanted to tell her but, for Haleine, Bronagh would have found a way to make him.

"She sleeps still?"

The voice startled her. She turned to see who had spoken, and Lord Omur appeared in her view. She fell out of the chair and into a curtsey.

"My lord," she said. "I am sorry. I did not hear you enter."

"There is no need for apologies." Omur approached the bed. "I have only come to see how the queen fares."

"She sleeps still," Bronagh said, shifting her position to stand between Lord Omur and the queen. "I feel she is quite out of her senses. I cannot be sure she even knows where she is. When she is awake, she mostly speaks nonsense."

"Mostly?"

"She does recognize those in the room."

Omur nodded. "It is curious how she came to be here, returned all the way to the palace without any seeing her before you."

"My lord?"

"It is what you've claimed happened, is it not?"

"It is, but I know nothing of those who found her, how they did so or how they managed to bring her here unnoticed. I confess I did not ask questions. I was too relieved by her recovery to think clearly, my lord."

"You did not summon the physician directly."

"There was so much blood, I only thought to do what I could. I was afraid to wait. I feared what the loss of too much would mean for her life."

"The queen is fortunate to have someone so loyal serving her," Omur said. "Given the utter chaos in this palace these past days, she may not have lived had you acted differently."

Bronagh bowed her head but did not say anything. He hadn't asked her a question, and she didn't want to offer any information for which he did not specifically ask.

"You do not wish to speak with me," Omur said next.

Bronagh looked up. "My lord?"

"My appearance here has made you nervous," he continued. "The queen does not like me and, by extension, neither do you.

Your man is gone, your mistress's children possibly threatened, and now here I am. You're afraid, I know, but there is no need for it. I am not here to cause your mistress nor her sons harm. When your man has finished boxing the ears of his negligent page, he'll return and I shall be gone."

"Why are you here?"

"I want the rebels stopped. I want them dead," he said. "I want you to help me."

"Why would you think I could help you?"

"Because I know the truth, Bronagh. I know the heirs to Lira's throne are bastards. I know their true father is the man fighting against the one who calls himself their father. I know the queen has spied on me, on her husband, and fed the information to her lover. I know you and your man, among others, have helped her."

She stood absolutely still. Inside, her stomach was churning.

"But here is what I want you to know, and pay close attention, Bronagh, for I shall only say this once," Omur said. "I have no interest in punishing the queen for her crimes."

Her stomach leapt into her throat, but she stayed quiet, afraid to open her mouth. Was he trying to trick her into saying something?

Omur sighed. His impatience with her was blatant. She blanched inwardly.

"I am not trying to trap you, girl," he said. "I am trying to destroy the rebels. I thought you might share a similar desire."

She did. She couldn't deny that. She blinked. "If I did believe you, what sort of help would you require of me?"

"You would presume I lie? That is very bold for someone of your stature. Shall we blame Michaela for instilling such fierce loyalty in someone so absolutely unworthy it emboldens her to overextend her place?"

Bronagh didn't budge.

"Very well. You will want proof of my good faith and, as a courtesy, I shall provide it," he said. "If you open the balcony doors, you will have it."

She didn't move. Her palms were sweating and she pressed them against her dress. Omur smiled and laughed softly. He crossed the room and opened the balcony doors himself. She neither saw nor heard anything at first. Then her stomach, already in knots, tightened as the sound of a body being whipped reached her ears. A man's screams followed. She looked to Omur.

"I've provided you with a much needed story to explain your queen's sudden reappearance," he said. "The men assigned to recover her mangled it badly, as did everyone involved. Everyone, I should say, except you. You look very well in this story, and the king is grateful for your competence. You'll receive more than a hovel against the castle wall for this, Bronagh."

She looked at the sky. She didn't know what story he had told. She didn't want to know.

A woman's scream came next. Bronagh gasped and Omur nodded.

"Ah, yes. I have also given you Sabine."

"What?"

"I had her found to be a spy. It was well known that Dana had one within these walls, and instead of giving Maddox the queen's name or even yours, I gave him hers. I suppose he decided to start her torture with a flogging."

Sabine screamed again, and tears filled Bronagh's eyes. She refused to let them fall.

"Does the screaming bother you?" Omur asked. "It won't for long. You won't hear anything once they move her to the dungeon. The walls there are too thick. Even so, I don't imagine she will live long anyway. Not with what Maddox will do to her."

"How do I know she truly matters to you?" Bronagh asked.

Omur's face changed. "Oh, she matters."

She didn't think she could believe him. She thought he would use Sabine like Bronagh would use Sabine—or anyone she had to—in order to gain what she wanted. She wanted Haleine safe. Omur wanted Dana dead. Bronagh wanted that, too.

"Come, Bronagh," he said. "You know this is what you should do. Help me and purchase for your mistress a pardon."

She didn't look at Haleine again. "What do you want me to do?"

"I've been trying all this time to kill the rebel leader, the legend," Omur said. "I want you to help me kill the man."

Bronagh nodded. "Aye. I can help with that."

"I know you can. I want you to give me something," he said. "Proof of the man's presence in this room."

Her first thought was the dagger. It had never been said, but she knew from where it had come. At Haleine's insistence, Bronagh had hidden it in the vanity. As much as she hated the one who had given it to Haleine, she couldn't say she didn't want Haleine to have it.

She wouldn't give it to Omur, but there had to be something that would appease him.

Perhaps the cloak. Haleine had been returned wrapped in it, but it didn't belong to her. Bronagh didn't know why she had kept it. She didn't know why she hadn't burned it. Surely that would have been the wise thing to do, but instead she had folded it and tucked it into the bottom of a chest.

"Bronagh?"

"Yes," she said.

She went to the chest and knelt in front of it. She raised the lid and removed the cloak that did not belong to the queen. It was in ruins, filthy and torn. It was barely recognizable, but she had kept it. She now laid it in her lap and touched it carefully, smoothing out the wrinkles in the fold. She closed the chest and returned to Omur.

"Here," she said as she offered the garment to him.

He took it and shook it out. "What is this?"

"It's not the queen's."

Omur looked at the cloak again, tilting his head to the side as he did so. After a moment, he smiled and draped it over his arm.

"Thank you, Bronagh," he said. "I think this shall do quite nicely."

She nodded. Omur left the room and Bronagh returned to her chair and watched Haleine as she waited for Willem.

She was calm, more so than she had been in a long time. Her decision had been the right one. She knew it, even if she couldn't tell Haleine or Willem. Neither of them would understand if they found out. Haleine would be especially furious, and there would be punishment, but at least Haleine would be alive to give it.

Willem returned, telling her all was well in the nursery. She nodded.

"Did anything happen here?" he asked.

She shook her head and kept her eyes on Haleine. "No."

⸺⁓⸺

Upon his departure from the queen's chambers, Omur went to the courtyard to seek out Varro. It was emptier than before when Sabine and the others were taking their punishment, but Varro and a small group of soldiers remained, engaged in swordplay. When Varro saw Omur's approach, he gave orders to his lieutenant and came toward him.

"My lord," Varro said. "You have need of me?"

Indeed Omur did. He'd known when Revelin received word of an attempt on Haleine's life that the prince would respond in the form of an army thirsty for Dana's blood. Omur hadn't yet formed a more specific plan, but because of the amulet in Haleine's chambers and the maid's duplicity, one was coming together nicely. Without them, Omur never would have heard an unsuspecting queen reveal the rebels' greatest advantage.

"*They move in tunnels,*" she had said. "*It's why you never see them.*"

The maid hadn't understood but Omur had. It explained much, and so simply that Omur was ashamed he hadn't considered the possibility sooner. The goddess and her minions drew their power from the earth and its elements; the unicorns would have the ability to alter the earth. Naturally they would have used the earth to their advantage.

"When you are finished here, gather your maps," Omur said. "Mark the locations where the rebels have been known to disappear. On our progress to the rebel camp, we will leave men in those places. When Dana learns we are coming for him, he will evacuate all those unable to fight, if not the entire camp. We may find those refugees there. Say nothing about this to anyone else, Lord Coileáin included, should you see him."

"I already have," Varro said.

"He was here?"

"Watching the men train," Varro said. "He says my men are soft."

Darian had been scarce since his arrival in Eluned, holding a near constant vigil at his eldest daughter's bedside. To hear he had approached Varro but not himself was a surprise. Omur thought, with all he knew about Darian, that the man would have been to see him sooner.

Omur had become aware of Nathan's military pet years before when the alliance between Lira and Tanuba was nothing more than a proposal. He had heard it said that in order to convince Nathan of anything, one must first convince Darian Coileáin, a man so highly valued by the Tanubian king that even his physical distance from court didn't diminish the weight of his opinion. Omur was curious to meet this man, for he had much hinging on the alliance and needed to know—if such a thing became necessary—whether Darian could be bribed to do as Omur wanted and, if so, with what. And if Darian could not be bought, Omur needed to know how easily the man could be killed. He received word from spies in Tanuba claiming Darian was neither corruptible nor killable. Omur didn't relish dealing with a man with such apparently rigid morals but did not believe Darian unkillable. Every man could be killed when the right weapon was used.

But he never found out what weapon would be most effective against Nathan's advisor, for Darian never made an appearance at the negotiations. He was chasing some rebel faction from one part of Quatara to another. In his absence, the alliance was formed, Haleine became the central figure in the pact, and Omur didn't come face to face with Darian until after the man had lost his king. Then he was still driven, still determined to carry out Nathan's wishes. His new liege lord became Revelin, also wholly devoted to his father's will, and Omur saw Darian as a man who would live to serve. Those were the sort of men Omur could appreciate. Those were the sort of men who could be counted upon to do the right thing for the exact wrong reason.

"What did he want?" Omur asked.

"He wanted to plan an attack, and I told him to seek you out," Varro said. "He should be in your chambers."

Omur nodded. "Then I shouldn't keep him waiting any longer. Don't take his censure so hard, Varro. The man's lost more than a sword at Dana's hands."

He left the courtyard and returned to his chambers to find Darian sitting in front of the fire, his back to the doors. The scent of the man's mourning was in the air, hanging there so thick it was nearly a wall. The loss of his king had not broken him, but it would seem the loss of his wife had. Omur smiled as he laid the cloak on a table. It was always the woman.

"My lord," Omur said.

Darian rose from his chair and inclined his head. "You do honor me."

Omur motioned for Darian to keep his seat, but the man remained standing. "The honor does belong to me. We are most grateful you have come to aid us in our time of need."

Darian clapped a fist against his chest, over his heart. "We of Tanuba hold true to our alliances."

"I would never suggest otherwise, my lord," Omur said as he sat.

"I have tried to speak with both your king and captain of the guard on the matter of the rebels. They directed me to speak with you."

"Yes. Maddox has been quite distraught since the attempt on his wife's life and has left me to deal with the rebellion in his stead. This is not a problem, is it?"

"You are no soldier."

"I am of sorts."

"Have you seen battle?"

"I have of sorts. I assure you I am quite capable."

Darian nodded. "I offer my apologies. If your king trusts you, I shall do the same."

"I am glad to hear it. Now shall we discuss what is to be done?"

"Yes."

Omur had never spent much time in the company of soldiers apart from ordering Varro from one task to the next, and he'd never sat through the process of planning a campaign with a career soldier such as Darian. He listened intently to the information Omur offered and made plans with such precision, Omur found himself appreciative of the man's skills and as impressed by a mortal as he had ever been.

Darian wanted to know everything. Omur declined to oblige but did make sure to mention everything he wanted passed along to Haleine, everything he knew Bronagh had hidden from her mistress. A conversation between the queen and her father was inevitable, and Omur looked forward to it. He wanted to hear what Haleine would tell Darian and what she would choose to keep from him. And, following that, Omur would care to know about Haleine's reaction to her maid's treachery.

"Can you tell me what this Dana looks like?" Darian asked.

"My lord?"

"This man murdered my wife. He very nearly murdered my daughters. I want to know who he is. What he looks like."

"Of course," Omur said. He sifted through the piles of parchment on the table until he found a small square piece bearing a sketch of Dana's face. He handed it to Darian. "We give these to the new guardsmen so they know for whom to look."

It was a lie, but Darian didn't question it. His grief was draining him completely. He took the parchment Omur offered and studied it.

"He is young," Darian said. "Are you sure he is the one responsible?"

"Yes. I'm sure your daughter can confirm his identity. He was one of her captors."

Darian nodded. "Would your king be much insulted should I slit this bastard's throat?"

"I think not, my lord."

"Very good, then," Darian said and crushed the parchment in his hand.

Haleine stood on the balcony. She stayed close to the doors and leaned against the wall because she knew her strength would give out soon. Only sheer will had carried her this far, but as long as it held out a few moments longer, she would be satisfied.

A gold chain hung from her fingers. On the chain was the amulet Maddox had given her. The amulet she had seen in her dream, if she could indeed consider it as such. She had to rid herself of that amulet. She didn't know why she was so driven, but it had been nearly her only thought since her awakening.

She hated her obsession with the object. She didn't know if it was justified. Faolan could have told her had he been there but, as Bronagh told it, he had been gone for more than two weeks. Something must have happened, because he told her he'd never leave her.

No, she reminded herself. He said he'd always keep her safe.

And he hadn't even done that.

She pushed off the wall with enough momentum to reach the other side of the balcony. There she leaned against the rail and looked at the necklace. The gold shone in the sun, but it didn't register with her eyes. She focused instead on the blood-red stone. Its center was an even deeper red, and it was with consternation, not surprise, that she both saw and felt the stone pulse in regular intervals. She could feel herself getting lost in it, her arms and legs growing heavier as though she were being lulled to sleep. It was dangerous and, with great effort, she tore herself away from it to look at the dizzying landscape below. She didn't look long. The land came rushing up to meet her, making her feel as though she would or should slide over the railing's side. The decision was made for her when an unexpected lurch sent her plummeting.

She fell, but when she should have slammed into the ground, she found herself in her bed, looking at the angel-adorned ceiling as she suppressed the urge to cry.

Her days and nights had become a tangled mess, and her ability to distinguish between what was real and what was dream was so muddled, she never could tell the difference. She couldn't even be sure how many days or nights had passed, for they all bled together, one into the next. The only constant between them all was that damned amulet.

When she was awake, she lay on her side and stared at it resting on the corner of her vanity, the gold chain dangling over the side. When she was asleep, she dreamt of lying on her side and staring at the amulet resting on the corner of her vanity. People filtered in and out at all times. She never knew if they were truly there. Some sightings, like her mother, were obvious. But her husband, Omur, Sighle? She didn't know. Bronagh was real. Mayhap Willem as well, but he wasn't supposed to be there. He was supposed to be with her sons. She had a vague memory of the two of them telling her her sons were safe, that Willem's place was with her, but she didn't know if it was to be believed.

But now she thought she was lucid once more. It wasn't the first time she had had the thought only to discover her mind was wandering yet again. There was only one way to be sure, she supposed.

She pushed herself up. It was slow. It was painful. Her head swam. She waited until it settled. When Willem took a step toward her, she thought she could feel his concern.

"It's all right, Willem," she said. "Where is Bronagh?"

She heard him turn immediately for the servants' passage.

"No," she said. "No. Please don't."

He stopped. Uncertainty was creeping over his face.

"What I do now will be easier without her presence," Haleine said, inching toward the edge of the bed.

He wanted to ask her intentions. She knew it, though she did not know how. The question was at his lips, on the tip of his tongue, but he refused to give it voice.

"I don't know what I do. It may be nothing," she said, looking at the amulet. "But it may be everything."

She sat on the very edge of the bed now. Willem stood in front of her. He wanted to force her to lie down again. She smiled at him.

"Fetch me that amulet," she said, indicating it with a nod. "Please."

He hesitated but moved toward the amulet, as he couldn't see the harm in such a simple request. When he returned, she held out her hand to receive the necklace.

It was such a small thing, yet the weight of it in her hand was great. It could have been nothing but she knew—she just knew—it wasn't. These visions—seeing Zaide Romanza wearing it around her neck, the flash of that woman tangled in the sheets with her husband—couldn't be ignored. Somehow, there was truth behind her dreams. Somehow. She didn't understand it, but if Faolan believed it, she currently required no other evidence.

She stood slowly and Willem took her elbow. She appreciated his foresight, as her legs quickly started to buckle. His eyes pleaded with her to return to the bed. Haleine smiled again and gently shook her head.

"Thank you," she said as she let go of him. "You may return to your post now. I shall call should I have need of your aid."

He didn't move.

"Please," she said.

He nodded and bowed before drawing away. She shuffled her way to the balcony. Her progress was maddeningly slow. Wherever Bronagh was, she wouldn't stay away for long. But even more pressing than that was knowing that if Zaide Romanza was connected to the amulet, it stood to reason Omur was connected to it as well. What if he knew of her intentions? What if he was coming for her? Her stomach constricted and she urged her legs to move faster. She wanted to believe Omur wouldn't—or couldn't—come. Faolan said he'd keep her safe. Faolan said he wouldn't let Omur touch her again.

But Faolan wasn't there.

She slipped onto the balcony and leaned against the wall. She was exhausted already. Her strength wouldn't last; she couldn't wait any longer. When she pushed off the wall, she walked with more purpose than she thought she could have mustered. She dangled the amulet over the balcony's edge, being careful not to look directly at it. She kept her eyes firmly fixed on the sky and released the amulet, throwing it as far out as her bindings would allow.

And then there was nothing to be heard nor seen nor felt. She remained on the balcony. She did not awaken in a sweat-drenched bed. Lucid again, it would seem.

She stumbled to the balcony doors before needing to rest. When her breath had been sufficiently recovered, she worked her way into her chambers and raised her head to call for Willem's aid. She stopped short when she saw who stood in the center of the room.

Her father. Dressed in black. His sword hanging at his side.

"It's you," she said.

She stared at her father a moment more before her legs gave out, and she crumpled to the floor. Darian helped her back to the bed.

"What were you doing out there?" he asked. "What sort of servants have you? Why would your man let you do this? Has he no sense?"

"He has a great deal of sense," she said.

"Your presence on that balcony suggests otherwise."

"He has more sense than to argue with me about such a stupid matter," Haleine said.

"That is ridiculous. You shouldn't be out of bed. I'll summon your maid and—"

"Don't," Haleine said. "Willem, please wait in the hall."

"Haleine?" her father said.

When Willem had left, she looked again at her father's sword. He had carried it into battle for as long as she could remember. How did she not recognize it before?

"You've come to make war on the rebels," she said.

"They didn't tell you?"

"No. They didn't tell me."

"And you haven't seen your sister?"

"You brought Sighle here?"

"She didn't want to remain behind."

"She never should have come in the first place."

"You think I don't tell myself that every day?"

"I don't think you've ever had a thought in your head a member of the royal family didn't put there first."

"Haleine—"

"Oh aye, decorum should be observed above all," she said. "You're right. Forgive my lapse in judgment. I mean you no disrespect, Father. You and Mother, cut from the same cloth."

"Haleine—"

"I should command you to stay."

"You wouldn't."

"I wouldn't have Sighle suffer the loss of her father."

"And what of you?"

She shook her head. "He has been lost to me for quite some time now."

"Haleine, I have put off this campaign for as long as I dared, hoping I might speak with you before I—I would not leave it like this."

"Then don't leave."

"You ask me for that which I cannot do."

"No," she said. "I don't."

"I have to do this, Haleine," he said. "I have to do this for your mother, for you."

"I don't want this."

"For Sighle," Darian said. "Do you know what that child survived? Did they tell you that?"

Her survival had been inadvertent. Haleine knew that. Had Omur sent someone more vigilant, or if her sister hadn't been so quick to hide herself, there would have been a different outcome.

"Aye," she said. "I know. I know what she survived, I know what I've survived, and I know what you won't survive should you leave to pursue the rebels."

"I am not a novice at the art of war, Haleine. You do give me too little credit."

"I don't doubt your prowess. I fear you have given your opponent too little credit."

"I've dealt with rebels before."

"You've dealt with Einar. You've dealt with the man whose country you stole."

"And now I deal with the man who stole from me your mother."

"You work alongside him," she murmured, "and you know it not."

"What did you say?"

"I said you do not know what you undertake. They will know you come, and they will be ready for you."

"How will they know?"

"They have spies," she said. "They know everything said within these walls."

"Not any longer."

Hearing the words was like being doused in cold water. She cocked her head and braced herself for what would follow. "Not any longer?"

"They've not told you that either?"

"No."

"There were spies found, rebel spies, within the employ of this palace. Men and women in the kitchens, maids—"

"Maids?"

"Yes. From what I understand, one of them, just a young girl, was recently put to death for her treason."

"What young girl?"

"I do not know her name," Darian said, sounding surprised that she had asked. "Some others have died, but they're still interrogating the rest. The king's men are working them—"

"Stop," Haleine said. "Please stop. I don't want to hear more."

Omur had declared war on the rebels. It was an odd thought for they had been fighting for nearly a year now, but war all the same had been declared. Omur wanted to crush them now. He wanted her to lose. He wanted Dana to lose.

And they wouldn't know. The rebels wouldn't know Tanuba had sent men bent on their destruction. She had no one to tell.

"Haleine?"

She looked at her father. She'd seen the duel, the death dance, over and over. There was Dana, the bloodied, fearsome warrior, and her father—aye, her father—the dangerous other. She had watched it over and over but never had seen the ending.

"Don't go," she said.

"Haleine," her father said, his voice sounding small. "I must."

After a miserable moment, she nodded.

"Lord Omur said you were in their camp," Darian said.

"Aye, I was," she said. "I hope you are prepared to extend your war to women and children because that is what you will find there."

"It happens."

"Someone else's wife? Someone's daughter? Do you not see—?"

Darian sat in a chair, studying the floor. "Do not do this."

"What? Act as your conscience?"

Her father stood and walked toward her. "I will not seek out the innocent, Haleine, but if they interfere, I will do what I must. I want Dana and Dana only but, by God, I will kill them all."

"It won't bring her back."

Darian ignored this. "You have met Dana. He was one of your captors, yes?"

Her only captor. Haleine looked away.

"What can you tell me of him?" Darian asked.

"He is a man who entered this rebellion with nothing to lose, yet, somehow, seems to have lost more. I have known none quite like him. I doubt I ever will."

Her eyes filled with tears, and she ducked her head to hide them from Darian. He noticed them anyhow and came to her side. He lifted her chin.

"I will make this right, daughter," he said. "I will fix this. For Sighle. For you."

"Don't go," she pleaded. "For Sighle. For me."

He backed away, shaking his head. "I have to do this. I have to make it right."

"Killing yourself won't do that."

"That's not what I do here."

She thought of a dream of a summer's day. Of her and her lover and their son. She watched her father bow out of the room, acutely aware of how different their next meeting would be. There was truth to what she saw. Somehow, there was truth to that.

"You're wrong," she said to the now empty room.

She didn't know how long she sat there afterward, sitting in such absolute silence that it became an oppressing force closing in around her. The sensation ended when she heard the servants' entrance open. She didn't look, already knowing it was Bronagh.

"You're awake," her maid said.

Haleine nodded. It would appear she was, indeed, awake.

"Where is Willem? Why didn't he tell me?"

"I asked him not to," Haleine said.

"Where is he?"

"The hall."

"Why is he in the hall?"

"I asked him to go."

"Why?"

"My father was here," Haleine said.

"Was he?"

"He's come to make war on the rebels."

"Of course he has. He thinks—"

"I know what he thinks," Haleine said. "Who was she?"

Bronagh's confusion showed on her face. "Who?"

"The girl put to death for treason. Who was she?"

"How did you—?" Bronagh looked at the floor. "Sabine. It was Sabine."

Haleine hadn't expected that. "Sabine? But she was—how—why would he—?"

Bronagh shrugged. "I don't know."

It was a lie. Haleine saw it plainly. Bronagh knew much more than she claimed. She always did.

"Sabine was his lover," Haleine said.

"Aye."

"You couldn't have given them her," Haleine continued. "You couldn't have told them she was a rebel spy. Omur would have known the lie. It wouldn't have worked if it had come from you. He would have had to make the claim himself or endorse whoever did say it. But either way, he invented the claim she was the spy and had her killed for it. Why?"

"I don't know. Maybe he'd grown tired of her."

Realization dawned. Sabine was payment.

"Oh Bronagh, what have you done?" Haleine breathed.

Bronagh looked sharply in her direction. "I don't know what you're talking about. I haven't done anything."

Haleine met her maid's eyes. "He came and asked you to tell him what you knew, didn't he? He asked you to help him kill the rebels. How did he word it? Did he tell you it would save me? Save yourself?"

"He knew everything. About you. About your boys. I did what I had to."

Haleine shook her head. "I don't know what you might have told him, what you thought you knew, but it'll be for naught. He'll not be content. He'll come for me again. What will you do then? Who will you throw in his path next? Nonna?"

"Sabine was far from innocent."

"Nevertheless, she did not deserve the end she met. That girl's death is on your hands."

"No, it isn't. But if it were, I wouldn't care," Bronagh said. "And when he does come again, I will find someone else. I swore to Michaela I would protect you, and I have, even if it is from yourself."

"You were to help me."

"I have. I am now, though you do not see it. And I'll not beg your pardon either, your majesty, because I won't help you kill yourself."

"That's not what I do."

"It is what you do. Aligning yourself with that man signed your death warrant. *Lying* with that man—"

"That man is not the villain here!" Haleine shouted. "He fights to preserve this land and these people from those that would see it destroyed. He's done so much good. You know he has."

"Aye, I know of the good he's done. I've seen the good he's done you."

"He's done naught to me."

"Look at yourself!" Bronagh exclaimed. "You haven't been out of bed for two weeks! You haven't stayed conscious more than a handful of moments that entire time!"

"That was none of his doing."

"That was all his doing," Bronagh said. "And aye, I would give them Dana if I could. I hope I already have!"

The doors to her chamber opened, and the room plunged immediately into silence as Willem entered. He appeared as stoic as always, only his eyes betraying his concern. He closed the doors behind him and stood in front of them, his gaze fixed on Bronagh. Bronagh stared back for a moment before turning once again to Haleine.

"Willem would have done the same," the maid said.

"No, Bronagh, he wouldn't have. Willem is my man through and through," Haleine said. "Your loyalty lies with a dead woman."

The trumpets sounded then as they always did when the army marched, but this time, her father was among them. Her eyes drifted to the balcony.

"And yours lie with a dead man," Bronagh said. "You didn't see the army below. You didn't see the size of the force that rides to crush your lover, but you can hear it now, and you know. You know what will happen when they find him. But you can't even warn him, can you? You can't warn him of his doom because he's gone and abandoned you yet again. Oh aye, tell me of the good he's done."

She had abandoned him. Haleine listened as a cadence filled the silence. Theirs was a death march, and she had abandoned him.

"Out," Haleine said, but the maid was already gone.

More than two full weeks had passed since Haleine had taken her leave of him in the darkest part of the night, just before the dawn. Dana had awakened to find her gone and would have thought it had been naught but a dream except for the presence of her gown, discarded, likely deemed too unwieldy with which to be bothered. He had spent each night since waiting to wake up and find her defection hadn't been real.

"I said I'd take her back," he murmured.

"Dana, did you say something?" Ilya asked.

He looked at her and shook his head. She would know he lied but would be polite enough not to say so in front of the others. She might say something later on when they were alone; it wouldn't be the first time. She'd corner him somewhere, probably his own tent, and chastise him in the tone she usually reserved for James. He'd let her rant without comment because she was right.

"My mistake," Ilya said and returned to her report.

She was recounting patrols that had seen nothing. Next Lucius would talk about what was happening in the palace. Neither of them would mention Haleine—Lucius perhaps purposely—and Dana didn't care to hear about anything else.

He walked to the entrance of his tent. Ilya's voice faltered slightly as she waited to see if he would walk out. He didn't. He stood just inside and lifted the flap to survey his surroundings.

The air around camp had changed. It was the calm before the storm, but he couldn't say just how close the storm was to breaking. Everyone else knew it was coming, too. He could see it in everything they did, no matter how minor a task. It was especially obvious on the training field. People were there from dawn to dusk, and even well into the night, honing their skills.

James was among them. He had gone back to trying to beat everyone into the ground. His anger at the royal family hadn't diminished any, but now Dana suspected there was an equal share directed at him. Let James be as angry as he wanted. Dana didn't care. Ilya did.

"Send him home," Dana had said to her after she had complained.

"You send him home," she'd snapped in response.

But he didn't. He had avoided James since their confrontation in Hanah's tent, and James did the same. It was unusual, this animosity between them; it was wrong. He thought several times about going to James, interrupting his warmongering and making things between them right again. He considered it but never took a step in that direction, irritated with himself for pondering supplication in the first place.

That was Haleine's doing, her influence. Questioning actions and decisions, entertaining uncertainty—he'd never done any of it before her.

How would it have been different had he not stumbled through her window that day? Maybe he wouldn't be estranged from James, but Haleine's help had been so vital in those early days. If he hadn't fallen, his rebellion might have done just that.

But she was gone now. She'd left. She'd walked away from him to spare him the task, to avoid another fight. Did that make her the stronger of the two? She'd fought with him to return. It was the only way to protect him and his people. A true queen, he thought, put her people before herself. She walked away knowing he wouldn't be able to let her go.

Could he? Could he let her go even now?

People started to push past him, their reason for being there done. He backed away from the entrance and let them exit unhindered. When the last had gone, he turned and saw not everyone had left after all.

Ilya remained, her arms folded across her chest. "Did you hear anything of what he said?"

Dana thought she meant Lucius but couldn't say for certain. But she already knew that, didn't she?

"Well, hear this," she said. "Something's happened at the palace. Those who spied for us are gone."

"Gone?"

"Taken. Aye."

"Dead?"

"Some of them."

"And the others?"

"Not dead yet."

"Then how—?"

"Everyone speaks of it."

"And Haleine? Do they speak of her?"

The question annoyed her. She adjusted her stance and placed one hand on her hip.

"Dana—"

"She's a part of this. She's spied for us, and if Omur's gone after them—"

"We've heard naught of her." Ilya sighed. "Can you not ask Faolan?"

"No," Dana said. "I can't."

He couldn't ask because Faolan also had been in camp the past two weeks. Dana wasn't sure why because Faolan had yet to tell him, but Dana suspected something had happened to Laorans. He'd seen the change in the unicorns. He'd seen the change in Luisiúil. The mare's sheen had dulled. It was an unsettling transformation.

"Dana," Ilya said. "Something's coming."

"Aye."

"You know?"

"I feel it."

"Then get yourself together."

He wanted to say something biting, something to make her back down. He hated the way she looked at him, but even more so he knew he hated how he had given her a reason to look at him like that.

He nodded. "Aye."

They looked at each other a moment longer, their stare broken only when the frenetic sounds of someone calling his name shattered the silence. They both stepped outside.

Owain, and a pair of other boys, ran toward them. Only Owain shouted his name, doing so over and over again until they reached Dana. Owain bent over to catch his breath, his hands on his knees. The other boys mimicked him. Their faces were flushed and their eyes afraid.

"What is it?" Dana asked.

"Army," Owain gasped. "There's—there's an army."

"Where?"

"Every—everywhere. All the patrols are seeing them. Sent me and them"—Owain gestured to the two boys behind him—"to tell you."

"It's all right," Dana said. "Our wall will—"

The wall will not hold.

He turned slightly to see Luisiúil standing at the edge of the clearing. Her blue eyes held his for a moment.

"Raise an alarm," he said, still looking at the unicorn. "Everyone who's able, tell them to prepare."

"Dana?" Ilya asked.

"Do it," he said.

She shouted orders at Owain and the others. They ran, and she jerked Dana away from Luisiúil to make him look at her.

"What's happening?" she asked.

"Find out how many there are. Find out how far away they are. If they'll attack tonight or wait until tomorrow," he said. "We'll have to make cover of some kind. There's precious little of it here."

"Dana—"

"The storm's breaking, Ilya," Dana said. "Here and now. The wall will not hold. We have to get everyone who can't fight out through the tunnels to somewhere safe and—"

Omur is among their number.

Dana stopped. He didn't turn to look at the unicorn this time, but Ilya understood the reason behind his hesitation and glanced at Luisiúil herself.

"What?" she prompted.

"Omur is among the soldiers. We have to—" he paused. *Run* was what he wanted to say. They had to run. "We have to send the unicorns away, too."

"Dana, we'll need them. Our numbers—"

"I know. But they're weak, Ilya. Faolan is weak. The goddess is weak. I don't know why or how or what it means except that they're vulnerable now, and Omur must know it. We can't expose them to him. We fight this one on our own."

Ilya considered that. Dana thought he could see the scenarios and numbers whirling in her head. None of them would make her happy.

"We will need our leader, then," she said. "Will he be among our number?"

Dana didn't hesitate. "Aye, he'll be there."

CHAPTER 23

Haleine had rid herself of the amulet. Omur sat his mount in the midst of the king's army and fumed silently at the girl's initiative.

From where had it come? And why now? She was supposed to be drowning in despair, not fighting him. How had she even known? Who would have told her? The pegasus was the only being in her circle who would have possibly recognized it as something more than the necklace it appeared to be, but he had not been in the queen's presence for some time now. It couldn't have been him.

The elimination left only one plausible possibility. Haleine had dreamt it. Her nighttime visions had alerted the pegasus to other things, perhaps now they had compelled Haleine to expel Omur's magic from her presence.

He was not pleased by this. He didn't care about the amulet. He'd known when he gave it to Zaide Romanza that its use would be short. The pegasus would sense it eventually, and it would have met the same end, but the pegasus had not sensed it at all. It had been Haleine.

That meant whatever magic the girl possessed was advancing of its own accord. Haleine was still ignorant to it all. The pegasus had told her as little as possible about the prophecy, only claiming she may have been implicated within it somehow.

Omur did not know why the pegasus would think that. It might have been he suspected the queen's bastards. Zaide Romanza suspected the same, but Omur was certain they were both mistaken. If Haleine's sons were the two of the prophecy, his lords would not have shown such great indifference toward their conception and birth. Haleine, they had told him, was a means to an end. Why did the pegasus think she was something more? What did he know that Omur did not?

"Is it much farther to the rebel camp?" Darian asked.

Omur looked at the man now riding beside him. He had a habit of interrupting. It would become a problem when they were closer to the camp and Omur's attentions would be needed to bring down the spell protecting it. He would have to speak to Varro about ensuring his privacy.

"My lord?" Darian asked.

But Omur didn't respond. Instead he looked around the forest in sudden realization. The goddess was weakened. She was *dying*. Omur hadn't known it before, but now that he was drawing closer to the heart of the rebellion, he could feel it. The magic protecting the camp was complex and strong but starting to crack. He could almost see it in the air. The fine winding tendrils were appearing in the blues and greens and browns of his surroundings. It would be easier to break now. *She* would be easier to break. He allowed himself a small smile.

"Not much farther," Omur said as he remembered Darian still waited for an answer. "We should stop and make camp soon."

"I shall give the order."

When Darian had ridden on ahead, Omur turned in his saddle and motioned to Varro, who rode just behind him. Varro came alongside him.

"Send your fastest riders back to the men we've left behind," Omur said. "There may be unicorns among the people. If so, I want your men to capture as many as they can. Forget the people and take the animals."

"Unicorns, my lord? We'll never get close enough."

"Send the word, Varro. I think you'll find their luck has changed."

"Yes, my lord."

"Tell your messengers should they wish to participate in tomorrow's festivities, they should hurry," Omur said. "We will, without fail, attack at dawn."

Varro pulled back and shouted the names of the men he would send. They extracted themselves from the ranks and pulled away from the others.

"You're not telling me everything," Darian said, returning to Omur's side. "Don't think I haven't noticed."

"Nothing that will affect tomorrow's plans," Omur said. "I ask you, my lord, for a small amount of latitude on this."

Darian watched the men now riding away from them and nodded. "My daughter tells me Dana is a man with nothing to lose."

Omur contemplated what discussion had prompted Haleine to offer such information. He had not been privy to her reunion with her father, nor anything else said in the queen's chamber, for as soon as Haleine had awakened, she had rid herself of the amulet. What dream had driven her to do that? His ire with the unknown encompassed him.

"With all due respect to your daughter, my lord," Omur said, "she is mistaken. Dana is a man who does not realize how very much he truly has to lose."

Darian nodded. "Men never do."

———⁓⁓⁓———

The army was vast. Dana had gone with Ilya and James to see for himself the men Omur had mustered in the name of the king. The soldiers, both mounted and on foot, stretched, it seemed, for miles. It wasn't miles, he knew, but they would be so badly outnumbered the exaggeration didn't matter. The soldiers were setting up camp now. Dana was glad to see the distance between them and the rebels' own camp. It would buy them the night.

"Why so far away?" Ilya asked.

"Omur's dismantling our defenses," Dana said. "When our wall comes down, he can't let the soldiers see."

"Good God," James murmured. "We'll be overrun."

"What are those colors there?" Ilya asked, pointing. "I don't recognize them. Those men can't be Liran."

Dana didn't need to look. "They're from Tanuba."

"Well, we finally got them involved," James said. "I'm so glad. You make it through this, Dana, be sure to thank your lover for that."

"This isn't what she intended."

"Are you sure?" James asked.

Both Dana and Ilya looked at him. James grunted and walked away, moving silently through the brush.

"We will be overrun," Ilya said when he was gone. "We need the unicorns, Dana. We'll drown without them."

"We won't have them. We either find a way to survive on our own, or we drown."

"Whatever you do, don't make that your speech on the morrow," Ilya said. "What do you want us to do?"

"I want us to prepare," Dana said.

As neither Omur nor the king's soldiers were aware of what exactly lay behind the magical barrier, it was the rebels' only advantage. The camp had been made in a flat, open glen perfectly suited for living but was now an ocean of abandoned tents. Men and women were emptying and tearing them down. Those who were leaving loaded their possessions onto mules and horses. Those who stayed gathered whatever weaponry they could from the stores. Goodbyes were said and plans were made.

Dana set them to defacing the terrain. The trees surrounding the camp would limit the army's movements, force them to bottleneck and make them easier prey for archers. Dana wanted to carry that protection into the camp itself. If they could keep the soldiers contained as much as possible for as long as possible, if they could thin the numbers, if they could incapacitate the front lines, maybe more of his own would survive. If. Maybe.

They dug trenches: some deep, some not. They filled deeper trenches with the trunks of smaller trees sharpened to a deadly point. The shallow ditches were filled with wet wood, hay, canvas, anything and everything that would burn when the time came and, more importantly, create smoke. Smoke would create cover and confusion. They dug other holes and ditches at random throughout the rest of the camp. They did anything to make it harder for the mounted knights. If they could force them to abandon their warhorses, they would stand a better chance. Maybe it would work. Maybe it would help. Maybe more of his own would survive.

They worked in shifts the entire night. Only Dana refused to rest. He did everything he could think of—everything anyone else could think of—that could make a difference. He was in constant contact with the spies set to watch the king's army. He knew everything that happened in the army's camp. They ate, they drank, they whored. They laughed and sang, joked about the slaughter that would come the next day. Eventually, their gaiety died down as they turned to sleep. The idea came then to steal entrance to the unsuspecting camp and do what damage they could.

"No," Dana said immediately. "He'll know. We wait."

Dawn was just breaking when word came that the army was stirring once more. Dana knew it was time to ready themselves for what was to come. He gave the order for his people to start arming and returned to his tent, the last still standing. Throughout the night, it had been the site of countless conferences as they coordinated their efforts to strengthen their defenses, but it was empty of people now, as well as most everything of value, anything not easily replaced. He lit the lantern on the table and began to dress.

Throughout the war, the rebellion had been collecting weapons and armor. It was never much but always more than with which they had started. Dana thought too much armor weighed a man down in battle. As he feared losing his mobility, he limited his protection to a mail shirt and a leather breastplate. He had a helm taken off a man in Trutina but never wore it. He kept it, though, for the same reason he kept Varro's sword. The pair normally sat in a corner of the tent, but when he glanced over at them, he saw the sword was missing. He knew exactly where it had gone and merely looked at the lonely helm before pulling the mail over his head. He was attempting to straighten it when Hanah entered.

"What are you doing?" she demanded.

"Preparing."

"And making a mess of it, I suppose," she said. "Here, let me."

He wasn't making a mess of it but recognized her need. It surprised him. Hanah had never been that sort, but he stopped what he was doing and allowed her to fuss over him. She straightened the mail and reached for the breastplate. He watched her hands tremble.

"You're afraid," he said as she fastened the breastplate in place.

"You're not?"

She took a step back and he tested the armor's tightness. The fit was as perfect as it ever was.

"No," he said.

"Well then," she said, holding out his sword. "You're a fool."

He smiled as he took the weapon from her. "You're not the first to think so."

Faolan came in and landed on the table. Dana nodded at him and buckled the sword belt around his waist.

"They're almost out," Faolan said. "Everyone you wanted gone."

"And the unicorns?" Dana asked. "They're to go as well."

Hanah's eyes widened and she looked at Faolan. Dana didn't want to argue, so he turned away to search through the remaining weapons in the corner.

"Dana, you'll need them," Hanah said.

"Not this time," he said. "Faolan will take care of it. Tend to everyone else, Hanah. See if you can get Owain and the other boys to go with you. I'd like to spare them this if I can, but if they want to stay, if they want to fight, you're to let them."

Hanah nodded. "We should all leave. Let the soldiers find nothing but an empty camp."

"No."

"Why?"

"Because they'll know, Hanah. *He'll* know. Because they'll follow and they'll destroy wherever we do go. It has to happen, and it has to happen here."

Hanah made a sound but did not speak. Dana slid a dagger in his boot and another in his belt and looked at her.

"You won't be the last to call me a fool," he said. "And not just because Faolan will assuredly do the same as soon as you've left. Go now and get yourself and the others away from here. We'll call for you when it's over."

"How will you—?"

"The unicorns will know," Faolan said. "Trust them."

Hanah looked at him for another moment. Dana didn't want to meet her eyes; he didn't want to prolong her presence in the tent. Instead, he searched for his bow. It rested on his bedroll, and he picked it up and adjusted its strings until Hanah left.

"Do you want to tell me what's happening?" he asked.

"There's an army coming to destroy us," Faolan said. "You didn't hear?"

Dana put the bow down. "Omur's with them this time, and our wall won't hold. What's happened to the goddess?"

"What makes you think—?"

"We were supposed to be safe here. Omur wasn't supposed to be able to find us, but now he's busy dismantling the wall protecting us. He's been at it all night," Dana said. "What's happened to the goddess?"

"She's weakened tremendously. To explain how or why takes more time than we currently have available to us."

"Is that the reason Omur's here now? Or is his presence here the reason why she's weakened?"

"I don't know about the first," Faolan said, "but it's not the second."

"What is his taking the wall down doing to you?"

"Nothing now."

"What's it doing to him?"

"Weakening him tremendously. It's a complicated spell he's breaking. He'll feel it. Magically or physically, he won't be much good when he's finished."

"So we let him break it," Dana said as he sat down. "Are we going to be able to survive this?"

"I don't know the future."

"Are we going to be able to survive this?"

"Maybe some."

"It's not good enough."

"It'll have to be," Faolan said. "It's all there is."

Dana looked at his bow. He should bring it along. It would be better to have it. He stood to retrieve it.

"James thinks Haleine was involved in this," he said. "That she's betrayed us. Me."

"Of course he thinks that."

"But not you?"

"And not you either," Faolan said. "You didn't see her, Dana. She wasn't telling anyone anything. She couldn't."

"Even if she wanted to."

"She didn't want to. She had nothing to tell them anyway."

Dana picked up the bow and quiver and walked to the tent's entrance. "She should have stayed."

"You think the outcome would have changed? You think we wouldn't have an army sitting outside our walls then? They would have come for her."

Dana nodded. "Aye. You should go."

"No."

"You can't keep the wall up, and I don't need you to take it down."

"You'll still need me."

"Will I?" Dana asked. "If the goddess is vulnerable now, so are you. Get out of here."

He walked out of the tent in time to see the wall as it came down. There was surprisingly little to it. A crack like thunder came first; a flash like lightning followed. A rumble ripped through the earth. Those around him cringed and flinched and fell into each other. Dana stared right at it and swayed with the earth's movement. He wondered what it looked like from the other side. He didn't wonder for long because the sound of a drummed cadence filled the air. They were coming. He moved forward to take his position at the front of their lines.

His people had started the fires, and the smoke was serving its purpose. It also obstructed his view of the army's approach, so Dana walked through the opening they'd left for the army and out of the camp. He stopped just outside of it and watched the horizon. Lucius and Ilya, with Owain as their shadow, came and watched with him.

When the army appeared, the trees broke up their line. They stood, at most, five men abreast. The mounted knights took up more room. If he hadn't already seen them, he never would have known how many there were. Three horses broke out amongst the ranks. One of their riders carried a white flag. Lucius and Ilya turned away, shouting something. Dana didn't know what. He watched the three horsemen.

"Dana?" Owain said.

"I see them," he said and handed Owain his bow.

"Don't you want someone to go with you?" Owain asked.

"No," Dana said and walked out to meet them.

The three men wore black armor and black cloaks over it. It wasn't until he was closer that Dana saw the Maoilriain crests over their hearts. Revelin's men. The two on either end were the lower men. Their weaponry and steeds confirmed it. They were guards to the third, so Dana focused on the man in the center. Older, strong, capable. Revelin's finest knight, no doubt. He rode a solid black stallion. The horse pranced and snorted as Dana approached. It was high-strung and vicious. It had been bred for war. Much, Dana thought, like his rider.

"Come to surrender?" Dana asked when he was close enough to be heard.

The man in the center laughed. The stallion danced more, and the man easily brought the beast under control.

"I've come to offer safe passage to the women and children in your camp," he said. "And any others who will renounce you and your madness."

"Have you now?" Dana asked. "No taste for killing the innocent?"

"Not when it can be avoided," the man said. "Does that make me a lesser man in your eyes?"

"On the contrary," Dana said. "It does, however, make me question your choice of allies."

"Don't."

Dana nodded. "Right. Well, it is kind of you to show concern for the women and children here, but it's an unnecessary gesture. You'll find none among our ranks unable nor unwilling to fight you."

"There are women. There are children," the man said. "That boy, for instance, who now holds your bow."

"He has earned his right to stand alongside me this day."

"And when he perishes here?"

"*If* he perishes here, his death will be on your head. You'll have to make peace with your god on that account."

"My god?" the man asked, his eyes resting on Owain for a moment. "You are outnumbered. You will be overrun. There is no hope to be had for those who follow you."

"There is always hope."

"Not for you. Nor for them should they engage in this fight. Give yourself over to my men and they will be shown leniency."

Dana smiled. "You really don't know with whom you're in bed, do you? Leniency is a word they do not understand," he said. "Thank you once again, but I think you'll find we'd rather fight."

"You're a fool."

Dana started back. "It's been said."

"When I find you on that field, I will kill you!" the man shouted before turning his mount and returning to his own men.

"That went well," Owain said when Dana returned.

"Always making new friends," Dana agreed. "He's worried for your soul."

Owain looked across the field and spat. "My soul is for the goddess," he said. "And with it, I shall purchase my revenge. In this life or the next."

Dana nodded. "That's what I told him you'd say. Get in position, aye? Tell the others as you go. They won't be long in coming now."

Owain held out the bow. When Dana took it, the boy turned and ran through the smoke. Dana followed and heard Owain making his way down the line of men and women, shouting for everyone to take positions. Ilya stepped up beside him.

"If they've ever needed a speech, Dana," she said, "it's now."

Dana rotated to see his followers, all of them with weapons at the ready, all of them watching him.

"Listen to me!" he shouted. "Listen to me now, for this you have the right to know!"

The already near-silent camp fell into an absolute stillness.

"The king's army has come here today to offer the women and children among us safe passage and leniency to any of the rest of you who abandon me to my inevitable fate. There is no need for you to die, they say, and die you surely shall should you choose to stay and fight alongside me. It is a good offer, far better than any our loved ones ever received from these same men. When did they ever show Cinna mercy? Or Trutina? Enimode?" Dana asked, not seeking but finding James's eyes. James held his gaze only briefly before nodding and looking away.

"Where was their mercy then?" Dana continued. "Where? They have run rampant over this country, run rampant over your villages, your lands, your mothers and fathers, your sisters and brothers, your sons, your daughters. Where was their offer of clemency then? Where was their offer of forgiveness for those that were truly guiltless?

"Why make the offer now to those of us who are anything but innocent? We lost our innocence the day we lost all which we held dear. We came here to the forest to recover something of what we lost. We came here to fight the tyranny that has become the law of this land. And now that evil is here at our borders, once again threatening all we have left.

"We are not a threat, they say. We have no hope, they say, for they are many, and we are few, and they have strength where we have none. They say this day will be our last. They say we have seen our last dawn and yet," Dana said. "And yet, here they are, on our borders, offering us mercy. Offering you mercy. And do you know why that is? Do you know?"

"Fear!" someone shouted.

Dana didn't know who had said it but pointed in the direction from which the answer had come and nodded. "Fear," he said. "Aye. They fear us. They fear you. They fear the loyalty you have shown to me, the goddess, each other. Such loyalty is foreign to them, and they do fear what they do not understand. They've wrapped their fear in a blanket of pity, hoping we will not see it for its true self, hoping we will not know them for the cowards they are.

"But they will find we know their faces anywhere. They will find we know them for their evil anywhere. Their cowardice cannot be disguised, cannot be obscured by a burial shroud masquerading as a flag of truce. Accept their offer if you'd like, but know you will receive no more quarter with these men than those whose lives they have already taken.

"Now, the men of Tanuba are new to us. They do not fear you. The men of Tanuba have come here seeking retribution for some perceived slight. They think they have suffered. They think they know what it is to lose, but we will show them today that they are wrong. Let us show them today what it is to suffer. Let us show them today what it is to lose. They think this dawn will be our last, but we will prove them wrong. We will show them this dawn has been their last, that they are the hopeless here, not us. We will crush them. We will grind them into the ground because they would do as much to us if they could, so I say this to you: cut them down before they have the chance. Make them rue the day they presumed to march into this glen and rule us. Make them understand what loss truly is."

He was met with resounding cries from every direction. He turned once more and looked at his army until he came face to face with Ilya.

She smiled. "That'll do."

"Take your archers," he said. "Get into position."

Trumpets sounded, announcing the advancement of the king's army. Ilya turned and ran toward her archers. James herded another group of their best shots in the opposite direction. Lucius and Dana stayed on the front line and waited.

The smoke prevented them from seeing the effect the archers were having, but they could hear it. There was the twang of the bow strings, the swoosh of arrows in the air, the thud arrows made when hitting their targets. Screaming followed, some human, some not. Occasionally, a cluster of arrows shrieked through the smoke at them, but since the shots were unfocused, they hit very little Dana cared about.

He readied his own bow when he saw the first of the army crossing into the rebel territory. Lucius called the order to the others. Dana took the arrows from his quiver and stuck them into the ground. He fitted one in his bow and fired when Lucius called for it. A line of men fell. The next climbed over them and continued forward. Dana took another arrow and another, firing in rapid succession, knocking one man down and the one who took his place.

When he ran out of arrows, he threw his bow to the ground and drew his sword. On either side of him, men and women did the same. They ran—screaming names of their families or villages—to meet the soldiers. Dana walked, his sword held low and at the ready.

A soldier charged him. Dana parried the first blow and thrust his blade into the man's stomach. He pulled it free and swung to his right to repeat the pattern with a second man. A third and fourth fell in a similar manner.

They kept coming. He kept killing, working his way farther into the fray. He deflected a mace aimed at crushing his skull so it only caught the side of his head. He fell and drew the dagger from his belt. He stabbed the foot of the man responsible and wrenched the mace from his hand. When the man bent to pull the dagger from his foot, Dana used the mace to kill him and reclaimed his dagger and returned it to his belt. The mace he took with him, holding it in his left hand. He dragged the sleeve of his tunic across his forehead, wiping away some of the blood.

"Come on!" he screamed to the still-advancing soldiers. "Come and meet your death!"

The battle continued. Dana caught snatches of his people, some dead, some wounded, some still fighting. He saw Owain briefly, the boy weaving his way through the chaos, bloodied but not badly enough to slow him. Lucius took an unchecked blow to the head. The man crumpled immediately. Dana set his sights on the attacker, pushing and stabbing and clubbing his way through countless others. He heard someone scream his name and turned in time to see a man wielding an axe about to overtake him. Dana moved, but the blade still caught his shoulder. The mail shirt took the brunt of the blow, but the force still tore flesh and drove Dana to his knees. Dana swung the mace at the soldier's knees and knocked him to the ground. He used his dagger to finish the assault.

Soon after Dana had resumed the fight, trumpets pierced the air followed by a cry for retreat. Dana stood frozen for a moment, not daring to believe it. The command was shouted again and again. Dana looked around and saw Varro, his sword in the air, screaming for his men's withdrawal.

"Captain Varro!" Dana shouted. "Surely you're not leaving so soon!"

Varro spotted him and stalked over. "We've gotten what we wanted."

"Have you?"

"With the exception of your head and my sword, yes."

Dana followed the man's eyes down to his bloodied blade.

"Oh, I don't have your sword," Dana said. "You'd best hope the man who does wield it doesn't find you. He carries a bit of a grudge."

Varro looked around. "Perhaps he carried a grudge."

"If that is true, I will come for you," Dana said. "I carry a bit of a grudge myself."

Varro smiled and backed away. "Bring my sword when you do."

When Varro disappeared into the crush of retreating soldiers, Dana relaxed his hold on his weapons. He returned the sword to its sheath and wiped his forehead once again. He turned slowly to survey the damage done to camp. What exactly had Omur wanted?

"Dana!" someone roared.

He searched the sea of faces to find who called him now and saw the man in black, Revelin's finest, still astride his great war-horse and urging the stallion through and over the confusion. The man yelled his name again. Dana smiled, drew his sword and started pushing his own way through in order to meet him.

The horseman had just broken free of the thickest of the throngs when Owain flew in from the side and used his knife to cripple the horse. The stallion screamed as he went down. His rider rolled away from harm and was back on his feet impossibly fast. His own dagger was drawn and ready, but his target was no longer Dana. Owain lunged, but the black knight was faster. Dana couldn't see the individual movements, but it ended with the man holding Owain by the hair, with a dagger at the boy's throat.

"Are you going to kill the boy just to prove to me you can?" Dana screamed, shoving his way clear. "Because there's no need. I already know what a coward you are!"

The struggle stopped. The man kept his hold on Owain, but his eyes sought out Dana. The dagger wavered slightly.

"The boy can go," the man said, shoving Owain to the ground. "It's you I want."

Owain fell into the dirt. When he pushed himself up, his dagger was in his hand, and he dove at Revelin's man. Dana's breath caught as the man lashed out once again and kicked the boy in the face. Owain hit the ground and didn't move.

"Call me a coward?" the man asked, stepping over Owain's body.

461

Dana looked at the boy. "Was I wrong?"

"It is bold of you to call me a coward when you are naught but a murderer."

"Are you saying you've never killed a man?" Dana asked. "I can't believe that. What good would you be to Revelin?"

"You will leave my lord out of this."

"Gladly. I never wanted him in it."

"You are the murderer," the man said. "You murdered my wife. You nearly murdered my daughters. Do you not remember?"

"Well, you must forgive me," Dana said. "I have been accused of murdering so many wives and daughters, I can't possibly remember them all."

"Forgiveness is not an option," the man said. "I will kill you for what you've done."

"So you claim."

The man raised his sword in salute. Dana tossed aside his mace and returned the gesture. His challenger started the attack before Dana had lowered his sword. He was caught off balance and staggered back. Only with desperate maneuvering did he stave off a killing blow. He jumped sideways to avoid another swipe and prepared an attack of his own.

"Are you sure you have the right man?" Dana asked. He knocked the man to the ground with a solid kick to the chest and raised his sword as he prepared to strike. "I've never been to Tanuba."

Dana hesitated a moment too long, and the man's sword lashed out and bit into Dana's side. Dana cried out and pulled away before the weapon could do more damage. He passed his sword into his left hand and covered his wound with his right.

"Oh, I have the right man," the black knight answered as he got to his feet. "If indeed you can be considered as such, knowing the travesties you have committed."

"If you're looking for travesties, you didn't need to go any farther than Maddox's palace," Dana said. "You don't know the king of Lira very well, do you?"

He ducked to avoid another blow and then rushed the man. Their swords clashed and locked, bringing the two men face to face. They strained against one another, neither wanting to be the first to break.

"But I know you," the man said. "I know the sort of man you are. You assassinated my king. You murdered my wife. You—"

"Aye, I know. I nearly murdered your daughters. I'd hate to disappoint you since you traveled all this way just to kill me, but I don't hurt children. I don't kill the innocent."

"No, you exterminate them," the man hissed. "Like you have all your countrymen since the day Maddox ascended the throne."

Dana flushed anew with anger. "I am trying to save these people!"

"You are their executioner."

Dana took his hand from his side and backhanded the man. The force of his action knocked them both to the ground. Dana's sword fell from his grasp, but he picked it up as he rose to his feet. This would end now.

Faolan appeared suddenly, hovering in the air in front of him. "Don't kill this man."

"Get out of the way," Dana snapped as he lunged for his opponent.

Dana attacked with an unrelenting series of blows. The man blocked some, but not all, and tried to launch a counter attack. It failed, and the man fell behind to the point where he finally lost his sword. The weapon landed far out of his reach as the man dropped to his knees. Dana placed both hands on the sword for his final blow.

"Dana, don't!" Faolan shouted.

Dana didn't listen. He swung the sword and finished Revelin's black knight, decapitating him with one swift stroke.

"Oh Dana," Faolan said. "You shouldn't have done that."

Dana threw down his sword and went first to the fallen stallion. He used his dagger to end the animal's agony. Next he knelt at Owain's side and rolled the boy over. The kick had broken the boy's nose and crushed his cheekbone. He was unconscious but alive. For now.

"We're going to need Hanah," Dana said. "Get her back here."

Faolan did nothing but look at the man Dana killed.

"I had to do it, Faolan," he said. "If our positions had been reversed, do you think he would have shown me mercy?"

"No, but you don't understand. He's—"

"I showed him all the mercy he deserved," Dana said, leaning back to examine his bleeding side. "Get Hanah back here."

"Dana, you need to listen to me. You don't know who this man was, and you have to know—"

"Who was he?"

"Your whore's father," Omur said, reining in his mount along-side them.

Dana stood immediately, pain tearing through his side once more. His weaponless state wouldn't matter against Omur, but he searched for his sword anyway. Omur noticed the look.

"If I had wanted to kill you, I would not have called for a retreat," Omur said.

"Why did you call for retreat?"

"Varro didn't tell you? We got what we wanted."

"Whatever that was, it couldn't have been this," Dana said, gesturing to the man Omur claimed was Haleine's father. "You called for the retreat before he found me."

"It did push him to find you, though, but no," Omur said. "This was not it. I do admit it was my original intention. I knew one of you would kill the other, which would, in turn, cause the queen much pain, but then I found something I wanted more."

"Which was?"

"You'll find out soon enough. But thank you for this." Omur motioned to the body. "I shall enjoy informing the queen of what you've done."

"What do you want?" Dana asked.

"His body," Omur said. "The queen, I'm sure, would like to bury her father. She never did get the chance with her mother."

Dana didn't move as Omur motioned to two soldiers, who came forward and removed the man's body. When they had withdrawn, Dana looked back at Omur.

"Is that all?"

"Not quite." Omur pulled a crumpled heap of fabric from a saddlebag and dropped it. "Her majesty requested I return this to you," he said. "She thanks you for its lending."

He turned his horse and rode away, taking the rest of the king's men with him. Dana didn't move until the last of them had cleared from the remains of the camp. Then he walked to the nearest tree and leaned against it as he looked at what Omur had left behind.

"Dana," James said, appearing at his side. "Are you all right? I saw Omur and I thought—you're bleeding."

"It's nothing," Dana said. "You? Are you all right?"

"Aye. Lucius—"

"I saw. Is he dead?"

"Not yet. Has anyone sent for Hanah?"

Dana shrugged, his eyes still on the bundle of fabric. James finally noticed.

"What's that?" he asked.

"Omur left it. He said Haleine thanked us for its lending."

James picked it up and held it out for Dana to see. "It's my cloak. Or, it was. I gave it to the queen when I took her back to the palace. Kind of her to return it, don't you think?"

"It wasn't her," Faolan said. "She wouldn't have given it to him."

Dana looked at Faolan. "Was he telling the truth? Was that man her father?"

"Yes," Faolan said.

"You killed her father? The queen's father?" James asked, and Dana nodded. "You think she won't turn from you now?"

"I tried to tell you," Faolan said.

Dana touched the injured side of his head. "Not helpful," he said, wincing slightly. "I have to go to the palace."

"You're not serious," James said. "Dana, we need you here!"

"She needs to hear it from me," Dana said. "I have to be the one to tell her, not Omur."

James punched him. Dana staggered back against the tree but didn't fall outright. He put his hand over his jaw and looked at James.

"Your people died for you today, and more will die yet, but you still worry only about her," James seethed, shaking his hand. "What is wrong with you?"

James walked away before Dana could offer any sort of response. He shouted commands to those needing guidance. He did what Dana should have been doing, but the rebel leader didn't move. He stayed propped against the tree.

"You stay here," he said to Faolan. "Figure out how to better protect this camp."

"I won't be able to do anything without Luisiúil and the other—" Faolan stopped. Dana looked at him.

"The unicorns," Faolan said finally. "He has the unicorns."

"Something he wanted more," Dana said. "How?"

"Doesn't matter how," Faolan said. "I have to get to the palace."

Dana nodded. "I'm going with you."

CHAPTER 24

Following her confrontation with Bronagh, Haleine took to spending her days in the solarium. She really ought not to have been out of bed at all, as her physician told her daily, but Haleine went anyway. It was the only place Bronagh would not follow her.

Also missing from her entourage was Ceallach. When Haleine asked Nonna to investigate, the girl reported that he had been set to other things. No one Nonna asked seemed to know what these other things were, but Haleine suspected it meant Omur no longer considered her a threat.

And why would he? She was harmless. The most she could do was sit in whatever room she happened to be in. Everything else required help. Everything else required effort. By the time she reached the solarium, she was so exhausted, she sat there, half asleep and trying not to succumb to the urge completely. She wanted to know when they brought her the news. She wanted to hear Ceallach coming.

She would hear the trumpets first, as they announced the return of whatever remained of the king's army. She didn't have that warning when he came to tell her of her mother's death, but when he came this time, she would know exactly what he would say. She thought of her dream, of Dana cutting his way through a wall of soldiers.

"He'll come back."

Haleine opened her eyes. Sighle stood on her right. "What?"

"He'll come back," Sighle said.

Haleine nodded but said nothing.

Sighle sat down. "Do you think he won't?"

"I don't know."

"I do," Sighle said. "He'll come back."

Her sister picked up a bit of sewing her ladies had dropped and examined it as though it were more than a scrap of fabric. It had been only a couple of months at most since she last saw Sighle, but the change in her sister was remarkable. Haleine sighed and Sighle looked over.

"What?"

"You look so grown up," Haleine said.

Sighle shrugged. "Loss will do that."

Haleine nodded, unable to say anything. Loss would do that. So would waiting. It wouldn't be the first time either of them waited upon word of their father. Einar never rested long, and Darian was always riding from one end of the country to the other to put a stop to whatever Einar plotted. Every time Darian rode out, Rhoswen and her daughters would start their vigil. But Rhoswen had never been a passive woman. She always found something to keep her mind occupied. Once, she had a painter come, and her daughters had sat for a portrait. Haleine had been fourteen and found the exercise unbearable. Sighle, Haleine recalled, understood perfectly what was required and never moved until Rhoswen granted permission. Haleine remembered the annoyance with which she had thought of her young sister, as well as the irritation with which Rhoswen had regarded her eldest daughter. Haleine smiled and tilted her head to look at the ceiling.

"What?" Sighle asked.

"I was thinking of those portraits Mother had us sit for."

"Why?"

"I don't know. It feels as though we are doing the same thing now. Sitting, waiting, posing as the soldier's daughters we are. I remember before it was agony. I couldn't sit still. But you," Haleine said. "You never flinched."

"I never will."

Her sister's tone was odd. Haleine furrowed her brow and straightened so she could see Sighle. Their eyes met, and Haleine shivered so violently, a ripple of pain went through her body. She cried out, and Sighle's face was marred by a look of unmistakable fear. Haleine's ladies surrounded her, smothering her, calling for Rhys and shooing Sighle out of their path. Sighle backed away.

"Sighle, no, I'm fine," Haleine said.

"Open the window," Sighle said, standing near the doors. "You need some air."

"I'm fine. Would you please stop smothering me?" Haleine said as she watched her sister disappear from the room. "You frightened the life out of that poor girl. Would somebody please find her and explain the stupidity that is the lot of you?"

"Your majesty!" one of the younger women exclaimed and pointed to the window. "Your pegasus has returned."

Haleine turned her head and saw Faolan hovering in the air. "Let him in," she said. When none moved, she shouted the command. "Let him in!"

Still no one moved. Instead they stared. She could not blame them. She had become something to be stared at, to be marveled at. A soul unhinging from everything civilized.

She struggled to get out of the chair. "Oh, never mind. I will do it myself."

She couldn't have done it herself, with one arm slightly less useless than the other, but her activity spurred her attendants to complete their duty. One woman helped her to her feet while another woman opened the window and allowed the pegasus to enter.

"You're not well, your majesty," one of the older women said, laying her hand on Haleine's arm. "Allow me, please, to summon the physician to attend you."

Just as Haleine shook free of the woman's touch, the trumpets sounded. She closed her eyes as Faolan settled on her shoulder.

"He will have others who need attending more than I," she replied. "I require rest only, but please, do send someone to see to my sister."

Someone promised to attend to it. Haleine didn't know who. She didn't care. She pushed her way through her still-staring women to the relative emptiness of the hall where Willem waited.

She stood unmoving for a moment, looking at the floor and feeling Faolan's weight on her shoulder more than ever. She would know soon enough. As soon as she reached her chambers, she would know. She thought about returning to the solarium but raised her head and looked at her guard.

"This way, your majesty," he said and stepped in front of her. "What?"

"Follow him," Faolan said quietly.

She fell in step behind Willem and let him lead her below stairs into the growing chaos. Servants and soldiers ran in every direction. Willem stepped back and walked just behind her, his hand on her back, guiding her gently through it all. They left the castle and entered the courtyard now teeming with injured and dying men.

She had witnessed this scene before. This was not the first battle with the rebels, and every time the two sides had fought, men came back bruised and bleeding. Before that, there was her father's household. There were rebels in Quatara, too, and her father had fought them. Her mother had trained her for such a sight as this. She knew how to assess an injury, to determine whether a man might live or die, and staunch the worst of it until a physician could be sought.

But, apart from a visit to the hospital long ago, those lessons had gone unused. It wasn't expected of her here. The queen wouldn't be expected even to appear in such a place. No one had noticed her yet, but someone would soon. They would think she came for word of her father, but they would be mistaken. She knew why she was here and what that meant for him. Her eyes swept over the sea of hurt, settling on the cart bearing the bodies of the dead.

"I do not want to be here," she said.

"Just wait," Willem said, scanning the soldiers. He did not look at the cart.

"I do not want to wait," she said.

"Haleine," Faolan said so softly no one else could hear. "Just wait."

She shook her head. "No. I'll not wait any longer."

She left the courtyard before Willem could say anything about it. Faolan said her name again, harsher and louder this time, but she shrugged him off her shoulder and kept moving.

There was no time to wait. There were things to be done, arrangements to be made, a vigil to be held and a burial to be planned. Sighle needed to be told that their father indeed had come home for the final time. Never again would they wait upon word of his return because he was dead and gone, slain as their mother had been, and Haleine was the reason why.

How would she ever reveal that Darian Coileáin had gone to his death because his daughter had let him? She told him he was lost to her but didn't tell him what would happen if he were to go. She had seen it—so many times had she seen it—and still had said nothing. How did one explain such a thing? Especially to a girl still grieving for the loss of her mother?

"Your chambers," Faolan breathed, settling on her shoulder once again.

It was the only viable choice, for nothing could be done until Ceallach brought her the news of her father. She'd been wrong. Knowing was worse than not.

469

She walked through the halls, seeing nothing but the floor as she sought the shelter of her rooms. The sudden clanging of armor startled her, and she looked over her shoulder. Standing next to Willem and leaning against the wall was a soldier in ill-fitting and incomplete armor. Blood seeped out from beneath the man's dented helm. She glanced at the half-hidden blue of his eyes, his identity and intentions obvious. She knew what he would tell her. She didn't want to hear it from him.

"Willem, this man is injured," she said. "Dismiss him."

"No," her guard said. "He will continue on."

His disobedience should have been a surprise. He'd never defied her before, and she should have been angry, but she couldn't muster the emotion—nor any other—so Haleine turned away and continued walking. She moved as quickly as she could, a wild idea in her head of outrunning the men behind her, of escaping them. It was a design dashed when she reached her chamber doors and found herself incapable of opening them. Faolan said her name a third time, now trying to soothe her, and she shook him off her shoulder again.

Willem opened the doors and she rushed inside but stopped when she saw both Bronagh and Nonna standing by the fire. The two women stared at the newly arrived procession. Bronagh's surprise quickly became annoyance.

"What is this?" she demanded.

"This man's injured," Willem said. "Fetch supplies, Bronagh."

That turned Haleine's head. "No, Willem, no. Bronagh can't leave this room. You can't let her go, not while he's here. Send Nonna, please, but don't let Bronagh go."

"Nonna, then," Willem said. "Be quick about it."

The girl curtsied and disappeared into the servants' passage. Bronagh moved to follow her.

"Where are you going?" Willem demanded.

"I'm not staying here," Bronagh said.

"You are."

"You can't force me."

"I can if I have to, and if I have to, I will," he said. "Now come and help."

"No. I know who that man is, and I'll have nothing to do with him."

"Then sit yourself down until the queen dismisses you."

Bronagh stared at Willem, suddenly fighting tears. She turned sharply to look at Haleine. "Your man."

470

Dana collapsed then, his borrowed armor scraping and crashing against the floor. Both Haleine and Willem got on their knees to help. Haleine had a harder time with it.

"Your majesty, you shouldn't—" Willem began.

"But I am," Haleine said. "And I thank you for all you have done here, but I need you to go to the hall now and keep Ceallach from bursting through those doors unannounced. I do not know when he will come, but come he will. You will need to stop him until it is safe."

Willem wanted to stay. Haleine could see it in his face. He wanted to argue but could see the sense to her request. He glanced at the corner where Bronagh now lurked.

"Help her," Willem said.

"No. I'll have nothing to do with this."

"Bronagh, your queen is on her knees," Willem said.

"My queen is in her grave."

"Willem, go," Haleine said. "Nonna will return soon enough, and we will manage until she does."

Her guard nodded and left. When the doors were once again closed, she turned her attention to Dana. He had removed his helm and now held it in his hands. She scanned his face, avoiding his eyes and what might be lurking there. He had taken a blow to the side of his head. That hadn't been her father. She didn't want to look at the blood anymore and shifted her eyes to the helm instead. She tried to take it from him, but her fingers couldn't hold the weight and it fell to the floor.

"Haleine," he said.

His fingers brushed hers. She looked at his rough, dirtied and bloodied hands. Nonna entered, and Haleine was spared hearing what he would say next. Nonna sat at Dana's side, put her basket of supplies on the floor and looked the rebel leader full in the face. The girl's eyes widened.

"Oh," she said.

"Nonna," Haleine warned.

The girl immediately lowered her eyes. She spoke as little as possible, instructing Dana to lift one arm, then the other so she could remove the breastplate. The mail shirt and his tunic followed. Haleine's eyes were drawn to the red stain low on his left side.

That had been her father.

Nonna examined all wounds and, after checking his shoulder and mopping the blood from his brow, deemed his side to be the worst. She asked him to lie back and helped him to do so. He put his hand behind his head. Nonna cleaned the wound tentatively, Dana wincing with every touch.

"Do you wish me to stitch it, my lord?" Nonna asked.

Dana's mouth twisted into a smile. "I am far from a lord." His eyes caught Haleine's, and the smile disappeared. "No. No stitching. Just pack it as best you can. Please."

"But the wound is quite serious."

"Just pack it," Dana said. "There's no time for stitching now."

"Oh," Nonna said again.

She set to work doing as Dana had requested and a pinprick of red broke the purity of the bandaging almost immediately. It soon became a full bloom, engulfing the white fibers completely. Nonna noticed as well and looked at Dana.

"No time," he said.

"But it—"

"It doesn't have to be perfect," he said, propping himself up on his elbows. "You've slowed the bleeding and saved my life. I think that'll do."

Nonna blushed as she looked at him. Any other day, any other time, Haleine would have been amused.

"Nonna," she snapped, "take Bronagh and go to the courtyard to see what other lives you might save this day."

"The other injuries," Nonna said. "Your shoulder—"

"It's nothing. They're nothing," Dana said. He started to sit up and Nonna helped him. "Thank you, Nonna. I truly am indebted to you for your aid this day."

The girl's face flushed again. She tossed her things back into the basket and scrambled to her feet. She curtsied quickly and left the room.

Bronagh slowly rose to her feet. "Not worried anymore what I might do? Who I might tell?"

"Run straight to Omur if you want. You won't tell him anything he doesn't already know," Dana said. "Get out."

"You can't order me about."

"I'm only repeating what's already been said. You're still here, yet Haleine dismissed you."

Bronagh smiled and walked away. "Aye, she certainly did."

When Bronagh was gone, Dana looked at Haleine. They were alone now. There would be no hiding any longer.

"You really shouldn't be down here," he said, reaching for his tunic. "Not in your condition."

"And one in your condition should not be gallivanting around the palace in his enemy's armor."

He gingerly slid the tunic over his head. "I never gallivant."

"Why did you come here, Dana?" she asked. "Please say it was not solely to tell me of how you killed my father. Please say there is something more."

Dana stared now. His lips parted but he didn't speak.

"Omur has taken the unicorns," Faolan said after a moment.

Haleine had forgotten about the pegasus. She broke off her stare with Dana and searched the room for Faolan. He stood on the vanity.

"How?" she asked.

"We don't know," Dana said.

He stood next to her now, his hand held out. She didn't want to take it, but she couldn't stay on the floor and couldn't get up without help. She nodded, and he slipped his hands under her elbows and lifted her. Her breath caught and she gasped. Dana's hands pulled back.

"Did I hurt you?" he asked.

She walked toward Faolan without answering. She didn't know how.

"He means to harm them?" she asked as she sat in her chair.

"Yes. It will cripple the rebellion," Faolan said, joining her. "But more importantly, it will cripple Laorans past the point of recovery."

Haleine glanced quickly at Dana. He stood where she had left him, looking as though he did not dare come closer.

"He holds them here?" she asked, focusing again on Faolan.

"I think so. He wouldn't want them too far out of his control."

"What is your plan to retrieve them?"

"We don't have one yet. First, we need to find out all we can about where they are and how he's protecting them."

"And for that you will need my help."

"Yes."

She nodded and looked again at Dana. He still had not moved. She didn't know what to do. Ignoring him only condemned him, but reaching out would absolve him. Neither seemed correct. She was relieved when a soft knock came on her doors and Willem entered.

"Lord Ceallach is here, your majesty," her guard said. "He wishes to speak with you."

Haleine nodded. It was time, then. Her stomach lurched, and she could taste bile in the back of her throat. She forced it back down.

"A moment, Willem," she said.

Her guard nodded and withdrew.

"I'll go," Dana said.

"Yes," Faolan said. "You do that."

"You will let me know if—"

"Yes," Faolan said.

She heard the scrape of armor against the floor and listened to Dana walk to the servants' passage. She didn't look; she couldn't. She stared at her lap and concentrated on breathing.

"Haleine," Dana said.

She looked at him before it occurred to her not to.

"I didn't know."

She closed her eyes and nodded.

"Haleine," he said again.

"Just go," she said. "Please. Just go."

━◦∞◦━

When Ceallach entered with word of her father's death, he kept his distance as he braced himself for what would follow. He expected tears and screaming. He expected anger. It was what he had received from her when he told her of Rhoswen's death. Why would Darian's be different?

But she hadn't done any of that. She sat in her chair and waited for him to say it because she couldn't say it before him. *Your majesty, it sorrows me to have to tell you this.* She sat, dry eyed, and waited. *Your father was killed in the battle. It was Dana, my queen. He did this.*

He said nothing untrue. She wasn't sure why she thought he might. What need would Omur have to lie when the truth would provide him all he wanted?

She nodded when Ceallach finished. She thanked him.

"I best find my sister," she said. "Sighle will need to be told what has happened."

"You needn't worry about that, your majesty," Ceallach said. "Lord Omur told me he would see to your sister personally."

The sentence nearly stopped her heart. She left the room immediately, shrugging off Faolan's attempt to follow. She left him behind
with Ceallach, leaving only Willem to accompany her to the chamber her sister had been given.

Sighle refused to open her door. Haleine lost track of how long
she stood in front of it, calling her sister and entreating the girl to
admit her. But despite her efforts and pleading, the door stayed
closed and her sister silent.

In her most desperate moment, Haleine considered having the
door broken down. There were men in the castle who would tear
down each and every stone if she commanded it; they would think
nothing of a single door. She looked to Willem and opened her
mouth to speak the demand, but her guard shook his head.

"Nonna," he said.

Haleine nodded. "Yes. Send for her, please. Tell her what I
require her to do."

When it was done, Haleine was resigned to waiting. She continued to stand at her sister's door until her injuries forced her to
concede her post. She slid to the floor and leaned against the wall.
Willem knelt in front of her.

"Allow me to help you back to your chambers," he said.

"No, I will wait for Nonna."

"She will come to you there."

"I will wait, Willem."

"As you wish, your majesty."

"Yes," she said. "As *I* wish."

Willem stood and backed away. She didn't move, wondering
only what happened behind that door. Omur would see to her sister personally. Sighle was the only family she had left. Did he now
come for her? To finish what he'd started with Rhoswen?

She looked to Willem again, the command to break down the
door on her lips. He started to shake his head yet again when Nonna
appeared. Willem helped Haleine to her feet.

"You've seen my sister?" Haleine asked as Nonna curtsied.

"Aye, your majesty."

"Is she well?"

"She's mourning, your majesty," Nonna said.

"As am I."

"Aye, your majesty, but, please, leave your sister be this night."

"I can't leave her alone."

"She's not alone. Some of your ladies are with her," Nonna said. "They were there when she received word."

"She prefers those women, those strangers, to me?"

"She does tonight," Nonna said. "They don't need to talk about your father. She's afraid you do."

But Haleine didn't. She didn't want to talk about Darian at all, but she nodded and dismissed Nonna after bidding her to stay close to Sighle. Nonna curtsied once more and withdrew, leaving Haleine alone with Willem.

"Your majesty?" he said.

"Sighle should have guards," she said.

"Your sister is in no danger."

"I want Sighle to have guards," she said. "You set men to watch my sons, now I want you to set men to watch my sister. My family has come under attack, Willem, I do not know if you've realized this, first my mother, now my father. Sighle is all that remains, and I will see her safe, so when I tell you my sister should have guards, the only thing I want to hear you say is 'I'll see it done, your majesty.'"

"I'll see it done, your majesty."

She nodded and looked away, feeling the anger dissipate inside her. Why couldn't she hold on to it?

"I want to see my father," Haleine said next.

"Your father?" Willem asked. "But your majesty, you shouldn't—"

"I will see my father, and I will see him now."

"You should rest now," Willem said. "You're hurt, you're exhausted, and your father will still be there in the morning. He's certainly not going anywhere now."

Haleine looked at her guard in astonishment. Willem's eyebrows furrowed slightly, indicating she was not alone in her surprise.

"You've been rather disagreeable this day, Willem. It is unlike you," Haleine said. "Take me to my father now."

Willem bowed his head and brought her to the room where her father's body lay. She waited in the hall while Willem cleared the room of those who had been tasked with preparing her father for burial. When the last of them were gone, Haleine went in alone.

The last time she had stood in this room was when Amatheon and Michaela had been killed. That had been more than a year ago. How young she had been then and how very stupid. She was different now, but what she was, she did not know. Perhaps there was no word for it, for her.

Darian's body lay on a slab at the far end of the room. His was the only one there. She kept her head down as she walked. She approached with apprehension, knowing she was about to see the end of the dream which had plagued her for months. When she stood in front of the slab, she placed her hand on the edge and looked at what Dana had wrought.

It was awful. It was grotesque. She pushed off from the edge and backed away as quickly as she could. She tripped on her skirts and fell, landing on her back in the center of the room. The urge to vomit forced her up again, and after she had purged, she sat, her legs tucked under her, staring at her father's body.

"Disturbing, isn't it?" Omur said from behind her. "The violence of which men are capable, the evil they do. You didn't know he had it in him, did you?"

Haleine didn't turn around. She hadn't expected his appearance, but neither was she surprised by it. "What have you done to my guard?"

"Nothing he'll remember."

"What have you done to my sister?"

"What makes you think I've done something to your sister?"

"Ceallach told me you would see to her personally. I took it for a threat."

"Why would you do that?"

"You've killed my mother. You've killed my father—"

"Dana killed your father. I thought I told Ceallach to mention that."

"What are you doing here?"

"So suspicious, Haleine," he said. "Perhaps I have come to pay my respects."

He started to circle her, but she didn't look at him. She kept her eyes fixed upon the slab bearing her father's body.

"But you haven't," she said.

"No, I haven't."

"What are you doing here?"

"Satisfying curiosity."

"Looking to see me cry?"

"Not tonight. I've sensed your mood. It does not lend itself to tears."

"What do you know about my mood?"

"Nothing, I confess. But I can tell you of how your sister cried when I told her of your father's death. Or if you'd prefer, I can tell you of your father's mood as he rode to the rebel camp. I can tell you neither you nor your sister were far from his thoughts. He wanted so much to remedy your recent tragedies. He wanted to save his daughters and avenge his wife. I found it interesting you did not tell him all you knew. It might have saved his life."

"Is that what you are curious about?" she asked. "What I did or did not tell my father?"

"No."

"Then ask me what you will, so you may go and leave me be."

"I had been told your father was unkillable." Omur stopped when he stood in between her and her father. "Dana certainly proved my source wrong, though I suppose anyone would be hard-pressed to survive the loss of his head. Oh, my queen, you should have seen it. The spray of the blood and bone and sinew, your lover nearly burning in anger. Your father begged him for mercy."

"No, he didn't."

"No, you're right, he didn't. It was the pegasus who begged. It was the pegasus who begged Dana to spare your father's life. Your lover wouldn't hear of it."

That she could believe. She could envision it. She saw Faolan shouting for Dana to stop; she saw Dana pushing past him; she saw the spray of blood and bone and sinew. She retched again. When the moment passed, she wiped her mouth on her sleeve.

"Do you love him still?" Omur asked. "Can you after what he's done? Do you forgive him the slaughter of your father?"

Why did he pose the question like that? Why was he concerned with her absolution of Dana? The more cutting question would be to ask if she could forgive herself.

"He didn't know," she said.

"And that would have made a difference?"

She didn't know. Darian had wanted Dana dead. He would have only wanted it more had he known what Dana was to his daughter. He wouldn't have backed down. He would have come at Dana with everything he had, and Dana would have had to defend himself. But if he had known it was her father he faced? If he had heard Faolan? She thought of Dana's face when she asked him why he had come and later when he said he hadn't known. There was no lie behind his eyes.

"Yes," she said. "It would have."

"You are naive to think that."

478

"Perhaps. But that must satisfy you. I have answered your question, and now you can be on your way."

"How eager you are to rid yourself of me. Why?"

"I am in mourning."

"As you may well be." Omur knelt in front of her. "But not for your father."

She had to work to keep her face stoic. She struggled to keep from looking at her father. He was right; she hadn't cried for her father. She'd vomited, twice now, but because the sight had been truly sickening, not because the soul that had once inhabited the body had been the one to give her life. She bit her tongue as hard as she could manage. Blood trickled down her throat, and tears spilled from her eyes.

"There," she said, looking at Omur at last. "You've now seen my tears. Surely you can want no more of me."

Omur stood. "If you bit your tongue any harder, it would have come clean off."

"And what if it had?" she asked. "Would that please you? Is that why you hound me? It is not tears you want but blood?"

"If I wanted your blood, Haleine, I would have spilled it long before now. I have no desire to cause you physical pain."

"Nor any of your enemies it would seem," she said. "It is little wonder why you have been at this war for seven hundred years and why you shall continue to do so for seven hundred more. You do not understand the fundamentals of war."

"You think because you are a soldier's daughter, you know better than me?" Omur asked. "You think because you are a rebel's whore, you can school me in the art of war? Well, your lover once thought to do the same. He didn't understand the true art of war any better than you. Humans are always incapable of grasping the nuances of anything larger than themselves."

She smiled at his agitation. "What do you want with me if I am, as you have said, incapable of comprehension? What is your true purpose for being here?"

"The king gave you a necklace," Omur said after a moment. "It seems to have gone missing."

She laughed. "You will have me believe your puppet so concerned over a lost trinket that he would send you to seek me out here in the dead of night?"

"He gave it to you out of love."

"He doesn't know why he gave it to me."

"Do you?"

She didn't. But she could guess.

"Somewhere in your seven hundred years, some ancient gave a prophecy," she said. "This prophecy named me as someone who, despite her detested humanity, has great value to the gods you serve. Your necklace was used to spy on me."

She wasn't looking directly at him, but she could still see his expression change. His smug certainty was gone. She bit her tongue once more to stop herself from smiling.

"You don't believe in prophecy," Omur said.

"You do. Your gods do. And you don't want my blood because they don't want my blood." She smiled. "I used to think my husband was the impotent one."

"You don't know anything about it," he said. "The pegasus didn't tell you."

"How are you so sure what has been said? Your amulet is gone, your man is gone, my maid is gone. How do you spy on me now?"

"My man?"

"Ceallach. You set him to watch me."

"You believe Ceallach is one of mine?"

"Isn't he?"

Now Omur laughed. "No agent of mine would have delivered that wretched beast to your side."

"Then what is he?"

Omur shrugged. "He is human. I do not know what that makes him."

"Apart from worthless?"

"Apart from that," Omur agreed. "You're wrong, you know, about my gods not wanting your blood. They'd like it very much."

"Are you saying that in addition to being impotent, you're also incompetent?"

"What I am saying is that I have not yet finished with you," Omur said. "And when I am, when I have gotten from you everything I want, I will—"

"Bleed me dry," Haleine said without knowing why.

"Worse," Omur said.

He said it because he didn't know any better. All he could offer were empty threats because he was blind to everything but his gods' will. They wanted her, they needed her, so all Omur could do was bluster at her like a rough wind. He didn't know what they'd planned for her. He didn't know how it happened. But she did.

She looked up, looked through him. In the wall above her father's body, she saw appear a stained glass window bearing the likeness of an unknown dark-haired woman with the bluest eyes she had ever seen. The light behind it was so bright, her eyes hurt, but she didn't look away.

Nor did she turn her head when she heard the sound of fast-moving water. It lapped against her, its frigid temperature numbing her legs and fingers before creeping up and freezing her arms. The water continued to rise and lifted her off the floor. She floated on her back, as her father taught her, and stared at the window until the woman's effigy cracked. Her chest first, right over her heart, then moved north, splitting the face in two. Light poured out of the broken window like water. It was too much; it hurt. Haleine closed her eyes and let the darkness pull her down.

Her chest ached, her lungs burned. Something somewhere inside her was screaming for breath, for fight and for life. She tried to push her way clear of it. She wanted to drown it.

Haleine.

Haleine did not open her eyes, but it did not stop the blue-eyed woman from appearing in her line of sight. She was no longer made from now-shattered glass. Her body was flesh and bone and bathed in light. The woman reached out to her.

Open your eyes.

Haleine gasped for breath and opened her eyes. The water was gone, the woman was gone, and everything was as it had been before. She saw her father first before glancing at Omur. He was how she had seen him last, unaware any time had passed.

"You are a terrible liar," she said when she could.

"Only when the lie doesn't matter," he replied. "What have you done with my amulet?"

"What have you done with the unicorns?"

"Nothing yet."

"Where are they?"

"In the stables. If you could convince the guards at the entrance to allow it, your lover could visit them himself," Omur said. "He must be very concerned for their welfare. Without them, his rebellion amounts to nothing more than a group of angry farmers with pitchforks. And as terrifying as those farmers may be, I think I'll survive. Now, what have you done with my amulet?"

"I threw it over the side of my balcony, and where it is now, I cannot say," Haleine said. "But I suspect you already know that, just as I suspect you truly want to know how it was I knew to rid myself of your jewel."

"How did you know?"

"I didn't. I hate my husband and I didn't want his damned necklace any longer, so I threw it away. A protest, delayed and worthless as it may have been, but a protest nonetheless."

"You are a terrible liar," Omur said as he swept from the room.

Haleine looked at her father's body. "Only when the lie doesn't matter."

———

After Haleine had left him alone, Faolan began the task of determining how much damage the rebellion had sustained. He knew the human causalities would be great, but he was more concerned about the unicorns. If they were lost, the rebellion would follow. He tried connecting with Luisiúil but couldn't find her. He tried Lorcan next, but he, too, was missing. Fáinne he found. She remained in camp.

Where are Luisiúil and Lorcan? he asked.

Taken, was her answer.

By the humans? How?

They were waiting for us. They captured Luisiúil first, Fáinne told him. *It was easy for them; you know how weak she is. When Lorcan saw they had her, he gave himself over to them, to protect her. He ordered others to do the same—twenty in all—but he ordered Bearach and me to return to camp to wait for you.*

They didn't notice the sudden surrender? Faolan asked next.

They're humans, Faolan, Fáinne said. *Humans who believe they are in the right. There is no creature more blind than that.*

He was still dealing with the battle's aftermath when Haleine returned. He opened his eyes and watched her settle by the fire. There was something different about her. Faolan contemplated her stillness before joining her.

"The unicorns are being held in the stables," she said when he landed in front of her. "We will go there in the morning."

"How did you—?"

"I asked Omur."

"You asked Omur?" Faolan said. "When did you talk to Omur?"

"Just now. He came to pay his respects to my father."

"No, he didn't."

482

"Of course he didn't. He came to taunt me," Haleine said. "Why did you let Dana come here?"

"He wanted to tell you himself," Faolan said. "He didn't want you to hear it from Omur."

"You should have told him I already knew."

"I didn't know you already knew."

"I knew before we went into that courtyard, before you appeared at my window, before a single blade had been drawn in battle, before my father even left this castle," she said. "I knew when he sat in a chair at my bedside and told me of how he would kill Dana."

"How?"

"I told you of my dream, of Dana dueling a man in black. That man was my father."

"You said you'd never seen the ending."

"Oh, I saw the ending. I saw what Dana did."

"In your dream?"

"On a stone slab in the bowels of this castle."

"Then how did you know your father would die? If you hadn't seen it before?"

"They're not all dreams, are they?"

"I don't think so."

"How do you tell the difference?"

"I don't know."

She nodded. "I had another dream. I told you about it."

"Of Dana teaching your son to ride."

"Aye."

"And that's how you knew."

She nodded again. "What did you do to Willem?"

"What do you mean?"

"I mean the man has barely spoken two words to me the entire time I've been in Lira, and never once has he failed to grant any request made of him. Yet he spent much of today speaking to me as you would have and arguing with me the very same way. What did you do to him?"

"How do you know it was me?"

"Who else would it have been? What did you do? Cast a spell?"

"Of sorts."

"Of sorts?"

"When you think of spells, you think of candles and rhymes," Faolan said. "It's what you were taught when your priests told you about the evil and subversive nature of magic. What you don't know is that while some beings need to resort to such crude tactics to invoke higher powers, I don't. My skills are more advanced."

"Then what did you do?"

Faolan took a moment before answering. "I accessed his mind and took control of his actions."

"Is that not an evil and subversive thing?"

"Probably not for me to say," Faolan said. "Omur's likely done something similar to people, most notably Maddox, and I'd prefer to think he's far more evil and subversive than I am. My intent wasn't to harm anyone. I only briefly used Willem to help protect you and Dana. It wasn't hard. The man's rather devoted to your protection anyway. I just had to guide him."

"And speak for him."

"When I needed to."

"Need?"

"Haleine—"

"Do you do this often? Take control of another's actions?"

"No. It's not always easy and can be quite difficult to maintain. I only do it if I must."

"Have you ever done that to me? To make me help you?"

"No," Faolan said. "You've always wanted to help, so it was never an issue."

She was quiet, but the conversation wouldn't be over. He didn't know what she would ask next but anticipated hearing Dana's name come off her lips. What answer would he give her?

"And if it had been an issue?" she said.

"You're not susceptible to my magic."

"How do you know?"

"I tried protecting you in the forest by creating a shield around you. It wouldn't work."

"Is that common? One who is immune to your skills?"

"No."

"Then what does that make me?" Haleine asked. "Something less than human?"

Faolan shook his head. "Something more."

She looked at the fire. Desperation took up residence in her eyes.

"We should—we should talk about that," he said.

"Yes, we should. But not tonight," she said. "I am in mourning."

CHAPTER 25

There had been a moment when the battle at Trutina had ended where James had stood in the middle of the village, in the center of the dead and dying. A taunt and a drawn sword had been the start, but this was its finish, and the rebels had won. He hadn't known it then, but to win at war seemed to be nothing more than to win the right to bury the dead and tend the wounded. James had done it before, more times than he had cared to count, and now he'd do it again.

There were perimeters and prisoners to guard and a new camp location to be found. Supplies needed to be inventoried, and new provisions had to be obtained. They sorted the able-bodied from the injured and the dead from the dying. There were frighteningly few in the former and all too many in the latter. And thus was a victory at war.

Nothing was simple, but caring for the injured was a task made easier when Hanah and the others who had made the exodus at her side returned to camp unharmed.

"An ambush," she told him. "They were waiting for us. I don't know how, but they knew right where to find us."

James knew exactly how the soldiers had found them but said nothing to Hanah. Those were words meant for Dana's ears, for whenever he showed himself again.

That moment came late into the night when Ilya nudged him awake. James didn't even recall having stopped to rest, but now he pushed off the cloak covering him and sat up to see he was one of a small sea of people taking rest and shelter when and how they could.

"What is it?" he asked.

"Dana's back," she said. "Thought you'd want to know."

He nodded and got to his feet. "Where is he?"

"With Hanah. He looked to be injured."

"He was. Have you slept any?"

"Some."

"And Lucius? How is he?"

"Still with us. Hanah says if he makes it through the night, he stands a good chance."

"Owain?"

Ilya shook her head. "He was just a boy. He wasn't strong enough."

James's stomach tightened. "When?"

"Not long ago," Ilya said.

James swore and ran his hands through his hair. "We never should have—"

"There may be many things we never should have done," Ilya said. "Don't count this fight as one of them."

James looked at Ilya for a moment and nodded. "With Hanah you said?"

"Aye."

James crossed the camp to where Hanah had set up, surveying everything as he walked. They were recovering well, he thought, or as well as could be expected. It would be harder in the morning when they began to bury the dead. His head started to turn toward the spot where the bodies had been laid out, but he stopped himself and looked ahead. It was better to keep moving.

When he found them, Hanah was helping Dana remove his tunic. James sat on a log across from the two of them and waited. Dana acknowledged him with a nod. Hanah didn't.

James supposed she was still upset with him over his initial refusal to allow her to care for their prisoners. They'd never had prisoners before. The only men Varro ever left behind were either already dead or so close to it no amount of effort on Hanah's part would have changed their fate. This time, there were ten men in Tanubian colors. All of them had sustained some degree of injury but none so badly that they wouldn't, with proper care, survive. James had killed the captured men in Lanval and was considering doing the same here when Hanah arrived with the intention of seeing to the prisoners' wounds. James refused.

"They would do as much to us," he said.

"They would do worse," she responded. "But no matter what you think you are, we are not our enemy, and I will tend these men. You will stand aside and let me."

"If any of our people die because you've been tending this lot—"

"If any of our people die, it will not be because I have given these men clean bandages," Hanah said. "Now, unless you intend to take me prisoner as well, move out of my way."

He moved, agitated with her for fighting with him. He was agitated still and almost smiled to think that she was, too.

"Who did this?" Hanah asked Dana now.

"One of Haleine's maids," Dana said. "Don't be too hard on her. She was nervous."

"You're lucky not to have bled to death. It needs stitching."

"As she told me repeatedly," Dana said. "There wasn't time for stitching then."

Hanah nodded. "Well, there's time now. I'll fix you proper."

Dana sat. Hanah patted his cheek and frowned as she noticed the bruise on Dana's jaw. She took his chin and turned his head at an angle.

"It's my own fault," Dana said.

She looked doubtful. "Let me get a potion for the pain."

"Nothing that will make me sleep," Dana said.

"You'll want something."

"Not if it will make me sleep."

Hanah nodded once more and walked away. James had a feeling whatever she brought back would render the rebel leader unconscious but didn't say so.

"Did you find the unicorns?" James asked instead.

Dana shook his head. "Faolan will do it."

"Is he going to involve the queen? Has he already?"

"He thinks she'll be needed."

James didn't want to start a fight in front of an audience of the dying so he shook his head and said nothing.

"Did Hanah say what happened out there?" Dana asked.

"Ambush. They knew about the tunnels. They knew where our people would come out, and the king's men were lying in wait for them. By all reports, they hit hard and fast. We're fortunate not to have lost more."

"What of our losses here?"

"Have a look around," James said. "You'll see our losses."

"I know you're angry. I know you wanted me to be here, but I had to go to the palace," Dana said. "The unicorns—"

"You didn't go because of the unicorns."

"Not entirely, no."

"Not at all."

"You have to stop fighting me, James."

"I fight those who do harm to this rebellion, to these people."

"That's not me."

"Isn't it?" he asked. "What about your lover? It's a terrible coincidence that the king's army finds out, after all this time, about tunnels they never knew existed, just after the queen herself returns to the palace with that same knowledge."

"It wasn't her."

"Then who was it? Faolan? They're the only two who knew."

"She didn't tell—"

"Dana!" James looked at the ground. "She told someone."

Dana was quiet for a moment. James lifted his head and saw Dana nod.

"I know."

James walked away, the look on Dana's face and the tone of his voice making him sick. He didn't look where he was going; he just walked away from the light and life in camp. He stopped when he stood in front of rows and rows of the dead. A taunt and a drawn sword had led him to kill his first man. Others had followed, but never had James thought he would one day include Dana in that number.

The next morning, Faolan found Haleine to be more taciturn than ever. She ignored his attempts to speak to her and languished in bed until maids appeared. She bathed and dressed and picked at the breakfast brought for her. She sat silently through the physician's visit. She only nodded when Nonna arrived to report on Sighle's well-being and didn't do anything but stare out onto the balcony when Ceallach arrived to speak to her on the matter of her father's burial. When she offered no answer, he moved on.

"What are your plans for the day?" he asked.

"I plan to stay here," Haleine responded. "I need to rest. I charge you with keeping away those who would wish to disturb me."

Ceallach bowed and left. Haleine dismissed the maids next and sent Willem out to the hall, asking him to succeed where she was sure Ceallach would fail. They were alone, but Haleine still didn't move. Faolan stayed on the vanity and waited. When she was ready, she searched the room for him.

"Shall we find your unicorns, Faolan?" she asked.

She rose from her chair with surprising grace. She crossed the room, walking as though her injuries were never there. He thought of her the day before, the trouble she had getting out of a chair, and wondered what it was Omur had said to her.

She opened the servants' passage and looked at him. "I do not know these halls."

He settled on her shoulder. "I do."

She nodded and left her rooms. Faolan immediately started casting spells to find approaching souls. When one was found, he gave the person a gentle push in another direction. The longer Haleine could go undetected, the better. They moved quickly through the deserted corridors, talking only when she required direction. Haleine didn't speak at all until they entered the empty kitchens. There she stopped.

"This castle is full of people. Normally, you trip over them all, but somehow we've not seen one single person. Where is everyone?"

"They conveniently had to be elsewhere."

"Meddling with minds again," Haleine said. "I thought so."

"How did you—?"

She shrugged and walked toward the exit. "This way?"

The courtyard was harder to manage. There were more people, too many people, for him to control. He diverted the most immediate threats and had to hope someone wouldn't alert Willem or Bronagh to their location. He needed more time.

He didn't bother tampering with the two men standing guard at the stables' entrance. They would be Omur's men, and Omur already knew both he and Haleine would come. For whatever reason, Omur wasn't concerned about losing his quarry.

The reason why was obvious before they had gone too far inside. The residue of magic was like a battlement. Faolan left Haleine's side and flew ahead.

The unicorns were at the very end of the building. The magical barrier forced him to stop well before he reached them. He hovered and examined the situation. The individual stalls had been altered to become one. Luisiúil pushed her way to the front of the herd, Lorcan following close behind. Faolan nodded to them, suspecting their only means of communication would be visual. Lorcan returned the gesture, but the mare wasn't looking at him. She focused on Haleine.

Faolan looked away when Haleine passed him and the point where he had been forced to stop. She continued right up to the corral and looked Luisiúil in the eye. Luisiúil returned the stare. Faolan sank a little lower in the air.

Omur had no idea what Haleine was. Faolan didn't know for sure what she was or what power she might have possessed, but he understood better than Omur. The mage never would have allowed her such unhindered access if he had.

But how would Faolan tell her of her destiny? Months ago she had asked him questions he could not answer, and he swore he would find the truth for her, but he hadn't done that. He'd lied because he hadn't known how to tell her of his suspicions, and now the truth was standing before him, only he still didn't understand what it meant.

How could he have known what she was? The prophecy Haleine was evidently a part of had been in existence for more than seven hundred years, each one of those years spent waiting for her birth. There hadn't been a being like her before and, if she hadn't borne sons, Faolan would say there wouldn't be one after her. There would be no way to know the extent of her abilities without seeing it firsthand. But how would he tell her that? If he wanted her to accept it, she would need more than speculation.

There was a sudden flash of light brighter and louder than lightning. The entire stable shook, and Haleine was lifted off her feet and thrown away from the unicorns. She landed on her back in the center of the stable, arms and legs splayed at concerning angles.

Faolan looked back at the unicorns in time to see the shield repair itself before disappearing from view once again. Luisiúil caught his eye.

She's the one. The first.

The unicorn's voice was faint but there. Faolan nodded.

—◦◦◦—

Bronagh sat in the kitchen, wringing the necks of chickens, when three servant boys tumbled in from the courtyard. They wrestled their way across the room, laughing and joking. One of them acted out what she thought to be a woman fainting. One of the others saw her and hit the other two. The three fell suddenly into silence.

"What are you lot going on about?" she asked.

They looked at each other and then at the floor. She set her chicken on the bench and stood.

"You'll tell me, and you'll tell me now, or I'll see you cleaning garderobes and chamber pots until you're gray."

"The queen fainted," the first said.

Bronagh looked at the ceiling. For a moment, she considered sitting back down and finishing with the chickens. Then she rolled her eyes, cursed herself and started toward the stairs.

"She ain't there," the second boy said.

Bronagh turned, and the boys seemed to shrink in size. "Where is she?"

"The stables," the third offered.

"What was Willem thinking, letting her go there?" she muttered.

"Willem ain't with her."

"Then you find Willem, wherever he is, and you tell him what you've told me," she said.

"We're supposed to find the doctor," the third said.

"You find him, too, send him to the queen's chambers and wait there with him, but you find Willem first," she said. "And God help him if he isn't dead or near to it."

They nodded and ran up the stairs. She went in the opposite direction, through the doorway and arches that led to the courtyard. The sun was bright, more so than in days past, and she put her hand up to shield her eyes.

A crowd gathered in front of the stables, everyone standing on their toes and craning their necks to see what transpired. She ran across the yard. When she reached them, she started to pull them away from the scene.

"Worthless, all of you!" she shouted. "Get yourselves back where you belong!"

Some scattered but more stayed. A path opened up for her, so she left them alone and went inside. After the brilliance of the sun, she was forced to stop and let her eyes adjust. When they did, she saw the unicorns penned at the far end. She stared.

"What are you—?" a voice said. "Oh. It's you. Well, come on."

Bronagh looked away from the unicorns and saw two guards. One came toward her while the other knelt beside the queen. The pegasus hovered nearby.

"What happened?" she asked, going to Haleine's side.

"We don't know," the kneeling guard said.

"What do you mean you don't know?" she asked. "Weren't you watching?"

The guard shrugged. "Wasn't our job to watch the queen. We were watching the entrance to keep people from coming in."

"How did she elude you?" Bronagh asked. "Abandon your post, did you?"

He laughed. "Lord Omur set us here. You don't fail that man. He's the only one around here scarier than you."

"Then how—?"

"He said the queen might come. If she did, we were to let her pass. She came, so we let her through."

Bronagh looked at Faolan. The pegasus stared back at her.

"Here's your man now," the guard said. "Gonna ask him about abandoning his post?"

Bronagh looked away from the pegasus, glad to have a reason to do so. Willem had entered the stable. He walked toward them, looking at nothing but Haleine. He knelt to pick her up and carried her out. Bronagh trailed behind him and the pegasus followed her. They moved quickly through the palace to Haleine's chambers where Rhys and the three boys waited.

"Lay her on the bed so I may examine her," Rhys ordered. "These boys tell me she was in the stables. Why was she there?"

Willem set Haleine down and caught Bronagh's eye as he straightened. He left the room, signaling the boys to follow him. Bronagh glanced at the pegasus as he settled on the vanity.

"She wanted to take some exercise," Bronagh said.

"The next time our queen wishes to take some exercise, I suggest you keep her on her own balcony. The distance will be far—"

Rhys stopped talking. Bronagh rounded the other side of the bed to look at his face.

"What?" she asked. "What is it?"

He had removed the splint from the queen's wrist and now scrutinized the arm closely. "She's not hurt."

"What?"

Rhys removed the bandages from Haleine's shoulder next. Bronagh inhaled sharply at what she saw. Everything was healed as though Haleine had never been hurt at all.

"She's not hurt," Rhys repeated.

Bronagh looked at the pegasus. "What did you do to her?"

"A new—a new poultice," Rhys sputtered. "That is all. I do not know what you—"

"Well, it worked," Bronagh said. "We should be pleased about that. We *are* pleased about that."

"Yes."

But Rhys frowned as he continued his examination. Bronagh searched for something she could use to distract him. She couldn't let him think too much about it. Willem provided the necessary diversion when he opened the doors and came inside.

"You have been summoned," he said to Rhys. "Some of the soldiers from the battle are worsening."

"Yes?" Rhys asked. He took one last look at Haleine and nodded. "Well, everything seems to be in hand here. Nothing more than exhaustion, I think. You will send word when she wakes?"

Bronagh nodded and curtsied, though she would likely do no such thing. Rhys left, and she shared a lingering look with Willem before he returned to his post. Bronagh sat in the chair by Haleine's side and put her head in her hands.

She didn't know what had happened in the stables but knew Haleine had only gone there because of Dana and his rebellion. She lifted her head and looked at the pegasus. Haleine wouldn't be safe until Dana was gone. Sending an army after him didn't work. She would have to find something else that would.

"Where am I?" Haleine asked.

Bronagh stood. Haleine gazed at the ceiling.

"In your bed, in your chambers, which you ought not to have left in the first place," Bronagh said.

Haleine's eyes found her. "Willem must be so angry."

"He's not pleased."

"And you?"

"I don't know," Bronagh said. "What were you doing in the stables?"

Haleine looked back at the ceiling. "I was lost."

"No, you weren't."

"No, I wasn't," she said. "Fetch me some wine, Bronagh, please."

"I'll fetch you some tea."

"Very well. Tea, then," Haleine said. "Is Faolan here?"

"He's here," Bronagh said. "Will you be all right while I fetch your tea, or shall I summon Nonna first?"

"No, not Nonna, not anyone." Haleine closed her eyes. "I'll be fine alone."

"Will you still be here when I come back? Or will I find you in the stables again?"

"Do not scold me, Bronagh. I asked for tea, not a lecture."

"You asked for wine."

"So bring me wine."

Bronagh sighed and walked away. She opened the servants' passage and had almost closed it fully when she heard Haleine speak.

"Faolan?"

"I'm here."

Bronagh froze. She held the door still, opening it only slightly more. She waited to see if she had been noticed. When Haleine continued, she knew she hadn't.

"What happened?"

"You don't remember?"

A pause.

"No," Haleine said. "I was speaking with the unicorn and—"

"What did you talk about?"

Another pause.

"I don't remember," she said. "Did you hear?"

"No," the pegasus said. "She healed you. Do you remember that?"

"She healed me? How?"

"Magic," the pegasus said. "Haleine, I have to leave for a while."

"Leave? Why?"

"I need to get Dana and bring him back here."

"Dana? Why?"

"Do you trust me, Haleine?"

There was another pause, a longer one than before.

"Yes."

"I'll explain everything when I come back. I promise."

"All right."

"Can you keep Bronagh away from here?"

There was no answer this time. She imagined Haleine nodding her consent.

"I will come back as soon as I can, Haleine," the pegasus said. "I promise."

Bronagh heard Haleine get out of bed. She heard the balcony doors open and close. Bronagh closed the servants' door completely and leaned against it.

Dana was coming, and Haleine wouldn't be safe until he was gone. She wouldn't be safe until Bronagh made sure he wouldn't come back. *Couldn't* come back.

She pushed off against the door and ran down the hall. She swore, she made a promise to Michaela to keep Haleine safe, and Haleine wouldn't be safe until Dana was gone.

She ran to the library and pushed her way inside, past the two guards standing there. She fell to her knees.

"What is this?" the king asked.

She lifted her head and saw the king standing in front of her. Lord Omur sat in the corner, looking at her with interest.

"What is it?" he asked.

Bronagh checked to make sure they were alone in the room before answering.

"He's coming."

———

That night, Dana made love to Haleine. They lay together in her bed from dusk until dawn with no worry apart from the giving and receiving of pleasure.

Later, basking in the glow of the morning's light, he lay on his back, Haleine on top of him. Her hair was unbound, encircling him like a curtain. He twisted a piece around his hand and pulled her down to kiss her.

"Do you know," he said, their lips still touching, "how much I love you?"

She smiled and kissed him gently. "I do."

She pulled away from him and climbed out of bed. He tried to prevent her from leaving, but she skirted his attempt and laughed as she reached for her robe and slipped it on.

"Wine, I think, for the both of us," she said. "You'll need your strength."

"Will I?" He grinned as she crossed the room. "And for what will I be needing such stamina?"

When she turned to look at him, her smile was gone.

"For this," she said and opened the doors to her chambers.

Soldiers marched inside. Another moment and they were coming in the servants' entrance too. He rolled out of bed, but there was nothing for him to do but allow the soldiers to take him into custody.

"Haleine," he croaked. "Why?"

Her answer was delayed by the arrival of her husband. Her face lit up as she went immediately to his side.

"I told you to leave once," she said. "Do you remember?"

Maddox drew her close to his body, and she kissed his cheek. She looked at Dana and smiled. "You should have listened."

Dana woke then and found himself squinting at the midday sun. His temper was as raw as his side felt.

"Welcome back," Hanah said, her face appearing between him and the sun.

"You said that potion would dull the pain."

Hanah helped him sit. There was a tightness in his shoulder he hadn't expected. He reached back to feel a linen bandage covering the skin there. He looked down and saw the bandage wrapped across his chest.

Hanah shrugged. "Did you feel anything?"

"I didn't want to sleep," he said, almost growling.

"My mistake." She raised an eyebrow at his abrasive tone. "I decided to take care of your shoulder, too."

"My shoulder was fine."

"No, it wasn't," she said and held out a cup. "Here, drink this."

He looked at the cup. "I don't think so."

"It's only water."

"Laced with what?"

He found his tunic and started to pull it over his head. The bandaging on his shoulder made the task difficult. Hanah sighed and put the cup down to help him.

"Fine. Don't drink the water. Go thirsty if you want, but even if you didn't want it, Dana, your body required sleep," she said. "Not that it's done your mood much good."

He looked at the wounded surrounding him. "Tell me Hanah, how good should my mood be?"

"Well, I didn't mean—"

"Where's James?"

"You have to stop fighting with that boy."

"I have. It's done. Now where is he?"

Hanah sobered. "Seeing to the dead."

"Then that's where I should be."

"Dana, you shouldn't—"

"I'll manage."

He got up and walked away before Hanah could argue with him further. He found James and five others, spades in hand, working next to the rows of the dead. Two spare spades rested on the ground. Dana went to claim one and paused as he spotted Owain's body. He knelt beside the corpse and laid his hand on the boy's chest.

"What are you doing here?" James asked.

Dana stood. "I came to help."

James gestured to Dana's side. "Are you sure you should?"

Dana looked at Owain. "I'm sure."

James didn't seem convinced but nodded, and Dana set to work. They finished one grave, carefully lowered a body into it, covered it, and started the next. They hadn't been working very long when Faolan arrived. Dana saw his approach but chose to ignore it. Faolan coming here meant something else had gone wrong, and Dana didn't want to know what it was.

"The unicorns are in the king's stable," Faolan said. "Haleine asked Omur where they were, and he told her. We've confirmed it's true."

Dana stopped digging. "When did she talk to Omur?"

"Last night," Faolan said. "She was mourning her father. He came to taunt her."

Dana attacked the ground again. "About me. About what I did."

"Yes," Faolan said. "And since we're already talking about Haleine, we have to get her out of the palace."

"Why?" Dana asked. The spade stuck in the ground, and he left it there. "What happened?"

"She's not safe there anymore," Faolan said. "We have to get her out as soon as possible."

Dana laughed and ran his hand through his hair. "It wasn't that long ago, you realize, that she was here and not in the palace."

"I know."

"She wasn't safe here. She had to go back to the palace because she'd be safe there," Dana said, and Faolan looked away. "And now you're telling me the opposite is true. What changed?"

"Do you remember, Dana, when Omur attacked you?" Faolan asked. "Do you remember the dome in which you were imprisoned?"

"Aye," he said and walked away from the graves. Both James and Faolan followed.

"What happened when you touched it?" Faolan asked.

"I told you this before," Dana said. "It burned my hand. It knocked me off my feet when I tried my sword. Why?"

"Omur has a similar spell protecting the unicorns," Faolan said. "Only this one is much more powerful than the first. So much so, I couldn't even begin to unravel it. But Haleine walked through it as though it wasn't even there."

Dana stopped walking and focused on the ground. James stepped up beside him.

"What does that mean?" James asked.

"It means we need her. It means without her, we'll lose the unicorns," Faolan said. "Without them, we lose the rebellion, and without the rebellion, it means your parents, James, will have died for nothing."

Dana looked up. "Faolan."

"You're not going to tell me that harlot holds the key to our success," James said.

"I'm not talking about success," Faolan said. "I'm talking about survival. If you want to keep your head off a pike in the very near future, you'll get her out of there."

"What about the unicorns?" Dana asked before James could counter.

"Haleine can help with that. All you have to do is ask."

"Ask Haleine?"

"Yes."

"Faolan," Dana said, rubbing the bridge of his nose. "I killed her father."

"I know. I was there."

"And you were there in her chambers when she couldn't even bring herself to look at me. She won't want to help me."

"Yes, it is possible she won't want to help you."

"Aye, more than possible," Dana said. "How do I ask for a favor after what I've done?"

"You say 'Haleine, do this for me.'"

Dana shook his head. "She'll say no."

"She won't."

"She might," James said.

"She can't," Faolan said. "Dana, she can't say no to you. Don't you see that? She's done everything you've ever asked her, regardless of the cost. You are her weakness."

"More reason to stay away."

"More reason?" Faolan asked, looking at James. "What reason was there before?"

As much as he didn't want to have the current conversation, Dana knew he wanted to avoid this new topic even more. He watched the remaining gravediggers bury another body before responding.

"Nothing," he said. "No reason. I just—I killed her father, Faolan. I thought—I thought she might need time alone. Away from me."

"You're not doing this. You might be her weakness, but you're also her strength, and right now we need that more than you know," Faolan said. "The moment she walked through that shield, Omur would have known it."

"Why does it matter who Omur thinks broke his barrier?" James asked. "He's always known, hasn't he, that the queen is your ally?"

"If he recognizes her for who she is—who she really is—he will kill her," Faolan said. "And if that happens, you can start digging your own grave."

"Who is she?" Dana asked.

"She's the one," Faolan said. "The first."

"The one what?" James asked. "The first what?"

"I told you about a prophecy, Dana, that spoke to the fall of the goddess and the rise of the dark gods."

"You told me nothing more than that."

"I'm telling you now," Faolan said. "It claims there are two who will bring this about: the first from moon and the next from dark. Haleine's the first."

"Well, she must be some sort of sorceress, the way she's inveigled you both to follow her so blindly," James said. "How do you know she's the first? How do you know she's not the second? How do you know she's anything at all?"

"Luisiúil healed her. She's an excellent judge of character, and I trust her not to waste perfectly good magic on an enemy fated to kill her."

Dana smiled. "She said it was fate."

"Who said what was fate?" Faolan asked.

"Haleine. When we first met, when she was—and I fell through her window, she said it was fate, our meeting. She said she wouldn't turn her back on it."

"Good," Faolan said. "Come to the palace and remind her of that."

"Does that mean you've already asked her?" James asked. "Has she already said no?"

"No. I haven't told her anything about this," Faolan said. "Luisiúil may have, but I don't know and Haleine claims she doesn't remember."

"You say that as though you think she's lying," Dana said.

"I do think she's lying."

"What reason would she have for that?" James asked. "If she's as loyal to you as you say, why would she lie?"

"Because I told her once that if there was a choice between saving the world and saving Dana, I would choose the world," Faolan said. "I suspect she's reluctant to listen to me because she suspects I'm choosing the world over her."

"Aren't you?" Dana asked.

"No," Faolan said.

"I think so, and I don't even *like* the queen," James said.

"No," Dana said, ignoring James's comment. "You want me to do it for you."

"She'll listen to you."

"I won't send her to her death."

"That's not what you do here."

"Isn't it?" Dana asked. "You said your prophecy tells of the goddess's downfall. That would mean those who serve her as well."

"You don't include yourself in that?" Faolan asked.

Another grave. Another body. They would reach Owain next.

"I don't care what happens to me," Dana said.

"Haleine does."

"And I care what happens to her."

"Which is why you need to hear what I'm saying," Faolan said. "Prophecy can be thwarted. It can be rewritten. It can be altered, but what can't be changed is Haleine's part in this. She has powers, Dana, powers that can sustain this fight, and Omur will know it soon if he doesn't already. If you don't act now, that girl you claim to care so much about is going to die. Take her out of the palace, give her a chance to discover who she really is, and let her write her own destiny."

Dana stared at Faolan. Somewhere on his right, he heard James blow out an exasperated breath. Dana understood his frustration. He thought whatever concessions made the night before would be lost now. Dana thought maybe they were weakened but not lost. Not completely.

"This is the only way?" Dana asked.

"Yes."

"Then I'll go," Dana said.

"Dana!" James exclaimed.

"It's our only chance to get the unicorns back," he said. "The state we're in now, we'd never be able to mount an assault on the palace itself. If we're to get them back, it'll have to be with Haleine's help. So I'll go."

"Dana," James started.

"But not alone," Dana continued. "Gather everyone we can spare, James. I'll need you to be there in case anything should go amiss."

"It won't be many," he said.

Dana nodded. "It'll be enough."

"What exactly do you think will go amiss?" Faolan asked once James had left.

"Have you stopped to wonder how Omur found out about the tunnels?" Dana asked. "How he knew where the unicorns would be?"

"Haleine wouldn't have known about the unicorns. That was a decision made when she was long gone from here."

"But she did know about the tunnels," Dana said. "Because you told her."

"You shouldn't listen to James."

"Are you certain?"

"Dana," Faolan said. "Why are you doing this?"

Dana watched as Owain's body was delivered to a grave. "Because she told someone."

CHAPTER 26

Haleine lay in bed as she waited for Faolan to return with Dana, as she waited to hear what Faolan would tell her about what she was now, about what she was that she hadn't been before. She stared at the ceiling, at the clouds and cherubs, until she didn't know what she looked at anymore. Then she rolled onto her side to better hear her heart beat. The strong rhythmic sound was the same as it had always been, and yet, she was different. Not human, but something more so.

How such a thing could be possible, she didn't know, but at the same time she recognized it as truth. Even though she was born to decidedly mortal parents, even though she required air, water or food the same as any, even though she bled and cried the same as any, there was something else within her, something beating as regularly as her heart which marked her as something else. Something, the unicorn had claimed, that had always been within her.

So many times Haleine had heard about Lira's unicorns but had never seen them, apart from their likeness in tapestries or the country's crest. Even her time within the rebel camp had yielded no glimpse of them. But then she stood in front of them in her husband's stables. She had done naught but gape at them until *she* made her way to the front. Luisiúil.

The unicorn's eyes were blue. It was the blue of the lake where her father taught her to swim. It was the blue of the eyes she had seen in a stained glass window that didn't exist. Haleine was drawn to them; anyone would have been. She walked right through the gossamer veil shrouding the unicorns, passing through it as though it were not there at all. Faolan stayed behind, and for that Haleine was glad. He didn't belong there.

Your eyes are her eyes, Haleine had said.

The unicorn tilted her head. *And yours as well.*

I cannot see it.

You will.

Haleine slid off the bed and walked onto the balcony. Eluned was gray today, and the land surrounding it. It was always gray, the whole damn country. She knew that hadn't always been true; there had been a time when the land was green and beautiful and alive. She didn't know when that had changed, but it was gray now. She spent day after day looking over it all, and never did the palate change.

Do you know who I am? she'd asked the unicorn.

Do you? had been the reply.

She was Haleine. She had to be Haleine, daughter of Darian and Rhoswen, sister to Sighle, lover of Dana and mother to his sons. She didn't know how she could be anything else.

Do you know what I am?

The one, the first.

The sky wasn't gray. It tried hard to be blue. Apart from a paled sun, the only thing in the sky was a pair of golden-brown hawks soaring on the air's invisible currents. She watched them ascend and plummet and rise again.

What does it mean to be the one, the first?

Not one among us knows.

Knowing there was a name for it, for her, was frightening. Knowing there was nothing but mystery surrounding it was worse.

Not Faolan? He knows naught?

Faolan has tried always to protect you. Let him.

Faolan tried always to protect his cause. He took what he wanted, used what he needed and sacrificed what he must. Two men in Tanuba. Her mother. He would sacrifice Dana as well if the war came to that but said he never expected to have to make such a choice with her. Would he have said as much to appease her? Just as he had once told her he would find the answers she wanted and explain all when, it would seem, there were no answers to be had?

How do I tell truth from lies?

Your heart will guide you. You must trust its lead.

Her heart had led her parents to their death. Her heart betrayed her constantly. She could not trust anything less.

Her heart also told her to lie. It was not often she lied to Faolan, and maybe she hadn't now. There was a look about him when she said she didn't remember that suggested he didn't believe her. But he went anyway, despite his cause hanging in the balance, to fetch Dana, to have her lover tell her what sacrifice he needed her to make now because the pegasus would choose the world over all else, but she wouldn't.

What choice would Dana make?

He will ask for your help, the unicorn had said. *It may well be you are the only one who can help us now.*

She watched the hawks continue their elaborate and effortless dance. They were drawing farther away now, and soon they would be gone from her sight. She wanted to disappear with them. Her heart told her that, too.

Fight or flight? Flight or fight? It didn't matter how afraid she was. There was still a war to be fought, and she would do whatever she had to. Dana would ask, and she would say yes. She always did.

"What are you doing?" Bronagh asked then.

Haleine turned around. "Wishing I were a bird."

"What?"

"Nothing." She came back inside. "I'm doing nothing. What are you doing?"

"Nothing," Bronagh said and gestured to the tray. "Well, I brought you tea."

Haleine looked at it. "I asked for wine."

"Well, I brought you tea. Are you sure you should be out of bed?"

"No," Haleine said. "I need you to find Ceallach for me. I would like you to tell him I have decided on the matter of my father's burial."

"Oh, I'll tell him you want to see him immediately."

"I don't want to see him. I don't want him anywhere near here. I want you to tell him what I wish him to do."

Bronagh's eyes flashed. "And what is that?"

"Tell him to take my father's coffin across the ocean to Tanuba. His heart is there, his heart was always there, and his remains should lie alongside my mother's."

"Of course."

"My sister should be allowed to say her farewells before the ship sails, but do not allow the coffin to be opened," Haleine said. "I do not wish her to see what this war has done to her father."

"Yes, your majesty."

"One thing more, Bronagh." Haleine walked to her desk and picked up the letter she had written earlier and held it out to her maid. "Tell Ceallach this is to be placed in the hands of Prince

Revelin. If I hear any but he has fulfilled this task, I will not be pleased."

Bronagh took the letter. "I will tell him."

"Stay with my father until his coffin is loaded on a ship pulling away from the harbor."

Bronagh stiffened. Haleine walked past her and sat down by the fire.

"I trust you to do this in my stead," Haleine said. "I know you will not fail me."

Bronagh curtsied. "Of course not, your majesty. I'll see it done."

Haleine dismissed the maid with a wave of her hand. Bronagh walked out of the room, her irritation showing in her stride. Haleine didn't know what the woman was upset about now but wasn't concerned. She'd know before long. Bronagh's anger always managed to boil over.

The sun was starting to set when the servants' passage opened once more and Dana walked in. She still sat in her chair, watching the logs in the fire slowly crumble to ash. Faolan drifted into her line of vision and landed on the table.

"Should you be out of bed?" he asked.

She looked away from the fire. Her eyes passed briefly over the pegasus and settled on Dana. He kept his distance on the far side of the room. Fight or flight.

"Your unicorn healed me, did she not?" Haleine said.

An act of faith, Luisiúil had called it as she dipped her majestic white head. They stood so close, the creature's horn grazed her cheek before coming to rest over her heart. Haleine wanted to move away but was held in thrall by the other unicorns before her. Every beast there looked at her the way Luisiúil had, seeing the something within her that Faolan saw, the something the goddess needed. She held their gaze for only a moment when all was replaced by a sudden white-hot flash. She woke in her bed, looking at that damned ceiling.

"She isn't my unicorn," Faolan said.

Haleine looked at him. "You like to do that, don't you?"

"Do what?"

"State the absolute truth of any challenge made to you, no matter how minor."

"Haleine—"

"You must always be right. You must always be in control."

"I do prefer it to the alternative," Faolan said. "Are you sure you—?"

"How you must hate this," she said. "You must hate knowing that everything you've worked for these seven hundred years somehow now rests in the hands of someone you think perhaps you cannot control. You must be concerned."

"Well, not until just now," Faolan said.

"That is a lie," she said. "You are concerned. He would not be here otherwise."

Faolan looked at Dana. She did as well, and he looked back. He was wary, like a deer in the forest, assessing the threat posed to it and prepared to bolt at the first sign of trouble. What had Faolan told him? Had he said she was the one, the first? Had he explained to Dana what that meant? Did it frighten him, too?

"Haleine, did something happen while I was gone?" Faolan asked. "Did Omur—?"

"Omur has done nothing."

"Was it something Luisiúil said?"

She looked away from Dana. "I told you I don't remember what she and I spoke of."

"I know you did, but you were lying. What did she say to you?"

"She said you are a liar. She said I am the one, the first, and she said there is not one on this earth who knows what that means. Are you the liar, or is she?"

"Luisiúil never lies," Faolan said. "And while I have been known to tell the occasional fib, I've never lied to you about this."

"Then what answers would you have given me when there are none to be had?"

"Not very good ones," he said. "I can only tell you what I suspect to be the truth about the prophecy and—"

"I do not want to hear about prophecy," Haleine said. "I put no store in such nonsense."

"You did once," Dana said. When she looked at him, he went on. "You said our meeting was fate. You said you wouldn't turn your back on it."

"Faolan told you to say that."

Dana nodded. "He did, but it doesn't make it less true. You've yet to turn your back on this. You've kept the rebellion going—you've kept *me* going—from the very start, no matter what it cost you, because you wanted to see the evil ended," he said. "Has your father's death changed that?"

The unicorn had posed the very same question. Had Darian's death changed her so much?

Should I not be changed? Haleine asked in response. *The man did give me life.*

And you brought him death.

Haleine nodded. She did do that.

Why? Luisiúil said. *It is the question Omur did not ask.*

Why didn't he?

He didn't know he should.

Why do you ask?

Because it is in your mind.

And you know what is there?

The unicorn could not smile, but Haleine could see it in her eyes. *We have been talking at some length for some time, Haleine, but you have yet to speak. Yes, I know what is there.*

Then tell me why I let him go.

The same reason you threw yourself in front of Revelin's sword. The same reason you let your mother carry a letter. The same reason you—

Stop.

War is about sacrifice, Haleine. You know this. We sacrifice what we think we must as an act of faith that what we do is just. That what we do is necessary to win our fight. Our war. Do you still wish to fight?

Haleine nodded then, and the unicorn dipped her head to perform her healing magic.

An act of faith.

Now, Haleine looked at Faolan, standing on her table, nervous but resolved. She looked at Dana, standing in the room's darkest corner, standing where she, believing him to be forever lost, had once sought refuge. An act of faith.

"No," Haleine said finally. "I want it to end."

"Then help me free the unicorns," Dana said. "Help me keep this fight going, at least for one more day. You're the only one who can."

"Because I am the one, the first," she said.

"Aye."

"I do not know what that means," she said.

"No one does," Dana said. "But we will find out together."

She looked at him and found herself lost in the azure eyes she had long loved. They had brought her heartache and pain. They had brought her hope. Life.

You think perhaps you should not love him, not after all he's done.

I never should have loved him.

But you did. You still do.

She did.

"Haleine," Dana pressed. "Do this for me."

He will ask for your help. It may well be you are the only one who can help us now.

She watched Dana but saw Faolan give a small nod of approval. The choice was made. She nodded as well and then, not knowing why she did it, turned her head to look at the chamber doors.

"Haleine?" Faolan asked.

"You shouldn't have come," she whispered.

The doors opened and Willem came inside. He threw the doors closed and stalked across the room, shooting a tense glance in Dana's direction. "Go."

Haleine stood as Dana bolted for the servants' passage. The door there opened and soldiers flooded inside, forcing Dana back. Willem did the same to her, pushing her around the chair and to the side of the fireplace.

"For your life, keep quiet," he said, turning and drawing his sword.

Over his shoulder, she saw more soldiers invading her chambers. They came through both entrances now. They surrounded him.

"Dana—" she started.

Willem whirled around and clapped his hand over her mouth, crushing her against the wall. When Willem dropped his hand, she fell to the floor.

"Quiet," he hissed. "Not one sound."

She nodded, but he had turned before he could see it. She huddled on the floor and listened as Dana was taken into custody. They wouldn't kill him. Not here. Not now. They would want it to be public. They would want to send a message; they wouldn't kill him here. There would be time for rescue, for *something*. Faolan could—

Faolan. Where had he gone?

"Bring him forth so that I might look upon my enemy."

Maddox. Haleine struggled to stand. She finally grabbed the hem of Willem's tunic to help haul herself up. He bore her weight and put out his arm to keep her behind him. She clung to him and watched as the men holding Dana presented him to her husband.

"Whatever happens, whatever they do," Willem whispered, "stay quiet."

She gripped his arm tighter as she considered what they would do. They would hurt Dana—oh aye, they would, but they wouldn't kill him. Not here. Not yet.

"Where is my wife?" Maddox asked.

No. Willem tensed more and adjusted the grip on his sword. The soldiers standing in front of them parted.

"Here." She released Willem's sleeve. "I am here."

She stepped around her guard, avoiding his eyes. He was afraid for her, but he didn't know better. They wouldn't kill her, either. Omur's gods didn't want it. Not here. Not yet.

Maddox's captain caught her elbow and dragged her forward. Willem moved to follow, but Haleine heard the other soldiers stop him before he could make it far. Varro dropped her on the floor at Maddox's feet.

"Now, Varro, that will never do," Maddox said. "I'll have her treated with more respect than that. It is, after all, my lady wife's doing that we are all gathered here this day. It is because of her I can now do this."

Maddox drove his fist into Dana's face. Once, twice. Someone cried out. Blood sprayed as her lover's head snapped back. The blood hit her dress, her neck, her face. The men holding Dana staggered but quickly recovered their balance and thrust him forward again.

Maddox held out his hand. "You gasped, my dear?"

Did she? She did not remember it. She supposed she was fortunate it had not been an outright scream. She got to her knees and looked at Maddox's hand. The knuckles were raw and bloodied.

"Concern for you, my lord." She took his hand. "You have hurt yourself."

She kissed his knuckles. Maddox twisted his hand free and laid it on her cheek.

"It does not concern you?" Maddox asked. "My striking this man in your presence?"

"This man is the reason my parents lie in pieces," she said. "What is a little blood when compared to that?"

Maddox raised her up. "I will have more when I am through."

She nodded. "You will bleed him dry."

He smiled. He twisted her head to the side and licked Dana's blood off her cheek. He was aroused now. Another moment, and he'd take her here and now, in front of all. She braced herself for it, but he only turned her face back to him and used his thumb to part her lips. He glanced at Dana before kissing her. She closed her eyes during the kiss and, when Maddox pulled back, forced herself to look at Dana. There was nothing behind his eyes.

"You shouldn't have come," she whispered.

"I see that now," he said, his tone as dead as his eyes.

"Bring him below," Maddox said. He searched the room and pointed at Willem. "You stay with the queen. The rest of you will come with me."

They left then, just as abruptly as they came. The doors closed behind them and she heard the click of the lock before moving to stand in front of them.

"Are you all right, your majesty?" Willem asked. "Are you hurt?"

She placed one hand on the door, then the other. She rested her forehead between them and closed her eyes.

"Are you hurt?" Willem repeated. "Your majesty?"

He took her arm and pulled her back. She looked at him and shook her head. No, she wasn't hurt. Willem's expression softened, and he released her arm to place his hand on her cheek instead.

"He knows," Willem said. "He knows why you did it. He understands."

She wanted to believe him, and maybe she would have had she not seen Dana's eyes. Those beautiful azure eyes that had once brought her hope had brought it crashing down. She turned away from Willem and retreated to a dark corner to wait.

———

The night the king and queen had been joined as man and wife, James sat in a borrowed room and made an ill-received jest about kidnapping the woman with whom Dana was obsessed. *Kidnapping the bride on her wedding night certainly would've been one way to make our mark on the kingdom*, he'd said. Now, a year later, he stood in the same room, looking at the same palace and thinking about everything that could have been avoided if they only had done just that.

He should have gone with Dana inside. They all should have. Gone right up to the queen's chambers and carried her out, regardless

of whether she wanted to come, before anyone even knew they had
ever been there.

But both Dana and Faolan refused, claiming a need to move
cautiously, so James and the others he'd brought from camp stayed
at Orla's and waited. Most of the men who had come with him
were now in the barroom and keeping watch outside of the tavern,
but James, Rhydwyn and Gair stayed in the room to watch the
palace.

When he first spotted Faolan, he didn't realize what he was seeing. When the pegasus grew closer, James turned from the window
and barked out an order for Rhydwyn and Gair to rouse the rest.
He was gathering his weapons when Faolan flew inside and landed
on a table.

"They have Dana."

"I told you she was a traitorous bitch," James said.

"We can talk later about who is or is not a traitorous bitch,"
Faolan said. "First, let's get Haleine and the unicorns out of the
palace."

James stared at the pegasus with narrowed eyes. "Let's get
Dana out of the dungeon, you mean."

"I'm sorry," Faolan said, "but no."

James sat on one of the beds. "They're going to torture him."

"Quite a lot, I'd think."

The agreement was so offhand, James wanted to slap him.

"They're going to kill him," James said.

"Eventually," Faolan said in a tone that suggested that if he
could have shrugged, he would have.

"Faolan!"

"James?"

He shook his head. "You did it, didn't you? You chose the
world over Dana."

"I did that a long time before now," Faolan said. "It had to be
done; it couldn't be helped. We can survive now without Dana if
we have to, but I can't say that about Haleine or the unicorns. We
get them out first. We take care of them first. Then we worry about
Dana. If he's still alive."

"If he's still alive?"

"Provoking Maddox to kill him will be less painful than the
torture."

"What happened in that room?"

"Not what you think."

511

"Really?" James said. "I'm sure Dana's in the dungeon right now trying to get Maddox to kill him because his whore's done nothing."

"Or because he knows this could be just the opportunity we need to get Haleine and the unicorns to safety."

"Dana's death will never be an opportunity."

Faolan nodded. "And that's why Dana's the leader and you're not."

"Well, I'm the bloody leader now, aren't I?" James said, standing to better confront Faolan. "And I'm telling you, I'm not going to leave him there. Neither will those men I have below stairs do a damned thing for *her* without my or Dana's say-so."

Faolan was quiet for a moment. "And you certainly won't say so."

"No, I won't."

"Well, then, we should probably go. We have a lot to do," Faolan said, "especially as we're starting with a suicide mission in a heavily guarded dungeon."

"Meet us outside," James said, ignoring the pegasus's tone as he headed for the door. "The queen's pet can't be seen in the barroom."

"It's good to know you're back on Dana's side," Faolan called after him.

James closed the door behind him. "I never wasn't."

———

Dana did not fight the men holding him. He allowed them to drag him through the palace halls and down to the dungeon. They threw him on the floor of a cell. He didn't move.

"Chains," Maddox said.

Chains were brought and attached to rings. They lifted him off the floor and shoved him against the wall. Iron cuffs were clasped around his wrists and ankles. His arms were raised above his head. Hanah's careful work was being ripped to shreds. He was bleeding again, but he did not care. When the men released him, Dana slumped down. The chains prevented him from falling to the floor outright.

"Leave us," Maddox said.

The men left. Dana kept his eyes fixed on the floor. He heard Maddox's approach and saw the tip of the man's boots. There was a flash of color, and Dana found himself without breath as Maddox's fist lodged itself in his gut. He gritted his teeth and let out no sound. The next blow was harder and in the same place. It was hard to keep silent. It was hard to keep from vomiting. The third blow was to his head. Maddox, using the flat of his palms, struck Dana's ears and forced him to look up.

"Just making sure I have your attention," Maddox said.

"Oh, I'm sorry," Dana said as best as he was able. "Did you want something?"

"You've always amused me. Do you know that?" Maddox said. "I don't know what I'll do once I've ripped out your entrails."

What did entrails matter?

"I'm sure you'll think of something," Dana said.

"I'm sure I will," Maddox agreed. "You seem upset. Did you truly love my wife as much as that?"

More. He didn't say it aloud, and his lack of response inspired Maddox to strike him again, this time in his freshly bleeding side. Dana barely transformed the scream into a loud, short burst of laughter.

"Did you love her?" Maddox demanded.

Faolan would protect her. He'd get her out of harm's way, if he hadn't already.

"Loved to fuck her," Dana said.

Another punch. Another scarcely choked cry.

"Did that make you angry?" Dana gasped. "What will you do when I tell you what a good whore she made?"

The answer was to punch his side once more, but this time the king let his fist linger and grind into the wound.

Maddox dropped his hand. "Only as good as I told her to be."

That gave Dana pause. Maddox smiled when he saw it.

"Quite the actress, isn't she? She nearly had me convinced the sons she bore were actually from my seed. But I know better. They have the eyes and hair of a man who is not me."

Those children could be mine, he'd said to Faolan.

They're not, had been the reply.

Dana slumped as much as his chains would allow.

"Oh," Maddox said. "She didn't tell you that, either?"

It wasn't true. The king was trying to save face.

"I think I'll go and throw them in a well when I'm done here," Maddox said.

"Oh, don't lie," Dana said. "We both know you'll keep my bastards because you've already given them claim to your throne. If you came out now saying they're the offspring of your enemy, begotten on your wife, everyone will know you for the useless coward you are."

"Coward am I?"

"You run away. You always run away. You've never fought me. You've never met me on a battlefield. Instead you send others to run away in your place."

Maddox hit him again, this time across the face. "I'm not running now."

"That wouldn't have anything to do with me being chained to the wall, would it?" Dana spat out blood. "Because that doesn't make you craven at all."

Maddox drew a short dagger from his belt and plunged it into Dana's gut. Dana screamed. There was no way to avoid it. The pleasure in Maddox's face was unmistakable. He gripped the blade's handle and drove it in deeper. Dana hung his head and laughed. Maddox's hand jerked in surprise, and the blade cut him further, but Dana only laughed harder.

"You dare laugh?" Maddox asked.

"Oh, I dare," Dana said, looking up. "I do."

Maddox ripped the dagger out and held the blood-drenched blade at Dana's throat. Dana nearly passed out.

"Go ahead and laugh now," Maddox growled.

"My lord king!" Omur shouted. Maddox paused and turned his head toward the sound. "You do not want to do this. Not this way."

Maddox stared at Dana as he contemplated the validity of Omur's statement. The dagger didn't move. A moment passed and something changed in Maddox's eyes. Omur had intervened. Maddox pulled the knife away and sheathed it. Dana laughed and Maddox lashed out, his hand grinding into Dana's stomach until Dana screamed again.

"You should have stayed dead," Maddox said.

Dana hung his head. "You might be right."

Maddox left but Omur stayed behind. He lingered in the cell's doorway.

"Your dog almost slipped his leash," Dana said. "You should be more careful."

"I should say the same to you. One in your precarious situation shouldn't taunt the king like that." Omur stepped inside. "If I hadn't been here to stop him, he might have killed you just then."

"As opposed to killing me later? After days of unbearable torture?"

"What do you think that belly wound will be?"

"Don't plan on living long enough for that," Dana said.

"I hate to see you giving up the fight."

"Don't stay."

"Why the rush to die? Don't think anyone's coming to save you?"

"No one is."

"Because your pegasus wants Haleine more?" Omur asked. "That must hurt after all the years you two had together."

"Well, she is an awfully good tumble. I can't say I blame him."

"You don't have to continue this persona with me, you know," Omur said. "I bear no amorous feelings toward the queen, so talking so crudely about her won't provoke me to do anything."

"I'm not trying to provoke you to do anything."

Omur walked forward, stopping just in front of him and examining him for something as yet unknown. Dana stared back, not wanting to give Omur the satisfaction of looking away. Omur smiled.

"The king's very good at torture when it comes to whips and chains and hot pokers and whatnot. He likes to hear his victims scream. He likes to see them cry, but he loves to watch them bleed," Omur said. "And he'll do all that to you. You'll scream, you'll cry, you'll bleed. Everyone does, and he hates you more than most. It will be agony. I'd say you'd plead for death before the end, but you're already doing that."

"I haven't begged him for death, and I won't start."

"Not in those precise words, no, but pleading for death, begging for death, you are. A master of torture, a reveler in the art of pain, is our king, but he doesn't realize the most exquisite source of pain is found here." Omur laid his hand on Dana's chest, right over his heart. The mage's fingers dug into his flesh as though he meant to rip it out. "You're already bleeding more than you show. His words cut you worse than any blade ever could."

"His words were nothing but lies."

"Most of them, yes," Omur said, dropping his hand. "He was, as I'm sure you suspect, trying to salvage some sense of pride. No man likes to be made the fool of by a woman, especially his wife. Maddox knows, as do you, that no matter the ending to this messy affair, she did love you once."

Once?

"You probably thought it was Bronagh who betrayed you to the king," Omur said. "She certainly hated you enough, but then she's always hated you. With all the hate and all the opportunity, why would she ever wait until now?"

"If you don't mind, I'd prefer torture by hot poker."

"I'm sure you would," Omur said. "Her defection started after her mother's death, if you'd care to know. I do not know what happened in the forest that night that chased her back here, but whatever it was, whatever you did, I should thank you, for when that girl awoke, she was ready to spill her secrets. Tunnels, cloaks, daggers—"

Daggers? He looked at Omur who saw the question in his eyes and nodded.

"Yes, I know of the dagger you gallantly left your mistress to help protect her. She didn't give it to me when I asked," Omur said. "I wonder why. Perhaps it meant her betrayal of you didn't come as easily as it seemed."

Her betrayal. It had to be a lie. Faolan would have seen it; *someone* would have seen it.

"Well, at least not until you decapitated her father. It was that, I think, which turned her completely. They were at odds, I hear, when it happened, but I am also told there is a difference between being at odds with your father and not caring when someone cuts off his head. Did you know I saw her that night? Did she tell you? I saw her sitting in front of his corpse, looking about as lost as any one person could."

This man is the reason my parents lie in pieces, she'd said. *What is a little blood when compared to that?*

"You went there to taunt her," Dana said. "About what I'd done."

"Yes, she would think that, but I went there to pay my respects," Omur said. "I rather liked Darian. I appreciated him. I knew when I saw him kick in that boy's face I would be sad to lose his acquaintance."

"What are you trying to provoke me to do?"

"Nothing."

"Why are you here? Why did you stop your dog from killing me?"

"Did you really think I'd let you go that easily?" Omur asked. "No one is coming to save you, Dana. No one. You're going to die, and it will be brutal, and it will be horrible. And when you're screaming and crying and bleeding and lying in your own filth, praying for that last breath to leave your body, I just want you to know how it came to be."

"You hadn't mentioned the filth before," Dana said after a moment. "The king enjoy that, too?"

"Provided you're dead at the end," Omur said. "And you will be."

"Everyone dies someday."

"Not everyone," Omur said. "You should have surrendered when you had the chance."

"This only would have happened sooner."

Omur shrugged. "She wouldn't have hated you. You wouldn't hate her."

"I don't."

Omur smiled. "Who is the liar now?"

Dana didn't answer. Omur laughed quietly and walked away. The door closed and the jailer locked it. He tested the door with a firm shake and disappeared as well.

Dana slumped again, letting the chains support him. The shackles dug into his skin, hurting his wrists. He could feel the blood running down his arms. How long would it take before he lost feeling there? How long before he lost feeling everywhere?

The dungeon was strangely quiet. There was the occasional shout, a prayer to nameless gods for salvation, a cry for mercy, for food, for water, for rescue. Dana shouted nothing. He continued to slump and listened to the blood pounding in his ears. He would pass out before long.

Some of the prisoners were howling now. Screaming and yelling. He threw his head back and looked at the ceiling. He wrapped his fingers around the chains keeping him up. It made the pain return, worse than before, but he didn't care. The sooner he was unconscious, the better.

"Well, locked in and chained to the wall. The king really doesn't like you, does he?"

Dana released the chains and saw James standing at the cell door. He understood the howling now. He heard the jingle of the jailor's keys and the sudden click of a successful match. James pushed the door open and stepped inside. He was blood-spattered and grinning slightly.

James had seen it. He knew her for what she was. *She'll be the end of you,* he'd said.

"And you had such high hopes for the opposite," Dana said. "What are you doing here?"

"Rescuing you," James said. "What do you think?"

"You weren't supposed to—"

"Well, I did. What, you want me to leave you here?"

Yes.

"No," Dana said. "Get me out."

James nodded and set to work finding the proper key for the chains. "Faolan didn't say what happened. Did she—?"

"Just get me out."

James nodded again. They didn't speak again until both sets of chains had been removed. Dana leaned against the wall, his hand pressed against his side.

"Where is everyone else?" he asked.

"With luck, they're still holding our way out. Without luck, they're either dead or in irons on their way here."

"And Faolan?"

James shrugged. "Don't know. Off plotting my capture, maybe. He didn't want me to come."

Dana hadn't wanted James to come either but only nodded. "The queen? Where is she?"

James looked at him for a moment and shrugged again. "Her chambers, I suspect. I told Faolan we wouldn't do anything for her without your say-so. We still won't. But if you say we need her..."

She'll be the end of you.

"No," Dana said. "We don't need her."

CHAPTER 27

The Lady Sighle hadn't wanted to bid farewell to her father at all. She remained sequestered in her chamber, so the body of Lord Darian Coileáin left the Liran palace without regard from either of his daughters. The coffin was loaded into a wagon and Bronagh rode beside it to the harbor. There, she walked alongside the coffin as it was carried aboard the ship meant to bear it to its final resting place. It was stored in a corner of the cargo hold. Bronagh was left standing alone, looking down upon it.

Haleine sent her here, to get rid of her at the pegasus's request. *I trust you to do this in my stead*, Haleine said. *I know you will not fail me.* Bronagh laid her hand on the coffin. No, she would not fail her.

"Bronagh?"

She quickly drew her hand away and turned to see Ceallach standing behind her. She bobbed a curtsey and he acknowledged her with a nod.

"The captain intends to depart," Ceallach said. "Unless the queen meant for you to travel to Tanuba as well, you will need to disembark now."

She thought about saying yes, the queen did mean for her to make the journey to Tanuba. She considered leaving everything to resolve itself without her. The voyage would take days—nearly a fortnight there and back—and it would be over by the time she returned.

She looked at Ceallach and the letter tucked in his belt. "No, I need to return."

She stood on the dock and watch the men cast off the lines. When the ship was well on its way, she climbed in a wagon headed for the palace. She rode with the other servants sent to attend to the queen's father. They spoke of missing a meal, hoping there would be something warm waiting for them. Bronagh did not think of food. She thought of Haleine and whether the scene set to play out in her chambers had yet ended.

She knew the moment she entered the courtyard. Everyone was talking about what had happened in the queen's chambers. The rumors that had circulated for so long had been confirmed. The queen, the rebel leader and the king. A terrible triangle that would, for certes, result in bloodshed. They feared for the queen. Bronagh didn't. Omur had only wanted Dana, and now he had him. Haleine would be safe.

Bronagh made her way to Haleine's chambers. Two guards stood in the servants' passage, in front of the door. She hadn't expected them and stopped to stare. They weren't Willem's men. One of them nodded at her and moved aside so she could pass. She nodded back and walked inside.

Haleine's chambers were darkened, the only light coming from the fire. She saw the pegasus near there. Haleine sat in the opposite corner, Willem crouched in front of her. He looked at Bronagh briefly when she entered, saw she wasn't a threat, and turned back to Haleine.

"He knows," he said. "He understands."

"What happened?" Bronagh asked.

Willem ignored her but Haleine turned her head sharply.

"Why do you ask what you already know?"

"I don't—I don't know."

"Liar."

Haleine turned away again. Willem held out his hand to her and, after a moment, she took it. He squeezed it gently. Bronagh took a step back, surprised by the sight. She'd shared a bed with him for years now, and never once did she think she'd seen a gesture as intimate as that one. She walked away, suddenly cold, to throw another log onto the fire.

Bronagh stood near the balcony doors, listening to Willem's continued murmurings, when the servants' passage opened again. This time, Willem was immediately on his feet, his sword drawn. He shielded Haleine but lowered the weapon when Dana entered. James followed behind him. Dana carried no weapon, but James's sword was out and bloodied. She looked past them to the opened doorway they had come through. How many men had died upon that blade this night?

Haleine gasped when she realized who had come. She lurched to her feet and pushed past Willem to reach Dana. The rebel leader was bleeding again, worse than before. Bronagh took account of his wounds. She didn't know how the man was still standing but couldn't imagine he would be doing so much longer. Haleine hadn't yet noticed his injuries. She threw her arms around him and clung to him. He swayed but maintained his balance. He tolerated her embrace but made no movement to return it.

"Dana, what's wrong?" Haleine asked, pulling away from him. "Oh Dana, look at you. Oh, you're hurt. What did they do to you? Come and sit. There must be something here to use to slow the bleeding. If we just slow it down, it'll be all right. The unicorn, Luisiúil, she can heal you as she did me. I'll do whatever Faolan says I must to get her out, and she can heal you as soon as we're away from here."

"You're not coming," Dana said.

His tone was low and guttural. Haleine shrank from him. Bronagh did the same. This wasn't the way it was supposed to happen.

"I'm not?" Haleine asked.

"She's not?" Faolan said.

"That's not what I'm here for," Dana said.

"Then for what are you here?" Haleine asked.

"The truth. They said you betrayed me," Dana said. "Maddox told me you lay with me at his command, that it was all at his command."

"He lies," she said. "Dana, you have to know that he lies!"

"He says your boys are my sons. Does he lie about that, too?"

Haleine hesitated, not for long, but for long enough. Dana took a step away from her.

"You never told me," he said.

"I couldn't," she said. "I had to keep that secret. I had to, to protect them, to protect you, to protect me."

"My sons!" He pounded his chest with his fist. "*My* sons."

"Yes, your sons," Haleine said. "Sons you could not bear to know. Sons you shunned from the moment you learned of their existence."

"Is that when it started, Haleine?" Dana asked. "Omur thought it came with your mother's death, but was he wrong? Did you turn from me when our sons were born?"

"I never turned from you."

"All evidence points to the contrary."

"Evidence?" Haleine breathed. "What evidence is there?"

"He said—"

"His word? You would take his word over all I have done to help your war?"

Dana backed away. "He has no reason to lie."

"He has one," Haleine said, following him. "Dana, don't do this. You're hurt and you're not thinking clearly. They fed you lies; they forced you to swallow them and made you believe, but it isn't true. You have to see that."

"Don't do what you're doing, Haleine," Dana warned.

"You can't ask me that. You can't ask me not to love you because I can't help it," she said, her eyes now brimming with tears. "The heavens know I've tried to stop it. The heavens know I've had every reason to, and yet, I'm still here, my heart bleeding for love of you."

She reached for him, but he caught her wrist and pushed her away. She stumbled back, lost her balance and fell. Willem moved forward and Haleine put her hand out to stop him. She got to her feet and stood again in front of Dana.

"Ready to die for you, he is, just as I was once," Dana said, glancing at Willem. "Spread your legs for him, too, did you?"

Haleine, tears now spilling over, slapped him. Dana responded in similar fashion, and the sound reverberated through the chamber. Haleine crumpled to the floor. Bronagh choked and started forward. Willem immediately bolted toward the queen, his hand already on his sword's hilt, but was stopped just as suddenly. James stood with his arm outstretched and his sword across Willem's chest.

"Lower your arm, boy," Willem said.

"Not bloody likely," James responded.

Willem's next move was so quick, Bronagh never would have known what he had done if she hadn't before seen him teaching the technique to new members of the guard. He grabbed James's sword hand with his left, and with his right, Willem rolled James's shoulder, disarming and flipping James onto the floor. Willem threw James's sword to the side and drew his own, causing enough noise to draw the attention of both Haleine and Dana.

"Willem, no!" Haleine cried as she got to her feet once more. "Stop it!"

Bronagh held her breath. Willem hesitated as though he were tempted to ignore her command. He looked at Haleine with more anger in his eyes than Bronagh had ever seen, but she doubted

Haleine noticed. Haleine walked forward and placed herself between the two men. Willem relented and took a small step back but did not sheathe his weapon.

"I *never* turned from you. Even when I should have," Haleine said to Dana. "Get out."

"James, get up," Dana said without taking his eyes off Haleine. "We're done here."

"Yes," Willem said. "You are."

Dana looked at the guard in silence. His expressionless eyes remained as such. James's mouth twisted into an unfriendly smile as he stood and recovered his sword.

"Faolan," Dana said as he walked away. "Let's go."

"No," the pegasus said.

Everyone stared at Faolan. Willem hadn't known the pegasus could speak and now gawked at the little beast. Bronagh remembered she wasn't supposed to know, either, but it probably didn't matter anymore.

"Faolan," Dana repeated. "We're leaving."

"Yes, I can see that," Faolan said. "You do what you have to do, but I'm not coming with you. You're on your own."

Dana nodded. "So be it."

If the pegasus's defection threw him, Dana didn't show it. He just walked away without another glance at any of them. James followed, and the servants' passage closed behind them. For a moment Bronagh felt as though they had taken all the air in the room with them. When she recovered, she looked at Haleine.

The queen stood motionless where Dana had left her, her face stricken and her eyes dry. Her hands hovered above her stomach, fingers clutching at her gown. Haleine swayed as though about to faint and Willem caught her. She rested against him, then shook her head and pushed away. She moved unsteadily across the room and sank to her knees in front of the fire.

No one moved. Haleine stared at the flames and Bronagh and Willem watched her do it, waiting for her to guide them. The pegasus didn't look at Haleine at all. Bronagh could feel his eyes on her. He must have known what she had done. She took her eyes off Haleine long enough to glare at Faolan to let him know she didn't care.

And she didn't. It had to be done.

"Bronagh," Haleine said eventually. "I want you to fetch me water for a bath."

"You want a bath now?" Bronagh blurted.

"Yes."

Bronagh stared at the back of Haleine's head but still saw the pegasus tilt his head. The request concerned him. Bronagh knew it and didn't move.

"Bronagh," Haleine said. "Now."

She relented and passed Willem. She opened the servants' passage and was about to step inside when Haleine called the guard to her. Bronagh stopped to watch. She hated him and his blind devotion in that moment. She hated that Haleine loved him for it. The queen would only hate Bronagh even though she had done more than anyone to keep her mistress safe.

But she knew that would happen. And she didn't care. She didn't. It had to be done.

Willem knelt at Haleine's side and the queen turned her sad face toward him.

"I have to ask you to do something," she said. "Something you will not like."

"I am yours to command, your majesty."

"I need you to go—I *want* you to go and watch over my sons," Haleine said. "I want you to protect them as you have me. I need to know they are—I need to know your last breath will be spent in their defense."

Willem nodded. "I will see it done, your majesty."

"Yes, I know you will." Haleine kissed his cheek. "If their father should come for them—"

Her voice faltered. Willem reached out and put his hand on her cheek.

"I will see it done, your majesty," he repeated.

She nodded and he rose. He brushed past Bronagh without a word. He stepped over the bodies of the fallen guardsmen without breaking stride and disappeared down the corridor. Bronagh looked at the dead men and followed Willem, leaving Haleine alone with the pegasus.

Bronagh went to the maids' quarters first. She expected to have to rouse them to prepare the queen's bathwater, but none in the room were sleeping. They sat on pallets and stood in groups, talking about the queen and the rebel leader and the king's anger. She stood in the doorway, unnoticed, and listened to them.

"He's gonna kill her," a woman named Frann said. "You mark my words."

"He won't," Bronagh said.

The gossip came to a halt as everyone looked at her. Frann smiled and came forward.

"That girl made the king a cuckold," she said. "He won't suffer that."

"That girl's your queen," Bronagh said.

Frann nodded. "But not for much longer, aye?"

"He won't kill her," Bronagh said.

They didn't believe her, and she didn't know why they would. They all looked at her in silent accusation. *You've lost another, Bronagh. How could you?* They didn't know. They didn't understand.

"The queen wishes a bath," Bronagh said.

"What?" Frann asked. "Now?"

"Aye, now," Bronagh said. "See to it."

"If it's what the queen wants," Frann said.

"It's what she wants," Bronagh said. "There are two men outside her rooms. They're—you won't tell anyone about them. Not yet. Not if you care about her."

"We're fond of the lass," Frann said. "All of us."

"Then keep your mouth shut."

"Bronagh," Frann said. "The king—"

"He won't kill her," Bronagh said. "Bring the water."

She turned and let the whispers chase her from the room. She went to Omur's chambers next and found the man awake and standing in front of the balcony doors. She wondered if he ever slept.

"It is late to come calling," he said without turning around. "Have you brought me something new, Bronagh?"

She should have been surprised that he knew her without seeing her. It should have bothered her.

"No," she said. "I just—Have you gone back on our deal, my lord?"

"What deal is that?"

"The rebel leader for the queen's life."

"Oh," Omur said, turning around. "That."

"Aye, that," Bronagh said. "You said if I helped you get Dana—"

"I no longer have Dana, now do I?"

If he knew, why hadn't he done anything about it? No alarm had been raised, no soldiers called. What was he waiting for?

"That was not my doing," Bronagh said. "Nor the queen's."

"How can I be sure? You were willing to sell out your mistress, why not me?"

Bronagh shook her head. "I didn't. I haven't. You said, my lord, you said you had no interest in punishing the queen."

"I still don't," Omur said. "However, I believe the king might have different plans."

Bronagh felt ill. "Do you mean he'll kill her?"

"I would be surprised if he didn't."

"But you can—you can stop it," Bronagh said. "You can stop him. You have to."

"No," Omur said, turning his back. "I don't."

Knowing she'd been used and dismissed, Bronagh went back to Haleine's chambers. She wasn't wanted there any more than she was wanted anywhere else, but she didn't know where else to go.

Haleine sat at the vanity, looking in the mirror as she tied off her braid. She had discarded her gown in favor of a robe. The other maids must have been there earlier, but now the only other soul in the room was the pegasus, standing near the fire.

"I would ask where you've been," Haleine said, "if I did not already know your answer would be a lie."

"What?"

"Did you go to Omur and tell him how I am weathering this latest storm?"

"No," Bronagh said. "I went to him to ask the extent of your husband's anger."

Haleine stood and turned around. "I imagine he is furious."

"He is. He thinks you've done—"

"Exactly what I have done."

"Aye. You should not have sent Willem away. He is your protection."

"Not anymore," Haleine said. "That time has passed."

She walked to the bathroom and closed the door behind her. Bronagh looked at Faolan.

"It was me."

Faolan didn't respond. He looked at her blankly.

"It was me," she repeated. "I told them Dana was coming."

The pegasus continued to do nothing but look at her like the stupid beast she'd always thought him to be.

"What is wrong with you?" she demanded. "I know you talk."

"Oh, I know you know," Faolan said. "And I know it was you. I was just trying to decide why you thought I might be interested in having a conversation with you."

"I'm trying to save the queen. I thought you might be interested in that."

"You're trying to save the queen?"

"Aye."

"Interesting claim," Faolan said. "How long have you been Omur's lackey?"

"I'm not anyone's lackey."

"How long?"

Bronagh looked down. "After the Lady Rhoswen died. After the queen was hurt."

"Did you approach him, or did he approach you?"

"He came to me. He said he knew everything, the treason she'd committed. He said he only wanted Dana. He said he had no interest in harming the queen."

"And you believed him?"

"What was I supposed to do?"

"Not believe him."

"I thought I was saving her."

"You weren't."

"I know that now," Bronagh said. "Maddox is going to kill her."

"He's going to try."

"And what will stop him?"

"Too soon to say."

"What does that mean?"

"It means it's time for you to run along now, Bronagh. Your services here are no longer wanted."

"But I can help."

"You can help?" Faolan said. "I have to be honest. I don't want your help."

"I'll go to Dana, then. I'll tell him it was me. I'll tell him she's innocent."

"Why would he believe you?"

"I'll make him believe me. Just tell me where he is and—"

"You want me to tell you where he is?" Faolan said. "I don't think so."

"He's in the city. I know that. The gates are closed and he can't get out until morning. Tell me where he is—"

"No."

"Tell me where he is so I can go and convince him of the truth. Then I'll help—"

"No."

"I'll help you and Haleine—I'll help all of you get out of the city tonight."

"By way of the king's dungeon?"

"Stop that and listen to me," Bronagh said. "You have to get out. You have to get *her* out, and you have to do it now. Omur knows Dana is gone, yet no alarm has been raised. He's waiting for something, and she can't be here when that happens. I can help you."

"How?"

"There's a passage, like the one in the kitchens, but in the city walls. It's unguarded."

"Does Omur know about it?"

"He might," she said. "But he doesn't know that I know."

"How do you know?"

"Willem told me."

Faolan nodded. "All right. I'll take you to Dana."

"Wait," Bronagh said. "You're going to leave her alone?"

Faolan looked in the direction of the bath chamber. "She's not alone."

———

Haleine leaned against the door. She could not hear what Bronagh and Faolan were talking about, but she could feel their argument all the same. Let them quarrel all they wanted. She did not care.

She looked at the bath the maids had prepared for her. The scent of lavender and chamomile filled the air. Did Bronagh request the herbs be used, or had it been someone else who had heard the gossip of what she'd done and thought she might now be in need of calming?

Regardless of how they came to be there, the herbs were unnecessary. She was calm. As calm as Dana had been when he walked out of her chambers. He wouldn't be back.

Do what you have to do, Faolan had said, and Dana had done that. Now she would do the same.

She looked at the window, at the glow of the nearly full moon. She crossed the room to stand in the light. She pushed open the glass and closed her eyes as the night breeze caressed her face.

When the wind grew more insistent, she opened her eyes and found herself standing on the edge of a great jutting promontory. Behind her were the mountains and the forest. Before her was the moon and below lay the ocean, deep and vast and silver in the night. What color would the water be in the daylight? Blue like the eyes of the moon or gray like Lira, gray like everything that stayed in this place too long?

There was only one way to know, only one way to be sure. Haleine glanced at the moon.

"Laorans," she whispered. "Are you there?"

She took a step forward, off the edge, but instead of falling, the wind caught her and threw her back. She struck stone and fell forward, landing on the smooth stone floor of her bath chamber. She looked at the window and saw the pale, dark-haired woman standing before her, robed by light.

"I am here."

A single tear escaped and slid down Haleine's face. "Is it true, then? Am I what they say I am?"

"You already know the truth."

"Still, I would hear it from you."

"You are the one, the first, Haleine. You are my one trueborn daughter."

"That is no small thing to be."

"Indeed not."

"That is no easy thing to be."

"You are not a thing at all, Haleine."

Wasn't she? Wasn't she some elusive, mythical creature, like the unicorns, like Faolan? Wasn't she more than that? Nothing was known about her apart from her name. Neither the unicorns nor Faolan could share that claim. She was the one, the first, always the same, and always spoken in that manner as though it were the name of a deity. Even when spoken by one.

"Why do you think you are alone when you are not?"

Haleine didn't answer. Offering a response of any sort—be it truth or falsehood—would lead only to more lies, more empty words designed to elicit her aid. Faolan had done it, as had the unicorn. Why would their goddess be different? They needed her to keep their war going, to survive another day. They wouldn't want the next sunrise to be their last. They would say or do what they had to because she was the one, the only one who could help them now.

"Do not think so ill of me, Haleine. It is true that I am desperate, but to manipulation I have not yet fallen."

"Your agents practice it freely."

"As have you, I think."

There was truth in that. She had spun quite a few tales of her own. Her husband, her mother. She was no better than the rest of them.

"I did it for him," she said.

"They do it for me."

"And you are worth that?"

"They believe so. Just as you believed."

"What if I no longer believe?"

"If that were true, you would not have called upon me."

"Why did I call upon you?"

"You already know the answer to that. You do not need me to tell you. You've known precisely what you meant to do ever since you entered this chamber. Why do you delay?"

Haleine shrank back as far as she could, ducking her head and drawing her knees to her chest. She wanted to make herself as small as possible. She wanted to crawl deep within herself, where perhaps it was safe. The dam within her, so carefully constructed so long ago, was damaged beyond repair now. She couldn't be who she was without him. Neither did she know how to let him go. She felt the goddess's eyes upon her and lifted her head to meet the stare but turned away and looked at the bath instead.

"I am afraid," she said. "I do not know what will happen."

"No one does. What you do now is—"

"An act of faith. A damned act of faith."

"Yes. It always comes back to faith, Haleine. Always."

"My faith was in him."

"I know."

"I didn't betray him."

"He will know it soon enough."

Damn him. Damn him for this, for everything.

"He should know it already," she murmured. "I never turned from him."

"I know."

"Even when I should have, I didn't."

"Will you begin now?"

There it was. Would she begin now? It smacked of the manipulation Laorans thought herself to be above. It was the same treatment she had received from the unicorn. From Faolan. From Dana. For one spiteful moment, Haleine thought about saying yes. Yes, she would begin now. She would turn from Dana, from Faolan, from Laorans, from everyone. She wouldn't be used; she wouldn't be exploited again. Damn them all for thinking otherwise.

Haleine looked back at the goddess, at her eyes, and the moment passed. She shook her head and dried her tears. The dam would hold a little longer.

"Tell me what you would have me do," Haleine said, "and I shall see it done."

———

Dana leaned heavily upon James as they stumbled together through the city streets. James sang snatches of songs and maintained a steady stream of nonsense so they would appear to any passing patrols as nothing more than a pair of drunkards making for their beds. The other men James had brought were scattered, some gone on to Orla's to summon the alewife to their need, some lurked just ahead and others behind, all seamlessly blending into shadow. No one else would have ever noticed them.

When they reached Orla's, someone held the door for them. Two men came inside while the others stayed outside to keep watch. Dana raised his eyes to see the barroom unexpectedly empty and terribly quiet.

"You look like you're seeing a ghost," James snapped.

Dana shifted his gaze to Orla. She stood in front of her bar, looking as though he was, in fact, some sort of apparition.

"Am I?" she asked.

Dana didn't respond. He didn't know what she saw. He didn't know what was left. What had stayed behind in the palace and what had survived?

"He's not dead," James said. "Where is everyone?"

"Kicked them out when your lad told me you were coming," Orla said. "He didn't tell me you were this bad off though, Dana. We'll get you above stairs, and I'll send for the doctor."

"You'll send for a doctor?" James asked. "You can't send for a damn doctor!"

Orla's hands went to her hips. "Where's your knife?"

"What?" James asked.

"Where's your bloody knife?"

"What do you want with—?"

She spotted the blade tucked in his belt before he could finish the sentence. She pulled it free and dragged it across her forearm before dropping the knife on the floor. Dana watched blood fill the gash.

"There, I've cut myself," Orla said. She turned to look at one of the tavern boys. "Go and fetch Midhir. Tell him I need his help."

The boy ran. Orla stooped to pick up the knife. She wiped the blade on her skirts and tucked it back in James's belt.

"Who's Midhir?" James asked.

"A man who knows how to keep quiet," she said.

James looked at Dana, searching his face for a sign as to how to proceed. Dana knew Midhir and summoning the man posed little threat, but he still didn't want treatment. But to refuse would require him to speak, and he didn't want to do that either. Dana kept his focus on Orla's arm. James's eyes turned there as well.

"You didn't have to do that," James said.

Orla shrugged. "Come on, let's get him into bed."

"All right," James said. "Let's go."

Together, they helped him above stairs and into the room with a view of the palace. They lowered him onto one of the beds. He groaned before he could stop himself, and Orla's eyes glistened. He closed his eyes so he wouldn't have to see.

He fell into darkness then and dreamed of Haleine. They lay together on her bed, sinking into the softness of the mattress. He lay on his back and she on her side. One hand supported her head. The other traced lazy circles on his chest.

"I don't want to dream of you," he said, wrapping a lock of her hair around his hand.

"Then don't."

"I don't know if I can control that."

"The leader of the rebellion needs always to be in control."

"Am I that still?"

Her fingers trailed down his chest to his navel. "Faolan will return," she said. "He'll come back to you."

Her hand pressed on his stomach and he cried out. He came awake suddenly. Haleine was gone, and Midhir hovered over him, his hand on Dana's stomach.

"You're awake, then?" Midhir said with a faint smile. "I must say I've seen you looking better, lad."

Dana nodded and turned his head toward the window. James stood there, watching both the exam and the palace.

"Nothing," James said when he saw Dana looking. "There's nothing. Maybe they don't know yet."

They knew. Their escape had been much too easy. Omur let them go. Maybe it meant nothing. Omur, after all, now held the unicorns and Haleine. The rebellion was helpless without them— why bother chasing him down? Perhaps Omur was planning something else, but Dana didn't want to think about that. He couldn't change it, nor could he stop it. Let it come and finish him. It would be easier. God, it would be that.

"The side wound only needs to be stitched again," Midhir said. "But the belly—it is quite serious, I'm afraid."

Dana nodded again. "Just do what you can."

"I'll give you a potion—"

"No," Dana said.

"But the pain," Midhir protested.

"What about the pain?" Dana said. "No potion."

"But—"

"You heard him," James said. "He doesn't want it."

Midhir looked at James. Dana didn't. How was there still loyalty there? He didn't deserve that.

Midhir relented. He cut away the remains of Dana's tunic and set to work. He cleaned the side wound first. When he started to stitch it together once more, Dana closed his eyes.

This time Haleine waited for him in his tent. She sat in a chair next to the table, her hand tracing the outline of a map of Lira. He stood just inside the entrance.

"I don't want to dream of you," he said.

"I don't want to dream of you," she returned.

He stepped fully inside and walked to the other end to stand behind her. Her eyes followed each step he took. When he stopped, her head turned away and she once again focused upon the map.

"Is that what you do now?" he asked. "Dream?"

"I don't dream anymore. Mayhap I never did."

"I don't understand."

"As if it were a matter of that."

Her hand left the map as she stood. She didn't turn to look at him.

"Where are you going?" he asked.

She walked to the entrance. "You'll know soon enough."

"You broke my heart," he called before she could leave.

"That was bound to happen, a love like yours."

"A love like mine," he said. "What happened to us, Haleine?"

"The same thing that happens to all fools in love. The dream ends, and the world that doesn't want them spits them out."

He nodded. "I can't dream of you anymore."

She looked over her shoulder. "Then open your eyes."

He did and found himself back in a room above Orla's tavern. His cheeks were wet, and his entire torso felt as though it had been scraped raw. He tentatively felt the bandages and lifted his head. Midhir was gone. James sat in a chair by the window.

"How long have I been asleep?" Dana asked.

"Not long," James said.

Dana lowered his head. "Where's Midhir?"

"Tending to Orla's arm. He did what he could for you, but he says the belly wound will likely—"

"Kill me."

"Aye."

Dana sat up. "He's right."

"I don't think you should..."

Dana stood next. He went to the wall and leaned against it. "I don't think it matters, do you?"

A knock at the door spared James from answering. It opened slightly, and Orla's face appeared.

"Dana," Orla said. "Faolan's here."

Faolan? What did Faolan want with them? *You're on your own* had been the pegasus's last words to him. The finality of the tone had been unmistakable. Dana was done, he was out. Out of favor with Faolan, with Laorans, all of them. What had brought Faolan around? And why had he bothered going through Orla?

"Dana?" Orla said.

Dana nodded. "Let him in."

Orla opened the door wider and stepped back. Faolan flew inside, followed closely by Haleine's maid. Dana looked away immediately. James stood.

"What is she doing here?" he asked. "Did you bring the royal guard along, too?"

"*She* came to talk to Dana, not you," Bronagh said as she closed the door. "You can leave."

"He'll stay," Dana said, turning toward her. "What have you to say to me? Your mistress send you here to beg me on her behalf?"

"No."

"Then why are you here?"

"She didn't betray you."

"Ah," Dana said. "She sent you to lie for her."

"No. She doesn't know I am here at all," Bronagh said. "She didn't betray you. It was me. I told them you were coming. I told them everything. She didn't know I overheard."

"You told him everything? You gave him a cloak?"

"Aye."

"And the dagger I gave her? You told him about that, too?"

Bronagh looked uncertain. "Aye."

Dana lowered his eyes and focused on a knot in the floor. "Now you lie for her."

"No, I—" Bronagh sighed. "Of course I lie for her. I've lied for her, and to her, and done everything else I've thought was right to keep that girl safe. It's why I'm here now, begging for your help, when I can hardly stand the sight of you."

"What do you think I will do for you? Or her?"

"Save her. Come back to the palace with me and—"

"The next time I go to the palace, it'll be for my sons and my sons only," Dana said. "I'll do nothing for her."

"Your sons? Willem guards your sons now. Did you know that? And you'll never get near them. Not without the queen."

"He can't keep me from them."

"He's going to take great pleasure in doing just that," Bronagh said. "He watched you rip that girl's heart out, and he would've killed you where you stood if she hadn't stopped him."

"I ripped her heart out?"

"You crushed her."

"She lied to me!"

"So did I," Faolan said.

Dana looked at the pegasus. He'd settled himself on a small table near the door.

"She didn't tell you those boys were yours, but neither did I. I lied first even," Faolan said. "When I first told you she was pregnant, I lied. You asked me if I knew the father, and I said I didn't know, but I did. And the night they were born, I looked you right in the eye and told you they didn't belong to you."

Dana turned his back on them. He put his fists against the wall and laid his head upon them. He clenched his teeth. The downpour had become a maelstrom. He didn't know how he'd be able to keep his head out of the black much longer. He didn't know why he should bother. He lifted his head slightly and pounded the wall once and then a second time, harder than before.

"Dana, please," Bronagh said. "You have to take her away. Get her out of the palace and get her somewhere safe."

He had done that already. He fucked her in the forest, made her squeal, made her sob. He told her he loved her over and over and over, and still she walked out on him. Still she returned to her goddamn husband. He hit the wall a third time. A fourth.

"Whatever happens now," Dana said, "she brought it upon herself."

"You brought it upon her. Everything she's ever done has been because of you, and now you abandon her. I'm not surprised," Bronagh said. "Never once have you acted in her best interests, only your own. I don't know why I thought you might change now. You do not deserve my lady's love."

Dana whirled around. "Your lady's love is poison," he spat. "I wouldn't wish it upon my worst enemy, which is ironic since I think she does love my worst enemy."

"Since I think you are your own worst enemy," Bronagh said, "I am forced to agree."

Dana grabbed the back of a chair and threw it to the floor. "Get out of here," he shouted as he advanced upon her. "Go back to your whore of a mistress and you—"

He was interrupted by something sounding like an explosion. The tavern shook, sending Bronagh tumbling into him. He caught her instinctively as he looked to Faolan.

"What is this?" he asked. "Is this magic? Who's doing it?"

Faolan didn't respond. He was riveted to the window. Dana started to look as well, but a sudden flash of light forced him to avert his eyes.

"Faolan," he demanded. "What's happening?"

"Dana," James said. "You should—you should probably see this."

He pushed Bronagh away, but the woman stayed on his heels as he went to the window. James stepped aside to allow him access. Dana saw the expression on James's face and hesitated, afraid to know what had happened. Bronagh was not bothered and pushed them both out of the way. She gasped, and Dana finally stepped to the window to see why.

A beam of light coming from the moon surrounded the palace. It hurt to look directly at it, but Dana didn't look away. Horror swallowed him, and he used the wall to steady himself.

Dana knew little of magic, never caring to know more, but he understood that that was what was happening here. The one responsible was a mystery, though, as he could not imagine there were many with the power to perform a spell of this magnitude. Luisiúil came to mind, but Faolan claimed she was locked in an impenetrable spell of Omur's doing. A nearly impenetrable spell, Dana reminded himself. There was one other, one who had walked through that spell as though it had not existed.

There was a second explosion then, smaller than the first, and the unicorns were suddenly free. They broke through the palace gates and stampeded through the city streets. It stopped his heart to see it.

She'd done it. She'd done it for him. She'd done it in spite of him. His eyes watered, and still, he didn't turn away.

"Witchcraft," Bronagh whispered. "Sorcery."

When the last of the unicorns disappeared from his view, Dana stepped from the window and looked at Faolan.

"She's not wrong," the pegasus said.

CHAPTER 28

Seven hundred years Omur waited and plotted and planned. Seven hundred years he bowed and scraped and kowtowed to an increasingly numbing line of mortal men, the next always weaker than his predecessor. Seven hundred years he spent walking an invisible line between being entirely indispensable and altogether forgettable. Seven hundred years he had done this, and done it gladly, so his lords might once again move unencumbered over this land.

Seven hundred years were suddenly gone, lost in the span of a single breath.

The first blow had been a fist to his gut. The second knocked him to the floor. Omur struggled to respond, to fight back and stop the intrusion, but the attack had come so swiftly and so unexpectedly, there was no true chance for recovery.

He did what he could against it, against her, but it had not been enough. She had broken him, and now he lay stricken in front of his balcony doors, drenched in the light of a brightly burning moon.

The orb's brilliance stood as testament as to how badly he had failed. He stared at it, unblinking. His lords would be rather more than displeased with him now. He was quite honestly surprised they hadn't already swooped down upon him to finish what Haleine had started. Seven hundred years gone in the blink of a girl's eye. It was far from his finest work.

He had underestimated her. He did not think her stupid. After all, she had survived thus far. There was intelligence somewhere within her. He never doubted that, but he had thought her weak. He'd thought her too knotted with fear and doubt. He had thought her too entwined with the rebel leader to be an effective threat. But now he lay helpless in her wake. Did she know what she had done? Could she begin to grasp the magnitude of her actions? Did she realize how close she was to destroying everything?

Well, he could not wait to find out. Left alive and unchecked, Haleine would finish what she began. The pegasus would get to her if he could, and he would tell her that which Omur didn't want her to know. If she didn't already know it. Left alive and unchecked, Haleine would destroy them all.

So he wouldn't leave her alive. Yelsneh had requested it, and Omur never meant to disobey, only postpone for greater gain. He thought he had seen the end of his long-traveled road and had grown eager. He'd grown impatient, forgotten the lessons learned from his masters and rushed that which should not have been hurried. Now all he had gained was lost, and all he could hope to do was recover something from the ruin.

Laughter erupted from deep within him. How low had he fallen that he now relied upon hope? But he would do just that; he would do anything necessary to salvage something of his plan. His survival—his lords' survival—depended on it.

So he would hope.

What he could not do was see to Haleine's demise himself. He would have to trust Maddox to see it carried out, for even if Omur were not so stricken, he could hardly face Haleine so soon after his defeat. She would not fear him as she once had. Omur remembered a day where he held her against a wall, his fingers wrapped around her pale, slender throat. She feared him then. He heard her tell the pegasus so, but she was afraid no longer. She knew she could cause him pain. She'd done that before, although she did not know it. Her swift, angry slap that day months ago burned him, but she walked away without seeing it. Sabine's mortal tricks had done well enough to cover the scars ever since.

He fingered the scars now, pausing to wonder if Maddox would be enough. Would Haleine succumb to him? If he released the beast, would the lamb remain as such? Or would she recognize the power she could now wield against a long-abusive husband? And if she did, what would he do? He had to know. He had to be prepared. The rebel leader and the pegasus both would come for her, and Omur could not afford to lose her.

She is a means to an end, Yelsneh had said.

She was more than that, Omur realized now. Had his lords always known? He thought of his orders, of Yelsneh's unspecified special interest in the girl. No, they had to have known. And for whatever reason they had not told him, he could not deny what was plain before him. Haleine was a child of prophecy, of their prophecy, his scripture. She was—she *had* to be—the first. There was no other explanation.

Two from one, the prophecy started. *They'll come, they'll come. The first from moon, the next from dark.*

The first, the servant of the moon, of Laorans. The next, the second, was a child of Yelsneh, Lamak, Azia and Gargon, of dark and malice, of pain. If Haleine was the first, who was—

"My lord?"

Omur lifted his head to see who entered. A guardsman stood there, his head bowed.

"What?" Omur said.

"The Lady Sighle is here. She requests an audience with you."

The Lady Sighle. Two from one. Perhaps he owed Darian more than his appreciation. Omur smiled and stood, leaving the moon to her own devices. He brushed off his robes.

"By all means," he said, "let her in."

Haleine sat with her back against the wall and looked at the moon, suddenly shining brighter than that to which she thought it had a right. Swelling with the return of her faithful flock, the goddess had left to tend to them. The goddess had gone, and Haleine was alone.

But she wouldn't be for long.

They were coming for her. Both of them. Her lover, awash with guilt, came at the request of his conscience. Her husband came as well, blind with anger, coming unknowingly at the request of his master, for he was too weak and limp to see to her death himself.

This will not be easy, the goddess had said as she held out her hand.

Haleine looked at it, the smooth perfection of the pale skin, the elegantly slender fingers. They had been hers once. But that was true no longer.

This will not be easy, the goddess had said as Haleine took the proffered hand. *He will try to stop you.*

He will fail, Haleine promised.

And he had. He tried, he failed. Her hands, once beautiful and refined, bore the proof. Red, angry, blistering welts began at her fingertips and traveled up to her elbows. She could not see them past her wrists—the robe covered them—but she could feel them. They pulsed but did not hurt. She knew they should, but she supposed she was too broken, too hollow for something so human.

She told her mother once of this. Dana would leave her for the final time, she claimed, and that day would mark her end. She said it to shock Rhoswen, to make her mother cringe to think of the degradation and weakness to which her daughter had fallen victim. She had not meant it as prophecy, yet the truth it had become.

The very moment she'd taken Laorans's hand, the very instant she gave herself over to the goddess, she ceased to be Haleine. She became an instrument, a weapon incapable of feeling pain, incapable of feeling anything. A weapon, used and set aside, sheathed until needed again.

There would be time before that happened. Omur had expected a fight. That was obvious from the moment she had set foot in the stables. But he had not expected her. That, too, had become obvious.

Before, when she had gone with Faolan, the shield surrounding the unicorns was nothing more than a curtain sewed from sheer fabrics and as easily defeated. It was different now. Omur knew someone, something, had passed through once; he didn't want it to happen again.

The shield now was a sterner consistency, solid, but still fluid, milky white and difficult to see through. She could barely make out the unicorns on the other side but could see their shapes, amassed at one end and watching her as they had before. Luisiúil stood at their head, her eyes piercing everything.

"I will release you," Haleine said.

But how to go about it? She didn't know any spells. Faolan said some beings required rhymes and chants, but he was not among them. It would stand to reason she would not require such tools either.

Reason. It was ridiculous to think of reason and magic within the same breath. It was ridiculous to think of reason at all anymore. It had been long abandoned and lost.

She stared at the shield. She could hear the heat, feel the words and see the whispers holding it together. She could reach in as though it were a pond and snatch a word and pull it out like a small, silvery fish, wet and wriggling and fighting.

She put her hand out but stopped just before she made contact. She slowly curled her fingers inward and drew her hand away. If she touched it, Omur would know. She couldn't stop once she began.

If she did, if she hesitated even for a moment, he would destroy her instead. There would come a time when she wouldn't care about that, but it wasn't now.

"I will release you," she said again, this time not looking at Luisiúil.

She would do it to show Dana she could. He thought he knew what it was to hurt, what it was to be hurt, but she would prove he knew nothing. Faolan had gone to his side, so Dana would know what she was about to do was not of Faolan's doing. So Dana would know that his precious goddess had her precious beasts back because of Haleine and only her. She would see him hurt. She would—

No.

She would do it because it needed to be done.

She thrust her hands into Omur's shield. The heat burned her, searing her skin. Her fingers curled around the words, tearing them apart. The heat, the life, his anger, came rushing back, fighting and pushing into her, scorching every part of her it touched. She responded with all she had left. Everything she'd kept behind the wall poured out. Love, hate, grief, the cold, the emptiness, the death within her heart. She forced it onto him, into him, freezing the spell and turning his shield to ice. The words were dying. The whispers were shouts, outrage and pain. Omur was not dying, not yet, but he hurt.

The shield hardened beneath her touch, and she lifted her hands from it. The air was still and cold. One last shriek fought its way free, and she reached out without thinking and snatched it from the air. She closed her fingers around it and crushed it. She felt it die, and when she opened her fist, nothing was there. Luisiúil now stood in sharp focus. A stallion pushed his way to the front and stood just behind the mare.

"Do it now," Haleine said. "Do it and be free."

The stallion inclined his head and turned. As he prepared to kick the shield, the other unicorns backed away. Only Luisiúil stayed, watching Haleine.

The shield shattered easily when the stallion struck it. Shards washed over her like sand. She closed her eyes and let them. Her eyes reopened when the first of the escaping unicorns knocked her back. She stumbled into an empty stall to avoid being trampled. A luminescent Luisiúil was the last. She stopped in front of Haleine, the stallion back in the shadow created by the mare's brilliance. Her head dipped, and Haleine jerked away before she could be touched. She swayed, hollow and exhausted, and fell back, but instead of landing on a pile of soiled straw, she collapsed on the bath chamber's floor. She lay there for a while before sitting up to lean against the wall. She hadn't moved since.

But now they were coming for her: one thinking to save her, one meaning to kill her. Omur didn't want to make the same mistake twice. He didn't want her to catch him unaware again. He wanted her destroyed before she finished what she'd started. But sending Maddox for her showed the mistake already had been made. Maybe he thought he was loosing the hawk to dispatch a sparrow. Maybe he thought she couldn't fight back, but he was wrong. Fight back she could.

She turned from the moon and looked at the bath. The water would have lost its warmth by now, but that didn't matter. Its purpose would still be served. She tried to push herself up, but her hands refused to support her. She looked at her legs, ungainly sticks, and willed them to move. They resisted, stubborn and mutinous bones, atrophied and useless. They had forgotten how to move, and she had forgotten how to make them.

But their laziness was unacceptable, and she could not allow it further. Too long had she wasted already while Maddox and Dana came ever closer. Anger and guilt so thick, it choked her. They were coming, and she did not wish to be found by either one. She wanted to be far from their reach before they even set foot within her chambers. She couldn't wait any longer.

She fell to her side and rolled onto her stomach. Her arms were reluctant to work, but they obeyed, dragging her across the small room. It was only when she reached the white marble that her legs seemed to remember their purpose. They lifted her so she could lean over the side and peer down at the water. Its smooth surface acted as a mirror, and she looked at her reflection briefly before seeking to distort it with her burnt fingers.

The moment's serenity was broken when Maddox's boot pressed against her back, hitting her with enough force to cause her legs to buckle. Her chest hit the bathtub's edge and forced the air from her lungs. Maddox lifted his foot, and she slumped to the floor. He didn't move again except to right his stance.

"My prisoner seems to have disappeared," he said.

She faced him. "I had nothing to do with that."

"Do you expect me to believe you?"

"No."

"Where did he go?"

"To hell, one hopes."

"To hell?" Maddox asked. "Have a falling out with your lad, did you?"

"You should know," Haleine said. "You orchestrated it well."

"Yes, I did." Maddox grinned. "Upset your lover didn't prove to be the unfailingly steadfast boy you thought him to be?"

"That hardly matters now."

"Why is that, love?"

"Because you're here to kill me."

Maddox cocked his head. "You seem very sure of that."

"More than I have been of anything before."

"Really?" He straddled her. "Well, I do hate to disappoint."

His hand closed around her throat. She gasped for breath but did not fight him. He picked her up and threw her to the side. She had barely hit the floor when he was on top of her again, dragging her into the bedchamber. He dropped her in the center of the room and circled her.

"But how could I kill you now?" he asked. "Oh, I admit I am tempted to do so, to snap your neck, rip out your spine, when I think of all you've done to wrong me."

Do it, she wanted to say. She wanted to scream it at him, but instead she laughed. He wouldn't just do it. He would need encouragement.

"Do you know what I do when I think of all I've done to wrong you?" she asked.

Maddox froze and glared at her, his eyes flashing.

"I laugh," she said. "And then I laugh some more. You are so stupid, so very stupid. I can't help myself."

Maddox didn't move. She stood and took a step toward him, thinking he would lunge at her, but he remained motionless. She looked at his eyes and saw Omur looking back at her, studying her with curiosity.

"Do you want to know why I don't kill you?"

The question was asked in her husband's voice, but she didn't know if the words belonged to him or the mage. She didn't know why either was suddenly concerned with keeping her alive. Maddox's eyes flashed and became his again, but she couldn't be certain of Omur's departure.

"You're not man enough for the task?" she asked.

"Do you question my abilities?"

"No more than usual."

Still he did not move. She didn't understand why.

"I am man enough for this, for everything."

"Oh," she said. "That must be why a person cannot take two steps within this palace without tripping over one of your offspring, true born or otherwise."

"I don't know what you're trying to do, Haleine, but—"

"I'm trying to understand how a man who sows his seed as much as you can continue to yield no crop."

"The fault does not lie with me."

"There are two golden-haired boys in this palace who say different."

Maddox moved now. He came straight at her, grabbed her arms and pushed her back. She cried out as his fingers dug into her damaged skin. It hurt, which made her laugh. Maddox growled. She looked in his eyes, almost certain he was the one looking back at her. He was the one pushing her now, hurting her. Omur, for whatever reason, had held him back before but was now losing his hold. She had weakened him, and he wouldn't be able to keep Maddox's nature in check.

"Going to kill me now?" she asked.

"Not while you're begging for it. It's disgusting. Your lover," he spat, "begged me as well. But I'll kill you no more than I killed him."

"Because you can't," she said. "You had him in your dungeon, wounded and bleeding and *dying*, and still you could not do it. Still he lived and walked away from you. It is no wonder he gave me two sons while you never could."

"We'll see about that, won't we?" Maddox said. "You gave him two sons. You'll give me more."

"I'll give you nothing," she said, "you weak, worthless waste of—"

He struck her before she finished speaking. She yelped. He turned her around and threw her face down against the bed. She heard him fumbling with his breeches and felt him raising her robe.

She laughed. "Go ahead. Rape me. Fuck me until you're bloody senseless if you'd like. You have before, and the only thing you ever made me was ill."

He drew away from her. For a moment, there was nothing. Then there was a sharp crack and her knee gave out. She screamed in shock and pain. She started to collapse, but Maddox grabbed her hair and held her, yanking her head back.

"You'll not talk like a whore!" he hissed.

"Why not?" she asked. "I am one."

"You are my wife!"

"I can't be both?"

He threw her down again. She clutched at the bed as she fell, but the coverlets gave way and slid to the floor with her. Maddox hovered over her.

"You like playing the whore so much, mayhap I should strip you down and give you to the men of my army. Would you like that?" he asked, his lips pressed against her ear. "All those men lined up to have their turn on you? One cock after another sliding in and out of you? Would you like that?"

"Better them than you," she said.

He screamed. He hit her. He kicked her. She closed her eyes and let him.

"What's wrong, Haleine?" he asked as he continued his assault. "Why won't you fight me? You used to fight me all the time. I would lie in bed each morning, fondling some pretty young wench and imagine what gauntlet you might throw down that day. But you don't do that anymore." He suddenly stayed his hand and crouched in front of her. "Have I done it? Have I finally beaten the spirit out of you?"

He had asked her that before, in some sort of half world made of dream and nightmare. Then she had walked through him because he wasn't there. Now she rolled so she could see his eyes. Their icy blue stared back at her.

"No," he screamed and jerked away. "I cannot be provoked; I will not kill you!"

Maddox struggled against himself. He fought to return to her. He could be provoked; he had been and wanted nothing more than to finish beating the life from her. He didn't understand what prevented him from doing just that. She watched, feeling pity for the dumb animal before her. He finally gave in and collapsed on the floor. She pushed herself up and leaned against the bed, waiting for him to stir.

When he did, he moved slowly, like a newborn foal just learning to walk. His head snapped up and black eyes focused on her. The eyes were not his, but neither did they belong to Omur.

"If you want to die, it won't be by my hand," the thing in her husband's body said. "Not yet. Not until I will it."

She didn't watch the shell of her husband walk away. The strain of holding herself up was too much, and she slipped back to the floor. She laid twisted, half on her side, and stared at the ceiling until even that was too much work. Her eyes slid closed, and in the darkness, she listened to the life drain from her body.

It wasn't going to be enough. Dana was still coming for her, and when he appeared, she would still be lying there, waiting for her life to seep away. He wouldn't let her go either.

She opened her eyes and forced herself off the floor. Her eyes swept over the room, stopping only when they caught sight of her vanity. She heard the echo of her husband's voice.

If you want to die, it won't be by my hand.

She would have smiled if she'd remembered how.

"Then my own hand will have to do," she murmured.

―⁓―

In the end, it was decided that James and Faolan, accompanied by Rhydwyn and Gair, would go to the palace for the queen. Dana, subject to his injuries, would stay behind with the rest. The rebel leader did not argue with the decision.

Since it was certain the entire palace would have been roused by the spell, they went in unarmed except for daggers hidden in boots and belts. Orla had given them clothing for the queen, as they couldn't very well smuggle her out of the palace dressed as she usually was. Bronagh carried the garments as she led them through the passages. She didn't look back, just pushed her way through whatever was in her path, determined to keep her mistress from harm.

They reached the queen's chambers without trouble. The two guards James had killed earlier that night were still on the floor. Bronagh stepped over them without stopping. James followed.

The room was darker now. The fire had died down, and most of the candles had gone out. His eyes swept over the room, searching for her, but he did not find her anywhere. Bronagh came out of a side door carrying a candle which she used to light the others as she moved through the room. Light returned, but still the queen was not to be found.

Bronagh screamed, the sound cutting through James to his soul. They were too late. God, they were too late. He bolted for the maid and grabbed the candle from her hands as she started to sink. He looked at the floor and saw the queen lying there in a rapidly spreading pool of her own blood.

He had slaughtered animals before on the farm, pigs and sheep and deer, and the amount of blood produced by the act was always immense, but never had it made him flinch. He cringed now and couldn't help but wonder how anything that small could hold so much blood. He saw a dagger lying on the floor, just out of her hands. Dana's dagger.

"James," Faolan said. "James, she's not dead."

James glanced again at the queen. "Are you sure?"

"She's not dead."

James dropped to his knees, set the candle down and rolled the queen over. The wound, over her heart, jumped out at him. He pulled a blanket from the bed to cover it and placed his fingers beneath her jaw. He felt her life beat there, faint but present.

"God, she's alive," he breathed.

He looked around the room, formulating a new plan. He motioned to the men behind him and heard them come closer.

"Gair, watch the entrance. Rhydwyn, tear up the bed sheets," he said. "Bronagh, give me the dress."

The two men immediately did as they were instructed. Bronagh stayed as still as before and stared at him. He yanked the dress from her hands. She moved then, looking at her empty palms before meeting his eyes.

"You have to help me, Bronagh," he said. "She's not dead, not yet, but we have to get her out of here, and quickly. Just the same as before, only now we don't have to argue with her."

"There's so much blood," she said.

"She's not dead," he repeated. "Help me."

"I'll get the doctor."

"No," James said. "No doctor. They did this to her, Bronagh. They won't help save her. Only you can do that, so help me dress her."

The sheets were shredded into strips by this time, and James accepted them readily. He handed the dress off to Rhydwyn and pulled back the blanket covering the queen's chest. He untied the robe and stripped it from her body to fully expose the wound. He stuffed the sheets in and around it, packing it as well as he could.

"Faolan," he said as he worked, "we're going to need a little divine intervention here. Where is Luisiúil?"

"On her way back to camp."

"The queen won't make it to camp," James said. "Tell Luisiúil to find us in Enimode. Can you do that?"

"Yes."

James lifted the queen off the floor and instructed Rhydwyn to help him dress her. The man had barely touched her when Bronagh yelped again.

"He can't lay hands on her!" she cried. "Not like that! It's not proper!"

"Neither is letting her bleed to death," James said. "If you don't want him to do it, get over here and do it yourself."

She stepped around to the other side and knelt down. She snatched the garments from Rhydwyn and helped James dress the queen.

"A blanket," James said when they had finished. "We need a blanket, Bronagh. We need to keep her warm."

Bronagh nodded and turned away. When she had, James looked at Rhydwyn.

"The dagger," he whispered. "Fetch it."

Rhydwyn stepped around to where the bloodied weapon had been discarded. He picked it up and tucked it into his belt. James nodded. He didn't want to leave any trace of Dana in that room. He thought the queen and the dagger would be the last of it.

"All right, Bronagh," he said as he picked up the queen. "Get us out."

He waited until Bronagh was well ahead of him and turned to Rhydwyn once more.

"The maid will want to come with us," James said quietly. "When we're out of the city, you and Gair make sure she stays behind. Don't harm her, just—we can't let her follow."

"Aye."

"When you're free, take the other lads and make for camp. Give your report to Ilya. Tell her everything that's happened here, and tell her I'll return as soon as I can. She's not been abandoned."

"Aye, Captain."

He nodded. "Good. Now watch my back."

There were no problems in leaving the palace. The servants they came across merely looked at the woman in James's arms and moved out of the way. The few servants in the kitchens fell into total silence at their appearance, but none made a move to stop them. They slipped through the passage there and into the city.

Dana and the others waited a short distance away. Dana was mounted on horseback, looking away from them. His head snapped in the other direction as he heard their approach. His eyes scanned the group before him and settled on the bundle in James's arms.

"What happened?" he said. "James, give her to me."

James looked at Dana, barely sitting a horse because he lacked the strength to stand. He was preparing for an argument when Faolan interjected.

"It'll be all right," he said. "I'll make sure of it."

James nodded and moved toward Dana.

"What happened?" Dana asked as James passed the queen to him.

"I'll tell you later," James said, pitching his voice low to keep Bronagh from overhearing. "We're bound for Enimode, you and I and the queen. Luisiúil will meet us there."

Dana nodded.

"Bronagh," James said, turning toward her. "Our way out?"

"This way," she said.

Dana urged his mount forward and fell in line behind Bronagh. James moved to follow and someone pressed his sword back into his hand. He took it and called for Dana's as well. He buckled his sword around his waist and slung Dana's across his back. Next someone placed the reins of a second horse, the mount meant for the queen, into his hands. He took them and led the animal along. The rest of the rebels trailed behind.

The path Bronagh took was isolated and dark, lit only by the moonlight. He recalled her telling him the passages existed for the protection of the king and queen. The cover of darkness would serve that purpose well. When they reached the end of the path, they stood facing the stone wall of the city. This part of the wall had been long overgrown with vines and various blooms. James dropped the reins and bent to pull his dagger from his boot. His hand was on the hilt when Bronagh spoke.

"You won't need that," she said, pushing aside some of the vines to reveal a well-concealed door. She found the latch and opened it. "It's secret."

She stepped to the side and allowed Dana to ride through. James gestured to the others to go next. When everyone had gotten out of the city and into the forest, he turned to Rhydwyn.

"Give me the dagger," he said under his breath, "and see to the maid."

Rhydwyn pulled the dagger from his belt and handed it to James. He put it in his own belt and glanced up at Dana.

"You all right?" he asked and Dana nodded. "Then let's go."

"Wait!" Bronagh said. "Dana, wait!"

"Go," James said. "Faolan, you with him."

They left immediately and disappeared into the trees. Bronagh rushed up to him, but James turned his back and prepared to mount his horse.

"I have to come," Bronagh said. "I have to come with you."

James swung into the saddle and looked at her. "Not this time."

"You have to take me with you," she said. "I can't go back there. They'll know I helped you."

He shrugged. "Don't go back there."

"I have nowhere else to go!"

"That's not my problem."

"What am I to do?" she asked as Rhydwyn and Gair closed in on her.

"You'll think of something," James said.

———◈———

Bronagh stopped struggling against the men who held her when Dana and Haleine were lost in the trees. When the men saw the fight leave her, they released her and nudged her back toward the city wall.

"Get on with you, now," one of them said to her.

He was one of James's hand-selected men. Rhydwyn or Gair, she thought. She didn't know which one he was, but she supposed it didn't matter what he was called. He wasn't going to let her follow them. He motioned to the others who had stayed behind with him, and they started to melt into the forest. He stayed the longest, standing in front of her, staring her down.

"Bastards," she said. "If she dies, I'll kill you all."

The man smiled. "You'll have to find us first."

He left, too, then, and she stood alone for a while before going back into the city. She closed the door behind her, taking care to rearrange the flora so no one could tell the door had been opened.

She returned to the palace, stumbling on the path where she hadn't before. The walk was somehow shorter than the walk from the palace had been, and she soon found herself standing at the entrance to the kitchen passage.

But she didn't go inside. She looked toward the city instead. She could wander there. She could leave the city and wander the country. She looked back at the palace. She could go to her little house and stay there until they came for her.

And they would come for her. She thought of Sabine, imagining she could hear the girl screaming with each lash that bit her bared back. She looked over her shoulder at the path that would take her to the city wall. She should've disappeared in the forest, too, and taken her chances out among the people. There were other estates. She could find a position in some household somewhere. It wouldn't matter how menial the task. She'd done it before, and now it would save her life.

But she didn't go. She went back into the palace. She entered the kitchens, and the people at work there stopped and stared again.

"What are you looking at?" she asked.

None answered. It irritated her and she repeated the question. They still didn't answer, only one by one turned back to what they had been doing.

"Now, Bronagh, don't be too hard on them," Frann said, appearing from the far corner. "They've never seen a dead woman walk before."

"Tell them, did you?" Bronagh asked.

"None of us said anything," Frann said. "For her sake, not yours."

"Then how—?"

"Do you really think anyone had to tell them anything?" Frann asked. "They know, Bronagh. They'll come for you."

Bronagh let Frann and the others watch her walk away. She left the kitchens and walked through the halls, wanting to find Willem. Anyone she passed snuck looks at her. Curious what had happened to the queen, curious to see her still there, curious as to what would happen to her now. When she arrived at the nursery, two of Willem's men stood in front of the entrance.

"You have no business here," one of them told her.

"Is he in there?" she asked.

"I don't see how that matters to you."

She pursed her lips briefly. "I don't suppose you would. I'm going in there. Run me through if you must."

They didn't draw weapons. They moved aside so she could pass. Whatever orders Willem had given in regards to her, they didn't extend to physical harm. The thought offered her small comfort.

Willem stood near the two cradles. The nurses were near the fire, trying to settle their charges. They nodded at her as she entered. Willem did nothing. Bronagh crossed the room and stood in front of him, but he adjusted his position to keep Haleine's sons in his view.

"How many men are posted outside that door?" she asked, gesturing to the nursery's main entrance.

Willem didn't answer.

"How long are you going to stay here?" she asked.

She did not expect a response and Willem didn't surprise her. She sighed and looked at the floor.

"I let her go," she whispered and felt Willem's eyes on her. "I gave her to them. He tried to kill her, and I didn't know what else to do."

Willem grabbed her chin and forced her head up. He didn't speak, but she understood what he wanted to know.

"Not Dana," she said, more mouthing the words than speaking them. "The king, I think."

Willem nodded, took her elbow and led her from the room. Out in the hall, he released her and sent the two guards inside to take his place.

"What happened?" he asked, his voice impassive.

He moved away from her, still keeping his distance as though she were something revolting. Because she was the one tainted, and he didn't want her stench to touch him. She looked at him for a moment and nodded.

"I told them Dana was coming. I told Omur. I told the king because I thought if I gave them him, they would spare her. I've only ever tried to protect her, I did, even though you think I betrayed her, even though she thinks it."

"I don't—"

"I went to Dana to explain, to make him come back for her, to save her," Bronagh said. "I thought there was time. Omur was waiting for something—I *know* he was waiting for something, and I thought there was time."

"What happened?"

"There was so much blood," she said. "I've seen her bleed before, too many times have I seen that, but this—"

"You tell me what happened," Willem demanded, grabbing her arm. "You tell me now!"

"Why?" she asked, pushing him away. "What are you going to do about it? Kill the king? No, it can't be that. We both know you're going to die in that room behind you because she asked you to."

"Bronagh, you tell me what happened."

"Too little, too late, that's what happened," she said. "We killed that girl, you and I."

Willem didn't like that. He started to protest but she wouldn't let him.

"I know you don't see it. You can't see it any more than she could," Bronagh said. "She loved you for your blind loyalty and your damn obedience, but she didn't need a bloody lapdog, did she? She needed someone to save her and we failed her. *You* failed her. She didn't know how to survive and you didn't show her."

"Bronagh—"

"You shouldn't have waited."

"I don't—"

"If she asked," Bronagh hissed. "If she asked, you said, you would kill the king, you would do whatever you had to to keep that girl safe. Well, she was asking every damn day, and you never heard it!"

Willem didn't say anything. He stared at her.

"Are they out of the city?" he asked finally.

"Aye."

He nodded and hit her in the face. The movement was so efficient, she didn't realize what he'd done until he drew his fist away, revealing his bloodied knuckles. Her blood, she realized, tasting it as she started to sink.

"When you wake, you tell them the rebels came for the queen," he said before she fell forward into nothing.

———※———

Thanks to an irrepressible moon, they made good time through the forest. The light managed to stream through the otherwise impenetrable canopy of trees. Faolan's doing, James thought, or the goddess's. They kept the light coming and Dana going.

They also kept the wolves at bay. He could hear them in the dark, running alongside them, snapping, growling, howling. They smelled the blood. No doubt they knew what an easy kill traveled the path, but they never appeared upon it.

They only provided an unnerving escort to Enimode, pulling off a few at a time when the sun started to show itself. Soon the wolves were gone, but the moon stayed with them. It was too bright for the emerging dawn. Someone would notice the oddity of its appearance. *Everyone* would notice it. None of them, however, would know what it meant. He wished he could count himself among their number.

When they rode upon the outskirts of Enimode, he forgot about the moon. He hadn't seen the village since he buried his parents. He'd known they'd rebuilt what they could; Dana had told him that. There were structures in various states of construction. He reined in and looked at it for a moment.

It was too much, he thought. Too much to be here now, after all this time, after all he'd seen and done. There was a serenity to the village that rankled him. He could feel it reaching out for him. He pulled on the reins until the horse backed up a few steps, as if that would change anything. Somehow, Enimode was blanketed with a peace that eluded him. He didn't begrudge them that. He couldn't. But he didn't want any part of it.

"James?" Faolan said. "Are you coming?"

He nodded and looked away from the village. "Where's Luisiúil?"

"The pond," Faolan said.

When they got there, the unicorn was pacing at the water's edge. She stopped when she saw them. The horses were skittish. James dismounted and dropped the reins. He didn't care if the horse stayed. He grabbed the bridle of Dana's mount and settled the beast before reaching for the queen. Once his arms were empty, Dana swung from the saddle. His tunic was soaked in blood.

"Dana," James said.

The rebel leader shook his head and took back the queen. "It doesn't matter."

"Lay her on the ground over here, Dana," Faolan said. "And uncover the wound."

Dana did as he was directed and stayed at the queen's side. Luisiúil came and stood beside him. She dipped her head closer to the queen. Everything was still. James held his breath, afraid even something so slight might disrupt what the unicorn attempted.

Suddenly, Luisiúil swung her head, her horn connecting with Dana's gut. The rebel leader screamed and James leapt forward.

Dana crumpled to the ground before James could reach him. Luisiúil disappeared into the forest.

"What did you—what happened?" James gasped.

"He'll be unconscious for a while," Faolan said. "You'll have to carry Haleine to the house."

"Faolan—"

"He'll be fine," the pegasus said. "Luisiúil healed him. This is just part of the spell's aftermath. When we have Haleine situated, we can come back for him."

"Why did she heal him and not the queen?" James asked. "If we truly need her more, why did—?"

"Luisiúil's healing magic is entirely contingent on the intended's will to live. Dana still has one," Faolan said.

"The queen doesn't?"

Faolan shook his head.

"I should have listened to you," James said. "I should have gone for her first, like you wanted."

"Yes, but that doesn't matter now," Faolan said. "Let's get her to the house."

James removed Dana's sword from his back as well as his own sword belt before wrapping the blanket around the queen and carrying her from the woods. He emerged on his family's land, looking at the homestead he'd left behind. Aaron was just coming out of the house. His brother scanned the landscape and froze when he saw who approached.

"Aaron," Faolan said when they were close enough. "Be a good lad and track down the physician, would you?"

Aaron ignored the pegasus and focused on his brother. "You've come back. It took bloody long enough."

"Aaron?" Faolan said again. "The physician?"

Aaron wouldn't take his eyes from James. "If you want the physician, find him yourself. I've work to do."

"You'll go now," Sarai said, appearing at the door behind her grandson.

Aaron glowered as she nudged him forward, but he disappeared in the direction of the village. Sarai watched him go and shifted her gaze to James.

"Where is Dana?"

"He'll be along."

Sarai nodded and backed through the door. "Come on. Let's have a look at what you've brought."

James carried the queen inside and laid her on the bed Sarai herself used to occupy. He knelt beside the bed and pulled back the blankets. Sarai hovered over his shoulder and gasped.

"Good God," Sarai breathed. "She looks just like the queen."

"Probably because she is," Faolan said.

Sarai looked sharply at James. "What did you do?"

"Killed her or saved her," he said. "We'll find out."

Sarai pushed him aside. James didn't protest. He was all too glad to let her take control. He stepped back and leaned against a wall, his eyes burning with sudden fatigue.

"What happened to her?" Sarai asked.

"Someone stabbed her," James said. "Her husband, I think."

"He did more than that. Why?"

"She's been helping us," James said.

Each word was a weight around his neck. Sarai nodded and kept her head bent over the queen. James couldn't look at the queen anymore and stared at the wall instead, waiting for other questions to follow. Sarai would ask where he'd been, why he'd stayed away, why Dana had come and he never had. He waited, but Sarai never said a word.

Aaron arrived with the physician. James didn't recognize him and looked warily at the man. The physician stood in the doorway and returned the favor. He ran his eyes over James, lingering on the blood-stained clothing, and went to Sarai's side when she beckoned him closer. He took a step back when he saw who lay upon the bed.

"What is this?" the man asked.

"Your patient," James said. "Do your work."

James went outside. Faolan followed and landed on his shoulder. A moment later, Aaron brushed past, knocking his shoulder too hard for it to have been an accident. James reached out to grab him.

"Let him be," Faolan said.

Too tired to argue, James let his arm drop. He walked to the empty corral and leaned against the fence. As he watched Aaron enter the barn, Faolan left his shoulder and perched on a fence post.

"Luisiúil couldn't heal her," James said. "What do you think a physician will be able to do?"

"Buy us time."

James caught sight of movement within the trees and lifted his head to see Dana coming out, carrying both swords. His anger showed in his walk. He was furious, but he was also alive and unharmed. He stared hard at James until James gestured to the house.

"Why did Luisiúil heal him?" James asked once Dana had gone inside. "You said he was on his own. You meant it."

"I hold grudges," Faolan said. "Laorans doesn't."

James nodded. "What do we do now?"

"I'd suggest prayer," Faolan said. "I know you've never been much for praying in the past, but we're pretty desperate now. It might be worth a try."

James laughed. "And to whom would you have me pray? If the goddess could have saved her, wouldn't she have done so already? No, Faolan, tell me true. What do we do if the queen dies?"

Faolan didn't respond.

"There has to be something else, *someone* else," James said.

"There isn't."

"So the queen dies, and that's it? We all die?"

"Maybe."

James took a few steps away. Aaron was coming out of the barn now, leading a pair of horses. One was Sarai's mare. The other he didn't know. He watched Aaron turn them loose in the pasture.

"No," he said. "That's not it. It can't be it. There's something else, something you're not telling me. Faolan, it just can't be—"

Her name is in the air again, Faolan. It is time. For better or worse, it is time.

It was a woman's voice, and one he didn't recognize. James looked every which way for its source but saw nothing. He finally looked at Faolan.

"What was that?" he asked. "Who?"

Faolan sighed. "That was Laorans. That was her way of making sure I tell you this even though she knows I think this isn't the right course of action."

"Laorans?" James asked. It wasn't the first time he'd spoken the name, but suddenly it felt strange on his lips. "The goddess Laorans?"

"Yes."

"Oh." James looked skyward momentarily. "What does she want you to tell me? Whose name is in the air?"

"Haleine's sister. Twin sister."

"The queen doesn't have a twin sister."

"She does, actually. Most people just don't know it. Haleine included."

"How does she not know?"

"I'd say that was a question for Haleine's parents," Faolan said.

"How do *you* know?"

"That's a long story."

"Is it?" James asked. "Well, you'd best start talking then, haven't you?"

Faolan nodded. "All right. Tell me what you know about neruals."

About the Author

Armed with a deep and lasting love of chocolate, purple pens, and medieval weaponry, M.J. Fifield is nothing if not a uniquely supplied insomniac. When she isn't writing, she's on the hunt for oversized baked goods or shiny new daggers. M.J. lives with a variety of furry creatures—mostly pets—in New Hampshire. Visit her online at mjfifield.com.